BROTHERS

Bernice Rubens

A DELL BOOK

Published by
Dell Publishing Co., Inc.
1 Dag Hammarskjold Plaza
New York, N.Y. 10017

This work was first published in Great Britain by Hamish
Hamilton.

Dell ® TM 681510, Dell Publishing Co., Inc.

ISBN: 0-440-10847-0

Reprinted by arrangement with Delacorte Press
Printed in the United States of America

First Dell printing—April 1985

For Joshua and Dashiel Lilley, brothers.

The Bindel Family Tree

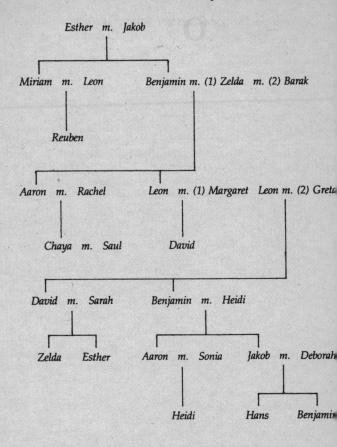

BROTHERS

PROLOGUE

Come stranger. Welcome to our Passover table. In the spring of each year we celebrate our flight from the bondage of Pharaoh. But this Passover festival of ours is much more than a homage to our history. Indeed it seems not history at all, for there is something disturbingly modern about its story, a story that has a sour currency, as if no lesson had been learned from history at all. In the *Haggadah,* which is the service for the Passover eve, there is written a phrase that is the very core of the thanksgiving. "In every generation each man must regard himself as if he himself had gone forth from Egypt." Alas, we need no such reminder. Pharaoh has sundry names, and Egypt dwells in many lands.

Come stranger, and hear the story of our constant flights from bondage and of that minstrel who sings the song that orchestrates our survival. A song that was heard almost a century and a half ago in a small tavern in the ghetto of Odessa.

Come stranger, and warm yourself by our fire, for outside it is snowing.

PART ONE

❦

The Book of Benjamin and Reuben

It must have been snowing.

Whatever else we know about czarist Russia, whatever events punctuated its history, we can be pretty sure that it was snowing at the time. Snow fell on almost every Tolstoy page. Gorki's childhood was grievously gloved. Alexander Nevsky subdued the Teutonic knights in a celluloid battle on ice. The norm in Russia was snow. All else was expedient deviation. So we can safely assume that, on the day that the milk-brothers were born, it must have been snowing.

In fact, we know with absolute certainty that the temperature was well below freezing. We know it because it was historically recorded. Not that the birth of the milk-brothers merited a chronicle of any kind, but they chose to make their appearance on that very day in the winter of 1825 when Czar Nicholas the First succeeded to the throne of Russia. On his inaugural way to the Palace of St. Petersburg, it is written, one of the many horses drawing the royal carriage stumbled and fell on a mound of snow that had been carelessly left on an otherwise cleared roadway. As a consequence, the royal carriage was delayed, a delay that did not improve the new Czar's habitually sullen temper. The negligent shoveler, leaning on his spade, was stationed by the wayside along with crowds of other pageant-fanciers, excited at the prospect of pomp and ceremony. When he saw the carriage falter, and realized the cause, he slunk away, with a haste and a tool that marked him as undeniably guilty. Poor Ivan Vassilevitch was the first casualty of the many thousands that littered Nicholas's reign, and before the royal carriage had reached the palace, his powder-peppered body had been shoveled away to the side of the road together with the mound of snow that he had so dearly neglected. By evening, a vulture—at that time there were many such birds in the Russian skies—would have gnawed poor Ivan out of recognition.

No czar had ever been good for Jews, and Nicholas the First upheld that tradition. He was a military man, with an unsurprisingly narrow vision, and in the course of his inaugural speech that day he made reference to that time-honored irritant to the Russian soul. "The Yids run everything here," he said. "They are merchants, contractors, publicans, mill owners. They are regular leeches, and suck our unfortunate provinces to the point of exhaustion." So it would have seemed audacity, to say the least, that on that very day, and in the very echo of his words, yet two more affronts surfaced on the Russian soil to vex the Czar's mighty person.

The milk-brothers were born in snowbound Odessa with ten minutes and one rickety story between them. The first appearance was that of the only male offspring of Jakob and Esther Bindel, that partnership having already produced four daughters. Esther was forty when the boy was born. Her husband, two years her senior, knew that the child would be the last of his issue. Jakob Bindel, who all his married life had prayed for a son, cursing God behind his hand every time a girl dropped from Esther's fertile womb, now felt himself entitled to the status of Patriarch, and in keeping with his forefather, whose name he bore, he ordered the boy, this last child of his, to be called Benjamin, "the son of my right hand." He kissed his wife and left her bedside, making his way to the front part of the house, to that section which served as his tavern. It was five o'clock in the morning. Only one customer sat there—Faivel the insomniac, Jakob's closest friend.

"*Nu?*" Faivel said as Jakob entered. There was little hope in his voice. A woman like Esther Bindel did not have the sinew for a son.

"Benjamin," Jakob said softly, and he poured two glasses of kvass.

A tear fell from Faivel's eye. It might have flowed from sheer fatigue or from the two glasses of wine he had already drunk. But whatever its source, he meant it for joy. "*Mazeltov,*" he said. "*L'chaim.*"

Jakob raised his glass. "To Benjamin," he said.

Esther Bindel put little Benjamin to her breast, and listened to her daughter's laboring cries from above. Sofia was with her, her oldest, still unmarried child. Esther began to sing softly, a song of joy and celebration, as much to welcome her own son as to herald the arrival of her first grandchild. Then she heard a piercing cry, and she knew that the Bindel line had nudged itself a little further into eternity.

At the moment of her grandchild's birth the child's father, Leon Wolf, was in the shed behind the tavern milking Devorah, the family cow. When Miriam had gone into labor, her sister Sarah had volunteered to replace him at milking time. But the cow had kicked and whined at the touch of an unfamiliar hand. Leon was happy enough to be called away from the thrashing bedside. He could not bear his wife's pain, or the embarrassment that the ensuing event would inevitably cause him. Leon Wolf was a shy man, and he was happier alone, his head resting on Devorah's warm flank as he pumped her teats to relieve her. When he heard his wife's piercing scream, and shortly afterward the undeniable cry of a newborn child, he quickly finished the milking, nuzzled Devorah's nose, and returned to his wife's bedside. Miriam had borne him a son, and as his father-in-law had called the last of his line by the traditional Benjamin, in that same manner Leon's firstborn was to be named Reuben, which translated means "Behold a son." Leon kissed his wife and went to join Jakob in the tavern. Man's work it was to toast one's sons.

Sofia ran to tell her mother of her new grandson, and returned to Miriam with the news of her baby brother. Both children, oblivious of their strange and almost synchronized kinship, sucked happily at their mothers' breasts.

Or at least Reuben did. Downstairs little Benjamin was having a tougher time. He sucked a little and then he stopped. He sucked again, and again he paused, wondering why his hunger was not assuaged. His mother was aware of it too, and without surprise. With her last child, Zena, she had heard the hollow echoes of a dried-up well. She clasped her newborn tightly to her breast, kissing him on his puckered bewildered brow. Then she wrapped him in a blanket. "Your sister will suckle you," she whispered. Then she handed the bundle to Sarah, who took it to the room above.

Miriam put her brother to her breast where he suckled till his brow was smooth. His nephew fed on the other side. Both children's eyes were closed. They neither saw each other, nor did they touch. Between them there was no sibling blood, but the bond of milk that coupled them nurtured between them an enduring and compelling love, a bond that was to remain unbroken throughout their lives.

On the eighth day the children were to be circumcised, and Jakob, who had never before been granted the privilege of such a ceremony, was determined to make of it some celebration. He was, too, for the first time, a grandfather, a cause that on its own account called for commemoration, so he sprinkled sawdust on his tavern floor, set up sundry wines and schnapps on his counter, and fussed about the stove as his daughters baked cinnamon cakes, honey rolls, and pots of peach and raspberry jam.

"Can we dance, Papa?" little Zena asked. "Is it allowed?"

"We shall dance," Jakob said. "The Bindels shall dance and the Wolfs shall dance. Whether it is allowed or not," he whispered to himself. There were enough restrictions already on their daily lives, enough "Thou shalts and shalt nots," whether they came from the Czar or from the rigid tenets of their own faith. More and more Jakob Bindel resented the restrictions that the elders of the community forced upon the ghetto congregation. Their taboo on the learning of anything but the scriptures, their insistence on speaking Yiddish, their sheer contempt for the Russian tongue. But he must refrain from argument. Esther got very nervous if he aired his views. They would be coming to the ceremony, some of those black-robed men of God. Jakob Bindel would hold his tongue. But, nevertheless, he would dance. And so would the women.

"Will you dance with me, Sofia?" he said. Sofia was his favorite. Of all the daughters she, being the first, was the only one whose gender was forgiven. He wished he could see her married. But there were impediments to that, terrible obstacles that he dared not think about. She was different from the others, headstrong, like himself. She would be no man's lackey. Besides, she was cleverer than any young man he knew. She spoke and read Russian. She dreamed of getting out of the Pale. She even dreamed about Palestine. "Russia isn't home," she told her father once. "It's exile." He did not gainsay her. She needed that target.

"Will you dance with me?" he said again.

"Dance with an old grandfather?" she teased him and, although she hugged him, pulling playfully at his beard, he felt her separateness for the first time.

Although it was not the Sabbath, the guests had put on their

Sabbath clothes. The custom of circumcision, of cutting a covenant with the Lord, was a deeply religious act that called for appropriate attire. The men wore long black caftans with their brushed sable hats, and the women wore silk shawls under their woolen wraps. Reb Schlomovitch was the first to arrive, his wife three respectful paces in his rear. Crooked in her elbow she carried his bag with the tools of his trade, his prayer book and shawl, his knife and his roll of lint. Reb Schlomovitch was also the cantor in the synagogue, with a voice of operatic splendor, whose dulcet sonorous tones were occasionally at odds with the duties that were part of his calling. Appropriate as it might have been for weddings or other joyous celebrations, it jarred with the wielding of his knife.

Reb Schlomovitch sat down heavily on a corner bench and eyed the kvass on the counter. But Jakob made no offer. Reb Schlomovitch was getting old. His hands were already shaky.

"Afterward, Reb Schlomovitch," he said, "we'll drink like czars." Then he went to the door to welcome Faivel. His friend's eyes were red-rimmed, a thirst for the sleep that forever eluded him. His wife brought up his round-shouldered rear. One earful of Raisl explained Faivel's insomnia. It wasn't that she was an incessant chatterer. In fact she spoke little. But it was the tone of her voice. Its sound was of measured, monotonous tedium. It was like a continual drip that, given time, would wear away rock. Poor Faivel, Jakob thought, and he dragged him behind the counter and slipped him a measure of kvass.

From his stand, he caught sight of Mendel Meisels as he negotiated his large ungainly body through the tavern door. As always, when he saw Meisels, Jakob's spirits were clouded with foreboding. He did not like the man, and for good reason. Jakob owed Mendel a favor. And not just any favor. The nature of Mendel's payoff was quite specific, though Mendel himself had never spelled it out. But he would drop hints at every meeting and usually with a lecherous grin, so that it was clear to Jakob that there was only one means of squaring the debt. And that means was very costly. Sofia. Jakob owed Mendel Sofia, and nothing less than Sofia would satisfy him.

Mendel Meisels was the head of the Jewish community organization, the *kahal*. This body acted as liaison between the government and the ghetto and was responsible for collecting the crippling taxes and executing the sundry restrictions that the

government thought might help efface that ubiquitous eyesore on
their landscape. Some years before, Alexander the First, the then
Czar, had ordered that Jews could no longer be licensed as tavern-keepers. Many lost their homes and livelihoods. But Mendel
Meisels had turned a blind eye on the Bindel holding. Government officials were always bribable. Part of the *kahal*'s funds
were earmarked precisely for that purpose. On his occasional
visits to the Bindel tavern, Mendel Meisels had caught sight of
Sofia. And for many years, since the death of his wife, and even
before, if he were honest with himself, he had coveted her. But he
had to admit to himself that he had little to commend him in
Sofia's eye. He was older than her father. His body was ungainly.
He had nothing but money and position and she would be attracted by neither. He needed Bindel in his debt. He needed
Bindel beholden. Sooner or later Bindel would have to pay his
due. Neither man ever referred to the nature of the payoff. Jakob
was totally silent on the subject, but Mendel skirted around it
from time to time, voicing his paternal concern with Jakob's
daughters and inquiring as to their marriage prospects. "Now
that eldest one of yours," he would occasionally say, with positive avoidance of her name, "she's not getting any younger, you
know." And Jakob would cover his smile as his heart soured with
the thought of what Meisels had in mind.

So when he saw him standing at the tavern door, he looked
quickly around the room for Sofia, as if with his glance he could
protect her. And she, ignorant of the sacrifice that was expected
of her, was approaching the door to welcome him, as she would
any guest, with her smiles and greetings. Mendel eyed Jakob behind the counter. Sofia took his hand. She led him to her father.
Jakob stared at Sofia's fingers, willing them to be disjoined from
his guest's. The look was not lost on Mendel.

"How's business, Bindel?" he said, which was a reminder that
he was beholden to him to be in business at all, whether his
profits were large or small.

"Business is good," Jakob said, "and today even better. For I
have two heirs who will make it prosper." He thought it as well
to remind Meisels of the purpose of the gathering.

"As long as the tavern remains in Bindel's name," Meisels said
with a smile. He tightened his grip on Sofia's hand, and Jakob
saw how she pulled it away, giggling a little to hide her embarrassment.

"Are we all ready?" Reb Schlomovitch sang from his corner. His eye had fallen on a dish of cinnamon rolls that Zena had carried to the counter. He was anxious to get on with the job and let the festivities begin.

"We're waiting for the Pinskis," Jakob said.

"Then we'll wait forever," Reb Schlomovitch groaned.

The Pinskis were notorious for their lack of punctuality. But for the most part they were forgiven because, as Jakob pointed out, they were artists and were therefore licensed to find the notion of time irrelevant except insofar as it referred to immortality. The Pinskis were music teachers, Dov of the violin, and Rosa of the piano. Almost every child in the ghetto had, at one time or another, passed through their kitchen/studio, and most of them without payment. Many of them were talented, but there was little in those days that a Jewish performer could achieve outside the teaching profession, and often the Pinskis regretted that they had uncorked a talent that had been better left dormant and at peace. The Pinskis were much loved in the ghetto, and pitied, too, because they were childless.

Little Zena ran to the door and looked down the street.

"They're coming," she shouted, excited. "And somebody else is with them."

"It must be that nephew of theirs." Raisl's tubular voice tunneled through the tavern, turning the room into a vast echo chamber. "He was driven out of his village."

It took a little while for Raisl's reverberations to subside, by which time the Pinskis and their companion had reached the tavern door. Jakob caught sight of Sofia's face as she herself caught sight of the stranger's in the doorway. It was as if two stars had glided into her eyes and, in an instant, had singed her childhood. He knew then that he would lose her, but he felt no sorrow. At least, not until he caught Mendel's eye, and then his knees trembled. He looked to the tavern door.

Yosif Pinski was probably Sofia's age with a beauty that matched her own. In the restless line of his eyes and mouth there dwelt an equally unquiet spirit. The magnet that coursed between their two glances was almost tangible. Sofia did not move from the counter, nor Yosif from the door, even when the Pinskis moved into the tavern apologizing for their tardy arrival.

"Dov was giving a lesson," Rosa explained. "The Boks' little girl. So talented. We didn't notice the time. This is Yosif," she said, almost in the same breath, and looked around for him. "Yosif," she called, "why don't you come in?"

And so Yosif was obliged to move and he lowered his eyes, as if their mutual and compelling gaze could contend with nothing but stillness.

"This is Dov's brother's boy," Rosa said.

"God rest his soul." Reb Schlomovitch put in his kopek's worth. The boy's father was a no-good, a drunk and an idler, who'd been stupidly killed in a tavern brawl. But villain as he was, Reb Schlomovitch thought that he was still entitled to some blessing, perhaps even more so than those who had led virtuous lives, insuring their souls along the way. "How's your poor mother?" he asked.

"She's not well," Yosif said. "The journey was hard for her." When Sofia heard his voice, she lowered her eyes for the first time. Its gentleness was almost unbearable.

"On Shabbos they did it. Of all days." Raisl's pneumatic drill of a voice was at it again, and it shattered the caress of his voice that still echoed across the tavern.

"In the middle of the Shabbos service," Dov Pinski said, "they stormed into the *shul* and told everybody to leave the village. Just like that. No warning. Nothing. They walked out of the *shul* and took to the road."

"It's getting worse and worse," Faivel said. "Where do they expect them to go? The ghettos are overcrowded already."

"What do you do for a living, young man?" Jakob said, and Sofia blushed for it was the time-honored question of a father to a possible son-in-law. But Jakob had only meant it for conversation and he realized too late how others might interpret it.

"You lose no time," Reb Schlomovitch laughed.

"I'm a farrier by trade," Yosif said.

"In Odessa we have more farriers than horses," Jakob said, smiling. "You'll have to look for something else."

"I know Russian," Yosif said. "I could teach it."

"Russian?" Mendel Meisels sneered. "Yiddish isn't good enough for you? To learn Russian is the first step to baptism."

"I don't agree," Yosif started, but his uncle quickly interrupted him. One didn't argue with Mendel Meisels. One day you might need favors of him.

"Go and get the children, Sofia," Jakob said quickly. And for the first time since Yosif had arrived at the tavern, Sofia moved

from the counter. Her step was unsteady. Her knees were trembling, and she stiffened them, walking slowly, her head bowed,
anxious to hide the rapturous confusion in her heart. But once
out of the tavern, she held her head high. "He is for me," she
almost sang. "Yosif is the man I shall marry." She repeated it
over and over again, until she reached the back room, then
paused at the door to whisper it to herself yet again.

She opened the door. Her mother was holding both children,
who were sleeping, blissfully unaware of the price they were
about to pay to be one of the chosen. "You look so beautiful,
Sofia," her mother said, catching the glow on her face. "I've
never seen you more beautiful," she whispered. Then Leon came
and gathered the children in his arms, and still they were not
disturbed. Sofia opened the door for him, and stayed behind with
the women while the men got on with man's work of going about
God's business. Suddenly Miriam began to cry and rushed to her
mother's side for comfort, but Esther, with all her mothering
years behind her, was new herself to this man's game and was
holding back her own tears. It was Sofia who embraced them
both with the strength and the love with which Yosif had wordlessly flooded her.

Leon carried the babies into the tavern. Benjamin, who was the
elder of the two, was the first to be initiated. Leon was to hold
him as Reb Schlomovitch performed the rite. It was considered
an honor to present a child in such an offering, but Leon could
have done without it. It seemed to him to be a fruitless act of
mutilation. He was a God-fearing Jew, but he couldn't understand that his God could seriously demand such dire payment for
His friendship. But he had never voiced any opposition. He cradled Benjamin in his arms, and he shut his eyes. He felt that if he
was not a witness to such a procedure, he could not be held
responsible. "God forgive me," he whispered to himself, though
it sounded ridiculous to ask forgiveness for obeying a command-
ment. So he emended his prayer. "I forgive You, God," he said,
and he held the child in his outstretched arms.

Reb Schlomovitch smeared the baby's lips with a little kvass,
his small concession to anesthesia. Then, holding the knife in a
surprisingly steady hand, he sang a prayer and did what had to be
done. Benjamin woke with a scream of affront, and as they linted
his wound he squirmed with reproach. He had been initiated not
so much into Judaism as into the concept of pain, which, as he

was to learn during the course of his life, added up to much the same thing. Leon gathered him into his arms and moved away, not wishing to see his own son submit to the ordeal.

Reuben had already awoken, warned no doubt by Benjamin's cries. He struggled a little in Jakob's arms, sniffing Benjamin's blood and knowing the pain that was now his due. Jakob took a gulp of kvass, and kissed his grandson on the lips. Then, with joy, he held him out for the sacrifice. Reb Schlomovitch wielded his knife once more, accompanied by the same prayer. Reuben was silent. Not a whimper escaped him. Benjamin had wept for both of them, as Reuben would have done had he been first on the knife.

And so it was done. The knife was put away and the children removed to their mothers. It was in order for the festivities to begin. Leon returned from the back room behind the tavern with his accordion. Sofia and Jakob poured the wine, and Zena and Sarah handed around the cakes. Jakob held his glass high. *"L'chaim,"* he shouted, and he looked around for his friend Faivel with whom he shared everything. But Faivel, who had, with half an eye, witnessed the first cutting, had closed it with disgust and desolation. He would die rather than witness another. And at that moment God gave him sleep, and in that sleep, He hoped, a little understanding.

Jakob leaned over the tavern counter. Faivel was sprawled on the sawdust floor, his arm crossed over his chest, and blowing through his parted lips a gentle childlike snore.

"A miracle," Jakob whispered. "Faivel is sleeping."

"It's a good omen," Raisl rasped, staring at her man with astonishment.

"Sh," Jakob said. The last thing Faivel would want to hear, and possibly the only thing that would wake him up, was his wife's voice. "We'll have some music," he said. "A lullaby."

And as Leon stretched his concertina into a gently spread chord, Yankel the *schnorrer,* as if on cue, appeared at the tavern door. His arrival was greeted with warmth and a certain relief, for no Jewish ceremony was complete without its attendant *schnorrer.*

There were four professional beggars in the Odessa ghetto, and Yankel was the doyen of them all. He was well over sixty, and his years, if not his calling, provoked a certain respect. The other operators were relative newcomers to the district, and to the trade as well. Over the past years, they had been expelled from their villages and from their livelihoods and, out of necessity and with a certain initial shame, they had taken to begging. Until their arrival, Yankel had had no competition, and their poaching posed a real threat. Moreover, they tarnished his profession. He had been a highly trained *schnorrer* all his life. So had his father and his father before him. It was a calling that demanded qualifications, skill, and apprenticeship. But Yankel was a generous man and he could not deny others a living. He knew it had to be orderly and noncompetitive, so he called them all to a meeting and together they formed what might loosely be called a *schnorrer*'s union. They debated whose territory belonged to whom, and the rules pertaining to trespass. But most important of all was the principle that, whatever charity was offered, no services must be rendered in return. That code was unbreakable. A good *schnorrer* was one to whom it was a privilege to give, and that privilege, and that alone, was the only permitted form of return. In view of Yankel's age and experience, he was accorded the larger slice of the charity cake. He was allowed to take his choice of weddings, bar mitzvahs, circumcisions, and funerals. In his line of work, there was always demand. Whatever the political or economic climate, wherever a Jew celebrated or mourned, wherever joy or sorrow dwelt, guilt was its eternal bedfellow. The most convenient and handy outlet for guilt is charity, and Yankel was always on the spot for the purposes of mitigation. A Jew in joy will always question what he has done to deserve such happiness, and that same Jew, in sorrow, will often blame himself. Guilt in the ghetto was a ubiquitous shadow.

"Welcome, Yankel," Jakob shouted from the counter. "Take a glass of wine with us and drink to our sons."

Yankel kept his stand at the door. A glass of wine would be brought to him. He knew his place, and it was part of his professional skill to keep it at all times. Socializing was no part of a *schnorrer*'s pursuit. And the guests knew their place too. Apart from the initial welcome, there would be no further conversational exchange. A *schnorrer*, after all, was almost a divine messenger, a broker from God, as it were, sent for the relief of them all, and his calling would brook no familiarity. Yankel would stand sentry at the door till the festivities were at an end.

Leon struck up an old Chasidic folk song, and Jakob rose to his feet. He was a tall man, of rocklike stature, and as he spread his arms to invite his guests to dance, it was as if he would embrace them all. He clasped Reb Schlomovitch's shoulder and danced him to the center of the floor. Dov Pinski joined them, and Yosif, unaware of Meisels' hostility, took his ungainly arm, and linked the circle. Then each man took out a white handkerchief and waved it to the rhythm of the song. The women sat around the circle and clapped their hands. That, according to ritual, was the limit of their participation. Sarah, Zena, and Sofia stood at the counter, their feet itching to dance. If they'd been alone, with just their parents and the Pinskis, they could have danced too. But the presence of Reb Schlomovitch and, even more forbidding, that of Mendel Meisels, chained their feet to the floor. Leon was playing his heart out and the singing grew louder and the dance more frenzied. At its dizzy circling height, Dov Pinski waved his arm in Sofia's direction. "Come," he said. "Join the dancing."

Suddenly the circle lost its momentum. It was Mendel Meisels who skidded it to a halt. He stood stock-still, horrified at Dov Pinski's suggestion, and he made to withdraw, not only from the dancing but from the tavern itself.

"But it's not every day we have two sons," Dov protested, looking to Jakob for some support.

Had it been anyone else but Meisels who had taken offense, Jakob would have stood by his friend. But to Meisels he was beholden, and today, the presence of Yosif Pinski was a sad reminder of that debt.

"It's not done, Dov," he said quietly, begging his friend to understand.

But Dov did not know of Jakob's obligation and he was more bewildered than hurt. He shrugged his shoulders and made to get on with the dancing. But now the music had stopped too, and Jakob had rushed to the counter to refill glasses. He sent the girls around with the trays of cakes, anxious to rekindle the light of good cheer that till that moment had filled the tavern.

"Play," he shouted to Leon, but Leon was already drinking. It took very little wine to render Leon incapable. Jakob looked at his concertina shriveling on the floor, and he knew that Leon would not play again that day. He looked over the counter and saw that Faivel was still sleeping. He wished he would wake up. Suddenly Jakob Bindel felt very alone.

At the tavern door Yankel had missed nothing of the proceedings, and had overheard Dov Pinski's outrageous suggestion, and in view of that he counted on a little extra from Pinski's pocket.

"Where are the mothers?" Rosa suddenly asked, and Jakob realized that he had forgotten about them. He went out to the back room. He was sad at the turn that the festivities had taken. He hated Meisels. The thought of him brewed an implacable rage in his heart. He wished him dead, and he did not even ask God for forgiveness. Meisels' demise would be just and honorable. There were others in the ghetto who were bound to him in misery. The thought even passed through Jakob's mind that he might kill him himself. He shuddered. He went into the back room and gently embraced his wife. Hers was a cleansing love and it soothed his troubled spirit.

"Is Meisels still there?" she whispered.

He nodded.

"Has he said anything?" she asked.

"No."

"What should he say?" Miriam said.

"Nothing," Jakob said quickly. No one except him and Esther knew of Meisels' blackmail. And Faivel. Jakob kept no secrets from his friend. "Come," he said. "The guests are waiting." He led them back to the tavern.

All the women had gathered together and Jakob led the mothers to their table. Their arrival was an excuse to propose another toast, and Jakob welcomed it, for it might well sweeten the scowl on Mendel's face and soften the bewilderment in Dov Pinski's eye.

"To Esther and Miriam." Jakob raised his glass.

Then Dov raised his glass and gave a toast to Reuben and Benjamin, who at that moment were nursing at Miriam's breasts. Then there was a pause while the guests searched in their minds for someone else to be toasted.

Then Mendel Meisels coughed and raised his glass. Jakob trembled.

"To Sofia," Mendel said.

There was silence. No one echoed his words, for they were all mystified by his choice. Only Jakob understood, and Esther too, and she lowered her head into her chest. For in that toast both of them heard his undisguised proposal of marriage.

Sofia laughed. She thought it ridiculous that such an old and

ugly man should toast her, but she thanked him out of kindness
and pity.

Mendel took her thanks as a sign that she was not entirely
indifferent to his offer, and translated her laughter as an embarrassed girlish giggle. He sat down and took another glass of wine.
Let that Yosif feast his eyes on her, and she on him. Sofia was his,
or she, with all the Bindel tribe, would be out on the streets, the
tavern door closed firmly behind them. No, he would not be
moved by pity. Solomon Zemach, another innkeeper on the edge
of the ghetto, was also beholden. It was true that he had already
handed over to Meisels a large proportion of his monthly profits,
but Zemach also had a daughter. Not as young as Sofia, and
certainly not as pretty, but a woman for having children. But as
he looked at Sofia, he knew that no one could ever match her,
and that he could settle for nothing less. He would even offer
Bindel to take her without dowry. He raised his glass once again.
"A toast to our future," he said, addressing the company in general, then slowly edging his glass in Sofia's direction.

At the tavern door, Yankel made a note of the movement. He
did not like Mendel Meisels and his hypocritical piety. They
spelled out nothing but his lechery. If men like Meisels heeded
their consciences, men like Yankel would be millionaires. He
hoped that the festivities, such as they were, would soon end. He
had a wedding that afternoon, a rich wedding, a timber merchant's daughter, and it was a long and tiring walk across the
ghetto to the house of the bride.

"To our future." The guests were responding to Meisels' toast,
and Dov picked up Leon's accordion, and once again music filled
the tavern. But there was no longer any dancing.

"Sofia, sing a little," Dov shouted. He knew she had a good
voice. When she had come to Rosa for piano lessons, they had
discovered it and now he played what he knew was her favorite
folk song. Sofia blushed and lowered her head. Normally she
would have sung without any shyness. She was always singing.
An audience made little difference to her. But Yosif's presence
unnerved her. Yet she couldn't refuse for fear of betraying the
secret in her heart. So she went over to Dov's side, turning her
back on Yosif, singing to Dov's melody as if she were singing for
Dov and Dov alone. When they reached the chorus of the song,
Dov urged the rest of the company to join in. But only one voice
obliged, a voice as beautiful as Sofia's. Dov caught Rosa's eye and

they smiled at each other. At the tavern door, Yankel translated the smile. "They are made for each other," it said. Dov and Rosa Pinski, the matchmakers.

When the song was finished, the company cheered, and Sofia felt obliged to turn to her singing partner and acknowledge him. But her cheeks were on fire, and she dared not reveal to him such ardor. It was he who came to her. "Thank you," he said to her back.

Then she had to turn or else appear rude, and make a public issue of that very thing she wished to hide. But now everyone in the tavern knew how Sofia's heart was beating, and Sarah and little Zena didn't even bother to stifle their giggling. And all were happy for them both, but for Jakob and Esther, who knew the perils of such a meeting.

"We must be on our way." Reb Schlomovitch suddenly stood up, shamelessly stuffing what was left of the cakes into his large cape pocket.

"For the children," Mrs. Schlomovitch explained, as she did at the end of every function. She had been saying it for so many years that she had overlooked the fact that her children had long since left home and had children of their own. She waited as Reb Schlomovitch extracted a few kopeks from another pocket to pay his exit money to Yankel. Farewells were given all round, and Yankel straightened his back for his first customer of the day.

"I must wake Faivel," Raisl rasped, and made for the counter. But Jakob barred her way. He had an omen of an impending Meisels confrontation, and he needed his friend about him, even if his presence was a sleeping one. It would be a comfort to him, a silent support.

"Let him sleep," Jakob said. "He gets little enough. I'll send him home when he wakes. I'll bring him myself," he reassured her.

Nevertheless, Raisl insisted on at least looking at her man. Faivel in a state of sleep was such a rarity that it gave cause for anxiety. That perhaps it was something more than sleep, that Faivel had decided there was nothing left in his life to keep him awake at all. Raisl knelt down beside him and stroked his forehead. Then she bent over and kissed him on the lips. Faivel did not stir. Jakob thought he saw a faint smile on his lips and he was convinced that behind those still-closed eyes, his friend was as wide-awake and as tired as ever.

As Raisl left the tavern, Yankel bowed to her, letting her pass without payment. It was a principle of his never to take alms from a woman. Women had other ways of squaring their guilts. Harder ways. Money, as long as you had it, was the easiest thing in the world to give. Yankel looked to his next customer.

Mendel Meisels was putting on his coat. "Have another glass," Jakob said, anxious to delay his departure and the whispered demand that might well accompany it.

"No," he said. "I have business, and a little with you too, Bindel, if we could have a private word." He motioned him to a quiet corner of the tavern.

Esther trembled. She watched Jakob as he followed Meisels to the darkened corner. Meisels' back was turned to the room and Esther could only see her husband's face. It was clear that Meisels was doing the talking. At first there was a great deal of it, for Jakob said not a word. As he listened, his face was grave, and his lips parted, wider and wider, as Meisels had his say. Then he spoke a few words and it looked to Esther like a timid and futile protest. She hoped she would never see begging in his eyes. Then he was shaking his head, not with adamant refusal, but as a signal of total disbelief. Suddenly Meisels turned and made for the door.

As Meisels approached the door, his face beaming with confidence, Yankel had the distinct impression that he had it in mind to walk straight past him, so gently he shoved his foot forward and barred the way. Then he put out his gnarled hand. To his surprise, Mendel had his money ready, and big money it was too, as a first downpayment to insure his future. He put a rouble into Yankel's hand, neatly stepped over his foot, and went out into the falling snow.

Esther looked at her husband. His face was gray. At his feet lay Leon, stirring slowly out of his drunken sleep. Jakob squatted and lifted him gently to his feet, leaned him over the counter and pushed a beaker of water into his hand. He looked at Esther and shook his head with despair. Sofia was collecting the glasses and the empty cake dishes. He dared not catch her eye. He would never tell her. If she were to know the debt he owed, the debt for which he had never volunteered, she would settle it for him. She would not see him lose his livelihood. She was that kind of girl, his Sofia. So she must never know. Never. He smiled at her as she looked across at him. He saw the glow on her face, and her happiness broke his heart.

Dov Pinski took his arm. It was a gesture of goodwill to show that he held no grudge against his host for his lack of support against Meisels.

"I can explain," Jakob said, scratching in his mind for some excuse.

"It's not necessary," Dov said, "though I'd like to ask a favor of you."

"Anything." Jakob smiled, grateful for his friend's trust.

"It's about Yosif," Dov said. "You were right. There are more farriers than horses in the ghetto. D'you need help in the tavern? He's a good hardworking boy. If only for his meals. That would help. Times are hard."

Jakob shook his head. It hurt him deeply to refuse his friend, especially as he had, only that morning, considered taking on another hand. What with his growing family, he could do with another cow, and some chickens perhaps, and even a vegetable plot, all too much for Leon to handle. But Yosif was out of the question. He must not see Sofia again. Perhaps if she married no one else, he might keep Meisels at bay. "God forgive me," he whispered as he realized what pain such a suggestion would cause her. Again and without any plea for forgiveness, he wished Meisels dead, unmourned, unpardoned, and a relief to them all.

"I have nothing," he said to Dov Pinski and his voice was gruff and hostile, and once again Dov was bewildered, not so much at his friend's refusal, but at his manner.

Jakob put his hand on Dov's shoulder. "One day I'll explain everything," he said.

"Is there anything I can do?" Dov said.

"Keep Yosif away from the tavern."

The two friends stared at each other. "I can't tell you why," Jakob said after a while.

"I think he loves her," Dov whispered.

"And she him," Jakob said.

Dov moved away. "Neither of us can do anything to change it," he said.

Jakob watched and saw the Pinskis take their leave. He stood by and saw Yosif take Sofia's hand in farewell. He spoke words to her and she smiled at him. He was possibly requesting to see her again. Jakob looked on, helpless. He knew that if he had to choose between his own livelihood and Sofia's happiness, he would not hesitate. But he had to consider the rest of his family,

who would be homeless and without means of support. He
watched the Pinskis leave the tavern, paying their exit dues into
Yankel's outstretched hand. Then he himself went to the tavern
door. "You had a good day, I hope?" he asked, pressing money
into the beggar's hand.

"Good enough to insure a long life for your children," Yankel
said. Then, like a courtier, he bowed, and stepped backward to
take his leave.

Jakob returned to the counter. The tavern was empty now. The
women had gone to their quarters and only Faivel remained,
sleeping peacefully on the sawdust floor. Jakob watched him. He
remembered the stories they would tell each other as children,
impossible stories that stretched one's belief. The story that was
even now unfolding itself in his life would not have reached the
heights of their boyhood fantasies. For it was as banal and as
predictable as any hackneyed fairy tale. But it was actually happening under Jakob's roof, and its happy ending was in no way
guaranteed.

Jakob Bindel didn't know what to do. Despite the joy that the milk-brothers had brought to the family, a general gloom had settled over the innkeeper's house, a gloom that was generated by Sofia's despondency. No word was spoken about its cause, but conjecture centered around the name of Yosif, who had not been seen in the tavern since the celebrations over a month ago. The Pinskis had come of an evening, as was their custom, but always they were alone, and Sofia could have sworn that they were avoiding her eye. When Yosif had left her, he had asked permission to visit her again. She gave it to him with leaping heart. He would come the next day, he had said. She had dreamed of him that night, and all day she had waited and trembled. And every day since. Now she cried at night. Sarah and Zena could hear her sobs as she clung to the edge of the bed beyond their comfort. She feared he might be ill, but she dared not inquire. For if he were well, then there were other reasons for his absence, and those she dared not think about.

But Jakob thought about them. He thought of little else. Meisels had given him a week to apprise Sofia of his intentions. He proposed marriage within the month. Jakob had managed to get a stay of execution. He had explained to Meisels that it would take time to persuade a woman to make a decision that would have to hold for a lifetime. He pleaded that it would be grossly insensitive to drive her to a marriage bed so ill-prepared. He hinted that a move made with such unreadiness might well lead to disaster for them all. Mendel had relented. He had given Jakob another month.

There was barely a week to go, and Jakob's mind was in turmoil. Esther's too. They discussed it endlessly. At night when everyone was in bed, they shut the tavern door and talked in the darkness. The idea of marriage was unthinkable, but the alternative was even more sinister. It was an unsolvable dilemma that no amount of discussion could resolve. Yet they talked together well into the night, comforting each other with the belief that something would happen, some miracle, that would erase the villainy and leave no trace behind.

The following day was a Thursday, market day, and Jakob settled in his wagon and made for the center of the town. For the first time in many weeks, no snow fell, and Jakob took it as an omen, a good omen of change. The roads were still icy, and he urged his horse gently on its way. He heard himself singing, a cheerful song of harvesting, and he wondered why such a song had seeped from his troubled heart. Yet he took pleasure from it and the clean biting air that sliced through his beard and whipped his cheeks into a rosy glow. He felt the slippery surface under the wagon wheels and he slowed the horse down, mindful of its fears, and from time to time he interrupted his song to comfort and encourage his horse. As he proceeded at a snail's pace, with an unbidden song on his lips, he heard someone call him by name. He looked around. There were many wagons on the road, both to and from the marketplace, and it was difficult to decipher whence the sound had come. He heard it again, louder this time, and he stopped his cart. Then he saw Faivel. Faivel running. Running and calling his name. Although Jakob recognized him immediately, he could not equate his old friend with such an athletic pursuit. Faivel was always so tired.

"Jakob, Jakob," Faivel kept shouting, though Jakob was waving to him and he was barely twenty yards from the wagon. Still he called, shouting and laughing at the same time, as if he had pressing news to impart, and tidings of great cheer.

Jakob watched him, and his heart warmed to the recollection of their long and affectionate friendship. For they had been reared together in the ghetto, and each had taken over his father's trade. Old Max Bindel had founded the tavern, while a few steps down the road, which in those days had been no more than a beaten path, old Meir Poliakov, Faivel's father, plied his needle to the already threadbare suits of the poor. The small terrain between the two family holdings was their childhood playground. They had both been born in the same year, 1783, a year that still rumbled with the echoes of American independence and the stirrings of the French Revolution that was soon to come. In their growing years they sniffed at freedom, which in those days, even in Russia, could be more than just a dream. The era of Czar Alexander the First had started with a small measure of liberation for its Jews. They were allowed into high schools and universities. They could learn Russian, and both Jakob and Faivel had taken advantage of such liberalism. But such freedom was not to last. Their own children knew no alternative to the restricted life of the ghetto, and their fathers would reminisce about their Russianized youth in whispers, with nostalgia and a certain shame.

At last Faivel reached the wagon, and Jakob helped bundle him inside. And even before he settled himself on the bench, Faivel panted, "I heard a great story, Jakob, a story that will warm your heart. Let's go to Zemach's tavern."

"Why Zemach?" Jakob asked.

"Because Zemach," Faivel teased.

All that Jakob knew of Zemach was that his tavern too remained open despite the law of closure, and that most certainly Zemach must be in thrall to Meisels as well. This tenuous connection excited him and he was more and more impatient for an explanation from his friend. He stopped the wagon.

"Come on, my friend. What's it all about?" Jakob spoke to him in Russian as a reminder of the bond between them, a bond in which Zemach played no part. "Zemach can wait," he said.

"It's a very sad story," Faivel said, also in Russian in acknowledgment of the bond. "D'you still want to hear it?"

"You said it was good news," Jakob said.

"It's an ill wind," Faivel answered.

"Then I'll listen and affect a sympathetic ear."

Faivel smiled.

"Yesterday in Toloczka Street," he said. "Opposite the Pinskis' house, one of the horses in the timber yard cut loose and careered right down the street. There was no stopping it. It was quite wild, neighing, braying, and rearing on its hind legs as if it were going off to war. Then a man stepped out of Mintoff's bank. He was the only one in the street at the time, because everyone else had fled for safety. Well, this horse just made for him, poor devil, crashed him down and stepped on him." Faivel paused, then lapsed into Yiddish. He felt more at home in that tongue. "Then the horse lowered its head, and nuzzled the old man's beard. Then it sang out a muted bray, like a mourner's *kaddish,* and turned and went back to the timber yard at an orderly trot, as if its day's work were done."

"Who told you all this?"

"Yankel the *schnorrer.* He was on his way to the bank and he was hiding in a doorway."

"Was the man dead?" Jakob asked. His heart was singing, fluttering with a joy and excitement.

"As good as," Faivel said. "One of his legs was crushed. They took him off to hospital."

"Poor devil," Jakob said, and slowly he nudged his horse on his way.

There was a silence then between them, broken only by the clip-clopping of the horse's hooves and their distant echo through the cobbled streets.

"Someone we know?" Jakob dared to ask at last.

Then Faivel burst out laughing and took Jakob in his arms and hugged him. "God is good sometimes," he said. This last in Russian, for Yiddish was not the tongue of profanity. Russian could deal with all that. Let the language of their oppressors translate their curses, Faivel thought, and above all, their illegal joy. "Mendel Meisels," he whispered in Jakob's ear.

Jakob stopped the cart. A great weight dropped from his heart. "Will he die?" he asked softly. "Will he most definitely die?" This last in impeccable Russian.

"Yankel's already preparing for the funeral," Faivel said. "He told me that's one burial he couldn't afford to miss. The crowd and the pickings will be legion. Come, let's get on to Zemach's and bring him the good news. We'll all celebrate together."

But as they entered the tavern yard they already heard noises of celebration. When Zemach saw Jakob and Faivel at his door, he was surprised, for they rarely came to drink at his tavern, nor he at Bindel's. He afforded them both a great welcome, pouring them wine. Then he raised his glass to a nameless toast, and so did the others. Not once during the carousals was Meisels' name mentioned, but the object of their toasts was clear to them all.

It was well after midday when Jakob and Faivel left the tavern. By the time they returned to the marketplace, everything had been sold. Jakob saw old Max Blomski crossing the square toward him. Blomski was another member of the *kahal* and would no doubt have news of his colleague.

"You heard about Meisels, Bindel?" he said when he reached the cart.

Faivel and Jakob nodded their heads with as much solemnity as they could muster.

"How is he?" Faivel said with manufactured concern.

Blomski shook his head. "They saved the leg," he said, "but he's bleeding inside. He's not expected to last very long. Ach," he said, moving away, "we live in terrible times."

Jakob smiled to himself. Runaway horses didn't make the times terrible. It was riots, expulsions, restrictive laws, and taxes that made ghetto life unbearable. Most Jews died from one or another of these causes. That way they died with some measure of distinction. It was just like old Meisels to succumb to such a mundane way of departure. Unimaginative, Jakob thought, perverse, and an almost illegal way for a good Jew to die. But for Meisels it fit superbly.

He dropped Faivel off at the square, and made straight for the Pinskis' tenement. Once there, he summoned them to his tavern that very afternoon, and ordered that they should be sure to bring Yosif with them. Again Dov was bewildered, but by the look on his friend's face, he knew that the invitation was connected with celebration, and all no doubt would be explained.

Esther was waiting for Jakob in the courtyard, anxious because he was so late. But when she saw the empty wagon and smelled the liquor on his breath, her anxiety gave way to anger.

"No, I didn't go to market," he teased her. "And yes, I have been drinking. Me and Faivel. We've been celebrating."

"With all our troubles you found something to celebrate?" Esther said.

"All our troubles are over, Esther." He put his arm around her and walked her into a quiet corner of the tavern. Then he sat her down, and quietly and soberly told her the news. "Poor Mendel," Esther said, and clearly she was sorry for him. She was aware of the great fortune occasioned by Meisels' mischance, but she regretted that it was at such cost. "Well, poor man, he had no family at least." For her, the lack of mourning kin was a distinct advantage.

"I've told the Pinskis to come," Jakob said. "They're bringing Yosif with them. I shall explain everything."

"Are you sure?" Esther asked. "Are you sure he will . . . ?" She couldn't speak the word. It made her feel like Meisels' murderer.

"Blomski said he can't last much longer."

"Perhaps we should wait," Esther said.

"What difference?" Jakob said. "Today, tomorrow, or the next day. We are delivered, and so is Sofia. Where is she?" Jakob asked.

"In the kitchen."

He got up, acknowledged his few customers, and followed Esther to the back of the house. Sofia was bent over the stove and even though he couldn't see her face, he knew its desolate look.

He put his arm around her shoulder. "Sofia," he said softly. "Go and put on your best dress. This afternoon the Pinskis are coming."

She did not move. "Why should I change for the Pinskis?" she said to the stove.

"They're bringing Yosif."

Then she turned, her cheeks aglow. Jakob embraced her. "Everything will be all right now," he said. She rushed from him and out of the room.

Miriam was sitting by the stove, the milk-brothers at her breasts. He went over to them and took them in his arms. "My little tavern-keepers," he said.

Before the Pinskis arrived, Jakob took Leon aside and told him the whole story. Leon was to look after the tavern while the Pinskis and the rest of the family were being enlightened in the back room. Jakob was very fond of Leon, most fond perhaps of his timidity and shyness.

When Leon heard the story, he kissed his father-in-law on both cheeks. "At Sofia's wedding," he said softly, "there will be no one to stop us dancing." He took up his stand behind the counter, proud to be privy to such glad tidings. When the Pinskis arrived, Leon called to Jakob, who came out to the tavern to greet them. Yosif still wore his best and only suit. It had been much patched since Leon had last seen it, and it seemed to hang very loosely about its model. Yosif looked thin and pale, yet his eyes were feverishly bright.

"We're all in the kitchen," Jakob said. "Come," and he led them through the tavern to the back of the house. He allowed Yosif to enter the kitchen first, and from the door he viewed the wordless exchange that passed between them. Then he ushered the Pinskis inside and they all sat around the table while Esther drew the samovar.

"I want to tell you a story," Jakob began. Jakob was by nature and long practice a superb storyteller. He told a tale as if he himself were hearing it for the first time. He would tell it slowly, embroidering each event, sowing seeds of suspense and excitement in every turn of the tale. But he knew that the story he was about to tell lent itself to no elaboration, to no adventurous detail, and, above all, to no moral. He would tell the tale simply as it was, without judgment, without alibi. The narrative was quickly over, and its brevity, and the bare bones of its telling, seemed to sharpen its cruel dilemma. His listeners stared at each other, but no one said a word. The silence was finally broken by Sofia.

"Poor Mendel," she said, a remark that called for a silence even longer than the first.

"And poor Sofia, if he would live," Dov Pinski said at last.

"And poor Yosif," Yosif muttered. He took Sofia's hand. It was a public gesture for them all to see. The private proposal of marriage had been wordlessly made at their first meeting. Now Yosif was asking her family for Sofia's hand.

"God bless you both," Esther said. "We shall all dance at your wedding."

"We'll drink a toast," Jakob said, and he went into the tavern to fetch some kvass.

Leon was doing a brisk trade. News of Mendel Meisels' accident had by now spread right across the ghetto, and men had need of a meeting place to pick over his bones, even though they were as yet unburied. One brought a rumor that Mendel was already dead, but another had later news that spoke of his prolonged and painful dying. None was openly gleeful, but they seemed to be drinking more than was usual in the middle of the day, and a working day at that. They greeted Jakob with the news. He could not pretend he hadn't heard it, but he feigned indifference. He would not go as far as to assume regret. He whispered to Leon that he keep a sharp ear for the latest bulletin on Meisels' condition. Then, with his bottles, he returned to the kitchen.

"And how will you provide for this beautiful daughter of mine?" Jakob teased Yosif, filling his glass.

"I teach a little. I already have some pupils. I'll get more."

"One day, this tavern will be partly yours," Jakob said. "You should learn its trade. I give you Leon's job, and nobody will be happier than Leon for he will be able to go back to his cows.

We'll buy another cow and some chickens. You can start tomorrow."

And so toasts were given in quiet celebration.

In light of the circumstances, everyone consciously avoided discussion of practicalities, foremost of which was the date of the wedding. So they whiled the time away with endless toasts to people and to things that they invented on the spot, toasts to a good wine harvest and to little Zena's plaits. They drank toasts to the health of everybody but Mendel Meisels, whose recovery would have nullified them all.

At milking time the Pinskis left the tavern, and Jakob took over at the counter. Toward evening Max Blomski arrived, and when Jakob saw him, he prayed to God for forgiveness for the joy in his heart, for Blomski was by no means a regular customer and his arrival could only mean that he had brought news of Meisels' passing. For he looked doleful enough and in need of some sustenance to raise his spirits. He made straight for the counter. Jakob stiffened his knees and steeled his face to sorrow.

"Welcome, Mr. Blomski," he said. "And how's Mr. Meisels?" he said straightaway, as anyone would have asked, whether he wished Meisels to live or to die.

"It's bad," Blomski said. "He's fighting, the doctors say, fighting like a lion. But there's little hope. We must all pray for him."

When he's dead, I'll pray for him, Jakob thought, I'll pray for his rotten soul, and he wondered why Max Blomski was in such despair. He had never been Meisels' friend. Mendel Meisels had no friends.

But Meisels' death would mean Blomski's inevitable promotion on the *kahal,* and to be chairman of that association was a dubious honor that he could do without. To be a liaison between a vicious government and the people it oppressed was in itself a position of treachery. And even if one started in office with the most honorable of intentions, it was very easy to backslide into the bribery, blackmail, and corruption that attended the job on all sides. Over the years he had seen it happen to Meisels, though Meisels, aware of all the possible bonuses, had hankered after the post in the first place. Even at that very moment, lying so close to death, he was availing himself of one of the perks of his position. For he was lying in a private ward in a state hospital, well beyond Odessa's Pale. Blomski could do without such favors. He would sooner take his health chances in one of the almshouses of the

ghetto. "We must pray for him," he said again, and he downed an
unaccustomed glass of kvass.

"Are you going to visit him?" Jakob asked. Blomski, as a
member of the *kahal*, would be entitled to a visitor's permit.
Jakob needed someone for firsthand information. He could not
rely on rumor and hearsay in the tavern.

"He's not allowed visitors," Blomski said. "Not anybody. One
day soon, the black wagon will cross over the bridge, and it will
all be over."

The days passed, and no word or wagon left the big house on
the hill. In the tavern Meisels was still the main topic of conversation, and Jakob was glad of it, for as long as that name was
bruited about, his imminent death was possible, and Jakob himself would often promote it when that subject of conversation
threatened to flag. But after a month had passed, it became
harder to resurrect his name. Old Meisels was taking an uncon-
scionable time to die, and speculation as to how long he would
live was too shameful a subject for conversation. At about that
time, Zemach came to Jakob's tavern, a rare occurrence, and
Jakob knew well the purpose of his visit. But between the two of
them the name of Meisels was unmentionable. Blackmail, especially on the receiving end, was a private matter, no matter how
innocent the parties.

"How is business?" Zemach asked, a question that he hoped
was tangential to the matter that was pressing on both their
hearts.

"It's good," Jakob said, "but who knows how long it will go
on." Jakob had expressed the fears for both of them.

"Who knows indeed," Zemach said. He leaned over the
counter. "Come again to my tavern. We should keep in touch."

"I will," Jakob said, and intended to do so, for though he and
Zemach had little in common, Meisels had created a bond between them.

"You've taken on a new counter-hand," Zemach said, nodding
in Yosif's direction. His statement was an expression of admiration for Jakob's optimism. "I was thinking of expanding myself,"
he said. "But I'll wait. I'll wait and see."

"This is Yosif," Jakob said, putting his arm around Yosif's
shoulder. "Zemach keeps the tavern at the edge of town," he
explained. It crossed his mind to detail the introduction, to con-

firm Yosif as his prospective son-in-law. He knew that the suspicion was passing through Zemach's mind. Instead he said, "We must all of us have hope, Zemach. We must go on living as if we shall live forever."

"Not all of us," Zemach said. It was the closest either of them had come to the mention of Meisels' name.

The rumorless days passed. Yosif had settled happily into his work, and the tavern clientele increased under his caring service. Sofia kept her domestic place in the back rooms, and they would meet at the midday meal and look across the table at one another, and day after day the words multiplied between them. In the evening Yosif would take supper before going home, and Sofia would be left alone to serve him. The other women would tend the children, and Leon would be in the yard. At this hour Jakob would take over the tavern, a slow time for business, a change-over time between work and hard-won leisure. It was during one of these intervals that Jakob was in the tavern playing a game of chess with Faivel. There were no customers and the game was slow. It was Faivel's move. His chin rested on a clenched fist, and his eyes, never wide-awake, were almost closed. He was debating his next move, or so Jakob thought. Until he spoke.

"Any news?" he said.

Jakob shook his head. "I'm worried, Faivel. They say he's fighting like a lion."

"To retain his power," Faivel said. "That's the only reason people linger against all laws of nature. People don't fight for love, not when they're dying, for they know that loving and dying are often the same, and they yield gladly to death's embrace. Those who are monsters in life are monsters in death, too. A curse on him," he shouted. "I'll drink to his death," he said, raising his glass, "and to hell with the consequences."

It was at this moment that a stranger appeared at the tavern door. He was dressed in soldier's simple military uniform of low rank. Even so, his presence in the tavern inspired fear, and he leaned his young shoulder against the door with the arrogance of one who owned the place.

"Jakob Bindel?" he shouted with disdain.

Jakob trembled.

"Which one of you is Bindel?"

Jakob stood up and, for his support, so did Faivel, but his caring gesture only led to confusion.

"You can't both be Jakob Bindel." The soldier did not conceal his temper, whereupon Faivel sat down, inadvertently knocking over the chessboard.

"You were in check," he mumbled to Jakob, though lesser check, he thought, than his friend might be in now.

"I have a summons for you," the soldier said. "From the hospital. Meisels. Mendel Meisels. A Jew. He orders you to come. Here is your pass."

He handed over a yellow star, the obligatory badge for those few Jews who were permitted to travel outside the ghetto. "It is valid only for today," the soldier went on. "You should go at once." He pinned the badge on Jakob's blouse. "I'll have a kvass before I go," he said.

When he had gone, Faivel said, "I'll come as far as the river with you."

Jakob took off his badge and went into the back room to ask Yosif to take over the counter. He said he had urgent business in the town. His hospital visit would remain a secret. He returned to the tavern, replaced the badge and covered it with his coat, then he and Faivel climbed onto the wagon.

The journey was silent.

"D'you want me to wait for you?" Faivel asked after a while.

"I may be some time," Jakob said, though he knew that to offer his forgiveness to Meisels, or to accept his warning, would take roughly about the same time, and brief it would be. "Come to the tavern later," he said. "Who knows, we may have cause for celebration."

Jakob said it with little conviction.

At the bridge, Faivel stepped down from the wagon, and stood waiting as Jakob crossed over. At the end of the bridge he saw the sentry coming out of his box, and he watched Jakob get down from his cart, open his coat, and reveal his passport to beyond the Pale. Then he mounted again and drove into the distance. Faivel waited until the wagon was out of sight. Then he made his way home.

It was many years since Jakob had visited this now forbidden quarter of Odessa. When he was a child, there had been, as yet, no statutory law regarding the limits of the Pale, and the whole city was open to Jews and non-Jews alike. He had always lived where the ghetto was now confined, but often as boys he and Faivel would wander up the hill to view the harbor from the highest point in the city. Then they would run to the dockside, and watch the timber-laden boats put out to sea, and wish themselves aboard. As he drove his wagon up the hill, Jakob thought of those days, and how much less restriction had ruled their lives.

He remembered that the hospital was in a field at the top of the rise, but as the horse trudged uphill, he could see no greenery, and as he came closer to the top, he realized that the field was no more. The building that in his youth had been the hospital had swollen over the grass. There was not even a tree on its perimeter to mark the spot of Jakob's boyhood. The sight depressed him profoundly. He hitched his wagon where a turnstile used to stand, and recalled how he and Faivel would race toward it in an effort to vault it first. He walked along, looking for an entrance, but he noticed that there were many doors, and none of them were marked in any way. He was wary of asking directions. His Russian was heavy with Yiddish accent, and he would have to display his star to prove his legality. Many people passed him by without a glance. He listened to their Russian talk and, though he loved the language and understood each word, he felt a stranger there. He wanted very much to be back in his tavern, finishing his game of chess. Esther would wonder what urgent business had taken him away, and though she would never ask, she would guess that it was on Meisels' behalf. He prayed that he'd have good news for her on his return.

He opened one of the doors and found himself in a large public room where many barefoot men shuffled about aimlessly. They were dressed in gray hospital gowns, so they were clearly patients, and Jakob wondered why they were not in bed. They looked fit enough, he thought. Many of them were of good color, but a pall of hopelessness hung about the room, as if it were more a prison than a hospital ward. But for some reason, he suddenly felt freer in this place than he had since leaving the ghetto. He felt he could talk to these men without fear of his yellow star.

"Take your coat off, brother," one of them called over to him. "Make yourself at home."

Jakob opened his coat and the bright sun of his faith was plain for all to see. They stared at him. Then one of them spoke.

"Welcome," he said, "and doubly welcome. You are our first Yid."

Jakob was encouraged by his smile. "Who are you?" he dared to ask. "What is this place?"

"We are madmen," a voice said from the corner of the room. "This is a madhouse, and we are detained at the Czar's pleasure."

Jakob was puzzled. He had seen mad people. There were plenty in the ghetto shuffling wild in the streets or lurching along the cobblestones, mumbling their magic words, cleansing the air with their beautiful dreams. They were incoherent, untouchable, almost holy. Not like these men at all.

"What's mad about you?" he asked.

"We have spoken against the Czar," one of them said.

"But people go to prison for that," Jakob said. "They're called criminals, not madmen."

"But our Czar is generous," another man said. "He thinks that anyone who is opposed to his office must, by nature, be a lunatic and should be treated as such. He sincerely believes that. They give us medicines to love him with all our hearts and to have no other god."

Jakob permitted himself a small smile. "Are you getting better?" he asked.

"We shall die of our disease," one of them said, "and in this very place."

"But the door's open. You could walk away," Jakob said.

"There's ice on the ground, and they have taken away our shoes. And there are dogs outside who are practiced in our smell. But worst of all," he added, "we're used to it here."

Jakob was overcome with depression. He wanted very much to be out of the room, but he felt that leaving them would seem like betrayal. In many ways he was one of them himself. He hated the Czar with all his heart, and so did all those who lived in the ghetto. But it was a private, unpublished hate. It had to be. The Jews were the official victims. They were the legal scapegoats. They kept their mouths shut, as was befitting to their status. They survived only because they knew their place.

"What are you doing beyond the Pale?" the man asked.

"I was summoned by a patient to make a visit," Jakob said. "I thought this was the hospital."

"It is," the man said. "But this is the asylum. All the low buildings are part of the asylum." He returned to his seat in the corner of the room.

Jakob followed him. He wanted to be part of that circle of men. He felt them as brothers. Yet as he stood there among them, he felt himself a stranger. He was ashamed of his own rude health

amid their frailty, ashamed of his sheer height towering over their
shrunken despair. He saw the gray stubble of their shaven heads
and he was offended by his own protection of thick black hair.
But above all else it was his boots that shamed him, that passport
to the small freedom that he still owned, despite the confines of
the Pale and the prison of his yellow star. He spread out his arms
to embrace them.

"What can I do for you?" he pleaded.

Then they shrank away from him. There was nothing he could
do for them, and his concern disturbed them. His loving and his
caring reminded them of those loves and cares they had left behind, and stirred those longings that over the years had been
numbed in their hearts. Such feelings could find no accommodation in this place.

"The hospital is the old high building, the brown brick one, at
the end of the road," one of the men said. "Someone there will
tell you where to go."

They were giving him permission to leave, yet somehow Jakob
was loath to go. He wanted to offer them favors, some means of
communication with the outside world, but he knew that he
would be putting himself in jeopardy, for despite his yellow star,
he was still beyond the Pale, a Jew who, with a little patient
investigation, would be found in illegal livelihood. Then he remembered Meisels and the unknown purpose of his visit. He had
troubles enough of his own. Yet he didn't know how to leave
these men. "Good-bye" was too final. It was a confirmation of
their life sentence. "I'll come again" was impossible, because a
visit to these renegades would be no ground for a yellow-star
permit. Perhaps he should, after all, offer to do something for
them on the outside, no matter what risk there might be to himself. He opened his mouth to speak.

"You can do nothing for us," one of the men said, as if reading
his thoughts and his hesitation. "You and I are the same,
brother," he said. "We receive the same kind of treatment, but on
different sides of the Pale."

Jakob went toward him and embraced him. There were tears in
his eyes. His fears of the Meisels visit ebbed quickly away; his
own troubles were paltry and insignificant compared with the
lifelong deprivation of these men. He turned away, sadly, button-
ing his coat as he went, and he left the room without looking
behind him.

He went into the street again, and passed the row of single-storied huts. He shivered. The thought crossed his mind not to visit Meisels at all. Meisels was as much the enemy to those men as the Czar himself. Let him rot in his dying, he thought, or, at worst, stew in his wretched recovery. But he needed Meisels to stamp his pass, as proof that the purpose of his permit had been fulfilled, else he would have trouble with the sentry on the bridge. He trudged along unable to wipe from his eye the misted vision of that loose circle of men. He still felt on his shoulder the print of their touch. Brothers, he thought, as brother to me as I am to Faivel, as Benjamin is to Reuben, as all men are to each other in the terrain of love. Meisels was a stranger to that land. He would grant him nothing, Jakob decided, not even a dying wish, and he hastened his step, anxious to get the visit over and done with.

At the desk, he was directed to the third floor, where he was to ask directions once again. By the time he reached Meisels' ward, he was feverish with hate and indignation. He strode through the door. There were many beds in the ward, but he trusted his nose to sniff out the plague he was seeking. He stopped short, however, as he saw Meisels coming toward him, limping a little but otherwise with the air of one in perfectly good health. Jakob made no attempt to hide his disappointment. "You're better, I see," he said coldly. "You sent for me."

"My recovery does not please you. Come, sit down," he said. "This won't take long."

Jakob followed him to the table at the end of the ward. They sat opposite each other, and Meisels got down to business straightaway.

"I shall be leaving the hospital in two weeks," he announced, as if it were an order to lay the red carpet in the ghetto. "You will make arrangements for the wedding. I have settled money on your daughter and she will want for nothing. On Sunday in two weeks, I shall celebrate with my bride at your tavern. You will invite all the members of the *kahal,* and we shall dance through the night. The men, that is."

Jakob stared at him vacantly.

"D'you hear me?" Meisels whispered.

"Yes, of course," Jakob said. He did indeed hear him, his voice, that is, and the sounds of his words, but he had long ceased listening. He got up to leave. "I shall put everything in order," he said. "The wedding will take place on Sunday in two weeks."

And he meant it, with all his heart. On Sunday, in two weeks, Sofia would marry Yosif. They shook hands on what Meisels believed was their trading.

"I'm glad you're better," Jakob said. He no longer minded if Meisels lived forever, for never again would he figure in his life or livelihood.

He hurried out of the ward and down the steps and out of the hospital. His wagon was at the far end of the complex and he almost ran toward it, slowing down when he reached the low-slung huts. "Brothers," he whispered, and the word halted his step. He stood there for a while and muttered a short and, he knew, futile prayer for their well-being. Then he mounted his wagon and drove toward the bridge. He handed over his badge and his pass to the sentry. He felt it as an act of cleansing. Now he could go home to his own kind. The whole of his life lay on the far side of the bridge. All but that small loose circle of men.

Halfway across the bridge, he caught sight of a lone figure on the other side, and on approaching, he slowly recognized Faivel, leaning his back on the iron rail. Jakob's heart was joyful. He would tell Faivel everything. And only Faivel. To Esther and the rest of the family, he would say nothing. They did not know that he had been summoned to the hospital. And Faivel would tell no one. They could all go on assuming that Meisels was nearing the end of his rotten days.

Faivel climbed onto the cart. "I'm glad to see you," Jakob said, and they drove for a while in silence. "He lives still?" Faivel asked after a while.

But Jakob had forgotten all about Meisels. He wanted to tell Faivel about his brothers in the circle.

"I saw some men," Jakob said. "D'you remember that field we used to play in. That turnstile? It's all gone now. All gone. The hospital has spread over the whole field. It's an asylum. I went into it by mistake."

"Where we used to make up stories?" Faivel asked. "That field?"

Jakob nodded. "They built a madhouse on our dreams," he said, "and inside I heard the most terrible story of all."

Faivel recalled the field and the game they always used to play. He was usually the winner. He would fly into fantasies of horror, leaving Jakob incredulous at his side. "I'm listening," he said. He pulled the blanket more firmly across his knees. It was beginning to snow again.

"There are men who are called lunatics," Jakob said. "They don't have abnormal illusions; they don't think they're God or Jesus. They're not deeply depressed or jumping-crazy, and they don't scream or mumble." Jakob listed the categories of lunatics he had encountered in his life. "None of those," he said.

"What makes them mad, then?"

"They're against the Czar," Jakob said simply.

"That makes them mad?" Faivel laughed aloud.

"They actually get medicines for it," Jakob said.

"God in heaven," Faivel said after a while. "Who in the world is sane?"

It was getting dark and there were few people on the streets.

"It's your turn for a story," Jakob said.

Faivel was silent. Even he had no tale to match Jakob's vision of horror. He kept thinking of that distant, cowslipped field on which their boyhood dreams had spawned the most fearful nightmare of them all. He pulled the blanket over his shoulders. Although it had stopped snowing, he was feeling bitterly cold. He shut his eyes, though not for sleep but to raze that charnel house to the ground and sniff once again those innocent childhood lawns.

They were within a few yards of Faivel's dwelling, and then he spoke again. "And the villain lives still?" he whispered. He, like his friend, now understood that one villain was very like another, that between the Czar and Meisels there was very little to choose. Jakob stopped the cart.

"Not only does he live," he said, "he is better. He is walking about. In two weeks, he will be back among us."

"What did he want from you?"

"He ordered me to arrange his wedding with my Sofia. On Sunday, in two weeks."

"What will you do?" Faivel asked.

"I shall do as he asks," Jakob said. "I shall arrange a wedding on that exact day. And in my tavern. But Yosif will be the groom."

Faivel clutched at his friend's arm. "And after the wedding?" he said.

"We'll find something. We can all work. Each one of us."

"But where will you live?"

Jakob shrugged.

"It will be hard on all of you," Faivel said.

"D'you think I don't know?" Jakob shouted at him. "D'you think I haven't thought of all that? But I think of Sofia's life too, and of those men I just saw on our field. We have to live with some kind of truth, Faivel," he pleaded.

"I'll help you all I can," Faivel said.

Jakob urged the horse forward once more, and stopped the wagon at Faivel's home. "Not a word to anyone, Faivel," he said. "Not a word about the hospital visit. We don't know how Meisels is. We assume he is still in the business of dying."

Faivel nodded and folded the blanket away. "I'll come later and finish that game," he said.

Jakob watched him into his house. "Thank you for waiting," he shouted after him. Then he turned his wagon in the direction of the tavern.

It was the Thursday before the wedding was due to take place. And, as was his custom, Jakob was driving the wagon toward the marketplace. The horse moved slowly, unurged by his master, who was in deep contemplation. By now it was possible that Meisels had had rumor of the coming event that would seal the rejection of his suit. Jakob had heard from an excited Blomski that his chairman was due to return that very day. He dreaded the evening and a possible confrontation. But he had no doubt in his heart that he would brazen it out and take the consequences. Then he fell to thinking about what those might be, and as he tried to put such thoughts from his mind, he heard someone call his name. He remembered how Faivel had called him one market day not so long ago and had brought him those glad tidings that had turned out to be not so glad after all. He looked around expectantly, and there, to his joy, was Faivel yet again, in the middle of a workday week, bursting with news of great import.

"Jakob, Jakob," he shouted when still some distance from the cart. "Have you heard the news? We must go at once to Zemach's tavern."

Meisels is dead, once and for all, Jakob sang to himself. He hoped that Faivel in his excitement would not forget himself and scream the good news abroad, and thus publicize their joy.

"Get in first, Faivel," he shouted. As he waited for his friend, the thought crossed his mind that Meisels' funeral would coincide with the wedding. There was a certain poetic justice in that, he thought, though it would pose a dilemma for poor old Yankel, who, skilled in his profession as he was, could not hope to stretch his hand between graveyard and tavern.

He helped Faivel up onto the cart and when he'd settled down, Jakob took up the reins once more.

"No. Don't let's move," Faivel said. "This is important. I want you to listen to every word." And Faivel came straight to the point. "The ukase regarding Jews and innkeepers has been rescinded. As of today. Our Czar, God rot and bless him, is full of whims." He grasped Jakob's shoulder. "You're free, my friend," he said.

"Where did you hear it?" Jakob asked, unbelieving. "Who told you?"

"Blomski. It's written in their bulletin. He showed me. Signed by Nicholas himself. To Zemach's," he shouted.

And so once again they made for the shortcut through the woods, singing their shameless joy to the trees.

"Old Meisels should live forever," Jakob sang.

"For ever and ever," Faivel chorused.

"What a wedding we shall have," Jakob said.

And so once again Jakob missed the market, and once more without fear of Esther's rebuke, for this time the news was good; and its value was irrevocable.

In the few days that remained before the wedding, Jakob kept himself indoors. He did not wish to risk an encounter with Meisels. In many ways he pitied him, and it was more for Meisels' sake than his own that he avoided a chance meeting. None of the customers in the tavern made mention of his return, or reported sight of him in the streets, so Meisels, too, was probably keeping himself indoors, stewing in a fury that Jakob dared not imagine.

The wedding took place in the ghetto's oldest and smallest synagogue. The Bindels did not want to advertise their triumph, and they did their best to call but small attention to their celebrations. But once the ceremony was over, and the tavern doors closed on the wedding guests, the festivities were loud, long, and without scruple.

The long table in the tavern was laid out with meats and savories. Faivel's Raisl, who was something of an expert in flower arrangement, had gathered a wide variety of dried grasses that grew in the fields behind the tavern and had arranged them as

harvest offerings. The guests crowded inside. Apart from Jakob's
close friends, there were officials of the community, entitled by
their standing to be invited to all joyful occasions, and though
Jakob knew some of them only slightly, he accorded them an
equal welcome. By this token, most of the members of the *kahal*
were present but for their chairman, whose absence was dis-
creetly unobserved. The thought of Meisels soured Jakob's joy.
He thought of him, crouched over his stove, brooding and seeth-
ing in his misfortune. He hoped some time would pass before he
would see him again. In the corner he noticed Zemach, his wife
and daughter at his side. He had been happy to invite Zemach to
his celebrations. Between them, over the last few weeks, there
had grown a firm bond based on their common hopes and curses.
He went over to them and urged him into his circle of friends.
Some of these had brought their hobby instruments, and the bala-
laikas outnumbered the accordions. Leon gave them all his cue
and dancing started on the floor. Even Miriam rose from her
accustomed nursing position, and waltzed the milk-brothers
around the floor, while they slept, the two of them, their faces
turned into the darkness of her flesh. And then Yankel arrived,
sealing, with his presence at the tavern door, the legitimacy of the
occasion. When Jakob saw him, he felt relieved. He called for
little Zena, and sent her with a plate of food and a beaker of wine
to the tavern door. Yankel acknowledged it, and raised his beaker
to his host.

For many hours they feasted and wined and danced. The
Bindels were celebrating more than a wedding, and though none
of the other guests, apart from Faivel and Zemach, suspected that
there might be other cause for celebration, the Bindels' exaggerated joy was infectious, and Sofia and Yosif's wedding feast
would be recalled in the ghetto for many years to come. And not
simply for its joy of celebration. For one other event was to make
it memorable.

Dusk was falling. The music was soft and soothing, and the
guests spoke almost in whispers. They had returned to their seats
to drink the various toasts of the day. The honor of the first toast
had been given to Faivel, who was to propose the health of the
bride and groom. He stood up and raised his glass. As he opened
his mouth to speak, Jakob noticed that his friend turned suddenly
pale. His wide astonished eyes were on the tavern door, and Jakob, together with the rest of the party, followed his gaze.

And there, in the true tradition of any fairy tale, the villain of the piece stood on the threshold, screaming his revenge. Mendel Meisels' large ungainly frame filled the tavern door, and poor and patient Yankel was forced inside the tavern, his right and proper place usurped. It was this displacement that disturbed Jakob even more than Meisels' sudden appearance, for it was as if, in Yankel's eviction, the whole natural order had been destroyed. Faivel put down his glass and stared at the late arrival, and so did all the others, and all were afraid, for his sudden raging presence was clearly uninvited and it seemed from the fire in his eyes that he had come to curse them all.

"You will pay, Jakob Bindel," he shouted. "Mendel Meisels will bide his time, but the day will come when he will surely destroy you." Then he turned, and was quickly gone.

And in the ensuing silence, the milk-brothers stirred and woke together; and together they started screaming.

Mendel Meisels waited. As he had promised them, he bided his time. He was a patient man, which was just as well, for he had to wait ten long years before an opportunity presented itself for his revenge. Much happened in that time. Sarah and little Zena married, and both brought their husbands to the tavern. Behind the back of the inn, Victor and Yuri had planted a vegetable garden and its produce fed the increased family and reaped a modest profit in the Thursday market. Between them they had five daughters. Sofia and Yosif contributed two children to the Bindel table, daughters too. It was as if the birth of the milk-brothers had sapped all trace of male inheritance. The tavern was still the central meeting place of the ghetto and rang with the laughter of a new generation, despite the fact that in those days there was little enough to laugh about. The Czar's attitude had hardened toward the Jews. The Pale of Settlement was narrowed down, and expulsions from towns and villages continued at a greater pace. The Czar's intention was to make the holy earth of Russia Jew-free. It is possible that the word *genocide* passed through his mind, and if not the word, then certainly the thought. But he did not consider it in the light of total annihilation. The Czar was still of the opinion that wholesale baptism could purify the Russian soil. To "Russianize" the Jew, to wean him from his Talmud and his Jewish gabardine, were steps in that direction. And to do that, there was only one course of action—conscription into the Russian army.

Until 1827 the Russian Jew had been exempt from military service and was obliged to pay heavy taxes in lieu. The 1827 ukase annulled these taxes and in their stead gave Jews the dubious honor of serving under their tormentors' flag. Jewish conscription was thorough and brutal. Unlike the Russian soldiers, Jews were required to serve for twenty-five years, and again unlike their Russian counterparts, they were recruited at the age of twelve. This last clause in the law was a veiled permit for child murder.

It was the duty of the *kahal* to provide the conscripts, or *Kantonisti,* as they were called, on the basis of ten for every thousand of the Jewish population. In the Odessa ghetto, grossly overcrowded as a result of village expulsions, and overburdened with the very young and the very old, the toll was especially punitive. And it put a burden on the *kahal* too, for if it did not fulfill its quota, its members were liable to fines or conscription. On the other hand, it was a sordid opportunity for the extortion of bribes, and few members of the *kahal* would forgo such gifts. So, unsurprisingly, it was the poor who had to pay the terrible price. They would often run away in fear and hide in the forests and the *kahals* would employ huntsmen, Jews themselves, to track them down. Thus a man like Mendel Meisels was kept very busy, filling his quotas and lining his pockets at the same time. Over the years, since the passing of the conscription law, Meisels had accrued wealth. But his appetite for revenge on Jakob Bindel did not cool, and he willed himself to live until such revenge were possible. The conscription law might well provide him with the key. Every week in the synagogue he had seen the Bindel tribe, and noted how the milk-brothers were loved and cosseted on all sides. They were now ten years old, and Mendel had sworn in the middle of the Sabbath prayer, on that consecrated ground, that they would not live to see their bar mitzvahs.

It was the week before Passover, and Meisels' quota was almost due. He was sitting in the *kahal* office, drawing up his conscript list, when a woman, black-shawled and weeping, stumbled into his room. Mendel was irritated. He was too busy for visitors, especially the poor with their endless complaints and pleadings. He had work to do. But the woman had already sat down on the chair in front of him, and deposited a large bag on his desk.

"It's about my sons," she blurted out. "They're all I have. You're sending them to the army. I've come to beg you, honored Mr. Meisels. There." She pointed to the bag. "Look inside. It's all I have."

Meisels looked at the leather case with disdain. He wondered whether it was worth his while even to bother to open it and look inside. The woman must have read his thoughts, for she leaned over and opened the clasp herself, spilling the contents of the bag onto his desk. Four small bundles of rouble notes.

Meisels looked at them with contempt. "You value your sons lightly," he said.

"It's my life's savings," the woman answered. Then she began to cry.

"What is your husband's living?" he said, ignoring her tears.

"He was a tailor. He's dead these ten years."

"And what do you do for a livelihood?"

"I sew, I bake, I do people's washing. Anything in the house," she almost pleaded.

Now it seemed to Meisels that she had something more interesting to offer than her miserable savings. A bribe paid in terms of service was always more exciting than one paid in simple coinage. It was more oppressive. "Stand up," he said to her. "Let me look at you."

The woman rose from her chair, trembling. She stood in front of him, straightening her body, holding her head high, even offering him a timid smile, for instinctively she knew that, whatever test she had to pass, it was related to her womanhood.

Meisels looked her over. "Take off your cape," he said, enjoying his command and her obedience.

The woman dropped her cape from her shoulders, letting it slide to the floor. It was an instinctive and totally unconscious gesture of seduction. But she wanted to please him, for his pleasure might benefit her sons.

"Turn around," Meisels said. "Turn slowly." And when she obeyed, Meisels trembled with a specific sense of authority that he had never experienced before. He eyed her carefully. The woman was clearly beyond childbearing, but she still had a good thigh on her.

"You will come to me every day," he said, "and serve me as housekeeper."

"And my sons?"

"I shall cross them off my list," he said.

The woman got down on her knees and crawled toward him. "You have my lifelong gratitude, sir," she said.

He trembled at the "sir." Life held great joy in store for him. "What's your name, woman?" he said, pocketing her life's savings.

"Lascevitch," she said. "Rachel Lascevitch." She was still kneeling at his feet. She would stay there until his questions were over.

"And your sons?"

"Judah and Lev Lascevitch," she said to his boots.

Meisels scanned his list until he found their names. "Look," he said.

She peered over the top of his desk, and saw how his manicured finger circled her sons' names. Then he took a pencil and deleted them.

"Go home," he said, "and sleep in peace. Your sons are safe. As long as you serve me," he added. "You will start early tomorrow, and make my house fit for the Passover."

The woman rose and pulled her cape around her. He handed her the empty leather bag.

"I shall never forget you," she said, making her way toward the door. "I shall speak your name in my prayers every night." Rachel Lascevitch would thus join a thousand other voices in the Odessa ghetto, but not to beg for God's blessing on Mendel Meisels, but His curses, loud and long, for having robbed them of their sons and their livelihoods.

When the woman had gone, Meisels laid out his list before him and counted the names. Now with the loss of the Lascevitch boys, he needed two more to complete his quota. Once again he went through his second list of eligible recruits, but he had already exhausted them by either blackmail or bribery. He was in something of a quandary. He had heard that in some cities of the Pale, the *kahals* were kidnapping eight- and nine-year-olds in a desperate bid to fill their quotas. Or sometimes, he had heard, they didn't even bother to kidnap them. They would forge a new date of birth on their papers, and recruit them legally. They were doing it in Vilna, Vitebsk, and Poldava. He had heard it on the *kahal* grapevine. What was so special about the Odessa *kahal* that it could not avail itself of the same maneuver?

Mendel Meisels had no problem with the selection of the two quota-fillers. Their names had been on his unforgiving lips for ten whole years. Their destruction had been in his nightly prayers. God had lent him His ear, and was now granting him a means for their annihilation. It paid to be a religious man, Mendel thought. He took out a clean sheet of official paper and dipped a new nib in the inkwell. And in his neatest and most official hand, he

wrote, "For the attention of the Recruiting Officer." He could as
well have donned a black cap and pronounced the death sentence
on them all. Dipping his pen once more, and licking his lips, he
headed his list with the milk-brothers' names. Then he put down
his pen. He would complete the list in the morning; he had already done more than a day's work. He had brought to fruition
the result of ten years' travail, of carefully keeping his wound
green. A decade of unrelenting rancor had at last come to an end.

It was the eve of Passover. The ghetto streets were deserted,
and candlelight flickered from every window. The Seder service
was about to begin, the feast that heralds the eight days of the
Passover. Every household in the ghetto was celebrating, as they
did every year, remembering with prayers and symbols the expulsion of the Jews from Egypt and their forty years' wandering in
the wilderness. The Bindels were holding their Seder in the tavern, a room large enough to accommodate their family and
friends. Miriam and Leon sat at the end of the table. The milk-
brothers were seated in pride of place at the head of the table,
Jakob and Esther beside them, together with the Pinskis and
Faivel and Raisl, whose children had long left home. Esther lit
the candles and said the blessings. All was in order for the ceremony to begin. The tavern door was firmly closed. After the meal
it would be opened, as would all the doors of the ghetto, in order
to allow the entrance of Elijah, that prophet of redemption,
whose full cup of wine shivered to the brim. Jakob rose to sing
the first blessing of sanctification, and all those around the table
drank the first of the four glasses of wine. It was time for the four
questions, traditionally asked by the youngest member at the table. This year the duty fell to Shoshannah, Sofia's youngest, who,
though she could not read, had learned them by rote. Sofia
proudly lifted her onto her chair. Shoshannah needed little
prompting. Her cheeks were flushed with excitement. She took a
deep breath, as she had been taught to do, and the first question
was posed loud and clear.

"Why is this night different from all other nights?" she said.
As soon as the question was out, there was a loud banging on the
tavern door, as if the caller, whoever it was, had brought the
answer.

And answer it was of a kind, of an updated history, from a
minion of another Pharaoh, of an Egypt that was now called

czarist Russia. Jakob paled. He knew that whatever was behind that door on such a holy night could only augur ill. Faivel too feared the worst, and so did Dov Pinski and Leon, and all three rose to support Jakob in his fear. Shoshannah burst into tears, her long-rehearsed recital so rudely interrupted. The milk-brothers stretched out their hands to each other, and clasped them. They too rose, so that only the women were left seated.

"We must be calm," Jakob whispered.

There was more banging at the door. "Open up," a voice cried. Jakob waited for some identification, though he knew from the authoritative and self-assured tone that it belonged to an official, and a hostile one at that. He turned and went to the tavern door.

He opened it wide, as if he had nothing to hide, displaying the Seder table in all its quiet solemnity, hoping to indicate to the caller the peace he had shattered. But beneath his apparent calm, Jakob was trembling, for he recognized on the intruder the hated uniform of the recruiting officer. And in the same moment he confirmed to himself that he and Leon were beyond recruiting age. Victor and Yuri carried forged papers, and were still officially registered in the village from which they had fled. That left only the milk-brothers, who, even according to that terrible law, were still minors. Over the years since the enforcement of the law, he had not unduly worried about them. He was rich enough to buy their exemption. But he had not reckoned with Meisels. Even Meisels, he considered, could not be that cruel. But Meisels must have lied about their age. For what other reason could this officer be standing at his door? He pictured the two children swamped in army greatcoats. "No, no," he pleaded.

The officer handed him a document with the Czar's red seal emblazoned across the vellum. The summons was penned in Russian, and translated into Yiddish in Meisels' gleeful hand. It ordered the appearance of Reuben Wolf and Benjamin Bindel at the conscription center at eight o'clock the following morning.

"But it's a Holy Day," Jakob mumbled, knowing how irrelevant was such a plea.

"A *Jewish* Holy Day," the officer almost spat. "Here we abide by Christian law."

Jakob reread the summons, and the lie of the milk-brothers' birth date. "But they're only ten," he pleaded.

The officer looked at the document. "Not according to the *kahal,*" he said. "*Your* people. Your honest leaders." Then he

bent his mouth to Jakob's ear. "Are they really only ten?" he
whispered. His voice was gentle, as if he too were a father, and
from it Jakob gleaned a measure of hope.

"I swear by all that's holy that they are ten."

"The *kahal*'s word is law," the man said sadly. "There's nothing I can do. In Vitebsk, they're taking them at eight. Hold their
look, father," he said, "for it is a gaze that must last you for some
twenty-five years. I hope you will live to see them again."

Now Jakob broke down completely.

When the recruiting officer had gone, Esther came quickly to
Jakob's side, and took his arm. She shut the door and led him
back to the table.

Shoshannah was persuaded once more to be the Seder questioner. She stood high on her chair, but the old self-confidence
would not return. She had to start once more at the beginning,
since, having learned all four questions by rote, she could not
pick them up at random. "Why is this night different from all
other nights?" she asked again. But now everybody around the
Seder table knew the answer, even little Shoshannah.

Jakob answered the four questions in turn, outlining the story
of the Egyptian bondage, and the ten plagues that God visited
upon the oppressors. And as they spilled one drop of red wine for
each plague, Jakob prayed that each one be visited upon Meisels.
"Blood," he mouthed, "and frogs. Vermin and murrain; noxious
beasts and boils; hail and locusts. And darkness. Let it shroud
him for the rest of his days."

A drop of wine trickled on his finger to pronounce the last and
most terrible plague of all. The slaying of the firstborn male. That
curse he could not put upon Meisels, for Meisels had squarely
laid it at his own tavern door. He stood up, his *Haggadah* in his
hand, and pointed with his blooded finger to the phrase that was
the very heart of the Seder. "In every generation," he sobbed, "let
each man regard himself as if he personally had gone forth from
Egypt." Then he sat down. He could pray no further.

Esther announced that they would eat, but that they would
forgo the eating of the bitter herbs, for they needed no reminder
of the bitterness of bondage. It dwelt with them now at that very
table. The meal that had been prepared with such care and such
joy was consumed in sad silence. After the meal, Jakob was to say
grace. But he rose from his seat and left the table. He was in no
mood to thank God for the blessings of his house. He strode to

the tavern door, and suddenly a flicker of life sparked within him.
He opened the door wide, as all the ghetto celebrants were doing
at the time, and he shouted the verse from the *Haggadah* into the
silent cobbled streets.

"Pour out Thy wrath upon the heathen who will not acknowledge Thee and upon the kingdoms that invoke not Thy name, for
they have devoured Jacob, and laid waste his dwelling."

Then he closed the door softly, and leaned his head on the
lintel, sobbing as if his heart would break.

The guests dispersed in silence, and all the children were sent
to bed. Then the men of the house sat around the Seder table, and
made plans for the milk-brothers' flight from bondage.

Sofia had withdrawn to the kitchen with the other women. She
knew that Meisels had maneuvered the recruitment, and she
knew why he now sought his terrible revenge. She could not help
feeling that she and she alone was responsible for the milk-brothers' sacrifice. "I shall walk in the garden a little," she said to
Zena, who was sorting the dishes at the stove, and she threw on
her cloak and left the tavern. The ghetto streets were deserted.
Candles still flickered through some of the windows and from
time to time she heard the closing songs of the Seder service. She
made her way to Meisels' house. She had no idea of what she
would say to him or whether indeed he would receive her. But
she knew that she had to go to him, to show herself to him in the
hope that her beauty could still move him.

She waited for a while before his door, shivering as she recalled
his ugliness and cruelty. Then she knocked with a strength and
anger that astonished her. She heard his slippered tread behind
the door, and she prayed that he was not already in his night
attire. She heard the bolt slipping inside and she caught sight of
his white nightgown in the crack of the door. She was terrified
and wanted to run quickly away, but her fear rooted her there.
Meisels gasped when he saw her and he stared at her for a long
while. Her fear and trembling served to enhance her frail beauty,
and his heart, withered as it was, opened to her, and in that
moment he would have granted her anything. But only for a
moment. For then he realized the magnitude of his loss.

"What do you want, my child?" he asked, though he knew well
enough. He took her arm and guided her into the house. He tried
not to notice how she shivered at his touch. She would not move

beyond the hall. She did not seek a greater intimacy. She was neither a guest nor a casual visitor. She was a supplicant.

"You can't take the milk-brothers," she shouted at him. She regretted the hate that rang so clearly in her voice. She needed a favor from him, and favors were pleaded for in gentle tones.

He took offense immediately. "And why not?" he said. "It's the law."

"That's not your reason," she shouted at him again. "It's your revenge. You know it is."

She was crying now and Meisels clenched his hands behind his back, for the urge to take her into his arms was overwhelming.

"What can I do, my little Sofia?" he said.

How dare he address me in such a manner, she thought, but she held her tongue.

"What can I do?" he said again. "I need to fill my quota."

"There are others," she said, and hated herself for saying so, but she could not bear her father's pain.

"Oh, yes, there are others," he said. "I can think of one at least."

"Then . . . ?" She looked him in the face for the first time, her tearful eyes full of hope.

"I'll make a bargain with you," he said. "I'll strike the milk-brothers off the list and replace them with the one I know. My quota will be short, but for your sake, I'll take that risk." She fell on her knees then, and whispered her gratitude to the hem of his nightshirt.

"How can I thank you?" she said.

He raised her from the ground. Then he put his arm around her waist, and in that moment she knew that the price of his bargain was more than she would bear.

"I'll give you the milk-brothers for Yosif," he said.

She stared at him unbelieving. He was bargaining for a twenty-five-year tenure on her body. No more. No less. Her mouth welled with saliva and this she gave to him, spitting squarely into his terrible face. Then she hurried to the door, fearful of a whipping, and let herself out into the street. She ran through the ghetto trying to muffle her footsteps on the cobbles, and she did not stop until she reached the back door of the tavern.

The following morning the Bindel household rose very early. Esther had packed a portmanteau of warm clothing and a store

of food that would last for several days. Apart from the horror of
the summons itself, its arrival was grossly ill-timed. The following day was a Holy Day in the ghetto. There would be no wagons
on the road, which limited the possibilities of flight. The only
avenue of escape open to the brothers was the forests behind the
tavern, the very spot where the *khapers* would go hunting. But on
the first day of Passover there was no alternative. On the second
day a few people would appear on the streets. Faivel had volunteered to cross the ghetto in his wagon and hide the brothers
under bales of cloth. He would take them to the forests behind
Zemach's tavern, where their whereabouts would not be suspect.
If, with God's help, they remained undetected, they could be
smuggled in a timber wagon to Vilna, where Faivel had a brother.
All night long, Leon and Jakob prayed together, and so, in their
separate dwellings, did Faivel and Dov Pinski.

At milking time Leon went to the yard, as was his custom, and
the milk-brothers followed him. There were now three cows in
the Bindel holding, and one was assigned to each of them. Both
Benjamin and Reuben had Leon's gentle touch and it was the
happiest time of their day when the three went together to the
sheds. The brothers were especially quiet that morning. They had
been told of their recruitment and the plans for their escape.
They could not help but feel excited at the prospect of such adventure, but they were also a little afraid. And sad, too, that they
must leave the tavern and the laughter it contained. But what
saddened them most of all was the desolate look in their parents'
eyes, betraying a pain that in no way matched their own.

"We'll be all right," the milk-brothers kept telling them, with
such confidence and faith that it pointed to a total ignorance of
how deeply their survival was threatened.

Leon finished his milking and lingered. He watched the milk-
brothers at work, and prayed for their deliverance. In his own
heart he held out little hope for their escape, and he turned his
face away from them and fought to hold back his tears.

"I've finished," both milk-brothers said after a while.

"I'll miss you," Benjamin said, nuzzling the cow's cheek, while
Reuben stroked his own farewell caress. Leon took their hands
and led them back into the tavern.

At the counter, Miriam and Esther were wrapping the parcel
of food. Jakob sat at a table, his head in his hands. When he felt
the children at his side, he lowered his hands and his eyes

lingered on their faces. He drank in the image of them, etching their gentle beauty in his mind's eye, for he did not think that he would ever look upon them again. After a while he beckoned them, and to the others he said, "Leave us awhile."

Leon and the women went to the back rooms, and the milk-brothers kept their eyes on the floor, because they could not bear Jakob's almost palpable pain.

Jakob gathered the boys into his arms. "Look at me, children," he said.

The boys shifted themselves and raised their eyes and stared at him, with a gaze of such intensity that they saw only around and beyond him, and thus avoided the film of tears that dimmed his eye.

"I want you to live," he said. He gripped their arms. "I want you to survive," he shouted. Then he paused, loosening his grip. "You may be caught in the forest, and then you will have to be soldiers. You will be taken a long way from home, and sometimes you will be very sad. But every day you must think of us in the tavern, and think of our love for you, and that will give you strength. Life will be hard for you," he said. "They will give you strange food to eat, the food of the Christian. They will offer you pig, and you will eat it. Do you hear me?" He was shouting again. "You will eat it because without food you will die." Then he sank his head into his hands and wept uncontrollably.

"We'll be all right," the milk-brothers whispered, and they kissed the top of Jakob's head and stroked his hair. He clasped their hands. "They will force you into baptism," he said. "You must not resist them. Let them sprinkle their holy water on your brows, let them flood your bodies with their purging priesthood. They cannot lay hands on your Jewish soul. You must survive, my children," he said again. "Listen to me." He took them both in his arms. "Beware of principles. Abandon them. You must if you are to survive." Jakob knew that they could have no idea of what he was talking about, but he had to speak out if only for his own sake.

"There is no cause on earth worth dying for," he said, "no God worth one's dying breath, no country worth one's martyrdom, no principle worth one's sacrifice. Only in the name of love is death worthy. And friendship. Therefore make no friends. Friendship seduces sacrifice. Avoid it."

The milk-brothers looked at each other, and Jakob thought for one moment that they might have understood him. Then he gathered them in his large embrace.

"You must survive, my children," he said again. "Listen to me. Love each other as you have always done, and give each other your protection. Never go to bed in a state of quarrel. Settle your differences before sleep. Remember us all and all the love that binds us together. That will give you strength."

Leon tiptoed into the cabin. "We must go," he said. "It's getting light."

Miriam and Esther stood behind him and the children rushed into their mothers' arms. No word was said. They held each other silently for a long time. Then Esther tucked the parcels under their elbows. They took Leon's hands and left the tavern.

And so they went into the forest, fleeing their own Pharaoh, their unleavened bread in their baggage, and terror in their heels.

Later that morning Jakob and the women went to the synagogue. Their absence would have been conspicuous. Meisels, especially, would have noticed it, and suspected its cause. He would note too the absence of the milk-brothers and he would surmise that his vengeance was complete. In the women's gallery, Miriam and Esther stared vacantly into space, holding back their tears. The service of the first day of the Passover was no occasion for mourning, so their tears, if they had flowed, could not be attributed to the solemnity of the prayer. Below, Jakob sat next to Faivel. Meisels sat in a front seat, and a mere turn of his head would have forced some exchange. Jakob, for his part, had no intention of avoiding Meisels' eye. He would face him with pride and dignity, despite the torment in his heart. But Meisels kept his gaze ahead. He had no wish to look Bindel in the face. Although he had no regrets for his actions, he knew that what he had done was terrible, that he had wrought a revenge of such magnitude that it was grossly out of proportion to the insult he himself had suffered. So he sat motionless, his eyes in the prayer book but with no prayer on his lips. In his heart he relished the thought of Rachel Lascevitch, and the festive meal she would have prepared for his lunchtime diversion. He started to mouth the prayers, thinking all the time of Rachel Lascevitch's thighs, and a small spittle dribbled down his chin. He had it in mind to leave the synagogue immediately after the end of the service, to forgo the usual parleying in the courtyard, and to give Bindel a wide berth.

Jakob's eyes were also in the prayer book, but the prayer in his

heart was not written on the page. In his mind he was following
the children through the forest, timing their progress, pacing
their flight. At his side, Faivel was doing the same. He cursed the
Holy Days. Escape on an ordinary working day, when the ghetto
thronged with crowd and activity, would have been so much
easier than the lonely route of exposed forest. He feared the
worst, and he clutched Jakob's arm in a gesture of support.

When the service was over, Jakob watched Meisels making his
quick getaway. "Come back to the tavern," Jakob said to his
friend. "We need company."

As the two men crossed the synagogue courtyard and met up
with their women, they noticed that many of the congregation
turned away their faces, and shifted their positions to avoid them.
News spread quickly in the ghetto, and there was no doubt that
Bindel's tragedy was known. Known too, or at least surmised,
was the attempt to escape, and it was the need to keep that a
secret that prompted Jakob's friends to avoid discussion. When
the children were known to be safe, they would go to the tavern
and share his joy, and if, God forbid, the children were caught,
they would make the same journey to share in his mourning.

They walked slowly through the ghetto streets. Almost seven
hours had passed since the children had left the tavern. The
longer they stayed in hiding, the better their chances of complete
escape. If only they could remain undetected until the following
day, they could be smuggled out of the ghetto and onto a wagon.
And once the shouting had died down, Jakob would apply for a
travel permit to Vilna, and hold the children in his arms once
more. A smile crept over his face at such a thought, but quickly
froze as he heard and saw the marching feet along the cobbles.
He rushed to his women and hid their faces in his cape, to shield
them from the sight of what he was convinced was a nightmare in
broad daylight. He tried to concentrate on the two uniformed
figures walking on each side of the street, the guns slung on their
shoulders. He stared at their faces, trying not to wonder why they
marched so far apart, blinding himself to the pitiful struggle that
squirmed and writhed between them. He kept his eyes on their
faces, and a lump rose in his throat as he recognized the scum
features of the *khapers,* and he wondered with disgust how they
could go about their rotten work on such a Holy Day. Then he
forced himself to look at his children, and he uttered a loud wail
of pain. The milk-brothers looked up and saw him and saw, too,

his protection of Esther and Miriam. And at once they ceased
their struggle and managed between them a wan smile. Jakob had
ordered them to survive. They straightened their bodies, and they
held their heads high, a pair of unhumbled *Kantonistis,* and they
fell into the *khapers'* marching rhythm.

Jakob watched them out of sight, and when they'd turned the
corner of the street, he unwrapped his cape and held his women
close. "They have died, our children," he wept. "We must go
home and say *kaddish.* We must mourn for them."

The tavern door was open, and through it Jakob could see the
hunched figure of Leon, leaning over the counter, his body
shaken with sobs. On the walls of the tavern the mirrors and
pictures were already draped with white sheets. Leon had prepared for the mourning. When he heard them come into the
tavern, he turned and went toward them. He linked his arms in
their mourning circle. "We didn't get very far," he sobbed. Then
they lowered themselves to the floor, as mourners do, humbling
themselves to God's solace.

"Magnified and sanctified be Thy great name in the world,
which He has created according to His will," Jakob sang, his
voice broken with anger and desolation. Faivel joined in, and
gradually a whole chorus of men from the synagogue, to whom
the rumor and the wailing had spread, and who now gathered in
Jakob's tavern to share in his sorrow.

"O Lord, what is man?" they wailed. "His days are of grass; as
a flower in the field, so he flourisheth. For the wind passeth over
it, and it is gone."

Suddenly Jakob rose, and made his stumbling way through the
back of the tavern. Once in the yard, he lifted his arms to heaven,
and he let forth a sobbing scream of such grief and affliction that
the fearful ghetto echoed with its sound, and was giddied by its
heart's turning.

After the synagogue service Mendel Meisels went straight
home. Mrs. Lascevitch was waiting for him. As he opened his
front door, she hurried toward him to help him off with his cape.
He tugged a little at the top button, thwarting her efforts. He
wanted her to work at his service, and also to tease her a little.
From the hall he could smell the aroma of her cooking and his
nostrils flared with appetite. He went straight into his dining
room and sat himself at the head of the large mahogany table,,

where Mrs. Lascevitch had set his place. He noted the shining
display of his late wife's silver that his new treasure had rum-
maged from the cupboards and returned, as new, to its proper
place. He noted, too, the bunch of fresh-cut flowers on the sideboard, the cut-glass vase reflected in its high polish. He sighed
with satisfaction. It was like being married again. At least in the
area of domesticity. The rest could be taken care of with a little
maneuvering. He unfolded his napkin, fingering its white
starched linen with relish. Then he spread it over his ample chest,
and waited to be served. After a while Mrs. Lascevitch came in
with a tureen of soup. She set it beside him and served him herself. He noticed her white apron smock that covered her long
black dress. The thought crossed his mind to order her to wear
thick black stockings, the uniform of the common servant of the
time. He watched her go back to the kitchen, her quarters, and
imagined her preparing the next course of meat, garnishing it as a
dish fit for her master. He slurped his soup noisily. Her borscht
tasted even better than his late wife's. He gave a passing thought
to Jakob Bindel and the blow that he had caused him to suffer
that day. He did not let it trouble him. He had no doubt that the
milk-brothers, poor devils, were safely in custody, and probably
by now kitted out for army life. He had known that they would
make an attempt to escape, and he had known too that on this
Holy Day there was no way of getting through the ghetto unnoticed. Which was why he had ordered the summons for that very
day. Tonight the *khapers* would come to him with their report,
and he would relish every detail of their capture. He smiled into
his now empty soup plate, and raised his head, carrying the smile
to Mrs. Lascevitch, who was bearing a dish of meats. Quickly he
wiped the smile from his face. Servants were not thus to be favored.

She served him deftly, taking care with the layout on his plate,
apportioning each item separately and heeding their symmetry.
Not once did she look at him or speak one word, and when she
was done, she turned her back on him and walked away. Had
Meisels seen her face, he would have noted a look of contemptuous disgust. But he only saw that stooped servile back of hers,
and he marveled at the sudden surge of youth in his loins, and
considered that never in his life had he struck a better bargain.

In the kitchen, Mrs. Lascevitch consoled herself with the
thought of her sons' freedom. That morning, on her way to Mei-

sels' house, she had heard from the butcher of the milk-brothers' summons. The news depressed her profoundly. She knew that at such a young age they must have been desperate quota-fillers for Meisels' monthly contingent. Her sons' exemption had forced those children's recruitment. She tried not to feel guilty. Straight after work she would go to the Bindel tavern with her shame, and on a low stool, she would mourn with them. For it could have been her own *kaddish* for her own two sons. Meisels was an evil man, she thought as she emptied the compote of fruit into a dish, and she hoped it would choke him.

She took it into the dining room. Meisels had cleared his plate, as well as the extra portion she had laid before him. He had a pig's appetite, she thought. She ladled the fruit onto his plate and left the bowl, so that he could not call her back.

"The fire is low," he said. "It needs another log."

Mrs. Lascevitch thought of her late husband, who would have seen to their fire himself. It was not women's work to carry coals. But she did not complain. Instead she concentrated on her plan to get herself and her children out of the ghetto and flee to Kiev, where she had a sister, and where her sons could hide unregistered. But for that she needed money. Both her sons worked as wagoners and it would take time to accumulate the wherewithal for travel and bribed papers. She herself worked well into the night on her dressmaking. It was a hard life, but Rachel Lascevitch was a woman who could count her blessings without any sense of abdication. She stole a glance at Meisels' wretched countenance. With all his wealth, she was better off than he. She had children and a host of good memories.

"Would you put on a log?" he said. "Before the fire goes out altogether."

She skirted the dining table and crossed over to the fireplace. That morning she had carried a pile of logs from the yard outside the house and stacked them on the side of the hearth. She bent down to lift a log and Meisels watched her. With joy he noted that she was wearing black woolen stockings after all. He knew and did not care that he could no longer contain his excitement. He lowered the spoon from his mouth, removed the napkin from his chest, fiddled with his buttons, and made to rise. He waited until she had placed the log on the fire and was poking it into position, and then, unable to restrain himself any longer, he leapt on her, grabbing her from behind. The astonished woman did not

move. Her hand stiffened over the poker, and she stared into the
fire in total disbelief. And in the flames she saw the flickering
image of the milk-brothers in army greatcoats, their linked hands
hidden. Then she knew what she had to do. She turned quickly
and stared at him. She was not in the least surprised to find him
unbuttoned. Then she struck him on the chest with the hot poker
that quivered in her hand.

Mendel Meisels fell backward, catching the cup of his neck on
the brass fire fender. She watched him fall, and she listened to his
howl of pain. "I am sent from the milk-brothers," she screamed
at him. She waited until his eyes rolled to the ceiling and his
writhing head lay still. Then she put the poker back in its place,
took her coat and bag from the hall, and left the house.

That evening the *khapers* came to Mendel's house to make
their report. They banged on the heavy oak door, and were surprised when there was no response. They thought Meisels might
be sleeping and they banged again. He had requested their report
most earnestly, so it was unlikely that he was away from home.
They knocked again, and their noise brought neighbors out of
their houses. But when they saw the *khapers,* they quickly went
indoors, for the sight of such officials brought fear and contempt
into their hearts. One of the men then opened a side window, and
through it he could see the dining table, and underneath a pair of
boots, which were, without doubt, attached to a lying figure. He
called to his companion. Between them they decided that this
was a matter that called for a witness of a higher authority than
their own, and they agreed to call on Blomski. So one of the men
stayed to keep watch, while the other went to Blomski's house.
The street was silent. The neighbors still kept themselves indoors,
but they peeped through their windows for any sign of change.
For it was clear from the expression on the *khapers'* faces, as they
looked through Meisels' window, that something was amiss in
the house, a house on which they had often prayed calamity to
fall. They were excited. There was an indisputable air of foul and
beautiful play abroad. They lay in wait for its final proof.

After a while the *khaper* returned with a worried Blomski hurrying at his heels. Blomski was invited to the window, and the
neighbors caught his look of fearful concern. Then he was seen to
nod, and one of the *khapers* opened the window wide, and
climbed inside. After a while the front door opened and Blomski
and the second *khaper* went inside. The front door closed on the

witnesses, and they waited hopefully for the blessed clap of thunder.

Once inside the house, the intruders hesitated in the hall. They smelled death there and each was loath to seek out its source.

"We mustn't touch anything," Blomski said, instinctively sensing that murder was afoot. A man like Meisels, with so many enemies, stood little chance of dying of natural causes.

The sight of Meisels' corpse came as little surprise. It was the fact that it was unbuttoned that astonished them. The *khapers* began to giggle. The sight of Meisels' pathetic purple member drooping between his legs was ludicrously incompatible with the power and the authority he had wielded during his lifetime. Blomski was silent and depressed. He already felt the burdensome mantle of chairmanship. He knelt down at Meisels' side, and buttoned him. "He was on his way to relieve himself," he said. "And he fell. He knocked his head on the fender. It was a fatal blow." Blomski was taking upon himself the role of coroner. He had to. He suspected murder. And possibly the murderer as well. He was privy to the deal Meisels had made with Mrs. Lascevitch, and his unbuttoned state had clearly given her a motive. But such possibilities should not be rumored abroad. The man was dead and should be allowed to lie in peace. He looked up at the *khapers*, challenging their possible denial. "It was an accident," he said. "There's no doubt about it. Go to Strachinsky's," he said to one of the *khapers*. Yossel Strachinsky was the ghetto undertaker. "Tell him what's happened. He should come with the doctor. You will stay here," he said to the other, "and let no one inside. I myself shall go to make the arrangements for the funeral."

He looked at the corpse for a moment. It was not a pretty sight. "Let us take off the tablecloth," he said, "and cover him." The *khapers* removed the remains of Meisels' lunch from the table, and one of them could not resist a spoonful of Mrs. Lascevitch's fruit compote. Then the other *khaper* followed suit, and though Blomski's mouth watered, he refrained, for it seemed irreverent to consume a dead man's meal.

"That's enough," he said, and he took the cloth and spread it over the corpse. "Let us go," he said.

The neighbors saw the front door open, but no news could be read on the men's faces. They watched them down the street, then turned away. But some of them lingered and, shortly after-

ward, were rewarded with the sight of Strachinsky's wagon, covered with a black cloth outlining the coffin shape beneath, and
there was quiet joy in their hearts. In the wake of the wagon came
the doctor and four men, recognizable as the ghetto washers,
those who cleansed and shrouded the dead before burial. They
watched Strachinsky as he unloaded the coffin and took it into
the house. The doctor and the washers followed him, and once
more the heavy oak door was closed.

Then the neighbors left their houses and gathered in small
groups on the street, whispering the good news abroad, scuttling
it across the ghetto. It skirted Jakob's tavern, for that was already
a house of mourning, but in its time it reached Faivel's dwelling.
And Faivel wept. Not for the monster's death, but for its brutal
ill-timing. Later on, when he went to the tavern, he said nothing
to his friend, but Jakob's heartache was edged that evening with
bitterness, and Faivel surmised that he had heard the news. But
neither man made mention of Meisels' name. It would have sullied the milk-brothers' memory.

But later on that same week Faivel broke the ghetto curfew,
and went out in the dead of night, and made his way to the
cemetery. And there, on his friend's behalf, he danced on Mendel
Meisels' grave.

Although Benjamin Bindel was older than his milk-brother by a mere five minutes, Reuben, the younger, regarded him as his protector. Even though Benjamin was the shorter of the two, Reuben looked up to his twin with adoration and respect. Benjamin was his leader, and he, his willing apostle. Reuben had a striking beauty, and his large, almost black eyes reflected that distant look of spiritual engagement that he took from Leon, his father. Benjamin, on the other hand was, like Jakob, of solid and stocky build. His mien and his gait spoke of utter reliability. When the boy was captured, it was Benjamin who stretched out his arms to shield his milk-brother, as if to offer himself to the *khapers* for both of them. On the way out of the forest Benjamin had whispered to Reuben to take his chances and run. He trusted that the guns their captors carried would not be fired on a Holy Day, and certainly not on one of their own kind. But Reuben did not want to leave his milk-brother. Even now, as their captors led them into the synagogue yard, Benjamin urged him to run, but Reuben whispered his refusal. Whatever hell lay in store, they would share it.

The *khapers* shoved the boys toward the synagogue door. The rabbi was just leaving, but when he saw the *khapers* he knew why they had come, and at what gruesome ritual he was expected to officiate. He took the boys' hands and led them into the synagogue. He sat them down in front of the Holy Ark.

"I won't be long," he said gently. "Everything will be all right." Then he disappeared through a side door.

The milk-brothers were not unduly afraid despite the sullen presence of the *khapers* behind them. Nothing untoward could happen to them in a holy place and they smiled feebly at each other, clinging still to that sense of adventure that had quickened their forest flight in the early hours, in that dawn which now seemed to them so many years ago. For since leaving the tavern, they had become old men, and now the rabbi reappeared with old men's clothes to confirm it. Clothes to which their young years were not entitled—long shroudlike robes, prayer shawls, and phylacteries.

"You must put them on," the rabbi whispered. "It's the law. It's a bit like dressing up," he added with a smile, trying to blunt the awful implications of the ceremony he was bound to perform. The boys donned the robes and shawls, and wound the phylacteries around their arms as they had seen their fathers do at their morning prayers. "Let me try them, Father," they had often pleaded. "Time enough," Jakob would say. "After your bar mitzvah." Now to wind them about their ten-year-old arms was a little premature perhaps, and there was some mischief in it and an element of adventure. They giggled and the rabbi was glad of it. There would be time enough in their young lives, if they lived long enough, to forget the sounds and tastes of laughter. He led them to stand by the Holy Ark. The *khapers* approached and stood one on either side of them.

"We are ready," one of them said.

Then the rabbi walked slowly and humbly to the Ark and drew the curtains. He was reluctant to let the holy Torah bear witness to the violence perpetrated against its children. "Now repeat after me," one of the *khapers* said. "One at a time. I, Benjamin Bindel."

Benjamin echoed his words, and with little understanding he repeated each phrase of the endless recital. "I promise, in the name of God, our Father, and of His son, Jesus Christ . . ." Benjamin hesitated and looked at the rabbi, as if to ask his permission. Imperceptibly the rabbi nodded, and raised his hand to shield the sacred Torah. Benjamin sputtered over the lifelong forbidden words, while the rabbi sadly nodded his encouragement.

"I hereby swear," the *khaper* went on, "an oath of allegiance to my Lord and Czar, Nicholas the First, to serve him in his mighty army, with loyalty and with courage, and with total obedience to his law." Benjamin echoed each word, without hearing or listening to the sounds, so choked was he still on the blasphemy he had uttered, and his bewilderment that the holy rabbi had sanctioned it. He was drained now of all hope of adventure. For the first time he sensed the reality of their heathen and godforsaken future.

When Benjamin was done with the pledge for life and death in

His Imperial Majesty's service, the other *khaper* started on Reuben. Reuben was prepared and, under his shroud, his fingers were crossed against the blasphemy he knew he would be called upon to utter. And when it came, so oily smooth out of the *khaper*'s mouth, he thought of his grandfather Jakob, and how he had urged them, at whatever cost, to make it their supreme business to survive. Perhaps the utterance of that name was part of the price of survival, so when it came, Reuben pronounced it loud and clear, as if it were a lifeline.

The rabbi patted the boys' shrouded shoulders, as if they had done their lessons well. Then he took up the ram's horn and put it to his lips.

Across the ghetto wailed the howl of lamentation, a mourning out of season, a requiem for orphaned sons, an elegy for fathers and mothers bereft, an anthem for an entire tribe. And as its echo died away, the people left their homes and made their way to Jakob Bindel's tavern.

But Benjamin and Reuben saw nothing of their own obsequies. They were quietly disrobed and hurried into a covered wagon at the back of the synagogue. They huddled together, smelling each other's fear for the first time. They rode in silence for a long while. Even the *khapers*, who were wont to chatter endlessly between themselves, now fell silent, their faces drawn with such desolation that the milk-brothers almost felt sorry for them. "This is the last time I'll do it," one of them said, and they were the only words spoken throughout the whole journey.

At last the wagon halted, and the *khapers* took the boys' hands. One of them actually said he was sorry, and Benjamin saw a tear start in his eye. "Don't worry," Benjamin said with a little sympathy. "Your Jesus will look after you." He was astonished at how easily his lips could shape the word, and he was glad of it, for it meant a numbing of the senses, a steeling of the heart, an inert armor that would enable him to endure all the deprivations his father had woefully prophesied. He hoped that Reuben's heart would harden too, all of it but for a small throbbing nest within, which would guard and shelter the love between them, and he prayed for that same sanctuary in himself.

In front of them was a low-slung building that was an army barracks. The *khapers*, anxious now to take their leave, directed them toward the entrance and hurriedly returned to the wagon without any word of farewell. The milk-brothers watched them

as the cart turned on its own axis and trundled out of sight.
Reuben took Benjamin's hand, but Benjamin gently withdrew his
support, smiling in an attempt to cover his cruel gesture. Reuben
had to harden himself for a hardened heart seeks no protection.

A drill sergeant met them at the gate and shouted a command
in Russian. The milk-brothers were fairly schooled in the
nonghetto language. Jakob had taught them, and occasionally
Faivel with his stories. They obeyed the sergeant's command and
rushed to his side as he marched them into the barracks and to a
counter where a line of young and new recruits were already
waiting. They turned when they saw the newcomers, eager for
conversation. Where did they come from? How were they taken?
Did they too have to utter that terrible word while the holy
Torah stared down at them from the Ark? The friendly Yiddish
tumbled from their frightened lips, and Benjamin and Reuben
were stabbed with such pangs of homesickness that both reached
for the other's hand. Only a few of the recruits were from Odessa.
Most of them came from the outlying villages and had been taken
in much the same way as the milk-brothers. But they told their
stories with no sense of adventure. From the very beginning,
amid the wailing and the lamentation, they had seen their own
deaths as inevitable. And as their parents in the villages were at
that moment lamenting their loss, they were mourning for themselves, tugging at their ringlet sidelocks for some measure of support. For all the village boys were orthodox Chasidic Jews, and
the ringlet was a mark of their sect. Though they were wont to
worship with joy in their hearts, their prayers a splendid glorification of God, there was little joy on their faces now and less expectation. Benjamin was wary of them. They were losers, the lot of
them, and he feared their contagion. He drew Reuben to his side.

"Why are we waiting?" Benjamin asked.

"They'll give us our uniform," one of them said. "What's your
name?"

"Benjamin."

"And I'm Reuben, his . . ."

He was about to say "nephew," but he was too tired to deal
with the confusion that would ensue. "His brother," he said, and
left it at that.

"I'm Yossel," the ringlet replied. "My brother's with me too,"
he said. "His name's Lev. He's got his uniform. They took him in
that room over there." He shook his ringlets in the direction of

the door at the far end of the barracks, and as they looked they
saw the door open, and a herd of young children, swamped in
noisy greatcoats, shuffled through the door. Their feet were invisible, but from the sound of them, they were clearly burdened with
great boots, many sizes too large. All that was visibly human was
a mass of tiny heads, each one seemingly like the other. It was a
grotesque spectacle.

Yossel gave a little cry. He knew that his brother was among
them, yet there was no way of knowing him. Any one of them
could have been Lev. He looked searchingly at the sea of unsmil-
ing faces, while one of the crowd shuffled toward him and feebly
shrugged his shoulders under the weight of his greatcoat. Then
he put his hand on Yossel's shoulder.

Yossel stared at him. "Lev?" he said.

Lev's features formed a smile and a glimmer of recognition
passed over Yossel's face. And his little heart heaved. He cringed,
drawing himself away from this gentle creature, this hairless head
and ringletless face. He clasped his own curls with each hand,
pressing them into his cheeks as if to groove them into his flesh,
to root them there, entrenched for all time. For his ringlets were
his very being, his inviolable entity, as much a part of his nature
as color is of negritude. He looked at his brother in horror. The
hairless Lev had already begun dying.

Reuben and Benjamin had watched the painful encounter between the brothers. Reuben put a sympathetic arm on Yossel's
shoulder, but Benjamin made for Lev, grasping him by the thick
wad of his shoulder pad and shaking him. "You can live without
hair," he shouted at him.

But Lev shook his head in abdication and Benjamin moved
away, dragging Reuben behind him.

Though the barracks were now full of children, there was
scarcely any human sound. Only the mourning murmur of greatcoats was heard, and the occasional shuffle of a large boot. The
door at the end of the barracks opened again and two sergeants
entered carrying boots and uniforms. These they piled onto the
counter and doled out to the waiting recruits. There was no consideration of sizes, for the recruitment of children had been a
sudden and spiteful official decision and, therefore, there was no
proper equipment. The uniforms had once clothed grown men,
whose looted corpses lay buried under snow on sundry battle-
fields. The children's feet would be lost and blistered in dead

men's shoes. When the whole line had been attended to, the sergeants led the boys through the barracks door and across a tree-
lined court, large and wooded enough to stifle whatever cries
might plead from the bathhouse to which the boys were now
being led. In the center of the vast hall was a large sunken tub of
gray water, layered with scum. The boys were told to undress, in
gestures rather than words, for the sergeant had long since
caught on to the village boys' ignorance of the Russian tongue.
But they were friendly, laughing as they mimed their orders,
trying to make an adventure of it all. Occasionally they helped a
small frightened boy to unbutton his blouse, and with great respect, tidily folded the prayer-fringes that circled his waist. Most
of the boys had never had a bath and were frightened at the sight
of so much water. They saw no fun in it. But Reuben and Benjamin, recapturing once more the smell of adventure, were the first
to immerse themselves, jumping boldly into the bath, splashing
each other and laughing all the while. They gave the village boys
courage, who, one by one, risked the two-foot depth. Once the
boys were in the tub, the sergeant tossed them slabs of soap. They
also mimed the instruction that they need not bother about washing their hair. A slow silence gathered across the tub as the children realized the implications of that order. And, as the whimpering gave way to wailing, the sergeants lost their playfulness.
They unhooked two hoses from the wall, and ordered the boys
out of the bath while they hosed them down. Then they were
directed to a pile of dirty towels and told to dry. Naked and
shivering, they were lined up before their uniforms, and told to
become soldiers.

The boys fumbled with their dressing, anxious to delay the
unthinkable sacrilege that awaited them. Yossel kept one hand
straddled across his face, pinning down his ringlets, while the
other hand struggled with his blouse. But at times he was bound
to use both hands in his dressing, and at those moments he
crouched in a corner and shut his eyes, and prayed that he was
invisible. And then from habit, he reached out for his prayer-
fringes, and so did the other village boys, who wore them night
and day like a second skin. The sergeant, who from experience
now knew the nature of their search, picked up a pile of prayer-
fringes and shook his head. Then he threw them unceremoni-
ously onto the fire that burned at the end of the bathhouse. The
boys turned away in horror. It was like setting fire to God.

Yossel drew on his trousers with his one hand. Now more than ever, it was necessary to cling to that self in him. Though he felt naked and unclean without his prayer-fringes, it was less part of him than his ringlets, those fingers of God that had caressed his cheek. Thus, one-handed, he managed to become a soldier, in a tunic that reached his knees, and breeches that hung over his huge boots. With one hand, he reached down to the floor for his cap. And many of the village boys were doing likewise, anxious to provide some protection for their locks. But the sergeant roared out an order, and mimed it too, so that it would be clear that, at this stage, caps were premature. And at once he lined up the ringleted ones, knowing that they would give the greatest trouble, and herded them through the bathhouse door that led to the clipping room. Reuben and Benjamin were the last to enter, and they leaned against the wall, viewing the hair-strewn floor.

"It's only hair," Reuben said. "Such a fuss about hair."

For those under the clippers were already screaming, and when the heads were fully shaven, the ringlets were clipped and dropped like large black tears onto the stone floor. Then the wailing grew to such a volume of lamentation that the sergeant was obliged to strike out at the snifflers and to remind them of the honorable uniform they were privileged to wear. Reuben and Benjamin were clipped together. Their tearless faces did not go unnoticed by the two drill sergeants, who automatically singled them out as favorites.

For the next five years the sergeants would be in charge of this motley crew. In the whole troop there were about two hundred children. Only a quarter of them were expected to survive their first year. When the winter snows came, they would drop like summer flies, those who had not already died of spring starvation and autumn fatigue. But those two smilers looked like survivors, the sergeant thought, especially the smaller one, whose large black eyes melted his knees with longing.

"What's your name?" The sergeant approached him.

"Reuben," he answered. "Reuben Wolf."

"And yours?" The sergeant turned to Benjamin.

"Benjamin," he said, "Benjamin Bindel."

"I thought you were brothers," the sergeant said.

"Well, we . . ." Reuben stopped. Again he felt the explanation too complicated to offer. In any case, what would these blunt peasant soldiers understand of milk-brotherhood? Yet Benjamin saw in the sergeant a possible ally. He gave him what his father had called his winning smile. The sergeant responded. In school, Benjamin recalled, the teacher's pet had been a hated creature, but he was willing to play that role, and so, it seemed, was Reuben. "We live together," Reuben said. "We're sort of related." He had managed the whole conversation in his simple basic Russian.

The sergeants were impressed. The boys could be used as a liaison to bridge the language barrier between them and their infant troops.

The shaven children, threatened with beatings, were now quiet and subdued, and the sergeants led them back into the barracks. Yossel and Lev found each other once again, and like the others, sought comfort in their common deprivation. Fatigue dulled the full realization of their plight. When the sergeant tossed straw palisses into their midst, they were happy to lie down where they stood, brother seeking brother, and friend, friend, and if without either, then a Jew like any other, hairless, fringeless, beyond the Pale of both Settlement and Torah. "God help us," they dared to utter, fearing how unworthy they had become. But the milk-brothers fell asleep without scruple. Reuben did not even stir as the drill sergeant folded the blanket around his shaven head. Throughout the night, the sergeants dozed on a wooden bench, occasionally waking at the cry of "Mama" or "Papa," a cry for home discernible in any language, and both of them stirred in their sleep, grateful that they had no children of their own.

In the morning, the children were woken by a crash of bells. They rubbed their eyes, looked at their surroundings, and slowly realized the calamity that had befallen them. In the cold light of morning it proved to be no dream, a thought that had comforted them during their sleep. Some of them began to whimper for home, but most cried for hunger, for none of them had eaten since breakfast the day before. And then they smelled what was in store for them. To most of them the smell was unknown, for, sheltered in the ghetto all of their young lives, they knew only the kosher odors of their own meat, fish, and fowl. This was an alien smell.

"You'll all feel better after breakfast," the sergeant said, and motioned to Benjamin to translate.

Benjamin was surprised at the order, and glad of it, for it already gave him a status that for a time would be unassailable.

He faltered with the translation, but it was clear enough to the boys that their hunger would soon be assuaged.

"A nice piece of roast pork," the sergeant went on.

Benjamin hesitated. It was all as his father had promised him. He looked at Reuben.

"You have to tell them," Reuben whispered.

"You do it," Benjamin said, more as a move to include Reuben in his new appointment than to shift the responsibility of bearing such a monstrous piece of information. Reuben was hesitant. He himself was sickened by the thought of it, and he was frightened of speaking the terrible word aloud. So he whispered it in a small offended croak that was all that he could muster.

"You must fill your stomachs," the sergeant went on. "We have a long march ahead of us."

Reuben translated and, before his words were out, the source of the blasphemous smell was evident in the barracks. Soldiers bearing trays of food and huge samovars placed the breakfast on the long counter, and ordered the boys to get into line. The sergeant put Benjamin and Reuben at the head. He expected his recruits to refuse the pig, and hoped that his two favorites would set an example. Benjamin was first. With little hesitation he took a slice of bread and placed the pork on top of it, then he lifted it high and showed it to the others. "We must survive," he said in Yiddish. "God will forgive us."

But the young recruits were not impressed. Many of them dropped out of the line altogether, and those who were left took only bread and a tin mug of sweet tea, and when breakfast was over, the table still groaned with the meat.

"Put some in your packs," the sergeant said to Benjamin, and Benjamin did what he was told, and urged Reuben to do the same, though both were retching on the devil's taste. They had forced themselves to swallow it and, after each mouthful, had asked God's forgiveness. For they knew that it was a terrible thing that they had done. Without doubt, it was a step into baptism and thus into eternal limbo.

The drill sergeants did what they could to marshal the boys into some kind of formation. There were too many of them to handle, but that fact did not disturb them. They knew that within a few days, with the slogging march ahead, their numbers would most certainly be halved and the troop become manageable. They herded them out of the barracks, putting Benjamin and Reuben in the lead, and marched them through the clearing onto the open road. They had gone only a little way when Reuben faltered and doubled up in pain. Then he rushed to the side of the road, where he freed himself of the devil that he had harbored. Benjamin followed him and did likewise, while the others stood and watched with little surprise, and were strengthened in their faith. But when the brothers rejoined the line, Benjamin took a hunk of meat from his bag, broke it in two, and gave half to Reuben. And with a preliminary prayer, both for forgiveness and for the strength to keep it down, they chewed on it numbly to the rhythm of the march. Not that there was too much rhythm. Most of the boys were stragglers, already weak from hunger. The sheltered ghetto lives they had led in no way equipped them for this unexpected and strenuous calling. They were mostly poor, ill-fed, and prone to infection. Whatever small energy they had, they used in prayer.

At noon they were allowed to rest for a while. Most of them fell asleep and did not care if they ever woke again. Lev and Yossel clung together in their misery, Yossel still clutching at his nonexistent locks, ashamed of his bald cheeks. When, an hour later, the drill sergeant called them to order, there were some who could not rise, their frail bodies shivering, their brows feverish in cold sweat. Reuben and Benjamin trudged down the line and forced them to stand on their feet, with promises of hot cabbage borscht at their next holding station. For that was what the drill sergeant had told them. And so they struggled on, the sorry line of them, some near death and mumbling that time-honored Hebrew prayer that was a visa to Abraham's bosom: *"Shema Yisroel, Adonai Elohanu, Adonai Echod."* At nightfall they reached the wagon trail, where soup and bread were brought to revive them. Then they were prodded into the wagons like cattle.

"Where are we going?" Reuben dared to ask.

"To the Eastern Provinces," the drill sergeant said.

The name meant nothing, but it sounded like the other end of the world.

They traveled for days, on a diet of borscht, black bread, and tea. Some of the village boys had compromised on the borscht. But most of the children took only bread and sweet tea, and there was much fever among them. A fever that at last had cooled, a pain that had found peace, and a longing for home that was

mercifully stilled. In all, twenty-three children died in the course
of one night. Nobody knew their names, and in their huge boots
and greatcoats and shaven heads, even in death they were identi-
cal. The survivors turned their faces away with not one mourning
tear, their features hardened with the effrontery of their abduction, and their hearts enraged with a bewildering adult fury. They
did not look at the sergeants as they wrapped the bodies in blankets and ordered the wagon train to halt. They waited while the
soldiers unloaded their burden, and were silent as they heard the
click of shovels outside. Then, when all was still, they began the
chant of *kaddish*. It was Benjamin and Reuben who led them in
the mourning prayer.

The terrible journey continued, but the deaths had wrought a
great change. Now, one after the other, during the course of the
next few days, children went to sleep and never woke again. It
was as if, with the first deaths, permission had been granted to
turn away from sacrilege, to subject the spirit to no further assault, and in all simplicity to die, without offense and without
malice. So it was that some weeks later, at the end of their
wretched journey, one hundred and three of the young recruits
had succumbed, and the wagon trail was punctuated by their
unnamed shallow graves. In the course of time—official time,
which ambles at its own uncaring pace—word of their deaths
would reach the villages. One hundred and three whispers would
give shape to their names and wail them aloud. God was cursed
in one breath, and begged for forgiveness in another, and grief
would wind its sheet around the ghettos like a shroud.

Among the young recruits who survived, there dwelt a small
sense of victory, as if in their first great battle they had acquitted
themselves with honor. There was hope now that they might
endure their twenty-five-year sentence. They had paid the price.
They had eaten of forbidden flesh, they had suffered themselves
to be shaven. From time to time they had even spoken words in
Russian, that language of baptism. They were convinced that the
worst was over. But they had no notion of the horrors that were
to come.

It was snowing. Every year on the milk-brothers' birthday it
was snowing. But this snow was different, and so was the birthday on which it fell. For on that day, the milk-brothers were
thirteen years old, bar mitzvah boys, without synagogue, without

covenant, prayer shawl, or phylacteries, and all such improvidence in a wilderness of alien snow.

Benjamin and Reuben lay entwined on their narrow cot, and woke together, as they did each morning. As was their custom, they whispered a morning prayer, which, over the years of their recruitment, had never varied. "Thank God," they said, their eyes still closed and bleary with sleep, "God be thanked that we have survived another day." Then slowly they opened their eyes and knew what that day was. They smiled at each other with remembered joy of Odessa birthdays, and knew that on this day they must do something very special to celebrate their entry into manhood.

"Where's our knife?" Benjamin said.

Reuben reached into the deep pocket of his greatcoat, took out the knife and extracted the blade. He knew what Benjamin had in mind. He made a small incision in his left thumb and handed the knife to his milk-brother. Benjamin cut his thumb likewise, then they clasped each other's hand.

"Now we are blood brothers," Benjamin said. "Happy birthday."

From the room beyond came breakfast smells of roasting pig, an odd aroma for a bar mitzvah feast. The boys sniffed, as they sniffed at it every morning on waking, sieving their nostrils of its blasphemy, flushing from their taste buds its profane desecration. For so long now they had eaten it, always with the same disgust, but with Jakob Bindel's injunction on their larded lips that they were to survive. They had never acquired a taste for it, and concluded that that must be God's doing. "Eat," it seemed He was saying to them. "Eat, but by no means enjoy."

Like most of the recruits in their platoon, the milk-brothers were billeted in a farmhouse, one of many dotted over the snow-covered wastes. They had three billet-companions: Lev and Yossel Abromovitch, who despite the thousand assaults on their bodies and spirits had managed to survive. And pray too, with daily fervor, while little Yossel still clutched at the nonexistent ringlets on his sunken cheeks. Each of them had celebrated his thirteenth birthday with prayer and mourning, and they had fasted throughout the day. Over the years they and the milk-brothers drew close to each other and a frightening bond of friendship grew between them. Each time brothers hugged brothers with the relief of being alive, Benjamin and Reuben would recall Jakob

Bindel's admonition: Make no friends, for friendship and love are the only causes worth dying for.

The fifth lodger in their billet was one Sergei Ash. He was fifteen years old and something of an outsider. He didn't sleep with the others. Farmer Pankov had allotted him a small space above the hayloft, so that his presence, even if it were a sleeping one, would deter thieves in the night. Unlike the others, Sergei had not been forcibly kidnapped. His parents were given no advance notice of his summons, and there had been no time to flee into the forest. But despite the poverty of his childhood and his illiteracy to boot, Sergei Ash was tough. Never in his three years of army life had he touched meat of any kind. He lived on bread, tea, any vegetables that he could find, and eggs. He was the most deft egg thief in the platoon. But most of all, he lived on prayer. He adjusted his orisons to the rhythm of his marching steps, to every maneuver of his drill. Sergei Ash talked a lot too and his subject was always the same. Food. Food was an obsession with him, a close second to his compulsion for prayer. When he talked about his parents or the people in his village, it was not about what they did or how they lived. It was simply about what they ate. Night after night he would lead his fellow lodgers on a gastronomic tour of his village that was wholly of his own invention. Caviar was the staple diet, heightened with blintzes, sour cream, and smoked sturgeon. When pressed to offer what exactly it was that he, Sergei, used to eat around his own family table, he would confess to salt herring and black currant tea. And at that moment his lips would salivate and tremble with longing. It was clear that for a mouthful of herring, he would have forfeited, such as it was, his entire kingdom.

One night, during one of Sergei's culinary recitals, the drill sergeant Likov, called in at the billet, ostensibly to give an order for the following day but, in truth, to feast his eyes yet again on Reuben's face, a vision that nightly haunted his dreams. He arrived in time to hear Sergei's dissertation on the inestimable value of the simple, garden-variety salt herring, and it sowed the seeds of a monstrous plan in his mind.

Orders had come from the highest quarters, in fact from the mighty Czar himself, to confront and to conquer the Jewish menace once and for all. And with the final weapon. That of baptism. The directions as to how this was to be done were clear. Baptism was to be propagated by persuasion, gentle but firm. And if that failed, force was to be administered. The mighty Czar would brook no Christ-refusal.

The matter was urgent and put the platoon commanders in a dilemma. It was all very well for the Czar to dictate orders from his royal palace in St. Petersburg, a million miles from the smell of any Jew and his intransigence. Could he conceive of the flesh and blood of Benjamin Bindel, Reuben Wolf, Abromovitch, Lev and Yossel, and Sergei Ash? Could he hear their monotonous prayers and sniff their stubborn resistance to Him they had crucified and Who had died for them on the Cross? But orders were orders. At first they tried the gentle persuasion suggested. "If you became Christians like the rest of us, life would be much easier for you. For one thing, you wouldn't have such trouble with the food," they tried.

The boys laughed in their faces. A drop of holy water on their shaven heads would in no way numb their taste buds, or release from their throats that gentile monosyllabic thrush. That night a priest came to the Pankov billet, ostensibly to pay a social call; the boys claimed a sudden ignorance of Russian, and tried to school him in the Yiddish tongue. The priest left in a rage of defeat and confusion. Every week another directive came from the highest quarters, stressing the imperative nature of baptism, that it was the bounden duty of every God-fearing Christian soldier to show the Yids once and for all that there was only one true way to heaven, and it was not via Abraham's bosom. As it became clear that apostasy was not to be achieved through persuasion, gentle or otherwise, stronger measures were ordered and prizes awarded for every conversion. A bonus of two roubles was promised for the saving of each Jewish soul. Fifty Jewish souls, retrieved from the wayward path, merited promotion in rank and extra privileges. It was the very spur that the men needed.

The night Sergeant Likov dropped into the boys' billet he listened once again to Sergei's salivating soused-herring stories. He put his arm around Reuben's shoulder, and as casually as he was able, he said, "Treats for you tomorrow, Ash. Herring for breakfast. Just like home."

"For us too?" Yossel's eyes brightened, and for one moment, with this sniff of home, he dropped his hand from his ringletless cheek.

"For all of you," Likov said. "It'll be just like being back in the ghetto."

That night, Sergei slept without dreaming, and when he awoke his mouth was already watering.

When the boys entered the kitchen, they were astonished to find that Sergeant Likov's promise was indeed fulfilled. The table was loaded with black bread and salt herrings of all kinds, ruled by the steaming samovar in the center. But most surprising of all was the presence of Sergeant Likov himself, already seated at the head of the table. Surprising too was the frightened face of Anna Pankov, the farmer's wife, who usually attended breakfast with a bustling air. Benjamin looked around the room and smelled conspiracy. He knew that the mouth-watering herring was bait and he must by all means urge his companions to avoid it. Reuben needed no persuasion. Lev and Yossel protested in whispers for a while, but finally bowed to the milk-brothers' judgment.

But Sergei was immovable. He could barely wait to get to the table. His mouth was screaming for a taste of home. And so they sat down and listened, as they did every morning, to Anna Pankov's thanksgiving prayer. Normally she tossed it out of her mouth while doling out the hot oatmeal and hunks of bread. But this morning she sat upright in her chair and said it with her hands idle, thanking God for what they were about to receive in a tone of deep earnestness. For the last time Benjamin tried to dissuade Sergei by silently shaking his head in his direction. But Sergei would not be diverted. After the blessing, Anna Pankov dealt out the bread and forked a juicy herring onto each boy's plate. Sergeant Likov was awarded two herrings, but she took care not to look him in the eye. He lifted up his fork and it was permission for them all to begin. Yossel and Lev and the milk-brothers concentrated on their bread, turning their faces from the seductive aroma on their plates. Their eyes watered with their loss.

"Don't you like herring?" Anna Pankov said, and there was an unmistakable measure of relief in her voice.

They shook their heads, begging her to understand.

"There's nothing else this morning," she said gently.

"Bread is enough," Benjamin said. "Bread and black currant tea." He glanced across the table and winced as the sergeant refilled Sergei's plate. "You're lucky," he said. "You can have their share," and he shoveled fillet after fillet before him. Sergei did not take his eyes off his plate. The look on his face had little to do with relish. It was as if he had undertaken the most impor-

88   BERNICE RUBENS

tant mission of his young life. After a while of feeding, he reached
out his tin mug for tea. And then the whole point of the exercise
became crystal clear. The sergeant shook his head vigorously,
and so did Anna Pankov, as she had been strictly instructed. She
opened the samovar tap and filled the tin mugs of all at the table.
All except Sergei, who looked at her at first with profound disbelief, and then with the realization of what torture he had brought
upon himself. Sergeant Likov drank his tea noisily, leaning over
and slurping it in Sergei's ear. Then he shoveled more herring
onto his victim's plate. Sergei feebly shook his head.

"You'll eat it," Likov shouted. "Every last bit of it." And he
picked up Sergei's fork and shoved it into his hand. "Eat," he
said, forcing his shaven head down onto his plate.

The others watched in silence, and Anna Pankov hid her face.
The terrified Sergei chewed and chewed, his soul crying out with
hatred for the food he had once loved so well. Each time he
paused, the sergeant stuffed another forkful into his mouth and
continued to do so, until only the perfidious smell of the herring
remained.

"You want some tea?" Likov asked.

Sergei nodded eagerly but with little confidence.

"If you go to the priest, he will give you tea. Lots of it. And
lots of cold water to quench your thirst," he slurped.

This last, Benjamin was forced to translate, though it was obvious from Sergei's crestfallen look that the message was clear. He
had just enough energy left to shake his head. And shake it again
and again until the tears rolled down his cheeks.

"It's herring for lunch, then," the sergeant said, "and for supper, and for tomorrow and for every day after that. There will be
no drink of any kind. Except at the house of the priest." He
looked around the table menacingly. "If any of you give Ash
water," he threatened, "you will be shot." He looked at all of
them in turn, including Anna Pankov, but when his eyes rested
on Reuben, he gave an almost imperceptible shake of his head.

They left the table and were marched to the drilling yard for
their daily routine. For lunch and supper that day, Sergei was
made to eat his herrings alone under the watchful eye of Sergeant
Likov.

At the end of the third herring day, Likov wondered how the
boy managed to survive at all. So did the Pankovs and their other
lodgers. But none of them knew that Sergei had found a watering

hole. If one could call it that. Outside the barn door that led to
the hayloft in which he slept, there was a permanent puddle. For
the most part it consisted of liquified mud and horse urine. After
each stealthy mouthful, Sergei suspected that it was more than
likely that he would die from the cure than from the disease. Yet
it was a juice of sorts, and temporarily assuaged the raging thirst
inside him, though its aftereffects were as nauseating as the thirst
itself. Each day Likov kept his startled eye on him and wondered
how soon he could collect his ransom. But Sergei plodded
through his herring-filled days. Six of them in all. And on the
seventh day, like any good Jew, he rested. And yielded, too. His
body was athirst, raging. In a faint dry whisper he asked to see
Likov, who took him gently by the hand and led him to the
priest's quarters. Sergei tried not to think that the day was a
Sabbath, *his* Sabbath, and in view of his impending baptism, his
last.

Reuben, Benjamin, Lev, and Yossel gathered in their sleeping
hut and silently prayed for Sergei's soul. He was still a Jew to
them, and always would be, whatever kind of water was poured
upon his head. And in God's eyes he would remain one of His
chosen, because the water could not rinse his soul. They would
wait for his return, untroubled by the length of his absence, for
they knew that neither a minute nor a thousand years could rinse
Sergei's gentle spirit of the Torah.

When he returned, they were at supper. Anna Pankov was
sitting silently, ashamed of her involuntary complicity, and when
she saw the door open, and Sergei's sudden presence in the
kitchen, she turned her face to the wall. The boys stared at him,
as if they expected a change in his appearance, a halo perhaps
about his head. Sergei looked at them warily, gauging their response. With one hand he was clutching at something around his
neck, and his white little fist was tight and angry and ashamed.

"Hello, Sergei," Reuben said. "Come and sit down."

He stared at them without moving. "I don't want to talk about
it," he said. It seemed that their silence was a condition of his
joining them at the table.

"Neither do we," Benjamin said, and went toward him and
took his arm.

Still Sergei clutched at the curse around his neck, and without
removing his greatcoat, he sat down. Anna Pankov served him a
bowl of soup and at the same time drew him a large mug of tea

from the samovar. Sergei gave her a feeble smile. "It wasn't your fault," he said, and Anna Pankov was so overcome that she knelt by his side and took him in her arms. "My little Jew boy," she said. "Always will be. Now get some food inside you," she said gruffly, fighting back the tears.

Sergei picked up the soup spoon with one hand, and was obliged to put it down every time he reached for his bread. His was clearly going to be a one-handed supper. The boys had a vague idea of what Sergei was at such pains to conceal.

"It doesn't matter," Benjamin said after a while. "Let it go. It doesn't mean anything. Just a string around your neck."

"A millstone," Sergei whispered.

Benjamin leaned over the table and held Sergei's clenched fist. "A string," he insisted, and gently he opened Sergei's hand. Sergei turned away as the metal crucifix fell from his throat and draped itself across his breast.

"Benjamin's right," Reuben said.

But Sergei would not be comforted. He could not erase from his mind's eye the smile on the face of the priest as he draped the cross over his wet forehead. "Now you will walk in the ways of Jesus Christ, our Lord," the priest had said, "and that way, and only that way," he said, "only that way will lead to Paradise." It was a vision that Sergei would carry for the rest of his life. Even the long glass of water that the priest had thereafter placed in his hand as a payoff for his newly cleansed soul gave him little pleasure. He drank it swiftly and asked for more, less to assuage his gigantic thirst than for his own desperate need for purification. He went to bed early. There was now no point in sitting around the fire and listening to Lev's and Yossel's village stories. They would only gnaw at the raging hole in his heart. Neither did he want to listen to their Yiddish songs. He no longer felt himself worthy of the tongue or of its melody. He lay down on his cot, clutching the Christ in his hand as if to hide it from his God's all-seeing eye.

The other boys retired early as well with little appetite for their nightly reminiscences.

In the morning Sergei did not appear at breakfast and Reuben was sent to the hayloft to wake him. At the top of the ladder, he hesitated. A sudden fear had gripped him and he wished that Benjamin were there. He peered over the edge of the loft and saw the silent hump of Sergei lying in the hay. He listened. He prayed for a small sound of breathing, a whispered sigh, but the loft was silent and as still as a tomb. He wondered whether he should run and fetch Anna Pankov, but he knew that what had happened in that loft was no outsider's business. He crept toward the greatcoated hump.

Sergei was lying on his back, his eyes staring wide at the overhead beams. His hands lay open on his coat, and in one of them the Christ lay, his chain broken and dangling in the straw. A manger death, Reuben thought, and he took up the cross and for no reason that he could understand he carefully mended the broken chain and laid it tidily on the straw. Then he closed Sergei's eyes with the palm of his hand, and rested his head on Sergei's chest and wept long and silently. He wept for Sergei, for Lev and Yossel, for Benjamin and himself, for all the children of his tribe so rudely weaned from warmth and comfort. He cradled Sergei's shaven head in his arms, and in his ear he sang the prayer for the dead. Then he covered his friend's young face, and returned to the kitchen and told them what he had found. They did not ask or wonder why young Sergei had died. They knew. The priest had injected Jesus into Sergei's stubborn little Jewish heart. He had simply rejected it. It was the least and the most that he could do. The cause of death was wholly natural; a fitting way for a Jew to die. And as a Jew, they mourned him. They insisted on their own burial rights, and they insisted too on their own mourning rituals. And Likov, who had already collected his bond, saw no reason to deny them, especially since it was Reuben they had sent as their spokesman. So they washed and prayed over their friend, and on the very next day they buried him in Farmer Pankov's fallow field. And for seven days, between their regular routines, they sat on the floor and they mourned him.

Sergei was not replaced in the billet, and the young recruits drew even closer together, bound now by their common bereavement.

Sergeant Likov did not look upon Sergei Ash as one of his failures. He ascribed his death to his overlong thirst, but at least, in his eyes, and in his pocket, Sergei Ash had died a Christian, despite all those incantations they sang over his grave. Besides, he'd had greater success, and certainly a better survival rate than in other billets, and the pieces of silver itched his greedy palm. He'd heard of a traveling fair that was due to arrive in a nearby village, and with a certain amount of maneuvering, he managed to give his troops a week's rest, confined of course to their billets, and to take himself off for a well-earned spree. On hearing the news, a delighted Farmer Pankov put the boys to work. Benjamin and Reuben begged for and were given charge of the cows, while Lev and Yossel were delegated to the kitchen to help Anna Pankov bottle her fruits and vegetables for the winter. It turned out to be the boys' happiest time since they had left home, so much snow, so many *kaddishes* ago.

When, years before, the farm had been commandeered by the army as a billeting post for young conscripts, Anna Pankov had been apprehensive. Her husband had petitioned the army commander to be relieved of the duty. Like any good Russian peasant, he hated the sight of Jews, who were the cause of all the troubles in Holy Russia, and he did not want them contaminating his land. Neither Farmer Pankov nor his wife had ever seen a Jew in their lives, so when the farmer, his petition denied, had been forced to reduce part of his holding to an army billet, he and his wife had waited hand in hand in their yard in fear and trembling for their first lodgers. When the bedraggled group arrived at their gate, they watched as the sergeant siphoned off five of their number and pushed them up the path.

"They're not too bad," Sergeant Likov shouted to the farmer, "and they speak a bit of Russian. We'll make Cossacks of them yet," he had laughed, and he had led the rest of the herd away.

The Pankovs stared at their uninvited guests, looking for some mark that by all accounts distinguished them from the rest of young humanity. But they could find nothing.

"Are you Yids?" Farmer Pankov asked after a while.

Benjamin nodded on everyone's behalf.

"Lift up your coats from the ground." Farmer Pankov was skeptical. He no doubt expected cloven hooves. The boys did as they were told, revealing only boots many sizes too large for them.

"Come in," Anna Pankov said timidly, and she led the boys into the kitchen.

Farmer Pankov followed them, sizing them up from behind and no doubt looking for tails. Then he sat down on a kitchen chair and ordered them to take off their coats. In their blouses and breeches they looked the same as any school child of the region, but for their shaven heads, the mark of conscription. Still he was not satisfied, and resolved to have them strip to discover the exact spot on their bodies where the devil had left his print. So he ordered them to gather around the fire and to take off all their clothes in order to wash themselves down. He bade his wife prepare hot water and he himself unhooked a large tin bath that hung on the brick sidewall of the hearth. The boys undid their buttons nervously, fearing the telltale mark that they knew he was seeking. They left their breeches till last, then, naked to the waist and barefoot, they had no choice but to drop their final defense. Farmer Pankov looked hard at their bodies, staring from one to the other. Then he took Benjamin's genitals gently in his hand and examined them closely. He did likewise with the others. Then he wiped his own hand down the side of his breeches, threw back his head, and roared aloud. "Anna," he shouted. "Come quick," he said, as if the vanished foreskin would suddenly reappear. "Come and look, Anna," he shouted. Anna Pankov bustled back to the kitchen, laden with steaming kettles. She put the pans down and stood by her husband's side. "Look," he roared, pointing to Benjamin's parts, and then to the others'. "Here and here, and here. That's why they're different. That's what all the fuss is about."

Anna Pankov blushed scarlet, as much for the boys' embarrassment as her own, and she busied herself filling the bath and reaching for the slabs of soap. The spectacle had put Farmer Pankov in good humor and he urged the boys to stand in the bath and to wash that thing on behalf of which a million of their kind in his Holy Russia had been tortured and slain. He splashed them gently as his heart filled with pity for their tribe. "We'll make Cossacks of you yet." He echoed the sergeant's words, but he meant them kindly. He was a simple man and he devoutly believed that to arrive at Cossackdom was the height of any good Russian's achievement. He knew it would not be hard to love his lodgers.

Anna Pankov rubbed down their backs and gave them her husband's white linen nightshirts to sleep in. As the boys settled in their cots that first night in their new billet, they thought that in some strange way, and in some alien land, they had come home.

After a week Sergeant Likov roared back into barracks, drunk and penniless. It was high noon when he struggled into Farmer Pankov's billet and ordered food and vodka. During their happy freedom the boys had forgotten all about him, and all that he stood for. His sudden reappearance cast a gloom over the farm and all its inhabitants. He drank himself into a stupor and dropped his head onto the table, snoring himself into oblivion. The boys withdrew to the kitchen and the cow shed, dreading his wrath on the following day. And as it turned out, they had plenty of cause for terror, though it was kept secret from them. For during the sergeant's absence, word had come from on high that His Imperial Majesty was by no means impressed by the conversion figures. The Czar expressed a wish for quicker results and on a larger scale. So the order went out for wholesale baptism. An enforced measure without preliminary persuasion. A rider was added to the effect that His Majesty would be visiting that region in a month hence for an inspection of his young recruits, and would expect to witness a widespread baptism.

The barracks were thrown into confusion. A visit from the Czar was a menacing prospect. They were not too worried about the baptism, for that presented few problems of organization. The River Ural was waiting and willing, and so were the priests. It was the inspection that was worrying. The children's drilling and soldiership were hardly up to the expected standard of His Imperial Majesty. So the drill sergeants went to work with a vengeance and the poor children couldn't understand the sudden brutalizing panic. The long foot-slogging marches were now unending, the dress parades, the marathon runs. Every night Anna Pankov would rub her boys' feet with spirit of alcohol to soothe their blisters and sores. Rumor of the Czar's visit had spread around the camp, and this increased the boys' terror. They had the impression that a raging battle was at hand and that the Czar was coming to lead his infant troops into the bloody fray. In the last week of their training, their rations were increased to feed the energy expended in such exercise, but at the end of the day their fatigue and apprehension had blunted all appetite; and the morning prayer of thanksgiving for their survival was as fervent and as zealous as if it were their last.

On the appointed day the Pankovs gave their boys a special breakfast, and embraced them as if they were seeing them for the last time. Sergeant Likov was meticulous in his troop inspection and clearly very nervous. When he was satisfied with their appearance, he marched them onto the barracks square. There the few hundred of them were assembled and stood to attention until the entourage of His Imperial Majesty appeared on the brow of the overhanging hill and led their sovereign to the platform that had been erected on the square. The children stared at him with a raging hate, seeing in his terrible person the cause of all their sufferings, and their trigger fingers itched on their unloaded rifles. And their hatred acted as a spur to their parade, each marching foot a revengeful treading on the tyrant's grave. The drill sergeant did not know what had so suddenly inspired them, and he could only imagine that it was the awe of Majesty. When the long parade was over, they were allowed to stand easy for a while in preparation for the marathon formation run to the riverbank some nine versts distant. But the Czar was impatient for the river spectacle, so the rest period was curtailed and the children ordered into formation.

The marathon run began. Sergeants and officers rode along the way, their eyes on the troop, while the Czar and his entourage were carriage-driven toward the riverbank. Benjamin and Reuben, Lev and Yossel, ran abreast, encouraging each other in low whispers, and it seemed to each of them that their drumming hearts would burst. Yet there was no letup. The officers urged them on from the sidelines, whipping the odd straggler into line. Occasionally a sergeant would number off their striding steps from one to four to keep them in running rhythm. After a while the little legs moved of their own accord, and left the heart to deal with its own agony. In the last spurt toward the river, some forward officers galloped to the bank and arranged themselves in a row to mark the finishing line, while the sergeants conducted and graded a tidy slowdown. At last the whole troop came to a halt, and in their ranks there were now noticeable gaps, once filled by children whose hearts could not bear the strain. Their bodies lay somewhere on the roadside, trampled on, dying, or mercifully dead. The roll call registered twenty-five missing. The news was transferred to the Czar's aide, who shrugged his shoulders with disdain.

After the roll call the commanding officer stood the boys at ease and told them that they had done well. And as a reward for their labors they were going to be given a treat.

"You can throw off all your clothes, and cool off in the river," he said. "Enjoy yourselves," he commanded, and gave them the order to strip.

For the young *Kantonisti,* that order, under whatever circumstances, spelled danger. They hesitated, suspicious.

"You can't go in with your clothes on," Sergeant Likov laughed. "I'm going for a swim. Follow me." And he began to unbutton. Thus encouraged, many of the children followed suit. But Reuben and Benjamin hung back. They knew that for a poor *Kantonisti* in the Russian Imperial Army, nothing was for nothing. Treats were always costly and they wondered now what price they would have to pay. Around them, naked children, holding their mark of difference, were running toward the water. But Lev and Yossel held back too, sniffing conspiracy.

"What shall we do?" Lev whispered.

"Just not go," Benjamin said. "It's a trap."

And his fears were confirmed at the sight of a troop of Greek Orthodox priests who loomed out of nowhere, earnest in their sacerdotal robes and wading into the shallows, their holy books held high above their heads. And what was His Imperial Majesty himself doing there on his horse?

"It's baptism," Benjamin whispered, and the four of them turned and walked away.

"Come on, boys." It was the commanding officer's voice and its tone was order. "Get undressed."

They turned and he himself walked toward them. "Just get into the water," he said.

There was no way out. Benjamin grasped at the means that, even in this extreme and terrible circumstance, might justify the ends. "It's in the name of survival," he whispered, then a little louder in Lev and Yossel's ears, "We have to survive. It's God's will."

Lev shrugged his shoulders as he unbuttoned his blouse. Not *his* God's will, he thought, nor Yossel's. He did not know what they were going to do, for both of them knew that Benjamin's price for survival was beyond their spiritual means. Yossel put his little hand to his cheeks, once again clinging to his nonexistent ringlets, a habit he had slowly grown out of in the last few months, while Benjamin, already stripped himself, undid the button of Yossel's blouse. Then the four of them walked slowly toward the river.

Sergeant Likov, paddling in the shallows, encouraged them into the water. The sight of so many children laughing and splashing was so innocent and so devoid of malicious intent that Reuben was heartened. He started to run, clutching Benjamin's hand. "It's all right," he shouted back to Lev and Yossel. "It's only water."

But Lev and Yossel were not pacified. In their eyes, Christians could pollute anything, and most of all, water. Especially water, by pretending it was holy. For them the river was no playground. The commanding officer yelled at them again, and they slunk, terrified, into the shallows.

The water was undeniably refreshing after their long run. They dog-paddled a little, encouraged by the joy of the other recruits around them, until the commanding officer ordered them to the bank. They looked up and saw a troop of soldiers line up behind a line of priests, their naked bayonets in their hands. And each child among them knew that God's back was turned.

The priests took them in turn. The priest bade each child immerse himself and, on his coming up for air, a prayer was recited over his head, and the sign of the cross was made as the final seal of conversion. After a while Reuben and Benjamin, hand in hand, reached the priestly line, and both were baptized simultaneously. They held hands all the while, and when it was over, they walked silently out of the water and sat alone on the bank. *"Shema Yisroel,"* they both began together. "Hear O Israel."

There was a small commotion on the riverbank. And much shouting. Two single shaven heads were seen across the river. "Come back," Sergeant Likov shouted. Yet he made no attempt to save them. The other recruits looked on, helpless. Then the heads were seen to move close to each other, as if the bodies were clasped together below. A terrible silence spread across the water as they all watched the Abromovitch brothers from the bank— the children not knowing whether to pray for their deliverance or their peace. Then across the water, like a ghostly spondee supplication, came the cry of the *Shema* as Lev and Yossel Abromovitch made their final covenant with their God, and its unconquerable faith echoed across the river and onto the heathen bank in a fragile peal of glory. The young recruits shivered with shame. They watched as the twin heads submerged, rose once, then again, and finally were seen no more.

"That's two Yids off our hands," Reuben heard one of the officers say, and the other by his side laughed.

"I wish their whole tribe would be so obliging," he said.

Benjamin and Reuben stared at the now peaceful patch of water that sheltered their friends, and from their throats yet again came the opening chorus of the *kaddish*, that mourning prayer which, over the years, had found a permanent lodging on their lips. The other recruits, baptized as they were, took up the song, and pealed it across the water. His Imperial Majesty was seen to turn away in anger. "Horsewhip them," he shouted, then he rode off to his carriage.

The commanding officer ordered silence and the command that the naked boys were not to move from their places. Then the drill sergeants took their whips and wrought havoc with their naked flesh. The Czar watched from the door of his carriage until satisfied, then he ordered the coachmen to drive away. The whipping ceased, and the boys, wincing with pain, yet sustained by their small triumph, crawled along the ground for their clothes.

That night Farmer Pankov and Anna wailed the loss of their children and clung to the milk-brothers in their common sorrow.

"We'll miss them," Anna Pankov cried.

"I hate them," Reuben suddenly said, his grief heaving with anger. "Both of them. My grandfather said there was no God worth one's martyrdom. They were not *supposed* to die."

"They made their own choices," Farmer Pankov said with his simple wisdom. "It doesn't make them heroes, and it doesn't make you cowards." He took them both in his arms. "Tomorrow is Sunday," he said. "We'll go together and look after the cows." He knew that was a possible source of solace for the milk-brothers. But they trembled. If tomorrow was Sunday, they realized, then, that today was the Sabbath. They had submitted themselves to baptism on their Holy Day, and on that same day, Lev and Yossel had committed the most cardinal sin of all. That Sabbath day had been offensively desecrated, beyond forgiveness or prayer.

It was snowing. Odessa snow. And once again it was the milk-brothers' birthday. Jakob Bindel woke early, knowing the day from his dream. He smiled on waking because he knew with absolute certainty that somewhere in the vast eastern territory of this hated land, two people whom he loved more than his own life had survived yet another year. He knew it because there was no reason to know otherwise. Every night since the children's recruitment, he had made his fearful way to the offices of the *kahal.* Over a year ago the *kahals* had been abolished, but their offices remained, staffed now by police and local officials, as corrupt and as bribable as their predecessors. Yet even now, after so many years, Jakob's heart soured with Meisels' memory as he approached the bulletin board and scanned the register of missing child soldiers. Few were over the age of thirteen, and though they were presented as having sacrificed their lives for His Imperial Majesty, those bereaved would find no honor in such citation. As the years passed, Jakob had read the list with less fear, for he knew his children were children no longer, and had learned to accept Christ. Jakob Bindel in their absence had lived with them daily. He had stood by their side in front of the Holy Covenant and had coaxed words out of their throats. He had attended their weaning from their home and with them had suffered all the terrible pains of withdrawal.

On the day of their bar mitzvah he had gone to the synagogue, and on their behalf had initiated them into manhood. He had feared their eventual baptism, and daily he had reasoned and argued and finally defied God in the name of survival. He felt the growth of their limbs, the stirring in their loins, and he prayed that their gross deprivation would not forever freeze love in their hearts. And each day he thanked God for their survival.

And of this he had proof. It happened at the end of the milk-brothers' bar mitzvah year. It was late evening in the tavern and he was playing chess with Faivel. A uniformed soldier appeared at the door. Jakob's heart faltered, as it always did at the sight of a uniform.

"Jakob Bindel?" he inquired from the tavern door.

Jakob stood. The soldier came toward him, and he put his hand into the inside of his greatcoat.

"I have a letter for you," he said. "From Benjamin and Reuben."

Jakob was forced to seat himself again. The mention of his children's names always overwhelmed him. Now they came from a stranger's mouth, and in such loving tones that Jakob was shaken with emotion. "Sit down," he said to the stranger, "and welcome to my tavern. Will you take a kvass with us? This is my friend Faivel," he said, almost in the same breath. "He knows the children well."

But Sergeant Likov was not disposed to stay. He had almost not bothered to come at all. But he was anxious to catch a glimpse of the family who had reared that boy who, with such sulking resistance, had given him so much pleasure. Nothing was for nothing. For when, before his leave, he'd promised the boy anything he could name in return for lying by his side, Reuben's simple request had been for him to deliver a letter to his family. Then Reuben had laid down his reluctant body and paid the price. In Likov's heart was the lingering memory of that love, unrequited as it was, and it was to rekindle that joy that he had turned his steps toward the ghetto. But he did not want to stay. Despite the years he had spent in Jews' company, he still felt ill at ease in their presence. Besides, he was beginning to find them human and that was not good for a Russian soldier who aspired to Cossackdom. So he declined Jakob's invitation.

"I must be leaving," he said. "I just came to bring the letter." Then he turned to go.

"Tell me about them," Jakob pleaded. "When did you see them? Are they well? Are they happy?" he dared to ask.

"Who is happy in the army, Mr. Bindel?" Likov laughed. "But your boys are well. I saw them only a month ago. They are a credit to you, your children," he said. "They know how to survive." He clicked his heels, nodded to both men, and left the tavern.

"They will survive," he said to Faivel as his finger trembled on the envelope in his hand. "I will open the letter with all my children," he said. "You come too, Faivel. I shall need a man's support," he laughed, and he led him into the back room of the tavern. The women were all assembled around the kitchen table, Miriam, Sofia, Sarah, and Zena and all their daughters, and Esther, who clung to Jakob's sleeve.

"I have a letter from Benjamin and Reuben," he said simply.

"They are alive?" they whispered.

"They are well! A credit to us. They know how to survive."

"Open the letter, Father," Sofia said softly.

They waited in silence as Jakob prised the envelope with his thumb, and when it was open, two sheets of paper were visible. Jakob rested as if after a long labor. The pleasure that lay in store was to be savored. It was almost four years since word had come from the milk-brothers, and the breaking of such a silence was to be relished slowly.

"Our dearest grandparents, parents, sisters, uncles, aunts, cousins, Faivel and Raisl, Dov and Rosa." Jakob paused again, and watched each smile around the table as they responded to their names. "And the cows, too," Jakob read on, and paused yet again, and smiled. "We love you all very much," he went on, "and we think of you every day. Life here is not so miserable. We live for the time being on a farm with Farmer Pankov and his wife who are very kind to us." At this point in the reading, Jakob had to pause to accommodate the lump that was rising in his throat. And for the surge of love he felt for those unknown, unseen peasants. "Sergeant Likov," he read on, "who is our drill master, has promised to deliver this letter when he goes on leave. Do not worry about us. We have come to terms with many grievances. We have whispered the *kaddish* many times for friends we have lost, but we know we shall live to see you all again. We kiss you all. Love from Benjamin and Reuben."

"Again, again," Esther said quietly for she feared a flood of tears around the table. And Jakob obliged quickly, and for the same reason. So they read the letter over and over again, each one in her turn until they all knew it by heart. Then Jakob withdrew the other sheet of paper. He looked at it quizzically, trying to connect the unknown signature with the handwriting he knew so well.

"It's from Farmer Pankov," he told the gathering, "and look,

Faivel," he said, showing him the paper, "it's written in Russian, but it's in Benjamin's hand."

"Translate, Father, please, quickly," Miriam said.

Jakob adjusted his voice to a formal tone that was very different from his prior reading of the milk-brothers' Yiddish. The sound was almost declamatory. "My respected Mr. and Mrs. Bindel," he recited, "and honored Mr. and Mrs. Wolf. I cannot read or write, but I want to talk to you in some way, and Benjamin will write down for me what I have in my heart. I love your two children as if they were my own. My wife Anna says the same. They have suffered much, but they are strong and enduring. They meet every obstacle with courage. Today was their bravest day of all. They submitted themselves to baptism." Esther gave a small scream, and the other women wailed in sympathy. Then suddenly Jakob raised his voice, and shouted, "Be quiet, all of you," with such anger and with such trembling of his lip that they were cowed by his fury. "Listen," he said. "Listen to the rest of it. They submitted themselves to baptism," he repeated, "but," he shouted the word as he saw the horror on their faces, *"but,"* he repeated, "they are still your loving sons." He looked around the table, and touched the women's hands. "They're alive," he whispered. "Isn't that all that matters?"

"They did it to survive," Faivel said. "We should all be proud of them."

Jakob picked up the letter again. "My wife and I send our respects to you and all your family, all of whom, from the children's stories, we now know so well. And we hope that the times will soon be better for all of us."

Benjamin had then signed Farmer Pankov's name, and underlined it as if to give it the importance and the dignity he felt it deserved.

Jakob laid the two sheets of paper on the table and they touched them in silence for a while. Then he wrapped the letters in a silk handkerchief and put them in a leather bag that he kept under his bed. And every morning since, he had taken them out of their silk wrappings, as he was doing now on their twentieth birthday.

Since the recruitment of the milk-brothers, there had been two landmarks in Jakob Bindel's year: the anniversary of their birthday, and the night of the Passover Seder, which in many ways was the anniversary of their death. And in the approaching Passover of that year, he ticked off in his mind a solid block of their ten years' absence. He did not think in terms of the fifteen soldiering years that still lay ahead, for the years that had passed, however small in number, were of greater achievement in Jakob Bindel's terms of survival.

During these pre-Passover days the women were busy preparing for the feast, and Jakob spent much of his time with Leon in the cow sheds, where Leon was most at his ease. Over the years Jakob had come to value Leon's silences, and the worth of his unspoken words. He spoke of the milk-brothers rarely, but when he did, it was as if he had seen two sudden pillars of fire. He loved to go about his work while Jakob hovered about him and spoke of their children, recalling memories of their childhood. From time to time he would nod, smile, and even laugh aloud, and in the extremes of his emotion he would caress his animals to subdue his rage. Then Jakob would leave him, and it was in those moments when Leon was alone, and Jakob, frayed with memories, returned to the tavern, that the two men came closest to loving and to touching each other.

There were rumors that Passover in the ghetto. Rumors of unrest. The ghetto dwellers heard tell of even more restrictions on their lives, higher taxes and the closure of Jewish schools. But they were used to the pre–Holy Days ferment. The Jew-hate that seethed in the Russian soul throughout the year was wont to boil over on Jewish feast days. Especially at Passover, when the old belief that Jews used Christian blood in the preparation of their unleavened bread once more found its seasonal credence.

That year in Odessa was no exception, for there was one who was more than ready to take advantage of that medieval belief. His name was Victor Pandowska and he was a serf on a large holding of an Odessa landlord. His daily life was miserable enough, and now made even more wretched by the misfortune that had befallen his daughter, Tanya, fifteen years old, who at that very moment was giving birth to a poor bastard a passing soldier had planted inside her. He'd hidden her lying-in in the tool shed, keeping watch from the outside and listening to her laboring cries. And when they ceased, he cocked his ear for a baby's cry. But none came. He waited, and still there was silence from behind the door. He peered inside. Tanya lay there on a bed of straw, her legs spread-eagled with a lifeless shape between them. He could not hide his relief that the child was dead. But where, in God's name, could he hide the baby? The sight of his daughter's weeping countenance filled him with pity and rage against all the injustices of his life, against all his deprivation and poverty. It was the Jews' fault. It always was. Let those rotten Jews pay for his daughter's shame, and the misery of his own life. He looked at the child and was pleased that it was a boy. He turned his back on his daughter and quickly he incised the child's member with his knife. It was a crude cutting. A little blood flowed and soon congealed, then he wrapped the baby in a tool bag that lay on the floor and left the shed.

It was almost dusk in the ghetto, a good light for subterfuge. Not that Pandowska felt that he needed any camouflage. In all his poverty and deprivation, he was still rich in comparison with these ghetto dwellers, for he at least was of the Christian faith. He lorded his feet over the cobbles, strutting like a master, a parcel of dead child under his arm. He had made no plan as to where to deposit it. One Jew as a victim was as good as any other. At that moment, he was passing a tavern and saw behind it a field, and in that field was a cow shed. He made his mean way over the grass.

The door of the shed was open and the cows were lowing in their stalls. He sought out a mound of hay and threw the parcel in that direction. It landed on the mound and was clearly visible from the door, so he stepped inside and buried it lightly in the hay. The act of interment stirred a prayer in his heart and he committed the child's body to the earth and returned its soul to God in the way of any priest. Then he left the shed and sauntered down the street.

Leon was making his way to the sheds. He was humming one of those songs they would sing at the Seder table. "Only one kid, only one kid, which my father got for two farthings," and as he sang it, he saw the milk-brothers' ten-year-old faces, and he tried to imagine how they would look now in their twenty-first year. But he postponed that until he reached his cows, when, sitting on a stool at their flanks, he would while away the milking time with storytelling. Leon's tales for Reuben and Benjamin grew more and more adult as the years passed by. It was in their thirteenth year that Leon had put away their childish things, and his tales became those of manhood. It was his way of being with them, of holding them close. But that night, when he entered, he shivered and did not know why. He sat on his stool and set to milking, but the cow was restive, and he heard the others lowing uncomfortably in their stalls. He continued at his work, but he could not begin his nightly tale. Or rather, he would not. He didn't want his children in the shed. There was malevolence in the air and his fear would give the children little welcome. So he spoke softly to the cows to calm them, though he himself was shivering with apprehension. He tried to reassure them with his caressing hand, but he noted how it trembled on their flanks. For the first time in his life, Leon Wolf did not want to be alone. He would go quickly to the tavern, he decided, and fetch Jakob, on the pretext of needing some help. Perhaps Jakob too would feel the evil eye about him, and find some explanation. He patted the cows once more as his signal that he would soon return. Then, sweating, he turned and made for the door. But when he saw the posse of police sergeants standing there and watching him, looking as if they had been there for some time, the sweat poured from his forehead, and in the Law's eye, each drop of it was a confession of his guilt. Two of them pounced on him, and held his arms rigid behind his back, while the others began a search of the shed.

Pandowska stood at the door, avoiding Leon's gaze, and watching the men as they scrambled the hay, resisting the temptation to guide them to their quarry. They were far off the scent, rummaging in the stalls as the cows lowed in terror. Pandowska shifted from one foot to another, impatient to be done with it, and to go back to his miserable hut and tend his daughter. He dared to steal a glance at Leon, who was ashen-faced and looked as if he was about to vomit. The police were impatient too, and wantonly damaged the stalls in their fury, kicking down the wood partitions, as if some treasure were to be found in the grain. Enraged, they destroyed all in foot's range, until one of Leon's keepers left his post and joined in the search. To Pandowska's relief, he went straight to the part of the shed that the others had ignored, and rummaging in the hay, he came across the quarry.

"I've got it," he shouted.

The others left their havoc and gathered around him, while the cows bellowed, full of fear and pain, their udders bursting.

"Let me milk them," Leon managed to whisper to his guard. Whatever terrible charge they held against him, whatever appalling evidence their booty revealed, he was concerned with the well-being of his animals.

"He wants to milk his cows," the guard laughed across the shed.

"He won't be milking cows for a long time to come," one of the policemen said.

"On the milky way perhaps," another laughed.

Then they stood aside and revealed the parcel's contents on the straw.

Leon stared at it, and the full implication of the accusation overwhelmed him. "Reuben, Benjamin," he shouted, and he broke into terrible sobs, knowing that never in his life now would he see them again.

"Is this what you saw?" one of the policemen asked their informant. Pandowska dared to enter the shed, keeping his eyes firmly on the ground. Then he looked at his parceled grandchild.

"That looks like the packet I saw," he said.

"You can go now," the officer said. "You have done a good service today."

"A true Christian," another said, and Pandowska touched his forelock and retreated, his back to the door. Then once outside the shed, he turned and made his hurried way back to his hovel.

The policeman rewrapped the parcel. "Murderers," he muttered. "The whole tribe of them," and he motioned Leon's guard to take him away.

Outside, the guard kicked Leon into the wagon, and the posse and their parcel piled inside. Then they clattered off over the cobblestones. Above the din of the wagon wheels, Leon could hear the cows bellowing.

He hoped Jakob would hear them.

Inside the tavern, Jakob looked up from the counter and caught sight of the police wagon as it passed the open door. He heard the cows bellowing, and he made the sickening deduction. He called to Victor and Yuri to go to the sheds, and he himself made his trembling way to the police station.

Yes, Leon Wolf was there, they told him, and in custody on a charge of murder. No, he was not allowed to see anybody. There were a thousand questions that gathered in Jakob's mouth. Who had been murdered? Where was the body found? Why Leon? But he was afraid of voicing them, so instead, he heard himself saying, "But he hasn't had his supper."

The officer in charge laughed. "Don't worry," he said. "We

won't let him starve to death. We're saving him up to shoot him instead."

"When is the trial?" Jakob whispered. "There will *be* a trial?"

"Holy Russia is a land of justice," the officer said with pride. "He will have a fair hearing."

"But when will it be?" Jakob insisted.

"When the body is claimed, and we have more evidence."

Jakob made no inquiries about the body. He already knew all he needed to know.

He walked home in an agony of despair. He could not keep the news from his family, and he could not bear their pain. His own he could contain. But Miriam? Poor Miriam. He recalled now that last Passover tragedy when the milk-brothers had been taken. And he cursed God aloud.

The family had gathered in the back room of the tavern and were waiting for his return. The agony in their faces spoke of the news that had already spread through the ghetto. Miriam was clinging to her mother's arm.

"We know," Esther whispered.

Jakob embraced them both. "There'll be a trial," he said tonelessly.

They could do nothing but wait as rumor spread around the ghetto and the joy of Passover preparation turned sour. In the Bindel tavern that year, there were no festivities at all. There seemed little point in celebrating a freedom of the past when the present was bound in chains.

Jakob went every day to the police station and after a week, and the end of the Passover, there was still no claim to the body.

"How long will you wait?" Jakob asked at the station.

"Until someone claims him."

"But the child must have been missed by now," Jakob said.

They were not interested in his opinion. One day some distraught woman would arrive, screaming for revenge on the murderer of her child. She had to, else their case was threadbare. But no such woman appeared and, after a month's incarceration, Leon was brought to trial. It didn't matter that no one had claimed the body. It was enough that the child had been found dead and mutilated in Leon Wolf's cow shed.

The prosecution's case rested heavily on Pandowska's evidence, and he went into the box and swore falsely his rehearsed tale. Pandowska gave the impression of being an upright Russian peasant, who didn't want to get anybody into trouble but at the same time felt bound to do his Christian duty.

The court was crowded, and most of the spectators were shrieking for blood. Jews were wary of attending such proceedings. But Jakob was in court, and so was Miriam. She had been adamant about attending even though Jakob had tried to dissuade her. She sat next to him under his protective arm, while on her other side sat Faivel, and their three faces were masks of gloom. Miriam kept her eyes on Leon. Occasionally he looked in her direction, but neither of them could manage a smile. He was barely recognizable. His face was gaunt, and his clothes hung about his wasted frame, no longer familiar with the contours that once gave them a shape and a form.

The defense, such as it was, offered no witnesses. Any testimony as to the whereabouts and the doings of the accused at the time of the crime could only be confirmed by his family. He was in the tavern, they would claim, and they were all preparing for Passover. But it was the mention of those preparations that Leon's defense wished to avoid for they only confirmed the suspicion that no Passover could be prepared without Christian blood. So it was only Leon who was called in his own defense. He was frightened, and his voice was barely audible. He had been in the tavern all day, he whispered. He was helping to bottle the wine from the barrels, he said.

"Red wine?" the prosecutor asked with a sneer, and the court tittered.

He was asked to give the timings of his movements. But Leon's life was not guided by any timepiece. He woke when he was no longer tired, he ate when he was hungry, and he milked his cows when they called for him. The only time that was scored by any calendar was the length of the milk-brothers' absence, and he could have told them that to the day. He looked helplessly around the court.

"I don't know about the times," he said, and he meant it in the general as well as in the particular. "The only thing I know is that I am innocent." He shuddered, and slowly he straightened his shoulders and held his head high. Miriam gripped her father's arm. A reddish glow suffused Leon's face as he opened his mouth to speak.

"I have two beautiful children," he said, "who at this moment

are serving in the Russian army. They were taken away from me
ten years ago, when they were ten years old. I do not know
whether they are alive or dead. It is your Czar who is in the
business of killing children," he said. "My hands are clean."

The court was hushed. Then the spectators began to hiss their
horror; and Jakob, Miriam, and Faivel knew that Leon had now
condemned himself from his own mouth—that gentle mouth of
so few words and of so many silences.

The judge called for order. Then the defense lawyer was called
to pick up the pieces and make what he could of his client's
blasphemy. But the man did not refer to it. He thought it better
to let it lie. Instead he concentrated on the threadbare case for the
prosecution, and particularly on the lack of a petitioner for the
body. The child was probably stillborn and unwanted, he suggested, and some villain had seen it as an opportunity for persecution, and had planted the body on the defendant's property.
His words were addressed to Pandowska, who kept his eyes on
the floor.

"Thank you," the judge said, and the defense lawyer sat down,
and it was clear to the crowd that the judge fully agreed with
what had been suggested. Jakob, Miriam, and Faivel clasped their
hopeful hands.

"But what about the Czar?" one of the spectators shouted, and
his indignant cry was taken up by the others, whose peasant lives
had been oppressed by that Majesty in whose name they were
now so outraged. The judge called for silence again, and set about
to sum up the case. He prefaced his remarks by congratulating
the prosecution in bringing the case to the attention of the courts.
One could not be too careful, he said, especially in the period of
the Jewish Holy Days. But in this case, he went on, there was
little evidence of guilt, and he was bound to agree with the points
made by the defense. He therefore concluded that on the charge
of ritual murder, the defendant Leon Wolf was not guilty.

Jakob held Miriam close as she broke into sobs of relief, but
Faivel, smelling the judge's rider, laid a restraining hand on
Jakob's arm. The Czar's name once more hissed across the court,
and this time the judge did not ignore it.

"However," he said, "I cannot overlook the supreme insult
against His Imperial Majesty, and for that breach of the law, I
sentence him to ten years' hard labor."

On the whole the crowd was appeased, and some of them even

cheered. Miriam rushed over the benches in an attempt to reach
her husband, to touch his hand with a ten-year hold, to print his
face on hers in a decade's etching, but they were already taking
him away. Leon turned and saw her and smiled.

"I shall live," he shouted, "and so shall the milk-brothers."

Jakob watched Leon down the stairway. "We'll wait for you
all," Jakob whispered. Then he turned and led the way through
the court.

By evening when news of the trial had spread around the
ghetto, Leon Wolf had become its hero. He had spoken for them
all. Together with the Bindels they would await his return, as
many of them already waited for their lost sons. The years would
pass, the birthdays, the Holy Days, and all the landmarks of the
year. And each new day would swell the sound of their distant
voices, and the passage of time would shorten the shadows of
their long march home.

But for Leon Wolf they would wait in vain. For nine solid years
he broke stones on the Siberian wastes. He worked alone, talking
to himself all the time, telling stories to the milk-brothers on each
backbreaking shift. Perhaps he thought that in their thirtieth year
they were already too old for his tales. For one day he sat down
on the rubble and laid down his pick, as a minstrel would put
aside his harp. He died because he had run out of stories, and his
own was too monstrous to tell.

It was snowing. Siberian snow, as mean and as unyielding as it had always been. But now it didn't matter anymore. On their wagon trail across the Siberian wastes, the milk-brothers were seeing it for the last time. For they were going home.

They still could hardly believe it. A few months before, there had been rumors in the camp. Nothing specific, just hearsay of an event of great import. It was said to have happened in St. Petersburg, and its very location gave it a certain urgency. It appeared that what had happened was cause for rejoicing, but that the cheers must be behind the hand, and the laughter stifled in the throat. And as it turned out, the news required just such a reaction, and when the milk-brothers heard it, they feigned sorrow, but their hearts were bursting with joy. For the tyrant was dead. His Imperial Majesty had proved his final fallibility.

Alexander the Second, who succeeded him, was a lesser tyrant of spasmodic liberalism. In one of his generous episodes, sundry restrictions on Jews and Jewish life were lifted. Child recruitment would soon be abolished, and, in pockets of the Czar's army, those who had soldiered twenty years were released from service. The milk-brothers had been given an hour's notice to pack their kit and to prepare for home. They were stunned. Unlike their family, who took account of their years of absence rather than the soldiering years to come, the milk-brothers had concentrated on the latter, and when suddenly, from one moment to the next, five whole years were knocked off their reckoning, in a strange way they felt cheated.

The phrase "We have survived" had hovered for twenty years on their tongues, awkward, unripe, unrehearsed. Now it was called upon for utterance and it withdrew in shyness and total disbelief. Others would have to say it for them, all those waiting for them at the tavern, and as they imagined the welcome they would receive, it did not occur to them that each and every member of their family would not have survived as well.

During the course of their homeward journey, they rehearsed their return to the tavern. Two days were spent in arguments for and against surprise. There were ways of letting the family know that they were on their way home. A few days' notice would give them the joy of anticipation and lessen the shock of their sudden arrival. But it would detract from the milk-brothers' pleasure. They analyzed each choice like two philosophers, stretching out the argument beyond its merits. For in truth, they were both apprehensive of their return. They had changed. They did not know how they could tailor themselves to a life that, in their adult memories, had become so alien. They had traveled in lands never inhabited by any Jew. It had been twenty years since they had celebrated a single Jewish Holy Day. They were without language. They had left Odessa with a ten-year-old's Yiddish, a language in which they wrote, spoke, and, most important of all, dreamed. They were returning with an adult's Russian, an alphabet they could not decipher, an imagery not of their blood. For many years now their dreams had been silent. The occasional nightmare had startled their sleep, but it was wordless, full of images of despair and sounds and smells of fear. Even now, as they neared their home, they spoke together in their flat Russian, as if this would exorcise the Odessa ghosts whom they no longer had a language to confront.

"It seems so long since I milked a cow," Reuben whispered one night, but even this childhood memory could not prompt his childhood tongue.

"How many cows now in that cow shed?" Benjamin said.

"I'll lay you a rouble on ten."

"Done," Benjamin said, stretching out his hand.

They looked at each other for a long while. Then Benjamin clasped Reuben's shoulder. "We have survived," he whispered.

They were woken by a sudden change in the wagon wheel music. Instead of cobblestones, the wheels were passing over wood, and Benjamin and Reuben peered into the dim light and saw the wagon's reflection in a dawn river.

"It's the Dnieper," a soldier behind them said. "By dusk we'll see the ships in Odessa harbor. How long are you from home?" the soldier asked.

"Twenty years," Benjamin said.

"A lifetime," the soldier muttered.

"And you?" Reuben asked.

"Four years," he said. "I've got a girl in Odessa. Said she'd wait for me." There was little confidence in his voice. "But by now she probably thinks I'm dead. Maybe she's married somebody else." He paused and peered into the half-light. "I'm a bit afraid of going home," he said.

They turned into their blankets.

"Will you marry, Benjamin?" Reuben whispered after a while.

They had rarely spoken about such things. In all the years of their recruitment, neither of them had known a woman, and Reuben's connection with Sergeant Likov was a secret that he had kept from Benjamin.

"I'd like children," Benjamin said. "Two boys like us."

"Then you'll continue the Bindel line," Reuben said, and there was such a relief in his voice that Benjamin found it disturbing.

"What about you?" he asked.

"I'll never marry," Reuben said. He had never admitted it even to himself, but now that it was out, he felt suddenly unburdened. He knew his decision was unnatural, and he knew its cause. The stain that Sergeant Likov had left on his body could never be wiped clean in a lifetime. He would not contaminate another with his guilt, and he thanked God that the shame had diminished his body's appetite.

"Why not?" he heard Benjamin say.

"I want to spend my life learning. I want to study the Talmud." His future ambition, now so freely stated, did not surprise him. He had lost out on twenty years of his inheritance, and with each day of his recruitment, that loss had been confirmed. Now he would go home and spend the rest of his life redressing the balance of language and heritage.

Benjamin put his arms around Reuben's shoulder. "Then I shall have sons for both of us," he said, "and between us we shall guide their growth."

Then they slept the whole day through, and were woken by the hooters of the Odessa ships. This time on waking they felt less fearful. The certainty of the future, in both the body and the spirit of the Bindel family, had given them peace. The wagon convoy slowed down as it reached the harbor and the screeching of the gulls almost drowned the groaning of the wheels. Then they creaked to a halt, and the milk-brothers inside stared at each other, rooted to their seats, unable to deal with that moment of freedom they had dreamed about for so many years.

"What's the matter with you all?" the coachman shouted. "D'you want to go back to Siberia?"

Benjamin and Reuben lifted their kit from the quayside and walked along the waterfront. They were a good six versts from the tavern. If they hurried, they would reach it by evening. After some time they reached the limits of the ghetto and there, their feet faltered. From open windows the suddenly familiar cooking smells teased them. But the more familiar the smell, the more alien they felt. They trod the cobblestones warily, like intruders on a foreign soil. They matched nothing in their surroundings. Everything was out of joint and out of season, and the only fitting thing about them was their greatcoats into which they had finally grown, those same greatcoats that had swaddled their young limbs so many *kaddishes* ago.

"It must be near to suppertime," Benjamin said. He spoke in Yiddish, as if the ghetto cobbles had dictated that language. And Reuben responded likewise, plucking the syllables of their mother tongue into a distant familiar melody. And through those magic words they were gently shipped back into the past of their childhood, and its comforting sound eased their passage home.

It was Thursday, market day in the ghetto. That morning Jakob Bindel had woken in a mood of euphoria for which he could find no cause. As was his habit, he took the milk-brothers' letter out of its silk wrapping, and as he unfolded it, he was startled to find that the folds of the letter had split in two. The breakage did not dismay him, for in some way he felt it connected to his feeling of elation. He wound his phylacteries about his arms and made his peace with God. He saw the broken letter as a sign that he need not pray on the milk-brothers' behalf anymore, but that he must pray for himself, and give thanks for his renewed faith.

"We must cease suffering this day," he announced to the family table. "The year of mourning for Leon is over. We have all wept enough. We need to tutor our talent for joy in order to welcome our children home."

"You still hope for them," Esther said sadly. "There's been no word of them for seven years."

"I don't ever want to hear talk like that," Jakob said. His anger

reddened his face, and his clenched fists were white under the
knuckles.

"We must restore order in our lives," he shouted.

Then he left and hitched his wagon and made his way to the
market.

On his way, he made a detour to Faivel's. His friend was stitch-
ing away on the pavement outside his shop. Though he would not
admit to it, Faivel's sight was failing, and whenever the weather
permitted he would take his work outside and profit by the light.

"Come, Faivel," Jakob shouted. "Come with me to market.
We'll spend the day together."

Faivel caught his friend's happy mood. He wrapped up his
sewing and wheeled his machine indoors. Jakob waited while he
made his excuses to Raisl, and he heard the echo of Raisl's rasp
as it dogged Faivel's fluttering steps from the house. He shrugged
his shoulders in mock despair and hauled himself onto the
wagon.

"To Zemach's?" he said, his eyes twinkling.

"Of course to Zemach's," Jakob said. "But first we must go to
market."

Jakob found himself buying food far in excess of his weekly
needs, but he did not wonder at it for it seemed naturally dictated
by his continuing high spirits.

"Are you expecting an army?" Faivel asked, helping to pile the
provisions onto the wagon.

Jakob looked at his friend. That word was no accident, he
thought. "To Zemach's, Faivel," he said, "and we shall tell stories to while away the time."

"I dreamed of the milk-brothers last night," Faivel said suddenly. Jakob stopped the wagon and clutched Faivel's sleeve. "Is
that the truth, my friend?" he said.

"Have I ever told you a lie?"

They journeyed in silence. Outside the entrance, Zemach was
sitting, a white tablecloth tucked into his collar. He was having a
haircut, and Zelda, his granddaughter, was barber. When he saw
Jakob's wagon, he jumped up to give him welcome, and Zelda
scolded him for the disturbance.

"It will wait, my little cabbage," he said. "Friends are first,"
and he strode toward the wagon.

"What news?" Zemach asked. "Is it a holiday that Faivel
doesn't work and that you don't return home from market?"

"It's not good to work all the time," Jakob said. They went into the tavern. "We'll open one of my best," Zemach said, and he went behind the counter and drew out a bottle of red wine, which he held up to the light. "It's from Georgia," he said. "It's rare in these parts. It's fit for a celebration." He paused and looked at his friends, and taking the glasses down, he asked, "What are we celebrating?"

"To life? To the future?" Jakob said. "Isn't that enough?"

"There's life and future in every day," Zemach said.

"But some days," Jakob countered, "they seem more possible."

Zemach poured the wine. "To life," he said, and so the three friends sat and celebrated Jakob's unspoken hopes.

That night the family supper in the kitchen was lighthearted and carefree. They had all been infected by Jakob's mood. Esther had cooked his favorite dessert, and he noted that she had made more than could possibly be eaten by the family. "You cook for an army, Mama," Sofia laughed, and as she said it, there was a muffled knock on the tavern door.

In that moment, Jakob understood each auspicious moment of the day. His knees trembled. They looked at each other around the table. No one moved into the tavern. Not that they were afraid, for there was nothing authoritative about the knocking. There was no summons in its tone, no punishment. It was gentle, like that of a child begging shelter. Once more they heard the knocks and then Jakob rose on his trembling legs and left the table. He moved through the tavern, the tears already starting in his eyes. When he reached the door, he would not ask who it was. One did not question the identity of one's own children. He leaned against the door before opening it, gathering his strength and wishing with all his heart that the gentle Leon were still alive. Then he braced himself and lifted the latch and opened the door wide.

The doorway was filled with greatcoat and he looked from the hem to the collar and then at their faces before he could allow himself to accept that his daily prayers had been answered. They looked exactly as he had imagined them, as he had seen them growing day by day. Reuben was the taller of the two. He looked very much like Leon, and Jakob was glad of it for it would help mitigate Miriam's loss. When he looked at his own, Benjamin, it was as if in a mirror. He stared and marveled, afraid to touch them.

They, for their part, saw an old man, and in his worn wrinkled features all the years of his parental loss. Then Benjamin spoke.

"We survived, Father," he said.

Jakob grasped them both in his arms. He could not speak and he would not sob, but he thought his joy would break him in two. They led him gently into the tavern, noting on the way how small it had grown, or how greatly their nostalgia had enlarged it. They hesitated at the kitchen door, and then stood still. They were too frightened and too excited to take a step farther. Jakob gently pushed them aside, and he himself opened the door and shut it behind him, while the milk-brothers stood outside and listened to his voice, which had the resonance of a prophet's.

"What did I tell you?" he thundered to the astonished table. And again. "What have I always told you? What? What?" The tears were streaming down his face. "Did I not have faith in it every day?" he whispered.

They stared at him.

"God is good sometimes," he said. Then he stood away from the door and opened it wide.

The milk-brothers stood on the threshold, their eyes slowly circling the table identifying brother, sister, niece, parent. And once again they surveyed the faces, their lips muttering each name they knew. Throughout this silent scrutiny, the painful gap at the table, that seat unoccupied, that space unstaked that seemed to stretch out its ghostlike arms for remembrance.

"Where's Father?" Reuben said.

Jakob wished that could have been saved till the last. That they all could have rejoiced in the homecoming, that they could have celebrated with untrammeled joy, and then, after that, and only after that, Reuben would have asked for his father. Jakob was suddenly seized with a rage against Leon because he had chosen not to survive.

"He's dead," Miriam said. "He died a year ago." She did not cry. She did not wish to give her son a cue for weeping. Leon had been gone from her life these ten years and she was used to his absence. He had been gone from his son's life for much longer. "Leon died a hero," she said, and she stretched out her arms for her son's embrace.

He moved toward her, as Benjamin did to Esther. Gradually

around the table, hands, small, large, and all trembling, touched the milk-brothers' faces, as the blind seek out and welcome their kin. For the rest of that evening, they sat together, silent for the most part, not knowing what questions to ask of each other. The milk-brothers' story would take time, time for rage, disbelief, and wonder. And finally time to prepare its proper place in their heritage.

The news of the miraculous return spread quickly around the ghetto, and the following night, after the beginning of the Sabbath, there were celebrations in the tavern. Like most close-knit families in close-knit communities, the Bindels kept their friends for life, and the guest list for the welcome-home party, with a few additions, was exactly the same as for the parties that had marked the milk-brothers' circumcision and Sofia's wedding. Death had carried off a few of their number. Reb Schlomovitch had gone to his grave and his wife had followed shortly after. There were no officials of the community present, for, with the abandonment of the *kahals,* there was no longer need to curry favor. The absence of Meisels was especially toasted, since, for all his malevolence, the milk-brothers had finally outwitted him. Over the years the true nature of his death had been discovered. Mrs. Lascevitch, his reluctant housekeeper, had courageously let it be known, and now Faivel told it as he had told it a hundred times before with much relish and ornament. As he came to the end of his tale, Yankel appeared at the tavern door. He was old now, and retired, but in the Bindel household he had graduated to the status of guest and it was in this capacity that he was now welcomed to the tavern and given a much-needed chair and glass of kvass.

The last to arrive, because they had the farthest to travel, were Zemach and his family, his daughter, her husband, and his grandchild, Zelda. Zelda went straight to Esther and kissed her, and then went to help with the dishes on the counter. Benjamin stared at her and wondered who she was, and by what right she was so readily accepted into the Bindel family. He resented her a little. She struck him as flighty and presumptuous. Jakob looked at Benjamin looking at Zelda, and so did Faivel and so did Zemach, and so, out of his long professional training, did Yankel, and all of them chose to misinterpret the look as one of curiosity that might well grow into love. They waited for Zelda to catch sight of him, and when she did, turning with a dish of honey cakes, her eyes were drawn by his staring, and for one second were caught. The witnesses were satisfied. The mere exchange of glances between Benjamin and Zelda was enough in their eyes to set in motion a marriage contract. It was only a question of time, and if they had learned nothing else in their lives, they had learned patience, in whose name this present party was being celebrated. In his corner, Reuben had witnessed it too, but he knew his milk-brother's heart, and he knew that, like his own, it was closed to loving. To open one's heart was to allow a breach in one's defenses, gleaned and honed by so many years of exile. It saddened him profoundly, more for Benjamin than himself. For his resolve never to marry had been strengthened by the news of his father's death. His mother had quietly told him the story of Leon's trial and heroism, and he had decided to devote the rest of his life to study of the Talmud and the Torah, for he knew that in their pages he would find some meaning in his father's silences and in the passion to which he had finally given tongue.

In the months following their return, the milk-brothers withdrew more and more from the family circle. Adjustment was not easy. Over the twenty years of their absence, their daydreams of return had become so vivid that they no longer allowed for the stark reality of a family reunion. Despite their faith in their own survival, both men had had moments of despair that only such an abiding faith can engender. That in truth, they would not survive at all. So each army night before sleep, as they knocked on the tavern door, and with triumph presented their survived selves, the image of reunion had become more and more magnified, more and more blurred, focusing itself out of any possibility of realization. But on their return all images had shrunk. The tavern door was narrower than their combined greatcoats, and scarcely higher than the top of their shaven heads, and behind it, the impudent truth of an old shriveled man, the wrinkles on his face notching each year of their absence, and in that focus so suddenly and so professionally sharp, they were rudely shunted into the truth of the twenty years that had passed. But the most damning proof of that loss lay behind the tavern door, through the dark hostelry, shrunk now to their boyhood, and into the back rooms beyond, where lay all the pent-up love that over the years had fed upon its fragile hopes and expectations, a love that given the smallest avenue of release, would flood the earth.

It was that love that the milk-brothers had not reckoned on. In their dreams the tavern of their return was a palace, and such love does not dwell in palatial dimension. Rather, it belongs to confinement. It knows no breathing space, no formality. Any time, any place will do for its artless release, undressed for all occasion. Confronted by this sudden surge of loving, the milk-brothers, for so long untouched, unheeded, longed to withdraw, and to express the only safe loving they knew—that of the one for the other. They were like two conspirators who share the filthy secret of survival, a secret they share with no other.

In the months after their return they withdrew in such fashion, taking endless and silent walks through the ghetto, each familiarizing himself once again with his past. But one day, during a forest walk, as they strolled through a clearing, Benjamin put a hand on Reuben's shoulder.

"We've lost the talent of loving," he said.

Reuben paused and stared at his brother. He nodded. Benjamin had fully spelled out the cost of their survival. The love that they had for each other was real enough; it was their inalienable property. It was based on a sharing of a past, a past that was shareable with no other. For, despite the endless tales with which they had regaled the tavern table, they remained only stories. In no way could they convey the cost of their telling. Sergei Ash had chosen to die, and so had the Abromovitch brothers, and those hundreds of ringletless boys who had dropped into Abraham's bosom by the wayside. But Benjamin Bindel and Reuben Wolf had *not* died, because that was not what they had chosen, and there was no story that could convey the shame and the guilt of their survival. And so they had to tell it to each other, over and over again, in quiet and private places.

"You should marry Zelda," Reuben said after a while.

"I do not love her," Benjamin said. "Zelda nor any other woman."

"I have watched her," Reuben said. "I have seen her love for you. Such love can open your own heart. Such love will give you children, and your children will justify your survival."

"And you?" Benjamin asked.

Reuben did not answer. He took his brother's arm and walked him across the clearing into the safety of the forest. But after a while Benjamin stopped and held his brother close. "How will you reconcile yourself to it all?" he asked again. "You have more to assuage than I."

Reuben stared at him. "What do you mean?" he said softly.

Benjamin guided him once more into their walking. Then he stopped under a tree. "I know about Likov," he said. "Anna Pankov told me. She saw you."

Reuben trembled. Benjamin's reminder thrust him back into that hayloft, the tabernacle where Sergei Ash had died. Likov had deliberately chosen that spot, and had led him there to desecrate Sergei's tomb. Reuben recalled hearing some rustling in the hay. At the time he had thought it was a rat.

"She went up there to get some preserving bottles," Benjamin was saying. "That night she told me."

"What stopped you from killing him?" Reuben asked.

"Survival," Benjamin said. He spat out the word with bitterness.

"Was it worth it?" Reuben said.

"It has to be, brother," Benjamin said. "For both of us."

Reuben smiled. A surge of relief overwhelmed him. Part of the pain of the Likov experience had been its terrible secrecy. All their lives he and Benjamin had shared everything. Likov had erected the first barrier between them, and it was this slow and threatening isolation that had pained him most of all. Now that his shame was known and understood, his body seemed to cleanse itself a little.

"I'm glad that you know," he said, though he knew, as well as Benjamin, that this secret only served to reinforce their isolation.

Over the next few months, Benjamin felt more and more the need to settle down and raise another Bindel generation. It became with him a survivor's obsession, and he sought out Zelda. On their occasional meetings in the Bindel or Zemach taverns, he had found her fickle, but she was fun-loving, and it was that very quality that attracted him. For Zelda, as yet, knew nothing about pain or loneliness. She couldn't understand Benjamin's preoccupation with guilt.

"It's all over now," she said to him. "It's all in the past, and you must think of your future," and she turned away to hide her blushing.

"Would you share that future with me?" he asked. He hadn't meant to propose to her. He was simply obeying the logic of her argument. But he made no attempt to withdraw.

"We'll marry in the summer," he said, and as he took her trembling hand, he prayed with all his heart that he would learn to love her.

So Zelda and Benjamin were married and, contrary to custom, they made their home not in the bride's house, but in the Bindel tavern. Benjamin was loath to live apart from Reuben. Besides, Zemach had no land, and Benjamin and Reuben had already enlarged the cow herd and had started a small trading in dairy produce. In many ways their way of life and way of work had become a repetition of their past, always together, ever dependent on each other, and almost always alone. But now it was a life without fear, and over the years they talked less and less about those evil days.

It was not until Benjamin's first son was born that he was able to open his heart to Zelda. She had promised him a future, and here was the fruit of that promise. He called the boy Aaron. A year later, a second child was born, another son. It was as if the milk-brothers' return, after such a lengthy female holding, had licensed the renewal of male dynasty. Reuben was still unmarried, and the possibility of a family of his own grew more and more remote. So Benjamin named his second son for his milk-brother, calling him Leon.

The two boys grew up in the tavern with all the privilege of a new generation. Every woman in the household was their mother, and each man their father, but it was to the milk-brothers that Aaron and Leon instinctively turned for parenthood. All their free time was spent in the cow sheds, and as Benjamin and Reuben watched them at the milking, it recalled for them their own pasts that were as yet untainted by survival.

When Aaron reached his bar mitzvah year, the Bindel family considered it cause for great celebration. Not since Jakob Bindel's own initiation over seventy years ago had the tavern celebrated that seal of manhood.

It was snowing. Aaron's birthday fell a few weeks before Christmas, a safe enough time, for no Jewish festival, of either mourning or rejoicing, fell within its shadows. The congregation, mindful of the very special Bindel celebration, filled the hall to overflowing. Aaron was nervous, and so was Leon on his brother's behalf. But most nervous of all were the milk-brothers. Not that they doubted Aaron's skillful performance of his role, but they were wary of their own. This ceremony was unknown to them. On the day of their own bar mitzvah they had breakfasted on Farmer Pankov's pork. Baptism was not far behind, and as they watched Aaron climb the platform to read his portion of the law, they were assailed yet again with that hungry need for withdrawal, to go together to a dark and secret hideout, and share their shame. But Aaron's song soared in their ears, claiming his entry into that realm of manhood to which he was now, by his years, entitled. His voice was strong and entreating enough to gain a tardy admission for the milk-brothers as well.

After the ceremony they returned to the tavern, where the women busied themselves with preparations for the evening's festivities. The men were ordered out of the tavern. Benjamin took his sons into the forest, and Reuben went with them. The forest was a favorite haunt for the milk-brothers. Aaron and Leon had their own use for it too, as a brothers' playground, but this was the first time that the milk-brothers had shared the forest with the children. It was not a deliberate choice. Their steps had turned quite naturally in that direction. Aaron and Leon took the lead, making for the part of the forest that was their habitual rendezvous. Benjamin and Reuben followed, and as they covered the route, their legs tingled with a strange recall. When they saw the huge oak tree where Aaron and Leon were resting, they remembered that it was that very tree that had marked the end of their escape. Aaron and Leon had never been told the story.

"Now is the time to tell them," Reuben said as they approached the tree.

"Till now it would have been a fairy tale."

They reached the oak and leaned against its vast trunk.

"Is this where you always come?" Reuben asked.

"Yes," Aaron said. "Don't we, Leon? We always end up here."

"Why *this* tree?" Reuben said.

"It's big. You can always find it."

"There's a story attached to this tree," Benjamin said after a while.

"A true story?" Aaron asked doubtfully.

"It's true," Reuben said. "Every word of it. It happened to both of us."

"Tell us, Papa," Aaron said eagerly, settling himself down on a fallen pine log nearby. He moved along for the milk-brothers to sit beside him. Reuben took Leon on his knee.

"We were younger than you both at the time," Benjamin began. "We were ten years old. I have to tell you a little of the history of that time."

Thus Benjamin Bindel let his children into his childhood, leading them through the dark and perilous journey that had robbed him and Reuben of their youth. As he told the tale, he wondered at it, and so did Reuben, marveling at the miracle of their survival. As Benjamin set the stage for their capture, Reuben saw

the lean and gentle back of his father, hunched with anxiety,
tiptoeing through the trees, turning occasionally to urge the children's speed and silence. When they'd reached the tree, he'd motioned them to sit and rest. "You must go to the river," he had
said. "It's about three versts from here. I shall come with you.
But if we get separated, you must make for the willow tree. It's
the largest tree on the bank, and its branches spread halfway
across the water. At that point, the water is shallow and you can
cross the river direct. There's a hut on the other side. Stay there.
Eat some food and wait till one of us comes for you." Then
suddenly, as he was speaking, they heard the distinct crunch of
footsteps through the leaves. Reuben recalled the sickly pallor on
his father's face. "Go at once," he had said, and he'd lifted them
both from the ground, kissing the tops of their heads and holding
them still for a moment to say good-bye. Then he'd pushed them
away, turning his back on them, holding his ground with courage
enough in his heart to stem an army. Reuben had taken Benjamin's hand, and heedless of the noise, they had scrambled
through the tress. After a few moments' running, Reuben had
turned and looked upon his father for the last time. Leon was
standing where they had left him, his legs apart, his arms spread-
eagled, his fists clenched, an immovable bulwark against any attack.

"You are named after that man," Benjamin was saying, taking
young Leon's hand, and the boy turned on Reuben's knee and
clung to his uncle's neck. Benjamin smiled at his milk-brother. It
was a proper sharing of fatherhood.

Benjamin continued his story. He told them of the recruiting
oath of allegiance, their kitting-out, and their long marches into
the eastern wastes. He told them too of Sergei Ash and of the
Abromovitch brothers, but there was no story about Likov beyond his name and station. The children listened in wonder. The
light in the forest was failing as he reached the last chapter of his
story—the knocking on the tavern door, and their grandfather's
joyful face in its frame. And when the story was fully told, Aaron
took his father's hand.

"How did you both survive?" he said, using for the first time
the word that day by day had colored the calendar of the brothers' long absence from home.

And then Benjamin realized that, although he had told the
whole story of their survival, he had not told them how that word

was first spoken, how it had reverberated in their childish ears, and out of whose angry and loving mouth it first thundered. It was because of Jakob Bindel and his farewell oratory that the milk-brothers had survived at all. And Benjamin had told his children the story without mention of its central theme. He wondered now whether he should give it to Aaron in answer to his question, to give him Jakob Bindel's farewell, which he and Reuben knew word for word. But the present times were calm. No racial threat lurked in their childish corners. Jakob's words would be less pertinent now.

"We were lucky," he told Aaron. That was all his son needed to know. "Come," he said. "It's time to go back to the tavern."

As they turned their steps toward home, they heard the sound of men's voices, and the crunch of fir cones on the ground. In the clearing they came face to face with a group of woodsmen, state foresters with the Czar's insignia on their green caps. Benjamin and Reuben looked at their faces, and in the echoes of their recent story, they saw the features of the old *khapers* who had hunted them down. The men stared at them sullenly, then turned back to their work, that of singling out the trees that would be felled for the Christmas celebration. But the milk-brothers and the children did not move. They could not. Some unnameable fear had frozen their steps. They watched as the men tapped at the tree trunks, and from time to time marked one of them with a chalked cross, marking the wherewithal to rejoice in His birth with the mark of His crucifixion.

"What are you staring at?" One of the men turned suddenly from his chosen tree. He turned on them angrily, as if they had caught him in a depraved act. Benjamin and Reuben were silent and afraid. The woodsman turned to his companions.

"The Yids don't like what we're doing," he shouted.

"Christ-murderers," another yelled back. "What d'you expect from them? Look," he shouted. He strode across to Benjamin and grabbed him by the sleeve. "Watch me," he ordered. "I'll do you a favor." He took his chalk out of his pocket and went to the nearest fir, and on its trunk he chalked the six-pronged Star of David. "Is that better?" he laughed. "Does that suit you?" he sneered, and he took his ax and notched each arm of the Star in turn, destroying story by story the mansions of their Father's house. Then he raised his ax as if to blind a seventh star, and strode toward the children. Aaron and Leon took to their heels, and Benjamin and Reuben, in their already practiced flight, ran after them, hearing the men's laughter die away in the echoing branches of the trees. No, Benjamin thought. The present times were not as calm as he supposed. Jakob Bindel's valedictory counsel was as pertinent now as it had been over thirty years ago.

They had reached the path that led to the back of the tavern. Benjamin called to his children, and, together with Reuben, the four of them sat on an old wooden bench not far from the cow sheds.

"I have to tell you something," Benjamin said. "You asked us how we survived those terrible army years. I told you we were lucky. But that was only a small part of it. We survived because your grandfather Jakob had shown us the way."

"How?" Leon asked. "And why didn't you tell us before?"

"Was it because of those men in the forest?" Aaron said.

Benjamin smiled. "There are always such men," he said. "And always will be. Wherever you are. As long as you are a Jew. Such men will attack you in many disguises. They will do it in the name of the Czar, or they will assault you in the name of freedom. They will use all kinds of ideologies, but whatever they are called, and with whatever sweetness, they are made, each one of them, of Jew-hate and oppression. Listen to me," he said. "When we went into the Czar's army, your grandfather gave us the equipment to survive. And I want now to give it to you, as you must give it to your children. Look at me, my sons," he said, as his own father had addressed them so many years ago. The children stared at him, wondering at the urgency in his voice. "I want you to live," he said. "I want you to survive."

Reuben echoed him, as if in a litany, recalling all those terrible moments when anything seemed preferable to the life they were being forced to live.

"Listen to me," Benjamin whispered. "In times to come, the enemy will force you into baptism, as they did to me and your Uncle Reuben. Do not resist them. Let them sprinkle their holy water on your brows, let them flood your bodies with their purging priesthood. They cannot lay hands on your Jewish soul. You must survive, my children," he said again.

Then he and Reuben recited together. "Beware of principles. Abandon them if you are to survive. There is no cause on earth worth dying for," they said, "no God worth one's dying breath,

no country worth one's martyrdom, no principle worth one's sacrifice. Only in the name of love is death worthy. And friendship.''

When it was over, Benjamin, like his father before him, wondered whether his children had any idea of what he was talking
about. But he had to speak out, for his own sake, as his father
had for his. From generation to generation there would be a minstrel to sing that stubborn song of survival, in ghetto streets, at
wailing walls, in synagogue choirs. Everywhere and at all times,
there would be a minstrel, and somewhere, someone would hear
his song. It was the least and the most that the milk-brothers
could bequeath their children. That song was their sure and sublime inheritance.

The next years in the Bindel household were happy ones. The tavern was crowded and over the years the men had built make-shift extensions to house themselves. The Bindel holding was by no means prosperous, but between the tavern, the cows, and the vegetables they managed to eke out a living for them all. Jakob still controlled each area of their livelihood, but his work was confined to the care of the cows. It was that work that he loved the most. Besides, it was the least demanding, for since the return of the milk-brothers Jakob had aged considerably. It was as if their miraculous homecoming had at last given him license to submit to the natural process of aging. Until that time he had punished his body in his struggle to survive, to live until they came back to the tavern. Now he allowed himself shrinkage as nature dictated. There was little left of his thick black hair. It was sparse and gray, as was his beard, which he tugged at from time to time.

There was a certain relaxation of laws pertaining to Jews, a greater freedom of movement beyond the Pale, and entry into certain professions. But these concessions only applied to those who were known as "useful" Jews, those who were wealthy and educated; Jewish society in general remained unaffected. Indeed, a certain schism arose in the community among those who prop-agated assimilation and those who stubbornly adhered to their faith, and it was the latter who remained the constant target of czarist oppression. Jewish schools were closed and those who taught in them lost their license. The wearing of ritual clothing was forbidden, as was the wearing of ringlets on the cheek. The Bindel family was not particularly orthodox. They were Jews because the notion of apostasy was treacherous.

The Czar's policy of "fusion" was plainly unworkable. The more he screamed "assimilate," the more the Jews cultivated and

found shelter in the Mosaic law, and awaited the coming of the
Messiah, and fed the Czar's fury with their stubborn intransigence. It now seemed to them that he was as great a tyrant as his
hated predecessor. But for forty million Christian serfs under his
rule, Alexander the Second *was* the Messiah, for in 1861 he freed
them, allowing them to rent or even own their land. For many
Jews this emancipation had drastic repercussions. In their livelihood as middlemen in agricultural goods, they were now superfluous. Some of the more prosperous ones invested in the growing
railway boom, but for the most, the prospects were pitiable. The
Bindel household managed to maintain a steady livelihood, but
Jew-baiting was a daily irritant in their lives, and no authority
interfered to hinder it. There was no law that sanctioned anti-
Semitic riot, yet equally there was no law that forbade it. Until
that time, throughout the Czarist regime, attacks against the
Jews had been unorganized and erratic. But in 1871 a new word
surfaced in the Russian language. In the years to come, its utterance would shock the ghettos of all the major cities of Russia,
where the blood would run cold in its echo. It would reverberate
in the synagogues of Elisavetgrad, Kiev, Brody, and Balta. Finally, it thundered in Kishinev and shook the world. The word
was *pogrom,* and it was born in Odessa.

That year the festivals of Easter and Passover did not coincide.
The celebration of Christ's death and resurrection would be over
and done with before the Jews celebrated their freedom. And in
that year, for the first time, the Bindels were to feast at Zemach's
tavern. Zemach celebrated his eighty-fifth birthday and Benjamin
took Zelda and their sons across the ghetto. She was going to
help her mother with the preparations. Benjamin and the rest of
the Bindel family were to join them for the Seder.

Benjamin drove back alone. It was the Sabbath eve. The streets
were quiet, with an ominous silence, Benjamin thought, broken
only by an occasional grunt that Benjamin at first could not identify. It sounded as if it came from a stray pig, but Benjamin
dismissed that possibility, because the presence of a pig in the
ghetto was too unlikely. Yet he was uneasy. Benjamin was very
restless that night and regretted his separation from his wife and
children. He heard Jakob's restless tread on the floor above him
and, next door, the continuous creaking of Reuben's bed. He was
glad when morning came.

It was Sabbath and it was their custom to go to the synagogue. The men of the family left early, leaving the women to follow at their leisure. On their way, Benjamin heard once again an isolated grunt. He looked at Reuben, who showed no reaction. Neither did Jakob. But each of them had heard it and smelled the warning in the sound. At the corner of the synagogue there was another omen, this one visible—in a group of furtive-looking men in the uniform of the members of the Sacred League. Among them was a face that startled Jakob with its familiarity. At first he couldn't place it. He stopped and stared, and the man caught his eye and quickly turned away. And then Jakob knew him for Leon's murderer. Pandowska, now in the uniform of Defender of the Czar. Jakob grasped Reuben's arm and shielded his grandson from his father's killer.

"Don't hurry," Jakob said as the younger men quickened their pace. "We must show no fear."

Inside the synagogue there was a loud murmur among the congregation, and its tone was not that of prayer. Jakob and his family took their seats as the rabbi stepped into the pulpit and called for order. He looked up to the women's gallery and seemed relieved to find that it was empty.

"Please listen, all of you," he said. "This is very urgent. They are preparing an onslaught on our people. The Greeks have spread the story that we have stolen the cross that decorates their church."

A sigh of fearful disbelief rose from the congregation.

"They are screaming that the Jews have penned up cattle in the Russian cemetery. But there is worse, my friends," the rabbi went on. "A rumor is abroad that a law has been proclaimed from St. Petersburg that allows these hordes to attack our people. I fear the worst," the rabbi said in a whisper. "Go home, all of you, and keep to your homes. Protect your women and children," he said. And he started to sing the hymn that normally concluded the Sabbath service, "Lord of the World."

There was no dawdling in the courtyard that Sabbath. Everyone was anxious to get home. As the Bindels neared the tavern, Benjamin heard the grunting once more. A large pig was snorting his way over the cobbles toward them. It moved its huge head from left to right, the advance guard of an approaching horde. Jakob hurried his family into the tavern, and there they remained all day in a state of siege, fearful of the silence in the streets outside, and more fearful still that that silence might be broken.

They were all afraid to go to their beds that night, and they sat in the tavern watching the gathering dark. As dawn broke, they heard the grunts again, and they peered out of the windows and saw a flock of swine making their way past the tavern, unherded, and with no command. And then the church bells tolled their Palm Sunday chimes, and as if their peals were a signal to attack, the Odessa pogrom began.

It lasted for one whole day and night, punctuated with false lulls and feigned retreats. The Bindels kept themselves indoors and watched the straggling hordes of peasants, laborers, and professional agitators march past the locked tavern doors. For the most part they were armed with crude weapons—sticks and truncheons and iron bars. They were singing national songs of Holy Russia with the kind of patriotic fervor that has to have an enemy in mind. Jakob held his breath while they passed the tavern, praying that they would ignore his family. But he knew that all their swagger, all their jingoism, must find a target. Some family or many would have to pay the price for the Bindel reprieve, but not Faivel's, he prayed, not the Pinskis', and above all, not Zemach's. And on exactly that account, Benjamin was fraught with anxiety. He had to find some way of being with his children. He knew it would be madness to risk driving through the ghetto and its invading army, yet he could not stay where he was.

"I've got to go," he said suddenly.

"It's madness," Jakob said. "But you must," he added quietly. "Your place is with Zelda and the children."

Benjamin looked at Reuben.

"I'm coming with you," Reuben said.

Around the tavern the lanes were empty. They drove off in silence, but not for long, for shortly they could hear the singing again, and the cheering cries of the mob. They saw smoke, too, in the distance, lying in the very path they had to take to Zemach's tavern. Yet they pressed on. Soon they saw the site of the fire, a group of small tailoring stalls that heralded the beginning of the main shopping street. The wagon was already in the shadow of the mob, when suddenly the horse, sniffing danger, pulled up sharply, and neighed with fear. Its bellowing alerted the rabble, a handful of whom turned swiftly and made for the wagon. Benjamin tugged on the reins in an effort to turn the horse, but it was obstinate in its fear. Benjamin and Reuben could do nothing but await the attack. There was no time to get down from the wagon. The first of the mob were already clambering on the wheels, while others set about restraining the horse.

"You won't need this wagon anymore," one of them shouted, while another beat Benjamin about the head with his stick.

Reuben, raging in fury, kicked the attacker in the groin, and he fell back onto the cobbles, groaning with pain. The others looked on, dumbfounded that a rotten Jew should dare to put up resistance. Reuben stood on the wagon, his legs astride, as if daring another challenge to his authority. He had, after all, served twenty years in their rotten army, and those years had bred in him a consummate skill in survival. He helped Benjamin to his feet.

"We don't want the wagon," one of the men shouted. "We'll just take the horse."

Reuben made a movement to grab the reins but Benjamin restrained him. "You don't die for horses," he whispered.

So they had to stand there and helplessly look on while the beast was roughly unharnessed. There was no point in trying to get down from the wagon. Their elevated position offered some defense advantage, and they would risk a mob assault were they to descend.

Benjamin and Reuben waited till the mob was out of sight, then slowly they descended and made their way to the tavern. Benjamin was distraught. Now, even if it were possible to get through the ghetto, they had no means of transport. "If we can get to Faivel's," he said, "we can borrow his wagon." But Faivel, God help him, lived in the heart of the ghetto, the area where fires were burning.

"Let's wait till nightfall," Reuben said. "It may be quiet by then."

So they waited, keeping watch at the tavern windows, and the silence and the emptiness outside was unnerving. Then suddenly there was the sound of hurried footsteps, which stopped for a while, and they heard a desperate panting and reaching for breath. The sound seemed to come from a fugitive seeking shelter. The watchers waited and they heard the footsteps again. Then they saw a ghostlike figure approaching the tavern. At first the lone runner was unrecognizable, yet there was something familiar in its silhouette. Jakob rushed to the door and unbarred it.

Faivel stood there, or rather, bent there, moaning with an anguish more related to sorrow than pain. Jakob clasped him in his arms and helped him into the tavern. Reuben reached under the counter for some kvass, and together they settled Faivel on a bench and tried to calm him. His breathing was easier now, but he kept mumbling in a demented fashion, as if it were his mind that was out of breath. Jakob put his ear to Faivel's mouth.

"What is it, my friend?" he asked.

"I must bury her," Faivel said. "I have to bury her. Do you hear me, Jakob?" He looked up at him. "I must bury her."

"Who must you bury?" Benjamin said.

There was a silence, and then Faivel said, "She's lying in the street. But the rabbi's dead, and who will bury her?"

They did not try to press him further. They sat by his frenzied side and held his hands. It was clearly a ghastly tale that Faivel had to tell, and he would tell it in his own time. They sat in silence for a long while until Esther came to the back door of the tavern, bringing food for the sentries. She saw Faivel sitting there, his old head in his hands.

"What is it, Faivel?" she said softly.

He looked up at her. The tears were streaming down his face. "Raisl," he managed to splutter. "They killed her. She's lying on the street. Next to the Pinskis."

Esther said nothing. She looked at the men, and they clearly shared her disbelief—Faivel was hysterical. He was frightened and hallucinating in his fear.

"I must bury her," Faivel said again.

They tried once more with him. "Tell us slowly, Faivel," Esther said. "Tell us everything that happened."

His hands were trembling and they filled his glass once more, and as he put it to his lips he shook his head in disbelief. "The shop is gone," he said slowly. "They burned it down and we ran into the street, where we thought it would be safe. One of them picked up Raisl and threw her onto the fire. I ran and dragged her away, but it was too late. She's lying in the street, and all her hair's gone," he wailed, "and I have to bury her." His voice was calm now, detached. "I ran away because there was nothing more I could do. I saw the Pinskis farther down the street. They were burned too. I passed the synagogue. It's on fire," he said simply. "The rabbi was lying on the steps outside. He must have gone inside to save the scrolls, because he was lying on the steps still holding them in his arms." He looked up at Jakob. "I think it's the end for all of us, my friend," he said. Then he turned away and wept.

Benjamin turned away and grieved too, for if the fires had reached the synagogue, there was no reason why the marauders should not be making their way through the ghetto to Zemach's tavern. At first he could not understand why the Bindel tavern was spared. Now he realized that the mob were saving the taverns till the last. So they would loot and pillage at will, and drink themselves into a stupor to celebrate their victory.

Reuben read his thoughts. "Is this why we survived?" he said.

"We should leave," Esther said. "All of us. We should go into the forest. I shall get the food," she said, "and gather the children." As she spoke, the church bells pealed the close of the Palm Sunday evening service.

"Perhaps it will be over now," Jakob said. "They started with the bells. And the bells are tolling the end of the pogrom. They will go home now," he said.

"But on their *way* home," Reuben said, "they have to pass the tavern."

"I think in any case we should go," Esther said again, and as she spoke, they heard the singing and the shouting in the distance, and they knew that it was now too late for flight.

"Bring the family into the tavern," Jakob said. "We must all stay together. To keep watch," he added. He knew that against a mob they were defenseless, but Jakob feared their end, and he wished his family together. Poor Benjamin, he thought.

The women set the table in the tavern, and the family assembled. The children had been brought from their beds and they sat bleary-eyed and bewildered at the table. When Jakob saw them, he regretted that he had taken them from sleep. He had opened their eyes only to witness their own deaths. "Let them go back to sleep," he said quickly, and he picked up two of them in his arms and took them to their beds. The other children followed, and Jakob watched them as they closed their eyes and he prayed that they would sleep right through the pain of Death's calling. He went back into the tavern, and sat by Faivel's side at the table.

"I must bury her," Faivel kept saying, over and over again, and nobody stopped him, because the words bandaged his wounds and kept the lifeblood within him.

Despite all the food that had been prepared, nobody ate very much, but the ritual of the blessings over the bread and the wine created an order in the chaos that surrounded them. It was to be their last supper. They could hear the shouting and the singing, though still at a distance, and occasionally the sound of shattering glass. And they waited, restive and fidgety, almost willing a swift and painless end. All except Faivel, who sat motionless, his face filled with the infinite calm and patience of one who has lost everything, and now has nothing more to lose.

The hours passed until the shadows of first light limped across the tavern walls. And then, as if fueled by the cold morning sun, the singing grew louder and the marching feet nearer, and the screaming was drowned by the crackling fires. And then, suddenly, the tavern was surrounded.

Jakob went to the window and crouched beneath the sill. The men were sitting on the grass verge in front of the tavern, at least a hundred of them.

"They're on this side too," Benjamin whispered from his stand at the back window.

"And around the sheds," Reuben said. "They've got torches."

It seemed that the whole invading army had gathered at the Bindel tavern as their last port of call.

"They will go away," Jakob said, trying to instill some confidence in his voice. "In time they will all go away. And then we shall go out into the streets and bury the dead." He went over to Faivel and sat by his side.

It was then that they heard the lowing of the cows.

Yosif automatically rose, but Jakob shook his head. "No one must leave this room," he said. He knew that the appearance of any one of them would be provocation. Then suddenly the singing stopped and all in the tavern held their breath.

"Go and see to the cows," one of the rabble shouted.

Yosif rose again, and again Jakob shook his head.

"Don't you rotten Yids care?" another voice bellowed through the tavern. Then there was laughter and the singing started again and muted the cows' lowing. But Benjamin and Reuben heard it, even through the raucous voices, and the thought crossed Benjamin's mind that if he went out and relieved the cows, God would save his children. Reuben stared at his milk-brother. Whatever Benjamin chose to do, he would follow him.

The time passed and the singing outside could no longer mute the cows' call for attention. They were bellowing now, with

moans of such anguish that the women stopped up their ears.
And in that moment, the three men rose from their seats, Jakob,
Benjamin, and Reuben, and had Leon been alive, Jakob thought,
he would have joined them. All their lives they had chosen how
to live and how to survive. How to die lay within their choice as
well. The three men left the tavern.

Outside in the half-light, they discerned a body of men leaning
against the shed doors. As they approached, the men dispersed
and bowed mockingly, ushering the milkers into the barn. The
noise inside was deafening. The men hurried to the stalls and set
to work, resting their heads on the throbbing flanks. Death was
near they knew. And like drowning men, they journeyed into
their pasts. Of them all, Jakob had the farthest to travel. Eighty-
eight years of survival. There was no chronology in his recall, but
each event had a clarity. He remembered the winter pram of his
infancy. He played with Faivel in the nursery lands between their
houses and then made snowmen on the field that now penned
men into sanity. Then Esther flashed across his eyes in her white
wedding dress that also had clothed Miriam and then Sofia. But
blotting the vision was Meisels, and Jakob clutched at the cow's
teats in rage. He looked across at the milk-brothers and he had to
calculate their age. As long as they had been in the army, he had
known their calender as intimately as his own, crossing off the
years they had served from childhood through adolescence to
manhood. Once they had been released, he considered them im-
mortal in view of the miracle of their survival, so he had not
bothered to count anymore. He had to drum his fingers on the
cow's flanks to tally their earthly years. Forty-six, he concluded.
His own father had died at almost twice that age. He recalled
now how they had missed him at breakfast, and how all around
the table had stared at Jakob, as if confirming his succession. He
had gone to the cow shed. There had just been one cow in those
days, Devorah, he remembered, the milk-brothers' favorite. He
had taken his time getting there, fearing what he would find. His
old father lay slumped on Devorah's half-milked flank, his lips
grazing the limp teat, as if in death he had closed his circle. Jakob
paused for a while as he held the image of his dead father in his
eye. He thought of Esther again and of all those around the
fearful tavern table, and how, after a while, they would wonder
about his return, and no heir could be sent to look for him. As no
heir had gone to the shed to look for Leon. And no heir would

seek out Benjamin or Reuben. That day would mark the end of the rugged Bindel line and he prayed for the lives of those in Zemach's tavern.

Benjamin prayed for them, too, as he recalled his life. He recalled his capture, but he would not allow himself to think of his army life. With Death so patently by his side, he would not give those years of his life the dignity of recall. "Aaron, Leon," he whispered, for they were the names he must etch into the future, to whom in his memories and his blessings he must give the gift of survival. His own father had given him that gift and he had done his best to honor it. If he were to die this day, he thought, he would have given almost half his life in the service of that power that was about to destroy him.

After a while, the three men moved to the other stalls and soon the cows stopped lowing and there was silence in the sheds. Reuben's face was calm, glowing with a peace that he soon expected to be his. Now he and his milk-brother were to die together. Soon, he knew, it would all be over. He looked at Benjamin by his side, and Jakob, too, and he knew that whatever journey awaited them, he could find no better companions. Death would stand before them, face-to-face. But with Aaron and Leon, because they were children, Death would stand behind their backs, and in one gluttonous embrace would consume four Bindel generations. God is thorough in His work, Reuben thought. He cast a sidelong glance at the barn door, and saw them all assembled there. Soon they would finish their milking, and there would be no more to do but to abandon once and for all their lifelong clutch at survival, and walk with calm and with grace to their lynching.

But the mob had something else in mind. They would wait for the milking to be done. They watched as the men put the buckets aside. Then three of them rushed into the barn and pinned the men's arms behind their backs. None offered any resistance. Three others, armed with knives, poured the buckets of milk on each man's head, as if to anoint him. Then they passed their lances across each throat and the blood mingled with the milk, bonding their deaths as it had their lives. Then the cows were led from the barn and no one bothered to close the doors.

The murder of the head of the Bindel household was the signal to destroy it whole—root and branch. The mob burst into the tavern and there lay the three targets for their violence—pillage,

rape, and murder. Although there was no one outside the tavern
to witness the slaughter within, one of the rabble closed the door
behind him. Perhaps for him it was a God-bothering moment, or
perhaps it was a gesture of politeness. Then he grabbed Sofia by
the waist, threw her on the floor, and tore her legs apart. Soon all
the women in the tavern were spread-eagled on the sawdust. Esther's heart had mercifully stopped before her violation, so she
did not know of the succession of men who took their pleasure
upon her lifeless body. Yosif, Victor, and Yuri and even Faivel
had grabbed bottles from the counter, and had managed to lay
low half-a-dozen men before they themselves were slaughtered.
And then, when all the Bindels were disposed of, or so the rioters
thought, the children gathered in the back doorway, woken by
the noises and screams.

"Go back to bed," one of the men shouted, and the children,
terrified by what they had already seen, fled to what they thought
was the safety of sleep. So they huddled all together on Jakob and
Esther's large and gentle bed, among the feather pillows on
which all of them had been born. They, too, like Jakob and the
milk-brothers, were completing their own circle.

Downstairs the mob was withdrawing, taking what was left of
the Bindel cellars. And they closed the door firmly behind them.
Then they gathered paper and oil-soaked rags, lighting them one
by one, and they placed them with a drunk's care at intervals
around the tavern. They stood back and watched as the flames
quickly fed on the tavern wood, and spread until a vast carnival
conflagration consumed it whole. If the children screamed, their
cries went unheard, drowned by the chanting and the cheering of
the mob, who saw in the Bindel furnace the climax of their long
day's toil. The pogrom was over, at least for the time being, and
slowly they made their drunken ways home, rehearsing the tales
they would tell their children.

When the bright morning light broke, the police, who had
stood by and seen order destroyed, now set about to restore it.
Those still alive in the ghetto stirred themselves, thanked God for
their survival, and dared the streets.

Among them was Simon Paritsky, ripe in his ninety years and
shamefully unscathed. Paritsky was the beadle of the synagogue,
everybody's willing lackey, who, in his menial role, had never
sought preferment or promotion. It was God's will that he should
spend his life in humble service. God's will, too, he supposed,

that He had spared him in that terrible day and night, so that he could be His chosen witness to the hell that remained of the ghetto. He wandered through it like a ghost close to the peace that he knew would soon be his. He turned his unsteady steps in the direction of the synagogue. On his way he noted that many of the small shops had been razed to the ground. A tailor's dummy stood idly against a broken wall, its canvas chest pierced with a farrier's tool. He shrank at the occasional body on the cobbles, and looked around for something to cover the dead astonished faces. He heard a wagon approach, and as it neared, he discerned old Zemach the innkeeper at the reins, with Zelda and her two sons behind him. He supposed they were making for Bindel's tavern. He turned the corner of the synagogue street and he wondered whether he had lost his bearings. For that same temple where he had become a man, where he had married, rejoiced, mourned, and all his life given service, was now a shell, blackened by smoke, doorless, windowless, deserted. On the steps a handful of pigs were lolling, taking the cold morning sun, and in their midst lay a body. Paritsky approached and saw the Scrolls of the Torah, which had rolled open down the steps. The pigs were feeding on its parchment and velvet trimmings. He looked at the body and, with a cry, he recognized the rabbi. He took what was left of the velvet covering and laid it over the old man's face, then he turned away. At the bottom of the steps he turned around and saw a pig gnawing at the rabbi's right arm. Then, in all his ninety years, he fell onto his knees and prostrated himself on the ground. And with Elijah's heartrending cry, "It is enough, O Lord," he whispered. "Now take away my life."

Some time later a large hearse wagon drew up by the synagogue steps and collected two bodies. In its wake came Zemach's wagon, moving at a hearse's pace with two new coachmen at the reins. Aaron and Leon Bindel. Behind them, on the wooden bench, Zelda, shaken with sobs and disbelief, laid her head on Zemach's shoulder. Her grandfather's great years had dried up his well of tears. He sat erect, dry-eyed, with no release for his grief. All he felt was shame that he had survived. In the driving seat, Aaron clutched tightly at the reins, his fists clenched, holding back the tears. His father's death had left him too old to cry. But Leon, at his side, could still afford to be a child, and he sobbed for himself and for his brother, too.

"What are we going to do?" he asked.

Aaron recalled his father's words in the forest. Everywhere, and at all times, he had said, there would be a minstrel, and somewhere, someone would hear his song. Aaron heard it now, loud and clear across the cobbles of the broken ghetto. He put his arm around Leon's shoulder.

"We must survive," he said.

PART TWO

❦

The Book of Aaron and Leon

There were only three of them now at Zemach's tavern. Zemach had died shortly after the pogrom. On his return from the Bindel ruins he had taken to his bed and willed himself to die. It had taken him less than a week, and with his dying breath he had thanked God for his passing. Zelda's mother survived a little longer, refusing all the time to believe that anything had changed in the ghetto. Even after her father's funeral, she had returned to her kitchen and continued to prepare for his birthday. Occasionally she grumbled that the Bindel family were late in arriving and she fretted for her honey cakes that grew stale and mildewed with the waiting. She was irritated by her daughter's tears and laughed at her plaintive claims on widowhood. The Bindel family had not arrived because they were lazy and insensitive, and she would prepare for them no more. Nevertheless she remained stubbornly in her kitchen all the day long and later on throughout the night, cooking and baking with a demented vengeance. Shortly after her father's death, she began to sing at her work in a tone of careless joy that would suddenly dissolve into one of mourning. And all the time she baked, stacking the shelves with a disordered array of cakes and tarts and cursing the Bindels for their tardiness. Zelda did nothing to hinder her. Her mother was crying in her own way. After a while her mother acknowledged that the Bindels would never come, that they had forgotten in their careless fashion, that they were celebrating in their own tavern. Then one day she suddenly closed the kitchen door behind her, and went, barefoot, into the woods behind the tavern. She wasn't missed until Zelda smelled burning from the kitchen. On the stove, a tray of honey cakes had charred to a cinder. Their ashes were her mother's final signature. Aaron and Leon found her in a clearing in the forest. She was asleep. Or so they had to think. Together with their mother they laid her on the bed, and Zelda closed her mother's eyes. The three watchers looked from one to the other.

"No more of us must die," Zelda said quietly.

So they linked their survivors' arms and once more went wearily to the burial ground. After the funeral they ate no sweetmeats, but they took the hordes of honey cakes and buried them at the back of the tavern. For the customary seven days they sat on low stools and they mourned, and when it was over, Zelda and her sons threw themselves into work and the bustling trade of the tavern. Now that the Bindel holding was no more, much of the drinking trade of the ghetto was diverted to Zemach's tavern. They worked hard, dividing the counter and the cellar between them. It was a bereaved life, with little laughter and many silences. But they were not disturbed when others broke that silence. Indeed, it was a relief of sorts when the tavern filled up in the early evening with the sound of men's singing.

One such evening a stranger came to the inn, a man in his middle years, unknown to any of the customers and clearly a newcomer to the ghetto. He stepped warily to the counter and ordered a kvass. Zelda served him.

"You're a stranger here," she said, "but you are welcome."

"I thank you," the man said. His voice, his manner, unlike his clothes, were elegant and well-turned. He had clearly known better times.

"My name is Khasina," he said. "Pavel Khasina. I am come from Kherson."

"I am Zelda Bindel," she said. "Bindel," she said again, caressing that much-buried name. "My husband and his family died in the pogrom. But these are my sons," she offered, calling Aaron and Leon to her side.

"They are fine boys," he said. "Too fine for the Czar's cannon fodder. What will they do when their time comes?" The man had voiced the burning question that the three Bindels had suppressed with their silences. It was a relief to them all to hear it spoken aloud.

"We shall survive," Aaron said, repeating his father's catechism, though he knew that such a phrase would find short shrift with the recruiting officer.

"They should leave," the man said to Zelda. "You too," he added. He looked round furtively. "As I am doing," he whispered.

"Where are you going?" Leon said, whispering too, under-standing that it was not polite to advertise desertion from the land of their Holy Mother Russia.

"To Wales," Khasina said. "I have a sister there. She was wise. They left some years ago."

"But you have somebody to go to," Zelda said.

"There are many of our people over there," Khasina answered. "They will welcome you." He paused and drank from his glass. "You must leave," he said, and there was no mistaking the ur-gency in his voice. "You have learned a hard lesson in Odessa," he said. "There are harder lessons to come." He reached into his pocket for a pencil and notebook and, tearing out a sheet, he wrote down an address. He took his time with it, concerned with its neatness and legibility, familiarizing himself for his own sake with the strange letters and shapes, so alien to his Russian hand. He handed the paper to Zelda. "Look after it," he said. "You will find me there and I shall help you." He downed his glass. "I take the train at midnight." He took each of their hands in farewell, then he turned quickly and left. The three Bindels stared at the space he had so recently occupied and all of them wondered whether he had been a fleeting vision. Yet they heard the echo of his warning words and saw on the counter the undeniable proof of his recent visit. They read the address without understanding it. Wales, he had said. A place in England, they surmised, which was where his train and his boat were taking him. Wales, they said to each other, laughing at its strange sound, realizing that this laughter was the very first they had given voice to since their bereavements. And in that laughter there was hope, as if the visitor had, with his calling card, sanctioned them to have faith once more. That it was not enough to chant, "We must survive," without finding the wherewithal to do so. That it was permissible to leave the graves of husband, parents, grandparents, that their memory lay not in tombstones but in the consummate imperti-nent act of their own survival. Zelda folded the piece of paper and put it in her blouse.

"He's right," she said softly. "Aaron has just over two years before he is called. In that time we must try and sell the tavern." She looked at them with little confidence. "Well, we must try," she said.

"But who will buy it, Mama?" Aaron asked.

"We must try," she insisted, though she knew that the possibil-

ity of a sale was very remote. Tavern-keeping was a Jewish trade,
and no Jew in Odessa would stake a future in that town. But she
must try.

"We shall make our future in England," she said.

"In Wales," Leon laughed.

She hugged them both. Their long mourning was over.

They started their departure preparations the very next day.
Aaron and Leon began to clear the loft and the cellar of all the
jumble that had accumulated over the years of Zemach's holding.
Every market day, Aaron would load the wagon with dispensable
pieces of furniture and household goods, and he would sell them
in the marketplace and marvel at his wealth on his return home.
Within a month the tavern was stripped to its bare essentials.
There was now nothing more to do but to wait for a buyer. Zelda
did not want to publicize the sale. With two sons nearing conscription age, there would be too many questions, and besides, it
would be bad for her business and goodwill if her clients suspected a change of management. But she would speak to the
casual customer, the irregular passing trade, and hope thereby
that word would spread beyond Odessa. But for a whole year
there was not a single inquiry. Every night before sleeping, Zelda
would unfold the piece of paper that Pavel Khasina had left behind, reading the address aloud, assuring herself that a safe and
hopeful future was possible. But as the weeks went by, she began
to wonder whether she would languish forever in this hated land,
grieving for her soldier sons. Many of her friends in the ghetto
had already left. Occasionally when she went to the synagogue,
she noticed their vacant places. But they had not been encumbered with property. They were tailors, bakers, and craftsmen
and they traveled abroad with their trade. That was their wealth,
their future, a portable skill that would insure them a living anywhere in the world. But she and her sons had no trade but that of
tavern-keeping, and such a skill did not travel well. It required a
new language, a knowledge of strange money, and in England,
she had been told, it was not a trade for Jews. She knew she had
to sell the tavern. Money was the only wealth she could acquire.

One day in early winter, a few weeks before Aaron's nineteenth
birthday, the vintner's wagon drew up in the courtyard of the
tavern. It was the first of the month, delivery date for the tavern
stock. Usually there were two porters on the wagon who would
carry the goods to the cellar. But this time Zelda noted a third

man, who, by his elegant dress, was clearly no porter but possibly
the vintner himself. Zelda stood at the door of the tavern and
watched as he alighted from the wagon, firmly setting down his
silver-knobbed cane in the crevice of the cobbles. He smiled as he
saw her standing there and came straight toward her.

"Mrs. Bindel?" he said.

She was nervous, as she always was with strangers. Especially
with men, and those who were so Russian and so secure of their
patriotism.

"May I speak with you?" he said.

She was frightened, frightened for her children, her livelihood.

"What's the matter?" she said. "What's happened?"

"Nothing's happened, madam. I just wished a word with you.
Your respected grandfather, Zemach, was a friend. It's many
years now since I have visited this tavern."

"Mr. Fedorov?" she asked, recalling the name from her childhood.

He nodded. "I remember you as a little girl."

She led him into her sitting room and offered him refreshment.
But he declined.

"I am here on business," he said.

She wished her sons were with her, but Leon was serving in the
tavern and Aaron was helping the porters. She presumed Mr.
Fedorov wished to increase his charges, and she was not confident that she could bargain with him.

"Shall I call my sons?" she asked.

"Let me state my business first," he said, "and then if you are
interested, you can talk to your sons."

She folded her hands in her lap, her knuckles clenched. "I'm
listening," she said.

"While I was arranging your order this month," Mr. Fedorov
went on, "it occurred to me that you might be relieved to find a
buyer for your tavern."

Zelda tried to hide her excitement. She knew she must not
appear too eager.

"It's a very hard trade for a woman, Mrs. Bindel," he said.
"Your sons will soon be in the army, and then it will be impossible for you." He paused, staring at her. He wanted to make his
position quite clear. He was doing her a favor. It was his mission
in life to concern himself with widows and orphans.

"Did you hear that I wanted to sell it?" she asked, keeping her voice steady, trying not to think of the three of them on board ship, spitting on the hated land that they would leave behind.

"No. I heard nothing," he said. "Why? Were you thinking of selling?"

"Sometimes I think I would like to be rid of it," she parried. "But only on some days. I've talked to people about it. Why do you want it?" she said. She was suspicious of the favor. Tavern-keeping was a Jewish trade. A Russian, and a rich one at that, would consider it unseemly.

"I'm concerned with your welfare," he said with a smile, and the smile told her he was lying. "Your family have been my good customers for many years. Besides, it's a good little business. I would expand it. Build a good restaurant as an extension. I would give you a fair price," he said.

"I must talk to my sons." Zelda half rose from her seat.

"Of course," he said. "There's time. But not too long."

"Would you like to see my accounts?" She went over to her cupboard.

"Of course," he said quickly, "but only when you have decided to sell." He had no interest in her accounts. He didn't care about her stocks or her goodwill. He was totally indifferent to the tavern and its trade. It was the land he wanted, that ground on which the tavern stood, which, according to his inside information, could well prove to be a gold mine. For among other voluntary activities, natural in a man of his standing, Mr. Fedorov was a member of the Odessa Railways Commission, and was thus privy to the decision that the Zemach tavern holding was to be the site of the new railroad station, linking the line from Kishinev to Odessa. Whoever owned that land owned a fortune.

"I'll come again next week," the vintner said.

Zelda was confused by his haste. He had told her there was time, but a week was hardly time enough to make a decision that would affect their whole lives.

"A week is not long," she said, knowing that delay would be a bargaining factor.

The vintner kept the smile on his face, but in his heart he was grossly irritated by this Jew-woman who wouldn't let him have his way. "I'm leaving for St. Petersburg next week," he lied. "I have to have your decision before I leave."

He rose and held out his hand. But Zelda did not take it. She was beginning to tire of the smile on his face. "I don't think my sons will want to sell."

"They will be making a mistake," he said, the smile at last fading.

In four days Fedorov returned. He'd brought his smile with him, and wore it fixed over his cheeks, masking his fury at the woman's delay. This time she had her sons by her side, and both showed a marked lack of enthusiasm for the sale. Zelda had rehearsed them in their attitudes, and both crossed their fingers as they expressed their indifference to his offer. But the vintner, crossing his fingers, too, decided to call their bluff. He knew those two Jew-boys were perilously near conscription age. He knew that they would shirk their patriotic duty and, like the rest of their rotten tribe, would run like rats to save themselves. But to run, they needed money. "I'm sorry," he said, his smile fixed. "I'd hoped we could do business together." He turned to go, and with unhurried pace, waiting for their recall. It came as he reached the door. "We might be interested if you made a larger offer," Aaron said as Zelda trembled in her chair.

The vintner turned. Now he had them, he knew, and he could play with them. "I think my price is fair," he said, not moving from the door. He was beginning to resent the offer he had already made. Why should he, a good Russian patriot, finance these Yids' desertion? He watched them look at each other and he smelled the hesitation between them. It was that hesitation that proved their bluff. And with total confidence he said, "My offer is more than fair. Yes or no." He spread the smile on his face a little to offset the finality of his terms. He put his hand on the handle of the door.

"All right," Aaron said after a while. "We agree, as long as you can complete arrangements within the month."

"My lawyers will draw up the contract immediately," the vintner said, and he returned from the door and took Aaron's hand.

"We shall drink a kvass on it," Leon said, uncrossing all his fingers behind his back.

And so the deal was done.

"Where will you live?" the vintner dared to ask.

"We will go to Kiev," Zelda said quickly. "I have a brother there." Now it was she who handed him a fixed smile.

Fedorov, in his own exploitative interest, kept his word. Within the month the tavern deal was completed. The transaction had

been so smooth and so swift that it left Zelda in a state of shock
at the realization that at last they would leave a land that offered
them no future, and it was many days before she left the tavern to
make arrangements for their departure. Her first call was to the
railway office. A woman traveling abroad with two friends, and
even on a single ticket, would be less suspicious than young men
whose bodies and spirits were mortgaged to the Czar.

"Where to, madam?" the ticket-seller asked.

"To Wales," she said.

"Where is that? I've never heard of such a place."

"Near England, I think," Zelda said, wondering whether Mr.
Khasina had lied to them.

"I can only give you tickets to Hamburg," he said. "From
there you can buy tickets to anywhere you like. England, America, even Wales," he laughed. "Will you be coming back?" he
said.

"Oh, yes," Zelda answered hastily. "I have two sons here."

"When do you want to go?" he asked.

"Tomorrow." She wanted her sons away, and quickly, for she
trusted nobody.

The official gave her three rail tickets. "I hope you have a nice
holiday," he said. "I hope you find Wales too."

She left the office quickly. That night she closed the tavern
early, and the three of them sat down to a celebration.

"To Wales." Leon kept raising his glass, and laughing, too, for
there was something faintly unreliable about a country that even
the ticket official had never heard of. That night they went to bed
early, and it was early morning when they took their leave. The
cocks were crowing as they left the tavern courtyard. Zelda spat
on the ground.

"Come for them now, you recruiting swine," she hissed. "Go,
find my children over the high seas." Her laughter was almost
hysterical. Indeed, it soon dissolved into tears. For there was
much to weep for. Not for the tavern, nor for the livelihood, nor
for the hated country that they would never see again, but for
those that cruel land had buried. They left the tavern courtyard
and, at no one's suggestion, made for the burial grounds to visit
the Bindel and the Zemach families for the last time.

They walked in silence and there they picked their way over
the stones to where Zemach held domain with all his kin. Zelda
held her children's hands, but she did not weep; she had already

given her family its due season of mourning. Together with her
sons she built a pyramid of pebbles on the Zemach graves. Then
when it was done, they turned their steps to where the Bindels
lay. Or rather, their ashes, heaped together under a stone that
listed the four generations consumed by the fire. Aaron and Leon
stood by the side of the tomb, holding their mother's arm, and
read the names aloud. They stayed by the tomb for a long while,
loath to leave, reluctant to yield that certain proof of their history. Now all they would have would be memories and a list of
alabaster names to tell their children. Now they themselves
would start a history in a new country, would create their own
dead for their children's memories, new monuments for their
myths, new legends for their inheritance. But one legend they
would bring from Odessa—that of Jakob Bindel and his catechism of survival. They crouched by the tomb and made a castle
of pebblestones at its base, each stone for a future visit they
would never make.

"We shall not be buried here," Aaron said. "Our bones shall
break new ground elsewhere."

They linked arms and together they left the cemetery.

It was still early morning when they made their way to the
wagon station. They were burdened with luggage and their travel
was slow. Food for the long journey formed the bulk of their
luggage. Zelda had diligently concerned herself with that provi-
sion. They had money, they had food, but only Zelda had a passport. She had received one directly on application. But it would
have been dangerous for the brothers even to apply. Their ages
would betray their intended desertion. So they busied themselves
with journey preparations, with food and drink, and blankets for
the crossing. But none of them spoke about passports.

The wagon trail left for Kishinev at midnight. There they were
to take the train across Galicia and into Prussian territory. It
would be early morning on the following day when the passport
problem could no longer be ignored. It was when they changed
from the wagons to the train that Zelda realized the enormity of
the move they were making. It was the train that first set off the
fear in her. As they gathered speed, the nature of the landscape
changed, and its strangeness confirmed the farewell they had
made to a land that, for all its cruelty, was at least known and
familiar. The houses they passed were strange too, and the people
who went about their business in the streets. Everything about

the terrain was alien. The Bindels avoided conversation with
their neighbors. None were Jews and they feared awkward questions.

In the early hours of the morning, the train came to a sudden
halt. After a while an official entered the compartment and told
the passengers to alight. They were within walking distance of
the frontier post. There they would be able to buy refreshment
and wait for the passport official. In two hours another train
would take them across the border and on to Hamburg. The
Bindels rose with the other passengers but, unlike the others who
renewed their interrupted conversations, they kept their silence.
They followed the other passengers off the train, and gathered in
a waiting room that adjoined a tavern. Aaron took a seaman's
cap out of his luggage, and placed it firmly on his head. Zelda
had never seen it before, and when she saw how it transformed
his look, "Russianizing" his features, she understood that he had
on his own account formulated a plan to confront the hurdle of a
passport.

Aaron left the room and dawdled for a while outside the tavern, watching the comings and the goings of the passengers and
railroad officials. From the occasional furtive inquiries he had
made among the taverns in Odessa, he had learned, and not to his
surprise, that all officials were bribable. Sometimes sailors came
to those taverns, and he would encourage them to tell stories of
smuggling and stowaways. Apart from the details of their stories,
their underlying message was always the same. Every official,
however petty, however powerful, was corruptible. But in no way
could Aaron elicit details of the measure of the bribe. It was of
vital importance that he find out, for to offer less than the expected sum might expose him to even greater peril. His age, so
close to conscription, would spell out the reason for his departure, and he would spend the rest of his life serving hard labor for
desertion. He had somehow or other to find out the current bribery rate. He straightened his cap and, with a rolling gait, entered
the tavern.

His Russian, though fluent, was laced with a Yiddish accent,
and he had decided to pass himself off as a seaman who had spent
most of his youth on the high sea, where his Russian sounds had
been scored to the accents of each port. He was on his way to
Hamburg, he would tell them, to pick up a ship. He ordered
himself a kvass, and the same for a lone neighbor who stood

beside him at the counter. Thus he was able to enter conversation with the stranger and he was delighted to discover that he was a railroad official whose job was to check passengers' numbers against collected tickets. Aaron slipped easily into conversation, remarking on the number of passengers who seemed to be taking holidays abroad. It was a fruitful opening, for his companion was a bitter man, who all his life had served with little reward, so full of envy that he needed little encouragement to vent his spleen on those who were better off than he.

"Plenty of rich people in this country," he said with disdain. "Landowners, bankers, and the rest."

Aaron trembled, waiting for the Yids to join the contemptible company. But the official was satisfied with the exploiters he had already mentioned.

"Living off my sweat," he said, "and thousands like us. When did you ever see the likes of me going on holiday?" he asked. "Or you, my friend?"

Aaron ordered another round of kvass.

His companion put an arm around his shoulder. "Come, my friend," he said. "This is a time for drinking. Let's get drunk together, you and I, and dream of the holidays we shall never take. Let's get drunk, my friend, and curse those who oppress us, the landlords, the bankers"—Aaron waited, his knees trembling —"and the Czar." This last in a whisper, followed by such seditious laughter that Aaron put his mouth to the man's ear, and, sealing their friendship, he echoed, "And the Czar."

If they had nothing else in common, no language, no tradition, they did at least have a common enemy, and his destruction was worthy of a toast. His companion drew a wad of grubby rouble notes from his pocket, licked his forefinger, and drew one note from the pile. "Enough of these pretty little glasses," he said, and shouted to the bartender to bring a bottle. Then, grabbing it, he took Aaron's arm and guided him to a table at the far end of the tavern into the midst of a crowd of revelers concerned with their own toasts and curses, all of which, in their raucous echo, were exactly the same. It took little time for Aaron to be accepted as one of their number. He hoped they wouldn't ask him too many questions. So, to preempt their curiosity, he himself was the questioner. He asked about their work, and once again brought the subject around to the other passengers.

"How do they all get passports? Do they have to buy them?" he asked innocently.

His companion laughed. "Anyone can get one," he said. "It's the ticket you have to buy."

"Except conscripts," another man joined in.

Aaron was delighted. The man had turned the conversation very neatly.

"But some of the ships I've served on," he said, "I've seen men traveling, men who ought to be in the army. How do they manage without a passport?"

"Everyone's palm itches," his companion said. "The passport official's itches to the tune of fifty roubles." He laughed and put the bottle to his lips.

Aaron smiled. Now he had the information he sought. One hundred roubles would see himself and Leon into freedom. "They must make a good living," he said.

"Money buys everything." A drunken reveler raised his glass in their direction. "Passports, exemptions from the army," he shouted. He was becoming aggressive and Aaron wanted to get out of the tavern.

"Landlords' sons, the rich scum of the earth." The man threw out the words with contempt. Then he crowned his shabby catalogue. "And Yids," he spat. "Always the Yids." He lurched over to Aaron's side, and grabbed his arm. "What d'you expect from them, my friend?" he asked.

"What indeed?" Aaron said. His father had told him to survive. "I've got to go," he shouted, trying to keep his voice steady. He no longer trusted himself with these men, and he regretted the warmth he had first felt toward them. They had nothing in common. Not even an enemy. For when the Czar was on a Jew-baiting binge, they would be firmly behind him. Not so long ago, his own father had been killed by such a mob.

"I'm going back to the waiting room. I left my girl there," he added, feeling the need to give some excuse for his sudden departure.

"You can be with your girl friend anytime," one of the men said, and there was troublemaking in his eye.

"She doesn't feel well," Aaron improvised. Perhaps they would make allowance for sickness. And they did, grudgingly, urging him to return with the latest bulletin on her health. He promised he would, and, smiling all the while, he made for the tavern door, disguising his haste. When he was outside in the open air, he breathed freely, as if he had escaped with his life. He made his way back to the waiting room, and there he apprised his mother and Leon of his findings.

Zelda turned her back on the waiting passengers, and extracted the bribe from her portmanteau. She handed fifty roubles apiece to her sons. Then suddenly, as if from a signal, the passengers rose and made for the door. The train shunted into the station. Aaron and Leon sent their mother ahead of them, while they themselves hung back, waiting for the crowd to thin. Already many passengers stood in line outside the passport shed, their passports ready in their hands. Zelda stood among them, with the occasional trembling glance at her sons. Aaron and Leon waited until almost all the passengers had crossed the barrier, and then they joined the line. Leon was insistent on going in front of Aaron, as a protective measure, with instructions to his older brother that if the bribe should not work and the official called the police, he, Aaron, would then disappear to escape arrest. Leon would take whatever punishment was meted out to him. At least he was well under conscription age.

Aaron's heart was thumping as Leon moved into his turn. The official looked at the ticket and then at Leon.

"Passport?" he asked.

The notes shook in Leon's hand. He offered them to the official. The man made no attempt to hide the bribe. Indeed, he flourished the packet, counting the notes aloud. When he had finished, he folded them and stuffed them into the back of his boot, and Aaron noted that the space between the man's sock and the boot lining was already packed with bribery. Then it was Aaron's turn. The official looked at him, then back at Leon. "Brothers?" he asked.

Aaron nodded.

"Passport?" The man's voice was far from friendly.

Aaron handed him his fifty roubles, and again he counted them out loud. Then he smiled and put his hand on Aaron's shoulder. "What's your name, son?" he said gently.

Aaron smiled at him, melting with his gesture of friendship. "Aaron," he said. "Aaron Bindel."

The smile lingered on the man's face, but he tightened his grip on Aaron's shoulder. "Yids," he spat. "It's a pleasure to be rid of

scum like you." Then he stuffed the money in his shoe, and
booted Aaron through the barrier.

Leon took his brother's arm, anxious to distance themselves
from the official.

"We're through," he whispered. "We're safe. No one can insult
us like that anymore."

"D'you remember what Papa said in the forest?" Aaron reminded him. "There will always be men like that as long as there
are Jews."

Zelda was leaning out of the train window, scanning the platform, and when she saw them, she called their names aloud, shrill
and clear. "Aaron, Leon," she shouted, and for good measure,
"Aaron, Leon Bindel." For the first time since leaving the tavern,
she felt the rising fever of freedom.

They rushed onto the train and settled together in a crowded
compartment. The character of the train seemed suddenly to
have changed. The faces were different, the talk was loud, laughing, and above all, unguarded. And it was Yiddish, all of it,
unashamed and free. Each passenger had a tale to tell, and was
intent on telling it, even if nobody listened. It was enough for
themselves to hear it in affirmation of their newfound freedom.
Among them, sitting alone in the corner, was a middle-aged man
holding himself rather aloof from the others. Zelda stared at him,
and so did Aaron and Leon, and all for the same reason. He bore
an uncommon resemblance to Benjamin Bindel. A little younger
perhaps, but with the wisdom of Grandpa Jakob about the eyes,
and with Benjamin's squareness of build and the same laughing
mouth and stern chin.

"He looks like Papa," Aaron said, for it was a fact easier to be
declared between them than privately considered and contained.

Zelda smiled and Aaron saw a look of joy on her face that he
had not seen since the days before the Bindel tavern fire. She
leaned across the space between them. "Where are you from?"
she asked.

"Kiev," he said. "But that's of the past." There was a finality
in his voice, as if he was unwilling to dwell on what was gone
forever.

"We're from Odessa," Leon tried, anxious to keep the conversation alive.

"You must forget it," the man said, almost angrily. "Odessa,

Kiev, Balta, Kishinev. Every rotten syllable of them. For us Jews, they were regions of hell."

The man spoke in learned Yiddish. He had the self-assurance of an educated man, and the smoldering fire of an orator. "In the whole infested country," he declaimed, "in all that rotten blood-soaked soil, there is but one holy spot."

The man's eyes began to water. Aaron and Leon watched as the tears stood on the rim, immobile, becalmed, aloofly declaring themselves before going back where they came from. Aaron and Leon stared at him. Grandpa Jakob had sometimes cried like that, with the same stubborn stagnant tears, when nudged by the memory of a sorrow. Then Grandpa Jakob would speak of it slowly and with well-armed detachment, as if it were a story that belonged to somebody else. And in such manner did their fellow traveler tell his tale. "So so many years ago it was," he said. "My son Uri. They took him for a soldier. He was twelve. Can you imagine? Twelve little years of life, and they took him for a soldier." He paused, wiping the sleeve of his coat across his dry eyes. "Somewhere between Kiev and the Eastern Provinces, there's a small piece of holy ground. His mother died of mourning," he said. He folded his hands across his lap. "It's over," he said. Then he turned his body into his small corner and stared out at the passing landscape.

In the course of his story, the rest of the passengers had fallen silent. It was as if he had spoken for them all. And above all for Zelda, who heard in his words the final validation of their flight into freedom.

The night passed. It was late morning when the train drew into Hamburg station and its weary passengers boarded the wagons that would take them to the harbor.

The dockside was like a marketplace, but more in sound than in sight. For there were very few stalls, but innumerable traders who stood about and proclaimed their wares. Those of the passengers who had Yiddish as their mother tongue heard faint rings of familiarity in the German sales talk of the traders. For they were languages from the same root. Certain words were picked up and understood: soup, blankets, beds, hostelry, and, above all, tickets. Almost every trader it seemed was selling tickets for the boats and they shouted out a choice of destination. *"America, England,"* they sang, wandering through the marketplace. But Zelda, who never trusted a bargain, especially when it came from an unofficial source, made straight for the licensed ticket booth, dragging her sons after her. There she purchased three single tickets to England. She was given no choice of class. The boat carried only steerage, but the agent assured her in his broken Russian that the accommodation was adequate. The boat would not leave until late afternoon, he told her, but they were permitted to embark at their leisure. There was little else for them to do. They had no need to buy provisions. The sight of the ship was not a heartening one. It was little more than a cattle boat, and although it was not due to sail for some hours, it already appeared crowded. They made their way up the gangway. A seaman directed them to the steerage cabins, shrugging his shoulders as he watched them go, no doubt wondering where on earth they would find to seat themselves, and for how long they could bear the stench of those nightmare quarters.

It hit the Bindels as soon as they entered the cabins, like a wall of foul-smelling heat from the bodies of the emigrants as they lay on the wooden benches, their clothes torn, their faces haggard and yellow with dirt. There were many children among them, but all of them looked like old men. Zelda shrank back at the entrance.

"We'll get used to it," Aaron said as he urged them forward and sought out a bench for them to sit on. He found space enough at the very end of one of the platforms, where the boat narrowed. They sat down, their luggage on their knees. Except for the money valise, which Zelda held forever at her side. Over the platform an oil lamp was slung, and in the semidarkness it illumined the terrible shadows of the figures sprawled around them. It was like an entrance into hell. But for many of those who lay there, the present circumstances were paradise to what they had endured over the last few months. For, unable to pay for trains, they had walked their way to freedom, picking up a generous wagon here and there, some from the far Ukraine, others from Poland, robbed on their journey of their money and possessions. The roads had been full of pitfalls. Frontier towns were the worst, for the peasants had learned to exploit those illegal migrants without papers. Having come so far, the travelers could hardly return, so they were easy prey for the swarms of parasites. When they had run out of money, they offered their luggage and possessions, and perhaps after that, one dared not speculate, except perhaps that they sold that as well. At Aaron's feet a woman lay sleeping, her body draped in faded and torn finery. She seemed to have sold everything, yet her face was innocent still.

Crowded as it already, was, the newly embarked passengers continued to squeeze into the cabin area. On their faces was a look of dismay at the sight that confronted them. Some made to turn back, but the sailors forced them through, for the open decks were only available to passengers during the daylight hours. And so the cabins burst with the stream of passengers, all fighting for what little space was still available. Among them, Zelda caught sight of their fellow traveler on the train. Despite the horror of the surroundings, he still maintained his air of self-assurance. Indeed it seemed to be heightened, for there was actually a smile on his face, a smile filtered with rays of hope. He looked around for somewhere to place himself. Then his eye caught Zelda's and she waved to him, signaling him to come over to their small territory. Somehow they found room for him, and he settled himself with great dignity, then turned to thank them.

"The past is over," he said. "There is now only the future." He dug into his pocket and brought out a small bottle of grappa. He unscrewed the top, which acted as a cup, and he poured a measure. "We will drink to freedom," he said. "Madam." He handed the cup to Zelda, and as she raised it to her lips, he said, "To America. Our new world."

Zelda looked at her children. "To America?" she said.

"We're going to England," Aaron said.

"But this boat goes to America," their companion insisted, while the cup of cheer idled in Zelda's hand. Then Zelda opened her portmanteau and gave a ticket each to her sons.

"What does it say there?" she said, nervous now that the ticket official had cheated her, which explained why there were so few clients at the licensed booth. Aaron read the legend on the ticket. It was simply a permit to embark at Hamburg, but it gave no port of call. Their companion's ticket was the same.

"It goes to America," he said. "The ticket man told me in the marketplace. This boat goes to America. No doubt about it. Lots of people were buying tickets from him and they all came on this boat. I've got a brother in America. It's the only place I can go."

The Bindels were wary of the man's confidence. They did not wish to go to America. That was a land that, over the past years, had been granted no mention in Zemach's tavern. It was the sound of England that echoed daily in the inn and Pavel Khasina was their anchor there. It was in Wales, under Khasina's patronage, that they would settle. It was there that they would marry and raise their children, and where, in their due season, their bones would be laid. All that was arranged. America had no part in it.

"It can't be true," Aaron whispered. He rose and made his way to the end of the cabin, where a group of seamen were gathered, admitting the passengers who were still embarking. He managed to get their attention.

"Where does this boat go?" he asked.

"To London," one of them said, then seeing the confusion on Aaron's face, he clarified. "To London. England."

Aaron returned to his family with the news. Zelda, far from being relieved, was now deeply concerned for her companion. "How much did you pay for your ticket?" she asked.

"It was a bargain," he said. "The trader said it was half the official price."

"How much?" she insisted.

"Fifty roubles," he said.

It was more than she had paid for the three of them. She was enraged. "Come," she said. "We shall find him in the market-place. We shall demand your money back." She now felt herself part and parcel of her friend's campaign. "What's your name?" she asked, feeling it was time that she knew the identity of her companion-at-arms. She hugged her money portmanteau to her breast and took his arm.

The man took time to raise his hat. "Rubinov," he said. "Barak Rubinov."

"Leon, you come with me," Zelda said. "Aaron, you will stay and keep our seats."

Aaron rose. "Good-bye, Mr. Rubinov," he said. "I wish you well," and to his mother, "Come back soon. We sail in an hour."

"Don't worry," she said. "You just hold our seats." She was anxious to be away, to right the terrible wrong that had been done her friend. For now he was more than that. He was a cause, and she was going to fight for it, come what may. Leon looked at Aaron and shrugged his shoulders, then he followed his mother and Mr. Rubinov into battle.

They fought their way down the gangway. The fresh air was an astonishing relief.

"You are very kind, madam," Mr. Rubinov kept saying, trying to keep up with his crusader, for Zelda was tearing along the dockside with a vengeance. When they reached the marketplace, it was, unsurprisingly, deserted. No unscrupulous trader would hang around to take the consequences of his cupidity. Zelda stood in the empty marketplace and seethed with fury.

"There's nothing we can do," Mr. Rubinov said. "I shall stay in Hamburg and tomorrow I shall find him. You must get back to the boat." He took Zelda's arm. "You are a good woman," he said. "What a pity that we go our separate ways."

Leon instinctively stood to one side, as if not wishing to eaves-drop on what threatened to be a proposal.

"Perhaps one day you will decide to come to England," his mother said.

"D'you know what's so terrible?" Mr. Rubinov said after a while. "The man who sold me the ticket. He spoke a good Yid-dish. He was a Jew. He told me so. He called me brother." It was clearly that aspect of the deception that pained Mr. Rubinov most of all—far more than the extortion of his money. "Come," he said. "I'll take you back to the boat." He took Zelda's arm

with the ease of a long-standing escort. "What a pity," he said
again, "that we are to part. And I don't even know your name."

"Zelda. Zelda Bindel," she said. "I am a widow. My husband
was killed in the Odessa pogrom." She was surprised at how
calmly she had related an event that had shattered her life. For
the first time since her widowhood she knew that perhaps now
her life was not beyond repair. "My husband was a *Kantonisti,*"
she said. "Like your little boy."

"And in the end they conquered him," Mr. Rubinov said. "I'm
very sorry."

They walked the rest of the way in silence, and when they
came to the gangway they found that an official had taken a stand
at the dockside and was examining the credentials of the late
passengers. Zelda and Leon had their tickets at the ready. Zelda
gave Mr. Rubinov her hand. "I'm glad we met," she said, then
she handed her ticket to the official. He clipped it and let her
pass. It was Leon's turn. His ticket presented no problem, but for
some unknown reason the official asked for Leon's passport.
Leon called to his mother. "He wants my passport," he said.

Zelda paled. She opened the bribe bag and handed the official a
few rouble notes. The man ignored them. "Passport," he insisted.

"I haven't got one," Leon said simply.

Zelda took a few more notes out of her bag and pushed them
under the man's nose. He flicked away her hand with disgust.
"We Germans cannot be bribed," he said.

Zelda wanted to scream at him about what his compatriots
were doing in the marketplace. But she didn't have the language
to make herself understood.

"What shall I do?" Leon said.

The official shrugged. "Go back where you came from," he
said, "and get yourself legal papers."

Leon froze. The official smiled at him. He shouldn't have
smiled, Leon was to recall later. If he hadn't smiled, Leon would
never have raised his gentle hand. But it was the smile that armed
him, armed him for every struggle of his burning Bindel inheritance. It armed him to avenge Grandpa Jakob's death, to avenge
the monstrous service that his own father and uncle had given to
the Czar. It armed him to settle the account of the Bindel fire and
the four generations that had been consumed in the flames. It fed
a sweet revenge even on that swindler in the marketplace, and on
all the oppression and anger that drove one Jew to persecute his

brother. It was a titanic vengeance that he sought. He felt a tingling pain in his hand and his shoulder and at his feet he saw its cause. The official lay on the dockside, his nose bloodied, his eyes closed. Out of nowhere a posse of officials appeared, and rushed to his side. Mr. Rubinov, who had stood by and witnessed, took Leon's arm. Zelda rushed down the gangway to her son's side, and within seconds they were all surrounded. A wagon drew up alongside, and the three of them were herded into the cart, while a stretcher bore away the injured body of the official who should have known better than to smile.

On the boat Aaron paced the spread of his small territory. He was now restless indeed. The sailors had withdrawn from the cabins and he feared that the ship was about to sail. He feared too that if he left his spot, he would lose his holding, to say nothing of their provisions and luggage. He turned to a man who sat alongside. "I must go away for a minute," he said, "and look for my family. Will you look after my things?"

The man stared at him. He looked at the space and its furnishings, as if trying to assess their value. "It will cost," he said coldly. "Fifty kopeks."

Aaron would gladly have struck him. But he had no choice but to accept the deal. He nodded. "I'll pay when I come back," he said.

"Now," the man said, holding out his hand.

"We're Jews," Aaron said. "Both of us. You can take my word. My mother has the money."

"When you come back," the man agreed. "And then, no money, no space."

Aaron fought his way onto the deck and was surprised at how dark it was. He went to the ship's rail and to his horror he saw the gangway being shunted along the dockside. He heard the ship's hooter and his heart froze. Apart from a few officials and sailors the quay was deserted. One of them raised his hand as if in farewell, and even as Aaron stood there he felt the boat move on its creaking way. He panicked, not knowing what to do. Then he realized suddenly that, although he had the food and all their clothing, it was Zelda who held all the money.

A sailor came toward him and ordered him off the deck. He went down the wooden stairway to steerage, and as he entered the cabin he caught sight of his creditor. The man stretched out his hand, awaiting his due. "I've lost my mother," Aaron said. "I don't know what's happened to her."

In answer the man stretched his whole body over Aaron's holding, as if he would commandeer his luggage as well as his site. Aaron contemplated the two days' and nights' journey that confronted him and he wondered how he could survive. Then he remembered. "I have some food," he offered.

The man smiled and shifted back to his own small site. Aaron opened the food portmanteau. In his anxiety he himself had lost all appetite. He handed his companion a hunk of bread, a cucumber, some cheese, and an apple. The man was more than pleased with his payment. "Thank you, brother," he said. "I've not eaten for some days." And Aaron immediately forgave him, for hunger, he knew from his father's tales, could drive the gentlest of men into malice.

"Won't you break bread with me?" the man said.

"I'm not hungry." Aaron would not allow himself to believe that his mother and brother were still in Hamburg. He talked himself into believing that they were somewhere on the boat, that they had found a more comfortable cabin. But he feared that if they had reembarked, somehow or other they would have found each other. He kept his eye on the steerage door, but with little hope of their arrival. He could not understand what had happened to them.

"Don't worry, my friend," his companion said. "You will find them again. Have you schnapps in your bag?" he asked.

Aaron nodded. "Then drink some," the man said. "Drink of it well. Drink yourself into a sleep. Our people deserve forgetfulness for a while."

Aaron was glad to take the man's advice, for he could not bear his terrible imaginings. He poured a measure for his neighbor and he himself drank from the bottle. They finished it off and both fell into a drunken and merciful sleep. But for most of the passengers, unnumbed by alcohol, fraught with fears of the future, the night passed with appalling slowness. Although the seas were calm and the weather fair, the boat heaved and rolled with the misery of its cargo, and in the morning the stench of sickness, sweat, and human despair was intolerable. Aaron woke to it and wished to sleep again, but the thought of his missing family, which had never left his mind even during his drunken sleep, now drove him on deck in the vain hope of finding them. His bedfellow was still half-asleep, and Aaron whispered into his ear. "Keep our places," he told him. "Stretch out. I'll be back soon, and we'll take something to eat."

The man grunted, gratefully stretching his body over Aaron's vacant space, and he fell back into sleep. Aaron picked his way through the groups of crouching passengers. His own body was stiff and painful. His brow was fevered and he was afraid. Above all, he needed his health and, like a small boy, he longed for his mother. He reached the deck and leaned on the rail, gulping the fresh air. His eyes watered with the wind. Then suddenly his mind envisaged Khasina's address on the small card he had left on the tavern counter. Pavel Khasina, 24 Bute Street, Cardiff, Wales, England. He repeated it in the phonetic version they had taught themselves in the tavern, over and over again, then screamed it aloud across the sea, as if apprising his sponsor of his arrival. The recollection of the name much heartened him, and he turned from the rail and walked briskly about the deck. He had little hope of finding his mother and brother, but he scanned the deck for them all the same. He fretted less now about their absence. He had no doubt that somewhere soon they would find each other. He felt a little hungry, so he returned to the cabin and his breakfast companion, who was still stretched out over their holding. Aaron shook his shoulder.

"Aren't you hungry, friend?" he asked.

The man stirred at the suggestion of food, roused himself, looked around, and once again closed his eyes.

"Well, I'm hungry," Aaron said, "and you're lying on the food."

He sat him up gently, picked up the food hamper, and sat himself down. As he opened it, he was conscious of a sudden silence around him, and he knew its cause. He regretted now that he had so brazenly displayed the layers of rolls and cheese and honey cakes that Zelda had packed with such loving care. He looked up and saw the eyes staring, or rather the mouths, salivating with astonished and rude appetite. He gauged the amount of food in the case, and the number of traveling hours ahead. They would reach England in two days, so a sailor on deck had informed him. There was certainly not enough food for everybody. There was no question in his mind, however, that he must share it. His problem was how to ration most fairly. While he was

debating his allotting method, a man crawled to his side. He
looked up at Aaron, his eyes begging.

"I have something to exchange," he said. "It cost me my last
rouble, but I'll give it to you in exchange for food for my children."

"The food is for the children in any case," Aaron said. "We
have to share it as fairly as we can."

"You are a good man," the traveler said, and he drew a small
knife from his pocket and handed it to Aaron. Then he helped
him divide the food. Aaron cut small portions, on the premise
that a little food was better than none at all, and as he did so, the
children, urged by their mothers, crawled toward him, their little
hands outstretched for their portion. When they were all provided for, Aaron was glad that there was food left over, but he
did not touch it himself. There was still one more bottle of
schnapps. He would keep it till nightfall, he decided, then share it
with others desperate for sleep and oblivion. He returned the
knife. The man still crouched at his side.

"I'm Aaron Bindel," Aaron said, holding out his hand.
"What's your name?"

"Abraham," the man said. "Abraham Bok. From Vilna." He
smiled. "What a life this is," he said.

"What was it you paid a rouble for?" Aaron asked.

"Letters on a piece of paper," Bok said. "Here." He dug his
hand into his blouse pocket. "I will give it to you."

"I cannot pay," Aaron said.

"I give it to you in any case. Because I want you to live. A
good man must survive." He handed the paper to Aaron. It
looked like an address.

"What is it?" Aaron said.

"You must copy it out and keep it until we arrive. Then you
must show it to an Englishman."

"Yes, but what is it?" Aaron insisted.

"It's the address of the Jews' Temporary Shelter in London.
They keep it a secret and you have to pay to get it. It will save
our lives. It will give us money, somewhere to live, work with
which to earn a living, and a synagogue where we can pray."

"You *paid* for that?" Aaron asked. "Who sold it to you?"

"A Jew," Bok said. "A brother Jew. He probably paid fifty
kopeks for it himself. My friend," Bok said, laying his hand on
Aaron's arm. "Nothing surprises me anymore. Did I not try and

sell it to you? You, a brother Jew? And if you were hungry and your children were hungry, you would sell it too, and for the highest price. We are all in the survival business, my friend," he said, "and it is the most cutthroat business of all." He handed him a pencil. "Have you paper?" he asked.

Aaron searched his pockets. His ticket was the only paper. On the back of it he copied the letters of Bok's one-rouble lifeline.

"I know how to say it," Bok said. "A sailor taught me," and he ran his finger along Aaron's lettering. Then, like a child reading his first lesson, he pronounced slowly, "The Jewish Temporary Shelter, Leman Street, Whitechapel, London, England."

Aaron smiled. The sounds were similar to his sponsor's dwelling place and gave him reason to hope that Whitechapel was close to Wales.

Bok rose. "I must go to my wife. Perhaps we shall meet again," he said.

Aaron looked at his companion by his side. He was sitting upright but still fast asleep. At his feet the young girl stirred herself, she whom Aaron had noted the night before, dressed in torn silks, faded clues to a better time than now. She sat up and shivered. Aaron took a blanket and put it around her shoulders. "Are you hungry?" he said.

She nodded with an attempt at a smile.

He delved into the case for a roll of bread and gave it to her. She did not snatch at it, but took it daintily, and ate it with grace to hide her hunger.

"What's your name?" Aaron asked when she had finished eating.

"Ida," she said.

"I'm Aaron." He stretched out his hand.

She took it in hers, and he noted how each finger of one of her hands was ringed, some twice over. He stared at the dazzling stones.

"It's everything I have," she explained, as if in apology.

"Are you alone?" he asked.

"Yes," she said. "We came from Kiev, my brother and I, but we were caught at the frontier. He's twenty. So they took him back. But they let me go. I had rings on the other hand then," she said. "I was lucky. They only took the rings. Honestly," she said. "D'you believe me?" She was eager for his approval.

"Of course I believe you," he said. "But if they had taken more, it wouldn't have been your fault."

She gripped his arm. "They did," she said. "On the train to Hamburg. They offered me a ticket. I thought they were being kind, but I had to pay and they didn't want rings. I don't mind," she said shrilly. "It's not so terrible."

Aaron put his arm about her. "Of course it isn't," he said feebly.

She turned to face him, her eyes blazing. "What do you men know about it?" she screamed at him, and she took his hand and bit it with all her rage. He forced her head away and laid her down once more. He didn't know what more he could do, so he moved away and went once more on deck and longed for his mother and Leon. He felt more and more alone, and totally ill-equipped to deal with all the injustice that he met at every turn. Once again he repeated to himself Mr. Khasina's address. He took his ticket out of his pocket and tried to spell out the location of the Shelter. He could make nothing of the strange lettering. But it was enough to look at it, and to see in its strange hieroglyphics some kind of haven, a place for food, sleep, work. And above all a place where his mother and his brother could eventually find him.

He turned back to his cabin, and when he reached his site, the space on the floor was empty. He scanned the benches all around him but could see no sign of her. All that day she didn't return, although Aaron stayed there trying to convince himself that he was not waiting for her. At evening the children drew around him, knowing his corner as a source for food, and he rationed out what was left in the portmanteau. He himself took a drink of schnapps from the bottle and shared it with his companion, who all day had sat at his post, sleeping, waking, and preferring to sleep once more. Between them they finished the bottle and Aaron was weary with hunger and numbed with drink. Most of the passengers were sleeping more calmly now, more resigned perhaps to the hunger and the thirst they could not assuage. And soothed perhaps with the hope that the morrow would bring a new land, and hope for the future. When Aaron finally closed his eyes, she still had not returned. During the night he thought he saw her, or the faded silk of her dress. He heard it rustling at the cabin door. And he thought he saw a sailor's blouse in its folds. Or perhaps he was only dreaming.

When morning came, the passengers woke from their fitful sleep, and noticed that the boat was not moving. The sickness of the night, and days before, had suddenly left them. The sailors were moving along the compartments of the cabin, urging the passengers to leave the ship. They needed little encouragement, but many were weak with hunger. They shuffled to their feet, collecting their children and their scant luggage, and allowed themselves to be pushed and shoved to the cabin door. Once there, some of them tasted their first fresh air in two terrible nights and days, and they reeled with the blow of it, hanging on to the rails for support. Somehow or other they stumbled to the gangway and the surge of the mob carried them to the quayside.

Aaron stayed for a while on the boat, leaning over the rail. He still hoped for a miraculous appearance of his family among those who disembarked, and from his vantage point he watched each and every passenger. And as they touched English soil, he wondered how many of them, hoodwinked on the Hamburg marketplace, thought they had arrived in America.

The dockside was bustling with activity. He saw many stalls, but from where he stood, he could not decipher their wares. But he heard a lot of shouting from the traders, most of it in Yiddish. And then he caught sight of Ida. She was standing alone on the quayside. A man approached her, raised his hat, and bowed politely. A few words passed between them, then he took her arm and guided her through the crowds. For a moment Aaron lost sight of her, but he was glad that there had been someone to meet her, someone concerned who would look after her and heal the terrible wounds of her journey. Then he caught a glimpse of her again. Her escort was helping her into a carriage where there were four or five young girls already seated, and Aaron knew instinctively that that carriage was not good for Ida and he was no longer glad that she had been so graciously met and accommodated. The boat was quiet now and it seemed that most of the passengers had disembarked. Aaron turned from the rail and made his way to the gangway.

He must have been the last off the boat, for the crew were coming off at the same time. As he reached the end of the gangway, a man approached him and asked in Yiddish if he wanted some hot soup. The question reminded him of his raging hunger. He nodded his head weakly and the man took his arm and led him to one of the stalls.

"I have no money," Aaron thought fit to tell him before he was served.

"It's free from the Jewish Board of Guardians," the man said, and he pointed to a banner with that legend above the stand.

Aaron accepted a bowl of soup and a large hunk of bread. He took it slowly and relished the taste. He didn't know what or who the Jewish Board of Guardians were but he knew that he would be indebted to them all his life. There were other emigrants enjoying the Board's hospitality, and all were too engrossed in their food for conversation. Aaron stood alone and thought of Ida, then quickly put the thought of her from his mind. And as he did so, a woman approached him and asked him in Yiddish if he was enjoying his soup. He nodded, smiling and glad of company. She was a middle-aged woman with a gentle voice. Her hair was gray and wound in thick plaits about her ears.

"Have you lodgings?" she asked. "Work? Relatives?" She was offering him all that a man could need.

He shook his head, hope singing in his heart.

"If you come with me, I can give you shelter," she said. "Come unto me," she dared to add, "and I will give you rest."

But Aaron, whose schooling had not included the New Testament, was ignorant of her allusions. He put his empty soup plate on the counter. "Thank you," he said with overwhelming gratitude. He bent down to pick up his portmanteau.

"I will help you," the woman said. She stooped to pick up his valise, and as she did so, a pendant slipped from inside her blouse and dangled in Aaron's line of vision. He gasped when he saw it and deciphered the figure at the end of the chain. The Christ swung between his eyes. He raised himself and so did the woman at the same time, his valise in her hand. Then she noticed the mark of her calling that had so rudely and so untimely revealed itself, and she blushed with shame. Aaron took the valise from her hand, and without a word he turned his back on her and moved away, trembling with the joy of one who has been saved. He smiled at the woman's sheer audacity, that under the very banner of the Jewish Board of Guardians, she was plying her Christian trade. He looked about him, not knowing now where to turn. But he was no longer depressed. His body's needs were sated for the time. Then he heard someone call his name. He knew it could not be Leon because it was "Bindel" that the voice

called, and he turned around and saw his one-rouble friend Bok
running toward him.

"They are here," he cried ecstatically. "The Shelter have come
to meet us. I came to find you. That was a waste of a rouble," he
laughed. He put his arm around Aaron's shoulder. "Come," he
said, "they are waiting."

They began to walk toward the dock gates. Aaron looked
around and saw the Christ lady accost an immigrant as he relished his Board of Guardians' soup.

"Wait a minute," he said to Bok. He put down his cases, and
rushed to the immigrant's side. "Come," he said. "The Jewish
Shelter is waiting. Finish your soup and come."

Aaron and the rescued immigrant went back to where Bok was
waiting.

"It's a new life," Bok said, taking their arms. "We should all
have joy of it," and he helped them into the horse-drawn bus that
would take them to the shelter. I'm in England, Aaron thought
as they drove through the strange streets of east London. Occasionally he saw something that reminded him of home, a sewing
machine on the pavement, an old man's foot on the treadle.
Shops had Yiddish signs painted on their windows and groups of
Chasidic boys, their ringlets brushing their young cheeks, carrying large loaves from the bread stall. He could have been back in
Odessa. He thought perhaps that in whatever country, in whatever tongue, Jews were much the same all the world over, and
that thought comforted him a little, and blunted the edge of his
loneliness.

The massive exodus from Eastern Europe began in earnest in the late 1870s, and continued until the passing of the Aliens Bill in 1894. During the first wave of immigration, of which Aaron Bindel was a part, the Jewish Temporary Shelter was able to cater to all the needs of the new immigrant. There were beds, food, clothing, holy books for prayer, and help in finding employment. For many of the immigrants the Shelter was used as a stopover until relatives could be traced. Aaron fell into this catalogue, for though Mr. Khasina was no relative, he was a known *landsman,* or fellow countryman. So, after a day's rest and feeding, Aaron was given enough money for his travel to Cardiff and the address of the Jewish Board of Guardians in that city. He had told the officials at the shelter about his mother and brother. They assured him that contact would eventually be made. The shelter was inevitably the center and postal address for all new immigrants. They copied the address of his Cardiff sponsor and wished him well. A shelter official took him to the station, and instructed one of the train guards to put his passenger off at Cardiff.

The journey took many hours. The other passengers in the compartment were very talkative and they tried to include him in their conversation. He shook his head and told them in Yiddish that he didn't understand. Whereupon one of them set about giving him his first English lesson, the names of colors, features of the face and body, and all manner of emotions that they affected with charade. By the time he reached Cardiff, he had been equipped with a minimal vocabulary. One of the passengers offered to take him to Mr. Khasina's address. It was dark when they arrived in Cardiff and Aaron feared that it might be too late to make such an unexpected call. But his companion indicated that he need not worry and urged him along the narrow streets—checking the numbers on the doors against the piece of paper in

Aaron's hand. At last they reached Khasina's dwelling. Aaron
bid farewell to his companion. Then he pulled the bell at the side
of the door. He listened as the echo died away, but he heard no
footsteps. He wouldn't ring again, he decided. He was about to
turn from the door when it opened. A man stood there, slippered,
Aaron noted, which accounted for the silence of his approach.
Aaron gave his name and asked for Pavel Khasina. The man
smiled and turned his head indoors.

"Pavel," he shouted. "A *landsman.*"

Shortly afterward Pavel himself appeared at the door and scru-
tinized the caller. After a while he cried out, "Odessa. The tavern. The widow. Two sons. Come in, my friend. You took my
advice."

The welcome was lavish. They led him through the front room,
which Aaron could discern as a shop of sorts, but it was dark and
it was difficult to decipher what was being sold. At the back of
the shop were the living quarters, not unlike the layout, Aaron
thought, of Grandpa Jakob's tavern. And the kitchen was similar
too, where all the living took place, the cooking and the eating,
and there was even a small truckle bed in the corner.

"For you," Pavel Khasina said, and he took Aaron's bags and
put them on the bed. Then he introduced his sister, Hinda, his
brother-in-law, Max, the slippered one who had opened the door,
and two or three friends, "*landsleit* too," Khasina explained. And
just like at home, the samovar stood in the center of the table.

All were eager of news of home. They knew no one in common, no friends, no relatives, but that was not where their interest lay. Their nostalgia was for the land, the language, even the
cruelty; they needed to hear about it, to reminisce each chapter of
their own survival and to celebrate the fact that they were now
beyond its reach. But they kept silent. They wanted him fed and
fortified. Then, when he was sated, they could sniff out the land
on him, that land which had borne and bred them, hated and
abused them, and in which they had left their dead. Aaron ate in
a watchful silence and when he had done, Pavel poured wine for
them all, and they drank a toast to his welcome.

Then "What news of home?" one of them asked, giving Aaron
an opening. Aaron had only his own personal story to tell, but
that was general enough, for it could have happened to any of
them. He told it from the beginning, backtracking occasionally
when questions were asked that called for clarification from the

past. So that when the long recital was over, he had told them not only his own tale but that of his father and Grandpa Jakob's as well. During the telling they nodded with signs of recognition because many of the events had colored their own lives too. They drank another glass of wine together, and then they spent much time speculating on what could have happened to Zelda and Leon. Their prognoses varied, but fundamentally they were all the same. "Soon you will all be together again," they said.

The phrase had a familiar ring. From the stories Grandpa Jakob had told him, it was with exactly those words that he had bade farewell to the milk-brothers. But had not the gentle Leon used that phrase too, the Leon after whom his brother was named? It was that hope and conviction of family reunion that Leon had shouted from the dock before his Siberian journey. And his own father had said it as he kissed them and sent them off to Zemach's tavern to prepare for his eighty-fifth birthday. "Soon we shall all be together again," he had said. Aaron did not like that phrase, and he wished that those around the table had not voiced it. "Please God," he whispered. Perhaps if he appended a prayer, it might come true.

The following morning Aaron was awoken by the bustle in the kitchen. Hinda was making breakfast for the family. Two little girls materialized; they had obviously been in bed when Aaron had arrived. They stared at the newcomer on the cot, then turned away, giggling. Aaron rose and dressed quickly. Soon Max came to the table, and Pavel. Aaron was invited to sit between the children, who were chattering freely in English. Pavel explained that in front of the children only English was spoken. The children were their teachers and would be Aaron's teachers too. So for Aaron it was a silent meal until the children left for school. Then it was Yiddish again around the table, with plans for Aaron's future. His first move, they suggested, should be to go to the Jewish Board of Guardians and register his immigrant status. They would help him with money until he could find work. His lodgings on the kitchen bed would be free, they assured him, until he could make his own way. The board held classes for English, too. It would be somewhere to go during the day. As to the prospect of work, Pavel offered to train him in the job that he did himself. Pavel was a credit draper. This was a trade most favored by those immigrants who did not have a particular skill. Its great advantage was that it required little initial capital, and even that could be credited. The trade itself was concerned with the sale of clothing at the minimum payment of a shilling a week, and the main hunting ground for such clientele was the Welsh mining valleys. The tallyman would buy his goods on credit from the wholesale merchants, then make the rounds of his customers. The profit margin was narrow, the hours long and arduous, but it already provided Pavel with a living, as it did many of his *landsleit.* Some of them, after a year or two, had bought their own houses, and some, like Max, had used the profits to set up a shop of their own.

Max's shop was sited on the long, busy thoroughfare that led to the docks. The docks at Cardiff were a harbor for cargo from all over the world, and the wagons of imported grain would pass the outgoing coal wagons as they trundled to and from the dockside. The area was rich in passing trade. Many of the early immigrants had set up small businesses there, catering to the needs of sailors and ship personnel. Max's shop sold men's clothing and luggage, and wooden chests and tin trunks stood on the forefront. Tailoring establishments were sandwiched between alehouses and brothels. At first sight the area could have been any port in the world. Only the line of coal wagons shuttling down Bute Street gave a clue to its Welsh location.

It was into this confusing and alien thoroughfare that Aaron was thrust on his first morning, a carefully drawn map in his hand, to make his way to the Jewish Board of Guardians. As he walked he worried about Zelda and Leon. Perhaps he should go back to Hamburg. But even if he had the money to get there, where and how would he start looking? Perhaps the Jewish Board had a representative there. He quickened his pace, and from time to time he checked on the map in his hand. He was so concerned about his family's welfare that he had little curiosity about his strange surroundings.

In time he reached the offices of the board, where a member, noting his immigrant garb and confusion, spoke to him in Yiddish and welcomed him. Aaron sat down on the chair that was offered, but he declined a glass of lemon tea. He was anxious to apprise the official of the loss of his family, to seek his help in finding them. The official was baffled by the story. But he would make inquiries, he promised. He then concerned himself with Aaron's personal financial needs and gave him the address of a school where every evening he could attend classes in the English

language. Aaron left the offices of the board, his spirits lightened.
Now someone else, someone in authority, would share with him
the responsibility for finding his family.

That evening he attended his first English lesson. There were a
dozen or so pupils and most of them were older than Aaron. A
newcomer was assured of welcome because the smell of home still
lingered on his gabardine, and although most of them, as it
turned out, hailed from Poland, their mother tongue was common, and all had fled from oppression. One of the group, the
youngest, was a girl who introduced herself as Rachel and who
had recently arrived from Lodz. She offered Aaron a seat on the
bench beside her. It was a rule in the class that once a lesson had
begun, no Yiddish was to be spoken, so for Aaron it was a silent
hour. But he was able to learn a little and to begin to draw the
letters of a strange alphabet. When the lesson was finished, he
found himself walking into the street with Rachel at his side. Out
of politeness he offered to see her to her home, an offer she accepted on condition that they speak no Yiddish on their way.
And so it was, night after night, after the English lesson, until in
time, as the weeks passed, he was able to talk to her, and to share
with her his cares. And with words now between them, he began
to grow fond of her.

A few weeks after his arrival in England, he accompanied Pavel on his valley rounds. The job required little skill except that of
bookkeeping. Its major demand was on one's physical strength
and endurance. Pavel set out on his journey encumbered with
large parcels. He would travel by train to the central town of the
valley, and from there would walk or wagon along the roads to
the outlying villages and hamlets. It was backbreaking work, and
especially hard in the winters. But there was always a welcome in
the valley and the friendship and warmth of the mining communities. As Pavel's companion and apprentice, Aaron was slowly
accepted into their circle. In time he would have his own round.

It was about three months after his arrival that he returned
home from his English lesson to find a letter from Hamburg.
Over the past few weeks his family had ceased to be his waking
thought. That place had been taken by Rachel, and he hadn't
realized until that moment that any displacement had occurred.
He stared at the letter, chiding himself for his negligence. He was
wary of opening it, and he sat for a while staring at the much-

marked and redirected envelope, while Pavel and Max stood behind him eager for its news. Then after a while they realized that
Aaron wished to be alone and they withdrew. The writing on the
envelope was in his mother's careful hand. The address was clear,
but the town of Cardiff was omitted, which explained the delay in
its delivery. He slid his thumb slowly under the envelope flap.
There were two closely written pages inside, and both in his
mother's hand. He looked in vain for his brother's scrawl, then,
fearful, he spread the pages on the table and began to read.

His mother prefaced the letter with her deep love for him, her
concern with his penniless condition, and a plea for a swift reply
to an address that was written with great clarity at the top of the
page. Then after such preliminaries she gave him the explanation
for their absence, and each stage of it was spelled out factually
and unadorned. She wrote of the unfortunate incident at the
dockside, stressing their good luck that the official had only been
slightly injured. However, Leon had been taken to court and
charged with assault, together with illegal entry. This latter
charge the court was willing to overlook, and his mother thanked
God for that because Leon could well have been returned to the
border. But on the charge of assault, their judgment was severe.
Leon had been sentenced to one year in prison.

Aaron put down the sheet of paper. His mother's method of
narration had cushioned the shock. She was at pains to stress that
matters could have been much worse, so that the year's sentence
when it came seemed less devastating. But when Aaron began to
think about it, he could not help but reduce it to months, and
then to weeks and days, and after that to calculate how much of
his sentence his brother had already served. It had been three
whole months, and, like his Grandfather Jakob before him in the
milk-brothers' absence, Aaron concentrated on those months,
ticking them off in his mind, rather than admitting to the many
months to come. He pictured his brother in his cell, and his heart
heaved for his solitude and his despair. He hoped that Leon was
sleeping. How could his mother be faring on her own in a strange
land? He turned again to the letter. And again it was full of hope
and even a measure of excitement. She wrote much about Mr.
Rubinov. They had returned to the marketplace, she wrote, to
retrieve the money he had spent on his ticket, but everyone had
disappeared. He had been most helpful in dealing with the police
on Leon's behalf, and had decided to stay in Germany, at least

until Leon was released. He had found a small house near the prison so that they could visit Leon regularly. They found Leon well, she wrote, and in good spirits. Meanwhile Mr. Rubinov had found work in his old furrier trade. She wrote that she found him a wonderful companion and that they spent much time together. There were many beautiful things to see in the city, she wrote, and their pleasure was only marred by Leon's incarceration. *The language is not difficult,* she added. *It is so much like our own.*

There followed another passage about Mr. Rubinov's helpfulness and solicitude and the letter ended with practical matters. She was anxious to send him money but wanted first to make sure where he was living. She wanted to know everything about him, and quickly. She loved him with all her heart.

Aaron put the letter down. *All* her heart? he wondered, when so much of it was on its way to Mr. Rubinov. He was glad for her. His mother was still a young woman with much love to give and much grief to overcome.

But around the thought of his brother there was nothing but sadness; Leon's isolation from any possibility of happiness, such as he and his mother had found, gnawed at Aaron's heart. He took pen and paper and set immediately to writing. He described to her his journey to England, his night at the Shelter, and his eventual meeting with Pavel Khasina. He told her about his life and his work and his English lessons. But he made no mention of Rachel. Most of his letter related to his concern for Leon, urging her to write to him after each prison visit and tell of his brother's condition. He wanted no money, he wrote. Soon he would be earning his own living. He sent his regards to Mr. Rubinov and his thanks for taking care of his family. He did not reread the letter, needing to post it immediately. He was anxious that his mother know about him. Anxious, too, that she should write again, and quickly, for in his next reply he would tell her about Rachel. He went out immediately and posted the letter and when he returned, he told Pavel and Max and Hinda, who were hovering in the kitchen, all the news that he felt they were entitled to. He did not mention Mr. Rubinov and afterward, when he was in bed, he wondered why he had omitted his name.

One evening, shortly after the receipt of the first letter, Pavel and Max suggested it was time that Aaron started his own drapery round. They showed him a map and circled an area that was as yet untouched by tallymen of their kind. Aaron read out the

village names with difficulty. They were the mining villages of
Caerphilly and Senghenydd. The following morning he took the
train with Pavel, who was traveling in the same direction. He
carried no parcels. His mission was to find his first orders. He
was nervous as he walked up the strange valley road. On his way
he rehearsed the speech he would make at his first door. When he
reached the summit, he saw the now familiar sight of the pithead
and heard the grinding toll of its wheel. In his apprenticeship
days with Pavel, he had met some of the men who worked below
the ground, deaf to the wheel's turning, their ears cocked for
other noises, hearing hopefully only those they made themselves.
Alert too for the canary's song in its cage and in its melody the
assurance that they were safe. He'd warmed to those men he had
met, for he had smelled courage on them. Their poverty was
extreme, yet he did not pity them. Their pride forbade pity. They
held the rich in splendid contempt, but those who struggled like
themselves would find friendship among them. They accepted
Pavel because he too struggled for a living. Aaron hoped that
they would extend the same trust to him.

He knocked on his first door, and when it was opened, all the
words of his rehearsed speech deserted him. The woman called
him in after he had managed to mumble the purpose of his visit.
She sensed his shyness and his need. He was handsome, too, she
thought, with a face unlike any other in these parts. She was Mrs.
Williams, she said, one of ten Mrs. Williamses in the village and
none of them related. "You'd better call me Myfanwy," she said,
and a cup of tea was made ready to ease the frightened words
from his throat. There'd never been a tallyman in the village
before, she told him. There were insurance men and salesmen for
food and furniture, but none like him for clothes. But they'd
heard about clothesmen from the other valleys. Yes, they needed
clothes. All of them. Four children she had, and all dressed in
charity hand-me-downs, with nothing for a Sunday, and a wedding coming in the village and a family christening, too. But how
could she pay for all these things? She was asking his advice,
some magic maneuvering of her budget. She took herself a cup of
tea and sat at the table opposite him. And with no hesitation she
told him of her husband's earnings. Aaron took a pencil and
paper and wrote a column of her weekly expenses. She was poor
indeed, Aaron thought. She could hardly afford to invest in a pair
of shoes. He worked out a small savings budget for her, and

offered to let her have the clothes on a higher credit than was normal. She was his first customer and she might well bring him luck. He knew that he had chosen a business in which he would never make his fortune and the realization did not in any way trouble him. Mrs. Williams gave him a list of the village women who would be interested in his call. She herself accompanied him to the first house. Aaron fared better with his second customer, also a Mrs. Williams, who had savings put by for such a purpose. By the end of the day, Aaron had a full order book and he returned home lighthearted and in time to attend his evening lesson. When afterward, he took Rachel home, she asked him for the first time to come inside and meet her parents.

Rachel's father was a tailor, a trade he had brought with him from Lodz. Mr. Ruboff had a brother in America who had emigrated from Lodz some years before, and it was to America that the family had intended to travel. Like most immigrants from the east, they had set sail from Hamburg and it was possible that Mr. Ruboff was served by the same trader on the Hamburg marketplace who had misrouted Mr. Rubinov. Mr. Ruboff had not uncovered the swindle at the time. Indeed, he had walked the streets of Whitechapel for almost a week, under the impression that he was taking the air of New York. When apprised of his misconception, he had taken it in stride and had made for Cardiff, where he had *landsleit.* He and his wife spoke very little English, but they were proud of Rachel's achievement. She was their only child and they looked to her for interpretation of the strange ways they daily encountered. They invited Aaron for a glass of lemon tea. The talk was Yiddish, the language of home. Aaron told them of his life in Odessa and of their flight from the city. He told them of the events in Hamburg, and his present situation. In return Mr. Ruboff gave his own story, much of which Aaron had already heard from Rachel. But Mr. Ruboff's account was of a different style mainly because he shared the narration with his wife, who filled in those details that she felt would highlight the drama. It was a poet and peasant recital, which betrayed a marriage of initial inequality but one that, over the years, had, through tolerance and affection, found a level of harmony. The evening passed with ease and pleasure and as Aaron was leaving, they asked him to come again.

It was a few days after this visit that a second letter arrived from Zelda. Aaron was loath to open it, for any reminder of his

brother's deprivation could only cloud his own happiness. He put
the letter in his pocket and walked to the harbor, where he could
find some privacy. There he found an empty bench, and though
the docks were noisy, raucous with sailors, it suited Aaron well
enough, for those around him had no curiosity or concern for his
state. He looked at the date on the envelope. It had been on its
way only ten days. Whatever news his mother would reveal
would be new indeed. He slid his thumb under the envelope flap
and spread the two pages on his knees, holding them down
against the wind. The opening phrase of the letter heartened him.
Good news, my dearest, his mother wrote. As a result of Leon's
appeal, his sentence had been reduced by half. He would be free
in two months' time. His mother spent almost the whole of the
first page rejoicing in this piece of news and sharing it with her
eldest son. The second page began with words of urgency and
importance. *There is something which my heart bids me to do, and
for which I very much want your permission.*

Aaron looked out on the sea and let the wind fan his face.
What impressed him was that she asked for permission at all, and
he was reminded again of his status in the family and the duties
that attended it. He thought of the death of his father and of the
confusion as well as the grief that it had wrought, how it had
upset the natural order, turned mothers into children and given
sons the power of permit. He turned back to the letter.

The mention of Mr. Rubinov did not surprise him, nor did the
fact that, during the course of the letter, his mother referred to
him as Barak. He was kind, gentle, and lonely, and he had asked
her to marry him. For her part she owned a true affection for
him, and gratitude, too, that he had sustained her during Leon's
troubles. He had enough money, she added, for their comfort,
and his business prospered. They had it in mind to make their
home in Germany. She had made no mention of his proposal to
Leon, for she felt that Aaron as the eldest son should be the first
to be told. She eagerly awaited his reply. Whatever his decision,
she declared, they could look forward with joy to a family reunion in the near future. She sent her best wishes and her thanks
to Pavel Khasina and his family. *My son,* she wrote, *I am happy
for the first time in many years.*

Aaron folded the letter and quickly put it in his pocket. He was
anxious to get home, to write to her quickly, to give her the
permission she sought, to wish her joy of her future. But most of

all it was the news of Leon that so heartened him. He would write her of that, too. And when all that was written, he would tell her about Rachel. He ran all the way down the dock road, and when he reached home, Pavel, Max, and Hinda, as he expected, were hovering at the door for the news. But first, he explained, he had to write a letter, and only when it was done and posted could he tell them. He told them, in the order of his mother's priorities, of Leon's reduced sentence, and of his mother's intended remarriage. But he kept silent about Rachel, and would remain so until his mother was privy to his news.

He waited daily for her reply, for in telling her about Rachel he was seeking her permission for his eventual marriage. It was three weeks before the letter arrived. He was too impatient even to seek privacy, and then and there, on his truckle bed, while the family were preparing supper, he read of his mother's joy in the prospect of his engagement. *We shall be together soon,* she wrote, *to celebrate your marriage and Leon's freedom.* She added that she and Barak would marry quietly in Hamburg. She hoped then that they could arrange to come to England, at least for a little while. Aaron pocketed the letter and smiled at the hovering faces around him. "All is good," he said, then he put on his best suit, pomaded his hair, and took himself to Rachel's house to talk with her father.

On his way down Bute Street he rehearsed his address of proposal. He knew he had little to offer Rachel in terms of material goods. He had entered a trade in which he could see little financial reward. He had no home of his own and little prospect of one in the near future. He loved her, and his love was all that he had to offer. He wondered whether in her father's eyes that would be enough.

Rachel was not at home when he arrived, a fact for which her father apologized when he welcomed Aaron inside.

"But I can offer you my company," he said. "Come into the workshop. I'm pressing a suit."

"It's you I've come to see, Mr. Ruboff," Aaron said to his back as he followed him upstairs.

"Then take a seat," Mr. Ruboff said without surprise, "and talk to me while I work."

The steam rose from the heavy iron, and from time to time it cast a mist over his face and it was not easy for Aaron to put forward a serious proposition to a face that swam in and out of clouds of vapor. It was like talking to a ghost. He fidgeted in his chair.

"I remember when I was a boy in Lodz," Mr. Ruboff said. "I used to sit in my father's workshop and watch him at his sewing machine. Sometimes he let me turn the wheel or he would give me a box of buttons, and I'd sort out the sizes. That's how I learned how to count." Then, without a pause, and with the heavy steam masking his features, he said, "You've come to talk to me about Rachel." Then he put the iron aside, the smile on his face now slowly coming into focus. "Come, my friend," he said, "say your piece."

"I want to marry her," Aaron said, heedless of his rehearsal.

Mr. Ruboff moved away from the pressing table and clasped Aaron by the shoulders. "My blessings on you both," he said softly. Aaron opened his mouth to list his inadequacies, his lack of livelihood or position, and to state his willingness to wait for their betrothal. But Mr. Ruboff did not let him speak. "I know," he said. "You have no living and you have no house. But all these you shall have in time. I would like to teach you my trade. There's good business in tailoring," he said. "Think about it. There's time. Come, we'll make ourselves tea. Rachel will soon be home."

They went downstairs to the kitchen, where Mr. Ruboff busied himself at the stove. "You know," he said, "when I wanted to marry my wife, I was afraid to ask her father. He was a great rabbi, full of learning, and I felt I was not good enough for his daughter. For a whole year I tried to give myself courage. Then one day the old man came to me himself. 'In the *Haggadah* that we read at Passover,' he said, 'there is the story of the four sons, the wise one, the wicked one, the simple one, and the one who does not know what or how to ask. You are like that fourth son,' he said, 'and I shall answer you as the *Haggadah* instructs. To the son who does not know what to ask, the *Haggadah* says, "Thou shalt open the subject to him." ' Then he put his old hand on my shoulder and he said, 'You want to ask for my daughter's hand. You have asked and it is given.' "

Mr. Ruboff took the pot from the stove and topped up the samovar on the table. They heard the front door open and footsteps in the hall.

"David?" Rachel's mother called.

"We're in the kitchen," Mr. Ruboff shouted.

Rachel followed her mother and when she saw Aaron sitting there, and her father's face wreathed in smiles, she blushed and turned her face away, hiding it in the large shopping bag that she was carrying. Mrs. Ruboff, too, sensed a gentle conspiracy between the men, and she too knew its matter.

"Only tea?" she said, "for such an occasion?" and she went to the cupboard and brought out a bottle of schnapps. "Rachel," she said, "get the glasses."

Thus Rachel was forced to turn, and Aaron dared to go to her and take her hand. As he did so, he realized that, of all the words they had shared over the past months, marriage had not been one of them.

"Your father has given his blessing on our marriage," he said. He spoke in Yiddish for her parents' understanding. She smiled at him, then kissed her father and mother in turn. Then without a word, she took the glasses and held them for her mother's pouring.

"To our children," Mr. Ruboff said, raising his glass, taking his wife's arm, and they drank together.

"To you both," Aaron said, raising his glass in his turn. He could not call them his parents. His mother was still alive and his father was irreplaceable. It was possible that Mr. Ruboff read his thoughts, for he raised his glass once more. "To the memory of your father," he said, and with that toast he endowed their joy with the solemnity that was proper to the occasion, for at a celebration of continuity, at each avowal of the future, there must also be an acknowledgment of the past, a homage to those who have made the present possible. For the rest of the evening they sat in quiet reminiscence of that past, of both Aaron's and Rachel's. Despite the grief and the rage that had attended almost every event in their history, these events were remembered now with quiet acceptance. For the first time since he had left Odessa, Aaron felt himself free to let his father lie quietly in his grave.

That night, when he reached home, Aaron wrote immediately to his mother, telling her of his evening's visit. It was a short letter, but he enclosed a longer one to Leon, asking that it should be delivered to him in the prison. To his brother he wrote little of Rachel. He still felt unentitled to his own happiness. His letter

was a confirmation of the fraternal love he bore him, of all his
hopes of the future that they would share. He reminded him of
stories of their childhood; he talked of their father. He tried to
infuse his brother with the peace and serenity that he himself had
suddenly found in his father's memory.

For the next few weeks Aaron met with Rachel every day, and
every day, too, he went on his round to Senghenydd. He had not
yet decided on Mr. Ruboff's offer of tailoring apprenticeship. His
little credit drapery was prospering in a small way, and he wished
to consolidate it. When he thought about it, he knew that he was
doing it for his brother's sake, that he was establishing a foothold
for Leon, who would eventually make his home in Wales. Once
Leon was settled, Aaron could begin his tailoring apprenticeship.
   His mother wrote of her remarriage. Aaron replied, addressing
the envelope to Mrs. Bindel. Then he realized that, in truth, he
had not given her permission to remarry at all. So he took a new
envelope, and with a careful hand he wrote "Mrs. Zelda Rubinov" and it was as if he were writing to a total stranger. He began
to be apprehensive of their reunion. Leon was due to be released
in two weeks. In less than a month they would all be together
again, and though he longed for it, Aaron was nervous for its
success. In the last months the Bindel family had lost much of its
cohesion. The fact of living together under the same roof, as the
Bindel family had always done in Odessa—such a fact was crucial to family cohesion. For a moment Aaron dreamed of a huge
house in Bute Street where the Bindels would regroup once more,
and live out their lives in shared joy and sorrow. But when he
envisaged them in such a setting, with the stranger Rubinov at
the head of the table, with his brother, with whom he had not
shared those first steps into exile, and with his own Rachel,
whose childhood was known to none of them, it seemed to Aaron
that there was little left that could hold them together. The songs
of the Bindel tavern in Odessa did not travel well. They belonged
to the discords and harmonies of an era that had passed. Aaron
had accepted that passing. His love for Rachel had enabled him
to put it aside. Perhaps his mother, for like reasons, had done the
same. But there remained in Aaron's mind the figure of Leon in
his cell. He hoped, as always, that Leon was sleeping, but not,
Aaron prayed, dreaming of the Bindel tavern, hearing its songs in

the hope of ever hearing them again. He must help Leon to tune his ears to other songs and voices. Aaron was overcome by a sudden longing to take his brother in his arms, and it was this thought that helped him allay his fears of the impending family reunion.

Aaron had decided against going to London to meet the boat from Hamburg. What little money he had managed to save he had put by for his marriage. Pavel was insistent on making a reception to welcome them, and Max and Hinda were more than happy to open their home to new *landsleit*. The Ruboffs had readily offered sleeping accommodation. Aaron was dispatched in good time to the station to meet the train, so he had to idle nervously on the platform for an hour before the train would arrive. He took himself to the nearest hostelry and ordered a beer, which he had been told was the national beverage. It was the first time since his arrival in England that he had been into a tavern. Often on a Friday night the mining men of Senghenydd had urged him into the corner public house, but he had always pleaded his haste to be home. He liked the miners' company, but he had no taste for their beer, and now he wondered at himself for ordering the glass of ale that was by his hand. He remembered the last time he'd been in a tavern, adjacent to a railway station on the Russian border. He recalled his battle for survival. Now all that seemed a continent ago. Since that time there had been much confusion. His mother was no longer a Bindel, and both he and his brother had passed through adventures unshared. He felt profoundly alone. He lifted his glass in unspoken toast to the stranger beside him. He downed his ale and left the tavern.

The platform was now peopled with those waiting to meet the London train, and Aaron was glad of the company. Their presence might help dilute the intensity of the reunion. In the distance he caught sight of the signal pointer, its arm extended. Then suddenly it dropped and there was now no reason why a train should not approach the platform. He heard the train's hooter and saw the high column of smoke as it belched skyward. He planted his feet firmly together and stiffened his limbs to still the tremblings in his body. When the train creaked to a standstill, he stood rooted to the spot, unable to move. In the distance he saw them distinctly, Mr. Rubinov first as he held out his hand to help his mother from the train. And some moments after, his brother Leon, lagging behind as if he were a lone traveler. The crowd on the platform surged forward to greet those who had arrived, and it was only their movement that propelled Aaron into stirring. He allowed himself to be swept along the platform until he found himself face-to-face with his kin. Mr. Rubinov stepped aside, as if knowing his place, allowing a mother-and-son embrace. His presence affected the proceedings with some formality. When the embrace was done, they separated and Zelda stepped aside for Leon. One look at Leon's face told Aaron that in his brother's eyes he was already a stranger. Leon's look was cold, angry and bitter. Aaron put his arms around him, in that embrace that had so often scored his daydreams. But Leon's hands hung loosely by his side, with no attempt to seal that look that would secure their brotherhood. Aaron was saddened by the lack of response. On the whole of Leon's face, there was no hint of a smile.

"Hello, Aaron," Leon said, and his voice, too, was that of a stranger.

Aaron didn't answer. He just took his brother's hand and held it in both of his own. I understand, his caress was meant to say. I understand it all.

Aaron helped Mr. Rubinov with the luggage. He noticed that they had brought little with them, an indication that they did not have it in mind to stay very long. Aaron was ashamed of his relief. But not Leon, he thought. Leon must stay, and Aaron would help ease the pain that troubled him. He was frightened that his brother might be ill. He wanted desperately to talk to him, but he feared that Leon would give no clue. In any case, his instinct told him that Leon's recovery would take time. He reached out to his brother's arm and held on to his sleeve, and the cold rub of serge had caught the torpor of the limb it clothed.

As soon as they were settled on the tram, Zelda took Aaron's arm. "Now tell me," she said. "I want to know everything." She gave no pause for his reply, but proceeded to regale him with an account of their journey from Hamburg, detailing all the trivia of their passage. She seemed to be talking for the simple sake of filling the space between them. She feared that Aaron might whisper a question concerning Leon and whatever question he had in mind, she knew she could not answer. She told Aaron about her marriage and about the rabbi who had performed the ceremony. She described the house Mr. Rubinov had bought, itemizing every room and piece of furniture. It was a large house and in her manner took some time to survey, and by the time they alighted from the tram in Bute Street, she was almost hysterical with her catalog. Aaron longed for silence. When they arrived at Max's house, he made introductions all round, then withdrew quickly into the darkness of the shop. He needed to be alone, to rinse out of his ears the echo of his mother's chatter. After a while he returned to the living quarters and was not surprised to find his mother holding court with a recital of her life and times in Hamburg. Perhaps, Aaron thought, there was nothing wrong with Leon at all. It was Zelda who was out of countenance. Mr. Rubinov took his mother's arm and Aaron noted his look of concern. As he touched her, his mother slowed her tale to a halt. Max took advantage of the interval to pour wine into the glasses already set on the table and Hinda passed around the cakes.

"The Ruboffs are late," Max said.

In his anxiety, Aaron had forgotten that his future family were to be present at the welcoming reception. Now he heartily wished that they would not come. Much as he wanted to see Rachel, he did not look forward to presenting her to his family. And moreover, they were to stay in the Ruboffs' house. He heard the bell-pull in the hall. It was altogether too much for him. He felt like a child in need of protection, but those to whom he would have naturally turned were themselves afflicted.

He felt a cold presence by his side. He looked up and saw Leon.

"Let me stay here with you," his brother said. They were the first real words that Aaron had heard from his brother's mouth, and he wanted to embrace him, just for the sound of them and for their great gift of contact. Then he wondered what they meant. By staying, did Leon mean forever, and in Wales, or just that night in Pavel's dwelling place? He put his hand on his brother's shoulder. "Of course," he said. "You must. There's no question of it." Then he followed Pavel into the hall to greet Rachel.

The Ruboffs entered the room shyly, unused to strangers' company. But they were all *landsleit* of a sort, and some of them would soon, by marriage, be related. It was Mr. Rubinov, in many ways more of a stranger than the others, who eased the company into conversation. He was eager to ask Mr. Ruboff of his background and his immigrant experience. Mrs. Ruboff slipped easily into the conversation, and stretched out a hand for Zelda to join them. Aaron urged his way into the circle, putting Rachel by his side. He wanted at that moment to avoid a face-to-face meeting between his mother and his intended bride. Pavel had approached Leon, and Aaron strained one ear to listen to whatever conversation would ensue, while with the other he monitored the tenor of the women's exchange. Between the two he kept his perilous balance, fearfully anticipating a breakdown on either side. But for a while both parties seemed at ease, and Aaron felt that it would be safe to move to Pavel's side and perhaps through him to engage in conversation with his brother. But what conversation there was, was mostly one-sided, with a hard-pressed Pavel reminding Leon of their last meeting in the Odessa tavern with very little response or encouragement from Leon's side. For Pavel's relief, Aaron contributed his own elaboration of the scene. When it was done, Pavel scratched in his mind for a new topic of conversation. Suddenly Leon said, "I'm so very tired."

Both Pavel and Aaron knew that Leon's weariness had nothing to do with fatigue.

"When they are gone," Pavel said, "you can be alone here."

For the first time since their reunion, Aaron saw the smallest hint of a smile on his brother's face. He clutched Pavel's arm in gratitude for his understanding. Then Pavel turned to the company. "I think our guests must be very tired. I shall prepare the wagon to take the Ruboffs home."

"Have you spoken to Rachel?" Aaron asked his brother.

Leon shook his head. "Tomorrow," he said.

Aaron nodded and made to move away, when Leon touched his sleeve. "She's beautiful," he said.

"It's important to me that you should like her," Aaron said. "It's the most important thing of all." He smiled at his brother with the relief of the conviction that nothing was wrong with him. A man couldn't spend six months in prison and expect to emerge smiling. Gradually around his person there would be a gentle thaw. He looked at the group of women. His mother was silent and had been so since Mr. Rubinov had wound her down, and though her eyes darted from one face to the other, it was clear that she was not listening. He went over and took her arm, linking the other with Rachel's, while Hinda and Mrs. Ruboff compared their housekeeping problems and marveled at the strange English ways. After a while Pavel announced that the wagon was ready. He would first load the luggage. Capes and cloaks were donned, thanks and farewells were given, and it only remained for Pavel to return. In that waiting time was silence.

"He won't be long," Max said after a while, and there was silence again. Aaron wished that Pavel would return quickly. Then suddenly a small voice pleaded, "He doesn't talk to me anymore."

It was the voice of a ghost and Aaron wondered whether only he had heard it. But Mr. Rubinov put his hand on his wife's arm.

Max looked questioningly at Hinda and Rachel looked at the floor. And then Leon turned his back and walked from the room.

Then Mr. Ruboff spoke. "You're very tired, Mrs. Rubinov," he said. "Tomorrow all will seem different."

Then mercifully Pavel reappeared. Aaron kissed his mother good night. "We shall talk tomorrow," he whispered. "When you are rested."

"I have no sleep in me," she said.

"Come, my dear." Mr. Rubinov held her hand and she squeezed it like a child. Aaron saw them all to the door and helped them into the wagon and watched it out of sight. On his return, he called Leon's name.

"I'm here," Leon said, and his voice came from the corner by the window. Aaron groped his way to Leon's side and sat beside him, silent for a while, accustoming himself to the half-light in the shop, lit by the gaslight outside the window. He did not particularly want to talk or ask questions. It was enough for him to have his brother at his side. The silence between them was no embarrassment. Then after a while Aaron spoke.

"D'you like Barak?" he asked. He suspected that Barak, kind and concerned though he was, was the core of both his mother's and his brother's discontent.

"Barak is fine," Leon shouted, and his extreme protest could not mask his jealousy.

"He makes her happy," Aaron said, and as he heard his own words, he heard the lie of them too.

"You call that happy?" Leon mocked.

There was a silence then between them, and after a while
Aaron asked, "Then what do you think's the matter with her?"

"She's murdered her past," Leon said, "and she doesn't know
what to do with the body."

Aaron was astonished at his brother's turn of phrase. His solitary confinement had nurtured in him a philosophical frame of
mind.

"It was all right before she was married," Leon was saying.
"She was a widow, honorably widowed by our history, and the
past had its proper untainted place in her heart. Grief had made
her strong and independent. She had no need to marry again."

"Is that why you're angry with her?" Aaron asked as gently as
he could.

Leon turned away. "I cannot go back to Hamburg," he said. "I
must stay here." There was no pleading in his voice. Not even
anger.

"Of course you will stay. You will make your home here. With
me and Rachel. And there is work, too. There's a good life here,
Leon. We are safe here. We can all die in our beds."

"I would like to talk to Rachel tomorrow," Leon said tonelessly.

Aaron held him in his arms. He no longer minded the almost
imperceptible stiffening of his brother's shoulders in his embrace.
In his long and alien isolation, Leon had become untouchable.
But he would learn to love again. "We shall sleep now," Aaron
said, "and tomorrow we shall all begin again."

Pavel had offered to make Aaron's round collection during the
visit of his family, and the following morning he offered to take
Leon with him and show him a little of life in the valley. Leon
gratefully accepted his offer. It would be a relief to be freed for a
while from the constraints of his family. So the two of them left
for the valley by the early train, sharing the parcels between
them.

Aaron made his way to the Ruboffs'. He was surprised to find
his mother still in bed. Mrs. Ruboff had decided not to disturb
her. Sleep was remedial, and though she did not know the nature
of Zelda's condition, she was certain it needed cure. But Mr.
Rubinov seemed bright and eager to walk and talk with Aaron.
Which Aaron welcomed. As non-kin, his stepfather could admit
him to his mother's heart without any sense of betrayal. Aaron

spent a few moments with Rachel before leaving, and as he turned to the door she said, "Don't worry about your mother."

"But I do," he said. "I can't help it. With what miracle can she be cured?"

"Forgiveness," Rachel said.

"But she has done no wrong."

Rachel put her hand on his arm. "She thinks otherwise," she said.

"Then who can forgive her?"

"Only herself, but with our help."

Aaron kissed her on her forehead. "You are a woman of worth," he said.

Mr. Ruboff's house was situated on the riverside, and they walked in silence along its embankment to the steps that led to the bridge. From there they crossed over the fields and had a clear half mile in front of them before they reached the main thoroughfare.

"The Ruboffs are fine people." Barak broke the silence between them. "When will you marry their daughter?"

"I have to save first," Aaron said. "We need somewhere to live."

"Your mother has money for you," Barak said. "And you must take it. It would be your grandfather Zemach's wish. Your father's, too."

"But my mother has need of it," Aaron said.

"We have enough," Barak answered him. "My business prospers. It's not money that your mother needs." Barak dug his stick into a small clump of grass at their feet. For a moment he kept it there, screwing it deep into the soil. Then he sighed and retrieved it and walked on in silence.

"What does she need, then?" Aaron asked, though he knew the question was unanswerable.

Barak shook his head and continued walking. Aaron grabbed his shoulder. "Tell me," he said. His voice was almost weeping. "What's the matter with her?"

"Survival," Barak said. He stood still and turned to face Aaron.

"For some people," he said, "like you, like your father, and his father before him, survival is a state of health. For others, like your mother, it is a disease. They are maimed by its symptoms. My own wife died from survival," he whispered.

"I don't understand." Aaron was bewildered.

Barak took Aaron's arm and guided their steps over the fields. "Let me explain it to you," he said. "Your mother is consumed with guilt, and it gives her no peace. She blames herself for everything. She insists that Leon's imprisonment was her fault. She should never have left that boat in Hamburg, she says. If she had sailed to England with you, with no care of my dilemma, all would have been well."

"But she did care," Aaron said.

"Yes, I know. Your dear mother acted in accordance with her nature, but the consequences of her act were unfortunate, at least as far as Leon was concerned."

"And you?" Aaron dared to ask.

"I love her," Barak said simply, "but I am another symptom of her survival. I have replaced a man whom she refuses to accept as dead. So in our marriage she sees herself as an adulteress, and she must punish herself. That's how my first wife died," he said. "She too was convinced that she was responsible for our son's death, simply because she had survived him. Do you understand now?" Barak said quietly. "It is guilt your mother is suffering from. The guilt of survival."

"But how can she learn to forgive herself?" Aaron said, echoing Rachel's words.

"I talk to her a lot," Barak said. "I try to explain things to her. She knows the root of her despair. But there are two ways of knowing. Knowing with your head or knowing with the heart. We can do nothing for Zelda," Barak said, "except to love her."

The two men crossed over the main street and once again there was silence between them. When they reached the gate of the synagogue, Aaron stopped and turned to face Barak.

"My father would have called you friend," he said. Then he opened the gates and let his stepfather into the courtyard.

Morning prayers were over and the synagogue was closed. One could not just drop in on the Jewish God. Appointments had to be made. Appointments for morning and evening prayers, *kaddish* for the dead. "Let us sit awhile," Barak said, and they found a bench in the courtyard where they rested themselves.

"Leon told me he would like to stay in Wales," Aaron said after a while.

"I hoped he would want that," Barak said. "He needs to be with you."

"Will Mama be angry?" Aaron asked.

"I think she might be relieved," Barak said. "When we go back to Germany, we shall move. The fur trade is well-established in Leipzig. It is the center for world trade. With the money I have I could open a business there. The change would be good for Zelda, too. Hamburg has hard memories for her. And Leipzig, they tell me, is a beautiful city. You and Leon will come to visit us there when we are settled."

Then he rose, and both men left the courtyard and crossed the fields once more. When they came to the bridge, they paused and leaned over the rail, following the shallow waters of the River Taff.

"If you think about it," Barak said suddenly, "we are born with the status of survival. Out of the millions and billions of spermatozoa that flood the womb, only one can fertilize the egg. Can you imagine the struggle to achieve that victory? Yet each and every one of us on earth is a conqueror. We have, all of us, survived the others. And that victory, in the moment of fruition, pricks our consciousness with culpability. Man is *born* guilty, my friend." He turned from the rail. "Let us go to your mother," he said.

When Aaron returned that evening to Pavel's dwelling, they were all at supper. As he threaded his dark way through the shop, he heard laughing from the kitchen. And the voice that dominated all was that of his brother. He paused for a moment to check on his hearing. He waited for the laughter to subside before entering the kitchen, and when he did so, he saw his brother's smiling countenance and he was amazed at the day's transformation. Even when Leon saw Aaron, that link with his family, his smile did not fade. But when Aaron went to the table and embraced him, he tried not to notice the shriveling of Leon's shoulders. I must not touch him anymore, Aaron thought, not until he himself is ready to move toward me. Thereafter the conversation was subdued. Aaron's arrival had clearly dampened Leon's spirit.

That night when the brothers settled in their beds, Aaron made an attempt at conversation. But Leon pretended he was sleeping. Aaron tossed on his bed, sad and restless. And as was his custom at such moments, he thought of his father, then of Reuben and of the glorious milk-brotherhood between them. He and Leon were linked by blood, yet between them now was no fraction of the love that sustained the milk-brothers throughout their lives. More even than Rachel's love, he needed Leon's, and he feared it was that love that would elude him forever.

The following day Leon joined the family and in their presence he became again withdrawn. Zelda had set off on another unstoppable recital of their Hamburg life. Sometimes during her narration she dared to look at Leon, but each time he turned his face away and at each rejection, the pitch of her voice was raised. "You like Hamburg, don't you, Leon?" Zelda dared to ask.

Leon made no answer. He did not even shrug his shoulders. Aaron caught the pained look on his mother's face, and for the first time in his life he tasted the bile of hatred; to his horror it was directed at his blood brother. That night when they were alone, he again tried to talk to him, and again Leon feigned sleep. But Aaron ignored that ploy. He had to speak out, even if only to hear the words himself.

"Why don't you talk to her?" he hissed. "It's all that she wants. You can't hate her just because she married again."

Leon made no answer, but as Aaron heard his own words, he realized how threadbare a reason he had given for Leon's silences. The remarriage was nothing but a trigger for the pent-up anger that must have resided in Leon's spirit long before the Hamburg adventure. And his poor mother nothing but a convenient target for his spleen. And so Aaron set about to wonder at the source of his brother's rage. When he recapped their life since their childhood in Odessa, it could have been one of so many griefs that could have scarred Leon's spirit, griefs that he himself had endured without the consequent fury. But Leon's imprisonment was the only event of their lives that they had not shared.

Aaron got out of bed and went over to his brother's cot. "Leon," he whispered. Then, when there was no response, he shouted his name in his ear.

Leon turned on his pillow. "What d'you want?" he said sourly.

"What happened to you in that prison?" Aaron asked.

Leon sat bolt upright in his bed. "Nothing happened," he said. "I was in prison. That's all. Now let me get some sleep." He laid his head on his pillow and closed his eyes.

"Something happened," Aaron insisted. "Why don't you tell me?"

Leon turned over on his cot and put his hands over his face. Aaron was weeping with anger, and despite his decision not to touch his brother, he gripped one of his shoulders and shook him violently. "Why don't you talk to our mother?" he shouted at him. Then he heard Leon's muffled sobbing. He knelt down by the bed.

"What's the matter, brother?" he said softly.

Aaron waited, for he knew that an answer would come. And when it did, he reeled at its blasphemy.

"Why do we have to be Jews?" Leon said.

Aaron remained kneeling for a long while. He did not trust his legs to take him back to his bed. He crawled to his cot and sat on the edge and tried not to think of what Leon had said. But it was impossible to rinse that profanity from his ear. So he crawled into bed and covered his head with the sheets, so that the thought of Leon's sacrilege should lie in the darkness where it belonged. Aaron did not believe that ever, in the whole line of Bindel heritage, had one single member of the kinship uttered such an oath. Though their history had been strewn with corpses and griefs of many a kind, they still considered it a privilege to be born one of the chosen. Aaron wondered where such a thought could lead, but he feared its conclusions, and tried once again to put it from his mind. But it lodged there, every syllable of its heresy, so that he had to face the question that would naturally follow. What, with or without the help of God, was to become of his brother? These thoughts were not such on which one could sleep easily, and he tossed and turned on his bed till the morning light filtered through the kitchen window. Then, as if that light had smoked out the unhallowed company of his bed, he fell asleep, and did not wake again, despite the kitchen preparations, until late morning. For the first time in many months, his waking thought was light-years away from Rachel and their love, but surfaced uneasily on Leon's loss of faith.

In the next few days they completed the arrangements for the engagement party. Zelda and Barak would return to Hamburg shortly afterward, and Leon would remain in Wales. His intentions were forwarded to his mother via Aaron. She seemed in no way upset that Leon was remaining, and Aaron noticed that she was at pains to hide her relief. Occasionally during her bouts of hysteria, she would turn to Aaron and whisper, "Why does he not talk to me?" But with such repetition the phrase had lost its meaning. For Zelda knew that Leon's communication would not give her peace, any more than her continued widowhood would

have eased Leon's distress. Both of them were escape routes, the
bypasses around the cities of their pain, circuiting that core of
madness and confusion that neither of them could face.

Most days Leon accompanied Pavel on his rounds and twice a
week they went to Senghenydd. Each time Leon returned with
light and laughter in his eye, which dimmed at the sight of his
brother. Since that night when Leon had declared his lack of
faith, the brothers had spoken little to each other. It seemed that
Leon's statement had frozen conversation forever.

Aaron was relieved when his engagement day arrived, for it
hastened his mother's departure. He loved her now no less than
he had before, but he could not bear her desolation, each sign of
which nurtured in his heart a hatred of his brother. Leon, for his
part, would gladly have spent the day in Senghenydd, where he
warmed to the unencumbered welcome that the families offered
him, especially the women. One of them above all would welcome him, and he her, though he did not know her name. In her
eyes was a knowledge of his longing, and in her fiery looks an
anger that matched his own. Pavel had to persuade Leon to forgo
the valley on that day. Leon gave in reluctantly and his face and
mien were more sullen than ever.

The synagogue hall was crowded with *landsleit*. An engagement, especially between immigrants, was a cause for everyone's
celebration. It spelled settlement, stability, and, above all, continuity. It took them back to synagogue halls all over the Pale.
They dwelt for a while in the land of their fathers, in Odessa,
Kiev, in Balta and Vilna, and they loved once again and were
loved in turn, and even if that love was now lost, or had, over the
years, turned sour, it was still good to remember that there had
been a time when it was alive and true. Mrs. Ruboff and Zelda
between them had prepared the food. Though each cuisine was
different, marginally influenced by the different nationalities of
the ghettos, they were basically the same: survival food, which
was the essence of Jewish cooking. So even when the pressures
were lifted, when there was no longer any need to run for one's
life, the prerequisites of the food remained the same. Preservation
and portability. Apart from the wines, the menu for Rachel and
Aaron's engagement differed little from the fare that Esther and
Miriam Bindel had packed for the milk-brothers for their vain
flight from the services of the Czar.

The conversation was nostalgic and reminiscent. The guests came from all the cities of the Pale. Among them was a family from Kishinev, Mr. and Mrs. Nekrasov, with their daughter, Galina. A celebration such as this one, which concerned itself with continuity, was a mise-en-scène for matchmaking. In those days there was little opportunity for social intercourse. At an engagement party, it was almost incumbent on the hosts to insure that the seeds of another such celebration would be sown. Mr. Ruboff, who knew the Nekrasov family through business, took upon himself the duty of effecting an introduction between Galina and Leon. He himself had little hope of a match between them. Leon was an unknown factor. He was withdrawn, given to melancholy, and seemed to find little pleasure in the company of others. Yet he would try to put the two young people together, and Mr. Ruboff made his way to the corner where Leon stood alone. "Come," he said. "Meet my friends from Kishinev." He took Leon's arm and guided him across the hall, steering his way through the dancers who had already taken to the floor. The Nekrasovs stood in a group with others of their countrymen, recalling weddings in the old country, and when Leon was brought into their circle, each one of them knew the purpose of the introduction. Galina blushed and looked away, even when Leon, out of politeness, took her hand to make her acquaintance. All were at pains not to let the conversation flag and they continued with the discussion that Leon's introduction had interrupted. Then, when a new subject was called for, they turned to him and asked him about himself, his background and his prospects. There was nothing amiss about their questioning, neither was their timing too hasty. It was clear to all concerned what business was afoot, and the questions were lighthearted.

Leon wanted very much to get away. All these people were reminders of home, and such memories sickened him. The death of his father, and his loving Uncle Reuben, and his cherished Grandpa Jakob, had only recently overwhelmed him. Until his lone sojourn in the Hamburg jail, he had considered himself merely an orphan, with an elder brother to look after him. It was in the nature of things that fathers, uncles, and grandfathers died, and he did not allow himself to think in their cases how unnatural that nature was. He had cried for their loss, but had sensed some exhilaration, too, in being a survivor. It was only when he was stranded, alone in his cell, that he realized the obscene pro-

portions of his loss. Not only had most of his family died, but
they had died burning. Every night, the flames appeared before
his eyes, stinging the tears on his face. And sometimes he could
even smell their burning flesh. The privations he suffered as part
of his imprisonment in no way touched him, for his nights and
his dreams were agony enough. After a few weeks of his incarceration, the pain eased and gave way to an anger of titanic proportions. And at the height of that anger, he asked himself the question What was it all for? Why did they have to be so different and
incur the hatred of others? Why couldn't they mix with proper
Russians, live and marry among them, and learn their ways?
Why did they persist in being Jews? His whole family had died in
that name. He himself languished in a cell on account of that
name. When was it all going to stop? Some weeks later, to ease
his pain, he began to hate them, all those ghetto martyrs, their
trappings and trimmings, their distinctiveness, their beards, their
ringlets, and their suffering gabardine. Over the remaining weeks
of his sentence he nurtured in his heart a hatred of all those who
had sired and loved him. By the time he was released, he had
achieved a rehearsed indifference to the whole of his tribe, both
dead and alive, and that indifference had served to ease his pain.
Until his arrival in England and his meeting with Aaron, for
when his brother had embraced him at the railway station, his
touch had acted as an importunate reminder of the old love. Leon
had tried to resist it; he knew that if he yielded, his surrender
would force him back into his family and the desperate cult of
suffering of their tribe.

And now, as he looked at the Nekrasovs, he sensed again that
old pull of home, and he wished himself away. But out of politeness he gave answers to their questions.

"Have you started English lessons?" they asked.

Leon shook his head.

"Galina has a very good teacher," Mrs. Nekrasov said. "She is
looking for new pupils."

Leon turned to look at her daughter. She had that very special
beauty that belonged to the Pale, that pallor of inherited suffering, the very beauty that symbolized all that he wanted to dis-
card. Her long black hair framed a face that was vowed to sub-
mission, a head bowed to God, man, and oppressor. There was a
frightening promise of pogrom in her eye.

"I would like to meet your teacher," he said, and Galina whispered that she would talk to her.

Leon was grateful when Aaron and Rachel joined their circle and in time allowed him to withdraw. And as he turned to leave, he came face-to-face with his mother.

"Leon," she said, without looking at him. "Are you enjoying yourself?"

He nodded, staring at her averted face. He felt deeply sorry for her. He understood why she had married Barak and he had forgiven her. But he had used her remarriage as an excuse to cover his withdrawal from the family. Both he and his mother faced the same dilemma, the problem of acknowledging the past. With a gesture that he felt he could afford, he touched her arm. "Are you enjoying it?" he said.

Zelda turned to look at him. For her part she did not hear the words he had said to her. She heard only the sound of his voice so patently for her hearing. She was overwhelmed by it, scarcely believing the sound she had heard. She nodded in her turn. "I grieve that your father isn't alive to see it," she said, and dared to touch him, then wished she hadn't, for his revulsion was unmistakable.

Her reminder of his father symbolized for Leon all the gloom that would darken her future. He didn't want that darkness. He wanted the light, to see where he was going. Such light would find no admission in his mother's ways. He was glad she was soon going back to Germany.

"Papa is dead," he said. "We have mourned him. We have left his bones behind. The past is over." Then he touched her again, hearing the cruelty of his words. "You must begin to live again," he said.

"And you, my son?"

"I shall find a way," he shrugged. He was glad when Barak approached them and, once again, escape was possible.

Barak had watched their encounter from the side of the hall.

"Are you all right, my dear?" he said, taking her arm.

She smiled at him, and as she turned her face to look at him, Leon slipped away. She watched him go. "He spoke to me," she said, as if in a dream.

"It's a beginning," Barak replied. He did not ask the matter of Leon's words.

Zelda and Barak were leaving on the following day, and the

newly engaged couple would follow them as far as Tilbury to see
them safely onto the boat. Leon was persuaded to accompany
them all to the Cardiff station. Farewells were difficult. In Leon's
mind his farewell to his mother was a leavetaking of all the history to which he was bound, the link with the past that he wanted
so much to break. They leaned out of the window as the train
drew out of the station, and the steam from the engine slowly
obscured their features and made them indistinguishable from all
the other faces on the platform. Leon raised his hand and waved
to them, smiling, in the safe knowledge that he could have been
waving and smiling at strangers. As the train moved out of sight,
those left on the platform turned and went away, leaving Leon
alone. The smile still lingered on his face, but now it was on
account of his sudden feeling of freedom. He was, for a short time
at least, unencumbered by family. Leon straightened his shoulders and breathed deeply, as if a great burden had been lifted
from his heart.

Some years went by before Aaron was able to marry Rachel. Their long engagement was not deliberate, but events took place that prompted the delay. Rachel's mother died suddenly a few weeks before their intended wedding. A year of mourning had to pass before it could be considered once more. Then Barak took ill in Leipzig and Zelda requested her sons by her side. Leon could not be persuaded to go, so Aaron bore the brunt of filial duty. Then when Barak recovered, it was Mr. Ruboff's turn to take to his bed, and his condition required Rachel's constant care. Meanwhile Aaron still lodged at Pavel's house and had grown proficient enough in the tailoring trade to maintain the business, while Mr. Ruboff dictated instructions from his bed, giving advice on cut and fashion. It was unlikely that he would work again.

Meanwhile Leon had found lodgings in town, and had established a solid connection in the valleys, with Senghenydd as his center. His English was by now so fluent that he was able to supplement his income by giving English lessons to new immigrants.

By the late 1880s there were many who sought his services. For the great wave of emigration from Eastern Europe had begun. In the aftermath of pogroms in Warsaw and Balta, Jews fled in mass exodus from the lands of bondage. Most of them had their sights set on the golden land of America. If they were lucky enough to find an honest ticket agent, they eventually found their way to that land. But thousands made the shorter journey to England, and many of them settled in Wales. The Bindel brothers were by that time considered by their newly arrived *landsleit* as regular Englishmen.

It was in the spring of 1887 that Aaron finally took Rachel for his bride, roughly at the same age as his father had taken his mother. The long years of their courtship had in no way dimmed

their love for each other. Barak was not well enough to travel to
the wedding, so the honeymoon was spent in Leipzig. Barak's fur
business prospered, though Barak himself, in his failing health,
took little part in it. Zelda cared for him with a loving tenderness.
When she asked after Leon, hungry for news, Aaron was again
filled with a deep hatred of his brother for the hurt he caused
their mother with his neglect. And Aaron resolved to confront
him on his return. But Leon grew more and more distant. When
Aaron moved into the Ruboff house after the honeymoon, he
invited Leon to lodge with them, and Rachel too did her best to
persuade him. But Leon declined their offer and kept to his own
strange quarters, and the *landsleit* community looked with some
bewilderment on this arrangement. They wondered yet again
what would become of that younger Bindel who shunned their
society and was not like a *landsman* at all. Their doubts were
confirmed when Leon finally moved his person into the valley.
With his savings and his share of the tavern inheritance, he
bought a small miner's cottage in Senghenydd, far from Jew or
synagogue, with only Pavel to keep a weekly eye on him and hold
his tongue when Aaron asked for news of his brother's welfare.
For such news was untellable.

   Leon had fallen in love with one Margaret Davies, not the
redhead of Leon's first exiled dreams, but one very much of her
kind. A coal miner's daughter, a million miles from Odessa, to
whom the word *pogrom* was meaningless and would remain so all
her life. Leon kept Margaret a closely guarded secret, except
from Pavel, in whom he confided. Leon was aware of the monumental sin he was committing, but he rationalized it as being his
personal method of survival. Even so, he feared Aaron's reaction,
and at Pavel's suggestion he resolved to see more of his brother
and repair those bonds of fraternity that were so frayed. So
thenceforth, every Tuesday when he traveled to Cardiff to collect
his goods for sale, he called at his brother's house. On one such
visit he was given news of Rachel's pregnancy. He rejoiced with
them both, but he was fighting envy in his heart. After each visit
to his brother's house, he was gnawed by feelings of jealousy. For
he too wanted a home and a family, and he wanted to make that
home with Margaret. He would propose to Margaret at their very
next meeting, and hope that she would accept him. He knew it as
his only way to happiness. Suddenly he thought of his mother,
and in that thought he understood the magnitude of his trans-

gression. Such an act would be forever beyond her forgiveness, and perhaps would finally sever the bond between them. He would keep his marriage a secret from her, for if the truth were told, she would mourn him as though dead. He loved her enough to keep that secret, and Aaron, out of the same love and within that same mourning, would do the same.

It was not long before news traveled to Cardiff, along the salesmen grapevine, of Leon's impending engagement. And everyone was at pains to keep it from the ears of Aaron Bindel. But Pavel was uneasy with his secret. He sincerely thought that if Aaron were told, he might be able to change his brother's mind. Moreover, he had a right to know, a right to intervene, and a right too to fail. One evening, his heart trembling, he made his way to Aaron's house.

They were at supper, Mr. Ruboff, Rachel, and Aaron. Rachel was already big with child, her face radiant with happiness. Pavel sat with them, wondering how on earth he could begin. He decided to wait until the meal was over, and then, in privacy, tell Aaron.

"Shall we take a walk?" he suggested to Aaron when the meal was finished.

Aaron was glad of it. At this time of the year, the river was at full tide and it was pleasant to walk along the embankment. They set off briskly. It was Aaron who dictated the pace, and Pavel was at pains to slow him down, for the news that he had to tell was not appropriate to speed. It fit, if it fit at all, with an ambler's pace, which could suddenly in total shock root itself to the ground.

"Slow down, friend," Pavel said. "We have time." Yet Pavel was aware of what little time there was. Only that morning he had heard that Margaret Davies was preparing for a spring wedding. They reached the bridge and crossed over to the fields that skirted Cathedral Road. It was a favorite evening walk for many *landsleit* strollers, who would cross the fields, circle the synagogue yard, and return home. But that evening there were few people about and Pavel was glad of it. Near the road's verge there was a wooden bench, and Pavel reached it and sat down. He motioned Aaron to sit by his side.

"I have something to tell you," he said.

Aaron noted the seriousness on his friend's face. "Not bad

news, I hope?" he said. It must be about Leon, Aaron thought, who saw more of Pavel than he saw of his own brother.

"Is something the matter with Leon?" Aaron asked fearfully. "Is he ill?"

Pavel decided to tell Aaron without preamble, for he knew of no overture that could make such news more palatable. "He intends to marry," Pavel said, then before Aaron could question it, Pavel gave him the object of his brother's intent. "Her name is Margaret Davies," he said, as steadily as he could. "A coal miner's daughter." He watched the color drain from Aaron's face, and he gripped his arm, fearing that he might faint away. After a while Aaron managed to speak.

"Our mother must never know," he said. Then he rose, leaning on Pavel's arm. "I'm grateful that you told me," he said. "Tomorrow I shall go to the valley."

That night Aaron did not sleep. All night he prayed for his brother's soul, and in the morning, telling Rachel that he was visiting a client, he went to the station and took a train to the valley. He had never been to Leon's house, but from his brother's description, he knew its location. He trudged up the hill. A woman was coming toward him, stumbling under a large basket of washing. He offered to help her, but she declined with a look of both amazement and gratitude. He asked her directions to his brother's house.

"Over by there," she said, pointing behind her with her head. "That one with the pink door. It's open."

He thanked her and went on his way. When he reached his brother's door, he knocked, but there was no reply from within. He went inside, calling Leon's name, then sat on a chair in the sitting room and waited. He was not interested in looking at his brother's house. He was in a foreign land, a land in which no Jew had ever lived, had ever prayed, had ever chosen to lay his bones. Yet this was his brother's land, and he prayed to God to give him strength not to hate him. After a while he heard footsteps on the cobbles outside. He opened his mouth but no words came, and shortly Leon appeared in the doorway of the sitting room and paled at his brother's presence.

"Aaron," he said, not moving from the doorway.

Aaron stood. "I wanted to see you," he said, and he was relieved at the steadiness of his voice.

"Would you like some tea?" Leon said.

Aaron shook his head, then regretted that he had declined the offer. A cup of tea between them might have softened the anger and hatred in his heart. Leon moved into the room and took a chair opposite his brother. "How is Rachel?" he said.

"You can't do it, Leon," Aaron whispered. "You just cannot do it." His voice was no longer steady.

There was silence then between them until Leon said, "I love her, Aaron."

"You delude yourself, brother," Aaron said. "How can you love someone who is none of our kind? Come away from this temptation, I beg you. You can live with us." His voice was raised now, and it gathered speed. "We have room. I have enough money. I can teach you the tailoring trade." He stopped. He knew what he was saying was futile, for his brother was looking at him with pity. "You're a murderer," Aaron screamed at him.

"Whom have I killed?" Leon said softly.

"You break all our hearts," Aaron said.

"Won't you at least meet her?" Leon pleaded.

"Never. She is not of our kind. Never," he shouted. "Is this how you revere the memory of our father, our grandfather?"

"It is time all that had a stop," Leon said as gently as he could. "I am marrying in order to survive. Our own father baptized himself for survival."

"But this isn't Russia," Aaron sobbed. "Do you read what's happening in our country? The hundreds who are murdered day after day? Is this how you pay them for their faith?"

Leon put his hands on Aaron's shoulders, feeling for the first time like an elder brother. "It's a payment that over the years will insure that such madness will never happen again. My children will not be the Chosen, by either God or the Czar."

Aaron shrugged his shoulders away. "Don't touch me," he said. Then he looked him squarely in the eyes. "You are dead for me, brother," he said, and he turned and walked from the room.

On his way down the cobbled street, he met the washerwoman. She smiled at him. "Did you find him all right, your brother?" she asked.

He had no smile for her, no words, and she knew that he had quarreled with that foreigner, Mr. Bindel. Leon came to the door of his cottage and watched his brother as he walked slowly down the valley. His back was hunched and he looked like a very old man. Leon turned and went inside, and though there was no one about to watch him, he shut the door and buried his face in his hands.

All the way to the station, on the train, and along the embankment, Aaron muttered the *kaddish* prayers. And when he reached home, he said them aloud, over and over again, as he took sheets from the linen cupboards and covered the pictures and the mirrors on the wall.

Rachel watched his wild grief. "Who has died?" she said.

"He who was my brother."

"Leon?" she screamed.

He turned toward her, then took her in his arms. "Never mention his name again in this house." He told her all that he knew, then he sat slippered on the floor and his father-in-law sat with him and shared his shame and sorrow. And thus Aaron sat for seven days. On the eighth day he went back to his workshop and his machines; he knew that his pain would never cease. Time would not heal such a wound, for though for a whole week of days he had mourned his brother's death, he had, every one of those days, prayed for his life, too.

Leon, who had known what his brother would do, waited for the period of mourning to be over. Then he took Margaret to the small registry office in Caerphilly and there he married her. For the first time in many hundreds of years of their wanderings, from the Ukraine to Bessarabia, a Bindel had married out of his kind. That same day, Rachel gave birth to a daughter. They called her Chaya, which, translated, means life. Her second name was Esther, in memory of Rachel's mother—but a name that also served to revere the memory of Aaron's paternal grandmother, Esther Bindel. As Aaron and Rachel rejoiced in their parenthood, Aaron mourned the loss of that person with whom he most wished to share his joy. And in the valley to which Pavel the messenger had brought the news, Leon asked for and was refused a sight of his brother's child.

Aaron wrote to Zelda about the birth of her first grandchild. She replied posthaste, urging them to bring the child. Barak was not well enough to travel, she wrote, and she was loath to leave him. Rachel and Aaron would have happily done so, but Mr. Ruboff was now too ill to be left alone. And they dreaded that Zelda should come, for once in the midst of family and community, the secret of Leon's sin would come out; Aaron dared not think of the consequences of that revelation. So he wrote to his mother of his father-in-law's indisposition, and urged her to wait until he had sufficiently recovered for them to leave him for a while. He sent his best wishes for Barak's health.

But Zelda was impatient to see her grandchild, and made arrangements for Barak's care in her absence. She wrote that she was preparing a visit in two weeks' time. *Give Leon my love, too,* she added. *I long to see him.*

On receipt of this letter, Aaron was greatly agitated, and he went straight to Pavel's dwelling place. He thanked God for Pavel, who, without any encouragement from Aaron, had appointed himself as a liaison between the two brothers. He knew of the love between them that a million words of *kaddish* could not destroy. Hinda and Max took a different view. They were sorry for Aaron, but Leon was dead for them. They had children of their own and they did not want his contamination in their house. And though Aaron understood them, he turned away from them in his heart.

Pavel was not one to give advice; he merely offered a suggestion. On his next journey to Senghenydd, which was to be on the following day, he would tell Leon and allow him to make the decision whether or not to greet his mother. If Leon should decide to come to Cardiff, then Aaron would have to compose himself to treat him as if nothing untoward had happened. That would not be easy for him, Pavel warned, but on no account must his mother be privy to the catastrophe. During her visit they would make sure that she called only on those who could hold their tongues. He promised that he would visit Aaron the following evening to inform him of Leon's decision. As Aaron was leaving, Pavel said, "How is the child?"

"Beautiful," Aaron said. "She sleeps all night without feed, and she smiles all day." He was itemizing all the tidbits of news that he knew Pavel would convey to his brother. He himself did not ask for news of Leon. Pavel understood the rules.

The following evening Pavel called at Aaron's, and Aaron took him to the workshop at the top of the house, where they would not be disturbed.

"He's not very helpful, I'm afraid." Pavel came to the point right away. "He's quite prepared to meet your mother, he says. Indeed, he would look forward to it, but he insists on bringing his

wife with him. Any acceptance of him must include his wife."
Pavel threw up his hands. "It is impossible," he said.

"What shall I do?" Aaron said helplessly.

"We must tell her he doesn't want to see her. It will hurt her
terribly, but it will be less hurtful than the truth. D'you know,"
Pavel said after a while, "I'm beginning to feel very sorry for him.
The other day in the clothing market, Goldstein turned him away
from his store. So did Lepcovitch. No Jewish merchant will serve
him. He is a pariah. He has to buy dear at the big emporium."

Aaron was sorry for him too, but his compassion was blunted
by his anger.

"His wife didn't agree with him," Pavel said suddenly. "She
tried to persuade him to go. She said it was a son's duty to his
mother. But he is stubborn, your brother."

"Will you come with me to the station to meet her?" Aaron
asked.

"Gladly," Pavel said, and as he went, he deposited a small
packet on the worktable. He did not refer to it, neither did
Aaron, for he knew it was one of Pavel's messages. When he had
gone, Aaron opened the package. A tiny pair of baby's shoes
wrapped in tissue paper. Aaron examined the wrapping. Each
fold was neatly turned and symmetrical. He pictured Leon measuring each fold with his thumb, donating as much love and care
to the wrapping as he had to the choice of gift. Aaron took the
shoes and rewrapped them. Then he hid them at the bottom of
his button drawer. Leon had spoken to him, but it was a voice
from the dead.

A week later he and Pavel went to the railway station. They
dawdled on the way, with little appetite for the encounter. As a
result, when they reached the station, the train had already arrived and Zelda was waiting bewildered on the platform. It was
not a good beginning. Aaron ran toward her and he hugged her
with genuine warmth. He was surprised at how happy he was to
see her. She looked well, and younger than he had remembered
her.

"No one would believe you were a grandmother," he laughed.

Then Pavel came forward and shook her hand, but she did not
look at him. She was staring at the empty space around him.

"Where's Leon?" she said, then, looking at their faces, regretted that she had asked. "He's all right, isn't he?" she panicked.

"Oh, yes." Aaron was quick to reassure her. The only good news about Leon was that he was alive, at least in a physical sense. And Aaron was at pains to stress his brother's well-being.

"Where is he?" She knew she shouldn't have asked. She knew that it didn't matter where he was. He simply wasn't at the station because he had no wish to see her.

"He's in the valley," Pavel said.

"Will I see him?" she whispered. Again it was a question better left unasked. It seemed she wished to torture herself with his neglect.

"I thought you came to see your granddaughter," Aaron laughed, and he picked up her portmanteau and took her arm. They hired a wagon to take them home, and during the journey Aaron and Pavel pumped her for news of Barak and Leipzig, their questions always at the ready. Zelda was happy enough to give them her news. Barak was comfortable. He went to the store only once a week, but he had a good manager there. The doctor had told him that he must take life a little easier. Leipzig was a beautiful city, and she enjoyed the peace of it after the noise of Hamburg.

"That prison," she said suddenly, "with its unhappy memories. It was all my fault."

"Of course it wasn't your fault," Aaron said, and ached to give her proof that on that score Leon had never blamed her. He suddenly thought of Margaret, thinking of her by name, by that same name that his brother no doubt called her with his love. The thought disturbed him. He could not afford to identify her by name. She was that woman, that anonymous one, who had set a cross before his brother and taught him how to kneel.

Rachel was at the door to meet them with Chaya in her arms. Mr. Ruboff had risen from his bed for the occasion. He knew the problems that attended her visit, and he intended to offer his company for Zelda's diversion. Rachel had brightened the home for her visit and the table was set for the Sabbath that evening with the unlit candelabra in the center. Zelda was delighted with the welcome and at once took Chaya in her arms. She stared at the child. "She's a Bindel," she announced. "She looks like Sofia. D'you remember your Aunt Sofia, Aaron? She was a rebel." She smiled. "She died in the fire," she added, "with the rest of them."

Wherever his mother went, Aaron thought, she took that fire with her, charring her heart along the way, as Barak took that holy piece of Russian ground where his son lay buried, as he himself portered his father's loss. All of them cleaved to their holy luggage.

It was Chaya's feeding time, and Rachel took the baby upstairs.

"I'll come with you," Zelda said, rising.

Rachel looked at Aaron helplessly, but there was nothing he could do. There was no reason on earth why his mother shouldn't spend time with her daughter-in-law and grandchild. The men watched her follow Rachel out of the door.

"Rachel won't say anything," Aaron said when they were gone.

The three men sat there in silence, no doubt expecting at any moment the clap of thunder. But all they heard was laughter, Zelda laughing as she played with Chaya, changed her, mocking herself with her clumsy handling.

"Aaron was such a good baby," she recalled.

"Tell me about him," Rachel said. "About when he was a child." She grasped at a neutral topic of conversation, anxious to avoid a silence.

But there was only one topic of conversation of interest to Zelda. "Have you seen Leon?" she said. She was casual with the question, concentrating on the pinning of the baby's napkin, as if the whereabouts and welfare of her younger son were of little matter to her.

"We see him sometimes," Rachel said, rummaging in the drawers to hide the lie that might show on her face.

"Is he well?"

"Yes," Rachel said weakly.

Zelda caught the hesitation in her voice. "What's the matter with him?" Zelda whispered. "You must tell me."

"Nothing," Rachel fairly shouted. "Nothing at all." And she was seized with a need to tell her mother-in-law everything. It was not fair that Aaron had to bear the brunt of the terrible secret. It needed to be shared. Besides, it was Zelda's right to know. But Rachel dared not speak. There was only one who could rightfully tell Zelda, and that was Leon himself.

With Rachel's insistent denial that there was anything amiss with her son, Zelda became more and more suspicious. She began to convince herself that he was ill.

"I wish I could see him," she said. To which there was no reply that Rachel or anyone else could give.

At supper that evening, when Rachel had lit the candles and Aaron had said the blessing, Zelda expressed her wish to go to the synagogue the following morning. It was the anniversary of the fire, she said, and she wished to join in the prayers of remembrance. Mr. Ruboff was quick to make an alternative suggestion. He knew that a visit to the synagogue was out of the question. There, without doubt, in the gossip of the women's gallery, far from the protection of the men below, the secret would be out. She would have more than the fire to mourn. Her heart was a wailing wall, into the crevices of which the worshiper sent messages to God. In that crumbling structure, she would find yet another cranny to accept her grief, a grief without anniversary, without calendar, a grief for all eternity.

"On Sabbath I take my one walk of the week," Mr. Ruboff said. "Rachel usually comes with me and I am allowed to wheel the pram. I thought that this week you would accompany me. I've looked forward to it."

It was an unrefusable invitation, and Zelda readily accepted it. "I would like that," she said. "We could go to Sophia Gardens. I remember them from my last visit. They are so pretty." What she most remembered about the gardens was their proximity to the synagogue. Perhaps Leon would stroll there on his way to prayer. But Mr. Ruboff had no fear of such an encounter. It was unlikely that Leon would enter a synagogue ever again.

They went to bed soon after supper, for Zelda was much fatigued after her journey. But Aaron lay awake all night and heard his mother moaning and tossing on her bed. Yet she looked bright on the following morning.

Aaron left early for the synagogue. He was not a regular worshiper, but he knew without any reminder from Zelda that this was the anniversary of his father's death. When she heard that he had gone, she was glad of it, for Aaron could pray for all of them. Without her knowledge Aaron would pray for his brother, not with the regular Sabbath prayers, but with the *kaddish* he would use for his father.

When Mr. Ruboff was ready, Rachel prepared the pram, and she set them off on their way, glad not to be with them but fearful of the perils of their journey. But as it turned out, their way had been smooth, as Mr. Ruboff reported at the lunch table. Chaya had slept all the way and they had been able to converse without interruption. Mr. Ruboff declared that he now knew Leipzig as if he himself had lived there, Zelda's description of that city was so graphic. He had also learned much about the fur trade. Both had reminisced on their respective departed spouses and had seemingly found pleasure in so doing. The sore matter of Leon's absence had not ruffled their companionship; Aaron had hopes that his mother had accepted Leon's neglect and that his name would not be mentioned again. That afternoon Pavel came to visit, accompanied by Max and Hinda, who had been well primed to silence. The afternoon passed pleasantly in conversation. Aaron ticked off in his mind one day out of seven that had passed without incident. But the day was not yet over.

When the visitors had gone, Zelda insisted on helping Rachel prepare the supper. The kitchen had never been the domain of Bindel men. So once again Rachel found herself alone with her mother-in-law, and quickly she put her to work—preparing the soup, in the hope that if she busied her hands, her tongue would lie still.

"Now I feel really at home," Zelda said as she pared the vegetables. Rachel busied herself with the meats. Until someone pulled the doorbell. Rachel froze. People often came to their door, usually customers for fittings or collection. But for some reason she feared the ring and moved over to the kitchen door to close it.

"Who could that be?" Zelda asked, and there was no mistaking the hope in her voice.

"Probably a customer," Rachel said. She strained her ear for some clue. Then she heard Aaron's footsteps in the hall and the unlatching of the front door. There were two suits ready in the workshop and Aaron expected either customer to collect. He was glad of it and went smiling to the door. But the smile faded. Leon stood there. On his face was a look of anger, of expected rebuff. He was alone.

"I've come to see our mother," Leon said. His voice matched his face with its gruffness, and Aaron thought his brother might be close to tears. Aaron had sworn that he would never see him again, yet in his heart he welcomed him. He was sorry that Chaya was sleeping. The thought crossed his mind that he should question Leon as to whether he was intent on telling their mother. But suddenly he didn't mind anymore. The burden of that secret was heavy, and it was with some relief that he invited his brother into his house.

He ushered him into the dining room, because Mr. Ruboff was in the sitting room and he felt that Leon would prefer privacy.

"Where is she?" Leon said without looking at him.

"In the kitchen with Rachel."

"Would you tell her I'm here?" he said tonelessly. "I'd like to talk to her alone."

Then Aaron knew that his brother had not come home at all. He had come simply to confirm his leaving. Aaron looked at him in horror.

"Why are you waiting?" Leon said coldly. He had not forgotten the last words his brother had spoken to him in the valley. "I am dead for you, don't you remember?"

Aaron left the room and closed the door behind him. In the hall he gripped the banister to steady his trembling. He knew that he no longer had any control over the situation. He opened the kitchen door. Rachel saw the pallor on his face and knew at once the caller's identity. She gripped his arm.

"Mama," he said, his voice breaking. "Leon has come to see you. He's in the dining room." He could not bear the look of joy on her face as she rushed past him into the hall. He took Rachel in his arms and wept like a child.

Zelda did not immediately embrace her son. She stood at the door and looked at him, savoring that face that haunted her dreams. As she looked she noticed the agitation about his mouth, his clenched fists. She went toward him, kissing him tenderly.

"I knew you would come today," she said. "You would not forget the anniversary of Papa's death."

"It's almost twenty years since Papa died," Leon said, and there was no mistaking the anger in his voice.

"You went to the synagogue?" she asked, knowing even as she said it that the question would not be welcome.

"No," he said. "I don't go to the synagogue anymore."

She feared what he was trying to tell her, sniffing the heresy in his evasions. "There's no synagogue in the valley?" she asked, offering him some excuse for his lack of faith.

"Mama," he said. "I have to tell you something."

"What's the matter, my son? Are you not well?" Now she knew that something was very wrong. That his health was failing.

That her son's days were numbered. Oh, God, she prayed in her heart. Anything, anything but that.

"I am married, Mama," he said.

Now she was in total confusion. Her son was not ill. He was not dying. She would not survive him. Had she not asked God for that? Then she must thank God for His deliverance. Yet what gift had He given her in its stead? Her son's health. Should she not thank God for that? And something else. Marriage. Was that not a gift too? Not this way, her heart faltered. Married without ceremony, without warning, and now with apology. Did Aaron know? Did Rachel? Then she could postpone her pain no longer. She sat down, trembling. "Who have you married?" she said.

"Her name is Margaret Davies. Her father is a coal miner." It was the kindest way he could tell her that his wife was not of their kind.

Rachel and Aaron heard the screaming. Rachel rushed into the dining room and held her. Aaron stood at the door, staring at his brother with a look of such hatred that Leon thought his mind unhinged. "She had to know," he said quietly. Then he made to leave. As he reached the door, Zelda found some semblance of a voice. In her heart she was screaming, though the sound was a whisper. "In time she will look at you and call you a dirty Jew," she said.

Leon shrugged and left the room, while Aaron and Rachel helped Zelda to her feet and took her to her bed. Rachel sat with her for a while, holding her hand. There was nothing she could say. But as she sat there listening to Zelda's grieving, she could not help questioning whether what Leon had done merited such sorrow. It was a blasphemous thought, she knew, and must never be spoken aloud. Aaron would disown her.

Zelda squeezed her hand. "My son is dead for me," she said. "Tomorrow I shall begin to mourn him."

But he is alive, Rachel thought, and his health is good. Was it possible that Zelda preferred God to her children? She sat with her until she slept, then Rachel crept from the room—disturbed by thoughts that were out of her time, her gender, and, most of all, her faith.

When Leon reached home, Margaret was anxiously awaiting him. When she saw his drawn face in the doorway, she knew that the meeting with his mother had failed. She was glad now that she had kept her news, had saved it for just this time.

"I am dead for her," he said from the door.

She kissed him, took his coat, and set him at the table where his supper was waiting. She took the pot from the stove and poured tea for them both and she waited for him to speak. But he said nothing about the meeting. He was staring at the teapot. Then after a while he said, "When next I go to Cardiff, I shall buy a samovar."

He had told her all she needed to know. She now feared for the baby inside her, but she held her tongue. The time that she had thought to be ripe seemed not so ripe after all. They finished the meal in silence. As she cleared the table, Leon buried his head in his hands. She sat beside him and held him close. Now was the time perhaps.

"Leon," she said. "We're going to have a child."

He raised his head and looked at her, and though she searched the map of his face, she could find no contour of a smile.

"Are you sure?" he said.

"The doctor confirmed it yesterday."

"If it's a boy, we'll call it Benjamin."

"Benjamin?" she said. "That's a . . ."

"That's a what?" he shouted.

"Well, it's so . . ." She hovered. "It's not Welsh," and she prayed that he would settle for that rationale.

Then at last he smiled. But it was not a smile of joy. It was a bitter recollection of his mother's parting words.

The week of Zelda's visit passed very slowly. Most of the time she kept to her bed, reading the morning prayers. In the evening, visitors came. It was a relief that the secret was out so friends could come and officially share her sorrow. Throughout this time Mr. Ruboff was a source of great comfort. He refused to share Zelda's anger, and without words he did not condone her grief. When Rachel looked at him, full of her own profane thoughts, she wondered whether they shared the same impious doubts. And she realized how little she knew of her own father. One night shortly before Zelda was to leave, when she and her father were alone, she dared to ask him.

"Is it so terrible, Papa, what Leon has done?"

"Yes," he said. There was no hesitation in his voice. "What is not terrible is that you have questioned it. For times will change and so will men's hearts, and then it will not be so terrible. But yes, yes," he said. "Now it is terrible."

"As bad as dying?" Rachel insisted.

"It's a death of a kind," Mr. Ruboff said. "It's the death of a life that we know and have suffered to preserve. When Zelda mourns Leon, it is her own small death that she mourns." He spoke to her in Yiddish, as he always did, and for a moment Rachel was glad that he had never wanted to learn the language of his exile, because the matter of his words belonged inalienably to his mother tongue.

Aaron had counted the days to his mother's departure and when it arrived, he didn't want her to go. More for her sake than his own, for she would be leaving for a land without family to comfort her. Barak would be sympathetic, of course, but it was not his family that had been so cruelly threatened. He could only hold her while she wept. It was out of this pity that Aaron offered to take her as far as Tilbury Docks, and it was clear that she was very grateful, for she felt more alone and burdened than ever. The night before she left, Rachel made a farewell supper and invited Pavel, Max, and Hinda. There was little to celebrate, but it was an occasion to confirm their friendship and their support. During the course of the meal, Zelda turned to Pavel.

"I don't want any news of him," she said. She knew that Pavel was the self-appointed messenger between her sons, and with her negative declaration she hoped to include herself in his service. He smiled at her. "I understand," he said.

That night before she went to bed, she took Aaron to one side. "How did he come to Cardiff from the valley?" she asked. She had already buried Leon's name.

"He came by train," Aaron said.

"He rides on the Sabbath?" she said. There was a hint of relief in her voice, as if she had discovered for herself a small sin on her son's behalf, a sin that God in time would find forgivable. For a while that sin could erase the transgression that was beyond pardon.

In the morning, Aaron and his mother took the train to London. They took a tram ride to Whitechapel, and there Aaron found a restaurant that he had noticed when he had first arrived in London. The restaurant was in a busy thoroughfare, and the area of pavement outside served as a kind of unofficial employment agency. People scurried about. Tailors looking for pressers,

bootmakers for seamers, bakers for kneaders, and the crowds of
workless looking for anybody who could offer them a living. And
girls, too. Lining the thoroughfare in their faded finery. As Aaron
guided his mother toward the restaurant, he was obliged to pass
the line. He tried not to look at them, but one face caught his eye.
He knew her. He had seen her before. When she averted her gaze,
reddening beneath her rouge, he remembered who she was. The
last time he had seen her was over ten years ago. Ida. He smiled.
She was, after all, a survivor, surviving in her own orphaned,
untutored way. Was she not the same as his own brother, who
had chosen his own way too? If he could look at Ida without
censure, he could surely forgive his brother.

"Come," his mother said. "Why are you dawdling?"

"I thought I saw Leon," he said, testing his name on her.

"Did you?" she asked anxiously. "Where? Where?"

"It wasn't Leon," Aaron said. "It was just someone like him."
He smiled, for now he knew that her son was no more dead for
her than his brother was for him. And once alive, he could be
forgiven.

The years passed and quietly the century turned. It was Easter Sunday in the spring of 1903, and the bells tolled all over the world in cathedral, church, and chapel. In the town of Kishinev in the Russian province of Bessarabia they were tolling too, and were a signal to the onset of the bloodiest pogrom of all. In his cottage in Senghenydd, Leon Bindel was aware of another event, for it was the bar mitzvah birthday of his son. They had called him David as something of a compromise. Margaret had drawn the line at Benjamin, insisting that it was no name for a son of Wales, so they had settled on David, which conveniently doubled for the country's patron saint and the king of Israel. They had had no more children, which Leon considered a blessing, for the marriage had begun to sour shortly after David's birth. Leon's fractured English, which had so attracted Margaret when they had first met, now irritated her. Every aspect of his foreignness was a source of her displeasure. The sharp differences between them, the tribal and cultural barriers, seemed more and more insurmountable as the initial passion waned. Leon had never sought to tutor her in his history, and had not insisted on a Jewish upbringing for his son. But he had drawn the line at baptism. Margaret had grudgingly acquiesced. Leon had done his best to become part of the life of the valley, of the mining community that, for the most part, accepted him. As his domestic strife became more and more acute, he often thought of leaving, but it was the mining community that kept him there. That and David, from whom he would not be parted. Besides, his pride forbade a separation from his wife.

He knew he gave Margaret little pleasure. His mood was usually gloomy. She did her very best to enliven him, but she couldn't understand his guilt and his sorrow. He would laugh only with David and in the Working Men's Club in the High

Street, she was told. But at home he was disposed to melancholy.
He went to Cardiff twice a week to collect his goods and always
returned in a sullen mood. He longed to see Aaron, but he was
too proud to call. Four years before, Mr. Ruboff had died, and
Pavel had brought the message that Rachel would be especially
pleased if he would attend the funeral. He had gone and stood by
the graveside. Nobody spoke to him. Aaron had shaken his hand.
He had not seen his brother since that day. Leon longed for a
meeting between Chaya and David, but he was too wary of refusal to drop hint of it in Pavel's ear. Leon had learned from
Pavel that his mother was well and sending him her thoughts. He
knew that only he could make the move to return to his family;
but his pride would allow no move in that direction.

With such thoughts he sat in his cottage that Sunday in the
spring of 1903 and wondered where Margaret and David had
gone. Sunday morning Margaret was usually at home cooking
the traditional Sunday dinner, and David was playing with a
school friend. That Sunday, Leon had risen late and had found
the house deserted. In the kitchen there were no signs of dinner
preparations and the breakfast things still lay in the sink. He
heard steps behind the door, David's hobnailed boots that she'd
insisted he wear so that he wouldn't be different from miners'
sons. They came into the kitchen and Leon noticed that she was
dressed in her best attire, her Sunday best, she called it, and
David was wearing his proper suit.

"Where have you been?" Leon shouted.

Margaret opened her frightened mouth.

"Our Mam took me to Chapel," David said. "For my birthday." He spoke in an accent a million miles away from Bessarabia, and the content of his words rattled untold Bindel bones, and
every nerve in Leon's body writhed with insult. He was white
with rage.

"For his bar mitzvah?" he shouted.

"Dad?" David said, thinking that his father's mind had turned.
But Margaret understood the word, for once in their courting
days Leon had told her of his own initiation in Odessa.

"What difference?" Margaret dared to say. "There's nothing
Jewish about him. He's the grandson of a Christian coal miner."

"Your father would understand my rage," Leon said. "Better
than you will ever know." And Leon was right. David Davies
had always been on Leon's side regarding the boy. "For God's

sake, no religion," he had sworn at his birth. Mr. Davies was a
socialist. Dai the Red, they called him in the valley. His time was
spent, in and out of the mine, in organizing his workmates into
some form of a union. He was a bit of a poet, too, and those who
did not like his politics but valued him as a friend called him Dai
the Bard. Between his poetry and his politics he had no time for
God, and though he sang hymns in the colliery choir, he did it
for the melodies.

"The way I bring up my son is none of my Dad's business,"
Margaret said. She stood her ground, unafraid. Her man was not
like those others from the pit, who beat their wives into submis-
sion. Leon had never raised his hand to her.

"It's my business, though," Leon said. "I didn't give up one
God to exchange it for another."

"You never gave up anything," Margaret said.

She was right, Leon thought. From the beginning he had
wronged her to invite her into his wilderness of faith. He had
given up nothing. His body dwelt in a Jewless village and his
heart still lingered in Odessa. Margaret was right. He regretted
how he had used her. He took his coat and left the house, wandering down the hill to the village square. He had it in mind to
walk to the head of the valley to the pithead. There he would
meet miners and their families who, despite the six perilous days
that they spent underground each week, would often view its
stillness on a Sunday just for the reassurance of safety. Only two
years before, eighty-one men on the night shift had died in a mine
explosion. Now those who survived and took their Sunday stroll
remembered the friends they had lost. Sometimes on a Sunday
the Salvation Army band would gather with their choir, and sing
hymns and songs of praise. Being Easter, they were there that
Sunday, and Leon dawdled for a while listening to the haunting
melodies, and turning away his ear from the name of Christ,
whom they praised. He recalled his father's stories of his recruitment, and how the utterance of that name had been his first bid
for survival. That taboo was part of his inheritance, the legacy
that he had chosen to forgo. Yet while he stood here on alien soil,
still that name jarred his ear. He smiled to himself. Whatever
past one had, one had to accommodate it as best one could. Once
again he had longings to go home, to embrace his brother and his
family, to sit in a synagogue among his own kind. But pride and

love of his son forbade him. He made his way to his father-in-law's house opposite the colliery.

David Davies lived in a row of terrace houses known as the Huts. They were one-story buildings with corrugated iron roofs, which had been hurriedly constructed just over ten years ago when the sinking of the Senghenydd colliery had begun. Their purpose was to house the men who were shaft-sinkers and those who worked on the railway extension that took the coal to Cardiff. David Davies had been one of the shaft-sinkers and he and his family now lived permanently in the Huts. The terrace was located directly opposite the mine. It was a dangerous siting, and often David Davies had thought of moving. But over the years the terrace of Huts had become the center of dissent and protest against the working conditions in the mines. David Davies was their spokesman, and a change of address would have seemed like a small desertion.

When Leon arrived at the Huts, he was given, as always, a great welcome. Mrs. Davies had always regarded him as a bit of a catch for a son-in-law. He had a clean, tidy, and safe job. He'd had an education and he could speak a foreign language. The fact that he was a Jew did not disturb her. She regarded the Welsh as part of the lost tribes of Israel. He was a good father to her grandson. He'd actually bought a piano and insisted that David have lessons. He wanted the best for the boy, but Mrs. Davies had to acknowledge that in Senghenydd the pit was the best there was. David would be a miner like the rest of them, and no shame in that, she kept saying to a protesting Leon. The salt of the earth down the pits, she would say. Men didn't come any better. You wait, she would insist. In two or three years conditions would improve. More money, more safety. "You just leave it to my Dai. They don't call him Dai the Red for nothing."

She welcomed him into the house. "Go in the parlor," she told him. "They're meeting now. Starting the revolution." She grinned and showed him into the front room, and the men rose to greet him. It was a deference that made Leon slightly uneasy, for it confirmed the difference between them.

"Sit down, Leon boy," Dai said. "And listen. You'll learn something." He drew a chair to his side and motioned Leon to sit by him. Before the meeting continued, he leaned over and whispered in his ear. "Morgan Jones here tells me his wife said our David was in Chapel today. I'll tan our Margaret's backside for her, I will," he said. "I promise you. Chapel, for God's sake. What next?" Then he returned to the business of the meeting.

Leon looked at the men's faces. Morgan Jones was a fireman in the pits and lived in one of the first Huts in the terrace. He had five children, all of them girls except the youngest, Gwylim, fourteen years old and a colliery boy working his father's shifts at his side. Morgan was a tenor in the Male Voice Choir of the valley, and every Thursday night at the Working Men's Club, Leon would enjoy their concerts. Richard Hunt sat on the other side of Dai. He was Dai's neighbor in the Huts and a collier, too. He was the youngest of the men, as yet unmarried, but he was courting Morgan Jones's youngest daughter, Mary. He lived with his father, once a miner in a nearby colliery but now confined to his bed, coughing away a silicosis retirement. The last man in the group was Gilbert Whitcombe, who lived in the last Hut in the terrace. His father and two brothers had been killed in the pit explosion two years before, and his concern in the protest group was as much for better safety measures as for improved wages. For every time a collier went below, he put himself at risk. Most of them accepted that risk as part and parcel of the job, and it was this very acceptance that blunted their protest.

At the time, miners' wages were based on a sliding scale that was regulated by the current selling price of coal. It was a deeply unfair system, since coal prices were an economic factor over which the miners had no control. It was a scheme that insured the management would always make a profit. For Dai Davies, the abolition of this system had become something of a crusade. Wherever he was, and whatever subject was under discussion, underground or in the village square, in the institute or public house, he would always make it relevant to the wage issue.

Leon listened and felt at ease in their company. In many ways he knew them intimately, as he did most of the colliers in the valley. For he had seen them naked. One of his collecting days was a Friday and he tried to time his calls shortly after their return from the day shift. On Friday they would bring home their pay packets. Leon would knock on the open terrace door. "Bindel," he would shout. Then, without waiting for an answer, for he knew he was welcome, he would make his way into the kitchen. The tin bath, brought in from the backyard, was filled with hot water from the kettles, and placed in front of the roaring fire. In it the collier would make a vain attempt to scrub the years' accumulated coal dust from his body. Whoever was available, wife, daughter, son, would scrub his back. But often the man would ask for Leon, whose touch was as gentle as a woman's. Once one has viewed a man's body, touched it, known its particular symmetry, one cannot help but care for that man. He looked at the men around the table. He had scrubbed each one of their backs in his time while waiting for their weekly shilling payments on trousers, coats, boots, or shirts—all of which had probably long been worn out of service. Often, during a short wage-period, Leon would forgo the payment, which was why after ten years of valley business he had managed to save so little. He didn't mind his poverty. He had enough to keep a decent home. He minded only for his son. He minded for his son's future and he knew that the only way to make that future bright was to get him out of the valley. But the opposition to such a move would be insurmountable. Margaret's roots were in the Aber valley through countless generations. She could no more leave it than Jakob Bindel would have willingly left his tavern in Odessa. Leon did not relish such thoughts and he tried to concentrate on the discussion around the table.

Dai was in favor of sending a representative of the miners to see Edward Shaw, the manager of the mine. There was no question of who that representative should be. Dai Davies was indisputably the miners' spokesman. But Gilbert wanted the matter of safety to be on the agenda of their discussions.

"My father and brothers needn't have died," he said. "Nor any of those they brought up from the bottom, or who are still there. It's a dry mine. That's why there was fire. It's *still* a dry mine. Shaw's done nothing about it."

The Senghenydd colliery was a comfortable one to work in simply because it was dry. But being dry made it less safe, more vulnerable to fire and explosion. After the inquiry following the most recent tragedy, the investigating committee had suggested that the mine roofs be regularly watered, together with the rail tracks that linked one district seam with another, and that the full coal trucks plying from seam to seam should be covered to prevent the spread of dust. That was two years ago and still nothing had been done.

"Do we have to wait for another explosion," Gilbert asked, "before he gets off his fat backside? What's the point in better wages if you can't live to enjoy them?"

As Leon left the Davies Hut, he felt the acute isolation of the outsider. These men in the valley struggled daily for their survival, as his father and grandfather had done. But he himself was safe. His life was not daily threatened and he stood a good chance of a non-Bindel death, that of dying in his bed of natural old age. He was not part of their struggle.

When he reached home, they were already at their midday meal. Margaret was clearly in a sullen mood. When she saw him at the door, she rose from the table and went into the kitchen, then returned with his hot dinner and put it at his place on the table. She had a stern look of duty on her face, a look not conducive to conversation. So the meal was eaten in silence.

"I'm going to work on my ship," David said when they were done. David had a hobby common to the pitboys in the valley, that of making models out of matchsticks. Most of the boys were content with making copies of their own cottages or the pithead wheel, sights with which they were familiar. But David had chosen to model something he had never seen, nor even the sea on which it sailed, and Leon thought that some insistent Bindel gene in him prepared him for flight. He made to go upstairs to his room.

"What about a walk in the woods afterward?" Leon said. "The bluebells are out. We could pick a bunch for our Mam and our Gran." Leon had picked up fragments of the Welsh vernacular and they always sat uneasily on his tongue.

"All right, Dad," David said. "When I've finished with the sticking."

When he'd left the room, Leon picked up his plate and made to take it into the kitchen. Margaret snatched the plate from him.

"I don't want any man of mine doing women's work," she said.

"Well, at least I got you to open your mouth," Leon said.

She went into the kitchen and he followed her. "Margaret," he said. "I want to talk to you."

She turned her back on him at the sink. "I'm listening," she said.

"I want us to leave the valley," he said, coming to the point straightaway. "I want us to live in Cardiff. There are better opportunities for our David there." He said it almost in one breath, fearing her interruption.

She did not pause to consider what he'd said, and said, "No," even before he'd finished. "You're not getting me to leave Senghenydd. David neither. He's staying with me and his Gran and his Gramp. He was born in the valley and in the valley he'll stay. If you want to go to Cardiff, then that's your doing. And I'm not going to stop you. But you'll go on your own."

She was shouting at him, and in his ears it sounded like an order to leave. He had often thought of it. But he would not give up his son. "Won't you think about it?" he said softly. "It would be better for you, too. There's more to do in a big city."

"I've been there once," she said, "and I hated it. It's full of noise and traffic and nobody talks to you. Anyway, I want to be with my Mam and Dad." She turned to face him. "I'm not going," she said. "They might be your people, but they're not mine."

They weren't his either, he thought, or if they were, they would not receive him. But there were schools there, proper high schools for David.

"And don't you try and take him," she shouted.

He smiled. He imagined an army of angry colliers' wives descending on Cardiff to reclaim one of their own. Abduction was out of the question. "What will become of him when he leaves school?" he asked.

"He'll go down the pit like my father does, and like his father before him."

"But I'm his father," Leon shouted. "And I'm not a miner."

"More's the pity," she said.

He stared at her, hearing the terrible reverberation of regret in her voice. "Did you make a mistake, then?" he dared to ask after a while.

"No more of a mistake than you made," she said. "It couldn't work from the start. We're different, you and me, and it's not just religion," she hastened to add, "whatever your narrow-minded mother and brother might have said." It was the first time she had spoken ill of either of them. Leon had always given her credit for her silence on that score.

"They haven't helped," she said bitterly. "My Mam and Dad took you in like one of the family. Our David's got a cousin in Cardiff he's never seen. Who do they think they are?" she screamed at him, the tears starting in her eyes. "The chosen bloody people?"

He turned away. He could not deny what she had said. She was entitled to say much worse.

"It doesn't work," she said. "We're both of us unhappy."

He loved her then, for all the words that over the years she had left unsaid. "If we lived in Cardiff," he said, "it would help us. They would come round eventually." He knew there was little likelihood of it, and he was being less than honest in suggesting it. He had the impression that she was going to leave him, and it disturbed him that it did not hurt more. It was only David he wanted, his share of him that she could not deny.

"What shall we do?" he said.

"I'm going back to the Huts," she said. "With David. We'll live with our Mam and Dad. You can come whenever you want. I've thought about it for a long time. That's why I went to Chapel today, to ask God for forgiveness."

Leon shuddered. The bleakness of his future blinded him. He was now tied to Senghenydd forever. "D'you want a divorce?" he said. He had heard of such a measure on very rare occasions. He knew it was a shameful thing to do, but both of them still had a chance for happiness.

She looked at him in horror. "There's never been that sort of thing in my family," she said with a certain pride. "I made my bed and I'm going to lie on it, but I'll lie on it in my Mam's house."

"But you're young," he said. "And still beautiful."

She laughed with a certain bitterness. "And soiled goods," she said. "That's what they call us women in the valleys. You're better off widowed. Not that I want to be," she said quickly. "I don't bear you any grudge. You always treated me well. But it's better for both of us if I go."

He didn't know what more to say to her. Perhaps he could keep her with a little persuasion but his appetite for their marriage was as sickened as her own. He went to the foot of the stairs and called David. "We'll pick some bluebells," he said to Margaret. "You can take them to your Mam." He was sanctioning his wife's departure.

"She'll like that" was all Margaret said.

They walked toward the woods at the bottom of the valley. At home David was a silent boy, though his school reports declared that he was very talkative in class. Leon knew most of his son's friends and had noted how they chatted endlessly with their families. Dai Davies said that when he came to the Huts, he couldn't stop talking. On and on he chatted, as if he were making up for many silences. Leon could only suppose that he himself was the cause. Even when they took walks together, David said very little and usually in answer to questions that Leon asked. But this time he was more forthcoming.

"We're going to live at Gran and Gramp's," he said.

So she had already told him, and he resented that breach. He tried to hide his anger.

"Will you like that?" Leon asked.

"Yes," he said. "But you'll come every day, won't you? Mam says you will."

"D'you want me to come?"

David gripped Leon's sleeve. "You've got to come, Dad."

It was a rare show of emotion from his son. Leon could see he was on the verge of tears. He took his hand, but at the same time quickened his pace as if to minimize a gesture that a thirteen-year-old boy might find embarrassing.

"What's the matter, Dovidle?" Leon said. It was his Yiddish name for him, the name his own father and grandfather would have used had they lived.

"I wish you were a miner, Dad," David said after a while. "So's I could go down the pit with you when I leave school."

"D'you want to go down the pit?"

"Of course," David said. "All my friends are going to." The thought of an alternative had clearly never occurred to him and Leon was careful not to suggest one. He was deeply depressed at the prospect of his son's bleak future. Perhaps he should have been more firm with Margaret, he thought. He had been weak in acquiescing to her decision. But during his long sojourn in the valley he had learned the strength of its women. "I'll have to ask my missus," was a phrase he'd heard countless times in the Institute or on his rounds. Under the earth the men reigned supreme, but above ground was women's domain. "You'll like it with Gran and Gramp," Leon said.

"Will Mam let me go to Cardiff?" he said suddenly. "Just for a visit."

"Why d'you want to do that?" Leon asked.

"See my cousin. Mam's told me about her. Chaya or something. It's not a Welsh name, is it, Dad?"

"It's Jewish," Leon said.

"Like you?"

"That's right. You've got a Jewish name, too. David was king of Israel."

"It's Welsh, too," David said. "Patron saint."

They had reached the woods. Through a clearing they could see a haze of blue, and David darted to its center and started picking. "You pick for Mam," David called, "and I'll pick for Gran."

Leon stood watching him and he trembled with sudden and total recall of the Odessa forest behind the tavern. The scene played before his eyes with such clarity, he actually heard his father's voice, undeniable, insistent, as if it dictated Leon's turn to hand down his survival legacy to his son. But this is Senghenydd, Leon thought, a sleepy village in the Aber valley, far from the Czar, a village in which Leon Bindel was the only Jew. What relevance was his legacy to a child for whom his bar mitzvah day was no different from any other birthday?

"We used to have a forest like this," Leon began. "Behind our tavern in Odessa." Leon had told his son very little of his own childhood. Beyond its geography he knew practically nothing. Margaret had never encouraged Leon's childhood tales. They only served to accentuate the differences between them.

"Did it have bluebells?" David asked.

"No," he said, rather sharply. He wanted to get on with the story. He could afford no diversion. "We went there once on your Uncle Aaron's thirteenth birthday," he said. "Just like yours is today. We had quite an adventure there."

"Well, go on, Dad," David said impatiently. "What sort of adventure?"

Leon went over to where his son was sitting. "Well, first I have to tell you a little of the history of that time." He started to pick the bluebells, which gave a rhythm to his story, and he told his son of his grandfather's childhood. When he came to the end, to the account of the milk-brothers' return to the tavern, David asked a question that echoed those very words that he and Aaron had posed in the Odessa forest all those years ago. "How did they survive?" he said.

Leon thought of Grandpa Jakob, and of that litany of survival that had been the milk-brothers' inheritance. The same litany that his own father in his time had bequeathed his two sons in the forest. And now the burden of that inheritance was his and his alone. For Aaron had no son, and in the Jewish ethic, survival lay in the male domain. He looked at David and wondered what he would make of Grandpa Jakob's bequest. Leon knew every word of it by heart, as Aaron knew it, and as Benjamin and Reuben had known it. It was a hymn that had to be heard from generation to generation, a hymn that would have no stop, that no one could stifle, and even a stray from the tribe could be its minstrel. He put his arm around his son. There was no point in declaring the threat of baptism. His son was already halfway to the Cross. But there was point, ample point, in entreating his survival. So mindful of the seeming irrelevance of his homily, its anachronism in place and time, he laid before his son, word by word, the Bindel inheritance. "You must survive, Dovidle," he said. "But beware of principles. Abandon them if you are to survive. There is no cause on earth worth dying for, no God worth one's dying breath, no country worth one's martyrdom, no principle worth one's sacrifice. Only in the name of love is death worthy. And friendship."

When he had done, Leon, like his father before him, and his grandfather, too, wondered whether his son had any idea of what he was talking about. But he had to speak out for his own sake, as his father and grandfather had for theirs. But to whom would his son bequeath that minstrel's song of survival? Now for the first time he realized the most monstrous penalty of his desertion from his tribe. Despite all his efforts, he was still inextricably tied to the burdensome Bindel inheritance. But he had cut off his son from all of his father's history. With his own desertion he had disinherited his son.

David put his hand on his father's arm. "You know Trevor, Dad? Trevor Evans, my friend?"

Leon nodded.

"Well, you know his dad was killed in the pit explosion?"

Leon nodded again.

"Well, Trevor told me," David went on, "that his dad was saved. Ready to go up in the cage he was. But he looked in the cage and he couldn't find his friend. John Llewellyn it was. Owen's dad. So Trevor's dad went back to look for him. Then there was a fall. Killed him it did. So Trevor said. Him and Mr. Llewellyn." He gathered his bunch of bluebells and stood upright. "Let's go, Dad," he said.

And as his Grandpa Jakob before him, and as Benjamin, his

own father, Leon thought that his son had understood him after all.

When they returned to the cottage, the table was set with the Sunday high tea. The fact that she planned to walk out on her marriage that day would in no way upset Margaret's routine. Her duties as a wife would continue as long as she and her husband shared the same roof. But it was their last meal together as a family, and, mindful of that, Margaret had put herself out to make it memorable. She had baked Welsh scones and pikelets, both Leon's and David's favorites, and tinned salmon cutlets, which were the staple fare for every Welsh high-tea Sunday table. Margaret put Leon's offer of bluebells in a jar and placed them in the center of the table. She would leave them there, Leon knew, not as a rejection of his gift but because she would wish him some cheer to take the edge off his loneliness.

"Can I go to Cardiff with Dad one day?" David asked suddenly. "Just for a visit," he added, seeing the look of dismay on his mother's face.

She relaxed a little. "As long as your Dad brings you back," she said, with a laugh masking her fears of his abduction.

"You know I'll bring him back," Leon said. "This is his home."

She was grateful for that acknowledgment. "It could have been yours, too," she said. "If you'd put your mind to it."

"It is mine now," he said. "It has to be."

She did not want to pity him, but she could not be indifferent to his isolation. "You should patch it up with your brother," she said. "He might welcome you. Even our David. Or at least half of him." She didn't want to hurt Leon, but she hated his brother for all the pain of his neglect.

She insisted on clearing the table and washing up before she left. She made no production of leave-taking. As she pointed out, they were only going down the valley and no doubt they would be seeing him in the morning. Leon offered to escort her, to carry her case. But Margaret declined. She was leaving of her own free will. She was not entitled to a porter.

Leon waved them good-bye from the doorstep, and when he returned to the empty cottage, he looked around and noticed the sudden absence of all her traces, her sewing box on the sideboard, her brown exercise book of recipes, her white Bible, things that before had never impressed themselves on his eye. He wandered from room to room. In the kitchen, he noticed that she had set out his breakfast tray. On it was a glass in a holder and inside the glass was a piece of lemon. It was the only concession she had ever made to his Bindelhood, one of the few Odessa legacies he himself had retained with ease. He filled the kettle and boiled it on the open fire. Then when it was ready, he made a very weak tea and poured it over the lemon. He opened the larder and found the only flavor that would transport him back to the Bindel tavern. Black currant jam. He spooned it into the cup, then he sat at the table and sipped it slowly.

He had made a decision. After so many years of fraternal silence, he would make a bid to see his brother again.

Pavel Khasina, the Bindel brothers' intermediary, had retired some years before from his drapery round. He was no longer strong enough to carry parcels and to make the strenuous uphill climbs in the valleys. With his savings, he had set up his own small store a few doors away from Max's in Bute Street. There he sold haberdashery and notions, soaps and powders and registered aids to health. He had sold the goodwill of his valley round to a *landsman* who had recently emigrated from Odessa. He had had sundry offers for his round, but Pavel was looking for a buyer who could successfully execute the message service for the Bindel brothers. So each applicant was assessed for his loyalty, his tact, and his aversion to gossip. The lot fell to a man named Victor Zubko, who carried out his tasks as go-between with diligence and skill. It was Victor who brought Aaron the news of Leon's estrangement from his wife and, some days later, of Leon's wish to see his brother again.

The news of his brother's separation from his wife did not surprise Aaron. Indeed, he wondered why it had taken so long. He did not consider it a matter for his concern or his compassion. But he was delighted that Leon had expressed a wish to see him again. This he conveyed to Victor, who then divulged the second part of Leon's message. He wished to bring his son with him. Victor was quick to note the look of displeasure that clouded Aaron's face at the mention of this request, but that look would not be part of his returning message. Over the years Victor had taken a liking to Leon and would not hurt him. In his heart he thought Aaron a stern, ungiving man. "I have to consider it," Aaron said. "I will let you know tomorrow."

Aaron consulted with Rachel.

"Of course," she said. "He must bring his son. Chaya has never met her cousin."

"Cousin?" Aaron said. The notion of blood between his wholly Jewish daughter and a child who, by Jewish law, was Christian, he found faintly displeasing. But he did not want to argue with Rachel. He had noticed in the past that on the subject of Leon, her thoughts were sometimes dangerously close to approval.

It was Rachel who, on the following day, charged Victor with the message that Leon and his son would be very welcome, and Victor would take that message back to the valley. Except that he would say it was Aaron himself who had issued the invitation. Victor knew the cost of Leon's request, the cost to his pride, his dignity and self-respect.

"Aaron would be glad to see you. And David," Victor said to Leon the following day. "He will make you most welcome." Then they sat together at the cottage table drinking black currant tea and sharing stories of Odessa.

Later that week, on Sunday, David put on his suit and tie and went with his father to Cardiff.

Leon was nervous and tried to hide his apprehension from his son. He had not seen his brother for almost five years. That meeting had been formal and fleeting at the graveside at Mr. Ruboff's funeral. He had not been invited to return to the house of mourning, though he had the impression that Rachel would have wished it. He had slunk away like a pariah, while the men about him whispered and the women turned their faces away. On his way back to the valley he had tried not to think ill of his brother. He tried to understand him. Over the past years Aaron had become something of a leading figure in the growing Jewish community. He was an official of the synagogue and an organizer of charities. He had a position to maintain. The acceptance of a tainted brother into his life could only threaten that position.

David, for his part, was agog with excitement. On their way from the station he had seen a trolley tram for the first time, and he gripped his father's hand in joy. Leon wondered whether Aaron had given Chaya instructions on how to behave, what names must not be mentioned, and what questions must not be asked. On his side, he had given no instructions to David. They had to accept him without apology. As they walked down the bridge steps to reach the embankment, Leon said, "You can see your Uncle Aaron's house from here," and he pointed it out from where they stood. He felt a sudden sweat on David's hand as he clutched his own. The boy stopped, suddenly nervous. "Do I look all right, Dad?" he asked.

Leon looked at him and smiled. "Fit to meet a king," he said, responding to the nature of David's fears. But Leon knew that, however David looked, Aaron would see him as that little half-Jew boy, in his posh Chapel clothes on his way to the pit like all of his kind. He put his arm around his son as a preemptive move of protection. David, by the same instinct, did likewise with his father. "We'll survive, Dad," he said.

They stood for a while before Aaron's door. David nervously patted his hair and pulled at his unaccustomed tie. "Let me pull the bell, Dad," David said. He came from the village of ever-open front doors, so he was in awe of this heavily barred and locked one. He pulled on the metal chain and listened to the hollow echo of the bell inside the door. Leon hoped that Rachel would answer, or even Chaya, whom he had never seen. Either would have been more reassuring than his brother. But it was Aaron who opened the door and bade them welcome. Through the doorway Leon could see a girl peeping around a door into the hall, and he sent David into the house so that he could be alone with his brother.

"I'm glad to see you, Leon," Aaron said, with what sounded like a rehearsed formality.

Leon embraced him and, at his touch, Aaron melted a little, and arm in arm they entered the house. Rachel was introducing Chaya to her cousin. Her hand was on the boy's shoulder in total and immediate acceptance. Then she greeted Leon. "Come and say hello to your niece. This is your Uncle Leon, Chaya," she said.

"Uncle Leon," the child repeated, two brand-new words in her little world, unheard before in this house. "Uncle Leon," she repeated and went up to him and took his hand.

Leon hoped that the children would stay with them, for their presence diluted the tension he felt between himself and his brother. Rachel led them into the dining room, where lunch was ready. David went to his father's side and stayed there, clinging. He was fiddling with his tie. "You can take it off if you like," Leon said. He realized that a tie would make little difference to their impression of his son. He noted that Aaron had not yet touched the boy or addressed one word to him. He felt David clinging to his sleeve as if to confirm their mutual outsiderness,

evidence of which was all around him. The white tablecloth on
the table, and all that silver. Perhaps food would relax them all,
Leon hoped, and he guided David toward the table.

Rachel sat David by Chaya. She meant well, but David was
loath to leave his father's side. The abundance of cutlery on the
table frightened him, and his total ignorance of all their uses
seemed to put him in his lowly place. He wished he were back in
Senghenydd at his Gran's table, where one knife and one fork did
for everything. He watched his father unfold the linen napkin and
tuck it into his collar. He did likewise, wondering how his Gramp
would have managed, whose neck was always scarved above an
unbuttoned shirt. He dared to sneak a look at his Uncle Aaron,
who was carving a chicken at the end of the table. He reminded
him of his headmaster. Leon, too, was looking at his brother. He
noticed how fat he'd grown, with a fat that sat ill on his naturally
lean body. It was a fat of prosperity and safety, and had thus
never framed a Bindel before.

"Did you have a good journey?" Aaron said, making conversation.

"Yes," Leon said. "David had never been on a train before."
He wanted to include his son in their exchange, making it clear
that the one was not acceptable without the other.

"Did you like it?" Rachel said, addressing herself to David.

He swallowed. His face was on fire. He did not trust his voice,
so he nodded in her direction and hoped that she would be satisfied.

"No tongue in your head?" Aaron asked. They were the first
words he had addressed to him, and they were by no means
friendly.

"He's shy," Leon whispered to his brother. "Give him a little
time." He dared to look across at his son and saw the tears in his
eyes and at that moment Leon, too, wanted to be back in the
valley. He sought in his mind for some topic of conversation to
divert their attention from his child, whose lineage his brother
clearly could not forgive. But before he could think of anything,
Aaron was once again at his questioning.

"What school d'you go to?" he said, not looking at him.

His name's David, Leon thought. His brother should have no
difficulty pronouncing it. It was Jewish enough to slip easily off
his tongue.

Now David had to say something. A nod or a shake of the

head would no longer do. He raised his head and decided to brazen it out. He looked Aaron straight in the eye and was glad that he wasn't his father. "Senghenydd Boys' School," he said, then he looked back at his plate and wondered how he could deal with the chicken leg that had suddenly appeared on it, without using his fingers. He looked across the table at his father and Leon gave him a smile that told him he had acquitted himself well.

"And what will you be when you grow up?" Aaron was relentless.

"I'll be a collier," David said proudly. "Like my Gramp."

Chaya giggled. She had not heard that word before.

"Like Zeder," Rachel explained, using Chaya's word for Mr. Ruboff. Then it was David's turn to laugh at a word as foreign to him as Gramp was to his cousin. Leon looked across at him tenderly. He's a true survivor, he thought. The score was now about equal around the table.

"There are better things to be than a miner," Aaron plowed on.

Perhaps he was trying to get near the boy in his own ham-fisted fashion, Leon thought.

"Like what?" David asked. He was now perfectly at ease. The smile his father had flashed him was ammunition enough to confront his uncle's hostility. Now he felt he and his father were hosts, and the others rank outsiders.

"Well," Aaron pressed on, "you could be a doctor or a solicitor or a dentist. You're young." His voice was raised in anger. "You can do anything."

David found his catalog of possibilities quite ridiculous. "That's daft," he said with no adornment. "I'm going down the pit with my Gramp."

"I want Chaya to be a teacher," Aaron said proudly.

David was not impressed. He wished his Uncle Aaron would stop examining him. He was hungry and he wanted to eat, and even he knew that you mustn't speak with your mouth full. He looked at his chicken, checked on the tool that his father was using, and did likewise.

"How's your business, Aaron?" Leon said, offering himself as a second front for Aaron's line of fire.

"I'm busy," he said. "Lots of new immigrants have settled in

Cardiff. Everyone wants a new suit and they all seem to come to me. There just isn't enough time."

"What a pity," Leon laughed. "I was thinking of placing an order."

Aaron looked up at him. "For you I'll find time," he said. "After lunch I'll show you some new materials."

He was slowly thawing. Perhaps soon he would be ready to talk about their childhood, a conversation for which Leon longed.

"We'll go up to the workshop," Aaron was saying, and Leon wished the meal quickly over.

"D'you have any hobbies, David?" Rachel asked, carefully waiting until his mouth was empty.

"Matchstick models," David said. "I'm making a ship. My Dad's been on a ship," he said proudly.

"So have I," Aaron said. It was a journey he would have preferred to forget, but he wanted to make himself part of Leon's adventure.

David was not pleased with that news, though he tried to hide it. He wanted his father to be special. If he couldn't be a miner, then he had to have done something that his friends' fathers had never done. Besides, he'd hoped that his father would have done something special that he didn't have to share with his brother. David had been in that house long enough to notice the inequality in the brothers' ways of life. Uncle Aaron lived in a big house. He was rich and he had a happy family. His father had none of those things.

"But your father's done something none of us has done," Aaron said. Leon trembled. He knew that Aaron meant well, but there was no way David could accommodate a jailbird as a father. "He's been in prison," Aaron went on.

David paled. "Dad?" he said, and there were tears in his eyes.

Now Aaron was confused and regretful. Was it possible that his brother had never mentioned this episode to his son? Then he realized that the cause of that imprisonment was part and parcel of the heritage that Leon had forsworn. Aaron tried to make amends. "It was for a good cause," he said. "Your father was very brave. Any brave man would have done what he did."

"What did you do, Dad?"

"I hit a man," Leon said. "A ship's officer. Because he made insulting remarks about Jews."

There was silence. It was clear that David did not think that was a good enough reason. Why should he, Aaron thought, since he had clearly been told nothing about the events that preceded the flight from Odessa. "There's a long, long story behind it, David," he said. It was the first time he had used the boy's name.

"Have you not told him our story, Leon?" his brother asked.

"No," Leon said. "Not all of it. But I have told him of Grandpa Jakob's legacy. I have told him about survival. He has inherited." Aaron touched his brother's arm and smiled.

"Tell him the whole story, Papa," Chaya said. She turned to her cousin. "It's full of blood and fighting and running away."

Aaron took a sheet of paper from his pocket notebook and drew a little map. "Come here." He beckoned the children to his side. "I'll show you where it all began."

And so the tale of survival unfolded. The brothers shared it between them, laughing at times, reminding each other of omissions, encouraged by the excitement of the two children. Much of it Chaya had heard before, but for David it was new. It was teatime when the brothers came to the end of the tale, to the event that triggered the telling of the story in the first place. The striking of the ship's officer.

"You should have killed him, Dad," David said with indignation.

Leon was glad that his son had so fully understood his father's history. And for the first time in many years he felt the relief of one who no longer lives a lie.

Rachel had made two cups of lemon tea for the brothers and they took them upstairs to the workshop. They sat by the cutting bench and sipped their tea in silence. Then after a while Leon said, "Thank you for helping me to tell him." He spoke in Yiddish, for it was the togetherness of their childhood that he wished to recapture.

"Come, let me measure you for a suit," Aaron said, also in Yiddish. He drew the measure round Leon's chest. "What are you going to do?" he said. "Are you staying in the valley?"

"I must," Leon said. "David is there. Margaret won't leave, and I won't leave David."

"But you're young," Aaron said. "You should marry again. A proper marriage this time."

"Margaret won't hear of a divorce," Leon said. "And it was a proper marriage. As long as it lasted. It wasn't a mistake at the time. I changed. That's what went wrong. It was not her fault."

"But she must free you." Aaron was insistent.

"A divorce would destroy her," Leon said. "There's nothing I can do about it. When David grows up and marries, then perhaps I'll come and live in Cardiff. But till then, I cannot be apart from him."

"Is he really going to go down the mine?" Aaron asked.

"You must try and understand him, Aaron," Leon said gently. "David has a history almost as long and as oppressed as our own. His grandfather was a collier, so was his father before him. The pit is the whole fabric of the valley life. It's what he wants. It's his only honest way of growing into a man."

"But aren't you ambitious for him?" Aaron asked. "If I had a son, I would want the world for him, but Rachel cannot bear more children."

"I'm sorry," Leon said. Then with a shock he realized that his son, his David, would be the only Bindel of the new generation. And that it was Leon who, out of his renegade loins, had sired him.

"If I had a son," Aaron went on, "I'd want him to have all the opportunities that we never had. But Chaya will be a teacher. I have decided on that. It's a prestigious profession. Of course, it doesn't matter so much with a girl. She'll marry and have children. But they won't be Bindels," Aaron said.

How different they both were, Leon thought. In many ways, he had stayed closer to the Bindel tradition than his brother. Freedom and safety had bred in Aaron ambition, a greed almost, for prestige and status. He had become a different kind of Jew whose priorities were no longer those of survival. Parental expectation was the crippling disease of freedom. He thought of the Odessa days. When Grandpa Jakob had said farewell to the milk-brothers, when his own father had spoken in the forest, neither had said, "Go, my sons. Be doctors, be teachers, be lawyers." All they had said, and with all their love, was, "Go, my sons. Survive." That was the limit of their parental hopes. To do that was to do more than enough. That was the only thing he wanted for his own son. Just the miracle of survival. Had Aaron learned nothing from their history, that history he knew by heart?

Yet despite all this, Leon had never felt so close to Aaron. He watched him circling his body, measuring and writing down the

lengths. He was humming to himself as he worked, as their father, Benjamin, would do at his milking, as Grandpa Jakob sang
softly to himself as he took the stock to his tavern cellars. "It's
good to be with you again," Leon said.

Aaron squeezed that part of his arm that was under the measure. "You must come every Sunday," he said.

Over the next few months, Leon and David came every week
to Cardiff and, with each visit, David gleaned more and more of
his inheritance. Like his father, he looked forward to Sundays.

Margaret willingly gave in to these visits. She and Leon often
met in the public house where she would go with her father. She
would drink a stout with them and the people of Senghenydd
slowly got used to their strange relationship.

One evening, the messenger Zubko called at Leon's cottage. He
brought news. Aaron had received a letter from their mother in
Leipzig in which she wrote that Barak had died. She had been
expecting it for many months. He had been in no pain and his
death was peaceful. He had left her very comfortable. During the
last months of his illness he had been cared for by a young nurse
called Greta, whom she now kept on as a companion. She was
anxious to see her sons once again, and announced that she and
Greta would be coming to Cardiff within the next month, once
she had cleared up Barak's business affairs.

"Are you sure she said sons?" Leon asked. "Not just Aaron?"

"Aaron had written to her of your separation," Zubko said.

"What did she say?"

"She's never mentioned it in her letters. But she did write
'sons.' I saw the letter myself."

"Then she will have to meet her grandson, too," Leon said.

When Zubko arrived at the cottage shortly afterward with
news of Zelda's arrival, Leon indicated that he would meet her
alone on the following day. It was almost fifteen years since he
had seen his mother and their last meeting had been bitter and
painful. In his move to reconcile with his family, he felt no dis-
loyalty to Margaret. She had, after all, left him. It was her choice,
and her leaving was almost an instruction to him to return to the
fold. He wore the suit that Aaron had made for him.

When he arrived at his brother's house, it was Zelda herself who came to the door. She embraced him right away. "Where's David?" she said.

"He's coming on Sunday," Leon said, delighted with her ready acceptance.

"Let me look at you," she said, holding him at a distance from her. As she appraised him, he did likewise with her. She had shrunk a little, but there was a brightness in her eye, and a general radiance about her features that was surprising in a face so recently bereaved. He knew that his mother had always had qualms about her remarriage, though her years with Barak had been happy. But it was as if his death had wiped her slate clean. Now she was Zelda Bindel once more, widowed in that name. He followed her into the dining room, where the family was assembled. Lunch was set, and Rachel urged them to the table.

"This is Greta," Zelda said, taking the hand of a girl who stood at the far end of the room.

Greta held out her hand, looking him squarely in the face. There was no shyness about her, and Leon had the impression that he was no stranger to her. She looked at Leon as if she knew his childhood, his rebellion. And although he found her attractive and friendly, he felt slightly at a disadvantage.

"Your mother has told me a lot about you," she said.

He smiled. He was glad of that, for now he knew his mother had never fully rejected him. Aaron was in a jovial mood and so were Rachel and Chaya, each taking their cue from Zelda.

"What a pity my grandson isn't here," she said as they all sat down.

"Sunday, Mama," Leon said.

"Three Bindel generations around one table," she said. "It's just like the old days in Odessa."

And that was the cue for nostalgia and a texture of conversation that Leon so delighted in. He felt strangely elated, a feeling not wholly due to their reminiscence. It was the presence of that girl who sat opposite him. Later when they withdrew to the sitting room, Zelda told them about her life in Leipzig and she sang Greta's praises for the care she had given to the ailing Barak.

"I loved him," Greta said. "He was like a father. Mine died when I was little. Oh, it's no cause for sorrow," she said quickly. "I have no recollection of him at all. Nor of my mother, who died when I was born. I'm an orphan," she explained.

Leon warmed to the girl and smiled at her. And Zelda noted

the exchange and was glad of it. The notion of Leon's divorce and
whatever problems it presented in no way ruffled her. In Jewish
law the marriage had been illegal from the start. She took no
account of the Christian law of the land. All their lives the
Bindels had broken that kind of law. Grandpa Jakob had run an
illegal tavern. Benjamin and Reuben Bindel had attempted army
desertion. Leon Bindel, blessed be his memory, had died in protest against the Czar's law. Her own sons had run away from
legal recruitment and their traveling papers were by no means
legitimate. Since the beginning of time, the Bindels had been
chronic lawbreakers, and she saw no reason why they should
change now. Her dream was that Leon should return to Leipzig
with both of them, marry Greta, and make his home there. "I
don't intend to sell Barak's shop," she said suddenly. "There's a
good manager there," she said, "and it brings in a useful income.
You must visit one day," she said, directing her remark at Leon.
"Leipzig is a beautiful city."

"I have a short end of a lovely suiting upstairs," Aaron said
suddenly. "It will make a suit for David." Now that his mother
had not expressed displeasure at meeting her grandson, he could
afford to publicize his acceptance of the boy.

"Can you imagine," Zelda laughed, "a son of mine a tailor."
Which set her to remembering the insomniac Faivel. And once
again they were back in the Odessa tavern.

The following Sunday David met his grandmother for the first
time. The encounter was less uneasy than Leon had expected.
The presence of the rest of the family eased the first moments
between them. "He looks like you, Leon," Zelda said, though
David clearly looked like his mother. Zelda put her hand on
David's shoulder. "You're a Bindel," she said.

He felt an awe in her touch, as if she had loaded him with an
enormous responsibility. "Your children shall be Bindels," she
added.

Leon realized how little his mother knew of his son, how the
boy, through his father's own straying, had left the tribe far behind.

After lunch David and Chaya went walking in the park together. It had become a Sunday habit with them. At first Aaron
had had qualms about letting them go off on their own. Yet he
could not voice his fears for fear of hurting his brother. Often the
children would wander as far as Llandaff field, and then they

would bring back flowers or leaves according to the season. Which left the adults alone in the house. Greta and Rachel cleared the kitchen, but Zelda hung behind, keeping her seat in the dining room, a position that, out of politeness, kept her sons at the table. Aaron pleaded a suit to finish and Zelda gladly excused him because she wanted to talk alone to Leon. Leon was nervous of such an encounter, though he knew it was unavoidable. His mother would ask questions and would not be pleased with their answers. He waited for her preamble, for she was not one to come straight to the point, especially when that point was controversial.

"You have a lovely son there," she said. "A very attractive boy."

He thanked her, and said that he was a good son and had always given him pleasure.

"What is his future?" she said. She was skirting, for it was his own future she wanted to talk about.

"He'll follow in the tradition of all his family. He will be a collier."

She gasped. "A Bindel a collier?" She was unbelieving.

"He is only half a Bindel," Leon said.

"And what about you, a whole Bindel. What's to become of you?" The gentleness had gone from her voice and Leon was glad of it for it now allowed his cruel honesty. "My future is bound up with my son's," he said. "I shall stay in the valley."

"You will bury yourself there," she shouted at him.

"What do you want me to do, Mama?" he said helplessly. He hadn't meant it as a question. It was a simple statement of his own lack of choice. But she took it as a request for her advice.

"I want you to come back to Leipzig with me. I want you to make your home there. Take over the fur business. It will be yours one day." She paused. "I want you to marry," she said. All of it, till then, had of course been a preamble, Leon realized. At last she had come to her point. At least she had not mentioned Greta's name.

"But I'm already married, Mama," Leon said, as gently as he could.

"That's not a marriage," she said with disdain.

He did not want to dislike her, and he prayed that she would not mention Margaret's name, for it would be a curse from her lips.

"You can get a divorce," she said.

"My wife won't give me a divorce," he said, and he dreaded her response. But she was clever enough not to malign her. "In Leipzig no one would know that you were ever married before."

He let that pass and asked her the unanswerable question. "What about my son?" he said.

She looked at him with infinite pity, and then to his great surprise, she put her arms around him. He had spoken words that had finally touched her heart. "How old is he now?" she asked.

"Thirteen," he said. Any other year would have been preferable, for thirteen in the Bindel tradition was heavily laden. "I took him into the woods, Mama, like Papa took us into the forest. And I told him what Papa told me, and what Grandpa Jakob told him. I told it to David, Mama. He has inherited."

"You know," she said, still holding him, "children grow up, they marry, they have children of their own. Will you stay with him then?"

He smiled at her. "No," he said. "Then I shall come to Leipzig."

That evening before he left, Leon asked Greta if he could show her a little of Cardiff during her visit. He would gladly come from the valley for that purpose. She was delighted to accept his offer. So over the remaining weeks of Zelda's stay, Leon came often to Cardiff for the sole purpose of seeing Greta. They walked a lot, and talked as much. Greta told him all that she knew about him from his mother. She knew the Bindel history so intimately, she might have been born in the tavern. It was as if his mother had laid the foundations for his wooing. Greta knew about his marriage, too, and she wanted to know about Margaret and his life in the valley. Leon was happy to talk about such things, for never before had he found a listener for that Senghenydd tale.

Slowly he grew more and more fond of her and, at night, alone in his cottage, he dreaded the day of her departure. He dreamed of taking David out of the valley, to Leipzig to learn the fur trade. But it would be too cruel even to suggest it to Margaret, much less to Gran and Gramp. David Bindel, however he had been sired, was a son of the valley. And like all its sons, in the valley he would live, marry, bear children, and lay his bones. Leon thought of Greta and knew that he would miss her terribly.

They were due to leave the following week and Leon had de-

cided to take them to Tilbury. Margaret gave permission for
David to take off from school and go as far as Cardiff to say
good-bye to his grandmother. But she drew the line at London,
fearing the docks and their wherewithal for flight. It was arranged with Aaron that David would spend two nights with them
and wait for his father's return. Margaret bought him a new pair
of pajamas. It would be the first night he had spent away from
home. "Will you miss your old Mam, *cariad?*" she asked him.

He nodded for her sake. He was excited at the prospect of
having a room of his own, of sleeping in his own bed, as he used
to do at the cottage. Now in the Huts he slept with Gramp, while
his Gran and Mam slept on the couch in the parlor downstairs.
He loved his Gramp, but sometimes when he was dozing off to
sleep, he wished he were alone.

His father called at the Huts early on Thursday morning and
David was waiting for him at the door. He was wearing the suit
that Aaron had made him and when Leon looked at him, he
noticed that he did indeed resemble a Bindel. When he looked
closer, he saw that Aaron had cut the suit in their childhood
Odessa style. The thought crossed his mind that he might spirit
him away to Leipzig. "Keep an eye on our boy, Leon *bach,*"
Gramp said suddenly as he appeared at the door. "I need another
man in this house," he laughed. That colliery chain was as sacred
and as unbreakable as that of the tavern.

When they arrived at Aaron's house, there was only time for
lunch before leaving for the station. The whole family came to see
them off. As the train drew out of the station, Leon saw the lone
figure of his son as he stood slightly apart from Aaron and his
family. He was frantically waving one of Gramp's white Sunday
handkerchiefs, and as Leon watched his small blurring figure, he
knew that his Leipzig dream would remain a dream forever.

They did not reach London till late in the evening, and Leon
booked into a hostelry that was well on the road to Tilbury
Docks. That evening, before going to bed, Greta and Leon
walked the silent cobbled streets in long and sad farewell. They
exchanged promises to write to each other, to hold each other in
their hearts. Such promises Leon made freely because they could
be honored. But neither mentioned his possible future settlement
in Leipzig. Greta, too, had seen David's lone figure on the Cardiff
platform and she knew that, despite the years that would pass,
Leon would forever stay by his son's side.

At the docks the following morning, Greta held out her hand in more formal farewell. But Leon took her in his arms while Zelda stood to one side. Then he gathered his mother in his embrace, and kissed them both.

"It's been the happiest time I've spent in many years," Zelda said. "Soon we shall all be together again." That phrase, that Bindel phrase through each generation.

The journey back to Cardiff was endless and depressing. It was late when he arrived, but there was still time to collect David and take the last train back to the valley. He hurried to Aaron's house. As he pulled the bell, he had a premonition of something amiss; his fear was confirmed by the stern look on Aaron's face as he opened the door.

"What's the matter?" Leon said as he followed his brother into the kitchen. David stood in the corner, white-faced, close to tears, his overcoat buttoned and his little cardboard case in his hand. He was clearly being sent away.

"What's happened?" Leon said.

"I don't want him in this house again," Aaron said. "You are welcome, but not your son."

"In that case," Leon said, "I am not welcome either." He wanted to get that very clear before investigating the cause of David's exclusion. "What has happened, Dovidle?" he said.

But Aaron gave him no space for reply, even if David could have made one. He came to the point straightaway. "He's been telling my Chaya stories," Aaron said.

Leon noted the possessive. Was his Chaya his possession, not to be touched by alien tales? "What sort of stories?"

"He learns them in his Scripture class, he says. You know, the usual stories. He told my Chaya that we Jews killed . . ." He hesitated then, and settled for the least incriminating name. He still had problems with the word that had stuck in his father's throat. "He says that we Jews killed his Savior," he said.

"Has she not heard that before?" Leon said softly.

But Aaron ignored him. "She's in tears," he said. "Rachel is with her. I can't have her exposed to such damage. I was too free with my hospitality in the first place."

Now it was all out, and Leon wondered whether he should stay to argue, whether he should plead David's youth and lack of understanding. But that would have meant apologizing for his son.

"That's what our Scripture teacher told us, Dad," David whispered from his corner. "I only said what she said."

"Come," Leon said. "We have time to catch the train." He took his son's hand. "Good-bye, Aaron," he said.

"You are always welcome in my house," Aaron said. His voice was almost pleading.

Leon looked at him. "I'm sorry for you, brother," he said.

For many months after that unhappy meeting, Zubko was frequently called upon to deliver messages from town to valley and back again. Both brothers feared that their break was final. Through Zubko's services Leon learned that his mother was well, that Chaya had passed a piano exam and, in Zubko's whispered parentheses, that she missed David very much. He heard too that the tailoring business was profitable and that he was always welcome in his brother's house. From the valley, Leon was selective about his information. He said nothing about his constant correspondence with Greta, but he did convey the news that David had won a prize for his model ship and that soon he would leave school and start as a colliery boy. In reply to each of Aaron's invitations, he sent his polite refusal. His missed his Sunday visits, and so, at first, did David, but Aaron's price for brotherhood was too costly.

It was a Tuesday in mid-October, Leon's day for his Cardiff buying and also David's first day in the mine. All week he'd been trying on his helmet and his overalls that Gramp had brought home from the pit store. On that Tuesday he would relinquish his boyhood, and opt for a manhood that would be imperiled with each shift and would never vary thereafter. Leon left his cottage very early that morning because he wanted to see David before he went underground for the first time. When he reached the Huts, David was ready to go, nagging his Gramp to hurry.

"There's time, Davy *bach,*" Dai Davies said. "You'll be down there soon enough. And every day of your life, too, bar Sunday, and Saturday, too, if I get my way with the management." Dai Davies was still optimistic about a miner's future, though in the past years he had made little headway on the wage issue, and none at all on the matter of underground safety. "Just wait for me to fill up my jack," he said.

The jack was the miners' metal tea-carrier. Dai's was scratched and misshapen from its long years' service, but David's was brand-new and was stopped with a champagne cork that the man in the ironmongery shop had given him for good luck.

"Come on, Gramp," David said again.

Leon wanted to kiss him, but what with his overalls and his jack and his helmet, he was too old for that sort of thing. So instead he grasped his shoulder. "Good luck, son," he said. He watched the pair of them cross the road and walk up to the pithead; and he saw Gramp take David's hand halfway up the slope. It looked like a gesture of partnership, and Leon watched them out of sight, then he made his way to the station.

He was early for his train, so he sat on a bench and reread the last letter he had received from Greta. She wrote of her daily life in Leipzig in the smallest detail. Everything she had done she wished to share with him. She asked him to write in similar detail of his own life in the valley and not to think that it was too ordinary or too mundane to record. *Nothing's ordinary,* she wrote, *if it is you who experience it.* He resolved to write to her that evening after he had seen David, and tell her about his son's first day in the mine. He put the letter away and looked up at the station clock. It read ten minutes past eight. He wondered why he did not hear its ticking as he did every time he waited for the Cardiff train. He had a strange feeling that time had stopped. Then he heard the hooter and his heart froze.

He had heard it before, that sound, some years ago when the pit had exploded. His knees seemed to be melting. He looked back at the village and saw a column of dirt and smoke rising from the pit and in its occasional clearance in the wind he saw the pithead winding gear like a black tombstone against the sky. Then he found himself running with the speed of a stag fearfully seeking its imperiled young. On his way to the pit he prayed with fervor. Please God, not David. Not my David. Along the railroad tracks he was alone for a while, and then suddenly and silently he found himself among a vast crowd stumbling up the slope to the pithead.

He was nearing the Huts now, and what he saw appalled him. They in no way resembled the buildings he had left only a short while ago. For what had been Dai Davies's dwelling was now a mass of rubble, wrecked by the blast of the explosion. Thank God David was out of there, Leon heard himself say, but then he realized what other hell David now dwelled in. He realized that somewhere, underneath that heap of stones, lay the woman for whom he had left his tribe. Her mother, too, since both of them were still in bed when he had called to say good-bye to his son.

The whole village was assembled at the pithead, mostly women and children. The men who were there were old and coughing and had seen it all before. Other men, those who had shortly before come off the night shift, had risen from their beds to go down once again in the hope of rescue. Three ambulances pulled up at the foot of the slope and waited. Back in the village, Jones the undertaker went into his timber yard behind his house, and silently took stock.

They whispered around the pithead, as if the lives of the men depended on their silence. The black and red uniforms of the Salvation Army filtered among them, but for the most part they were given a wide berth. It was too soon for that kind of comfort. Much too soon.

The first cage of men went down. In it Leon recognized the pit manager, Edward Shaw, whom he had once seen at a meeting. It can't be that bad, he hoped, if the boss is going down. He wouldn't put himself in any danger. The others took the same hope from the sight of him, and slowly they began to talk to neighbors, to break the silence that boded so ill. Leon looked down the slope at the Huts. A crowd of men were attempting to clear the wreckage. He felt he should go down and help them, but his heart was pinned to the pithead, where at least there was still some hope of life. Down there among the Huts, all hope had been abandoned.

They waited.

It was early in the afternoon when the first bodies were brought up from underground. The women waited, their feet itching to run to the stretchers, yet fixed by fear to the ground. Leon hovered. He did not have a woman's fortitude. He moved trembling to the stretchers. The bodies were long, too long for children, and he uttered a shameful cry of relief.

"I'll go home and tell his wife," he heard one of the rescuers say. Then the men saw her in the crowd, and hung back fearfully.

"I'll come with you," another said.

Leon saw them walk like mourners through the crowd. Then they stopped before a young woman, a baby in her arms. They said nothing to her for she knew the news they bore.

They brought up forty more bodies that day, and with the appearance of each sorry batch, Leon crept to the cage, his heart bursting. As night fell, rumor spread that there were fires below, unreachable, unquenchable. The west district of the mine was the worst. There, all ventilation was blocked. There was little hope of any survivors from that quarter. The women didn't know where in the mine their men worked. Underground was underground and all of it was dangerous. Now they did not care to inquire of the management where their men were stationed. Death could not be muted by its location. Only a little bit dead your son, Mrs. Evans. Not much suffocated your husband, Mrs. Williams. Whether in the west quarter, east, north, or south, *death* was a word that could not be gently spoken.

When night fell, a woman's cry of "Murder" rang through the crowd, for word had spread that the explosion had been caused by gas from a naked light. That in itself could have been controlled, but the fires were fed by the coal dust, that ominous word that for years had been on the tip of Gilbert Whitcombe's tongue, a tongue that probably now lay shriveled and charred in the dust.

The crowd thinned out. Women took their children home, numb with despair. Leon stayed. He would stay there until David came to the surface. He had nothing to go home for, not yet. He prayed incessantly. He prayed first for God to forgive him, to forgive his desertion, and his neglect. He needed to be pardoned for that, before he could ask for His favors. A lump rose in his throat at the thought that if David died, it was God's punishment for his own heresy. He waited and he prayed. His legs began to ache with fatigue and he realized he'd been standing all day. He made for a bench farther up the slope, and as he sat down a cramp shot from his ankle to his calf. He stretched his leg, then relaxed, and almost immediately fell into a sleep. He was woken by a gentle tap on his shoulder.

"What's happened?" he cried, his waking thought on his son. Had they come to tell him that he need wait no longer? It was still dark. He had slept only a little while and he peered at the Salvation Army lady who stood by his side, a bowl of soup in her hand.

"Have some soup," she said. "It will warm you."

He could have blessed her for having no news to give him. He took the soup and realized that he'd had nothing to eat all day.

"I'll bring you a ham sandwich," the woman said.

"No," Leon almost shouted. Not that. Never in his life had he touched the meat of the pig. When Margaret wanted to eat it, she would go to Gran and Gramp's, but she never brought it into the cottage. Then he remembered Margaret, and chiding himself for his negligence, he hurriedly drank his soup and went down the slope to the Huts. The wreckage was almost clear. A few men, working by the light of miners' lamps, were boarding up windows and doors. When Leon approached the light, they recognized him. Jenkins, the village blacksmith, was the only one who could look him in the eye. "She's gone, Mr. Bindel," he said gently. He didn't know how to call her. She hadn't been his proper wife for a long time. "She's gone," he said again. "Her and her Mam. Six of them died in these Huts."

"Where are they?" Leon said.

"In the funeral parlor on the hill. Nice and tidy. Couldn't have felt a thing. In bed they were. It was all sudden like."

"Thank you," Leon said, and he moved away. He wondered whether he should make arrangements for their funeral. But quickly he dismissed the thought. It was a husband's job to bury his wife, a father's job to bury his daughter. When Dai Davies came up from the pit, he would break the news gently and he would hold David in his arms and tell him about his mother. Though Leon had a deep affection for both women, his eyes remained dry and he was glad of it. Because in this agony of waiting, he did not trust his tears. He returned to his bench and accepted the cup of tea that was brought to him. Then he dozed fitfully until morning light.

Over the next hour the women of the village came to the hill and so began the second day's vigil. It began with hope. Four survivors stumbled out of the cage. They were black with smoke and coal and fear, and their cold unbelieving eyes, strained by the sudden light, told of the hell they had seen below. Some women rushed to greet them, and some plied them with questions. But they were silent, all of them. What they had to say was untellable. Leon watched them as they emerged. All grown men, and not a boy among them. Later that morning the reporters from the south Wales press converged on the pithead. They were seen to go straight to the pit manager's office. Then after a while they mingled with the waiting crowd, taking names that many were loath to give, but finally offering in return the information they had gleaned from the management office.

The fires were still raging. That was clear from the appearance
of fire engines and firemen who had come from all over the valley. Ventilation to the west district of the mine was still blocked.
Much rubble had been cleared. There was still hope of survivors.
And so the day passed. Many bodies were brought up that day,
and in several shifts. No one of the crowd counted how many, for
each of them was counting for her own—a husband, a father, a
son, a brother, or sometimes all of them, for mining in the valley
was a family pursuit. But rumor had it that over a hundred bodies came up that day, many of them charred beyond recognition.
As the earth gave up its toll, Leon tiptoed toward the cages, and
gauged the measure of each body. There were many boys among
the dead that day, and some of them unrecognizable. He wondered whether he should go to the manager's office. But he was
afraid. He would sooner wait and hope. During the day an official
approached a board in front of the pithead and pinned up a
notice. Then he walked away, ashamed. The crowd stared at it.
They knew what it was, and they did not want to see it. At least
not publicly, because their possible grief was private. But Leon
was drawn toward the board.

The names of the dead were in alphabetical order. So he did
not have far to scan for Bindel. It was clearly not there, but he
did not trust its absence. Perhaps Margaret had registered him as
Davies. A little farther down, the Davieses began. About twenty
of them, for it was a common name in the valley. There were two
David Davieses and either of them could have applied to his son
or Gramp, and Leon's heart froze. He looked quickly at the addresses in the opposite column, but both David Davieses lived in
Stanley Street. Then he scanned the address column. Only one
lived in the Huts. He looked at the name. Morgan Jones, the
tenor in the Male Voice Choir. He turned away, the tears flowing
freely now, and he did nothing to restrain them. He went back to
his bench and he waited. More men were brought up that day,
and a few of them were alive. Those who could walk were fortified by soup and tea, and besieged by reporters. But none of them
wanted to speak. For their own reasons they had joined the conspiracy of silence that reigned about events underground. Their
reasons were not those of the management, whose silence alibied
the long history of their negligence. The rescued men held a survivor's reticence, that silence of embarrassment and shame. They
took their women's arms and made their way home. But none of

them, either the dead or the living, were Dai Davies or David Bindel.

Leon waited. He would not leave the pithead. The waiting women came and went, for they had children to see to, meals to serve, brass to polish, doorsteps to scrub. Somehow or other, life had to continue. As they left, some burdened Leon with their waiting. "Keep your eyes open for my Morgan, my Trevor, my Gwylim," so he felt he was keeping vigil for them all. The Salvation Army lady kept a special eye on Leon. She plied him with soups and teas. Over the last few days she had learned his history, and once she had sat by him on the bench and offered up a special prayer for his son. The Almighty listens to all of us, she had said, and Leon had thanked her, hoping that his prayers and hers would not lead God into confusion.

On the third day, Mr. Shaw finally made an appearance. He stood on crates of orange boxes that the colliers had hurriedly erected in front of the notice board, and as he mounted the wooden platform, the women surged toward him. He had news, and they could no longer postpone its hearing.

Leon moved with them, taking the arms of two women to help them up the slope. It was the third day and they were still dry-eyed. They looked angry, defiant, and unafraid.

"I have to tell you," he began without any preamble, "that the prospect of any more survivors is very dim. The fires are still smoldering underground, and those districts that are accessible have already been cleared. We are doing our very best to tunnel through to the west quarter, and to unblock the ventilation areas, but we cannot any longer hope that anyone trapped in that quarter is still alive. I'm very sorry."

He stepped down quickly from the makeshift platform and made for his office as if he feared a lynching. Still they waited there, as if they had not heard one syllable of what he had said. After a while they heard the creaking of a cage, and they drew back, fearful of its cargo. They waited until the cage bar was lifted, and out of it two rescuers led a horse. It was unsteady on its legs and had to be urged along.

"The horses live," a woman shouted. "Men come cheap." She rushed to the poor animal and pounded it with her fists, until a Salvation Army woman restrained her, and led her away. Later on that day, they brought up more bodies and at nightfall another list was pinned on the board. Leon made his weary way toward it, peering in the light of the miners' lamps for the Bindel name. His finger trembled over the Davieses, but none of them lived in the Huts. There was still hope, he decided. He went back to his bench and he waited.

Night and day he stayed there, as the stubble on his chin grew bearded and the lists on the notice board multiplied. On the seventh day, he looked down over the valley and it was black with funeral. The women had begun to bury their dead. That day, the bodies of another eighty men and boys were brought to the surface, but no Bindel appeared on the lists, and no Dai Davies either. They were sticking together, old Gramp and little Dovidle, Leon thought. They would look after each other. Then he began to wonder how he would break the news to them that Gran and Margaret were dead. He would take them home first, he decided, back to his cottage, and he would make them sleep the day away. He wondered whether there were clean sheets in the linen cupboard and what was in the larder for them to eat. He would go shopping while they were sleeping, he decided, he might even buy a bottle of wine to celebrate their return. Then when they had toasted their survival, he would gently break the news.

All day he sat there waiting, while his fever grew and his nerve ends trembled, and anxiety and hopelessness gradually overwhelmed him.

When he woke up on his bench on the morning of the eighth day, it was already late, and he heard the noon chimes from the church bell in the valley. He had slept overlong and he chided himself. He had to go shopping. There was so much to do. The fever was still on him, and he shivered in its delirium. Another notice had been put up on the board while he was sleeping. He trembled at the silence about him. His eyes were still half closed and when he opened them wide he saw that the pithead was almost deserted. Even the Salvation Army had left; it was the final indication to Leon that all hope had been abandoned. He tiptoed across the slope to the notice board. Nothing. A rider was appended to the latest bulletin. It announced a tally of four hundred and six bodies recovered. Thirty-three bodies were buried underground in the west wing and could not be retrieved. All rescue attempts had been abandoned. A list of their names was appended; but that list Leon refused to read.

He refused to believe it. He returned to his bench and he

waited. And there he sat, most of the day, looking at the motionless winding gear of the pit, and the occasional collier who passed
by in the gloom. Late in the afternoon, one of them approached
him. "Mr. Bindel?" he said sadly.

Leon nodded.

"I'm sorry about your boy," he said. "I was down there. They
were in the west quarter. Him and his Gramp. Other men from
the Huts too. They didn't have a chance." He reached into his
pocket and thrust something into Leon's hand. "We joked about
it," he said, "when we were going down in the cage. I found it in
the rubble on the west side."

Leon opened his palm. On it lay the champagne cork that had
stopped up David's tea jack. Then he knew the truth.

"My David's dead," he said to the man. "And buried."

He would wait no longer. He clutched the cork and made his
way down the slope. He felt the fever leaving him, but his eyes
were still dry. He knew he must busy himself and drive his raging
body about the valley until it calmed itself. He went to the funeral parlor in the village, and made arrangements for the funerals of Gran and Margaret. Then he walked to the bluebell woods,
tramping his feet on the ground where they grew, insuring that
they would never, never grow there again. Slowly his rage was
spent and he returned to his cottage on the hill. He took off the
cloth and the flowers from the parlor table and placed the champagne cork central on the wood like a naked shrine. Then he took
sheets and cloths from the cupboard and covered the mirrors and
the pictures on the walls. Then, because he had no low stool, he
sat on the floor and offered himself to God. Thus in the Jewish
tradition, he began his seven days' mourning for his uncircumcised son. In the act of placing himself in God's hands, the tears
flowed freely and his fever abated. All night he sat, dozing from
time to time, and in his waking moments murmuring the *kaddish,* embracing all the lost of the valley in his prayer. When
morning came, he looked up and saw the figure of his brother in
the doorway. Aaron came toward him, and gave him the traditional Jewish greeting to one who is bereaved. "I wish you long
life," he said. It was an order to survive at whatever painful cost.
Then he crouched down by his brother's side, and took him in his
arms. Then Aaron broke completely and he sat on the floor by
his brother's side, and shared the days of his mourning.

During that week Zubko came from time to time and even

Pavel made the journey to the valley, and they recited the *kaddish* together. Women came too, many of them greenly widowed. They shared their own mourning with Leon. They thought his ways were strange, with the sheets on the walls and him, a grown man, suddenly bearded, sitting on the floor like a child. And his brother, too, whom they had never seen before, doing likewise. They saw the champagne cork on the table, and all of them knew its meaning, for the story had spread around the valley. But they were different from Leon Bindel. They had had the relief of burying their men and their sons. There were graves they could visit, and the good earth for flowers, stations of remembrance. But David Bindel had been buried without ceremony, with no hymn, with no prayer.

For seven days Leon sat there, and on the eighth day he rose.

"We shall go home," Aaron said, though he knew it was a meaningless term for his brother. For home is with one's kin, and a child is the closest kin of all. Leon picked up the champagne cork, then went to his room and filled his suitcase with his few possessions. Then he and his brother left the cottage, closing the ever-open door behind them. He stood on the threshold and took one last and longing look at the valley, that site of his painful rebellion. His eyes wandered over the dips and the climbs of the dales, but he did not look toward the woods. Then he closed his eyes as if to gather all his strength to imprint, forever on his mind's eye, his son's memorial. Then he turned toward the pithead and opened his eyes. He stared at it for a long time. Then he let his brother take his arm and lead him to the station.

Some years before, Barak had told Aaron that happiness would return Leon to his mother. Barak had been wrong. It was tragedy that drove Leon home. He had made his sad peace with his tribe. He went to Leipzig because it was a way of returning to his father's house, and to the mother who had never left it. He needed to see her. Unlike Aaron, she had accepted David with understanding and without reservation and now only she could comfort him. He stayed only a few days with Aaron, then he left for Leipzig. His brother took him to the station. "You're still young, brother," he said to Leon. "You will marry again and have children."

Leon nodded without a word. He means well, he tried to think, though his brother's advice was untimely. But Aaron was not one who could deal with another's grief.

"Come and see us soon," Aaron said as the train was drawing out of the station. But not too soon, he hoped, not until Leon had recovered from a grief that his brother did not have the courage to face. For it was he who had turned David out of his home, and because of that, he felt unentitled to the relief of mourning. Some wounds do not heal, even given an eternity. The scars they leave are permanent and can only be woven into the fabric of one's life.

Over the years that passed, Leon responded to such partial healing, and three years after his arrival in Leipzig, to his mother's boundless joy, he married Greta. Their first child, a boy, was born two years later and was called David. A year later, a second son was born and was named Benjamin. It was an affirmation of sorts, an act of atonement that would once and for all settle the differences between Leon and his compelling tribe.

The years passed. Once during that time, Zelda and Leon made a visit to Cardiff, leaving Greta behind with the children. There were many visitors to Aaron's house, among them Victor

Zubko, the brothers' erstwhile go-between, to whom Leon had bequeathed what was left of his Senghenydd drapery round. He came with much news from the valley, but Leon wanted none of it. There was no news Victor could bring of the valley's dead, and he had no interest in those who had survived. He declined Victor's well-meaning invitation to accompany him back to the valley; David's tomb was forever in his mind's eye, a memory that needed no nurturing. Though Aaron's welcome was lavish and unstinting, Leon was not at ease with him. Despite their reconciliation, Leon was ever mindful of its terrible cost. But what depressed him most was Chaya, and the sight of Chaya growing. David would have been about her age now, and each time he looked at her, he had to invoke God's blessing on her life, for he feared the evil eye in his heart. He was glad when they returned to Leipzig. He decided that many years would have to pass before he could meet with his brother again.

Events enforced his decision. A year after that visit marked the beginning of the first Great War. Aaron, for the first time since Chaya's birth, considered himself blessed that he had no sons. And in enemy country, Leon rejoiced in his sons' young years.

Neither Leon nor Aaron were greatly inconvenienced by the hostilities. On the contrary, Both brothers prospered. Leon's fur business was turned over to the making of army coats for the winter campaigns. Aaron, too, had obtained a similar government concession in American officers' uniforms.

By that time Chaya had qualified as a teacher. Her childhood years had not been easy. After David's death, she had slowly become estranged from her father. She became rebellious. She joined the woman-suffrage movement and actually took part in sabotage. She was caught cutting telephone wires and for this offense she was sent to prison for two months. During this time, Aaron kept himself indoors and resigned from all his community positions, so great was his shame. But he did not complain. He considered it as part of his atonement. After Chaya's release, the school reinstated her on condition that she play no more part in politics. This she agreed to do. She had made her point. Aaron heartily wished her married and off his hands. But Chaya was headstrong and independent, and few men could match her intelligence. When war had broken out, she was already of marriageable age, yet despite her beauty and her expected dowry, men were frightened of her. In their parochial orthodox eyes, her prison sentence had left a faintly whorish stain on her. Sometimes Aaron feared that she might marry out, and that thought drove him to despair. Rachel understood her daughter better than her husband, and was secretly very proud of her rebellion. But such pleasure she had to conceal from Aaron, and Chaya found herself caught between their conflicting loyalties. She was not a happy girl.

One day she was coming back from school, dawdling as was her wont, for she was never eager to reach home. Her relationship with her father was strained and silent and she avoided him as much as possible. Mealtimes were the worst, when confrontation was unavoidable. Her father's looks were a mixture of anger and despair, and her mother's verged on pity. Both feared for her future, but neither so much as she herself. Almost all her friends were already married, and though she had little time for their husbands, she was jealous of their married state. She envied them because they had been able to leave home. That for Chaya was an overriding ambition, and she knew that her only escape route was through marriage. But where could she find a husband? She had long since given up her dreams of an ideal partner, considering him now the stuff of fantasy, and she was beginning to accept that, with certain reservations, almost any man would do. It would be the most supreme betrayal of all her principles. But what use principles, she thought, if they could find such little expression in the stifling confines of her home. She looked up and saw a young man approach. He was wearing an American naval uniform and he was looking about him as if he were lost. He walked slowly, occasionally stopping to study a piece of paper in his hand. Chaya had time to appraise him. In the light of her recent decision, she imagined that he would be suitable enough. If he was nothing else, he was certainly very handsome. She thought she might smile at him, but despite her rebellious nature, Chaya was a shy girl, and deeply conventional. She lowered her eyes as he approached, and she was startled when he stopped to speak to her. She felt herself blushing at her previous thoughts, and she wished that he would go away. "Excuse me," he said, "but I'm a stranger here. D'you know where I can find this address?" He handed her the piece of paper. She did not look at it straightaway. She was still too surprised by the encounter. She was sorry that he had stopped speaking, for his accent attracted her with its promise of a thousand miles from home. He smiled at her, embarrassed by her lack of response. Then she was forced to look down at the paper, and what she saw there only served to make her blush again. She felt her heart racing.

"It's where I live," she said to the paper.

"Is your father the tailor?" he asked.

She nodded.

"And are you going home?"

She nodded again, and started walking.

"May I come with you?" he asked, walking by her side.

"If you like," she said. She hoped he did not notice the spring in her step or the infuriating blush that burned her cheeks.

"You're the first Welsh girl I've talked to," he was saying. "Are they all as shy as you?"

She did not answer.

"Not so fast," he said. "I can hardly keep up with you."

She felt two of his fingers on her elbow, and her skin seared beneath his touch. She slowed her pace and he dropped his hand.

"What's your name?" he said.

"Chaya."

"My name's Saul. Saul Weinberger."

What a relief that name would be to her father, Chaya thought. Her house was now in view and she hurried once again. "This is where I live," she called back at him.

He ran, laughing, and joined her at the door. She pulled the doorbell and hoped that her mother would answer. And when Rachel did, she caught the radiance on her daughter's face and welcomed the stranger into her house. "My husband's with a customer," she said, assuming from his uniform that he had come as a client. And then for Chaya's sake she added, "Won't you have a cup of tea while you're waiting?"

"I'll make it," Chaya said quickly. She wanted to leave her mother alone with him. She needed to know the answer to so many questions that, if she were to ask them herself, would seem brash and forward. Where did he come from? Was he on leave? Would he be going away soon? And would he ever come back? She could leave such queries to her mother. She took her time preparing the tea, then she carried the tray into the living room.

"A lawyer," her mother was saying. "And will you follow in your father's footsteps?"

He rose, seeing Chaya enter the room, and helped her with the

tray. "Probably," he said. "I'm interested in law. But the war has
to be over first."

"Are you on leave?" Rachel asked.

"Just a few days," Saul said, "and then I go on maneuvers for a
month. Which is why I hope for a fitting before I go."

"I'm sure my husband will find time for you," Rachel said.

They had barely started their tea before Chaya heard the front
door close on her father's customer. She hoped he would have
been delayed much longer. But he came into the sitting room and
joined them for tea. Saul told him how he had met his daughter
in the street and the happy coincidence of her address. Aaron
tried to hide his pleasure, so he appeared brusque and asked his
prospective customer how he could help him.

"I need an extra uniform, just like this one," he said. "I leave
at the end of the week. Then I shall be back in a month."

"In a month a fitting will be ready," Aaron said. "Then it will
be finished in a few days."

"I'm much obliged," Saul said. "You have been highly recom-
mended."

Aaron actually blushed with pleasure. He was always delighted
when his work was praised, especially in front of his daughter,
whose respect seemed so hard to win. He rose, as a signal that he
was ready to begin. "Would you come upstairs?" he said.

Saul rose, then hesitated, and addressed himself to Rachel.
"There's a small gathering at the Jewish Servicemen's Club to-
morrow night. It will be over quite early," he assured them.
"May I take Chaya with me," he asked, "if she is willing?"

"Of course," Rachel said, without needing to look at her
daughter.

He turned to Chaya. "Then I'll call for you at six o'clock," he
said.

And so the courtship of Chaya and Saul began. Chaya was at
first diffident. She did not wholly trust her feelings. She felt very
close to Saul and she questioned the ease with which she was
beginning to love him. Before meeting him, she would have settled for much less. Much less than his tenderness, his humor, his
intelligence. It seemed a miracle that he should have happened to
her at all. So at first she was wary. But Saul was patient. During
his first month on maneuvers, she missed him terribly, and when
he returned, she accepted in her heart that she loved him. Thereafter, he was often away on duty, and his leaves were few. This

heightened the tenor of their wooing. The eternal fear of his non-
return and the relief of his reappearance, gave an artificial color-
ing to their relationship. It was one of extremes and Saul often
feared that it might collapse under the strain. He decided to put it
on a surer footing. He asked her to marry him as soon as the war
was over.

For Chaya, the proposal was an overwhelming relief, for sometimes she dreaded the end of hostilities.

"I shall talk to your parents," Saul said.

"Where shall we live?"

"In America, of course."

"I'll miss them," she said, and meant it. But it pleased her
nonetheless, for she realized that through her own happiness she
had learned to forgive her father.

During the war years, there could be no postal communication
between the Bindels on either side of the front. But shortly after
the armistice, the first letter for many years came from Zelda,
crossing one that had been sent by Aaron. Zelda wrote that they
had suffered little in the war years except for the lack of contact
with those she loved. She expressed a wish to visit them very
soon. Leon and Greta were well, she added, and the two young
boys flourished. *It is strange,* she wrote, *but it is young David who
looks so like Benjamin Bindel.*

Aaron's letter told her of Chaya's impending marriage, inviting
them all to come share in the celebrations. Zelda was delighted.
She was now in her early eighties, and though still sprightly, she
knew that this would probably be her last journey to England.
She was anxious, too, for the reunion of her sons. She knew that
between Aaron and Leon there lay an uneasy no-man's-land, a
land of crossfire. Aaron, as the accused, was trapped, and there
he would remain until Leon, with his pardon, would give him
free passage. She urged Leon to make arrangements for the journey while she busied herself with her own preparations. But as
the days passed, she noticed that Leon made no move.

"I'll do it tomorrow," he kept saying when asked about train
tickets and boat reservations, arrangements at the store, and permission for the children to take time from school.

"It's only a week to the wedding," Zelda said one evening at
supper. "When *are* you going to get the tickets, Leon?"

"I'll do it tomorrow."

"You've been saying that every day," Zelda said.

Leon rose from the table. "I'm not hungry," he said, and he left the room.

"He doesn't really want to go," Greta said after a while.

"I know," Zelda said. "But can't you persuade him?"

"I wouldn't try," Greta said. "It's his own decision."

In his bedroom Leon looked at the empty suitcase that Greta had placed at the foot of the bed. But in truth he was reluctant to go to the wedding. It wasn't because of Aaron. He had forgiven his brother. His reluctance was related to Chaya. Chaya's growth. Every time a letter came from Aaron, Zelda would read it aloud at the breakfast table, and at the details about Chaya, Leon would stop up his ears. Her growth was a confirmation of each one of David's lost years. He was glad that she was soon to be married and go off to America. It was unlikely that he would ever have to set eyes on her again. He hated himself for such a thought. He did not know what to do. He knew that Aaron would be hurt if he did not share in his celebration, but he did not trust himself. For despite his happy marriage with Greta and the delight that he found in his sons, the memory of his first David—that child of his revolt—was at times as painful as it had ever been. Perhaps if he had been able to bury his boy, he could in time have overcome his grief. He had to find some way of burying David in his own heart. Then he realized that his only chance lay in a return visit to his memorial. He began to pack. He would go back to Senghenydd, and on his way he would attend Chaya's wedding.

And so they made that familiar journey from Hamburg to Tilbury once more. Familiar to them all, that is, except to David and Benjamin, who had never been on the sea before. They were very excited and once on board, Greta and Leon gave them free range to wander at will. Leon watched them. Both of them looked like Bindels; he was glad his first David had resembled Margaret. For the first time in many years, he thought about her. He had no difficulty in recalling her features, and he was glad of that, because his long neglect of her memory had always troubled him. He had loved her in his own way at that time. Now he knew in hindsight that his manner and his season had been out of joint; but Margaret was blameless in all that. He would go to her grave, too, he decided, and was astonished at the sudden relief in his heart. He went and joined his sons.

Zelda watched them from the rail. Leon was talking to them, and she presumed that he was telling them the story of how he had missed the boat from Hamburg so many years ago. But she was wrong. Most certainly it had crossed Leon's mind to tell them, but he had decided against it. For it was a story that could not be told in a vacuum. It had to be told in the context of the whole Bindel history, and that story he was reluctant to relate. Although it was his sons' inheritance, he was loath to bequeath it. Once already in his life as a father, he had assigned the burden of the Bindel history. Already he had bequeathed the survival legacy, which had turned out to be so futile. He was wary of repeating such a bequest. So instead he told them all that he could remember of their cousin Chaya, whom his sons would be meeting for the first time, in much the same way he had told his first David as they traveled together from the valley. He remembered how the boy had fiddled with his Sunday Chapel suit, forever straightening his tie and smoothing his hair, and how Leon knew at the time that no matter how his son appeared, he would never be clean and proper enough for Aaron. Now his sons, his David and Benjamin, with no care for their appearance and no fear of rejection, would, in their pure Bindeldom, be wholly accepted in his brother's house. I must not feel bitter, Leon told himself. His brother had been punished enough.

Aaron was waiting for them at Cardiff station. It was a joyful reunion. He especially welcomed David and Benjamin, giving them his exclusive attention on the way home, and since they had no common language, their exchange involved much mime and gesture.

"It's good to see you," Aaron said. "You don't know how happy I am that you came."

Leon left on the first train early the following morning, and as the train drew into the valley, he felt the excitement of one who, after a long absence, was going home. He had expected the sight of the valley to fill him with gloom, but his feelings were quite otherwise. It had been fourteen years since he had last seen the valley, and he did not recognize the faces that passed him in the street; and no one seemed to recognize him, either. He was glad of that, for he had not come on social business. He had two calls to make, two accounts to settle in his heart. He made for the pithead. From a distance he could see that the winding gear was

still, and he wondered whether the day was a holiday. As he
approached the slope, he noticed that where the Huts had once
stood was now a playing field. The slope of the pithead was covered with grass, and Leon's heart faltered as he caught sight of a
clutch of bluebells. Grass was growing where the manager's quarters had once been sited. It was clear to Leon that it was not a
working mine anymore. The bench where, for over a week, he
had trembled and waited was still there. He went toward it and
sat down in the silence and stared at the pithead. He was glad
that it was closed, that no man went down to tread on that burial
ground. The pit was closed, as closed as a grave could ever be,
and he was glad of it. He walked up to the pithead and stood at
the foot of the winding gear. There he recited the *kaddish* and for
the first time since David had died, he buried him and was able to
honor his grave. He stood there for a while, and looked toward
the valley. He followed the paths he had trod years ago, burdened
with parcels. His eyes wandered to the head of the valley, and he
dared to look at the bluebell woods, that futile schoolroom,
where his dead son had learned his lesson in survival. He walked
down the pithead slope, picking bluebells from the grass, and
made his way to the little cemetery on the hill, for he had to bury
Margaret, too. He wandered around the churchyard noting how
many hundreds of headstones bore the same date of death. *Died
in the explosion,* was the epitaph on them all. It took him some
time to find Margaret's grave. She was lying beside her mother.
He crouched on the ground and laid the bluebells between them.
The champagne cork, which had stopped David's tea jack, was
always in Leon's pocket. For fourteen years it had rested in many
linings. Leon would have felt naked without it. Now he took it
out and consigned it to where it belonged. With his fingers he dug
a gentle hole in Margaret's grave, and put the cork inside. It was
his final act of burial. Then he stood up, caressed the headstone
with his hand, and turned away.

As he walked along the adjacent path, his eyes caught a small
black headstone. It was graveless, and stood there as a memorial.
Its legend astonished him, and he read it aloud. *In memory of
David Bindel, aged fourteen, son of Leon and Margaret Bindel.
And of his Gramp, David Davies. Both killed in the explosion.
1913.*

Leon stared at it for a long time, reading its epitaph over and
over again. He wondered who could have put it there, and he

could only conclude that it was Pavel or Victor Zubko, executing their messenger service to the last. He was overwhelmed with gratitude and now he was anxious to get back to Cardiff, to meet them and to thank them and to tell them of the peace that he had found. When he reached Senghenydd station, he stood on the platform and turned to take a long last look at the valley; he knew that he would never have to visit it again.

When he reached Aaron's house, they were all busy with preparations for a prewedding supper. Rachel was in the kitchen and he offered to give her a hand. Quickly she found him something to busy himself with. They did not talk till suddenly Leon said, "Are Pavel and Zubko coming this evening?"

"Of course," she said. "They both look forward to seeing you."

"And I them," Leon said. "Very much."

"Has Senghenydd changed?" She broached the subject gently.

"Not much," he said. "The pit is closed."

"Did you go to the little cemetery on the hill?" she asked.

He looked at her, and she was smiling.

"Did you see it?" she asked.

Then he knew that it was neither Pavel nor Zubko who had placed that memorial. "Aaron?" he said softly.

She nodded.

Once again in his mind he read the epitaph. In it, Aaron had at last acknowledged his brother's marriage and, moreover, with *Gramp*, David's lineage. He could have done no more. Leon left the kitchen and went to find his brother. Aaron was alone in the dining room, arranging chairs. He went to him and embraced him. "Thank you, Aaron," he said. "You have helped me to bury him."

That night at the party Leon was able to talk to Chaya for the first time.

In the Cardiff Jewish community, Chaya Bindel's nuptials were the event of the year, and when they were over, Chaya and Saul left for their new home in America. Leon stayed on with his family for a week, and it was clear that when they left his brother would be very lonely. Zelda sensed it too, and she declared that she would like to stay in Cardiff for a while. Perhaps Aaron would make her a new coat, and she and Rachel could spend time together. Aaron was grateful for her offer, and they both enjoined her to stay as long as she wished.

At the end of that week, Aaron took Leon and the little boys to the station.

"Do you think of going to settle in America?" Leon asked.

"I don't know," Aaron said. "We shall miss her, of course, but I think the Bindels have wandered enough. It's a pity that we are all so far apart."

But that's the accident of Jewish history, Leon thought. Chaya was in America only because Saul Weinberger's father had found an honest ticket merchant at the Hamburg docks. Aaron was in Wales only because one night Pavel had dropped into Zemach's tavern in Odessa. Their locations were all accidents of history.

"Will you stay in Germany?" Aaron asked.

"It's my home, my accidental home," Leon said. "Like Wales is yours."

"And your children?"

Leon bundled the two boys onto the train. Then he embraced his brother.

"Don't worry, Aaron," Leon said. "We shall survive."

Then he, too, boarded the train. He held his children's hands. Thus David and Benjamin Bindel, the fourth of the generations of Bindels from the Ukraine to Bessarabia, from Odessa to England, and from England to Germany, set forth on their journey to a land where their time-honored minstrel would soon be screaming.

PART THREE

❦

The Book of Benjamin and David

Germany. The accidental home of the fourth generation of the brothers Bindel. Germany is not a good word for the Jews. And never will nor ever should be. Even when time has blurred and distorted history, that word will sear each Jewish tongue even if its cause is long forgotten. For what happened in that land in the fourth traceable Bindel generation was a pageant of horror beyond any human imagination.

But that pageant was yet to come. In the 1920s the country was suffering from a postwar depression. For Leon and Greta Bindel, who in their own and in their forefathers' time had lurched from one catastrophe to another, the deprivations were not unduly disturbing. Leon Bindel did not feel personally diminished by the defeat, as did most of his compatriots. For Leon had never been a patriotic German. If he felt patriotism at all, those feelings centered around the land of his childhood, for in that land lay the bones of many he had loved. Greta was of the same unpatriotic mind, and their life together was smooth, happy, and unfettered by the frustrations of the conquered spirit. The fur business, even in the postwar years, still earned Leon a good living. David and Benjamin were well settled in their school, and within two years they could look forward to David's bar mitzvah.

Only one event had marred the even tenor of their lives. A short while after Chaya's wedding, a raging epidemic of Spanish influenza had spread throughout the English ports, and Zelda, in her rugged health and prime, had been one of its first victims. Leon had returned to Cardiff in response to Aaron's urgent telegram. On the train, on the boat, and on the train again, he had prayed that she would keep her dying until his arrival. He had been deprived of farewell to his father, and that deprivation had prolonged his grief. He prayed to see her alive once more, so that he could hold her hand into her dying. To see that hand loosen as

her life ebbed away, to know, to hear, to feel, beyond any shadow
of future doubt, that his mother was dead. And then, in that
painful knowledge, to give time, time to heal. He'd reached his
brother's house, and the front door was open, so that no obstacle
should delay his arrival. The house smelled of mortality and he
nosed it out, rushing upstairs to its source. She lay there, strug-
gling and bursting with death, keeping it in until he came. Leon
took her hand and she gripped it, a small smile laboring on her
lips. "I love you, Leon," she said, and he watched as the smile
faded, and her hand grew limp, and her head turned and stared
unseeing at the wall. His mother had given him much to wonder
at in his life, Leon thought, her strength, her fortitude, and her
talent for joy. But the manner of her dying was the greatest and
most wondrous gift of all.

He looked up and saw Aaron and Rachel for the first time.
They were standing at the foot of the bed. Rachel held Aaron's
hand, and she stretched her arm toward Leon, and together they
embraced their loss. The following day they buried her. Now
Aaron no longer thought of joining Chaya in America. Once in
his lifetime he had left his dead. He would not do it a second
time.

When Leon returned to Leipzig, he found it hard to enter his
mother's room. But every day Greta left the door open, and over
the months she refurnished it, keeping those small intimate
things that Zelda had loved. The children began to play in there,
and slowly the room lived again.

Leon missed Zelda terribly, together with his first David,
whose death her own death recalled. But he took great joy in his
sons, and curiosity, too, for each was different from the other.
David was open, responsive, and affectionate, while Benjamin
maintained a reserve that could sometimes be construed as coldness. He was studious, too, far more diligent than David, who
treated school as a continuing holiday and did little more work
than was necessary to get by. David had many friends, and
whether or not his choice was deliberate, they were all Jewish.
The school was a state establishment and though the numbers of
Jewish pupils were small, they all seemed to congregate together,
in isolation from the others, in some sort of united front. But
Benjamin was a loner. He had one friend in the school, a non-
Jew. Hans Dreiser. Hans was the son of a truck driver, but it was
not Hans's intention to follow in his father's footsteps, although

Kurt Dreiser thought he could do no better. This intention little Hans shared with Benjamin, who was equally determined not to enter the fur trade. Benjamin had set his sights on becoming a doctor and Hans had decided on a career as a scientist. Each of them went their own lone ways, coming together from time to time in a state of firm and enduring friendship that Leon knew would last a lifetime.

Leon had noticed that when David's friends came to the house, Benjamin would withdraw to Zelda's room and stay there until they had gone.

"They think they're so special," Benjamin said. "They stick together. They're asking for trouble. They've just got to be so different from everybody else."

In his son's words Leon heard the distant echoes of his own futile rebellion, and it did not please him.

"Who are *they?*" he asked.

"Jews," Benjamin said, with no hesitation. He clearly felt no sense of betrayal. "Especially the religious ones. The *ostjuden,*" he added.

Leon shuddered. "Those *ostjuden,*" he said, trying to control the anger in his voice, "they're you, me, your mother, your grandfather. We are all of us *ostjuden,* Jews from the East, and if you despise them, you despise yourself." Yes, he thought, that in sum and substance was the lesson he had learned from his own tribal desertion. The alarming lesson of one's own identity. He had learned it well, and his return to the fold had been as un-equivocal and as assertive as his straying. Since the death of his pit-boy son, he had embraced Judaism with a passion, compensating for all those lost years. He looked now at his younger son, his Benjamin, that son of his right hand, and he sniffed the Jew-fear in him and it saddened him. He wondered whether this was the time to tell him Grandpa Jakob's story, and the story of his own grandfather after whom he himself was named. But Leon held his tongue. He would not burden his children with Grandpa Jakob's song of survival. Not again. There was no czar in Germany. Even in Russia the czardom and all its tyranny had been overthrown. His children would grow up freely and would survive in the natural order of things. So, instead, he held Benjamin by the shoulders and said, "You are a Jew, Benjamin. Remember that. In our history, there have been enough people who have hated us and persecuted us. That is no reason for Jews to hate

themselves." He held him in his arms. He could not be angry
with him, for those same feelings of self-hate and shame had
assaulted him in a Hamburg cell all those years ago. He did not
want his son to experiment as he himself had done.

Benjamin detached himself from his father's hold. "I'm going
over to Hans's," he said.

"Wear a scarf," Leon said helplessly. "It's cold outside." At
least he could deal with his son's bodily welfare. But he feared for
his spirit.

Two years later, in 1922, the family prepared for David's bar
mitzvah.

"It will be your turn next, Benjamin," Greta said as they all set
out for the synagogue.

"I don't want a bar mitzvah," Benjamin said. And then, with
some determination, "I'm not going to have one."

Greta looked at Leon and shook her head. There was no point
in discussing it. "Let's not spoil David's day, Benji," she said.

Once again Leon thought of Grandpa Jakob. Throughout the
Bindel generations, it had been the bar mitzvah day of the eldest
born that had timed the bequest of Grandpa Jakob's legacy. His
own father had taken his sons to the forest on Aaron's day of
initiation; he himself had taken his first David into the bluebell
woods on his thirteenth birthday. Now was surely the time to tell
his second David, perhaps more for Benjamin's sake than for
David's. But Leon was loath to speak those words again, for the
explosion had embittered each one of them.

After the ceremony, the party was held in the house. There
was a small sprinkling of non-Jewish guests, David's form master, who had been invited at David's request, little Hans Dreiser
and his parents, invited likewise by Benjamin. It was the first
time that Leon had met Hans's father and he warmed to him
immediately because of his resemblance to Dai Davies of
Senghenydd. Like Dai, Kurt Dreiser was a fighter, a strong union
man, and he lost no time in putting his case to the sundry furriers
and publishers around the buffet table. Any platform would do.
He found a ready if hostile ear in Dr. Georg Fuchs, the Bindel
family doctor, not a Jew, who bristled at any premise that hinted
of Communism. But he loved a good argument, and the two of
them spent some time together.

The other topic of conversation, confined to the Jewish guests,
was Palestine and Zionism, a relatively new and exciting move-

ment that fired the imagination and nurtured the seeds of whatever patriotism lay dormant in the heart of the exiled Jew. Five
years before had seen the Balfour Declaration, which favored the
establishment in Palestine of a national home for the Jewish people. There were those among the guests that night who felt that
the Jews had a duty first to the country of their birth. This notion
was held by those Jews who had been born in Germany, and their
fathers and grandfathers before them. But those of the Bindels'
history were of the opposite opinion. They knew all there was to
know about scapegoating in the land of one's birth. It was at this
point in the argument that Kurt Dreiser suggested that anti-Semitism had nothing to do with race or religion, but was simply due
to economic causes. "There's no anti-Semitism under Communism," he said.

Leon knew that Kurt Dreiser was wrong. "Even in a Communist country," Leon argued, "whenever anything goes wrong,
they need to find someone to blame and hold responsible. It's
usually the Jews."

Kurt Dreiser smiled. "On that," he said, "we must agree to
differ."

Almost a year later, in 1923, when Benjamin's bar mitzvah
approached, he was adamant in his refusal. Leon knew better
than to compel him. He could not learn to love his tribe by force.
But the course of events would force him to learn to love them, or
at least to belong to them. For in that same year of Benjamin's
refusal, a young man sat in a cell in a Munich prison writing a
book. And in that book, which he called *Mein Kampf*, he made it
clear that Benjamin and his kind would have little option but to
belong. That for non-Aryans, there would be no choices. But that
was a lesson Benjamin would learn much later and to his cost.

This basic difference of opinion between the two brothers was
only relieved when Benjamin left home to study medicine at the
University of Dresden. Young Hans went with him to study elec-
tronics, and in that same year, David entered his father's business.

During his lifetime old Barak had built up a profitable fur
concern. Under Leon's subsequent management the business had
further prospered. With Greta's help and encouragement, Leon
had discovered in himself an untapped talent that had for so long
lain dormant in his Senghenydd days. By the time young David

entered the business in the late 1920s, it was thriving, and the
Bindel household lived unsparingly on its profits. At about this
time, David met Sarah. Since his late teens he had been a member
of a group of young Zionists who met every week and debated
different aspects of Zionist history and discussed the possibilities
of settlement in the Promised Land. Already hundreds of pio-
neers from Eastern Europe had opted for a life on the soil, and
there was much romanticism attached to that pioneering spirit.
Already the young movement had gathered a repertoire of nationalist songs and it was the custom of David's group to meet on
a Sabbath to sing, to dance, and to dream of settling in their
ancient home. It was on one of these Sabbath gatherings that
David had met Sarah Biedermayer, daughter of a tailor who lived
in the poorer quarter of Leipzig. Her father, like David's, was
from Russia, and he too had ridden the train through Prussia to
Hamburg. There, the family had run out of money and had had
no option but to stay, and for Mr. Biedermayer to ply his portable trade. But there were hundreds of others doing likewise in
Hamburg at the time. Sarah's father had heard of the fur business
in Leipzig, and the shortage of fur cutters in that city. With a
little training, he could adapt his tailoring skills. So he had come
with his family to Leipzig. But he discovered that fur cutters in
Leipzig were as plentiful as tailors in Hamburg, so Mr.
Biedermayer had settled for a poor living in his old and known
trade. Sarah was his only child. She worked as a clerk in a printing firm.

The wedding was set for the summer, when Benjamin would
return from Dresden. Leon dispatched invitations to Aaron and
Rachel, urging them to share in his celebrations, as he had done
with them at Chaya's wedding. Aaron replied that they would
both be happy to make the journey.

It was a very hot day at the end of July. The synagogue was
crowded with the Bindel and Biedermayer connections. Though
there was much disparity in their classes, their common history
and tradition were so strong a binding factor that there was no
unease between them. When the marriage ceremony was complete, and David trod the glass under his foot, a great cry of
"Mazeltov" rang through the synagogue, and Leon was suddenly
troubled by that old and nagging concern. My son is married, he
thought, and he has not yet inherited. He will have children of
his own, and he will have no story to tell them of his past. In his

grandchildren's life, wherever they may be, a minstrel might well be singing that song of survival, and their ears will not be tuned to hear its melody. He was assailed by guilt.

They adjourned to the house after the ceremony. In Leon and Aaron's memories of the Odessa tavern, there had been many births to celebrate, but only one wedding. The fire had quenched all the loving that might have been. But as the brothers looked around the room, they thought that tavern celebration would have been much like this one, with the same menu of portable and durable food, the same timid segregation of the women and the men and the daring fraternizations of the younger generations who, in their own time and ripe season, would assume the separateness of their present elders.

The talk turned to politics and the inevitable discussion of the new Nazi party. Most of the guests preferred to dismiss it as an overnight phenomenon, but their dismissal was desperate and hid their fears of its possible success. For Hitler was a name no better for the Jews than the czar's. Those of the guests who were *ostjuden* refrained from discussion. For they had long been schooled in alarm and the recognition of omens and they did not want to disquiet their new compatriots who had lived on German soil for generations and who counted themselves as true Teutons. Benjamin, who until that time had stood on the sidelines of the argument, now voiced his opinion. "We would have nothing to fear if only we would assimilate," he said.

It was a courageous suggestion to make in such a gathering, and though many of the guests agreed with him and were attempting that very assimilation in their own private lives, they did not think the occasion was a timely moment for such an argument. Leon was incensed at his son's suggestion, and again he thought of Grandpa Jakob's legacy and again he put it aside.

"It takes two to assimilate," he said quietly. "In Odessa, those Jews who baptized themselves did not escape pogrom."

"But this is not Odessa, Papa," Benjamin insisted.

And then the glass shattered.

The guests did not move. But they turned their heads slowly and viewed the large bay windows, the huge brick that had landed on the buffet table, and the group of young Brownshirts framed in the shattered glass.

"Down with the Yids," they crowed, over and over again,

gloating over their handiwork and celebrating it with their chanting.

Miraculously no one was hurt. Most of the glass had fallen
back into the street.

"Rich bloody swine," one of the hooligans shouted, piercing
the silence.

Greta had left the room meanwhile, and returned with two
screens that Aaron helped her assemble to shut off the room from
the street. Then, when that was done, she removed the bricks
from the table and rearranged the food that had not been
touched.

Young Hans Dreiser had also left the room, and the guests
could hear him outside on the street shouting at the ruffians and
ordering them away. It took some courage, Leon thought, to go
out there alone.

"Jew-lover," they heard them baiting. "You'll get it too, when
the time comes."

"He ought to come inside," Dr. Fuchs said. "He'll get hurt."

Greta urged the guests to take more food and to carry on as if
there had been no disturbance, but it was difficult to pretend that
nothing had happened. David put his arm around his bride in a
gesture of protection. Benjamin was standing white-faced at his
side. David turned to his brother, and in the silence of the room
he shouted, "Go Benjamin. Assimilate."

"They're just a hooligan minority," Benjamin said. "It doesn't
destroy my argument."

Leon could contain himself no longer. The voice of Grandpa
Jakob and his minstrel song of survival rang in his ear. "Come
here, Benjamin," he said. He was at pains to control his voice,
which was trembling with rage. "Come here," he almost shouted.
"You too, David."

They went to his side, hearing the urgency in his voice and
fearing his wrath.

"Excuse us a moment," Leon said to the assembled company.
His eye caught Aaron's across the room. And Aaron, knowing
his brother's business, made his way through the guests and followed Leon out of the room. No Christmas-tree forest for David
and Benjamin, no bluebell wood, no tavern table. But location
was irrelevant to Jakob Bindel's legacy. Zelda's room as a setting
would do as well as any other.

The young men followed Leon inside. Aaron shut the door

after them, and with no preamble, Leon began to speak. "I have to tell you a story," he said. "It has to be told," he shouted, "and you're going to listen. Both of you. Especially you, Benjamin, d'you hear me?"

"I'm not a child, Papa," Benjamin said. "Neither is David."

"But you'll listen all the same," Leon said. "It's a story for grown men's ears as well as for children's. I should have told you years ago."

So he began, sharing the story with Aaron, and they told of the milk-brothers' years, of Meisels and the *kahals*, of the child recruitment and the milk-brothers' miraculous return. Leon looked at his sons and saw them once again as children and as he related the story of the milk-brothers' return to the tavern, he recalled his first David in the bluebell wood and the great light of wonder in his eye. That same childish light now flickered in the eyes of his grown sons, and for some reason it angered him, for it was no adventure story he was telling them. So he told them about the fire. When it was all finished, and only the Bindel ashes remained, he told them of Grandpa Jakob's song of survival. And they sat there, the Bindel brothers of the fourth traceable generation, and syllable by patient syllable, they inherited.

When it was over, they returned to their celebrations. The non-Jewish guests had left, leaving their hasty apologies with Greta. All except the Dreisers, who would not be counted among the deserters. Leon was grateful that they had stayed and he was mindful of young Hans's support, yet he wished now that they would go away. He needed desperately to be exclusively with his own people, to be silent with them, in a language that they all understood. For many of them, those who believed that it would never happen, had been deeply shaken by the events of the afternoon. What had troubled them most was not the actual act of vandalism. That could be ascribed to the barbarism of a lunatic fringe. It was the sudden and silent withdrawal of those gentiles whom they considered friends that disturbed them. They had sloped off in a pack as soon as the street was clear, fearing the stain of their acquaintance.

When the summer was over, Benjamin went back to Dresden with Hans. Leon took him to the station, and as they were waiting for Hans to arrive, Benjamin said, "I've been thinking about what Great-grandpa Jakob said, Papa, about friendship and love. Hans is my best friend, you know, and I firmly believe that he always will be. How would Great-grandpa Jakob have viewed Hans?"

"He did not confine friendship to those of his own faith," Leon said. "He was not that kind of Jew. If the time should ever come, God forbid, that Hans is to be tested, he will not fail. He, like any other friend, would be a cause worth dying for. But let's not be morbid," Leon laughed. Then, after a pause, "Have you got a girl friend, Benjamin?"

"I was going to tell you, Papa, but I was going to wait until after I am qualified. She's a nurse in the Dresden children's hospital."

The question burned on Leon's lips, but he dared not ask it. If, as he feared, she was not of their kind, he dared not decry it, for it would have been to deny his own Margaret and their son.

"She's called Heidi," Benjamin said.

Leon's heart sank. A name as alien to the tribal ear as Margaret.

"Heidi Chernick," Benjamin went on, and smiled. So did Leon, and from that name he guessed her background. Born in Germany of the first generation, he supposed, out of parents from the Pale. Her forename was their bid for security. Much good might it do her, he prayed, when and if a fire should rage.

"Why don't you bring her home next time?" Leon said.

Then Hans came panting along the platform as the Dresden train puffed behind him.

"Good luck," Leon said, shaking both their hands.

Benjamin qualified as a doctor in the following year, and in that same year he married Heidi. The wedding took place in Berlin, where Heidi's parents lived. Once again Aaron and Rachel came to join in the celebrations and to rejoice in Leon's first grandchild, Esther, born to David and Sarah a few months before Benjamin's wedding. Aaron was also a grandfather, for Chaya had borne two children by this time—a son and a daughter.

"D'you realize," Aaron said to his brother, "that we have both outlived our father in years?"

"Let us hope for a more peaceful death," Leon said.

"Why don't you come back to England?" Aaron asked suddenly. "It's not safe here. I have terrible feelings about this country. I haven't easily forgotten David's wedding."

"There's been nothing as bad as that since," Leon said.

"They'll never come to power. Besides, how could I leave here?
My children are here, my grandchild, my living, though like
you," Leon said, "I shall shortly retire."

"I don't mean just you," Aaron said. "I mean your whole
family. You are all in danger here."

"You worry yourself too much," Leon said. "We shall die in
our beds. Both of us."

Later, when Leon went back to Wales for Aaron's funeral, he
wished he hadn't said that. Dying in one's bed was to die of ripe
old age, and Aaron, at seventy-five, still strong and agile despite
his increasing weight, was still too young for that natural death.
Shortly after Benjamin's wedding, only a week after their return
home, Aaron, without warning, had suffered a sudden heart attack, and died before Leon could reach his side. They had buried
him next to Zelda, a further Bindel investment in Welsh soil.

"What will you do, Rachel?" Leon asked when the burial was
over. "You're welcome in our Leipzig home."

She thanked him. "There is nothing to keep me here now,
except graves. And I want to spend the rest of my life with the
living. I shall go to Chaya and be with my grandchildren."

And so, with Rachel's departure, the Bindel connection with
England was severed, as Leon's own flight from Odessa with
Zelda and Aaron had cut the cord. Leon prayed that once and for
all he could live and die in Leipzig, and that his children and his
grandchildren would never have to wander again. But as his train
drew into Leipzig station, he heard singing on the platform, and
looking out of the window, he saw a boys' choir waiting there,
their black jackboots gleaming in the sunlight, their swastika
armbands raised in Nazi salute. They were clearly there to greet
one of their leaders. Leon walked down the corridor to the back
of the train, and when it stopped, he slunk off onto the siding and
crept up the embankment to the road. What in God's name am I
doing? he thought to himself. Aaron was right. We should all get
out of here.

When he reached home, he was happy to see Benjamin there.
He had been offered a job in a Leipzig hospital. This news greatly
lifted Leon's spirits. He hoped that within the proximity of his
family, Benjamin would come back into the fold. For his younger
son still flirted with notions of assimilation. Heidi too, whose
feelings, at her parents' promptings, had always been much the
same as Benjamin's. They never went to synagogue, had few, if

any, Jewish friends, and moved almost exclusively in the rarer air
of Christian Leipzig society, to which, as a doctor, he had access.
Benjamin had ceased to argue with his brother, David, but he
mocked his attempts at Zionist fund-raising, and he pitied his
obsession with the Promised Land.

"It will lead you into trouble," he told him once, "if you're not
careful. And the rest of us as well. We're Germans," he kept
saying, over and over again, and David thought his endless repetition of that phrase was by way of convincing himself.

The next few months in Germany were a period of severe economic crisis. Unemployment rose to over six million, and many
businesses went bankrupt. David kept the fur store going, but the
Bindels had greatly to reduce their standard of living. Despite the
worsening conditions in Germany, and the growing popularity of
Adolf Hitler, they refused to believe that the Nationalist Socialist
party would assume power. Only Kurt Dreiser feared it, and
knew with certainty that it was possible. When Benjamin came to
visit his family, he brought Hans with him, as if for his protection. Hans was now one of the few non-Jewish guests who came
to the Bindel house. Leon did business with them still, or rather
David did, for nowadays the aging Leon rarely went to the store.
He and Greta spent much of their time indoors, except when
Greta went shopping for food. Then she would return with as
much as the shops could offer.

One day David approached his father with the suggestion that
they should all migrate to Palestine. In the shop on that very day,
a rowdy gang of Brownshirts had been his only customers. They
had stormed in and unhooked a sable wrap from the window
display, and one of them had modeled it, to the great amusement
of his colleagues. David had made a small effort to retrieve the
cape, but he was too frightened to do battle with them.

"It's my mother's birthday tomorrow," one of them said, and
his friend tossed him the wrap and they left the shop swinging it
between them.

David would not tell his father of the incident, but the threat of
it hung over him all day, and he felt it more and more imperative
that the family should emigrate, for Leipzig threatened to turn
into Odessa.

His father sympathized with his suggestion, but he sensed David's lack of urgent commitment to his proposal. "We're too old,

Greta and I," he said, "to uproot ourselves again. And Benjamin would never leave. But for you and your children. That is something you should think about."

"I would never leave you, Papa," David said.

The matter of emigration was not discussed again, although conditions in the country worsened. At about this time, Hans Dreiser was preparing for his wedding. His bride, Inge, was a hospital almoner whom he had met through Benjamin in their Dresden University days. The whole Bindel family were invited to the wedding. Leon and Greta were wary of accepting the invitation. They did not want to offend Hans, but the presence of Jews in a strictly non-Jewish ceremony would be something of an embarrassment to them all.

But Benjamin insisted that they accept the invitation. "His friends are not like yours, Papa," he said. "They have no prejudices. They are Communists, most of them, and anti-Semitism is just not part of their thinking."

Leon was doubtful. Communism had sprouted and flourished in the land of his birth, and he could not imagine that out of that hated soil anything beautiful or just could flower.

"He's my best friend," Benjamin kept saying, and on that account Leon could not deny him.

So the invitation was accepted. Benjamin was delighted and as he left the house that evening to return to his own, he said, "By the way, don't wear anything too showy."

He was at the door when he said it, slinking out on its echo, of which he was ashamed. Sadly, Leon watched him go. Despite his inheritance, Benjamin was still uneasy with his tribe, and it was only the undeniable and compelling family tie that kept him from rejecting them altogether.

In their bedroom, they dressed for Hans's wedding. The bed was strewn with outfits that Greta had tried and discarded. Benjamin's word *showy* rang in her ears. "Wear what you like," Leon suddenly shouted at her out of his own anger. "We must not tailor ourselves to other people's expectations, especially when those expectations are false and unjust. Wear your mink," he dared her. "Let Benjamin eat his heart out."

He took the coat from her wardrobe and laid it on the bed.

"What is Sarah wearing?" Greta asked nervously.

"She'll wear what she pleases," Leon said.

When they assembled downstairs in the living room, Sarah was

also wearing mink. Neither woman was fond of furs; they wore
them only for business occasions. But for this event their furs
were an act of defiance, at least on their husbands' parts, if not
their own.

"You look beautiful, Sarah," Leon said, and David compli-
mented his mother in like fashion.

"Are we ready?" Leon said. They linked arms and each of
them feared that they were going into battle.

They had bypassed the church ceremony. Never in his life,
even during his marriage to Margaret, had Leon entered a
church. David had inherited the same instinctive aversion, but
Benjamin had no such scruples. Indeed, he had consented to be
the best man at Hans's wedding and Leon wondered whether he
was kneeling with the rest of them, his eye on the Christ, unblink-
ing. He shuddered.

They decided to walk to the reception hall, for they did not
wish to arrive too early. None of them had any appetite for the
festivities, aware as they were of their own fears and Benjamin's
admonitions. When they entered the hall, the first person who
greeted them was Benjamin. On his face was a look of pained
disgust.

"There's a cloakroom downstairs," he hissed. "Take them off."

Sarah and Greta were ready to oblige, but Leon held their
arms. "Is it warm enough in there?" he asked.

"Everybody's left their coats," Benjamin said.

Leon let the women go, and he watched them down the stairs,
taking their coats off as they went.

Heidi was not at the ceremony. She was shortly to give birth
and, in Benjamin's eyes, looked too ungainly to make a public
appearance. Leon prayed nightly that Heidi would deliver a girl,
and thus release Benjamin from a decision regarding circumcision.

"Was it a nice ceremony?" David asked, feeling the need for
conversation, however trivial, for the three of them stood together in public view and were clearly, even without mink, outsiders. For the other guests swept past them. Leon very much
wanted to go home. Greta and Sarah reappeared and Benjamin
led them into the reception hall. Hans and his bride were waiting
to greet them. Hans introduced his wife and welcomed the
Bindels effusively. He left the receiving line and escorted them to

a group of people in the hall with whom he knew they would feel at ease.

"This is Dr. Luber," he said. "Benjamin's professor of medicine from Dresden. And Mrs. Luber." Then, having introduced a topic of conversation, he left them and rejoined his bride. Benjamin had left them too, and out of the corner of his eye Leon could see him, hanging on to the end of the receiving line, affecting a great bonhomie with Hans's parents.

"So you taught my son," Leon said to Dr. Luber.

"Indeed. I hope I made a good doctor of him. He and Hans used to come often to our house in Dresden."

Leon was surprised at Dr. Luber's German. It was no purer than his own and sang distinctly of the Pale.

"Where are you from, Dr. Luber?" he asked innocently, hoping for a firmer basis for conversation than his academic acquaintance with his son.

"I am from here, of course," Dr. Luber said with some indignation. "I was born in Dresden. So were my parents. And their parents before them."

"That's interesting," Leon said. He decided to let it pass. He did not think there was a Jew in the world who could trace three generations of ancestry through a single plot of soil. He was sorry for the man who had to lie so poorly about his own provenance. His question and Dr. Luber's hasty and indignant response had somewhat halted any further conversation.

"Are you living in Leipzig now?" David practically shouted, anxious to keep the Lubers at their side because the alternative was complete isolation. He, too, wished they had never come.

"No," Dr. Luber said. "We are here only for the wedding. No, Dresden's my city. I wouldn't leave it. I was born there, and I expect that's where I shall die."

He was really making quite a production of that false birth certificate of his, Leon thought, but he made no comment. "I suppose you could say the same for us," he said, "though I myself wasn't born here. Nor my wife. But no doubt we shall stay here all our lives."

"Well, as long as the lunatics don't take over, this will be a fine country to live in, given time."

"Is there any chance of that, d'you think?" Leon said.

"I sincerely hope not," Dr. Luber said quickly, "and certainly for your sake, Mr. Bindel. They are not so well disposed to your kind."

Then David had the courage to call Luber's bluff. "Are you not of our kind, Dr. Luber?" he asked.

Dr. Luber blanched. "You are mistaken, Mr. Bindel," he said, and he took his wife's arm and steered her away from their company.

"He was stupid to leave," Greta said. "It's only proof of what he's trying to hide. I'm sorry for Jews like that," she said.

"D'you think Benjamin ever denies it?" Leon asked fearfully.

"He is too much of a coward even for that, I'm afraid," David said, and Leon was saddened by the rift between his sons. He thought of Aaron then, whom he missed terribly, and of those painful years of separation. They had finally come together in some kind of loving, but the cost had been appalling. He prayed that David and Benjamin would not have to pay such a price.

Benjamin, from the edge of the room, caught sight of his family's isolation, and after some hesitation he joined them. "What happened to the Lubers?" he said.

"They went to talk to some friends," Leon said quickly. He was suddenly afraid of his son.

"Then come and have some food," Benjamin said. Their isolation would be less conspicuous if they were eating. He led them through the hall and to the buffet at the far end. To their dismay, the Lubers were standing there, eating alone, and David quickly deflected their passage so that they could station themselves at the other end of the table. Benjamin did not notice the diversion, or if he did, he refrained from any comment. He stayed by their side, and ate a little himself, feeling their need for his protection.

"Have you thought of any names yet, Benjamin?" Greta asked.

"Gretchen, if it's a girl," Benjamin said. "And Hermann, if it's a boy."

Leon swallowed. What a long way they had come from Bessarabia. Gretchen, the Aryan ideal. And Hermann. He said nothing. He just hoped for a girl, however she was called.

The Bindels spent a good deal of time eating, though none of them were particularly hungry. There were many dishes on the table that were taboo in their diet, and Leon noticed how Dr. Luber was making a feast of the suckling pig, but with little relish on his face. Luber's self-deception could not have given him much pleasure.

David was relieved when the speeches started. That was an occasion in which they could be occupied, at least as listeners. Almost everybody who proposed a toast used the platform as a means for political statement. Reference was made to the brown-shirt scum that threatened to take over the country. But there was no fear of that, the speakers said, for the Communist party was strong and united and would not be overruled.

In time, the celebrations came to an end, and it was late enough to leave decently and without excuse. They left without Benjamin. He stayed behind, not wishing a postmortem with his family. But Leon would not have wished that either. He hoped that Hans's wedding would never be a subject of conversation between them.

When they reached home, Greta fetched him his slippers.

"Oh, Greta," he said, "it must have been so much easier in the ghetto to keep a family together. When there were no doubts, no temptations from outside."

"But it was too costly," Greta said. "Besides, look at David. He has no doubts. They're not all like Benjamin." She kissed his cheek. "Anyway," she said, "you were a Benjamin once."

"I hope Heidi has a girl," Leon said.

"We already have one granddaughter," Greta said. "A grand-son would be welcome. Besides, there must be Bindels in the next generation."

But Leon had a terrible foreboding that the Bindel line would end in Germany. The encounter with the Lubers, at Hans's wed-ding, had deeply depressed him, far more than any outward dis-play of anti-Semitism. "If our own people are our enemies," he said to Greta, "what will become of us all?"

A few weeks later, Benjamin called his father very late one night to announce the arrival of his first grandson. Leon tried to hide the disappointment in his voice, and hoped that if Benjamin heard it, he would ascribe it to the lateness of the hour.

"What will you call him?" Leon asked.

"Hermann," Benjamin said. "And Aaron, after Uncle."

It coated the pill a little. "That pleases me," Leon said. Then he dared to ask about the circumcision, for with a name like Aaron, the rite could not be denied. He heard the hesitation on the other end of the line.

"I'll talk to you about it," Benjamin said.

Leon was sickened. "Talk to your mother," he said, and he handed the phone to Greta.

They tried to get back to sleep, but Leon's mind was feverish. He realized for the first time how deeply hurt Aaron and Zelda must have been by his rebellion. He wondered whether Dr. Luber was circumcised. The following day he visited the hospital with Greta. It was the hospital where Benjamin worked and he was beaming with pride when they came in. He rushed them excitedly to the bedside to view their grandson. Benjamin bundled him from his crib and proudly placed him in his father's arms.

Leon looked at the screwed-up little face. "Aaron," he whispered.

"We're calling him Hermann," Heidi made it clear from the bed. "Aaron's only his second name." She was confirming that "Aaron" was only for form's sake. "It's in memory of your brother," she said. Heidi would always do the right thing.

"I'm very moved by that," Leon said.

She stretched out her arms and took the child. "Hermann, Hermann," she whispered in his ear. She did not want her baby confused.

Leon looked at Greta. There was something different about her hair, he thought, and the change for some reason offended him. Normally her fair hair hung loosely about her shoulders. Now it was parted and severely plaited, as if in homage to the myth of Heidi, that eternal heroine of German schoolgirls. She, too, he thought, had turned from her tribe with a vengeance equal to his own in his valley days. Leon took Greta's hand and they sat there for a while, both avoiding the question of circumcision that cried out for answer.

"How long are you staying in the hospital?" Greta asked. The length of stay might open a discussion of that vexed question. The eighth day of life was the usual timing for the ceremony.

"About a week," Heidi said.

"Don't worry," Benjamin said. "The baby will be circumcised, but here. And a doctor will do it. We don't want a religious ceremony. It will be done medically, and simply for the sake of the baby's health."

It was a compromise, in the same way Benjamin had offered Aaron in the baby's name. Leon was not dissatisfied. It was the most he could hope for. So a week later, without rabbi and without a ceremony, in the sterile confines of the hospital ward, with

Hans Dreiser as godfather, little Hermann was cut for the sake of his health and cleanliness. And let no one think otherwise. But with all that camouflage, Leon thought, with all of Benjamin's apologies, he had done more for his son than Leon himself had done for his first David.

As the weeks passed, Leon grew to love his little grandson, and he nurtured a growing hope for the continuance of the Bindel line. The family drifted back once more into the state of complacency based on the conviction that nothing would change.

And then on January the thirtieth, in the following year of 1933, everything changed. They were all in the family house that night as they listened to the news on the wireless. The announcement was cold, detached, and unsurprised. Adolf Hitler had been appointed chancellor of the Third Reich.

Benjamin said that the Third Reich wouldn't last. He insisted on it. Germany was his home and always would be, and when a year later his second son was born, he named him Heinrich, as a testimony of faith in his German future. Hans was once again the godfather. Heinrich, like Hermann, was circumcised in the hospital for the sake of his health and cleanliness, and, like Hermann, was given a second name for family appeasement. This time it was Jakob, after the Odessa patriarch. David had increased his family, too, and now had two daughters, Esther and Zelda, who, because of their gender, did not qualify for Bindel inheritance. Women, it was considered, survived by osmosis. It was only man who needed the equipment.

In the first few months of the Hitler regime, there were rumors of many arrests and disappearances, especially among the intelligentsia.

One evening Benjamin came to his father's house with the news that Dr. Luber had been arrested. "They're rounding up the Communists," he said.

That same evening Hans came to the Bindel house. He was looking for Benjamin, and Heidi had sent him to Leon's.

"They've taken my father," he said. He was trembling and they made him sit down and gave him a drink. Then they asked him what had happened. About twenty of them had come to the house, he said. They'd broken down the front door and stormed straight into the living room.

"My father was reading the paper," Hans said, "and I was fiddling with the radio. They asked him if he was Kurt Dreiser. I saw my father tremble. Then they grabbed him and took him away. Just like that. Twenty hooligans to take one defenseless old man."

"Where have they taken him?" Leon asked.

"I asked them, but they wouldn't tell me," Hans said. "They just laughed. 'Keep out of trouble,' they said, 'or you'll go the same way.' "

"Dr. Luber was taken too," Benjamin said. "D'you think the arrests are connected?"

"They have to be," Hans said. "Could you come home with me?" Hans looked at Benjamin. "Inge and my mother are terrified. We need company. I need some help, too, with the front door."

Leon opened his mouth to urge Benjamin not to go. In these times, a house that was the scene of an arrest was a contaminated place. And for a Jew, it was especially dangerous. But Hans's plea was one of friendship, and Leon could not forbid his son from offering that. But he feared for him.

"I'll come, of course," Benjamin said. "You have never hesitated to come to my house. We are both lepers in this society."

It was the first time that Leon had heard his son admit to the offense of being a Jew.

"Inge and your mother can come here anytime," Greta said. "We criminals must stick together," she laughed.

As they left, David touched Benjamin's arm. "Be careful," he pleaded. "Please be careful."

Leon noted the rare sign of loving between his sons, and though it pleased him, he was sad that it was the stress of the times that had brought them closer together.

Benjamin responded gently. "Don't worry, David," he said. "I will survive."

A few days later, Benjamin visited again, with the news that Hans's father, together with Dr. Luber and many others who belonged to the same Communist cell, had been taken to a prison near Munich. It was called Dachau. Nothing more was known. The police at headquarters would give no information as to the charge and laughed in their faces at the mention of a trial.

Winter gave way to spring and early summer, and there was still no word of Kurt Dreiser. In May of that year there had been a great fire in Leipzig. The grand square was the scene of a great burning of books. Books concerning Judaism, or those written by Jewish authors, and those that were opposed to Nazism. The auto-da-fé drew a huge crowd. Those Jews who happened to pass by ran from the crowd as if their own flesh had been charred. David Bindel happened to find himself in the crowd that day, for

his fur store was on the corner of the square. He rushed back to
his shop, but he was afraid to stay there, so he bolted the doors
and shuttered the windows and left for home. In the morning, he
found the shop looted. The windows had been daubed with the
yellow Star of David. Once more he thought of going to Palestine, and once more he broached the subject with his father. But
Leon would not leave Benjamin behind, and David would not
leave Leon. Thus, in the name of their family bond, the Bindels
colluded in their own destruction.

Over the next few months there was a lull in anti-Semitic activity. Jews dared to hope that Hitler would lose his power, and that
things would return to normal. It was the hope of desperation,
for slowly and without violence, the Jews found themselves
forced into a state of isolation. For many German Jews, who had
always considered themselves patriotic Germans with an inciden-
tal Jewish faith, it was a terrible blow to be so ostracized.

Leon Bindel had never been such a German. He had learned
from his own history the lesson of the outsider. But Benjamin
Bindel knew no such lesson and so was deeply hurt one morning
when a letter arrived from Dr. Fuchs, their family doctor, requesting the family to find a practitioner of their own kind. It had
become inconvenient, he wrote, to include Jews among his patients. Benjamin was incensed, but there was nothing that he
could do. Leon received a similar letter; he read the news with
less anger, for it did not surprise him. For a long time he and
Greta had noticed how their few non-Jewish friends would cross
the road or look the other way when a meeting seemed inevitable.
He did not blame them. He was grateful at least for their embarrassment. Only Hans Dreiser and his wife continued to be regular
visitors to the Bindel house, and though Leon urged them not to
come for their own safety, Hans would not listen. His father had
been taken almost six months ago, and there was still no news of
a possible release. Every fearful inquiry at Gestapo headquarters
produced the same blanket response. He was being dealt with,
they kept saying. And the words smacked of maltreatment and
torture.

Then, on Christmas Eve of that year, without any notice, Kurt
Dreiser came home. His family did not ask him about his imprisonment. They looked at him and they knew it all. It wasn't just
the gross loss of weight. That they could have expected. It was
his sunken, abdicated eyes that told the story of how the Nazis

had tried to break his spirit. Indeed, had probably succeeded, Hans thought, but he didn't care, for his father was alive and home.

Hans suggested that they visit the Bindels. The Bindels had sustained the whole Dreiser family during the absence of its head, and Kurt was anxious to thank them. Besides, he was so overcome with seeing his family again that he could barely accommodate the strain, and he needed neutral ground and the presence of a third party to dilute those emotions that threatened to become unmanageable.

Benjamin and Heidi were sent for, but Benjamin came alone. Leon was not surprised. He knew from Greta's hints that Benjamin and Heidi's marriage was fraying. Heidi was an outgoing woman, highly dependent on social intercourse, and with the wave of ostracism, she had grown depressed. They had few Jewish friends and, having neglected them for so long, she was too proud to seek them out now. Whereas Benjamin was changing. He no longer had the confidence that all would be well. He had been dismissed from his duties at the Leipzig General Hospital and he was now working in the Jewish Infirmary. He had been lucky to obtain the post, for after the purification measures, the hospital had been besieged with applicants from discharged Jewish doctors. He was grateful that the members of the hospital board had offered him work. And though he still winced at their separateness, both in their manner and their dress, he no longer found them a threat to his own safety. Indeed, they had saved his livelihood.

But he had another problem. The house where he lived was tied to his old hospital post, and within a month he would have to find other accommodation. He did not have enough money to buy a house, and people were now wary of renting to Jews. It was logical that he should return to the Bindel family home, where there was room in plenty. Benjamin would have welcomed that return, but he dared not suggest it to Heidi. Nowadays he spent more and more time at his father's house, so it was an unspoken agreement that Hans should meet him there.

They decided that this was a champagne occasion and they toasted Kurt's return, and as they sipped the wine, Kurt was eased into telling his story.

"They are not of the human species," he began. "I don't know who makes them or where they come from. They are primitive."

He paused. "That really is the whole of the story," he said. "What more can I tell you? We got up at four in the morning, and there was a roll call. Even when it was over, we had to stand there, barefoot and shivering. Sometimes they made us kneel with the palms of our feet upward and the guards would run along the line behind us, beating our feet for their pleasure."

Kurt's wife uttered a small scream. "I don't want to hear any more," she said.

Kurt put his arm around her. "I'll tell you one more thing," he said. "D'you know where I was last night?" He was smiling and they couldn't understand what happy memory he could have of his incarceration.

"I was being wined and dined in Nuremberg," he said.

"Wined and dined?" Hans asked. He was not curious about the location.

"Julius Streicher," Kurt went on, "that beast who publishes *Der Stürmer,* he's the provincial governor there. He entertained twelve of us at dinner, twelve of us who'd been released that day. There were SS officers at the table. We were a kind of Christmas gift for them. 'Repentant racial comrades,' Streicher called us. And they sang 'Heilige Nacht' with tears in their eyes. It was nauseating. They are a strange mixture, our people, of cruelty and sentimentality."

"Did they talk about Jews?" David was bold enough to ask.

"No," Kurt said quickly.

Too quickly, Leon thought.

"Not a word," Kurt said, and then the Bindels knew that the future of their kind had been discussed at that table and they were afraid.

"Is there any news of Dr. Luber?" Leon asked. "Were you together?"

"He's still there, I'm afraid," Kurt said. "He's Jewish. The guards said they wanted to play with him a little longer. Those were their very words." Kurt put his hand on Leon's arm. "My friend," he said, "you must leave this country. All of you. There is no future for you here."

When the Dreisers had gone, David decided to profit by Kurt's warning and so he brought up once again the subject of Palestine. He pleaded with them. "We must consider going. All of us. You heard what Kurt said."

"Kurt is not necessarily right," Benjamin said. "It will never be so bad that we have to leave. In any case, people who work in commerce or the professions are essential to the German economy. They'll leave us alone."

"What's essential about the fur trade?" David asked.

"Exports," Benjamin said, but with little conviction.

"We have never exported," Leon said. "There's nothing essential about us."

"If you listen to Hitler's speeches," David said, "it's clear that Jews are dispensable whatever their profession. At least let our children go," he pleaded.

"I won't be parted from my children," Benjamin said.

Then David wondered for the first time whether he himself should send his children away, and the possibility appalled him.

"All my life I've been running," Leon said. "Running to survive. I'm too old now to run anymore. What do you say, Greta?" he asked.

"I think we must all stay together," she said. "Whatever we decide."

"Mama's right," Benjamin said.

"She said *whatever* we decide," David reminded him.

"Heidi will never leave," Benjamin said. "I am tied to Germany."

With a shock, Leon recalled a similar bond that had rooted him in Senghenydd. A father's love for his son. But now it was Benjamin's bond that fettered them all.

If the German Jews at that time were unsure of their status, vacillating between complacency and despair, the passing of the Nuremberg Laws in 1935 made their position clear. The laws deprived Jews of citizenship. They were deemed persons of inferior status, of impure blood. They were forbidden marriage or congress with an Aryan. It was only a matter of time before their property would be confiscated and their isolation would be complete. Once more David introduced the now weary subject of emigration, and once more it was Greta who ruled that they must all stick together, which, in view of Leon's years and Benjamin's marital strife, decreed that they would stay in Germany. Over the months, at regular intervals, David would air the subject yet again, needing to keep the possibility of flight in their minds. Not one of them, not even David, considered that, in time, it would be too late.

Benjamin's housing problem became acute. They had moved into an apartment building, but now that whole complex had been sold to a party official, and he wanted it *Judenrein*. The Jewish families who lived there were thus obliged to leave, and in many cases it prompted their emigration. But in Benjamin's case there was the alternative of the Bindel family home. It was the only alternative, since Heidi's family lived in Berlin. So, with much reluctance on Heidi's part, and much welcome on Greta's, Benjamin and his family moved into the Bindel home. Now in Greta's sense they were all truly together. But in many ways the togetherness they had enjoyed until that time was splintered by Heidi's presence. She found it difficult to adjust to the Bindel way of life. Greta had always kept a Jewish house. Zelda had been responsible for that. After her death Greta had relaxed the laws a little, but they still honored all the festivals and the Sabbath. The Friday-night ceremonial supper was the high point of the week, especially for David's children, who were allowed to stay up late. But Heidi sat at the table like a stranger, her children safely tucked up in bed, away from their grandfather's constant "Aaron" and "Jakob" that he insisted upon when he played with them. Her little Hermann and Heinrich were fast asleep upstairs, undisturbed by the odd behavior of these outsiders who insisted on their differences. Greta tried to reason with her, but she sulked and was silent. Between Benjamin and herself there was little communication, and it seemed that the marriage was virtually at an end. But they would stay together, as they would stay in Germany. Leon viewed it all with desolation, and in these times he often thought of Margaret.

Benjamin's children were in kindergarten, and David's in the primary department of the same state school. One day, Sarah went to collect the children, both her own and Benjamin's. Little Zelda appeared tearful at the gate, and seemed to Sarah to look somewhat lopsided. She had left home that morning with two bright plaits over her shoulders, and one of them was missing. Sarah knew immediately what had happened, and she knew too that there was no one to whom she could complain. She took the children home and comforted Zelda as best she could. She cut her second plait and gave her hair an equal length all around. She took care not to ask how it had happened. There was no need for Zelda to relive the experience. Zelda did not want to go back to school on the following day, but Sarah and David insisted, though they were not sure whether they advised wisely. That day it was Esther's turn. She came home with a torn smock and a bruise on her cheek. She wore her scar with some pride, for it equalized her with Zelda.

Meanwhile little Hermann and Heinrich remained unscathed. Heidi was triumphantly convinced that their names protected them, until one day letters came to both Sarah and Heidi from the headmistress of the school, suggesting that they withdraw their children for their own safety. She could not be responsible for any injury they would suffer. She added that she was very sorry, but that her powers were restricted. The letter came as a tremendous shock to Heidi. For the first time she realized her lack of immunity. The children had to be schooled elsewhere, and the only alternative was the Jewish school in the Jewish quarter of the city. For Heidi it was a terrible humiliation, and she tried to persuade Benjamin that the children would be better off without schooling. But Benjamin was adamant. For the first time he berated Heidi in front of his whole family. Leon dared not look at his son, for he saw a terrible hatred in his eye.

The following morning it was Benjamin who took the children to their new school across the city, and David went with him. They had to join a queue for registration. All over Leipzig, Jewish children had been eased out of the state school system. It was midmorning before Benjamin and David were ushered into the headmaster's study. He apologized for the delay, and expressed his regret that their children's schooling had been so rudely interrupted. Zelda and Esther were registered first, and then it was Benjamin's turn to give the names of his sons. As he spoke them aloud, he felt deeply ashamed.

"Have they got other names?" the headmaster asked him.

"Aaron and Jakob," Benjamin said, and in that instant he decided henceforth that was how they would be called, at home as well as at school, whatever Heidi's objections. He wondered whether he ought to leave her.

The children could not start till the following week, so they all returned to the Bindel house. David had hoped that he and Benjamin could talk on the way home, but the presence of the children in the car inhibited a private conversation. For he needed to talk to him, or rather, he wanted to give Benjamin an opportunity to talk, to open to him his confused heart. For confused he knew it to be. Assimilation, which Benjamin had once promoted, had

BERNICE RUBENS

now been proved to be of no avail, and he was faced with a total readjustment of his values.

When they reached home, Benjamin's children proudly announced their new titles. Leon refrained from showing his delight, but Heidi was appalled by the name changes that had, at one stroke, turned her children into strangers.

"No more Hermanns and Heinrichs," Benjamin said.

Thereafter Heidi never called her children by name, and when she needed their attention, she would gently prod them.

Greta suggested that Benjamin and Heidi take a holiday, leaving the children in their keeping. But Heidi would not trust her children to the elder Bindels. They would convert them totally beyond her recognition. But she did suggest that she'd like to visit her parents in Berlin, and take her children with her. Benjamin disallowed that with the excuse that the children should not miss school, but in truth he was afraid that once out of the Bindel hold, together with her children Hermann and Heinrich, she would not return.

Lately the men of the household, even Benjamin, had taken to going to the synagogue on the Sabbath. The need for community among the Jews was becoming more acute. The synagogue was the center for news and rumor of their brethren throughout the country. And that news was always depressing. But most depressing of all were the vacant seats in the synagogue. Week by week, they emptied. In the year of 1938, a law was passed that enforced the registration of all Jewish property; it was clearly a preliminary to total confiscation. Emigration increased day by day, and each Sabbath as Leon left the synagogue with his sons, he wondered whether they were being foolhardy to stay, and whether if he, as the elder, were to insist on it, even Heidi might be persuaded to go. He broached the matter at the Sabbath lunch. Heidi gave a rare laugh. "You go if you want to," she said, "but I'm staying here with the children."

Leon looked at Benjamin, hoping for some show of resolve. But Benjamin had little appetite for battle, especially in front of his family. Besides, he was not yet sure himself that emigration was necessary. He still clung to the hope that the real German people would see the folly of their acts and, in time, desist. But there were no signs that Germany was coming to its senses. In fact, it was preparing for war.

That year in the spring, Germany annexed Austria and anti-

Jewish measures became more oppressive and widespread. Synagogues were destroyed in Munich and Nuremberg, and passports
belonging to Jews were invalidated. There was no question that
events were closing in on German Jewry and that in time they
would be trapped beyond any possibility of escape. But the
Bindels stayed.

Hans Dreiser was still a regular visitor to the Bindel home. He
brought news that Dr. Luber had finally been released. He had of
course been deprived of his university post, and he was leaving
Dresden because he couldn't bear to be ostracized by his erstwhile friends. He was coming to settle in Leipzig. Hans also
brought news of his father, whose health was failing. Ever since
his release from Dachau he had had trouble with his lungs. He
had caught a chest infection while at the camp and it had never
cleared. Now there were days when he could barely leave his bed,
so labored was his breathing.

"Why haven't you told me all this before?" Benjamin said angrily.

"My father wouldn't allow it," Hans said. "He knew you
would insist on coming regularly, and the house is under constant
surveillance. It would endanger you."

"I'll take you home," Benjamin said.

Thereafter Benjamin visited Kurt Dreiser every evening after
his hospital rounds. He reported back to the Bindels that his
condition was worsening, and that he was not likely to recover.
One evening he told Greta that Mrs. Dreiser would be very
happy if she would visit and be with her for a while, and so that
same evening, after supper, Greta went to the Dreiser house.

It was the ninth of November 1938, which later would be
known as the *Kristallnacht,* the night of broken glass. The night
Greta Bindel did not return home. At midnight, the family
started to worry. Benjamin phoned Hans and learned that Greta
had left an hour earlier. "Perhaps she had to wait a long time for
the bus."

Benjamin heard anxiety in his friend's voice. "I'll go out and
look for her," Benjamin said.

Benjamin took the car and David went with him. As they
drove through the streets, the silence unnerved them.

"It's so quiet," Benjamin said.

"It's midnight. Everyone's in bed." That would explain the
stillness, David thought, the natural silence of sleep. But he, too,

was disturbed by it. It was oppressive, menacing. They were nearing the town center when the silence broke. It broke with the
shattering of glass. In the main thoroughfare, the center of the
fur trade, the pavements were littered with the shattered remains
of shop windows. Venetian shutters lined the curb. What remained of the Bindel shop, and the one next to it, was the bare
steel armature of its erstwhile design. Fires had been started farther down the street, and a crowd of looters helped themselves to
the pickings under the very noses of the police. Benjamin drove
through the crowd as quickly as he could. It was no place for a
Jew to be seen, and certainly no time to claim ownership of the
damaged property. There would be no redress or reparation. To
claim it would be to put their lives in jeopardy. Now their fears
about their mother's well-being multiplied. They suddenly didn't
know where to look for her. Benjamin pulled up at a phone box
in a deserted street to ring home to find out whether she had
arrived. A distraught Leon answered. There was no sign of her,
but a friend had phoned to say that the synagogue was on fire.
"What's happening?" Leon almost cried.

"I don't know," Benjamin said. "Don't worry, Papa," he said.
"We'll find her."

They drove toward the bus station, having to make many de-
tours on route, avoiding the mobs of storm troopers who seemed
to have taken over the streets. A group of them marched along
the shop fronts, pausing occasionally to splash a window with
yellow paint.

By the time the brothers reached the bus station, it was deserted. "Mama," Benjamin called into the darkness, as if she
might be hiding there in the shelter, fearful of the streets.

"Benjamin?" It was Hans's voice, and he came out of the darkness toward them. "She's not here," he said. "She must have
taken the bus."

"What's going on, for heaven's sake?" David said.

"It's a pogrom," Hans answered. He had no problem with the
word, no historical precedent that would have curbed his tongue.
"It's on the radio. I heard it in the bus station office."

"Have people been killed?" Benjamin asked. He was not concerned with the burning of property or synagogues. All that was
replaceable.

"Yes," Hans said tonelessly. "They didn't say how many."

What did numbers matter, David thought. Only one mattered to them.

"I don't know where to look for her," Benjamin said.

"Let's follow the bus route," Hans suggested.

They got into the car.

"We should call home first," Benjamin said, but he made no move toward the phone box. He was loath to hear his father's anxiety yet again. "You phone, David," he said.

Hans and Benjamin waited in the car.

"I'm frightened," Benjamin said.

"You should leave. All of you. Go to America, England, even Palestine. You can still get passports."

"You're right," Benjamin said. "But first we have to find her. Then we'll leave."

From the look on David's face as he returned to the car, it was clear that there was no news from home. Heidi and Sarah were doing their best to restrain Leon from going out himself and looking for her. David got into the car and they drove off.

It was difficult to get through the streets because of the flying glass and missiles. Besides, their journey suddenly seemed pointless, for Greta was unlikely to be walking the streets. The presence of so many ambulances was unnerving. They had to swerve to give one of them right of way. Hans told Benjamin to stop the car.

"This is useless," he said, voicing the thoughts of them all. "Was she carrying identity?"

"Of course," Benjamin said. "It's the law."

"Then let's face it," Hans said softly. "Let's presume the worst. If she's hurt, they would have taken her to the Jewish Infirmary. That's where we must go."

The hospital lay on the edge of the Jewish quarter. As they approached the central street of the area, Benjamin was obliged to park the car, for the road was strewn with glass. The windows of almost every house were broken. There was wailing in the streets, and, from the little synagogue on the corner, they could see the rabbi carrying the sacred scrolls to the comparative safety of his own home.

"This is what Odessa must have looked like," David said, "after the fire."

"This is not Odessa," Benjamin practically screamed at him,

not so much in defense of his German birthright, but in the memory of the tavern fire and its fearful aftermath.

The hospital courtyard was full of ambulances, and the foyer with crowds of frightened relatives seeking news of their kin. Benjamin, in his authority as hospital doctor, was able to bypass the reception desk and go straight into casualty. David and Hans followed him. On their way, Benjamin acknowledged a colleague who was hurrying past in the other direction. But the man did not acknowledge his greeting. Benjamin turned and rushed after him, for he knew that his friend's avoidance had to do with his mother.

"Michael," he shouted.

The man turned.

"Didn't you see me?"

Michael was flustered. "Yes," he said. "I just . . . God, this place is a nightmare." And he hurried on.

In his friend's hesitation, Benjamin suddenly knew that his mother was dead.

The reception desk in casualty was besieged by inquirers. He forced his way through. The girl looked up at him and paled.

"Dr. Bindel," she said. "I was just going to phone your home." Then he knew. "My mother?" he whispered.

She nodded. Then there was a silence between them.

"Where is she?" he said.

"In the morgue."

She rose from her desk, took his arm, and led him into the registrar's office behind reception. David and Hans followed him. "Dr. Bindel," she said as she opened the door. Then she let them inside, and returned to her desk, relieved of the burden of bearing his sorrow.

"What happened?" David asked the registrar. There was panic in his voice, as if the knowledge of how she had come to die would resurrect her.

"The reports are very confused, Benjamin," Dr. Segal said. "It seems that the buses couldn't get through and the passengers had to walk. The storm troopers were taking identities of all pedestrians. They beat her up, it seems. I wouldn't look at her if I were you."

"Well, you're not me," Benjamin cried, and he put his head in his hands. "I'm sorry," he said after a while, then, turning to Hans he said, "You don't have to come if you don't want to."

"I thought of her as my family," Hans said, and the three of them left the room and made their way to the basement of the hospital.

Benjamin had never worked in pathology and he rarely went to the morgue. The basement was a tangled network of corridors and anterooms, and there was no sign posted. A few orderlies were about, wheeling empty trolleys, but Benjamin was loath to ask directions. He didn't want to inquire of strangers where his mother lay. As her son, he should know and he tried door after door with his search. Then they heard the rattle of a trolley as it moved down the corridor. They followed the noise to the morgue.

Inside, the room looked like a vast sterile filing cabinet with long drawers along each wall. "Dr. Bindel?" the attendant said as Benjamin came through the door. He led them to the far wall and placed his hand on one of the drawer handles. He left it there for a while. "Are you sure?" he said.

Benjamin nodded. Then the man pulled out the drawer and gently withdrew the sheet around the face. David took Benjamin's arm, and Hans stood aside, feeling an intruder. David did not look at Greta's face. He saw the mirror of it in his brother's horror. Benjamin put out his hand to draw the sheet down over the body.

"No," David said. "We have seen enough."

"We must see it all," Benjamin said, and his voice was strangely calm. "We must know what they have done."

He drew the sheet away. It seemed that almost every limb in Greta's body had been broken. The flesh was bruised and bloody. He touched her arms and legs gently, smoothing them in a caress, as if to reset them. Both brothers knew that their mother's death had been terrible, slow, and infinitely painful. Benjamin lifted her up by the shoulders and took her in his arms. He kissed her, then he passed her gently to David. But David held her tightly, as if willing her to live again, and there was a terrible creaking of bones as he pressed her spine against his large hands. They had broken her to pieces, and her sad and bruised skin was a fragile wrapping for the fragments of shard and bone within. He laid her down on the drawer and covered her.

"I'm sorry, Dr. Bindel," the attendant said. "We live in terrible times." He shut the drawer and its echo clanged across the chamber.

"We must go home," David said, though neither of them knew how they would tell their father. Hans did not offer to go with them. In the beginning, their mourning would be private.

Benjamin parked the car a good way from the house so that Leon would not hear their approach. They walked slowly and silently along the street and almost tiptoed to the front door. As David reached for his key, the door opened. Leon stood there. He had sensed their coming. There was no need to say anything. He looked at them for a moment and smelled the mourning on them. David took him in his arms.

"We must leave this country," he said. "We must save ourselves, Papa."

Heidi appeared in the hall. "What's happened?" she asked.

"They killed her," Benjamin said. "The storm troopers. It's a pogrom."

"But those things only happen in Russia and Poland," Heidi said, protecting her native land from such sullied words.

"They're happening here," Benjamin said coldly. "And it's only a beginning."

But as it turned out, it was a beginning on quite a large scale. Synagogues all over the country had been destroyed. Seven thousand Jewish shops were looted and wrecked. Thirty thousand Jews were arrested and sent to concentration camps, and according to the official figures, ninety-one Jews were killed.

They buried Greta a few days later. Leon had asked for her to be laid next to Barak. She had always looked upon Barak as a father, and it seemed fitting that she should lie by his side. When they reached the cemetery, they were horrified by the devastation. The wreckage of the burial ground had been part of the *Kristallnacht* celebrations. Barak's headstone lay in two pieces on top of his grave, and each piece was painted with a swastika. At the graveside, the rabbi intoned the customary burial prayers and when it was over, he did not turn away but stayed and stared at the ground for a long time. Then he lifted his head toward the mourners and said almost in a whisper, "You must leave this country. All of you who can." Then he turned and made his way out of the burial ground.

The Bindels returned home and mourned for the customary seven days, and when it was over, David broached yet again the subject of emigration. "We must go, Papa," he said. "All of us. There is nothing left for us in this country."

"There are bones," Leon practically screamed at him. Greta's death tore at his heart. "There are bones," he said again. "Bones of one I loved. All my life I have run away from my dead. This time, I shall not run. Not even in the name of survival. I am old enough. In God's eyes I have survived already. I shall not leave Greta," he cried. "I shall be buried at her side."

A few days later Leon went to the offices of the burial board of the synagogue, and reserved for himself the vacant plot alongside Greta. But Leon Bindel was never to lie there. His tomb would be a wide trench, dressed in quicklime, hundreds of miles away from this place, and he would lie there with countless others of his kind, related only by their common faith and their jagged creed of survival.

Shortly after Christmas of that same year, Kurt Dreiser died. Hans mourned him as naturally and as deeply as a son would mourn a father he loved, and that mourning bred his appetite for revenge. Mrs. Dreiser insisted that the funeral be private. Kurt had had many friends, most of them party members, and Mrs. Dreiser did not want to put them at risk at a gathering. The SS were everywhere, with their wary eyes and notebooks. It must be a family funeral, she insisted. But she made an exception with Benjamin. She loved Benjamin as she did her own son. He had attended her husband daily during his illness. She regarded him as part of the family.

Kurt Dreiser was to be cremated according to his wishes and the ceremony was to be performed in the afternoon. Benjamin took time off from the hospital. He said not a word to his family. He knew that Heidi and David would try to stop him. It was better that he tell nobody. They gathered in the courtyard of the crematorium. Mrs. Dreiser, Hans, and Inge. A stranger was there who was introduced to Benjamin as Kurt's younger brother. There were also two sisters of Mrs. Dreiser's together with their husbands. Benjamin, the only nonrelative, completed the small party.

"Everything is ready," Hans said. "Shall we go inside?" He took his mother's arm and led her into the small chapel. Benjamin and the others followed. The mourners arranged themselves in the first row, a pew of concentrated grief. The coffin, wreathed in flowers, stood on its ball bearings directly in front of them. The priest stood at the lectern, his head buzzing with hurriedly acquired information about the deceased's life, much of which was politically unspeakable. All men are human, and deserving of God's grace, he kept telling himself. That would be the theme of his sermon. Meanwhile, echoing through the hollow chapel, came the sounds of a distant choir, and when the hymn was over, the priest asked the mourners to stand. While he was reciting the funeral prayers, there was a disturbance at the back of the chapel. The doors were flung open and were heard to close behind stamping feet. Booted feet, the mourners knew, and jackbooted, too, and each of them was afraid to turn and look at the intruders' faces. But they saw the priest look toward the door. His voice faltered a little, then settled into the comfort of the prayer. When it was over, he asked the mourners to sit, and he cast a second nervous glance toward the door. Still the mourners dared not turn. The priest spoke about Kurt Dreiser in the terms of a brother. The presence of the SS guards in this holy place angered him, but he was not afraid. Indeed, their belligerent presence moved his tongue to speak out on Kurt Dreiser's behalf, to celebrate and to applaud his life, his courage and his principles. And when he spoke in this manner, the mourners trembled. They were glad when his eulogy was over. "Let us pray," he said.

The Dreiser family knelt down in the pew. But Benjamin's knees stiffened with that time-honored resistance that had dwelt in the Bindel soul for so many generations. So he sat on his wooden seat and crouched a little, hoping to make his lack of genuflection less conspicuous. The prayers continued silently until a long and solemn "Amen" from the priest signaled their end. "Let us say farewell," he said, "to our brother Kurt Dreiser, who leaves us with our grief and the memory of his courage and his glory."

Slowly the coffin moved backward on its bearings, and the slow movement of a Schubert quartet filtered through the chapel. But only for its first opening phrases, for suddenly it was rudely broken. From the back of the hall came the loud yet harmonious singing of the Horst Wessel song, its words and its music a monumental affront to the memory of a man who, all his life, had fought against the evil of which it sang. *The flag is high, the ranks are closed,/The SS march with calm and steady stride.*

Mrs. Dreiser broke into sobs and Hans's face was purple with rage. Benjamin was glad that Hans had his mother by his side, to whom he must give comfort, on whose behalf he must control his rage. But Benjamin's fury was enough for both of them. He turned without fear and, with no hesitation, he walked to the back of the chapel. They were waiting for him, laughing. He went to where they stood.

"How dare you, you scum," he hissed at them. "Get out of here."

"Identity," one of them said, as if he hadn't heard, while the other two guards grabbed Benjamin by the shoulders and kicked him behind the knees. He fell to the ground.

"So you *can* kneel," one of them said.

Benjamin's ears were burning with pain and his hand trembled as he withdrew his card of identity from his pocket. The storm trooper snatched it from him, then the other guards took his hands and forced them upward behind his back. Hot tears of anger and pain rolled down his cheeks. He turned his head then and managed to see the tail end of the coffin as it rolled toward the fire. "Farewell, comrade," he whimpered.

The guard struck him across the face. Then he held the card up to the light. "A doctor," he said. "We need his kind. I know just the place for him. Take him away."

The two guards relaxed their hold and gripped Benjamin's arms.

"Where are you taking him?" Hans was suddenly at Benjamin's side.

"You'll be told," the leader of the gang said. "But it would be better for you and the likes of you if you don't inquire." He raised his hand in salute. *"Heil Hitler,"* he said, and he goose-stepped out of the chapel.

They bundled Benjamin into a darkened van and threw him onto the floor, while they sat one on each side of him, their boots resting on his neck. Benjamin felt his bowels empty, but he would not let it humiliate him. This place would do for a sewer, and the storm troopers for sewer attendants. He had to think that way, else he would have crumbled in his shame. He was relieved to be lying down, despite the yoke on his neck. He relaxed his muscles and tried to breathe deeply, and slowly his pain ebbed. He was sorry when the van came to a stop. He had begun to doze and he would have liked to sleep forever, for he dreaded what fate awaited him. They dragged him from the van, keeping their distance.

"God, he stinks," one of them said.

"What d'you expect?" his companion said. "He's a Yid. Smells like all of them."

They threw him in a cell and they left him. Benjamin lay on the stone floor and did not move, while his eyes grew accustomed

to the darkness around him. He could smell himself, and in a
strange way it comforted him. For the smell spoke of his indignation, his weakness, and his fear, and all that made him more
human than those who assaulted him. He would sleep in that
smell and wake in it too, and it would not offend him. He looked
at his watch and noticed that the glass was broken. He put it to
his ear and heard its comforting tick. Four o'clock, it said, and he
wondered whether it was morning or afternoon. Then he remembered the funeral, only a short time ago, it seemed, so he knew
that the darkness was only in his cell. He closed his eyes. When
he awoke, or rather was suddenly awakened, he felt he had slept
for hours. But his watch showed ten minutes to five. He heard a
voice telling him to get up, and when he tried, his knees buckled
once again and a sharp pain shot through his arms. But he forced
himself to stand and to look at his captors. There were two of
them this time, but he couldn't tell whether or not they were the
same as the ones before.

"We're going on a little trip," one of them said. "You'd like
that, wouldn't you?" He kicked him on his shins.

Benjamin breathed deeply, fighting the pain, and allowed himself to be dragged from the cell and into the blinding light of the
street. But not for long. For once again he was bundled into a
van, a different one this time, one with windows. And one with
company. For there were already many men standing inside,
pressing against each other for lack of space. And still others
came after Benjamin, forcing their reluctant way inside in order
to escape the kicks of their guards. Then soon the van doors were
locked and barred and the men stared at each other, but no one
spoke as they shifted from one foot to another to try and find a
firm hold on the floor of the truck. Then suddenly the van took
off, and they could not fall because there was no space, so they
rocked and lurched until, in that rhythm, they found from each
other's bodies some means of support. They wove themselves,
body by body, into a web of common fear and apprehension, and
still none of them spoke. They could not bear to think of what
would become of them.

They traveled for many hours. Benjamin, who was taller than
most, could see out of the windows, and as it grew dark, he
deciphered a signpost, lit by the headlights of a following car. It
signaled that twenty kilometers hence lay the town of Weimar, of
which kingdom, Benjamin recalled, Goethe had once been chief

minister. He hoped that they would bypass it, and go far, far
away, miles from that place that had once spelled out his country's glory.

The van turned into a side road, and after a few miles, the road
was unmade and the van heaved its way over the bumps and the
dips, while the web of men inside held to its perfect symmetry. It
was very dark now, and it was impossible to see the terrain
through which they passed. Benjamin caught sight of a lone star
and, for the first time since the chapel, he thought of home, of his
children, of his father, David, and Heidi. And for the first time,
too, he felt despair, not on his own account, but on theirs, for
their anguish and pain at his absence. He looked at the men
around him and he knew that all of them were thinking of home.
The night had urged that recall. Some of the men were crying.
But still nobody spoke. Nobody wanted to know his neighbor's
name, where he was going and why, for any speech would have
lent credence to their present situation. They preferred to consider it as a nightmare from which they would soon awaken.

The van pulled up sharply. The door was flung open and the
human web disintegrated. They were herded into a group outside
the truck. "Get in line," one of the guards barked at them.

They shuffled themselves into some kind of order, and then
were led through a clearing to a line of buildings at the entrance
of the camp. A few guards stood there and ordered the men to
run. Mercifully the distance to the barracks was short, and once
there, they were directed to a shed and told they could sleep till
morning. Work would begin at 4:00 A.M. For all the men, the
offer of sleep was a gift indeed, and though they needed food and
warmth, their need for oblivion was even greater. There were
serried rows of straw beds on the floor, but no blankets. The men
lay down and shut their eyes against the horror of it all. As the
guards were leaving, one of the men dared to ask where they
were.

"This place is called Buchenwald," he said, "and you're not
likely to forget it."

The Buchenwald concentration camp had been opened a year
before and was, at the time of Benjamin's imprisonment, in the
last stages of its construction. It was five miles distant from the
city of Weimar in the wooded area of Ettersburg. The site was
deliberate, for Weimar was the cultural center of Germany, the
hub of its humanist spirit. It seemed fitting to the rulers of the

Third Reich that the new spirit of Germany should be sited there. Thus Goethe's oak tree, the Goethe-Eiche, which had inspired Germany's greatest minstrel, became the central feature of the Buchenwald concentration camp, the only tree spared in that black wooden landscape. The job of the first prisoners had been to clear the jungle of bracken and roots in order to lay the campsite. They had started building a road and the construction of drainage was under way. It was backbreaking work, with inadequate tools, and it was this work that the new prisoners would be forced to undertake during their camp stay. Nobody knew when that stay would end or whether it would end at all.

Benjamin was excluded from this detail. He was designated "prison doctor" and in the morning he was called into the commandant's office. SS Colonel Koch was in charge of the camp, assisted by one Major Rödl and Captain Weissenborn. Benjamin was greeted with unexpected respect.

"Your work is vital to our organization," Colonel Koch told him.

Benjamin was horrified. He didn't want to be any part of their organization and certainly not a vital one.

"A doctor's work is important wherever he practices," he said indifferently. "I would like to see the hospital," he added.

The colonel smiled. "We are not yet so grand," he said. "We call it our medical room. But first go and collect your uniform. Then I myself will show you your work quarters." He raised his right arm. *"Heil Hitler,"* he said.

Benjamin stared at him. Did the man actually expect some response?

Colonel Koch smiled. "It's very simple, you know," he said. "You just lift your right arm to about a hundred and twenty degrees from your body. It's really very easy. Try it."

Benjamin didn't mind lifting his arm, but he was not inclined to the words that accompanied such a gesture. His hand lay limp at his side.

"Aren't you willing to try?" Colonel Koch said, and Benjamin noticed that the smile had gone from his face.

"My heart is not in it," Benjamin said, finding courage.

"Then Major Rödl will help move your heart," he said. He signaled to his assistant, who grabbed Benjamin's right wrist and forced his arm upward. "Now keep it there," he ordered, letting the wrist go.

Benjamin looked at his outstretched arm and imagined himself
as a policeman on point duty, and this image held his arm where
it had been ordered.

"Now say *'Heil Hitler,'*" Colonel Koch said.

But such a statement was no part of a traffic policeman's work.
Benjamin's lips were firmly sealed.

The colonel signaled once more to the major, who pinched
Benjamin's nose so that his mouth had to open.

"Now let the words out," Koch said. *"Heil Hitler."*

Still nothing came. Rödl twisted the nose so that the tears
started in Benjamin's eyes. His ears rang with his father's words
from the minstrel of Grandpa Jakob's legacy. Survive. There is
no cause on earth worth dying for, no country worth one's martyrdom, no principle worth one's sacrifice. Survive.

"Heil Hitler," Benjamin shouted with zeal.

Koch was impressed by his enthusiasm. "That's a good beginning, Bindel," he said. "What a pity you're a Jew."

A guard took him to the shower rooms. "A shower is a privilege," he told him. "It's only because you're a doctor. Not that it
will make much difference. You stink like a Jew."

Benjamin had forgotten the incident of his capture. He had
become used to his smell and no longer found it offensive. But the
prospect of a warm shower was heartening and he stood under it
and wiped the dried feces from his flesh. The guard took away his
clothes, promising their return on his release. "If that day should
ever come," he added. Then he took him to the storeroom.

He was given a torn vest, a pair of socks, and boots, with no
regard as to their fit. Then he was led to a counter on which lay
separate piles of jackets.

"Jew," the guard said to the attendant.

The man pulled the top jacket from a pile, one marked with a
yellow star. Benjamin looked along the line at the other piles.
Jackets with purple stars, with red, with green.

"What do those colors stand for?" Benjamin asked.

"You'll learn," the guard said. "All you need to know is your
own. He's a doctor," he added to the attendant, who then went to
a cupboard at the end of the storeroom and returned with a none
too white coat. He handed it to Benjamin. It was very much
larger than the jacket, and Benjamin noted that if he buttoned it
all the way up, it would hide his yellow star. So he purposely left
it open. He had nothing to hide in this place. Indeed, the yellow

symbol had given him some pride. He wondered whether an equal pride could be felt in the other colors.

He was taken into the barracks yard and told to wait for the commandant. It was very cold. The torn vest next to his body did little to comfort him, and he longed for his funeral suit, stinking as it was, for its warmth and familiarity. It seemed to him that he had spent years in this place and he had to remind himself that Kurt Dreiser had been buried only the day before. A line of men was waiting at the barracks. They were probably his companions in the van that had brought them to this place. He could not recall any of their faces. In any case, in their prison uniforms and now-shaven heads they looked very similar, and the only feature that distinguished them was the color of their stars. Benjamin wandered over in their direction. He stood apart from them, at a distance, ashamed of his white coat and its mark of difference. He looked at them keenly, not at their faces but at the jackets they wore. He was searching for another yellow star for his comfort. He smiled. All his life, he and Heidi had run from that identity, and here in this bleak and desolate place, he was seeking it out for friendship. But he could not spot one yellow star among them. Most of them were red, with the occasional purple. He was afraid to approach them. There were guards all around. At night in their sleeping quarters he would seek out their categories. He watched the guard as he moved them off. "Left, right, left," he barked at them, and they fell into some kind of marching rhythm, their stars flashing in the cold morning light. He watched them into the distance, and saw how some stumbled and fell, and how the guard whipped them upright, and how they fell yet again. He wondered whether any of them would become his patients. He went back to the spot where he had been told to wait. He scanned the perimeter of the camp, and he could see no building that could pass as medical quarters. He began to fear what his duties as a doctor might be. He saw Colonel Koch coming toward him, and as he drew near, he raised his right hand in salute. *"Heil Hitler,"* the colonel said.

Benjamin was glad that the other prisoners had gone, and that there was none of his kind around to witness his response. *"Heil Hitler,"* he said, raising his arm, and he was surprised at the ease with which he could react because he knew it guaranteed his survival. At least for the time being. Then he would find other means, he decided, no matter how base, how demeaning. He owed it to his Great-grandfather Jakob of Odessa.

"Come," Colonel Koch said. "I'll show you your working quarters. You will keep three paces behind me," he said. He called two guards to his side, and instructed them to walk in front of his prisoner. With all his power Benjamin thought, Koch is frightened, and the thought pleased him.

He was led to an outhouse on the perimeter of the camp. From outside it looked like a vast whitewashed shed, but once inside, Benjamin saw that it was subdivided into many rooms. There was little to indicate that it was a hospital. In one room, where they now stood, there was a table on which were spread out the rudimentary medical instruments. A blood-pressure gauge, a stethoscope, an eye-and-ear light, and a pile of swabs and a tongue depressor. In one corner stood a weighing machine. On a wall in a small annex to the chamber was a scale in feet and inches for the measurement of height. It seemed to be a room for preliminary examination, a diagnostic room perhaps, before the serious business of treatment began.

"These are your quarters," the colonel said.

"Where are the wards?" Benjamin asked.

"There are no wards. All treatment is given in here."

"But if people are ill and need beds?" Benjamin asked.

"Your patients will not need beds," Koch said. "In here they are given special treatment."

Benjamin shivered.

"Don't worry," Koch said. "I will show you how it works."

But he's no doctor, Benjamin thought. How can he tell me my job?

"I'll show you what you have to do," Koch said. "Come with me."

Once more Benjamin followed him, while the two guards placed themselves between the parties for Koch's protection. He crossed the room. The far wall was open at one end, giving out to an anteroom, the floor of which was covered with sawdust. The room smelled of death, like a morgue. But the most terrifying feature was the drain that ran through the center of the floor.

"What's the drain for?" Benjamin dared to ask.

"Blood," Koch said. "What else?"

"Whose blood?" Benjamin persisted.

"Criminals'," Koch said.

Benjamin knew that in Koch's opinion all men who were not Nazis fell into that category. The room could well be his own death chamber.

"It's all very simple," Koch was saying. "This annex is the killing room," he said. He was as phlegmatic as a real estate agent showing property to a prospective client. "And here, if you look closely at the wall, there is a hole large enough for the nozzle of a gun. Behind that hole is where the marksman takes his stand. You will place your patient alongside this embrasure, so that his temple is aligned with the hole. He will suspect nothing, for here, as you see"—he pointed to the wall—"is a measuring scale for his height. Rather neat, don't you think?" Koch turned to Benjamin. He was not asking his opinion. He was simply stating his admiration for an ingenious device.

"Of course," he said, "there will be certain formalities before the criminal is dispatched. Those formalities are your job. You will not bring your patient into this annex until you have weighed him, taken his pulse, his heartbeat and blood pressure. When that is done, and you have taken your notes, you will direct him to this annex, ostensibly to measure his height. When you have lined him up against the wall—there are three small steps here, you will notice—" he said, pointing to the floor, "you will have to adjust his height to the embrasure. And then you will say, 'Stand there for a moment. I'll get my notebook.' That will be the marksman's cue to fire. You yourself will have quickly withdrawn from the chamber."

He turned and walked back to the medical room. "Is that all clear?" he asked.

Benjamin stared at him, incredulous. "Why do you need a doctor?" he whispered.

Koch smiled. "Everything about our party, all our operations, are totally professional. Now I would like you to try out the scheme," Koch said. "The guard will stand in as your patient. You can regard it as a dress rehearsal."

"You"—he nodded to the second guard—"you will be the marksman. Go to your stand."

The guard withdrew to the shooting gallery, while the other waited for his examination.

"I omitted an important fact," Koch said. "It is imperative that you require all patients to strip naked before your examination. You will have a guard present at all times, and he will sort out the clothing and possessions after the patients' disposal. Now you may begin."

Benjamin did not trust the words that would come out of his throat, and when they came, they squeaked with fear and trembling.

"Would you undress?" he said to the guard. "Take everything off."

The guard made no move. He just smiled and looked at the commandant.

"A member of the Nazi party does not undress in front of a Jew," Koch said. "This is only a rehearsal, remember."

Benjamin walked to the table, stiffening his legs to hide his trembling. He picked up the stethoscope and hung it around his neck. Then he went toward the guard and made to open the buttons of his tunic.

"You don't have to touch him," Koch said gruffly. "I appreciate your zeal, Bindel, but this is only a rehearsal."

Benjamin put the stethoscope in his ears, and placed it over the guard's breast-button. He waited for a while, then he took it away and returned to the table for the blood-pressure gauge. "Would you sit down?" he said to the guard.

"What about your notes on his heart?" Koch said.

"I'm sorry," Benjamin said, and he picked up his notebook. It seemed almost obscene to apologize. He was angry with himself for not refusing this monstrous assignment. He kept thinking of Jakob, and wondered whether he himself had any notion of the cost of survival. Then he recalled the story of the milk-brothers, and the price they had been forced to pay. But had either of them committed murder, as he was doing?

"I'm sorry," he said again, almost to himself, but it sounded so grossly inadequate for the enormity of the crime he was about to commit in the name of his own survival. For a moment he was tempted to put down his sham tools and refuse to participate. But then he realized that he was replaceable a thousand times over, and that his refusal would not save a single life.

He wound the black bandage around the guard's arm and made as if to take his blood pressure. Then, with his light, he looked into his eyes and his ears, and with a tongue depressor he examined his throat, taking notes after each stage of examination, as he was directed. He dallied with his note-taking, delaying the denouement of his act, anxious to postpone his unpardonable collusion.

"Hurry up, Bindel," Koch said. "I appreciate your conscientiousness, but I have work to do."

Was this not his work? Benjamin thought.

"I'd like to take your height," Benjamin whispered, and he directed the man to the annex. Every limb in his body was trembling as he gauged the guard's height in relation to the opening. He instructed him to stand on the second step, and noted that he had rightly chosen, for the guard's temple fitted neatly against the hole in the wall.

"Well done, Bindel," Koch laughed. "Beginners' luck, perhaps," he said.

And then Benjamin realized he'd forgotten his line, that cue he was to give to the marksman. He turned to Koch. "I've forgotten what I must say," he said. There was no apology in his voice.

"It's the most important part of the procedure," Koch shouted. "Write it down, man, and learn it by heart. *Stand still for a moment. I'll get my notebook.*"

Benjamin turned back to the medical room to fetch his pad.

"You can write it down later," Koch thundered. "Just say it."

But it had gone again, so loath was Benjamin to utter it. He hesitated.

"Stand still for a moment," Koch prompted him, his patience sorely tried. Benjamin repeated the words in a whisper. *"While I get my notebook,"* Koch said, and Benjamin echoed the words.

"Now again. On your own," Koch said.

This time Benjamin remembered them, for their terrible echo still hung on the air. He looked at the guard's face as the cold nozzle nestled his temple. Benjamin was rooted to the spot.

"Get out of the way, man," Koch yelled.

"Bang bang," the marksman bleated from behind his screen. The guard fell to the floor, a huge grin on his face. The rehearsal was over.

"How many a day?" Benjamin dared to ask.

"It varies," Koch said. "Depends on how the prisoners adapt. Some, of course," he said, "are given a medical examination as soon as they arrive. We are not interested in their adaptability. But you will be here on duty, even when there are no patients. But I think we can keep you pretty busy. You start tomorrow," he said, and made to leave the room.

There was one question that burned on Benjamin's tongue. What had happened to his predecessor? But he was too frightened to ask. He knew that no man who had seen such things could be allowed to live. He thought of his children, but he could not recall their faces. Not their heights, their weights, their heartbeats, their pulses. Nothing. To recall all those things in this place would have been to confirm their mortality. All he could remember was the fact that they had not inherited, and that omission grieved him far more than the thought of his own death. Suddenly he felt very hungry, and he realized that he hadn't eaten since before Kurt Dreiser's funeral. He was ashamed of his sudden appetite.

"It's time for breakfast," the guard said, as if reading his thoughts, and he grabbed his arm and led him out of the quarters.

In all other ways Benjamin was treated like the other prisoners. He slept in the same barracks, covered by one thin blanket; he ate at the same slop table, and presented himself at roll call four times each day. Breakfast was a hunk of bread and some thin soup. The bread ration for the whole day was distributed the night before, but prisoners were so hungry that they often consumed it during the night. The work they were obliged to do was backbreaking. At the time of Benjamin's imprisonment, they were constructing the sewerage system, and the men, most of whom had never in their lives bent their backs to hard labor, were now forced to break stones and hump them by hand from the quarry. It was an exceptionally cold winter that year, and, for lack of food and warm clothing, it was unlikely that they would survive. If they must die, Benjamin prayed, let them die in the quarry. For no matter how painful that death, it was at least natural and clean.

He sat at the table in as isolated a seat as he could find. He did not ever want to see their faces, much less to know the nature of their pain. He did not want to learn of their work, or of their families that they had left behind. He wanted to know nothing about them. As they sat there, bent with their fatigue and their despair, each one of them showed the frightening symptoms of unadaptability. Any one of them, at any time, could be led into his medical room, with all the guard's solicitude, and offer himself for treatment. He dared not learn to know them, and through them the orphans and the widows he would make.

Yet Benjamin needed so desperately to reach out a hand for friendship. Perhaps if he could find a yellow star, that bearer of their common guilt, such a man would understand. But most of the stars in the barracks were red. He had to discover the colors' meanings. He would ask one of them, he decided. He would keep his eye on the man's star, but never once would he look into his eyes. A red one sat next to him, as intent, it seemed, on his separateness as Benjamin himself.

"What does the red star mean?" Benjamin asked, staring at the man's jacket.

"Political." The man gave a sideways whisper.

"Green?" Benjamin asked.

"Criminal."

"Purple?"

"Jehovah's Witness."

The conversation was over, and neither man would ever connect the other's voice with a face.

Every day Benjamin went to the medical room and waited, trembling at every footfall outside the door. He began to believe that Colonel Koch's little pageant was a huge joke designed to frighten him. So that when, on the fourth day, his first patient arrived, he just thought that Koch had carried the joke too far. But one look at the guard's face told him that he was at last in business, the serious business of extermination.

He heard the prisoner enter the room, and as long as he could he avoided looking at the man's face. The voice was young and trusting. Twenty-eight years old, it said. Profession? Married? Children? Any previous illnesses? Questions to put the man at ease, to authenticate the purpose of his visit, to erase from his mind any doubts or suspicions.

"Let's have a look at you, then," Benjamin said, as he would have addressed any patient at the Jewish Infirmary in Leipzig. Though in the hospital he would have known the man's face and the nature of his complaint long before the undressing stage. "Take your clothes off," he said. He looked at the man's attire as it dropped to the floor. He had been brought straight from the transport, so he wore no prison uniform, no star. Benjamin would never know for what so-called crime he was sending this man to his death. He looked at the young man's body. Uncircumcised, he noticed, and Benjamin was ashamed at the sudden surge of relief in his heart that he was not sending to his death one of his own kind. He put a stethoscope to the man's chest and was hurt at the rude health of the young heart. His blood-pressure pulse was like a boy's. No malady, no disorder.

"Let's see how tall you are."

"Five foot eleven," the man said.

"I must check it," Benjamin said helplessly. He took his patient's hand in a gesture of farewell. The hand was cool, fearless and trusting. Benjamin squeezed it as a token of his love. He instructed the prisoner to stand on the second step. Until that time he had not studied the man's face, but now he would have to look at it, to measure his temple's adjustment to that chamber of death.

"You'll see I'm right," the man said. "Five foot eleven."

Benjamin eyed the hole and found its adjustment exact. He did not smile at the man. Instead, he took both his hands in his own.

"Wait here," Benjamin said. "I have to fetch my notebook." He turned quickly away and shuffled back into the medical room. Then he heard the explosion and the thud of the falling body. "Well done," he heard the guard say.

Benjamin put his face in his hands and wept like a child.

"The first one is always the worst," the guard said. "You'll get used to it."

The whistle blew for roll call, the second of the day. He staggered out of the medical room, but the cold air of the morning brought no relief. The second roll call was always the longest and most punishing. The men, most of them unused to physical labor, had already broken stones since the cold dawn. They were hungry, too, and shivering. He waited while the names were called. In front of him a man fell forward onto his face. Benjamin knelt down by his side. "You must try to stand," he pleaded.

"Let me die," the man said.

"No." Benjamin was outraged. But what right had he to anger, he who had just sent a man to his death, who had, in all deception, prepared the body for that final celebration? Benjamin turned the man over and cradled his head in his hands. He noted the purple star on his jacket. A Jehovah's Witness. Where, in God's name, was his God witnessing now?

"Leave me," the man said.

Benjamin stood and returned to his place, turning his face from the jackbooted guard, clenching his teeth against the kicking on the ground, but forcing himself to watch, for after all, what he had done that morning was far gentler than this. He had touched no man's body except with love. He had gathered human hands in his own and had felt in their trusting pulse the very last throb of their earthly lives. He had listened with love to the curtain call of their heartbeat. His own face had been fanned by the patient's last breath. He had gone with him into death as far as he was able. And then he had turned away and tried not to hear, and to wipe from his eyes the vision of that face he had had to confront. I did not put the gun into the guard's hand, he kept telling himself. Yet he had put his target squarely and neatly, and oh, so skillfully, into the line of fire. What difference between him and the marksman?

The roll call was over, and the man fell at Benjamin's feet, shivering and crying and praying for death. As Benjamin made to kneel by his side, the guard laid a hand on his shoulder.

"Leave him," he shouted.

"But he will die," Benjamin said, and wondered why he was so concerned with the continuation of life, since they were all going to die in this place anyway. What point was there in prolonging a living death?

The guard led him back to his quarters. Once inside, he noticed how clean it was, how warm. The floor of the killing room had been respread with sawdust, and fresh water trickled through the drain. He sat at his desk and waited.

"There's a new transport tonight," the guard promised him. "Communists from Dresden. You'll be kept pretty busy."

That night, after dark, the van drove through the camp gates. There were seven prisoners. The men were kept in the van until their turn came, so that they were out of earshot of the guardsman's gun. "To spare their feelings," the guard told Benjamin.

That night Benjamin listened to seven hearts and seven pulses, and looked into seven innocent faces. He went to bed that night with eight murders on his hands, and he prayed to God for his own death. The following night the tally was twenty and no face yet blurred into another. As he closed his eyes for the sleep that would not come, each portrait loomed, separate, framed in the gallows of his mind.

For a whole week there were no new arrivals at the camp. Every day Benjamin was escorted to his medical quarters, where he waited for patients and prayed that they would not come. There was nothing he could occupy himself with. He was allowed no reading matter or writing materials, and all he could do was contemplate the instruments on the desk in front of him, which had, each one of them, become tools of fraud and deception. He doubted that, even if he survived, he could ever practice medicine again. At the end of the week Benjamin began to have hopes that the slaughter was over. Until that time, all his victims had been civilian-clothed. So he began to convince himself that at least his fellow prisoners would not be candidates for his fraudulent diagnosis. Perhaps now he could risk their friendship and dare to search for a confidant among them, one to whom he could confess his sins. And as it turned out, he was freed into their daily company. For after that week of idleness he was sent to work on the sewerage until new transports arrived.

He welcomed the work as one would a holiday. As he picked over the stones, his back aching with the unaccustomed work, he celebrated each moment of his absence from his usual quarters. Benjamin worked with zeal. Compared to his medical duties, he found the punishing labor, the searing cold, and the jeers and kicks of the guards something of a paradise. He covered for the other prisoners while they took rest from their labors. From time to time, and in whispers, he sang his inherited song of survival to them, a true Bindel minstrel in that desolate waste. But still he did not look into their faces.

He had been in Buchenwald for three whole weeks, and that night, after his day's backbreaking labor, sleep came swiftly to comfort him. The following morning he noticed that some of the beds were empty. Apparently some men had been released and sent back to their homes. Benjamin's heart surged with hope, and he dared once more to think of his children. For another week he worked in the sewers, and every morning, when he awoke, he noticed and blessed the absence of those faces he had not dared to view. Rumor spread that the camp would slowly be cleared to make room for a large contingent of prisoners that was expected after a nationwide political purge. They would need a doctor, Benjamin could not help thinking. But a white-coated guard would do. Each night he prayed for a day's work in the sewers. He would settle for that, even for a lifetime, rather than dispense one more diagnosis in his quarters. A week passed and the barracks slowly emptied. Roll calls were reduced to two a day, but still there were casualties who fell in the line.

"Hang on," Benjamin urged them in whispers. "Our freedom cannot be far away."

At the end of that week, marking almost two months of incarceration, he was told to wait in the barracks square at the end of the evening roll call. He dreaded the order for his return to the medical room. He stood alone on the parade ground, shivering with cold and fear. It was dark when the guard approached him, his personal guard from the medical quarters. "You will be released in the morning," he said. "You will go now to the storeroom and collect your clothes."

It was some time before Benjamin could move from the spot.

"Go on." The guard shoved him with his stick.

Benjamin ran to the storeroom. He waited at the counter while the attendant sifted through the piles of clothes. He withdrew a bundle wrapped with string, and checked on the label. "Bindel?" he shouted. "Doctor?" he sneered.

Benjamin would not acknowledge that profession. He had forfeited his rights to practice it. "Bindel," he said, and that was all. The attendant put the bundle on the counter.

"Thank you," Benjamin said.

"You're welcome to that stink," the attendant said.

Then Benjamin recalled his arrest in the crematorium chapel, and he longed for that smell again, the smell that had belonged to his last moments of freedom. He held the parcel to his chest. Then the attendant gave him an envelope with his wallet, his handkerchief, and his keys. Benjamin took them without thanks, and left the room. Outside the guard was waiting, and he escorted him back to the barracks. "I'll miss you, Bindel," he said. "You're different from the others. The last doctor we had was very unadaptable."

Benjamin refrained from asking what had happened to him.

Before Benjamin went to bed, he put on his suit. He wanted no delay in his freedom. He did not sleep that night. Once again he stalked his mind's gallery like a ghost, viewing the faces that time had not blurred. He prayed fervently for forgiveness. Suddenly the rumble of a lorry droned in his ear. Then he heard the screeching of brakes and the slamming of doors. No more doctoring, he prayed, and even as he whispered his prayer, he felt a hand shaking his shoulder.

"Patients," the guard's voice said. "Get up."

Benjamin could not move. He simply couldn't face that medical room again. The guard pulled the thin blanket off the bed, and poked the end of his gun between Benjamin's shoulder blades.

"Hurry," the guard said. "They're waiting."

Death will not be offended by their tardiness, Benjamin thought, and wearily he opened the medical room door and sat at his desk. Within seconds his first patient had arrived.

Benjamin fully expected that he would have forgotten the routine, and he was horrified by his total recall of every maneuver. The comforting questionnaire, the heartbeat, pulse, blood pressure, and the final alignment. He had lost none of his dexterity. His timings and his bearings were exact. Six more patients visited him that night. Six new bullets, six fresh sluices through the drains, six new layers of sawdust on the killing-room floor.

"One more," the guard said, "and that's the lot. Tomorrow you'll go home."

One more, Benjamin thought, and the nightmare would be over.

He heard the man enter the room, and he asked him to undress, keeping his eyes on the floor, as was his custom.

"Benjamin," the man said.

Benjamin trembled. It had been a long, long time since anyone had addressed him by that name. The voice was gentle, like his father's, and he thought he must be dreaming.

"Don't you know me?" the voice insisted.

Then Benjamin raised his eyes, and saw in the face of his last patient an old and respected friend. His former mentor, Dr. Luber. He could not stop the tears that burned in his eyes.

"You know this man?" the guard said.

"He is a friend," Benjamin answered, taking Luber's hand.

"Then be quick," the guard said.

His advice was gentle and exact, and Benjamin would have done well to heed it. But the shock of the encounter was devastating, and it took some time to recall those maneuvers that he had lately carried out with such consummate skill. He wanted very much to talk to Luber, or rather to question him. Why had he been arrested? Had he been charged as a Communist or a Jew?

"I'm in reasonably good health," Dr. Luber was saying as he undressed. "A little chest congestion perhaps, as you will hear. The tables have turned," he laughed, "that a pupil should examine his teacher."

Benjamin could not understand his professor's composure. Was it possible that he had no notion of what was to become of him? That the state of his chest, congested or otherwise, could grant him a reprieve? After all, the man had spent time in Dachau. He must be well versed in the lexicon of Nazi euphemism. Benjamin decided to say nothing, to recite the questionnaire, as if Dr. Luber were a stranger. Now, on the brink of his grave, was no time to renew their familiarity. He took the heartbeat, pulse, blood pressure, and weight, but all the time he looked him in the eye. It was the least he could do. He picked up his eye light from the desk and put it to Dr. Luber's eye, caressing his cheek as he steadied his light.

"You are very thorough," Dr. Luber said. "A credit to my teaching, I like to think."

How innocent he is, Benjamin thought. He has no notion of how I am so abusing all that he ever taught me.

"Why do you examine my vision?" Dr. Luber asked. "Is it necessary to know the opthalmology of a Communist? And my blood pressure? My pulse rate? Are they indications of my political stand? If my heartbeat is irregular, am I therefore unreliable? Does my vision affect my faith? If my pulse is racing, am I diagnosed as a fanatic? And my weight. What secrets does my weight reveal? Unless, of course," he laughed, "you are measuring me for the gallows."

He knows, Benjamin thought, and he is trying to make it easy for me. He turned back to his desk. This man taught me all I know, he thought. I know his wife, and I have played with his children. All the other patients were strangers. With them I obeyed orders. But this man is a friend. This is murder. Nothing extenuate.

Benjamin thought of his inheritance. Only in the name of love is death worthy, Great-grandpa Jakob had said. And friendship. But if he were to offer his own life now, it would be no replacement for Dr. Luber. Dr. Luber would die, no matter who placed him in the line of fire. I must not waste my death, Benjamin thought, for it will give life to no one.

"I must check your height, Dr. Luber," he said. He used his name. He wanted him to know that he was fully aware of sending a friend to his death. He was meticulous about the placing on the step. This alignment had to be exact, the death swift and painless. He looked him in the eye.

"I understand, Benjamin," Dr. Luber said. "You are innocent. You are innocent, Benjamin," he said again. "You must never believe otherwise. Never." He held out his hand in a gesture of farewell. Benjamin mounted the step and embraced him. Then he turned away. "I must get my notebook." He sobbed his due, then he returned to the medical room and waited for the explosion. When it came, he rushed back; Dr. Luber lay on the floor, his brains blown. He forced himself to look at what was left of his mentor's face, and he heard the echo of his merciful farewell.

"That's the lot," the guard said, and Benjamin suddenly realized that all the time a witness had been present. There was a rule that the doctor must not talk to his patients, a rule that until now Benjamin had been eager to obey. But the guard had obviously turned his ear from this last encounter, and Benjamin was grateful.

"Thank you," he said. He made to leave.

"Wait until the marksman leaves," the guard whispered, and Benjamin wondered why there was a sudden change of procedure, and he was frightened. The marksman strutted through the killing room, pausing for a while to view his most recent handiwork.

"A very brainy one," he said with disdain. As he passed Benjamin on his way to the door, he said, "You won't be needing your coat anymore, Doctor." Then he laughed. "Good luck, comrade," he said to the guard, and he sauntered out of the room. Benjamin took off his coat, and the guard threw it into the killing room. Benjamin shivered with the knowledge that shortly he would follow it. With little confidence and with melting knees, he made for the exit door, but the guard put a hand on his shoulder.

Benjamin trembled at the touch. He knew it as a gesture of authority, yet there was tenderness in the hold. He turned and saw how the guard drew his gun with his other hand. His first thought was one of gratitude that he would be killed with a semblance of affection and a hint of remorse. How stupid he had been to have ever believed in his freedom. They had to kill him, he knew, as they had no doubt disposed of his predecessor. After all he had learned in this place, how could they let his tongue loose? He thought of his children and the tears rolled down his cheeks. He was not ashamed of his weeping, but he felt he owed the guard some explanation. The man had shown consideration for him while they had worked together. Perhaps he, too, had children. "I have two sons," he said. "I was thinking of them."

The guard raised his gun. "This bullet is meant for you," he said. Then he leveled it at Dr. Luber's brain-spattered body and fired into his dead limbs.

"Go quickly," he said. "At the back of the hut there's a path that leads to a field. It runs parallel to the road. Creep along it and the sentry won't see you. I'll tell them I buried you with that one."

Benjamin stared at him. "Why have you done this for me?" he asked. The guard shrugged. There were a thousand reasons and every one of them would have sent him to the firing squad.

"I don't know," he said.

Benjamin grasped his shoulder, clutching that uniform that symbolized such gross inhumanity. Yet it clothed a man of great heart and unquenchable spirit.

"Go," the guard said. "There's little time," and he went to the door to ascertain that there was no one about. "It's clear," he said.

Benjamin took his hands and kissed them, then he stole through the darkness into the field.

When he reached the road, he stood upright. He was not afraid. He considered himself a dead man, and therefore he must be invisible. He remembered that, on that road, the van had swerved to the right for the camp. He turned left, and after a few miles he saw a signpost to Weimar. He walked in that direction. He was hungry, cold, tired, and, despite the official entry into the camp files, shamefully alive. He kept repeating to himself Dr. Luber's farewell. "You are innocent, Benjamin. You must never believe otherwise. Never." But no matter how often he repeated them, they gave him no consolation.

It was late in the afternoon when he reached a railway station, some miles from Weimar. He had just enough money to buy his ticket to Leipzig. He no longer worried about his hunger. It was now so acute that food would have sickened him. When the train pulled into the station, he found an empty carriage and slumped into a corner seat. "You are innocent, Benjamin," he said to himself, over and over again, until its repetition sent him into a merciful and dreamless sleep. He was woken by the guard who demanded his ticket.

Benjamin gave it to him and avoided his glance. The guard

looked at him and sniffed him, too, and thought it better to move
quickly away.

Out of the window Benjamin could see the factory buildings
that fringed his hometown. He felt no excitement or longing. In
many ways he never wanted to go home again. He didn't want to
see his father, children, brother, wife, all of whom, in their own
gentle ways, would smell the murder on him. Whatever Dr.
Luber had said, Benjamin wondered whether ever in his life again
he would be convinced of his innocence.

Many years before in the ghetto in Odessa, Leon's father, Benjamin, had told his sons the story of the milk-brothers' return from Siberia. He had told them of Jakob's premonition of that day, and his conviction that the brothers were alive and would soon come home. On the day of his son's return from Buchenwald, Leon Bindel had a like premonition. So when, late at night, he heard the key in the lock, he got up from his bed and went to the door.

"Benjamin," he called. It was no question, for he knew it was his son.

"Papa?"

He heard his son's voice and he winced at its pain. Carefully he made his way down the stairs, and, once in the hall, he stared at his son and saw that he was alive. It was only later, as he took him in his arms, that he knew of his hunger, his fear, and his shame.

"I love you, Papa," Benjamin said.

Leon started. It was not a phrase that came easily to his younger son. He had never doubted his filial love, but Benjamin had been unable to express it, and the fact that he did so now pointed to more than a declaration of affection. It was an expression of manic reparation. He knew that his son's declaration was a plea for forgiveness, so he held his arm and said, "You are innocent, my son."

Benjamin embraced him, his tears flowing. His father, with his forgiveness, had given him a license to loosen his tongue. He could, unashamedly, tell those he loved of all that he had done. It was the greatest freedom of all.

Soon the hall was filled with family. Benjamin ran to his children and passed the astonished Heidi where she stood at the top of the stairs. She had clearly never expected his return, and he tried to greet her without bitterness. David, Sarah, and their children leapt down the stairs to welcome him.

"You're hungry," Sarah said, appalled by his painful loss of weight.

"I need to bathe myself," he said.

"Then we will prepare a feast," Leon said. "And champagne, too." He was giggling like a child, unable to contain his joy.

"Not a feast, Papa," Benjamin said gently. "Just a little to eat, and a little more tomorrow, perhaps."

"Shall I come with you?" Heidi asked as he walked up the stairs.

"Bring the children," he said without turning. He was disturbed at the coldness in his heart for Heidi. Never once during his stay in Buchenwald had he thought about her. She belonged to that part of his life that had been a living lie, a lie that Buchenwald had more than confirmed. He wondered whether his absence had shaken her, touched that stubbornness of hers in any way.

"How skinny you are," she said as he undressed.

"We have to leave this country," he said.

She laughed. "You haven't changed at all," she said. "They won't take you again. No one gets taken twice."

He wanted to tell her about Dr. Luber, but he did not love her enough to share the story with her.

"Everyone says there's going to be a war," she went on. "Hitler won't have time to harass Jews. He'll be too busy fighting."

He did not have the strength or the inclination to argue with her. "Nevertheless, we're going," he said. He turned to go to the bathroom, where the children were waiting, fluffing the foam in the water.

"You can go if you like," they heard their mother shouting. "But I'm staying here with the children."

Benjamin shut the bathroom door behind him.

"Where are you going, Daddy?" Jakob asked.

"Nowhere," Benjamin said. He was distressed that the children had heard their argument. He would gladly leave Heidi behind, but never his children. But it was the children above all who must be saved, and he wondered whether he would have the strength to let them go without him.

Downstairs, Sarah had set the table with an assortment of light

foods for Benjamin's choice. They opened champagne to celebrate his return. Like the return of the milk-brothers, Benjamin's
homecoming was silent, and like the milk-brothers before him, he
was aware that nothing had changed in that past, nothing except
himself.

Later, Heidi asked him if he wanted to sleep alone. He was
grateful for her understanding. But he did not sleep at all. He
tossed on his single bed as Dr. Luber's farewell sang in his ear.
Toward morning he fell asleep, and when he awoke he looked for
his fellow prisoners, and when he realized where he was, he
missed them with an aching longing.

He got up and dressed. The children had already gone to
school and David had left for the store.

"Hans is here," Heidi said as she saw him coming downstairs.
Benjamin rushed into the living room, and welcomed his friend.

They embraced, and Hans tried to joke about Benjamin's spare
frame.

"You always wanted to lose weight, my friend," he said. Then
he looked at him and saw in his face the hell he had known. "You
needn't talk about it," he said. "Only if you want to. My father
didn't want to talk about Dachau." He paused, then after a while
he said, "I came to thank you for what you did at his funeral."

"Dr. Luber was in Buchenwald," Benjamin said suddenly. He
hadn't meant to speak about it. But Dr. Luber was a friend whom
he had shared with Hans, and Hans had a right to know his
story.

"Is he still there?" Hans said.

"He died yesterday." Was it only yesterday, Benjamin wondered, that he had measured his mentor for the scaffold?

"Did they kill him?" he heard Hans say.

Benjamin looked Hans in the eye. "I killed him," he said.

All this while Leon had been sitting silently in his armchair by
the fire. Now he suddenly shouted, "No, you didn't kill him." He
had known nothing of the Luber story until now. "If you killed
him, it was because they forced you."

"What happened?" Hans said.

"He was my last patient," Benjamin began, and slowly he unfolded the nature of his medical practice. He told the tale without
adornment. The simple facts of it were horrifying enough. When
he'd finished, he said, "Today I must go and tell Mrs. Luber."

"No," Hans said, and his voice was a command. "She'll be told

soon enough and she need never know the details. His death had
nothing to do with you. He told you so himself. You must begin
to believe him. Today you go back to the hospital and arrange to
start work as soon as you feel well enough."

"Hans is right," Leon said.

"We must leave this place, Papa," Benjamin said suddenly.

"*You* must leave perhaps. You and Heidi and the children,"
Leon said. "And David, too. But I am too old now to sow the
seeds of a new past. I am tired of running. I have done my surviving." Benjamin knew that he would never leave his father. Perhaps his father was right. He had done his surviving, and perhaps
Benjamin had done his surviving, too. Both had paid their dues
to their inheritance.

"What about some breakfast?" Leon said. "I've been waiting
for you. And Hans, too. He took the day off when he heard you
were home."

Benjamin put his arm around his friend's shoulder, and he
took his father's arm and they went into the dining room.

After breakfast Hans walked with his friend to the Jewish Infirmary. Benjamin was glad that he did not have to walk alone
into his consulting room and view all those instruments that he
had so lately abused. He picked them up one by one, handling
them with excessive care, concentrating on their orthodox use,
trying to wipe from his mind the fraud and the swindle that they
had so recently embodied. But one instrument he removed from
his room: the measuring rod with its irrelevant markings of
inches and feet. He put it outside his room for disposal. Then he
went to see the hospital director.

The director urged him to start work as soon as possible. Part
time to begin with, he suggested, until his health was completely
restored.

Benjamin thanked him. Then he and Hans took the tram to the
fur store to see David. From the outside, the shop looked closed.
The windows were boarded up, as was the front door. A hand-
written sign, declaring that it was open, was the only indication
that Bindel Furs was still in business. The shop was empty. David
sat behind the counter checking a ledger book. He greeted them
warmly, locked the door after them, and led them into his office
at the back of the shop.

"As you see," he laughed, "I'm not very busy. I don't know
that we can stay in business much longer. There are rumors in

any case that they are confiscating all Jewish property. Don't tell Papa, but I'm not buying any more stock."

"I think your father knows," Hans said. "He hears from other traders. But he says nothing."

"The fight has gone out of him," David said. "He is content to stay here until he dies."

"And you?" Benjamin broached the subject straightaway.

"How can I leave him?" David said. "But you could go. You could go with Heidi and the children."

"I wouldn't leave Papa," Benjamin said. "And Heidi won't go. We are all digging our graves in this place."

"Not all of us," David said. "I'm making arrangements to send Sarah and the children to Palestine. Her parents will go with them. But not a word to Papa. If only you could persuade Heidi, Benjamin," he said.

"I've tried," Benjamin said. "Besides, she won't leave her parents, and they are as stubborn as she is. They think that rich Jews will be exempt from persecution. Can you imagine such crazy logic?"

"How will they get there?" Hans said. "Entry to Palestine is illegal."

"There are ways," David said, "illegal ways. By the end of next week I shall have made all the arrangements. They shall leave within the month."

"So soon?" Benjamin said, imagining the emptiness of the house without Sarah and her children.

"There's not much time," David said. "By the end of the year, this country will be at war. And once that happens, we'll all be trapped."

"Shall I try talking to Heidi?" Hans volunteered. "I'm not Jewish," he laughed. "She might listen to me."

"I'd be grateful," Benjamin said. "But I doubt if you could move her."

"But the children, for God's sake." Hans was bewildered. He himself was childless. Inge had had a series of miscarriages and finally they had reconciled themselves to a life without family. Hans's marriage was a happy one, but both partners were sadly aware of their childlessness. All attempts at adoption had failed. Hans's political heritage was considered unworthy of parenthood.

In March 1939, German armies invaded Czechoslovakia. And still Sarah and the children lingered in Leipzig. There were hold-ups in the arrangements for departure. There was the problem of coordination. In the organization of *Aliyah Beth,* as illegal immigration into Palestine was called, there were a limited number of ships. Many of them were far from seaworthy, and all of them, when they sailed, were overcrowded. In panic, thousands of refugees were leaving Europe. Most countries had imposed refugee quotas, and the doors of many countries remained firmly closed. Only the gates of Palestine were open, or rather, illegally ajar, for British policy toward refugees was punitive. But despite these restrictions, boats sailed into Haifa harbor, or along the dark beaches, and with luck were sometimes able to disembark their passengers onto the forbidden shores.

One day, after weeks of waiting, news reached David that a boat would be leaving Venice in the first week of July. He had a month in which to make his final arrangements. With Hans's persuasion, he had decided to tell his father, and to tell him right away, so that he would have time to anticipate the children's absence. Leon welcomed the news, and urged David to go too. But David preferred to stay with his father, and in that preference he felt no sense of sacrifice.

"What about Aaron and Jakob?" Leon asked. "They must go too."

"Heidi refuses to leave," David said.

"Tell Benjamin to come to me," he ordered.

It was a Sunday, a day Benjamin liked to spend in the garden. It was planting and pruning time, a season that implied fruit and future. Since his return from Buchenwald, Benjamin spent many hours in the garden, hoeing a feverish stake in a future in which he would probably play no part. Nor even his children. Yet he planted, and nurtured, weeded and hoed, as if his life depended on it, and he was loath to leave his work when he heard David's call.

"Papa wants you," David shouted. He went out into the garden and they both returned to the living room. David had already told Benjamin of the impending departure, and now Benjamin had an inkling of why his father wished to talk to him.

"You want me, Papa?" he said.

"Heidi must go with the children. The Biedermayers will take care of them all. You cannot miss this opportunity. It won't come again." His voice was raised in anger, as if he anticipated Benjamin's objections.

"Heidi refuses to go," Benjamin said.

"So she stays," Leon shouted. And then, in a whisper, "But not Aaron and Jakob. David will take them to Venice with the others. When they have gone, you will tell her. The Bindels must survive."

At that moment, Leon was back in Senghenydd, standing at the pithead of his firstborn's memorial. He knew that there was no point in regretting one's past, but he knew, too, that one must learn from it, else all of one's history was folly. He knew now, in his present time, and in the autumn of his life, that he should have taken his first David and rescued him from the dangers of the valley. That he should have cared less for Margaret's feelings, that he should have insisted on the boy's future. Here now in his own drawing room, hundreds of miles from that memorial, so many griefs ago, was an exact reenactment of that drama. This time it had to have a different ending.

"They must leave," Leon said. "They must go with the others."

"Do I have your blessing to such a deception, Papa?" Benjamin asked.

"My blessings on you and your children," Leon said.

It took a little planning. Passports had to be applied for, and to that end they needed photographs. Benjamin could not take Aaron and Jakob to a studio, for they would have told their mother. So that afternoon, while the children were playing in the garden, Benjamin took pictures of each of the four children. The following day, he and David went to the passport office. There were many people waiting there and had been doing so for some hours.

"My God," Benjamin said. "I had no idea so many were leaving."

"We should bring Heidi here," David said.

"She would scoff," Benjamin answered. "Possibly she would call them cowards."

"You must try not to think ill of her," David said. "She loves her children."

"I know," Benjamin said. "I know, too, that I'm doing a terrible thing. She will never, never forgive me."

They waited and it was late afternoon before their turn came.

The official was gruff. He talked to his desk without once looking at their faces. But Benjamin could not blame him for that. He himself had used that manner of evasion out of his own sense of shame.

"How many passports?" the official asked.

"Five," David said. Sarah's parents were arranging their own.

The official took some forms from his tray. "Jews?" he asked his desk.

"Yes."

He took a large stamp and rolled it on a pad of ink. With it he stamped each form with the initial *J.* "Names?" he said.

David gave his list first. Names, addresses, ages, together with photographs. The official was slow. His writing was meticulous and he curved his tongue around each pothook and hanger. Then, when the particulars were noted, he stapled a photograph to each corresponding form and once again stamped the face underfoot with his *J.*

"You must sign here"—he pointed out the dotted line—"and your wife on the line below." Then he turned to Benjamin and repeated the same routine. He handed him the papers for his signature. "Your wife must sign too," he reminded him.

"I'll bring it back tomorrow," Benjamin said, knowing that he could forge Heidi's signature.

"She must bring it herself and sign it in front of the officer. Together with her own photograph."

"But she's ill," Benjamin quickly improvised. "Can't I do it for her?"

The official stared at his desk and shook his head. "Impossible unless she presents herself," he said. "You must wait until she gets better."

They took the forms and left the offices.

"They won't be able to go," Benjamin said. There was a measure of relief in his voice. But he knew that the relief was selfish, that however heartbreaking it would be to part with his children, it would be less heartbreaking than exposing them to the fire that he knew would burn out their future. "What am I to do?" he said.

"The Bindels have bribed frontier guards before," David said. "Let me take them anyway. It's worth taking that chance."

When the day of departure arrived, Benjamin awoke in terror. It was a school day, and the children were dressed in their school uniforms. Benjamin had surreptitiously packed a suitcase of his children's clothes and stored it in the trunk of David's car. They had breakfast together. Normally Heidi slept late, and the children would go to the bedroom to kiss her before going to school. But that morning Benjamin insisted on her rising, and she couldn't understand this sudden change of routine. But she came down to breakfast, not wishing to displease him. The children, too, were unnerved by Heidi's unaccustomed presence.

"Why are you up for breakfast, Mummy?" Aaron asked.

"Daddy wanted it," she said.

"Why, Daddy?" Jakob asked.

"I thought it would be nice if for a change we all had breakfast together." He was almost weeping with the shame of his deception. For a moment he weakened and decided that he would not let them go. Then he caught David's eye and his father's, and both conveyed an understanding of his pain.

"It's the same for me," David said.

"What's the same for you?" Heidi asked.

"My coffee. Black, like Benjamin's," David said quickly.

All the while, Leon had kept his eyes on the children, imprinting each image on his mind's eye, images to last him for the rest of his life. David saw tears start in his father's eyes and marveled that out of his sheer willpower, they did not drop down his cheeks. His restraint had a touch of nobility. When they rose from the table, he held them all in one embrace.

"Be good at school today, my children," he managed to say, then quickly he left the table and made his way through the French windows into the garden.

David gulped his coffee and rose from the table, and Benjamin followed him to his car. He did not want to witness Heidi's unknowing last farewell. He kissed Sarah good-bye, but said nothing, and when the children came toward him, he did as his father had done. He held them all, unable to let them go, knowing he would lose them forever.

"We'll be late for school, Daddy," Aaron said, and David touched his brother on the shoulder.

"We must go," he said.

He settled the children in the car, then came back to Benjamin. "It's for the best, brother," he said. "It means their survival.

Soon we shall all be together again." That Bindel phrase once more. Would there ever come a generation of Bindels when that phrase would not be called upon? Would there ever come a time when to leave was not to flee, when to part was not to die?

"I shall be back at the end of the week," David said, and he got into the car, and drove down the drive. Benjamin watched them out of sight, then he went quickly back into the house, grateful that Heidi was not to be seen, and he took his coat and made for the door. On his way through the dining room, he caught sight of his father in the garden. He was smelling the first of the roses, caressing them with his cheek, and Benjamin knew that his father's heart, like his own, was breaking.

He went straight to the hospital. Once there, he went to his room, locked the door, and allowed himself to weep. After a while, he rinsed his face and made his rounds of the wards. He tried not to think of Heidi or of the hour when the children would normally return from school. He was afraid to go home, yet he knew he must be there by the time school was over. Then he would break it to her. He watched the clock most of the day, timing his children's journey. The drive to Venice was almost five hundred miles. It would take two days of hard driving. They had been on the road for six hours. Allowing time to pick up the Biedermayers and to negotiate the center of Leipzig onto the main road south, Benjamin reckoned, they must have reached the Austrian border. There would be no trouble at that frontier. That country had been annexed to the Third Reich. It would be sometime around noon on the following day that they would reach the hurdle of the Italian frontier. At three o'clock, he left the hospital and made his way home.

Heidi was sitting in the drawing room. She told him that Leon did not feel well and had gone to bed shortly after lunch. She looked at her watch. "I must get the children's tea," she said. "They'll be home soon."

Benjamin did not look at her. Instead he went upstairs to see his father. He crept into the room and saw that he was sleeping. It would have been unfair to wake him up, so he tiptoed out of the room. Benjamin heard Heidi preparing the tea in the kitchen. Through the door into the dining room, he saw her set the table. He watched her and he could say nothing.

The time passed. It was after four o'clock.

"The children are late," Heidi said.

"They'll be home soon," Benjamin heard himself saying. He didn't know how to tell her. He did not believe that there were any words in any language to inflict such pain. He watched her out of the corner of his eye. She seemed composed, but after about ten minutes she began to get restless, and she walked to the window that overlooked the drive.

"I wonder why they're so late," she said.

"Traffic perhaps," Benjamin said.

"They've never been this late before," she said.

"Don't worry," Benjamin said, almost to himself. "They'll be here soon."

He trembled as the time passed. At five o'clock, Heidi began to panic. "I'm worried, Benjamin," she said. "You must ring the school. Please," she said.

"But the school's closed." Benjamin desperately played for time.

"Try them," she almost shouted at him.

He actually got up and made for the telephone. Then he knew that he could delay it no longer. He turned to Heidi and held her at arm's length.

"They're not coming back, Heidi," he said. The words were so simple, he thought, so easy to deliver, as easy as sliding an oiled dagger into an offered heart. It's over, he thought, and there was some relief in that.

"What do you mean?" she whispered.

"David took all the children to Venice. They'll take a boat from there to Palestine. Sarah and the Biedermayers are with them."

"They're not coming back?" The words were barely intelligible.

He shook his head. "It's only until all this is over," he said. "Then we shall all be together again."

Benjamin had murdered many people, but none of them had looked at him with hate. Now he saw on his wife's face a look of such abject loathing that it stabbed his heart with her pain. Then she let out a scream, so silent, yet so piercing, that dogs on the outskirts of Leipzig might have pricked their ears at her call. It was the same sound that Benjamin had often heard from women in the last stage of their labor. But this sound would have no end. He held her in his arms and she struggled like a wild creature to free herself. Finally he let her go. Whatever residual affection lay

beached on the shores of their tormented wedlock was now en-
gulfed by a tidal wave of loathing that swallowed it whole, and
without trace. She stumbled into the garden, then he saw her
pause by a rose bush. But she did not smell the blooms. Instead
she crushed them one by one in the palm of her hand, tearing her
skin on their thorns. Then she collapsed.

Benjamin went and gathered her in his arms. He carried her
upstairs to the bed and laid her gently on the pillows. Then he
took a syringe and gave her a sedative. He wanted her to forget
for a while the gross deprivation he had inflicted upon her. He
wanted to postpone the retribution that would surely come. He
covered her with a quilt and crept out of the room.

Once the children were settled in the car, David drove straight
to the Beidermayers', passing the school on the way.

"Where are we going, Uncle David?" Jakob said.

David couldn't answer.

"It won't take a minute," Sarah said, not daring to look at the
children. But when the Biedermayers stowed their luggage in the
trunk of the car, it was clear to them all that they would not go to
school that day.

"Where are we going?" Aaron wondered.

Sarah turned to face them. And she told them.

"What about Mummy?" Jakob began to cry.

But no one knew how to answer.

On the journey, the Biedermayers did their best to calm the
children with stories of the adventures that lay ahead. The long
boat-trip through the Adriatic and the Mediterranean. Then the
port of Haifa. They omitted any mention of the hazards they
would encounter on the journey. They had heard stories of less
than seaworthy boats that had been tossed through the Black Sea
and the Aegean, laden with refugees, dodging the attempts of the
British government to prevent their entry into Palestine. It was
on such a boat that they would travel, and they could only hope
and pray for safe arrival. So they told the children stories of
Palestine, a land that they themselves had never seen.

They crossed the Austrian border with no interference, and in
the early evening they stopped at an inn about ten miles outside
Vienna. That night when David took Sarah to bed, they made
love, fearing that it was possibly for the last time.

They set off early in the morning for the Italian border. As they approached it, David was more and more nervous. He had enough money for bribery, and he had heard that the Italian guards were happy enough to look the other way in return for grease on their outstretched palms. Even so, he was afraid. He slowed down and the car crawled toward the Austrian frontier post. The barrier was lifted without any questions asked, and he was soon two hundred yards away from the Italian hurdle. He thought of Heidi and her heartbreak, and of Benjamin, guilty and unforgiven, and for a moment he hoped that they would not let the boys pass.

"All out," the frontier guard said as the car approached the barrier. There were no other cars waiting, and plenty of guards about with nothing to do. It was a relief for them when a car came through and allowed them to busy their idle hands. One of the guards directed David and his passengers to the passport office on the side of the road. He asked for the keys to the trunk. Meanwhile, he told David, he would search their luggage.

David went first in the line, taking Aaron's and Jakob's hands. He allowed the Biedermayers to present their papers first. The official checked on their faces with a cursory glance and wished them a good journey. David approached the counter. He placed everything on the counter top—the passports, the car documents, and his wallet. He opened the wallet, as if he were looking for something inside; the wad of notes protruded from the pocket. David left it open and looked the official in the eye. But the clerk seemed to read no message in his display.

"Children with you?" he asked.

David nodded. They were invisible behind the counter. The man rose from his feet and came around to where they stood. It did not take him long to deduce that the number of passports and the number of children did not tally.

"Four children, two passports," he said, spelling it out as if it might come as some surprise to David.

"I know," David said, and he reached for his wallet and fingered the bribe in the pouch.

The official watched the gesture but said nothing. Then David was forced to speak.

"I can pay," he whispered.

"Pardon?" the man said, having heard well enough.

Then David knew that he'd had the ill luck to encounter an

honest official. Nevertheless he pressed on. "I can pay," he said, a little louder this time.

"I'm not in that market," the man said, "and I could well charge you for attempting to bribe an official of the Italian government. But I see your family are in a hurry."

"Thank you," David said, and he put his wallet away. There was nothing more that he could do. He must consider himself lucky that he was not charged.

"I don't know what to do," he said. "I can't leave two children here."

"Where are you making for?" the official said. "Apart from Palestine."

"Venice," David said.

"You could drive back to Vienna. There are trains direct to Venice from there." He retrieved the Biedermayer passports, and inserted a note that they had been stamped in error, so that there would be no problem when they recrossed the border by train. The official was very accommodating, with a courtesy that matched his incorruptibility.

They returned silently to the car, and David found himself relieved that he had failed. Although he would not now be able to see his family onto the boat in Venice, he would at least be taking Benjamin's children home. Sarah, too, was relieved, and overjoyed for Heidi's sake. "It's a good omen," she said. "It's a sign that they will survive."

"We could try another post," Mr. Biedermayer suggested. "We could go west through the mountains. It might be easier there."

"We would take a risk," David said. "And if we should fail, we risk losing the boat altogether. We have little enough time as it is."

On the way back through Austria, the Biedermayers told Benjamin's children that they would be going home to their mother after all. Aaron and Jakob feigned disappointment because that was what they thought was expected of them, but their hearts were leaping with joy and relief.

It was early evening when they reached Vienna's railway station. They had two hours before the Venice train, time for a farewell celebration. David had been to Vienna many times on business, and he knew the whereabouts of the Jewish quarter. They would feel safer there. He drove across the city and found the area without needing to ask directions. He was saddened by what he saw. Most of the shops were boarded up, and daubed with yellow stars. Some were in the process of renovation with the legend UNDER NEW MANAGEMENT across the hoarding. But they did find a restaurant that was open, with a brave proprietor beaming a welcome in the foyer. Or perhaps he wasn't brave, David thought. Perhaps he was an ostrich like Heidi, who would not allow herself to believe that anything had changed.

Apart from a couple at a table at the far end of the room, the restaurant was empty. The proprietor guided them to a large family table in the middle of the room and hovered for their order.

"Order anything you like," David said. He ordered wine to inject a little cheer into their farewell. David invited the proprietor to take wine with them. The presence of a stranger at their table loosened the tension between them, and they were able to talk of things that had nothing to do with the parting that, within the hour, would be over. Nothing, that is, until the proprietor asked them their business in Vienna.

"My wife and children and her parents are taking the train to Venice," David said.

"Palestine?" the man whispered.

David nodded.

"You're lucky," he said. "And very wise."

"You could leave too," David said.

"My mother is eighty-eight years old," the man said. "She is too ill to travel. How can I leave her? She has no one else. And my wife will not leave as long as I stay. But our son is in England. We advertised for a family to take him. He's in London. He goes to school there."

"My father won't go either," David said. "I stay for the same reason as you."

"Do you ever pray for him to die?" the proprietor asked. He had no shame in the question. It seemed to him that his mother was old enough to qualify for death from natural causes. He loved her without blame. He needed no more time for reconciliation. If she died that day, no guilt would prolong his grief. He simply could not understand why God was preserving her for the unnatural end that he feared awaited them all. He confessed these feelings to David, and in return for his confidences, David was able to admit, in a whisper, that indeed he did pray for his father's death, and for those very reasons.

"We will go to the fire because we cannot leave those we love,"
the proprietor said.

"Perhaps that is as it should be," David said, because, after all,
was that not the heart of the Bindel inheritance? The proprietor
was not an ostrich after all, David thought. He was a hero of
sorts, and he wondered how many old Jews in the Third Reich
were pinning their children to their invalid sides, through no
fault of their own, but through the invisible inheritance that
bound them, a reversed alimony from children to parents, the
loving payment of an account that nature was too tardy to settle.

For the rest of the meal, David kept his eyes on his two daughters. He knew now how Great-grandpa Jakob must have felt
when he said good-bye to the milk-brothers.

"We have to leave," he said. Now he wanted the parting over
and done with. He wanted very much to be alone. Then he remembered that Aaron and Jakob would be with him, and he was
suddenly glad of it. The house in Leipzig would not be childless.

They reached the station and David was glad that the train was
already waiting. He settled them inside. Sarah held him.

"Don't say anything," she said, fearful of the traditional Bindel
farewell. "I shall write as soon as we arrive. Then I shall write
daily, and so will the children. We shall all be together from day
to day," she said.

He kissed her, then held the children together with her in their
embrace. Then he turned and left the train and, holding Aaron's
and Jakob's hands, he waited on the platform and prayed that the
train would leave on time. Sarah hung from the window. It was
clear that she was smiling with great effort, that she too would
turn and, in the confines of the carriage, release her sorrow. The
guard blew the whistle and the train shunted slowly away. David
waited there long after it was gone from sight, viewing the empty
railway track and the distant clouds of steam.

Once on the road, he wondered whether he should telephone
Benjamin and let him know of his failure. But he decided against
it. Twenty miles out of Vienna, he found a small hotel where they
put up for the night. He settled the boys in their beds and was
glad at last to be alone. It was fitting for him to cry then, away
from Sarah and the children. He thought of Benjamin and he
knew that, for whatever reason—for the presumed loss of his
children, or for the shame of the hurt he had done—his brother
was crying too.

In fact, Benjamin was pacing the drawing room. He had had
no sight of Heidi since he had carried her from the garden. She'd
locked her bedroom door, calling out that she wanted to sleep.
She was deaf to Benjamin's constant entreaties. He wondered
how it would all end. He'd gone to the hospital that day and
thanked God for the work he was able to do. He worried con-
stantly about Heidi. He feared that, in desperation, she might
take her own life. So every half hour during the day, he telephoned and talked to his father or the housekeeper.

That same morning Leon had gone to the cemetery. Whenever
he was troubled, he would visit Greta's grave and find some solace there. It was summer and the flowers were in full bloom. He
sat on a bench alongside her grave. I'm eighty-one years old, he
thought. I'm strong enough in limb, and young enough in spirit
to run once more. For only in my fleeing will my children survive. For himself, Leon knew that his flight would be simply one
to a natural grave, and it seemed to him that Palestine was a
ridiculously long way to travel just in order to die. Yet when he'd
seen Heidi's face, he had felt full of blame, and that day he had
come to Greta's grave to say farewell.

He had made up his mind. He would go to Palestine together
with his sons and, he hoped, Heidi. He stooped and put a pebble
on Greta's grave, then another and another, until he had built a
small pyramid of remembrance. In Senghenydd, in Cardiff, in
Leipzig, he would leave a triangle of his loves. He sat down once
more and drew a circle on the gravel with his stick, his memories
absorbed in an old man's geometry.

On his way home, he began to grow excited at the thought of
David's return. He would ask him to lose no time in making
arrangements for the emigration of the rest of the family. He
quickened his pace and for the first time in many years, he recalled his boyhood spirit of adventure.

David began his homeward journey early in the morning. He
wanted to time his arrival with Benjamin's return from the hospital. They crossed the Austrian border at lunchtime, and were able
to take a leisurely meal before starting the last lap home. David
was surprised at his own cheerfulness and he knew it was because
of the children's company. He was glad that he had failed.

"Did Mummy know where we were going?" Aaron asked suddenly. He was barely seven years old, yet already he had a nose for deception.

David did not know how to answer the question. He did not want to presume on his brother's authority, or to tell a lie where Benjamin might have told the truth. "I don't know," he said.

"She'll be glad to see us anyway, won't she?" Jakob nudged his brother. Both of them clearly knew that their mother had been duped. "I bet you she's been crying all the time," Aaron said.

"We'll be home soon. Then you can comfort her," David told them. "Grandpa Leon, too. He will have missed you."

"Do we tell them where we've been?" Aaron asked.

"They'll know," David said.

It was just after five o'clock in the afternoon when they reached the outskirts of Leipzig, and the children began to get very excited.

"I've got an idea," David said. "When we drive into the driveway, you crouch down and hide, and I'll get out and tell them you've left. Then we shall surprise them." It was a ruse to keep them out of the way, to give David time to tell Benjamin.

As they approached the driveway, the children slunk to the floor of the car. David pulled up and went into the house. "Papa?" he shouted. "Benjamin?"

Benjamin rushed into the hall. He looked haggard, with the same guilt-ridden look he had brought with him from Buchenwald. "I have committed a crime," Benjamin said.

David shook his head. "It didn't work," he said. "They're hiding in the car." He smiled.

"*Heidi,*" Benjamin screamed, and he darted up the stairs. "Heidi," he shouted at the door. "Our children are home."

Almost immediately her door opened. Benjamin was horrified at the way she looked. Her hair was uncombed and the layers of stale makeup were caked with dried tears. She rushed past him down the stairs, breaking into a whimpering hysteria.

"Where are they?" she cried.

"In the car," David said.

Benjamin caught up with her, and managed to take her hand. David and Leon remained in the hall.

"We shall have children in the house again, Papa," David said.

"But not for long," Leon said. "You were right. You have been right all the time. I have decided to leave."

"Papa," David said, hardly believing. "We are saved. All of us."

They heard the children laughing in the driveway, and soon they were inside.

"Has Papa told you, Benjamin?" David asked. "He's decided to leave."

They all looked at Heidi. "It depends on my parents," she said. It was the first time she had offered an excuse for her stubbornness. "I'll think about it." It was the beginning of Heidi's surrender.

The following day, David made contact with his illegal immigration agent. The next sailing was due to leave just a month hence, or in the first week of September. Its port of embarkation was Naples. He advised David to prepare the family's passports and to realize what capital they could. David was satisfied. Within the month he should hear from Sarah of her safe arrival and of a base perhaps in Palestine where all the family could settle themselves. Over the next week, each member of the family waited in the long lines at the passport office. Even Heidi went, declaring that a passport was always useful and didn't commit her one way or the other. But she signed for the children without argument. Since their return, she and Benjamin had recaptured some of their former affection for each other. Indeed, they appeared to be very close. She had grown closer to Leon, too, and now replaced Sarah with her kindness and small services.

Meanwhile, David made an attempt to sell the fur business and the stock. But there were no buyers. It was clear that legal confiscation of Jewish property and businesses was only a matter of time, and no one would pay out good money for a concern that would soon be theirs by right of race and title. For the same reason, there was no interest in buying the large old family house. David realized what assets he could. He kept in regular contact with his shipping agent, and after a little while, was given the firm date of September fifth for a Naples sailing. It would be advisable, the agent said, to arrive one full day before the scheduled departure. The Bindels said no word of their leaving to anybody. Only Hans and Inge were told. Hans received the news with both sadness and relief. He would miss Benjamin profoundly. His children, too. And so, those last few weeks, they spent much of their time in the Bindel home by way of an extended farewell.

Toward the end of August, David received the long-awaited letter from Sarah. The postmark of Tel Aviv indicated that they had arrived and were safe, and he took the letter to the shop to read it privately. She wrote first of how she and the children missed him, and entreated him to persuade Leon and Heidi to make the move. Especially Heidi, she added, for Palestine was a land for children. She wrote about their journey, and although she said little, it was clear from her reticence that the voyage had been far from smooth. It had taken three whole weeks before they had sighted the Palestine coastline. There they had lingered for many days, dodging the British sentry boats that scoured the shore. Eventually they had beached along the sands of Haifa. They had been warmly welcomed and well accommodated. They had been housed all together in a kibbutz on the northern shores of Lake Galilee, a fishing settlement where work had been found for all of them. The children had started at the kibbutz school, and she herself was attending Hebrew classes. She missed him, she wrote yet again, and she hoped he would find some consolation in the thought that their children were out of harm's reach.

He put the letter away. Now he longed to be gone from this place, and he counted the days to their departure. Just over one week. He had not yet sold the house or the business, but Hans had been persuaded to move into the Bindel family home with Inge and his mother, and to hold it for them until a sale was possible. David could do nothing about the business, but he had packed the remainder of his dwindling stock and hoped to turn it into capital on arrival in Palestine. Now all they could do was wait. An uneasy waiting time, for rumors of war were rife.

Two days before they were due to leave, the German armies invaded Poland. The Bindels panicked and called Hans to drive them immediately to the station. When they were settled on the train that would take them to Naples, they firmly believed that they could safely get away. But they got only as far as the Italian frontier.

It was early morning when the train came to a sudden standstill and they were awakened by a crackling announcement on the station loudspeaker. England and France had declared war on

Germany. All transport out of the Third Reich was suspended.
This same train would return to Vienna.

For the Bindels the announcement was a sentence of death.
They were trapped in quicksand, beyond any means of escape.

And so it was that the Bindel family returned to Leipzig, and the fears that had prompted their flight were now magnified by their failure to get away. For with the borders open, there had always been the possibility of deliverance; with the borders closed, they were trapped beyond bribery or prayer. Over the next few months, oppressive measures against the German Jewish population were intensified. The fur store, like all Jewish businesses, was requisitioned by the government, and David was forced into idleness. He was profoundly depressed. He could no longer expect any communication from Sarah, and often he wondered whether he would ever see her again.

Every morning David took Benjamin's children to school. One day, as he approached the gates, he saw a number of children leave the building and make their way home. The headmaster explained that five of the teachers had been arrested and that the school could no longer operate. David drove home with a terrible premonition of what was to become of them all. It seemed to him that the Bindels, like all Jewish families in Germany, were submitting to house arrest by installments, to enforced idleness and fear. It was a dismal time for them all.

But Heidi flowered. She was not afraid, and no terrible rumors, confirmed or otherwise, would disturb her. Benjamin had never told her the details of his Buchenwald experience. Those he had shared only with Hans and his father. But Leon wanted Heidi to know them, and to know them in their gruesome detail. So in secret he told her everything. Her response was twofold. She grew even closer to Leon by virtue of his trust in her. She also finally understood that no one was exempt, and that one might as well fully espouse the Judaism of which one stood accused. So it was Heidi who urged the Bindels back into the orthodox fold. It was she who organized the regular family attendance at the synagogue, and no Jewish festival would pass without her celebration.

Among the Jewish community as a whole, the period marked a general return to the fold. The synagogue became the central meeting place, for the exchange of rumor, hope, and despair. On the Sabbath the Bindels would linger in the courtyard long after the services were over, finding comfort and a small security in the company of others in the same desperate plight. Out of this newly strengthened community grew a number of societies that concerned themselves with the study of the Jewish tradition. The Bindels began to attend Hebrew classes, and the children went on organized picnics, and sang songs and heard tales of Palestine. Each member of the community, old and young, now indulged in a dream that for most of them had come too late, a dream that would never be fulfilled.

The fate of the Bindels, like that of all German Jewish families, lay in the hands of the *Jüdische Gemeinde,* a council of elders that acted as a liaison body between the Jewish community and the government. The system was an exact replica of the function of the *kahals* in czarist Russia. While such a system functioned within its own sphere of community welfare, it performed a function vital to the cohesion of the Jewish group. But once interfered with by a hostile alien hand, it protected itself in ways that hitherto would have been unthinkable. Thus, like the *kahals* before them, the *Jüdische Gemeinde* became available to all manner of bribery and corruption. For despite the country's concern with the war, there had been no relaxation in the treatment of the Jews.

It had taken Germany only three weeks to conquer most of Poland, and stories that leaked from that Jewish community dared not be believed. By the summer of 1940, with the fall of France, almost the whole of Europe was Nazi-controlled. Jews went out and never returned to their homes. Sometimes the storm troopers came to collect them, and nothing was heard of them again. Nothing except rumor, too terrible to repeat, for its telling might give it some ring of credence. Often in these rumors one heard the word *Auschwitz.*

Toward the end of that year, when the war was raging in Germany's favor, David Bindel was invited to sit on the *Jüdische Gemeinde* of Leipzig. David was happy to accept the responsibility, for it would give him access to news otherwise restricted.

Above all, he hoped through their offices to find some means of communication with Sarah and his children. One of his first duties, on orders from the government, was to compile a census of the Leipzig Jewish community. It was a sinister directive. Even if there were to be an election, Jews were not allowed to vote, and the Jewish census was not part and parcel of a national survey. It was exclusive and its overtones were ominous. The SS had their own files on the Jewish population, but since the mass emigrations, they were somewhat out of date. This did not allow any loophole for cheating since the figures were checkable against the number of issued passports and traveling papers. It would be difficult to slip through their net.

But David Bindel was going to try. He planned to claim that his mission to Venice had succeeded, that Benjamin's children were well out of the country. If he should find their names on the list, he would erase them. He realized, of course, that if the time came for a roundup of Jews, and such rumors were rife, the children would have to be securely hidden, and David knew of no hideout or shelter.

The opportunity presented itself the following week when the preliminary lists were passed to David for his attention. Many names had been underlined, and the reasons were given in parentheses. *Deceased* or *Emigrated.* The Bindel family were listed in one group. Greta was the first to be underlined. David seldom thought of his mother. During her lifetime she had been much closer to Benjamin. She seemed to have donated her firstborn to Leon, and this was indeed the case, in memory of his first David, though David of course knew nothing of that namesake. But when David saw her name there, and the bracketed *Deceased,* he felt tears pricking behind his eyes. It was not so much her death that grieved him, but the manner of her dying. And that had been terrible.

He traced his finger down the Bindel line. His own Sarah, Esther, and Zelda were legitimately underlined as *Emigrated,* and that gave him a measure of comfort. He himself, Benjamin, Heidi, and Leon were all listed next as alive and living in Leipzig. For a moment he thought that Aaron and Jakob had been omitted. He did not at first connect them with the Hermann and Heinrich at the bottom of the Bindel list. That era seemed so many years ago. Tentatively he underlined their names. Those names were indeed dead. Even Heidi had long since ceased their use. The children themselves would now be startled by them, and probably very ashamed. At that moment he recalled their little faces when he told them that they would not be going on the ship to Palestine. That they would be going back home. And how they had feigned their disappointment.

In a careful hand, he wrote *Emigrated* after each of their names, and he prayed that the SS would take his word.

At the end of the following year, in 1941, the Japanese attacked Pearl Harbor and America entered the war. This new and formidable enemy changed the complexion as well as the course of the hostilities. Action was intensified on all fronts. Part of this intensification was the appointment of Reinhard Heydrich to organize and administer the Final Solution, and by the end of the year the mass deportations had begun.

The first roundup in Leipzig took place shortly after David had doctored the census. A directive came from the Town Council that fifty Jewish families were to assemble at the Leipzig bus station in two weeks from the date of the order. Guidelines were given as to how the selection was to be made. Those to be expelled were the unemployed, the sick, and the poor. Their destination would be a "Jewish Settlement in the East," where they would find work and comforts. The *Jüdische Gemeinde* was content to believe that such a residence was the point of the expulsion. And at least they could keep families together. They called a meeting for the painful discussion of selection. The Bindels were neither poor, unemployed, nor sick, so they did not qualify for the roundup. So David went to the meeting without fear but with a certain shame that he would be party to the expulsion of those of his own kind. None of the members of the board qualified either, and each of them nourished the illusion that they never would, whatever the conditions. But David was not deceived. Sooner or later his turn would come.

The list of fifty families was drawn up, and each member of the committee shared in that responsibility. Notices were sent out to each address, giving the time and the place of the assembly. Each family, according to the order, was permitted to take one suitcase, and this allowance confirmed their trust in the promise that they were indeed going for settlement.

On the appointed day, David went to the bus station. He could have wept when he saw them all assembled there, obeying the command, waiting in line, their cardboard suitcases, most of

them bulging and secured with string, at their feet. Most of them
were from the Jewish quarter of the town. Many of them were
from the very orthodox sect, bearded, ringleted and caftaned. A
group of storm troopers herded them into line, pulling the odd
beard if its wearer was tardy. There were no buses in sight and
David wondered as to the method of their transport. Soon afterward a large truck rolled into the station. David gauged its size.
There was hardly room inside for thirty people, but the contingent numbered over three hundred. The storm troopers ordered
the ramp to be lowered and they herded their charges inside. It
was soon full, and most of the families still lingered outside. The
troopers pushed them in, beating them on their backs to hurry
them. There were cries from children who had been separated
from their parents. Suitcases burst open in the crush and their
contents were kicked aside by the guards. David saw a pair of
black leather phylacteries roll into the gutter. He turned away,
appalled. He could hear cries, and then a barring of the truck
door. All was silent then, and he dared to turn and look again.
The bus station was empty.

David got into his car and followed at a safe distance. He
wanted to ascertain which road it was taking, whether indeed it
was going eastward or whether they were to be dumped outside
the city and left to suffocate in the transport. In any case, if they
were indeed going to the East in such conditions, they would
never reach it alive. He prayed that if they had to die, their
deaths would be quick and merciful. The truck stopped at traffic
lights and he was obliged to pull up close behind it. He turned
down his window and from the back of the truck he heard a
sound that curdled his heart. The mourning tones of the *kaddish*.
They were already celebrating their dead. The truck moved on
and David followed. They were approaching the road that gave
out to highways leading to the east and west. At the junction, the
truck turned westward. After a mile or two it turned down a side
road, and it was clear to David that it was making for the old
Leipzig railway station, long since out of service for passenger use
and used now only for cattle and freight. He stopped the car. It
would have been folly to allow himself to be seen as a spectator.
He swerved off the road and parked the car in a cul-de-sac of
warehouses.

Then he walked back to the station. He concealed himself behind a wooden fence that shielded the railway yard from the

road. He stood on tiptoe and peered over. A freight car stood on the sidings, its sliding doors open. The Leipzig truck had come to a halt, and the guards opened the doors. Bodies fell out, one on top of the other, and some of them rose and made their bewildered way into the fresh air. But some lay on the ground, either too weak to move, or simply dead. From where David stood, it was hard to tell, but he saw the truck emptying and the body of what looked like an old man on the floor inside. Someone had covered him with a prayer shawl. The children were crying, many of them lost. Families desperately regrouped themselves, finding in their kinship some sort of comfort. The group was littered with broken suitcases, and even now their owners sought to reassemble them, to retie the string with meticulous care. David saw one of them actually smile, an old rabbi, as he managed to get the sides of his case to meet and to secure them with string—displaying for all to see that great Jewish talent for parceling, learned over centuries of enforced and sudden flight.

David waited while the throng milled in the sidings, sniffing at one another's fear and bewilderment. He wondered where the other contingents had come from. They were not all sickly-looking, and many of them, by their mien and their dress, looked prosperous. Each remaining Jew in Germany would have his turn, David knew, and he trembled at the thought of their future. Most disheartening of all was the sight of so many children. Most of them were crying, and those dry-eyed stared vacantly with fear. They were all too young to have armed themselves with weapons for survival, too young indeed for that word to have entered their hearts and find some meaning there. Too young to survive, but old enough to die, they clung to their fathers' and mothers' hands, and wondered why those once so strong and reliable hands were now trembling.

The guards had begun to herd the deportees onto the freight car. They prodded them with their batons as if they were cattle. Those already in the van stretched out helping hands to the old and the frail. Mothers hoisted their children onto the van then climbed in after them. It took a long time to load them all. Most of them clung desperately to their suitcases, as if the ownership of tools, clothes, and prayer books would vouch for their future, a future in which to work, to take one's leisure, and to pray. At last no deportee was left on the siding and the heavy sliding doors were closed.

"Where's that train going?" David asked one of the guards.

"To hell," the man said. "One way."

David got back into his car and drove home. He would not tell his family what he had seen, nor any of the members of the *Jüdische Gemeinde.* If they had illusions about settlements in the East, it would be folly to shatter them. They would be forced to live in day-to-day dread of their future, to live with those fears that now plagued David every moment of his days and nights.

Some weeks later, another roundup was ordered, and this time the edict contained no directive as to the category of the selection. The request was straightforward and without reservations. Two hundred Jewish families. A meeting of the *Gemeinde* was called. David was loath to attend. The lack of specific orders for selection would make him party to choice. Yet he was afraid not to attend, lest his own family be part of the list. His presence at the meeting would at least delay their turn. Every member of the *Gemeinde* board were of the same disposition, reluctant to sentence another, yet fearful in their absence of their own sentencing.

They sat at the table with the copy of the order in front of them. Two hundred families. No more and certainly no less, ordered for employment and settlement in the East. No qualifications necessary. "How shall we choose?" the chairman of the board asked, though he expected no reply, for no one was willing to take the initial responsibility for the sentencing of others. There was silence around the table.

"We must think of some kind of system," the chairman said after a while.

"Have you any suggestions?" one of the members asked.

"We could select by streets," he suggested. "Or professions, or within a certain age limit."

But to David all these suggestions smacked of deliberation. They were guidelines as much as those they had received for the first roundup. Except that those qualifications were laid down by others. These they would be submitting themselves.

"Why don't we have a lottery?" David suggested. It sounded cruel to play with people's names as if they were dice, but at least their choice of list would be arbitrary. Even the hand that drew the name could not be held responsible.

They understood that David's suggestion would help assuage their consciences and they readily agreed. So they set about writing the names and addresses on separate sheets of paper. They divided the work between them, but even so, it took most of that day. By early evening the papers were folded and there was the question of a covered receptacle to hold them. They settled on a dustbin, an appropriate lodging, David thought, mindful of that gruesome sight at the railway siding. To most Germans, Jewish names were rubbish and waste, and their consignment to a dustbin, even in a lottery, was a fitting enough start to their journey to the dumping grounds. The dustbin was filled, the lid secured, and it was rolled on the floor to give every name a chance to lose. The chairman declared that the responsibility of drawing the names must be shared between all members of the board. Two hundred families. Ten board members. They would be obliged to twenty draws apiece.

The secretary took down the names as they were called. She herself enjoyed the same unspoken immunity as members of the board, but with each draw, she feared for the names of her relatives and friends. Forty families had been selected and it was David's turn to draw. All the names were strangers to him, but that was no comfort—for he felt they were part of his family. The last name he drew was Ernst Mayer, a member of their board. There was a ripple of consternation. Ernst Mayer slumped in his seat. The chairman was quick to invoke their privilege, now spoken for the first time. "We are exempt until the very last," he said. And to David, "Draw again."

Eventually the quota was filled. On the following day letters would be sent to all of them requiring their presence at the Leipzig bus station at ten o'clock in the morning that following week. The promise of work and settlement was the same and so was the suitcase allowance.

Once again David drove to the bus station at the appointed time and once again he was sickened by the deportees' obedience. This time he noticed that the suitcases were of a generally better quality and there was little string in evidence. But there was the same meek servility, a desire almost to please. After all, were they not being offered work and settlement? None of them wanted to make a nuisance of themselves. Some were even on the verge of gratitude. Like their predecessors, they were herded into a truck that could by no means accommodate them.

David followed them. The same road, the same bypass of the eastern highway. The same destination of the old Leipzig railway.

He parked in the same cul-de-sac and peered over the fence. Hundreds of obedient non-Aryans bowing to an Aryan code they dared not think was bad for them. Herded together, clinging to their kin, they already looked as poor and as ill as those who had gone before them. Like them, they shared the same obsession with their suitcases, their insurance for a future. David did not want to see them in transport. He was no longer curious as to the manner of their travel or their whereabouts. To have stayed to witness it a second time would have been to relish and savor his own survival. In time, all their turns would come.

At home, he dreaded every phone call, fearing a summons to another selection. After the second roundup there was almost a month's grace, and David began to believe that the Nazis had had their fill. Then, suddenly, they started again, and new and indiscriminate roundups were ordered every week. The committee used the same method of lottery, and each member was aware of the growing hollowness of the bin. Over the last few months the lottery had sent thousands of people to the sidings. In Nazi terms, Leipzig was almost *Judenrein*. At the end of one of their meetings the chairman said, "We have to face the fact that we on this committee can no longer escape our turn. We must prepare our families. I want to thank you all for helping me," he said. "Perhaps our next meeting will be our last. Ours has not been an enviable task."

The next meeting was indeed the last gathering of the *Jüdische Gemeinde*. Not a single Jew was to remain in Leipzig. The board met and sentenced itself to deportation. By that time, rumors from the East had confirmed the lie of "settlement." The members of the board had no expectation of a future. They knew that the suitcases were a mockery, that death called for no special change of clothing.

"We will meet a week hence at the bus station," the chairman said. "We will be the last Jews to leave Leipzig."

All but two, David thought, and suddenly panicked. The SS had not questioned Aaron's and Jakob's emigrated status. Now their discovery would be as dangerous as their deportation. He could no longer postpone telling Benjamin. He reached home in time to kiss Aaron and Jakob good night. I'll wait until they're asleep, he thought, and then I'll tell the family. By the time he'd told them a story—David's nightly task since the departure of his own children—it was suppertime. I'll wait till after supper, he thought. He had to tell them then. Tomorrow the official letter would come from the *Gemeinde* and they must not be caught unawares. Though it would come as no great surprise. On the last Sabbath at the synagogue, they could not ignore the empty pews, nor turn a deaf ear to the whispered rumors. They never pressed David for information, but they knew by his continuing silence that sooner or later the Bindels, like all the others, would be sent from Leipzig. Often during supper that evening, David opened his mouth to speak, but each time he swallowed his food on words that he couldn't find.

In the middle of the meal, the telephone rang. Benjamin went into the hall to answer it. From the dining room, it was difficult to hear his conversation. After a while, Benjamin summoned Heidi. It was her mother calling from Berlin. Heidi was some time on the telephone, and when she returned to the table, she was smiling. "D'you know it's our wedding anniversary next week?" she said to Benjamin. "Don't worry," she said, putting her hand on his, "I'd forgotten too. But Mother hadn't. She's sending us the silver candelabrum. You remember it, Benjamin? It was my grandmother's." A premature legacy, David could not help thinking, hardly merited by an ordinary wedding anniversary, and the news disturbed him. But what was to follow disturbed him even more. "They're going away for a month," Heidi went on. "To Wiesbaden. For the waters."

"A month?" Benjamin said. "That's a long time in a spa."

"I thought so too," Heidi said. "But Mother says they might stay even longer. Father needs a long rest, she said."

David trembled. Heidi's mother had telephoned to say good-bye. She, with Heidi's father, had an appointment at the Berlin bus station. They, too, were bound for "Eastern Settlement," which, for her daughter's sake, she called a spa in Wiesbaden. The legacy of the solid silver candelabrum was not so premature after all. Now was certainly no time, David thought, to broach the matter of the impending journey, else they might link it with Wiesbaden and wonder. They must speak of something else first, and David scratched in his mind for some topic of conversation. The war? That was rarely a subject of conversation in the Bindel household. Win or lose, it could make no difference to their present situation. They were fighting their own battle, and they knew it was a losing one.

"Would you look at my foot after supper, Benjamin?" Leon

suddenly said. "I tripped on the stairs today. I think I may have
sprained it."

David was dismayed. Now was no time for one's health to
falter. His father was eighty-four years old, but still young in his
years, and fit. David could not remember one day of sickness in
his father's life.

"Why didn't you tell me right away?" Benjamin said. "Let me
look at it now."

"It'll wait," Leon smiled. "After supper."

Now he could tell them, David decided. The echoes of Wiesbaden had been safely dispersed. Now was the time.

"Our turn has come," he said suddenly.

"Turn?" Heidi asked. "For what?"

"We are to be deported," David said. "We are on the next list."

"We won't be here for the candelabrum," Heidi said. "What
will happen to it?" Then she realized the implications of David's
statement. She shrugged her shoulders. "Well, it's only a candelabrum," she said.

There was silence then around the table.

"We have survived worse," Leon said after a while. "What a
pity about my foot. Look at it, Benjamin," he said. In his mind,
his foot had now become a hurdle to survival. It was imperative
that Benjamin cure it before his father's last battle would begin.

"All of us?" Benjamin asked, and he thought of his children.

"I took Aaron and Jakob off the register. I marked them as
emigrated. The SS accepted it. They don't have to go."

"But where . . . ?" Heidi whispered. Her face was white with
fear.

"They must be hidden," David said.

"That's impossible." Benjamin's voice was trembling. "Where
should they hide? We cannot ask anyone to hide them. Harboring
Jews is punishable by death. We've known it to happen. In Hol-
land, in Norway, in Denmark, they've been caught and publicly
hanged. We can't ask anyone to take that risk. We have to take
them with us."

"Hans?" Heidi dared to whisper. "He's their godfather."

It was astonishing, David thought, how she, whose former intransigence had prevented her children's flight, was now perfectly
prepared to hand them over. She must at last have understood
that deportation meant death. Her choice was very simple and
she was desperate to make it.

"Impossible," Benjamin said. "We cannot ask our closest friend to put himself at such a risk. Or Inge. Or his mother. It's impossible."

"They're coming over later on," Heidi said.

Almost every evening Hans would drop in after supper. Because of his specialized job in radar, he was exempt from army recruitment.

"We must say nothing to them," Benjamin said.

"But we must tell them we are leaving," David said. "We cannot just disappear from their lives without warning."

"Why not?" Leon said. "What is gained by telling them?" He was thinking of Heidi's parents' journey to the Wiesbaden spa. "They will understand," he said. "Now take a look at my foot."

He left the table and went into the drawing room, and Benjamin followed him. The doorbell rang.

"That'll be Hans," Heidi said. She made for the front door, then turned. "Do we tell him or don't we?"

"We say nothing," Benjamin said.

Hans was alone. Inge was tired, he said, and had decided on an early night. "I heard rumors today," he said as he took the armchair that Heidi offered him.

David went to the cupboard. "Would you like a drink, Hans?" he said. He didn't want to hear Hans's rumors. He knew well enough what they were. He poured him a brandy. "Your health," he said, giving him his glass.

None of them asked what the rumors were. Then Hans knew that they were true. "Are they sending you away?" he said.

Benjamin was examining Leon's foot. "Can you stretch it, Papa?" he said.

"Well, are they or aren't they?" Hans asked. His voice was raised.

"Yes," Benjamin said. There was no point in denying it.

"All of you?" Hans whispered.

"The house will be empty," Leon said. "And yours if you wish."

"Not mine," Hans said. "I'll just look after it till you return."

No one took him up on that. For it was clear to them all, including Hans, that they would not see Leipzig again.

"Is there anything else you want me to do?" Hans said. "Your investments, your dealings with the bank, insurances." He wanted tasks to perform, specific tasks that would presuppose their return.

"I shall put everything in order," Leon said, "before we leave. There's Greta's grave," he suddenly added. "I would like you to take care of it."

Hans went over to the old man and embraced him. "I'll come back in the morning," he said. "I'll help you with all the arrangements."

"What about your work?" David asked.

"That won't run away," Hans said.

It was clear now that Hans was in a hurry to leave. He was shocked by the news, and needed to be alone to assess his loss. They did not try to keep him.

"I'll see myself out," he said.

They heard the front door close.

"Poor Hans," Leon said, neatly shifting their own despair.

"What about the children?" Heidi said. The subject had lingered unspoken in the drawing room during the course of Hans's visit.

"There's nowhere they can hide," Benjamin said. "We shall take them. We shall all go together." He looked at Heidi. "I don't want to talk about hiding anymore. Tomorrow we shall tell them we are all going on a journey." He returned to the examination of Leon's foot. "It's sprained," he said after a while. "I'll put a bandage on it. But you must rest it as much as you can."

Benjamin went upstairs to the medical cabinet. He looked at the array of bottles and a terrible thought crossed his mind. In the hospital he had access to drugs that would painlessly and swiftly put an end to them all. But who would administer them? Who would dole them out to his children? "We will survive," he said to himself. "We must. All of us."

He took the bandage downstairs and dressed his father's foot. Heidi was clearing the dining room table and David was helping her.

"What must we take with us?" she asked him.

"We're only allowed one suitcase," he said. "For all of us." He didn't want to tell her that even one suitcase was superfluous. Yet he suspected she knew.

Over the next few days they would, each one of them, play the game of survival.

"You should go to bed, Papa," David heard Benjamin say.

"I'm not tired," his father said. He did not want to be alone. He needed the comfort of company even if that company was silent. When Heidi and David had finished in the kitchen, they returned to the dining room.

"Shall we have a nightcap?" David suggested.

The Bindels rarely drank unless it was wine with meals, but now seemed a time to break with custom, to question habits of a lifetime, to risk change since there was nothing to lose.

"I'll have a cognac," Leon said.

"Me too," Benjamin and Heidi said together.

David saw his father raise his glass and he trembled at what futile toast he had in mind.

"To survival," Leon said. "Of all of us."

They sat around the fire until the clock chimed midnight, and all were loath to leave each other. When the front doorbell rang, piercing the silence between them, they all trembled. Was it possible that the troopers had come for them—that even a week's grace would be denied them?

"I'll go," David said.

"Ask who it is," Heidi whispered.

But David did not want to know. Not until he had to. He opened the door.

Hans stood there with Inge.

"It's Hans," David shouted in the direction of the drawing room, and in their delighted relief they all came into the hall to greet him.

"Take your coats off," David said.

But neither Hans nor Inge made a move to disrobe. "We want to hide the children," Hans said. "Please," he added, anticipating their objections. "They'll be safe with us. And happy. As happy as we will be to have them. We'll move into the country. Near Halle. I will arrange everything."

"But it's dangerous for you and Inge and your mother. You know what happens if you get caught," Benjamin said.

"We've talked about it. Mother too. We know the risks. But we cannot stand by and do nothing."

"Take off your coats," Leon said.

Now they were prepared to do so, for it seemed that they might come to an agreement. David poured them a drink. Hans raised his glass.

"To Aaron and Jakob," he said. "And to your return."

Heidi began to cry. She cried with sorrow that they would soon be parted; she cried with joy that her children would live. There was no need for words between them, words of gratitude or comradeship. Inge put her arm on Heidi's shoulder. "Try to remember that they are alive and well, and to them you will always be their mother. And Benjamin their father. I promise you that. The war cannot go on forever."

"They will have to be called Hermann and Heinrich again," Hans laughed. "We're lucky that they're both fair-skinned. Don't worry. We won't send them to school. We'll teach them ourselves at home. We'll take no risks, I promise you."

"What shall we tell the children?" Heidi asked.

"We'll tell them the truth," Benjamin said. "We'll tell them all the truth we know."

David was glad then that he had not taken Benjamin to the railway sidings. The truth that Benjamin would, in all his honesty, tell his children would allow for their possible reunion.

When Hans and Inge had gone, all four Bindels were suddenly anxious to retire. It had nothing to do with fatigue, but rather with the need now to be alone, the need for each one of them to make his solitary entry into the land of grief and sorrow.

The following morning, Benjamin went to the hospital early. Rumors that the hospital would soon be closed had been confirmed in a letter from the authorities. Arrangements were being made to send all patients home, even those who would die if withdrawn from treatment. Benjamin did his ward rounds, comforting as best he could.

"I shall be going home tomorrow, Doctor," one of his patients called from his bed.

Benjamin went toward him. "You'll like that," he said. "You're getting your own way at last."

Mr. Zeider, a cancer patient, ignorant of his terminal condition, had daily begged to be sent home. And daily his ailing wife had visited the hospital and begged them to keep him, for she herself was not strong enough to care for him. If God were good, Benjamin thought, He would take them both into His keeping. But clearly in these terrible times, if there were a God at all, His back was turned.

He finished his ward rounds and was now anxious to get home. There were six days left before they had to keep their appointment, six days in which to print indelibly on his mind's eye an image of his children that would last until the day, he dared to hope, when they would be together again. But first he and Heidi must tell them about Hans and Inge and their new country home.

He let himself into the house and heard his children's voices from the drawing room. They were laughing. He followed the sound. They were sprawled on the floor with Hans, who was working their train set.

"Uncle Hans keeps calling us Hermann and Heinrich, Daddy," Jakob laughed as his father entered the room.

"Where's Mummy?" he said.

"She's making lunch," Aaron said. "Uncle Hans is staying."

Benjamin went into the kitchen. He was not surprised to find his father there too, and it heartened him. Ever since Sarah's departure, Heidi and his father had grown closer to each other. He was glad that however they would journey, and wherever their destination, the Bindels would at least be unburdened by family strife.

"How's your foot, Papa?" he asked.

"I've been resting it," Leon said.

Benjamin bent down and undid the bandage. The swelling had eased a little, but the pain persisted, Leon said, whenever he put his foot on the ground.

"It will go," Benjamin said, rebandaging. "Just keep resting it." He eased on his father's shoe. It was an ill-timed injury. They would all need their health and strength to weather the impending journey. The Eastern Settlements were hundreds of miles away and the journey would be wearisome. Then they would have to adapt themselves to new surroundings, new work, new friends. Sometimes Benjamin firmly believed the Nazi promise of happy resettlement and he would not admit to himself that there could be any other interpretation. Then why, he said to himself, am I leaving my children behind? He knew well enough, but would not give it voice. Such thinking was totally illogical, but he believed it fervently and so did the thousands of others who went to the railway sidings. Because, even with one's penultimate breath, death was something that happened to other people.

"When shall we tell the children?" Heidi asked. She took his hand and fondled it, knowing that there was little time to make up for the loving that had been lost between them for so many years.

He kissed the top of her head. "After lunch," he said.

David was called from the garden, where he had spent most of the morning sweeping the first of the autumn leaves from the lawn. For a time he had managed to forget about the impending journey, to concentrate on the leaves and their symbol of season. Their golden colors were herald to winter and the snow on the lawn—through which snowdrops and crocuses would insist on their time in their season. And this time next year he would sweep the leaves again to make way for the snows and the snow-drops and he would be part of nature's cycle for all eternity.

He was glad Hans was at the table, and the children were hanging on to each syllable of his stories.

"I've bought a house in the country," Hans suddenly announced.

"Oh, can we go there, Uncle Hans?" Aaron said.

"Please, Daddy," Jakob echoed. "Can we go and stay with Uncle Hans?"

The children were doing it for him, Benjamin thought, leaving on their own account. For a moment he thought that the suggestion of a holiday might be the only way to part from them. Yet it would be a monstrous deception, a trick that they might never forgive.

"Why not a little holiday?" Leon said, quickly picking up on that solution, and sanctioning its deception. "They could help Hans with the moving."

"We'll go on Thursday," Hans said. "Is that all right, Benjamin?"

"I think that's a lovely idea," Heidi said.

Was it all over? Was it all done? Had they orphaned their children so swiftly with this deception? To what home would they return?

"How long can we stay, Daddy?" Aaron asked, as if prompting the truth from his father's lips.

"Perhaps for a long time," he said. "Listen to me, children." He looked at them tenderly. Nine and ten years old, he had to remind himself. What could they understand of pogrom? "You remember," he said, "when you had to leave your old school, d'you remember why?"

"They didn't like the Jews," Jakob said.

"That's right. And now they're going to send all the grown-up Jews away. We don't know where, but it won't be very far, and it's only until the war is over." He was allowed a little license, Benjamin thought, for pity's sake. "You are going to stay with Uncle Hans and Aunt Inge, and you have to pretend that you are not Jews. That's why you have to be Hermann and Heinrich again, because they're not Jewish names." He stopped.

"Is Grandpa going too?" Jakob asked. His voice was tearful. It wasn't going to be a holiday after all.

"Yes," Benjamin said. "And Uncle David, too."

"Is that why Aunt Sarah went to Palestine?" Aaron asked.

Benjamin, David, and Leon knew at that moment that wherever they looked, it must not be at Heidi. They heard her sob-

bing. Perhaps for the first time she realized the terrible price of
her former stubbornness.

"Why are you crying, Mummy?" Jakob went to her side. "The
war won't last very long. Uncle Hans says so. We'll all be together again soon."

Leon shuddered. Was every Bindel born with that phrase on
his tongue? To hear it from the mouth of Benjamin's children, so
full of innocent hope and expectation, was to hear the lie of their
father's hopes. And he wondered whether they should not be told
the truth, that henceforward they were orphans and the only
living males of the Bindel line.

"Yes," Hans said, because he couldn't bear the truth any more
than the children. "You will all be together again soon."

And so the Bindel children were gently orphaned.

There were four days left. David, Leon, and Heidi did not
leave the house at all. Benjamin went to the hospital early each
day, until the last day, when there was no work for him at all. All
the patients had been sent home, and storm troopers had arrived
to commandeer the building.

It was the night before the children were to leave with Hans
and Inge. Heidi had packed for them, and made a celebration
supper. All of them were at pains to make it a festive occasion.
Tomorrow the house would be childless for the very first time
since Leon had returned to Leipzig and started his second family.
When the meal was over, the boys helped Heidi clear the table,
and while they were in the kitchen, Benjamin turned to his father.

"Papa," he said. "I want my children to inherit."

Leon smiled at him. "Let's go upstairs to Zelda's room." It
was in that place that he had bequeathed to his own children
Grandpa Jakob's litany. Of all the four traceable generations of
Bindel brothers, Aaron and Jakob were the youngest, and Leon
wondered what they would make of it all. He recalled the bluebell wood where he had bequeathed to his first David the prayer
for survival, and how, in all his thirteen years, the boy had understood. He recalled too the forest behind the Odessa tavern where
he and Aaron had inherited. He remembered that he had understood it at the time. And his own father, Benjamin, the milk-
brother, with his unleavened bread in his baggage and terror in
his heels, who in all his ten years had accepted the weaponry of
survival, and in time understood its power. He rose from the

table and called his grandchildren. "Come. Let us all go," he said. They went upstairs.

Leon began those familiar words. "First, I have to tell you a little of the history of the time."

So between them, Leon, Benjamin, and David, they told of the milk-brothers' years in the tavern, of Meisels and the *kahal*, of the children's conscription and the milk-brothers' miraculous return. Leon watched the light flicker in his grandchildren's eyes, with the wonder and the excitement that a fairy tale evokes. And suddenly he could not bear to break their spell. He could not tell them the story of that gentle Leon after whom he himself was named. Neither could he tell them the story of the fire. But he told them about survival in his own simple terms.

"Life is sometimes very hard," he said, "and sometimes we give in. We don't fight. I want you to fight to live, my children. Whatever names men may call you, whatever harm they try to do to you, you must always fight to live. We call that surviving. It is a difficult word to understand, and it is a word as long as the history of the Jews themselves. But as you grow older, you will learn its meaning. Aaron and Jakob," he said slowly, "I want you to survive. Now go to bed, my children."

They came toward him for his embrace, and he held them long in his arms.

"Grandpa," Aaron said. "You must survive, too."

Leon turned away his face; he knew that they had understood.

That night Benjamin took a large piece of paper and wrote in his best hand the exact words of Grandpa Jakob's legacy. On another sheet, he wrote the story of Leon and his Siberian imprisonment. And he wrote too the story of the fire. He folded them into a large envelope, which he addressed to his sons. In the morning when Hans came to fetch them, he put it into Hans's hands as his last will and testament. Hans put it away without a word.

No farewells were made until the children were settled in the car. They all came out into the driveway, and in turn they leaned into the car and kissed the children good-bye. Heidi was the last, and Benjamin held her body close to his to still her trembling. They smiled, all of them, as they waved the children good-bye, and Aaron and Jakob saw their mother turn her back and they wondered at it. The car reached the end of the driveway and turned into the street, the children still looking behind them.

Then Leon, David, Benjamin, and Heidi held each other close and returned to the house to begin their mourning.

When night fell, Heidi suggested that they organize their packing. With the allowance of only one suitcase between them, it was important, she said, for each one to choose his own essentials. David knew the fraud of those suitcases, but suddenly he was anxious to make his contribution. To go without luggage of any kind was to abdicate entirely.

"I'll take my new gray suit," he said. Not only would he pack, but he would be dressed for the occasion. Benjamin, too, decided on his best suit, and so did Leon. Benjamin took the suitcase down into the hall, together with his newly stocked medical bag, then he and David took their father to his room. Benjamin noticed that he was still limping.

"How's the foot, Papa?" he said.

"It will be better tomorrow," Leon said.

None of them slept that night. They tossed on their beds and wished for the morning. When it came, they rose, bathed, and breakfasted as if it were an ordinary day. They all put a package of food in their pockets, then they left the house together. David had arranged that Hans would pick up the Bindel car at the bus station.

They were early for their appointment, but when they reached the bus station, it was already crowded. They were horrified to note the number of infirm, those in wheelchairs or simply carried on the arms of relatives. And so many children. Benjamin caught sight of a mother whom he had delivered of a son only a week ago. The baby was feeding at her breast and on her face was a look of bewilderment at the world into which he had been born.

The trucks began to pull into the station. Four of them, David noted, many more than he had seen on his former witnessing, but still hardly enough to accommodate the growing crowd that frantically surged onto the platform fearful of missing their transport. The troopers began to load the first truck and there were those who rushed toward it, no doubt hopeful of better accommodation. But David held his family back. It was better to be last on the trucks. The danger of suffocation was less, for there was a small ventilation from the slats on the doors that could well mean the difference between life and death. They watched as the invalids were wheeled toward the ramp.

"No chairs," a storm trooper shouted as one old man was wheeled toward the truck. "You have to carry him."

His escort, probably his son, David thought, was old enough in years, and looked hardly able to carry himself. He looked around helplessly for some support. But those about him looked away. Benjamin made to go to his help. But Leon pulled him back.

The storm trooper grew impatient with the escort's feeble attempt to lift his patient. He pushed him aside, lifted the old man from his chair, and practically threw him into the truck. There was a scream of horror from the waiting spectators, but it was quickly stifled lest they themselves receive the same treatment.

David held his family back until the third truck began to load. He knew they would underestimate its capacity, even by their own cruel reckoning, and that it would be the last truck that would bulge with the uncontainable overflow. He waited until it was almost full, then he urged his family forward. Heidi took Leon's arm, and Benjamin noted again his father's limp. He took his other arm, and David took the suitcase on which he was now beginning to believe all their lives depended. They were fortunate to be the last ones on the third truck. There was room to shuffle about and to find some breathing space. Twice before, David had taken this route. He knew the road by heart, and when the truck swerved, he knew that they had bypassed the route to the East and were on their way to the railway sidings.

"It won't be long now, Papa," he whispered to Leon at his side.

"I'm fine, I'm fine," Leon insisted. "Don't worry about me."

He would not have said that, Benjamin thought, if there had been no cause for concern. His foot was hurting him and he was at pains to hide it. When Benjamin had rebandaged it that morning, the swelling had almost disappeared, yet still his father limped, as if he was in no hurry to meet his end. Death had lurked so often in many corners of his life. It could loiter a little longer.

There was silence in the truck, the hush of bewilderment and fear. A baby cried and was quickly put to the breast, lest its whereabouts be discovered. The truck slowed down and David could hear the gravel under the tires. It was drawing into the railway siding. Suddenly it stopped, and its frightened cargo girded itself to alight. But the doors remained bolted. David listened intently. He could hear no noise on the outside, though there must have been at least two truckloads parked on the siding. The storm troopers had changed their tactics and he felt cheated. Shortly afterward he heard the arrival of what he assumed was the fourth truck. He heard the grinding wheels on the gravel, the screeching of brakes, and again the silence. They waited. Then they heard the sound of heavy sliding doors and David knew that they were preparing the freight car for entry. Shortly afterward the truck doors were opened, and the deportees tumbled out, grateful for the air and reprieve, no matter how short its duration. But alas, it was short enough, for right away they were ordered toward the train and bullied inside. Again David held his family back, and for the same reason. He looked around. It was the same scene he had witnessed twice before from behind the fence in the cul-de-sac. Except that this time, there was a difference.

A crowd of spectators had gathered on the perimeter of the railway siding, looking down on the arena. Some were cheering and jeering; others were silent, drinking in each detail of that story that they would forbear to tell their children.

The Bindel family watched as the deportees were herded into the car. Soon those doors would be closed on all of them, on that stage of the drama that David had not witnessed. Until that time he had been able to guide his family along the lines of his own experience, but once behind those doors, they would all dwell in the same black ignorance.

He delayed their boarding as long as he could. Then a guard made his way toward their group, his baton raised. They dodged him, and hurried toward the car. Benjamin and David helped their father to board first, then Heidi, while the blows rained down on Benjamin's and David's backs, urging them to hurry. They were the last to board, and scarcely had Benjamin's foot slipped over the platform than the doors were slid shut and there was total darkness inside. The train shunted forward.

After a while they grew accustomed to the dark and they could see the faces around them. They shifted about, trying to find room for themselves. Benjamin sat his father on the suitcase, and David was glad that he had not advised them against baggage. For most of the cargo there was standing room only, and some held their children in their arms, for fear they might be trampled underfoot. Apart from the whimpering and the moaning, the truck was strangely silent, and Benjamin was reminded of his journey to Buchenwald, when the prisoners had kept that same silence, the silence that turns away from curiosity, lest the information received be unbearable. Everyone on the train knew enough about their present situation. Nobody wanted to know any more.

"Is there a doctor?" someone suddenly shouted into the dark.

"Yes. Here." Benjamin's response was automatic. "Where are you?"

"Here," a man's voice shouted. "By the wall. My wife's having a baby."

The people around Benjamin squeezed together to allow him a narrow passage to the wall of the train. He held his medical bag high above his head.

"Here, here," the man called, and guided him with his voice to where his wife was crouching.

Benjamin bent down at her side. "Lie down," he said to her gently. The people around made what room they could for her, and turned their faces away.

"It's our first," the father said, crouching by his side. Benjamin examined the woman as best he could. She was in the last stage of labor. He decided to stay by her side. She was a young girl, Benjamin surmised, probably twenty years old. Her body was healthy. She would survive. Her face was twisted with pain, but she stifled her cries, aware of her lack of privacy.

"Have you decided on a name?" Benjamin asked, wishing to engage her in conversation to allay her fears.

She shook her head. "We're waiting to see whether it's a boy or a girl. Will I be all right, Doctor?" she asked.

"Of course." Benjamin held her hand. "And so will the baby."

The girl gave a small scream that she could no longer contain. "It won't be long now," Benjamin said. "It will be painful, but during the pain you must keep in mind that soon it will all be over, and you'll hold a baby in your arms. If it helps you to scream, then scream aloud."

But her shyness overcame her need to cry out. She clenched her teeth and gripped her husband's arm. "It's time to push," Benjamin whispered in her ear. He prayed for a normal delivery. He had no equipment for any other. "Have you got a shawl of any kind?" he asked the father.

The girl's head was resting on their suitcase, and gently the man prised it open and withdrew a white woolen shawl. They had set out on their journey well prepared, full of hope and expectation of a new life, and a new life with whom to share it.

"Another push, my dear," Benjamin said. He had begun to love this girl, this total stranger who, in her quiet pain and labor, was gently affirming life, giving the lie to the death that lingered in the wagon. "Push," Benjamin said. "It's almost over."

He marveled at her silence. He even detected a small smile on her lips. He pressed his hands on her abdomen and saw the beginnings of the child's head. Benjamin had delivered countless children in his time, yet that very first vision of a newborn always appeared to him as a miracle. At the sight of this one, this impudently ill-timed arrival, he almost laughed with joy. "Push," he whispered. The head emerged. It was going to be a normal birth and he thanked God for it. He clasped the baby's skull with both hands, and carefully withdrew it from its nest.

"It's a boy," he whispered, and laid the child on her stomach. Then he cut the cord, thus giving the baby life on its own account, its inalienable separateness, its inviolate, untouchable solitude.

"*Mazeltov,*" he shouted into the car. "We have an extra passenger. A baby boy." As he spoke, he wrapped the child in the shawl, cleaned its eyes and ears with swabs of cotton wool, then handed the bundle to the mother. She was smiling. Her husband cradled her head in his arms.

"You must start thinking of a name," Benjamin said.

"What's yours?" the father asked.

"Benjamin."

"Then that's how he will be called. Benjamin, the son of my right hand."

"I'm honored," Benjamin said, and he embraced the young man. "I wish you joy of your son," he said, and meant it, although he was aware of how short-lived that joy might be. He poured a little brandy from the bottle in his medical kit. He urged the new mother and father to sip a little. And then the baby was toasted into a world bent on its destruction.

Benjamin returned to his family, and gave his father a sip of the brandy. He took Heidi's hand. "It's a lovely little boy," he said. "They've called it Benjamin."

"What's to become of us?" she whispered. Her eyes were full of tears.

He held her close. "Think of our children," he said. "We must live for them."

The train shunted along in the darkness, pulling up sharply from time to time, as if the driver were teasing his cargo. Toward evening, the real nightmare began. They sniffed at it in the darkness. The most private pursuit of all had, from want of privacy and facility, been publicized. And not a single one of them, in his or her own and natural time, would be able to escape it. During the night the smell was overpowering, and many were sick where they stood, and cried for air. There were some who cried for death, but they were quickly shouted down.

"We will get used to the smell," Leon said quietly. He was hungry, but he did not trust his digestion. The sight of food would have sickened them all. He dozed a little, leaning on Heidi's thigh, and for the first time in many years, he dreamed of Senghenydd and his firstborn. He woke with calm and peace of mind, knowing with absolute certainty that he would soon join him.

"Where can we be?" David whispered. By his watch they had been traveling for sixteen hours.

"If we're going east," Benjamin said, "we must have crossed the Polish border by now. Even though this train is very slow. It can't be much farther."

But Eastern Settlement as the Nazis had promised could, at that time, have meant Russia, too, much of which was already German-occupied. Benjamin dared not think of the distance they might still have to travel. He made his way to the wall of the car to see his namesake. He was suckling at his mother's breast between bouts of sleep. He asked her how she was, and explained about the milk. She offered the baby for him to hold, and as he did so he was overwhelmed by a sudden longing for his own children.

"I have two sons," he told her.

"What are they called?" she asked.

"Aaron and Jakob."

Benjamin returned the child to its mother and went back to his family. Heidi was crying. Her clothes were wet with her waste and her shame. He comforted her, and spoke to her words of love, and his tenderness frightened her.

"What will become of us?" she said again.

He poured brandy for them all.

Suddenly a cry was heard from the end of the wagon. Not a cry of pain, nor murmur of despair, but a chant of lamentation in which sound Benjamin detected a rogue note of joy. It was the *kaddish.* Someone in the car had died, and his death had been merciful. The song sounded like a thanksgiving. Gradually those men in the car began to hum, until the song was a chorus of glorification, a hosanna of praise. Benjamin looked at his father. His face was stern and his lips tightly sealed. "We must never celebrate death," he said, his voice breaking. "When one of our people dies, our greeting to the bereaved is almost an order. I wish you long life, we say." He raised his cup of brandy. *"Le'chaim,"* he said. "To life."

Night fell once more. Neither David nor Benjamin could sleep, but they linked arms and rocked against each other with the motion of the train.

"What are you thinking of, brother?" Benjamin asked.

"I have the same thoughts as you," David said. "We are both thinking of our children."

In the morning the stench in the car was overpowering, the odors of human waste now mixed with the smell of vomit. In time, Benjamin thought, the corpse at the end of the car would decompose. He wondered if one could ever get used to that smell. In the late afternoon, they heard the *kaddish* again.

"I wish you long life," Leon said.

Another night passed, and in the morning, waking to the stench, they wondered how long they could stay alive, and they marveled at human endurance, and began for the first time to have faith in their survival. Then suddenly the train stopped and did not start again.

"We shall have air," someone cried. "God is good," and the crowd echoed his thanksgiving. Suddenly the doors slid open.

They were blinded by the light and intoxicated by the air. Some fainted where they stood, and some were trampled on by those in the frantic rush to escape from the car. The Bindel family were among the first to climb down from the wagon, and they breathed deeply of the biting air. Benjamin waited at the doors, helping the passengers and waiting for the mother whom he had delivered. She came to the front of the wagon and handed him the baby. Then her husband jumped to the ground and lifted her down. "Where are we?" she said as she gulped for air.

Benjamin looked at his surroundings for the first time. They

reminded him of Buchenwald. For this was a camp too, though
on a vaster scale, its perimeters beyond the eyes' reach. And
despite the noise and cries of the new arrivals, as silent as the
grave. Some storm troopers leapt onto the wagon and hurried the
remaining passengers outside, beating them with their sticks.

"Where are we?" a woman asked, her eyes blinded by the light.

"Auschwitz," a guard said, and that was the first time that
many of the arrivals had heard the word. A place and a name.

"Auschwitz," Benjamin repeated to himself, the so-called Eastern Settlement.

He rejoined his family and they were herded into a line that
was moving slowly toward the gate. The Bindels kept closely
together. It was difficult to see what procedure was being followed on entry to the camp. Benjamin could see a group of
guards at the front directing the human traffic. As they neared
the gate, he saw that this traffic was being divided into two lines.
He noticed that one line consisted mainly of old people and children, while the other was made up of men and women who
looked as if they could work. By the time the Bindel family arrived at the gate, each of them knew instinctively that the divi-
sion of traffic was a very simple one. To the right meant to live,
and to the left meant to die. As they walked forward, Benjamin
noticed that his father was limping very badly. But worse still
that Heidi, on whose arm he leaned, was limping too, perhaps to
facilitate the support she gave to Leon. Her gait was not lost on
the guards. One of them shoved Leon's and Heidi's shoulders
with his stick.

"Left," he ordered.

Leon turned and looked at his sons as the guard prodded them
with his baton.

"Right," he shouted.

It was a clear moment of farewell, too sudden, too stark, too
terrible to believe. They looked across the space between them, a
no-man's-land. Benjamin looked at Heidi and tried not to convey
to her his fear. But she knew. She smiled at him. "Look after the
children," she said.

Leon was smiling too. "It's all so ridiculous," he managed to
say, then a guard prodded him on his last journey. Benjamin and
David watched them go. Then suddenly their father stopped,
turned, and shouted across the miles that separated the quick
from the dead.

"Remember Grandpa Jakob," he shouted at them, his voice cracking with the exertion. "Survive."

The word echoed across the camp and lingered on the foul air like a blessing. Benjamin and David watched them out of sight. No tears. There must be no tears. Survival was dry, without lament, without mourning. Benjamin turned to his brother. "I wish you long life," he said.

"And I to you," David answered, and because Benjamin had been twice bereaved, he added, "A long life twice over."

They stood as the death column moved slowly forward. Among them, the young mother Benjamin had so recently delivered, his namesake in her arms. She was alone, and her eyes were full of fearful wonder. Just about now, Benjamin thought, her milk would be coming through. He turned away, trembling. David took his brother's arm, and in a plaintive chant, they sang the *kaddish* together. "O Lord what is man," they prayed. "His days are of grass; as a flower in the field, so he flourisheth. For the wind passes over it and it is gone." They heard the echo of their father's words. "Survive," he had called out to them. From generation to generation there would be a troubador, a minstrel to sing that stubborn song of survival. And somewhere, someone would hear his song. Now it rang in the brothers' ears, though the minstrel, like the salmon that spawns its future and dies, had forfeited his life with his song.

Millions of people perished in the German concentration camps. And they died in all colors. Red for politicals, yellow for Jews, mauve for Jehovah's Witnesses, blue for emigrés, green for convicts, black for asocials, brown for gypsies, and pink for homosexuals. A pariah's rainbow.

Libraries have been written about them, based on the Nuremberg trials of the accused, or on the testimonies of those who survived, or on the diaries and journals that were found among the ruins. But millions of words were stifled. The basic lack of equipment—of a pencil and some paper—was one reason for the prisoners' silence; there was, too, the suspicion of one's own terrible words, that one could actually be dwelling in the hell of which one wrote. But above all else, the tale was untellable.

Out of that welter of unpublished alphabet, here follows the unwritten diary of one David Bindel, prisoner in Auschwitz, 1943. Aged thirty-four. Registration tattoo, 796702. Classification, yellow star. Jew. Inferior race. The pencil with which the diary is written never existed. Neither the paper on which it is recorded. For, in truth, there exists no pen for such calligraphy; no paper that would not ignite in the terrible fire of each syllable. But in God's sight, if His eyes were open in this place, every word is true.

It must be winter because it is snowing. Though which winter of what year, I am not sure. Hunger plays havoc with the memory. Perhaps it is the second winter in this place, because I remember being warm once, or was that a long time ago in the house in Leipzig? I must ask Benjamin. There is a calendar in the so-called hospital where he works. . . . I work in the munitions factory. I pack shell cases. There are hundreds of us in the plant. We say nothing but we think all the time of sabotage, for any Nazi enemy is our friend. Sonia talks about it to herself. I've noticed lately that she hides things under her blouse. Then she wanders off somewhere, hands clasped around her breasts. After a while, she comes back, her arms swinging, and she goes back to work with a smile. Ada does the same thing. Her tattoo is 131313. Three thirteens. She says she'll be lucky.

I shall have my picture in the paper. I weigh eighty-five pounds. They picked me out with seven others to be photographed for *Der Stürmer.*

Today Ada and Sonia keep wandering out of the factory when the guards aren't looking. There are four other girls doing the same thing. I don't know their names. But I wish they would all stop doing it.

I saw Benjamin today. He's been sent to work in the medical experiment center. Under a Dr. Mengele. He's obsessed with twins, Benjamin says. All kinds of experiments. Mainly injections for instantaneous death. He has this notion that if you inject one of the twins, the other will die too. Telepathic genetics, he calls it. He keeps trying but it takes an awful lot of twins to prove anything.
Dr. Mengele has children of his own.
Benjamin slipped some aspirin into my hand. He knows about my headaches.
He asks me if I ever think of my children. I think he was talking to himself.

I looked at my body today, and I wondered to whom it belonged.

I told them not to do it. At least I told Sonia and Ada. Tomorrow they're going to be hanged. Six of them. There's a prisoner that works in the gas chambers. He had a plan to blow them up. The girls were smuggling dynamite out of the factory. The prisoner was Sonia's husband. They buried him alive.

In the roll call area, they're rigging up a platform for the orchestra. They play while the gallows is being erected. The guards say we have to watch. It will teach us all a lesson.

Every morning outside my hut, there's a pigeon. It chooses to live in this place. It's a dove really, they tell me.

A dove?

At the foot of the gallows, I turn my head away. And so do many of the others. I'm beaten on the shoulders and forced to look. The orchestra plays the overture to *Meistersinger*. I am ashamed, but I confess to enjoying the music. I know it is the overture to hanging, but can I help it if the sounds please me? The spirit corrodes in such a place as this, and once corroded, it is divisible. Thus an SS guard will lovingly stroke his child's hair with one hand, while with the other, he scalps a Jew for a lampshade. It is possible.

Dear God, if that is so, let me not be made of Man.

To punish myself, I look hard at the girls as they are led to the gallows. God be thanked, the music sours on me. Ada is first, her three lucky thirteens hidden by the rope that ties her hands. Then Sonia. Then four others. I wish I knew their names. All of them are crying. All of them are afraid. Great-grandpa Jakob would not have applauded them. There is no cause on earth worth dying for. . . .

There are six guards on the platform, one for each noose. They string them roughly around each girl's neck. I think that's the extreme of injustice. They might be gentle, oh, so gentle, at such a time. It's quickly over. The band goes on playing and so do the guards, swinging the bodies to match the *Meistersinger* rhythm.

I don't know why I don't cry.

I don't know how I can sleep.

But I do.

I thought of my children today, and I wondered who sired them.

I am sent to the crematoria today to fetch back the towels for washing.

I can't write anymore.

Never forgive. Never.

There's a girl in the laundry. I think she's beautiful. She looks at me and I at her with a mutual remembrance of all those old longings that we can no longer translate with our hungry emaciated bodies. I want to hold her, to kiss her sunken cheek, to stroke her stubbled head. But kindness is cruelty in this place, for it is a reminder of our living past.

I saw Benjamin today. I notice that we cannot bear to look at each other. We see death in each other's eyes. But we touch each other. All the time. I have never loved him so much. He told me they had a selection at the hospital. Everyone is ordered out of bed. They have to strip, then the guards make the selection. They keep the pretty women, but the others they send to the gas chambers.

·I still cannot shed one tear.

I laughed today. I cannot remember why.

There are two women guards here. Bormann and Grese. Whenever I see Bormann, she's with two Alsatians. There's a party of women coming back from the leather factory. One of them walks slowly. She cannot keep up with the rest. Bormann sets the dogs on her. They lay her low on the ground. Then Bormann orders the dogs to the woman's throat. "Good dogs, good dogs," she says when they are finished. She actually nuzzles their noses with her lips. I walk away quickly. If you are to survive, you must not look at such things. I pass the spot later on, and the woman, or the pieces of her, still lies there.

I still cannot cry.

I have to start thinking of my children and my wife. Sometimes I cannot recall their names, and all their faces are a blur. Benjamin has children too, I think, though he never talks about them. I think of Papa all the time. I can remember *his* face very clearly. I think of the little jokes he played on us when we were children. That must have been why I laughed the other day.

Benjamin looks worse every time I see him. He told me about the sterilization. He has to pretend to give women internal examinations. While he's doing it, he has to inject a chemical irritant into the uterus. Dr. Mengele looks over his shoulder. They have women there with beards, he says, from Mengele's experiments. I'm glad I didn't study medicine. Poor Benjamin. We touch each other again.

Lately I dream a lot of Papa, Mama, Uncle Aaron. All dead.

In the morning when I awake, the air in the barracks is foul, infected by all our dreams.

Why don't we do something? Why do we let this happen? There are so many of us. But we are weak and hungry. Our hunger is greater than our rage. They are starving our vengeance. They are fasting our fury. For a meal, a bath, a change of clothing, many of us would, for a moment, forgive.

It is better we should starve.

Today a man tries to escape. He runs to the fence by the crematoria. He doesn't have the strength to climb the first few feet of wire. He *knows* he doesn't have the strength. He knew it when he started to run. He knew it even when the thought of running occurred to him. But he had to do *something*. He is a survivor who finds offensive his talent for endurance.

The guards look at him and laugh. His unfused, unearthed body, galvanized with current, burns spread-eagled across the wire. I still cannot cry.

Today I see Benjamin again. He says, "Don't worry about me," and I say the same to him. It is our way of declaring our love for each other.

Today in the munitions factory, the supervisor tells me I am a good worker. I will be promoted. Tomorrow I begin work as a *Sonderkommando,* a special attendant. Promotion.

Last night I didn't sleep at all. It pleases me, for I think my rage returns.

In the crematoria today, I learn how Papa and Heidi died.

Never forgive.
Never.

When I was a child, we had to write an essay on what our fathers did for a living. My marks were the highest in the class.

The teacher said it was because I went into great detail about everything. Detail. Cling to detail. Embrace particularity. It is an escape from what is real. For if I itemize everything I do in this job, I can shield myself from the horror of its totality. Itemize. Itemize without adornment. It is the only way to survive.

This morning outside the barracks, the pigeon isn't there.

My place of work. Birkenau. Part of Auschwitz.
Five crematoria.
Four gas chambers.
Each chamber holds fifteen hundred people.
Multiply.
Six thousand souls migrate in one firing.
Three firings a day.
Genocide.
The dressing rooms. Signs on walls in German, French, Dutch, and Danish.
Tie your shoes together.
Fold clothes neatly in a pile.
Authorities cannot be held responsible for loss.
One cake of soap per person.
One towel.
Hot coffee will be served after the showers.
Our generous captors.
Direct access from dressing rooms to "baths."
The bath.
Sprays all over the ceiling in parallel rows. Blessed clean hot water. Try not to look at the floor of the chamber.
There are no drains.
Heavy doors both sides of the "bathhouse."
Lock and bolt.
Hydrocyanic gas to be released through shower heads.
Estimated duration of dying. Three to five minutes, depending on the gas supply.
Causes of death. Rupture of the lungs.
Deaths out of season.
Unripeness is all.

So now I know how Papa and Heidi died.

Today I think of my children. I recall their names. For the
first time since I have been in this place, I cry. I do not sleep
and I am able to shed tears. Second by second my rage is fed.

I am alive once more.

But what can I do with all my rage?

My job. My promotion. I am part of the squad that services
the gas chambers.

Survive, so turn your ears from the screams and the
whimpers behind the bolted doors. Wait patiently until the
doors are opened.

Scan the bodies for any sign of life.

Watch it clubbed into peace.

Drag the bodies out.

Cut off the hair.

Place in neat bundles, according to color.

Examine all fingers for rings.

Remove them. Lead us not into temptation. Collect them in
bags.

Wait for dentists to extract teeth.

Stack bodies neatly in piles of ten each.

Shove each pile into furnace.

Time and motion study.

My job.

My promotion.

At night I lie awake. I think of all the millions of people in
the history of mankind who have died by others' hands. Every
day, I witness mass murder. Thousands of us go to our unripe
deaths every day. Probably by the time they've finished with
us, millions.

But why is this holocaust more offensive, more foul, more
malignant, more grievous than anything that has happened in
history before?

It is not a question of numbers.

Millions of black people have been slaughtered in their history.

Who can count the Armenians?

No. Not numbers.

This genocide is different from all others. It is different because of its sublime and obscene efficiency. Mass murder when not a minute is lost. Mass burial where nothing is wasted.

Human skin for reading lamps.

Human flesh for soap.

Human hair for pillows.

Man's teeth for investment.

No waste.

It is a system meticulous in every detail, premeditated, planned and coordinated, administered with the most sophisticated and satanic technology.

It is an artistry of murder, achieving a certain beauty in its symmetry.

That is the core of its obscenity. That is why it is different.

Dear God: Let no one ever forget that. Ever. Ever. Ever.

Yet how will we be remembered?

Those who survive will write about us. Even those who were never here will write about us too.

Some will say that silence is the only way to report this tragedy, and those who promote silence will be the most vociferous of all. In time, when the facts are exhausted, and repeated to the point of boredom and disbelief, we will become fiction. Sooner or later, we will be reduced to a rhyming couplet, or at best, a nursery rhyme, sung down the generations by innocent children long after its provenance is forgotten.

Finally we will become a myth. We have to. For in order to survive, man can find no other weapon but mythology to confront the flesh and the blood of our tragedy.

A new supply of gas arrives today. It is delivered in a Red Cross ambulance. Once again I laugh a little.

Another transport today. Those sent to the left at the railway terminal line up outside the dressing rooms. All unripe.

If the Allies bombed all those railway lines that lead to Buchenwald, Bergen-Belsen, Maidanek, Ravensbrück, Treblinka, Flossenburg, Mauthausen, Lublin, Sachsenhausen, Oranienburg, Theresienstadt, Sobibor, all these sad miles of steel cortège, there could be no transports. So simple.

Tomorrow there is to be another selection within the camp. The hospital is almost empty now. They won't be needing Benjamin anymore.

Today the sun shines in this place. Unashamedly. I feel it on my back as I watch the selection assemble. All in tidy lines. Obedient. My heart turns over when I see Benjamin in the line. I stare at him, but he does not look at me, although he knows I am at my usual stand. He does not look at me because he cannot bear my bereavement.

Great-grandpa Jakob's legacy. There is no cause on earth worth dying for. No principle worth one's martyrdom. No God worth one's sacrifice. Only in the name of love is death worthy. I shall not stay here. I shall not stay to sift my brother's gentle body from the carnage. I shall not shave his frail and beautiful head. I shall not tidy his bones. I go to where he stands and I take his hand.

I wonder where God is. *If* God is. I think of all those millions of people across the earth who kneel, lie, or simply stand at the invisible feet of one or another deity.

A universal deception.

A consummate swindle.

Now I know what to do with all my rage, with all my burning wrath. I hate God with it, with every shred of it, and that anger will see me through the chamber and annihilate my fear. *Shema Yisroel.* . . .

I squeeze Benjamin's hand as he moves toward the furnace. I know that somewhere in this inferno, there is a minstrel, although I cannot hear his stubborn survival song. Perhaps it is because I myself am singing it, crooning my quietus, like a swan. I pray to God that there are ears to listen. Somewhere, somebody will hear. Great-grandpa Jakob promised us.

We move into the dressing rooms and leave our clothes in tidy piles.

We do not bother with the soap and towel, Benjamin and I. We are old hands in the business of deception.

We say the *Shema* together as we go into the showers.

I see my children again, and by the triumph in his eyes, so does Benjamin.

Safe. Alive. The Bindels survive.

I feel a slow sickness.

Benjamin falters and turns toward me.

We embrace each other. Meeting of bone on bone.

We love each other in this moment as neither of us have ever loved before.

The soles of my feet tremble.

Benjamin's hand loosens in mine.

Shema Yisroel Adonai Elohainu. . . .

So ends the unwritten and fragmented diary of one David Bindel, prisoner in Auschwitz, 1944, registration tattoo, 796702, classification, yellow star, Jew, inferior race. Fourth of the traceable generations of Bindels, from the Ukraine to Bessarabia, from England to Germany, one of the millions who died in those camps, and one of six million of his own kind.

Never forget. Never.

It was May 1945, and the war was over. The conquerers moved in and divided the spoils. Much of East Germany fell to Russian occupation, and in among all the lootable terrain lay Leipzig, city of furs and fairs. Despite the war-weary misery of its citizens, the conquered came out onto the rubble-strewn streets and cheered the victorious Russian troops. Those who for years had hidden in lofts, attics, and underground now emerged from their hiding places, and viewed what was left of their city. Among them, two small children, brothers, eleven and twelve years old, who had grown to answer to the names of Heinrich and Hermann Bindel.

It was almost two years since the brothers had seen daylight. Their concealment under Hans and Inge's direction had been complete. Every night after dark, Hans would take them into the field behind their house in the country. They needed daily exercise, and they would run twice around the perimeter before going back into hiding. Even in the summer, when the light lingered, Hans had insisted on that routine, and it was often close to midnight before the brothers could go to bed. They slept in the attic of the house, which could be reached only by a ladder that, when not in use, was hidden under the stairs. The trapdoor to the roof was camouflaged with a false ornamental light-fitting that Inge or Hans removed for their constant access. The brothers spent almost all their time in the loft. It was in the attic that they ate their meals, and where Inge tutored them in daily classes of reading, mathematics, history, and French. In the beginning it had all been a game for the brothers, a game of continual concealment that seemed to have become a way of life. Until one day they began to question it and to have niggling doubts about their parents' safety. Where exactly had they gone? What were they doing? Why didn't they write? For a few weeks the Dreisers avoided their questions. The game continued and the brothers ceased to inquire. Then one evening when Hans went to collect them for their field exercise, he found them both crying on their beds. They didn't want to play the hiding game anymore, they told him. They wanted their father and their mother.

Hans called Inge to the attic and together they told them once again the story of their family's deportation. They had gone to a camp, Hans told them, many miles away, and they were not allowed to write.

"Why not?" Aaron said.

"Hitler doesn't like Jews," Inge told them. "He doesn't want to give them any pleasure. Like writing letters, for instance." It was the truth that they told the children, the truth that they knew, and within that limitation, the Bindel family were still alive. Hans said it with fervor, for he dared not think of any alternative.

But Inge was less optimistic and she tried to school the children for bereavement. "We hear it's a hard life in the camp where they have settled," she said. But she couldn't continue. She had already given them stuff for nightmare.

For the children, the game was over. All that was left was its fearful and monotonous routine. The brothers cried piteously that night. Inge took a camp bed into the attic, and for the next few nights she slept at their side to allay their fears and terrible dreams. For a while they began to hate their foster parents, as if they had abducted them from their reluctant family. They would not answer to those names they had been dubbed with. Hermann and Heinrich did not belong to that place where their parents had gone. They shouted "Aaron" and "Jakob" in their hideout, endangering their concealment.

This phase of their rebellion lasted only a few days, and it was almost a year before they inquired of their parents once more. By that time, rumors from the camps, which for so long had been hearsay, began to be confirmed. Camp guards came home on leave, and one of them lived in Leipzig. His brother was a laboratory technician, one of Hans's employees in the Halle plant. He was more than willing to relay his brother's stories, and though Hans was reluctant to hear, he encouraged him in his telling. His brother worked in a camp called Auschwitz, he said, one of the so-called Eastern Settlements near Cracow. Full of Jews, the technician said. Mainly from Poland, but there was a German contingent there too. "He told me stories you wouldn't believe," he said.

"I'll try," Hans told him, his heart sinking.

The technician warmed to an audience, especially one in authority, and he regaled his employer with minute details of gas chambers and mass killings.

Hans turned away.

"It's terrible," the man said, and for that, at least, Hans was grateful.

By the end of that week, fed by the same source, everyone at the Halle plant was talking of the gas chambers. All over Germany, camp guards came home on leave. All had fathers, mothers, brothers or sisters, and all of those had friends. A nationwide grapevine. Yet when the war was over, only a few Germans chose to know about the terror, and some to this day will deny that it ever occurred.

Hans did not tell Inge what he had heard. But now, when he looked at the brothers, he saw them orphaned and he felt ashamed that he should be privy to information that was inalienably theirs. For many weeks he stifled that guilt in his heart. Finally he told Inge. "Let us wait," she said. "There's still hope. They cannot kill them all." And although until that time, they had loved the Bindel brothers without reserve, now they began to love them with a protective passion, and the children sensed the change and they were afraid.

At about that time, early in the spring of 1944, old Mrs. Dreiser, who had been ill for many months, died. It was an event that put the Dreiser family and the children at risk. Hans's friends lived in Leipzig, and though some of them were very intimate, none of them knew of the hidden children. Hans, and Inge, too, had made a point of making no friends in Halle, for they didn't want callers. It had worked. No one ever came to the house, except the occasional tradesman. But a funeral could not pass unnoticed, without spectators or even a sympathetic caller. That day, the brothers were enjoined to absolute silence. They were sorry that old Mrs. Dreiser had died, though they hardly knew her. They saw her only occasionally, and usually in the dark in the cellar of the house during an air raid warning. She never climbed the ladder into the loft, and she was usually in her room when they sneaked into the field for their evening exercise. But they cried for her nonetheless. They were crying for Uncle Hans, whose mother had died. All day they sat in the loft, and not a whisper passed between them, and when night came, Inge

brought them a supper of all their favorite foods, and Hans
played with them till well into the night. Now with Uncle Hans
as an orphan, there seemed to be a new bond between them,
though they didn't know why, and thereafter they lost their fears
in Hans's and Inge's frantic embrace. They knew that things had
changed, that it was a new kind of loving, and it was that loving
that would score their future.

Occasionally Hans would go to Leipzig. Each time he would
call at the Bindel family home. He would linger in the large
house and remember the happy times he had spent there. He
would wander around the garden.

One day, on one of his rare visits to Leipzig, he went to the
house and found a number of government cars parked in the
driveway. He hid behind an oleander bush, trembling, and had to
accept that the house had been commandeered. It shocked him,
but surprised him less, for most of the houses and apartments,
especially the grand ones that had belonged to Jews, had long
since been taken over by party officials. This requisition depressed him profoundly for it seemed to confirm that Leon, Benjamin, Heidi, and David Bindel were no more. He went home,
but he did not tell Inge what he had found.

The tide of war was beginning to turn. In June of that year the
Allies invaded Normandy. It marked the beginning of the final
collapse of the Third Reich. Hans and Inge listened to each news
bulletin with growing and illegal excitement. After each broad-
cast they were tempted to convey the good news to the brothers
in the attic, that the war would soon be over and that they could
come out of hiding at last. But how good would they find such
news? Once out of hiding, to what should they return? So they
said nothing to the boys, afraid of what questions might ensue.

At the end of April there were rumors that Hitler was dead.
That he had committed suicide in his bunker. For many days the
rumors were hotly denied, and there was a total blackout on news
bulletins. The blackout was the rumor's final confirmation, and
when a week later Germany surrendered to the Allies, it could no
longer be concealed.

On the ninth of May 1945, Aaron and Jakob Bindel came out
of their hiding place and asked to go home.

Every week Hans went to the Leipzig Town Hall to make
inquiries in the missing persons department. They told him that
the Bindel family would take time to trace. The concentration

camp records, those that could be found, had not yet been collated. Months later it was the offices of the International Red Cross that gave Hans the final confirmation of the Bindel deaths. It was recorded that some time in November 1942, Leon Bindel and Heidi Bindel had been gassed at Auschwitz, and that in January 1944, David and Benjamin Bindel had suffered the same fate. The official showed Hans the names on the list. They told him nothing he hadn't already known in his heart, and now he could no longer delay telling the children.

That night he returned to Halle wondering to himself how he would break the news. There was no way he could cushion it, except to omit the details of their deaths. That, they would learn in their own time.

"When are we going home, Uncle Hans?" Jakob said at supper. It was his daily question. He had begun to ask it almost for form's sake, and always it was a source of irritation to his elder brother, who knew that there was no such thing as home anymore and never would be.

Hans didn't need any cue to break the news. "The house doesn't belong to you anymore," he said. "The Russians have taken it over."

The brothers paled.

"That's not fair," Jakob shouted. "It's ours."

But Aaron had understood the implications of the takeover.

"Mummy and Daddy are dead," he said suddenly in a loud and clear voice. "And Uncle David and Grandpa, too." He did not look to Hans or Inge for confirmation, but Jakob refused to believe one word of it. He raised his little clenched fists and punched his brother about the head.

"It's not true," he shouted, the tears running down his face. "It's terrible to say things like that. I'll tell Mummy and Daddy on you," he screamed. "You wait till they come back. I'll tell."

Inge took him in her arms, nursing his sobs. No one had denied what Aaron had said, and now Jakob knew better than to ask questions. They were dead. He would never see them again. He tried to remember what they looked like, but he could only see the backs of them as they had turned back into the house when they had driven away in Uncle Hans's car. He wished they would turn around so that he could see their faces. But his mother and his father had turned their backs on him and for a moment he enjoyed the relief of hating them. But it was short-lived. He went over to Inge and buried his face in her lap. In the future, Aunt Inge and Uncle Hans would have to do.

And so the Dreisers stayed in Halle, and day by day they felt the impact of the Russian occupation. They were issued new food cards, which entitled them to less than they had had before, but at least now they had one card for each person. There were daily roundups of Nazi leaders and those known to have had Nazi sympathies. People disappeared and were never heard of again. The Russians lost no time in implementing their ideologies. Farms were seized and collectivized. There was no freedom of speech or information. The one-party system controlled everything: the law, education, and the press, and when the German citizens chose to think about it, the Russian system of government was little different from the Fascist regime they had known.

Germany was almost without Jews. Those very few who had managed to hide out the hostilities left that hated land as soon as possible after the armistice was signed. But they were fortunate enough to live in the Western zone.

But those who lived in the East were now trapped yet again, for there was a ban on emigration, which affected all German citizens in the Eastern zone. This played a great part in the discussions that Inge and Hans had regarding the brothers' future. Among the Bindel papers, Hans found Sarah's address in Palestine together with the addresses of other Bindel relatives in America, and he wrote to both, informing them of the fate of the Bindel family. He expressed his desire to continue his role as the brothers' guardian until such time as the children could make their own choices about the future. Soon both Chaya and Sarah replied, each of them offering homes for the children whenever their travel would permit. Both agreed to Hans's continual guardianship with overwhelming gratitude, and they praised his courage and show of friendship.

As for the children, they never mentioned their relatives. They seemed happy enough to embrace Hans and Inge as their parents. They had settled in their new school, and had begun to make friends. The daylight still astonished them. So did their new names. "Aaron and Jakob are for keeps," Hans told them on their first day of school. "You will never change them again. And Bindels you will always be."

Their favorite lesson was Russian, a subject newly introduced into the school curriculum. Both brothers excelled in it, as if

nudged by their Odessa forefathers. Their French, thanks to Inge's tutoring, was far above the average standard of the class, as
was their history. Hans looked at their school reports with pride
and wonder.

"You are a credit to all the Bindels," he said.

He took every opportunity to include their dead family in their
lives, to hold their memories green. Now the brothers could talk
of their parents without pain, and often they would pore together
over old family picture albums and piece together the Bindel
lineage in all its European traces. It was at these times that Hans
wondered about the brothers' inheritance, how and when he
should bequeath it.

Life in East Germany was hard. There was a desperate
shortage of food, and potatoes, which had been a staple diet of
most Germans, were suddenly a luxury. The Russians seized the
crops for the distillation of vodka. The soldiers of the occupying
army and their families lived like kings. Members of the German
Communist party were also favored, and many joined their ranks
for the supplementary food allowances that went with the card.
But Hans made no move to affiliate. Though his father had died
in that cause, Hans had lost his appetite for politics.

The Siebel Aircraft Corporation, where he worked, had always
been under heavy guard and supervision. But nowadays it was
like a fortress and he had to show his identity at least a half-
dozen times before he could gain entry to his quarters. The place
was swarming with Russian technicians. Hans was asked many
questions about his work and from their inquiries, he was able to
deduce that in his own special field of radar technology they were
far behind. This fact gave him some small pleasure.

One day, on one of his visits to Leipzig, a friend told him that
the equipment of five large printing works in the city had been
dismantled and sent to the Soviet Union. Some of the most specialized technicians had been more or less dragooned into going
too. Hans returned to Halle that night and he began to have fears
for his own future. Fears that were confirmed, for during that
winter of 1946, it was known that hundreds of scientists and
technical workers were deported to the Soviet Union from East
Germany. And from the West, too, in a nocturnal wave of kidnapping. There were protests from the West deploring the Russian maneuver. So, to counteract those protests, the Russians
decided to found an organization that was legal within the area of

their own administration. Its name was Operation *Ossavakim* and it legalized the deportation of men and the shipment of machinery to their own country for full exploitation.

In the winter of 1947 the Russians reopened the trade fair at Leipzig. Many visitors came from all over Eastern Europe, and factory visits were organized for those visitors with specialized interest. The Siebel Aircraft Association in Halle was the focus of many tourists' attention.

So it came as no surprise when, about a month after the fair had closed, the removal men moved into the Seibel plant. At the same time, four hundred specialists who worked in the factory were given notices of deportations. Among the names was Hans Dreiser. Their families would be allowed to accompany them, the notices read. Their children would receive the best education, and each family would be provided with living quarters. The train would leave in two weeks from the East Berlin station of Friedrichsfelde. Removal expenses would be paid by the Soviet military administration.

The Dreisers prepared for their departure. The brothers were excited at the prospect of a new country, especially one that had belonged to their ancestors. They had none of the old Bindel scruples about deserting the bones of their forebears. Besides, apart from their grandmother's, the bones of those they loved were untraceable, of no marked grave or honored resting place. Somewhere in the "Eastern Settlements" their ashes had hovered on the wind for a while, without urn for memorial. Only *Yad Vashem,* a Place and a Name.

"What names will we use in Russia?" Jakob asked.

Was there anywhere in the world, Hans wondered, where the names of Aaron and Jakob would be given safe or even welcome passage? In Palestine perhaps, he thought, though now that possibility was remote. But they must not live a lie again.

"Aaron and Jakob," he said decisively. "And Bindel. That name will be forever."

Before they left for Berlin, Hans took the children to Leipzig to see their Grandma Greta's grave. During the war he had done his best to keep it in order. On every visit he had brought flowers, and built a pyramid of pebbles against the gravestone. Now Aaron and Jakob Bindel added to the pyramid, with extra stones for Grandpa Leon and their parents.

"Now we have buried them all," Hans said and he took their hands and left the cemetery for the last time.

The removal van came to Halle for their furniture and effects, and the following day the Dreisers and their adopted family took the train to East Berlin. Hans Dreiser was one of eight thousand men and their families who were forcibly deported to the Soviet Union under the aegis of Operation *Ossavakim*.

Thus Aaron and Jakob Bindel, fifth of the traceable Bindel generations, from the Ukraine to Bessarabia, from Bessarabia to England, from England to Germany, returned to the land where the bones of their forefathers lay, and hoped that they might call it home.

PART FOUR

⚜

The Book of Aaron and Jakob

It must have been snowing.

It was winter when the Bindel brothers of the fifth generation arrived in the land of their forefathers. It was almost a hundred years ago that they had been buried there. Much was different since that time, and much was still the same. Many changes had come about in the matter of names and labels. The country itself was now known as the Soviet Union. The name of Czar had disappeared too, and had been replaced by President. There was no longer any anti-Semitism in the country. That, too, had another name. In the fifth traceable generation of the brothers Bindel, it was called anti-Zionism, a label that somehow made Jew-hate more respectable. Much was different, but little had changed. What remained the same, immutably unalterable, were the Bindel names. Aaron and Jakob. Perhaps after all their bids at survival, the names resisted further change.

The Bindel brothers were now in their fifteenth and sixteenth years and they had still not inherited, a fact that disturbed Hans and Inge Dreiser. Year by year, as the brothers grew firmly in their Russianhood, the nature of their inheritance grew more and more irrelevant. For there was little Jewish about Aaron and Jakob Bindel. Since their enforced involvement in the Jewish school in Leipzig, they had not heard a word of spoken Hebrew. Jewish schools were not permitted in the Soviet Union. Neither of the brothers had been bar mitzvahed, nor had they entered a synagogue for many years. But on each of their identity cards was the word *Jew,* which proclaimed their inherited faith. When they viewed their bodies in the shower, they attributed their mark of difference to reasons of health, echoing their parents' alibi in their preorphaned years.

In 1948, Israel proclaimed its independence, and that event prompted illegal stirrings in the hearts of thousands of Russian

Jews. At the same time, the MVD, as the Ministry of Internal
Affairs was called, arrested four hundred and thirty-one Jewish
intellectuals, poets, writers, musicians, and party officials and
charged them with the crime of "national bourgeois Zionism."
They were put in chains and sent to concentration camps. When
Hans Dreiser first read the news, he hid it from the children and
hoped that they would not hear of it in school. He did not want
to frighten them, but at the same time he felt guilty of depriving
them of news that was theirs by a kind of birthright. Once again
he thought the time was ripe for their inheritance, and once again
he postponed it. Over the next few years he followed the story of
the convicted men wherever he could. There were rumors that
the majority of them had perished in the camps—rumors that
turned out to be sadly true, for when, four years later, the accused were secretly tried, only thirty or so were brought to the
courthouse, and all were found guilty and executed.

Still Hans held his tongue. He thought very often of his father,
and in many ways he was glad that he had not lived to see the
reality of that ideal in which name he had died. He was sickened
by the gross deception of his father's life, and sometimes for solace he would share his disappointments with Inge. But outside
the confines of their own home, he didn't voice them. He went
about his daily work at the aircraft factory where, over the years,
much progress had been made in his field of research. He was
satisfied with his work, and so was Inge, who had gone back to
her old profession as an assistant almoner. Their Russian was
halting and would never be fluent like that of their adopted children. At home they still spoke German so that Aaron and Jakob
would not forget their parents' tongue.

It was 1953, and in that year occurred one of the most sinister
events of Stalin's reign of terror. It was known as the Doctors'
Plot, and, unlike the earlier arrests of Jewish intellectuals, which
was secret and clandestine, this was given the widest coverage in
the press. A group of physicians, most of them Jews, were arrested on a charge of plotting to kill Soviet leaders. The newspaper *Pravda* claimed that the doctors were connected with an international bourgeois Jewish organization established by
American Intelligence with the aim of subversion. Widely publicized, it was the topic of conversation in factories, schools, and
party meetings. Aaron and Jakob Bindel, who at that time were

in their last year at school, listened to the vicious spread of anti-Semitism and the brothers intuitively suspected that they themselves were the target of such abuse.

At least so it seemed to Jakob. Despite his non-Jewish upbringing and his lack of inheritance, Jakob's ear was finely tuned to any aspersion on his patrimony. Like his father in his post-Buchenwald years, he could recognize a warning symbol. But Aaron took after Heidi and her intransigence. He would stand and hotly argue his rights, not as a Jew but as a human being, under the impression that in this golden land of equality, they were one and the same. Often the brothers would quarrel between themselves on the subject of their unpracticed faith and their talk would ring with bitter echoes of the old Leipzig dialogue between Benjamin and David.

"Why must we be so exclusive," Aaron would argue, "and think we're so different from everybody else?"

"But *they* think we're different," Jakob would say, "and nothing's going to change that. Jewishness is in the eye of the beholder. Maybe we *are* different," he would whisper, and then turn away.

At about that time a letter came from their Aunt Sarah in Israel announcing that she would be coming on a visit to Moscow. It was more than thirteen years since the brothers had seen their aunt. She had corresponded with them regularly, but for them she was part of a life that they rarely recalled, for it was the life of their parents and the memory of it was painful. Yet they were excited at the prospect of her visit. Especially Jakob, who wanted to learn about Israel.

A week before Aunt Sarah's arrival, Stalin died, and Aaron, along with his schoolmates, went into public and official mourning. But Jakob secretly rejoiced, as the milk-brothers had done almost a hundred years ago on the wild Siberian wastes, when the forbidden news had filtered through of Czar Nicholas the First's demise.

"Do not hope for too much," Hans told Jakob, taking him to one side. "There is no shortage of Stalins. Tyrants grow on many trees, whether they are called Czar, Chancellor, or President. In school you must feign sorrow, and mourn like the others. Stalin was their god, and they will punish you for any lack of respect."

The whole family went to the airport to welcome Aunt Sarah. "I've forgotten what she looked like," Aaron said as they

scanned the curious and bewildered faces of those who had come
to a land that half the world labeled Utopia. Through the glass
partition that separated the customs area from the airport foyer,
they looked for a woman who would be their mother's age had
she lived.

"There she is," Hans shouted. Sarah caught his eye and waved,
and then she saw the brothers alongside him. She held them for a
moment in her gaze, seeing in their faces the undeniable Bindel
image that her own children had not inherited. She stared at
them. Aaron, though older than Jakob, was the shorter of the
two, and took after his father, Benjamin. He had the same rigid
air, and when he smiled at her, she knew it was an effort.
Whereas Jakob's smile was swift and wondrous. True Bindels
they were, and in their amalgam Sarah saw David Bindel exactly
as she had seen him for the last time, when he had stood on the
platform at the Vienna railway station, holding those two boys
for his comfort. She rushed through the barrier, longing to embrace them. Wordlessly she approached them and held them
close, looking into their faces, hoping that the David she found in
their features would be in their hearts as well.

Sarah then turned to introduce her nephews to one of her traveling companions and out of the distant past, from the back row
of an enforced Jewish classroom in Leipzig, the brothers heard
the echoes of a strange tongue, a language they had thought dead.
"D'you remember that Jewish school?" Aaron said to Jakob,
smiling.

"They actually speak it," Jakob said, marveling at the sounds.

They shook hands with their Aunt Sarah's traveling companion, who greeted them in German. She, too, had come from Leipzig, she told them, and she remembered their father very well, for
he had delivered both her children. This reminder of their father
from a total stranger, and in their mother tongue, shipped them
back into their childhood and the remembrance of how quickly it
had soured. They knew that Aunt Sarah's visit would prompt
those memories in abundance and it disturbed them, for they
knew the price of their recall.

For in truth the Bindel brothers of the fifth generation had
been deeply damaged by their orphanhood. The deaths of their
parents had been unnatural enough, but in the eyes of the world,
or of those who cared to look, they were but two of six million,
and this continual promotion rather distracted from the particu-

larity of their loss. For Aaron and Jakob Bindel the Holocaust was the definition of the deaths of four special people, their parents, Uncle David, and Grandpa Leon, and they did not care to have them shrouded with six million others, for it somehow diminished their special sacrifice. Moreover, there had been those two long years spent in darkness, and in those shadows, for survival's sake, and in the names of Hermann and Heinrich, they had buried their Judaism. And though the brothers had survived, through the Dreisers' care and cunning, those remnants had remained in the German darkness. Yet their shadows still haunted the brothers, especially Jakob, who, when he recalled them, felt a sense of terrible betrayal. Now Aunt Sarah had come to invoke those spirits they had left behind, to nudge them into the open.

"Are we far from Odessa?" was Sarah's first question.

"About one thousand kilometers," Hans said. He smiled at her. She would lose no time in leading the brothers into their pasts on a journey of such terrible and rich confusion that it could well cause a small earthquake in their souls.

"I want to go there," she was saying. "I want to see where the Bindels began. David used to say that one day we would go back with Grandpa Leon. A pilgrimage, he said." She looked at Hans, smiling. "It's one of the reasons I came."

It was then that Hans decided that, during the course of Sarah's visit, the Bindel brothers would claim their inheritance.

And as it turned out, the opportunity for so doing presented itself that very evening. They had finished the festive welcoming supper that Inge had prepared. "I have photographs," Sarah announced, and she went to her case and brought out the family album. Inge gathered together her own assortment.

Aunt Sarah started with a display of her children from their Leipzig infancy to their Israel adulthood. Esther and Zelda resembled Sarah, and Aaron and Jakob were keen to know of them —of their likes, their dislikes, and whether they would ever come to Russia.

"Perhaps you should go and see them in Israel," Sarah said.

"What's it like in Israel," Jakob asked.

"I'll tell you about it later," Sarah said, turning the pages of the album. She did not want to dwell in the present. It was her David and the past she sought. "These are my wedding photographs," she said, stretching the double-page spread of the album.

Now is the time, Hans thought. He remembered David's wedding with meticulous recall. It was the day that Benjamin and David had inherited. He remembered his own part in the battle when he had gone out into the streets and faced the hooligans alone. He wasn't afraid at the time, but afterward he had wondered why none of the other guests had come outside to support him. When he'd returned to the reception he was in time to see a white-faced Leon manhandling his two grown sons up the staircase. Then and there, in their full-grown years, and one of them already a groom, their father had taught them the lesson of their history.

"It was an unforgettable day," she was saying. "You remember it, Hans?" she asked. "Look, here's a picture of you. You're not there, Inge."

"We hadn't yet met," Hans said. "But she knows the story. You tell it, Sarah. Tell it to Aaron and Jakob."

"The reception was in Grandpa Leon's house," Sarah began, and from the collection of photographs she pointed out and named the guests, and, as a codicil to almost every name, she added, "Auschwitz."

"What's the story?" Aaron said impatiently. He wanted no reference to that burial ground.

"That's all part of the story," Sarah said, and the tone of her voice was inflexible. "Auschwitz is only a name. A place and a name. But such places have many names. Babi Yar, the Katyn forest, Lidice."

Aaron and Jakob did not quite follow her, and they were unnerved by the zealous look in her eyes.

"You want to know the story of my wedding," she went on, "but first I must tell you a little of the history of the time." She spoke like any true Bindel, using that phrase that in each generation had prompted the bequest of the Patriarch Jakob's litany.

"It was in 1930," she explained, "before Hitler became the chancellor of the Third Reich. But for the Jews of Germany, the trouble had already begun." She told them something of the conditions that had favored Hitler's rise to power. She shared the narration with Hans, who had played a major role in the drama, and Aaron and Jakob were silent throughout the tale, in wonder not so much at the story itself, but that it could have happened so close to home.

"Why did Grandpa Leon get so angry?" Aaron asked.

"It was something that Benjamin said," Hans told them.
"Your father was a little stubborn," he said, smiling, "not unlike
you, Aaron, sometimes, but as gentle as you are."

"What did Papa say?" Jakob asked.

"He said that the hooligans were a trivial minority, that they
weren't important. And Grandpa Leon was angry. And there and
then, he took his two sons to Great-grandma Zelda's room, and
there they inherited."

"They what?" Aaron asked.

"It's a long story," Hans said.

"In every generation of Bindel brothers," Sarah said, "there
has been an inheritance handed down from fathers to sons. It all
began with Great-great-grandpa Jakob and the milk-brothers of
Odessa."

"Milk-brothers?" Jakob asked.

So Sarah started from the beginning. Like all the Bindel brothers, she knew it by heart, and she told it slowly from its Odessa
origins. She told the story, too, of Leon, that gentle martyr after
whom their grandfather had been named. Aaron and Jakob were
silent throughout, transfixed by the tale. It was late into the night
by the time she neared the end.

"Now it's your turn to inherit," she said, and slowly she recited the Patriarch's litany.

Hans and Inge listened with a sense of peace. Now they could
put away Benjamin's letter, that last will and testament that he
had pressed into Hans's hand as he bade farewell to his children.
Now these two brothers had inherited.

"It's time for bed," Inge said at last.

In the morning they were both too tired to go to school, and
Hans, who had always been very strict about school attendance,
that day relented. He said that they could stay at home in honor
of their Aunt Sarah's arrival, but in truth he hoped that through
sleep, they would gather the strength to accept the uneasy
changes that Sarah's story had wrought.

The brothers did not rise until late afternoon and the house
was empty. Inge had probably taken Sarah sight-seeing. Aaron
started on his homework, but Jakob was unable to concentrate.
He wandered about the house and stole into Sarah's room. His
aunt intrigued him. Though she was not of their blood, she was
more at home in Bindeldom than he. It was that home he wished
to enter. Aunt Sarah could help bridge the gaps between his or-

phanhood and his present state of alienation. She would tell him
about his parents, and revive in his memory Grandpa Leon's
stories. The photograph album lay on the table. He leafed
through its pages. Apart from those of Aunt Sarah and David's
wedding, many of the photographs were duplicates of those that
Hans and Inge had collected from the Bindel home in Leipzig.
But there was one that he had never seen before. It was a photograph that had been taken in a photographer's studio many years
ago. Its color was sepia and its edges were frayed. It occupied one
whole page of Aunt Sarah's album, and its subject was clearly of
some significance. There was no clue in writing as to the identity
of the subject of the portrait, and this omission, as opposed to the
meticulous labeling of the other photographs, added to its mys-
tery. The picture was that of a young boy, perhaps thirteen or so,
Jakob thought. He wore a loose brown boiler suit of sorts and on
his head was a tin helmet. In his hand he carried a small lamp,
and it seemed to Jakob that the boy was an actor playing his first
role. Jakob looked closely at the boy's face, and in his features he
saw distinct traces of the Bindel image.

That evening Aunt Sarah told them about her life in Israel.
Aaron excused himself, pleading fatigue, but Hans and Inge
knew that Israel was a subject Aaron dared not risk. It was part
of that Jewish exclusiveness that so disturbed him.

"Tell us from the beginning," Jakob said.

Sarah started her story at the railway station in Vienna.
"D'you remember that station, Jakob?" she asked.

He remembered it well, not so much for the farewell, but for
the passion with which Uncle David had held him and his
brother as the train had pulled out of the station. Jakob hadn't
understood it at the time.

But from the carriage window, Sarah had seen the embrace,
and though it was the beginning of her story, she knew then that
it was also its end and on the long and weary ride to Venice, as
her parents had tried to comfort her, she slowly gathered about
her the weeds of her widowhood, because she knew that she
would never see David again.

"The boat was already overcrowded by the time it docked in
Naples," she continued, "and there were hundreds of us waiting
to go on board. It took about three weeks to reach Israel, or
Palestine, as it was then called, and we stood on our feet most of
the way. It was a silent journey. Most of us were too ill to speak,

or we were listening for sounds of approaching danger—a British patrol ship that might turn us back, or the cracking of the ship's bows under its heavy load. But no one complained. We'd been given a chance to survive, and for that we were grateful. I really don't remember too much about that journey," she said, looking up at Hans and Inge. "It's easier to forget about it. But I remember the landing," she said. "It was at night, somewhere along the Haifa coastline. We'd been skirting the shore for days. It seemed the captain was waiting for a signal. And one night we saw lights flashing from the beach, and we knew that our journey would soon be over. Then it all happened very quickly. The boat beached on the sands, and I remember seeing pieces of wood splitting from the bows as we came to a stop. Nobody moved. Nobody believed that we had come to the end of our journey alive. We saw young people wading into the sea then, reaching up their hands to greet us and help us out of the boat. It seemed hours before we reached the beach and the row of huts hidden behind the trees. They were singing and dancing, celebrating our safe arrival, but all we wanted to do was to sleep. My father was not well and we asked for a doctor. They took him off in a truck to the hospital along with many others who were suffering from the journey. I remember seeing him lying in the back of the van and then we lay down on the grass and stretched our bodies for the first time since leaving Naples. Nothing on earth could move us. It was light when we awoke, and they led us to the trucks and drove us through the countryside, but we were all too exhausted and too astonished by our survival to look at the scenery. They took us to a kibbutz on the shores of Lake Galilee."

"A kibbutz?" Jakob asked.

"It's a communal settlement," Sarah said. "It was our first home and we stayed there for ten years."

"What happened to your father?" Jakob asked.

"He got better and joined us after a few days."

"And now?" Hans asked.

"Now we all live in Jerusalem. We have a little shop. Newspapers, sweets, cigarettes. That sort of thing. We all live together. But my parents are retired. I run the shop with an assistant. He's taking care of it now."

"And the children?" Inge asked.

"They're both at the university," Sarah said. "After that they have to go into the army. And then, who knows?"

It seemed that she had come to the end of her story, yet it seemed to Jakob that she had told them nothing.

"What about Israel?" he said.

She smiled at him. "It's too long a story," she said. "I'm tired. Tomorrow perhaps."

They knew she refrained because Aaron was not there, but they knew too that if the subject of Israel was raised, Aaron would continue to excuse himself.

"When am I to go to Odessa?" Sarah said suddenly.

"Can I go with you?" Jakob asked.

"You have school," Hans said.

"But next week is half-term," Inge reminded him.

"I'll wait till then," Sarah said. "We'll go together. Will Aaron come, too?"

"He usually goes camping at half-term," Hans said. "I don't think he'll give that up for Odessa."

"Then I'll take Jakob," Sarah said, and she was suddenly excited. On behalf of David, she would be exploring his past, and with a Bindel for company. The country of David's past that he had never seen, those bones of his forefathers that for him were the stuff of fairy tales.

The following weekend, they went to Odessa, and immediately on arrival at the station Sarah urged Jakob to inquire the whereabouts of the Jewish cemetery. He was nervous of such a request. To evince any interest in Jewish life was to betray some hint of unpatriotic allegiance. Sarah noted his hesitation. "Or let us ask for the synagogue," she said. Jakob shook his head. Such an inquiry would be a greater risk than that of the cemetery. A passerby might forgive an interest in the whereabouts of the Jewish dead, but he could not admit to his Russian consciousness the thought of living Judaism. Or any other religion, for that matter. The state frowned on competition of any kind, either from man or from God.

"I'll ask for the cemetery," Jakob said.

They walked a little, while he scanned the faces of the crowd for one who might be Jewish. But Jakob was not enough of a Jew himself to recognize others of his kind. At that moment, a bearded gentleman was seen to walk in their direction.

"There's a Jew," Sarah whispered.

"He could be Russian Orthodox," Jakob said.

"Well, at least he believes in God. Ask him."

"Excuse me," Jakob whispered as the man came alongside them. "Do you know the whereabouts of the Jewish cemetery?"

The old man smiled. "You are standing on it," he said. "The whole of Odessa is a Jewish cemetery. On the twenty-third of October 1941, nineteen thousand Jews were massacred here by the Germans. My wife, my children among them. Who knows where they are buried?" The old man took Jakob's arm and told him that he would lead him to where the dead Jews officially lay, those whom God had taken in His own and natural time.

"Come," he said.

Sarah followed them, nudging Jakob for explanation. He gave it to her in his childish German, regretting the loss of the old man's rage in his translation.

"Does your mother speak Yiddish?" the old man asked.

"She's not my mother," Jakob said. "My mother died in Auschwitz." He surprised himself. He had never in his life so openly confessed to his orphanhood.

"I'm sorry," the old man said. "She's a friend, then?"

"My aunt. She lives in Israel. Her husband died in Auschwitz too."

The old man stopped walking and turned to face them. "It all happened so many years ago," he said. "Yet we never cease to mourn. It's because we never buried them."

Jakob translated for Sarah. She smiled, nodding her head. The old man had exactly defined the nature of her sorrow. They walked on.

"Whose bones do you seek now?" the old man asked after a while. Jakob told him the story of his Odessa beginnings, and he was glad to tell it, for it was new to him, and he thrilled to the adventures of his forefathers.

"That will be the very old cemetery," the old man said, "though it has been desecrated many times, and most of it now is covered with long grass. I'll take you there," he said. "It's not far."

"You must not trouble yourself," Jakob said.

"It's no trouble. It's my pleasure. The history of one Jew is the history of us all. We must share it. I shall help you find your forefathers' bones, and I shall mourn them with you as if they were my own."

Jakob translated for Sarah. She was bewildered. "Has he nothing else to do?" she whispered. "Aren't we taking him away from his business?"

"He wants to come," Jakob said. "I think we're doing him a favor."

They walked together and the old man was silent most of the time. He walked slightly ahead of them, looking behind occasionally to check their progress. To a passerby he might have looked like a priest leading his small flock.

"Is it far?" Sarah asked Jakob after a while. "He's an old man. We should take a taxi."

Jakob passed his aunt's suggestion to their guide.

"It's not far," he said. "Just over the top of the hill. What's it like in Israel?" he asked over his shoulder.

Jakob translated for Sarah, and she was about to give a short answer when the old man continued.

"I wouldn't go there," he said. "I could not be a Jew there. The essence of our faith is the Exile. The Diaspora is the core of living Judaism. Only in our homelessness will the Jewish race survive."

Jakob stopped walking. He didn't understand the full import of the old man's words, yet he sensed that it was a point of view that required serious consideration. Slowly he translated it for his aunt.

"Some of us had no choice," she told him.

Jakob translated her response, but the old man was not interested. He hurried forward, anxious to dwell in the past as comfort for his loss, as proof of his history and stubborn continuity.

They reached the brow of the hill. The old man pointed out the burial ground, and from where they stood it looked like an overgrown field. They picked their way down the slope, and Jakob was wary lest the old man lose his footing and hurried forward to take his arm. But the old man snatched it away, as if offended by the support he'd been offered.

"I can manage," he said brusquely. He did not want to appear frail. Not in this place. He was dying, he knew. He was naturally old enough for that. But dying had nothing to do with death. He knew that. He had watched his own mother die for many years and when death came, it was a different experience. For dying is mortal. Only death can grant us immortality.

They reached the burial ground. It was less overgrown than it had appeared from the top of the hill and it was possible to decipher the headstones of many of the graves.

"What's the name?" the old man asked.

"Bindel," Jakob said.

The man wandered off among the stones. Jakob regretted giving him the name. He didn't want him to discover the Bindel bones. It was not his right, whatever he said about universal history. "I'll find them," he shouted after the old man. Sarah, too, had taken her own way and was pausing by the gravestones where the legends were still legible even though she could not read them. So Jakob, too, went on his private search, hurrying a little, fearful that the old man would poach on his Bindel past. Jakob looked across the sea of broken stones and saw him crouched beside a grave, in deep meditation, and there it seemed he was prepared to stay. He was in no race, and his old face was suffused with such peace that Jakob chided himself for his ungenerous thoughts.

Jakob looked up, and then he saw it. He was standing right in front of the Bindel tomb. He had seen the old man pause there, and pass it by. "Aunt Sarah," he called. "It's here."

She picked her way across the headstones, avoiding the graves with meticulous care. Then she stood by Jakob's side. "Read it to me," she said.

Jakob crept toward the stone, peering close. He read it aloud in the Russian that was engraved, and then he translated it for his aunt. "In Memory of Jakob and Esther Bindel, and of their children and their children's children, who died in the Tavern fire. Passover, 1871." He looked at his aunt and saw tears in her eyes. But they were not tears of sorrow, for she was smiling, too.

"It's just as your Uncle David told me," she said. "His grandfather is in that tomb, Leon's father, Benjamin, along with his milk-brother, Reuben." She sat down on the grass beside the grave and wept with such copious tears that Jakob wondered whether she had ever cried for her husband before. Perhaps in this place she was able somehow to bury him, and this ceremony had freed her tears. Jakob stood by and watched her and made no move to comfort her, for he sensed that she was comforted enough by her release.

After a while the old man called out to them. "May I join you?" he asked.

Jakob crossed over to where he sat, and helped him to his feet.

Then he led him along the path to his own history. The old man
stood and read the legend. "1871," he said, over and over again.
"Almost a hundred years ago. Yet they survive, and will survive
still, so long as their bequest is not destroyed. We owe them that,
as our children will owe us. Magnified and Sanctified be Thy
good Name in the world." The old man sang the first words of
the *kaddish*. Jakob listened in wonder, and though he had never
in his life heard that song before, the melody stirred a quaver in
his heart, and despite its mournful tune, he thrilled to a sudden
joy of awakening.

The old man had started to move away. He did not wait for his
fellow mourners, nor motion them to follow him. But as he
passed them by, Jakob noticed a small smile on his lips. He was
humming to himself as he made his way across the burial ground
and slowly up the slope of the hill. They watched him out of
sight, and then they made their way together, Jakob's arm in
Sarah's, without words, until they reached the crest of the hill.

"I am ready now to go back to Moscow," Sarah said. "We have
done our business here."

Jakob was happy to agree with her. The experience at the
burial ground had shaken him, and he needed silence and privacy
to contain it. They made their way to the station.

The same train that had brought them overnight from Moscow
was about to make its day journey back to the capital. They
boarded and found a compartment to themselves. Though they
had slept soundly on the train the night before, they were soon
asleep—overcome by an emotional fatigue that had drained them
both. It was as if they now called on sleep to seal the profound
changes in their hearts, to enclose and preserve them forever.

They slept for a long time, and the train was a mere thirty
miles out of Moscow before both of them awoke. Sarah's waking
thought was a resolve to tell the Bindel brothers all about Israel,
its life and its history, its struggle. For the first time since her
confused widowhood, she began to envisage a future. In that
Odessa burial ground she had visited the uneasy country of the
past. She need never dwell there again.

Jakob woke with the image of a photograph on his mind's eye,
the sepia portrait of the small boy in Aunt Sarah's album. He
knew that that, too, was a story that belonged to the Bindel past,
an unknown soldier of unknown grave. He needed now to know

it, for it was part of that lineage he had so recently discovered as
his own.

"I was looking in your album, Aunt Sarah," he began, "and I
saw a picture of a young boy. It's on a page of its own. He has a
sort of helmet—"

"David," she said, interrupting him.

"Uncle David?"

"No. That boy was the first David, after whom your uncle was
named."

"The *first* David?" Jakob was curious. "Who was he?"

"It's a secret," Aunt Sarah said. "But I shall tell it to you. You
shared the second David with me. Now I shall share the first with
you. You remember your Grandma Greta?" Sarah asked.

"Of course."

"It was she who told me. We were very close, your grandmother and I, and perhaps she felt she could unburden herself to
me, for it was a secret that she never told her own children. Your
father, Benjamin, and Uncle David died without ever knowing it,
nor had they lived would they ever have known."

Although they were alone in the compartment, Aunt Sarah
spoke in a whisper and Jakob leaned forward to catch her words.

"Before your Grandpa Leon married Grandma Greta, he had
been married before."

"To whom?" Jakob asked excited. "And where?"

So Sarah told Jakob the story as she had heard it from
Grandma Greta that day when Leon had returned from Cardiff
and Zelda's funeral. He had kept to his room in a black mood of
desolation. Greta knew that his mother's death had affected him
deeply, but she knew, too, that it was not only Zelda whom he
mourned. Her death had awakened in Leon's heart all the pain of
his firstborn's nonburial, and Greta did not know how to comfort
him. In her anguish she had told Sarah the Senghenydd story,
and Sarah remembered it by heart, and word for word, she gave
it now to Jakob. The train was pulling into Moscow as she came
to the end of her story. "He, too, is part of our past," Sarah was
saying.

When they reached home late that night, Hans and Inge were
surprised at their swift return.

"We did our business," Sarah said. "We saw what we had to
see."

"Did you find the graves?" Hans asked.

She nodded, but they did not tell him how, or of the old man who had led them to that place. Hans noted their reticence and he understood that both of them had undertaken a remarkable journey. With a certain relief he knew that Jakob had reentered his fold. He regretted that Aaron had not gone with them.

Over the next few days Sarah relaxed into a holiday mood. She visited Hans in his laboratory, and met many of the Dreisers' friends, and slowly she gathered the background against which the current Bindel brothers were growing into men. She thought of the old man's words in the Odessa cemetery. "Our past survives so long as its bequest is not destroyed. That is a debt we owe to our forefathers, and our children to us." His words seared her mind, for though she could in no way fault the care and the loving Hans and Inge had lavished on the brothers, she could not envisage their future as one that perpetuated the Bindel bequest. That day, she started to tell the brothers about Israel, and as each day passed she familiarized them with the land she hoped would one day be their home. Jakob never tired of her stories, but Aaron listened only out of politeness. Until his Aunt Sarah's visit, he had given the country of Israel little thought. Now it actually frightened him. Its sheer presence in his consciousness was a threat to his future. He was a Russian. The Soviet Union was his nationality, his faith, his land, and his living. Let Jakob do what he pleased. But he feared that Jakob's preference might cast a shadow on his own chosen way of life, that his friends would suspect the infection of brotherhood. But he did not question that fear, for the fear itself frightened him, and he secretly looked forward to his Aunt Sarah's departure.

When, at the end of the month, she left for Israel, she knew that her visit had wrought many changes in the brothers, and though such changes could not be harmful, she had a nagging fear of their consequences.

During the years that followed, Jakob and Sarah kept up a regular correspondence. Occasionally his Israeli cousins would write to him, but their letters, though friendly, were without enthusiasm and Jakob had the impression that his Aunt Sarah stood behind them while they wrote. But he was always glad of Sarah's letters, for in them she kept alive his curiosity and interest in a country with which he sensed an indissoluble spiritual connection. He did not consider that he would ever live there. The words of the old Jew at the Odessa graveyard had made a lasting impression on him. The survival of Judaism was guaranteed only by the Diaspora. But it had to be a dispersal in which the laws of Judaism were known and practiced, and Jakob had no means of learning them, and even less of putting them into practice. Among his friends at the university there were few who admitted to being Jewish, and though he felt close to Aaron on almost every other issue, that of Judaism continued to divide them.

At that time Jakob was in his final year as a student of mathematics at the University of Moscow. Aaron was due to qualify as a doctor at the school of medicine. Hans and Inge viewed them both with pride, both for their own sakes and vicariously on behalf of Benjamin and Heidi. But though they had done well, though both of them had inherited, Hans and Inge were still uneasy about the future of the Bindel line. So they were delighted when, one Saturday morning, Jakob announced that he was going to the synagogue.

Among the articles that Hans had collected from the Bindel family home in Leipzig was Grandpa Leon's prayer shawl, and this he now gave with joy to Jakob. As Jakob walked to Archipova Street, he thought of Leipzig and of the weeks shortly before his parents had been taken, when every Saturday the family would go to the synagogue. He remembered little of the cere-

mony inside the temple, but he recalled the recreation time in the
yard when the service was over, the games they played with the
other children. He wondered now how many of those children
had survived. As he approached the synagogue, he grew nervous,
and excited, too. He felt as if he were returning to his home after
a long absence. He quickened his pace toward the doors, donning
his cap and prayer shawl as he went.

But Jakob's heart sank as he entered the temple. A sprinkling
of very old men sat there, no more than a dozen in all. He raised
his eyes to the women's gallery, but it was empty. Now he wanted
to leave. He felt suddenly burdened, as if the whole future of
Judaism lay on his own shoulders. If he were to stay in this place,
he would be accepting that responsibility. As he turned to leave,
an old man called to him in a whisper and motioned him to come
and sit by his side. Jakob hesitated. It would have appeared rude
to decline the invitation, so, reluctantly, he made his way to the
pew where the man worshiped. The old man noticed that Jakob
had no prayer book, so he gave him his own and pointed out the
place in the service. Jakob looked at the left-hand page for the
Russian translation, that side of the page where the German had
been written in his childhood. But the language of the translation
was neither Russian nor German but in English, which Jakob
couldn't read. "It's illegal to print Jewish prayer books in Russia," the man whispered, seeing Jakob's consternation. "These
are smuggled in by friends from England and America. You must
learn Hebrew, my son."

"Where am I to learn?" Jakob whispered, though he was fast
losing his appetite for his return to the faith.

"Ask the rabbi after the service," the old man said.

But when the service was over, Jakob hurried from the synagogue, angry and disappointed. Judaism in the Soviet Union was
clearly moribund and it was certain that within a generation, it
would expire. Yet it lived in places like England and America. He
was thoroughly confused. He wished he was like Aaron, who was
never irritated by nudges from the past. He wished too that Aunt
Sarah had never come to visit him, and that he had never set foot
in that Odessa burial ground. He decided he would not write to
her anymore.

He noticed how the old men left the synagogue without even
pausing in the yard to exchange words with their fellow worshipers. Even that postservice conviviality did not exist here. Perhaps

that, too, would be frowned on by the authorities. He recalled the stories Aunt Sarah had told him about life in Odessa in Great-great-grandpa Jakob's time. The czars had been tyrants and anathema to Jews. Yet in their time Judaism had flourished. Synagogues were freely open and full, festivals were celebrated publicly and without shame, even in the awareness of the pogrom that might ensue. Yet in this land of equal opportunity, of fair shares for all, the spirit of man had been equalized too, and faith had become so diluted by equal distribution that it ceased to exist altogether. Jakob quickened his pace, anxious to avoid the old worshipers. He resented them for the monopoly they seemed to assume over his faith. He resented their neglect of bequest. But most of all he resented their old age, because their inheritance would be buried with them.

On graduation, Jakob secured a job at a middle school polytechnic in a suburb of Moscow. At about the same time, Aaron acquired a post in the Moscow National Hospital. The brothers saw little of each other in these days. As an intern, Aaron lived in the hospital and went home only on an occasional weekend. He and Jakob had little to say to each other, and those few words usually ended in argument. Since he had started in the teaching profession, Jakob had become more and more disillusioned. He himself had been through the Russian state school system, so he was not surprised by its methods. But as a mentor, he was beginning to question them. As a schoolboy, he had learned that a teacher's authority was unquestionable. A pupil would never argue with or doubt the infallibility of a teacher. During his schooldays, Jakob had conformed to the learning method with no thought of rebellion, but now he saw the shallowness and tyranny of the system. As a schoolboy, he had, from time to time, been publicly reprimanded and shamed by a teacher in front of the whole class. That, too, was part of the system, and he had, in great humiliation, accepted it. But now, as a teacher, he saw it as brutal and diminishing and he hated himself for being a part of it. But he kept silent.

Hans and Inge were sympathetic with his problem and commiserated with him. The subject was discussed again one weekend when Aaron was home.

"It's not only the schools," Hans said. "The schools are just part of the system. It's the system that doesn't work."

"Generally speaking, it does." Aaron was angry. "It's a good system. It's fair. Why shouldn't it work?"

"It may be equal," Hans said. "More or less equal," he added, "but it isn't free. Man is not free within it." He heard himself whispering. "See how I whisper," he said. "Man is not free in this country," he shouted, and shouted again, as if testing the gods to strike him.

"Be quiet," Inge whispered.

Hans looked at her. "See how frightened we all are," he said.

Jakob was amazed at the force of Hans's reaction. He had noticed how often now Hans would talk about his own father, and Jakob knew that somehow his anger hinged on those memories. Two years before, Hans had taken part in a small demonstration against Russia's invasion of Hungary and had spent two nights in prison for his pains. He had spent all that time thinking of his father, and how he had died for a dream that now seemed in his son's eyes to have turned so sour. He thought, too, of leaving, of taking his family to America, but to apply for an emigration visa was to risk refusal, which would jeopardize his future livelihood. Hans hated the Soviet Union with a passion, and unlike some of his Russian friends at the aircraft plant who were disillusioned in their own secret ways, he did not share their compensating love of the Russian tongue, of its drama, its landscape, and its poetry. Even Jakob, with all his disenchantment, could find some compensation in the Russian spirit. His language was perfect, and Tolstoy was closer to the tip of his tongue than Goethe. Sometimes Hans felt very isolated, even from his children.

"I've never felt any lack of freedom," Aaron said.

Hans turned toward him. "If you wanted to be a practicing Jew, you would feel the lack of freedom," he said. "If you wanted to stand up and protest against our system, you'd feel it too."

"But I don't want to practice as a Jew," Aaron said angrily. "Neither do I want to protest. I'm in total agreement with our system. I think all religions are a sop to the masses."

He's brainwashed, Hans thought, and sloganized, too, exactly as the Hitler youth had been in his German days.

"Let's go out," Inge said, anxious to avoid argument. "It's a lovely day."

The others were eager to agree. It was a bright summer Sunday, a traditional walking day for Muscovites, who would gather in parks and squares and mingle with the tourists. The nearest square to where the Dreisers lived was Mayakovsky and, as they approached it, they saw that a large crowd had gathered. On inquiry, they were told that a statue of the poet was to be unveiled, so they joined the crowd and watched the ceremony. After the formal speeches of Russian dedication to the arts, the statue was unveiled, and a group of poets on the platform began to read their verse. The crowd was silent, hanging on to each syllable, as if for the first time in their lives they had entered a new dimension of the spirit. Hans, too, was similarly affected and his sullen mood dispersed. By his side, Jakob listened with wonder, smelling a forbidden freedom in the event, not so much in the words themselves, but that they were being spoken at all. He was not surprised when, after the official readings, a number of poets among the crowd took their verses to the platform. The crowd roared their approval, eager for more, and the light was beginning to fade before they dispersed. But not before someone on the platform suggested that they meet again, and share their poetry with each other.

As the Dreisers left the square, Hans looked at Jakob and sensed a profound change in him. "Will you go again, Jakob?" he asked.

Jakob nodded.

"Poetry lifts the spirit," Hans said.

"It was more than a poetry reading," Jakob said. "It might well be the beginnings of a revolution."

It was a prophetic statement because after a number of such meetings in the square, the authorities smelled rebellion and read dissent between the spoken lines. Moreover, when the readings were finished, the crowd did not disperse but lingered in groups and talked of matters beyond the stuff of poetry. Mayakovsky Square had become a free Sunday club for those who longed to speak aloud. There were random arrests and warnings, until finally, after a few months, the readings were officially banned. But not before Jakob had found an avenue of release for all his questions, a camaraderie among those equally frustrated. These he found. And love, too.

He had been a regular attendant at the readings ever since the statue's unveiling. Each time, he had noticed a young girl standing at the foot of the plinth, her hand fidgeting in her pocket, possibly with her verses, Jakob thought, that she was too shy to reveal. Sunday after Sunday he watched her standing there, happy to keep his distance, and to feed on her beauty. She had long black hair, the style of which never varied. It was plaited into a thick pigtail that seemed to take off from the crown of her head, then hung in sheer perpendicular down her back. Her posture was strikingly erect and fearless. One Sunday he placed himself by her side, and in an interval between the readings he asked her if she herself was a poet. She trembled a little as she answered.

"I write a little," she said.

"Why don't you read them, then?" he asked.

"I don't carry them with me," she said.

He smiled at her. "Then what *do* you carry in your pocket?"

She withdrew her hand. Inside it was a small white mouse. She stroked it with the fingers of her other hand and looked up at him and smiled.

He was embarrassed by his poor guesswork. "Well, it's a kind of poetry, I suppose," he said. "What's its name?"

"Moses," she said.

Jakob trembled.

"It's Jewish," she said, and laughed.

"Doesn't look Jewish to me," Jakob said.

"Do I?" She looked squarely at him.

"How d'you feel?" he said.

"Jewish."

"So do I."

It was the beginning of their relationship.

It was the following Sunday that the police broke up the readings for the last time, but by then Deborah and Jakob had seen each other daily and had found their own meeting places rather more private than Mayakovsky Square.

Deborah was in her last year at the Moscow Film Academy. In the summer she would qualify as an editor and she hoped to specialize in documentary films. Despite the teamwork that her job necessitated, she was, like Jakob, a loner. And for the same reasons. She was a doubter, a questioner, and could find no one with whom to share her uncertainties. At the film school she had sought clues to frustration among her colleagues, but finding none, she had learned to hold her tongue, a habit encouraged by her parents out of fear for her future. She, like Jakob, had sniffed a promise of freedom in Mayakovsky Square. Deborah could retrace her heritage for five generations from the Magareks of Moldavia. Emanuel Magarek had dealt as a timber merchant in Kiev at the same time as the Patriarch Jakob Bindel had traded in his tavern in Odessa. The Magarek family had never left Russia. They had survived pogroms, wars, dispossession, and banishment from one province to another. But most had eventually returned to the Ukraine.

Deborah's parents had settled in Moscow because her father too was a film-maker and the center of that industry lay in the capital. Her parents were indifferent to the concept of Judaism. They celebrated no festivals, neither had they ever been inside a synagogue. The dilemma of identity played no part in Deborah's doubts, and she was surprised to find that it was the very core of Jakob's discontent. In the course of their daily meetings Jakob told her about his Aunt Sarah and her tales of Israel. He told her what he knew of Jewish history, but he refrained from taking her to the synagogue, for it had dampened his own willing heart. Deborah warmed to his stories of Israel, and slowly she began to accommodate the notion of Jewishness within the arena of her doubts and uncertainties.

Once she took Jakob to her cutting room at the film school. She was editing a government short on army training, and as the soundtrack boomed the virtues of defending the sacred motherland, with its notion of equality in all things, she put her finger to her lips, because there were others in the room.

"See what I mean?" she whispered.

He saw it exactly and he understood, too, that the silence he was keeping in his own classroom was the same fearful silence. It was a silence that could lead to collusion. They must fight against that, both of them.

Deborah was much at home in the Dreiser household. Hans and Inge welcomed her, glad for Jakob's sake that he had found a kindred spirit. Even Aaron was fond of her, despite her leanings toward rebellion. He even brought her a matching white mouse from the hospital laboratory. She would call it Aaron, she laughed, not for his sake, but because Aaron was Moses' brother. Likewise Jakob was welcomed in the Magarek household. Deborah's father was an established film-maker, highly thought of by those in the profession. As an artist, he was the recipient of many privileges unavailable to the ordinary Russian worker. His apartment was roomy. He was allowed far more space than the

eight square feet per person that was the state allowance for ur-
ban living. Its furnishings were sumptuous. Both the Magareks
were well-dressed, having access to the special department store
available to the privileged class. Food was plentiful on their table
and of a variety that Jakob had never seen before. There was
clearly no cause for personal discontent in the Magarek household, and Jakob wondered at the source of Deborah's rebellious
thoughts. Sometimes he talked to her father about the system
under which they lived, but Mr. Magarek felt himself in no way
indisposed. He was allowed to travel freely to film festivals all
over the world. He did not feel his freedom restricted. Of course,
he realized, he said, that he was one of the chosen citizens, and in
the same breath he urged Jakob to take into account the bonuses
of a system that was fair and equal for all. Mr. Magarek was not
a man one could argue with, but Jakob liked him well enough to
leave him with his illusions. Occasionally he would broach the
question of Magarek's Jewishness, but in this subject, too, it
seemed to Jakob that they were deluding themselves, for Mr.
Magarek asserted that he was a Jew only by accident. That he
was first and foremost a Russian, an identity that claimed his
total allegiance.

One day Deborah suggested that they go to the synagogue.
Because it was she who had proposed it, Jakob was not averse to
a second visit, and the following Saturday he took out his grandfather's prayer shawl once more and set out to give his faith
another chance.

Deborah had never entered a synagogue before, and had to be
conducted to the women's gallery by an old man, who looked at
her with some surprise. She was puzzled by his reaction, and
understood it only when she reached the gallery and found that it
was empty. She edged herself into a seat in the back row, but
once seated, she could see nothing of the proceedings on the
ground floor, so she sidled into a seat a few rows from the front.
She picked out Jakob first of all, sitting among a scatter of very
old men, their heads buried in their prayer books, and the sight of
Jakob among them marked him as a beacon, a torch to illumine
the future of his tribe.

And because of the love between them, she too felt that responsibility. She looked along the benches for a prayer book, but
found none. She listened to the rumbling from below, but she
could make no sense of it. Its sound stirred no lingering memory

in her mind. Yet she did not feel in any way alien to the strange
murmurings. Certainly not as alien as she had felt in a Russian
Orthodox church on the one occasion she had attended a friend's
wedding. She wondered what a wedding would be like in this
synagogue. She wondered, too, whether Jakob would ever ask her
to marry him. She looked at him again, and saw how his neighbor was pointing a gnarled finger along the lines of the prayer
book, and how Jakob nodded and smiled. But not once did he
look in her direction. Nor did any of the others. From long habit,
perhaps. Perhaps their womenfolk were dead, or they were keeping the home while their men kept the faith for both of them. She
fingered the mice in her pocket. Moses and Aaron. Closet Jews in
the dark, like these men in the temple mumbling their fearful
faith behind closed doors.

Jakob was standing now, along with the others, and singing.
Then she saw the men doff their shawls and fold them slowly and
carefully into velvet bags. And then Jakob looked up at her for
the first time, and signaled that they should meet outside.

"Would you come here again?" she asked as they walked down
the synagogue steps.

Jakob stopped and took her hand. "I'll come here again to
marry you," he said.

The two families gathered under the canopy. Aaron was the
best man. He was happy for his brother, and as he stood there,
clutching the ring, he began to wonder whether he himself should
take a wife, and he cast a sidelong glance to find Sonia. Aaron
had known her for almost two years, yet he had never brought
her to the Dreiser home. He was wary of Hans. Sonia was not
Jewish, and Aaron knew that Hans's welcome would be cold.
Not on his own behalf, but for the memory of Benjamin. Aaron
knew how acutely Hans felt the responsibility of fulfilling what
would have been Benjamin's wishes for his sons. He was grateful
to his younger brother for marrying within the faith, for it helped
to give him license to choose elsewhere.

He had no difficulty in picking Sonia out of the crowd, since
her beauty was remarkable, and those on each side of her sat
apart a little, as if to give her framing. She looked at him, but
without smiling, afraid that at this time and in this place, a smile
might be construed as a declaration of her own expectation. But

he smiled at her nonetheless. For he had made a decision. He would propose to Sonia after the ceremony.

He turned to look at Deborah, and he wondered where on her white pocketless person she had secreted Moses and Aaron, since it was known that she never went about without them. Then he caught sight of a small white silk purse, hidden in the blooms of her bouquet. The purse was wriggling, and Aaron was glad that they had come to the wedding.

Inge was crying a little, remembering Heidi and Benjamin, and Hans comforted her, saddened himself by the desolation of all their pasts. Then Jakob pledged his troth according to the law of Moses and Israel, and crushed the glass under his foot. A cry of *"Mazeltov"* rose from the congregation, and Hans sighed with joy and relief. The Bindel line could now nudge itself forward to a new generation. He was at peace with himself, having discharged the moral burden of the Bindel guardianship. Or almost discharged. He knew about Sonia and her friendship with Aaron. It would not please him if their relationship resulted in marriage, and when, later on at the reception, Aaron asked him to meet his intended bride, he tried to hide his displeasure. But Jakob had noticed it, and once the introduction was over, he took Hans aside.

"You look worried, Hans," he said.

"Your father would have been worried too. It is something that has never happened in the Bindel family in all its generations."

Jakob thought of the portrait of the young boy in Aunt Sarah's album, and of the story of Grandpa Leon. It was a secret between them, a secret that he had not even shared with Aaron. But seeing the look of pain on Hans's face, he knew he had to share it with him to lift the guilt from Hans's heart. So he took him aside and told him about Grandpa Leon's first marriage.

"So you see," he said when he had finished his tale, "it won't be the first time, and it certainly won't be the last. Yet we survive, we Bindels," he said, "and that's the whole of our inheritance."

"Does Aaron know this story?" Hans asked.

Jakob shook his head. "There's no need," he said.

"May I tell Inge?" Hans asked. "She has the same guilt as I."

"Of course," Jakob said. Then he put his arm around Hans's shoulder. "You have nothing to be guilty of," he said. "I have loved you and Inge as much as I could ever have loved my own parents. You know that. Aaron, too. He has more difficulty in showing it, that's all."

"He doesn't seem to trust me," Hans said.

"I don't think he trusts anyone."

But presumably Aaron trusted Sonia, for within six months they were married. Theirs was a strange coupling. Sonia's way of life represented all that Aaron had strived for. As an adolescent, Sonia had lisped her way through Tolstoy, Gorki, and Pushkin, writers whom Aaron read with a foreigner's secondhand relish. Her father was a high-ranking government official, a staunch party member, as was his father before him. Sonia's mother had died when she was a child, and Mr. Koskin had never remarried. In his privileged position he was entitled to a housekeeper and a governess for his child. He had had a series of mistresses who, after serving their terms, had been publicly discharged from their duties, usually on the plea that the party claimed his total allegiance. Or almost total. His love for his daughter was greater than any loyalty he owed to his party, a love compounded by the guilt of his neglect and his sundry infidelities. He would have forgiven her anything.

Aaron's first meeting with his prospective father-in-law had been cordial but cool. Mr. Koskin took no trouble to hide his disappointment that Aaron was not a party member. "We'll remedy that," he had said, but with little conviction. He refrained from inquiry as to Aaron's background and parentage, as if he feared that investigation into that quarter would not please him either. He toyed with the name of Bindel, finding it foreign and of dubious extraction. On the whole, despite the fact that Aaron was a doctor, he thought his daughter could have done better for herself. But he did the right thing. He welcomed Aaron into their small family in his well-endowed quarters facing the Kremlin, but he took care not to introduce him to his friends. To this end, he insisted on a quiet wedding. So Aaron and Sonia were married in a state registry office, in the presence of the Dreisers, Jakob and Deborah, and Mr. Koskin himself. When the ceremony was over, Sonia divided her bouquet into two sections, and with Aaron on her arm, took the bridal car to Lenin's tomb. There she laid half of her bouquet. They walked down the slope to the Tomb of the Unknown Soldier, where she deposited what was left of the flowers. She thus did her duty as a young Russian bride, in her homage to her past.

After the wedding, Aaron made little effort to maintain contact with Hans and Inge. From time to time Hans would drop into the hospital on his way to work, finding some excuse to talk to him. He was saddened by the distance that had grown between them. Only on the level of his work was Aaron willing to communicate, and Hans grasped at this thread to avoid a total estrangement between them.

Aaron had begun to specialize in immunology. He had his own laboratory in the hospital, and was slowly acquiring a reputation in that field. Once during a visit, Aaron showed Hans an article that had appeared in an American medical journal, written under Aaron's name. Hans was excited. He wanted to know the matter of the dissertation; he wanted it translated word for word, and Aaron did it for him gladly in his childhood German. Hans could understand very little of its technicality, but he understood the introduction, and he puffed with pride. "Aaron Bindel," it said, "at the age of twenty-seven, is a brilliant young immunologist whose future work in the field could well revolutionize present attitudes."

"Your father would have been very proud of you," he said. "As I am."

Aaron shrugged it off. To give to anybody, alive or dead, was for Aaron too burdensome a responsibility. But beneath the shrug, Hans could sense the anger.

"Aaron," he said. "I've never tried to replace your father. I have been your guardian. I have loved you as any father would his son. But you are a Bindel."

"I am happy enough to be a Dreiser," Aaron said.

How like his Granduncle Aaron he is, Hans thought, that stern, unbending man after whom he was named. And how like gentle Grandpa Leon Jakob was. Hans went toward Aaron and dared to touch him. "Your parents are dead," he said to him. "They died in Auschwitz. No one can give you proof. The only evidence is my guardianship." He paused. "I remember when Inge and I told you in Leipzig," he went on. "It was Jakob who cried. But you were angry with disbelief. You're still angry, Aaron."

"I know they're dead, Hans," Aaron said quietly, and Hans was moved by that so rare use of his name. "But it wasn't my fault. I refuse to bear the guilt of the survivor. That's what

Bindeldom is all about. That's our inheritance. Let Jakob carry the torch of suffering. It's not my burden."

Hans was deeply distressed at his words, and Aaron saw the sorrow on his face. And for the first time that Hans could remember, Aaron touched his guardian's head with a caress so tender that it seemed to make up for all the years of his cold indifference. "Why do I need anyone more than you and Inge?" Aaron said. Hans held him in his arms without fear, then quickly he left the laboratory. Thereafter Aaron and Sonia were regular visitors at the Dreiser household.

In these days Hans was a very contented man. Deborah was about to deliver her first child. That morning, Jakob, who lived close by, had borrowed Hans's car to take her to the hospital. Inge had waited by the phone all day for Jakob's call. Now it was evening, and Hans was with her, stifling his excitement.

"Have they talked to you about names?" he asked.

"No," Inge said. "But I suppose it will be Benjamin or Heidi."

"I hope so," Hans said.

Then the phone rang, and both hesitated before answering. Hans nodded to Inge, feeling that it was her prerogative. She picked up the receiver and Hans watched the smile break over her face as she listened.

"It's a boy," she shouted. "Everything's fine." She arranged with Jakob that they would go to the hospital in the morning.

The following day was one of celebration. In the morning they were to see their grandson, and in the afternoon, Hans and Jakob were going to Mayakovsky Square. After years of silence, the poetry readings were to recommence. The first reading was not advertised, but word of mouth from poet to poet and reader to reader would insure a large enough gathering. That Sunday in the spring of 1961 marked the anniversary of Mayakovsky's suicide, so it was an auspicious time to hold a reading that celebrated freedom. But it was a dangerous time too, for two days before, Yuri Gagarin had made the first space flight, and such an exploit was the cause of great celebration among the Russian people. The authorities would not look kindly on any event that might sour such an achievement.

In the morning, Hans and Inge went early to the hospital and were glad to find Aaron there. He excused his presence on medical grounds, but Hans knew that he had come to share in their happiness. "What will you call it?" he asked as he passed the baby to Inge and Hans for their inspection.

"Benjamin," Jakob said.

Aaron said nothing, and his lack of response signaled disapproval.

"That's as it should be," Hans said quickly. "It's the meaning of continuity."

Aaron let it pass.

"He's beautiful," Inge was saying, and she sat next to Deborah on the bed and asked for details of the birth and hospital care. They talked in whispers, and the men around the bed took the hint of the women's need for privacy and sought a subject of conversation for their own.

"I think there'll be quite a turnout at the square this afternoon," Hans said.

"You mean the reading?" Aaron asked. "You're not going, I hope. There'll be trouble."

"If we're orderly, there won't be trouble," Jakob said.

"But just being there, orderly or not," Aaron said, "is an anti-Soviet statement. You're asking for trouble."

"In what country in the world is poetry reading such a crime?" Hans asked, though he did not expect a reply. "You ought to come with us, Aaron," he said. "You would find it uplifting."

"I have better things to do," Aaron said. But he was smiling. "In any case," he added, "my father-in-law will probably have many friends there. Keep out of their way," he laughed.

Hans laughed too. He saw Aaron's joking attitude as a sign of a slight thaw in his stubborn patriotism.

"Well, maybe next time," Jakob said.

"If there is a next time, and I doubt it," Aaron said.

Inge had overheard the exchange. "Maybe Aaron's right," she said. "Perhaps you shouldn't go."

"Of course they must go," Deborah joined in. "What better way to celebrate? In any case, I want a firsthand report of what happens."

"Well, be careful," Inge said. "I'll stay with my grandson a little while. But come back here after the meeting. I'll see you here."

Jakob held his son for a while, then he left the hospital with Hans. Aaron accompanied them to the carpark, where they went their separate ways.

Hans and Jakob reached the square an hour before the proceedings were due to begin, but already the area was crowded with people. They recalled Aaron's warning, and knew perhaps that with such a crowd there could well be danger. Among the crowd Hans could spot those whom Aaron had called his father-in-law's friends. Plainclothes KGB men, but in all ways uniformed. For they were dressed alike in gray trousers and black leather jackets, and each carried a rolled newspaper. They were immediately recognizable. And indeed were intended to be, for their presence was meant to be a harassment as well as a warning.

Hans and Jakob mingled with the crowd and were quickly infected by their excited anticipation. The names of those who would be reading their works were whispered around. And Jakob recognized them as some of the foremost poets of the time. Then one of them was indeed seen to be making his way toward the plinth, followed by a group of men and women, their verses in their hands. A hush fell on the square as they approached the platform, and one of their number made a short speech of welcome. Then he called upon Anatoly Shchukin, the renowned poet, to open the proceedings. Shchukin's first poem, though untitled, was clearly about freedom, and with every syllable of each audacious word, he confessed to the crime of individualism. The words echoed through the loudspeaker and collided head on with the police cars at the entrance to the square. The officer in charge gave his orders through his radio set, and drove off. Shchukin got away with three more inflammatory verses before the snowplows, their shovel mouths agape with astonishment at such unseasonal duty, spluttered toward the square. Shchukin bravely went on reading, and most of the crowd, out of loyalty, stood their ground. But some panicked and tried to get out. In the scuffle, Hans and Jakob were separated.

Hans found himself on the plinth, and he shouted Jakob's name across the square. But not even he could hear his own voice, so raucous was the panic among the crowd. Then miraculously he caught sight of him, standing with his back to the gaping shovel mouth of the first plow that had entered the square. Jakob clearly could not hear its approach, for the din of the mob muted its rumble to a murmur. Hans looked at the gaping jaw with horror. He practically flew off the plinth and plunged through the mass of people to where Jakob stood. Then, with his two hands on Jakob's back, he pushed him forward, putting some distance between his son and the jaws of almost certain death. But in the great force of his propulsion, Hans himself fell to the ground, and seconds before he surrendered consciousness, he felt the steely and loveless embrace of the machine. Then he screamed aloud, but did not hear his screaming.

But Jakob heard, and all those who stood about him. They turned, and when he saw Hans's inert body in its iron nest, Jakob knew who had pushed him so violently and with so much love. And, oh, my God, he thought, with so great a sacrifice. The snowplow ground to a halt, and from nowhere two stretcher-bearers approached in the crowd. They bent down over Hans's body and murmured to each other. Jakob watched, unable to move, transfixed in terror. He watched the orderlies unfold a blanket. I'll wait, he thought to himself, and see how much of Hans they will cover, and if they cover his face, he decided, I shall kill them both with my bare hands. But they stopped short of Hans's sleeping countenance and tucked the blanket under his shoulder. Then Jakob stepped forward, full of love for those men who had not pronounced Hans dead. He walked alongside them.

"I'm his son," he said.

"We'll take him to the hospital," one of them said. "He's bad, I'm afraid."

Then Jakob saw the blood seeping behind Hans's shirt collar.

"One of the forks caught the back of his neck," the man went on.

"Murderers," Jakob screamed across the square. "Murderers."

Some of the crowd who followed the stretcher tried to comfort him. Jakob began to pray. He did not know what God was made of, nor indeed whether He existed at all. He did not want to pray to that same God who had turned His back on Auschwitz, yet he had heard that there was no other, and that His ways were mysterious. So he prayed fervently, or rather ordered, entreating Him to leave Hans to the living. "You've taken one father of mine," Jakob screamed into the depths of his soul. Then he felt the tears streaming down his face.

"Where are you taking him?" he asked one of the men as they loaded the stretcher onto the ambulance on the fringe of the square.

"To the National," the man said.

"I'll go and fetch my mother," Jakob said. "We'll go there together."

The man touched Jakob on the shoulder. "You'd better hurry, son," he said gently.

The National was where Aaron worked, but only now, for the first time since the accident, did Jakob think of his brother. It would be almost harder to tell Aaron than Inge. Inge's love for Hans was pure, constant and blameless. If he were to die, she would in desolation mourn him, but she would give time, time to heal the wound, for no guilt would prolong her grief. But Aaron's life would be shattered by a second orphanhood, by the death of one whom he had always viewed as a usurper to the Bindel throne, even though he himself found that throne so uncommodious and uncomfortable. But Hans would not die, he must not, Jakob wept inside himself, else for the rest of his life he would carry the blame of his demise. It was he who had insisted on their attendance at the reading. It was because he himself had so much wanted to go that Hans had accompanied him. "Oh, God," he prayed again, "let him live." As he prayed, he ran and ran, unaware of his speed or breathlessness. He turned the corner of the Dreisers' street and saw Inge coming out of the apartment building. She carried a bunch of flowers, clutching them in her hand on her way to see Deborah. Then Jakob, who for the last hour had forgotten his new status of father, now remembered his son. The Lord giveth, and the Lord taketh away. Blessed be the name of the Lord. He stopped, frozen by the thought, and waited for Inge to reach him.

"What are you doing here?" she asked as she approached him. Then she stopped and trembled. "Where's Hans?"

"There's been an accident," Jakob said, and put his arm around her. "It's all right, it's all right," he whispered. "He'll be all right. It was just an accident."

"What happened?" she screamed at him.

"We must get to the hospital," he said, taking her arm, and almost in the same breath, "It was a snowplow. They sent them into the square. It ran over him."

Inge stopped and forced Jakob to face her.

"How bad is it, Jakob?" she asked.

"It's all right," he sobbed, his voice breaking. "It's all right." He saw a taxi in the distance and with some relief, he flagged it down.

"To the National Hospital," he told the driver. Then in a whisper, "Please hurry."

But Inge had overheard him. She settled in the back of the car and put her arm around Jakob.

"Whatever happens, Jakob," she said, "you are not to blame. You must never think that. Never, never, never."

Then he put his head on her lap, as he remembered doing all those years ago when she had told him that his father was dead. He wept now as he had then, and as Inge had done in the Leipzig days, she cradled his head in her arms. They were silent for the rest of the drive, and by the time they reached the hospital, Jakob had steadied himself, and he took Inge's arm and ushered her into the waiting hall.

The receptionist lost no time in checking Hans's whereabouts, for she read the urgency in Jakob's eyes. They took the elevator to the third floor. The ward sister, learning of their kinship with her patient, was very solemn and told them as gently as she could that Mr. Dreiser was in a critical condition and was not expected to survive. The injury to his skull had been considerable. "But go and sit with him," she said. "He is semiconscious."

Jakob let go of Inge's hand and she went into the little annex where Hans was lying.

"I have a brother here, Matron," he said. "Dr. Aaron Bindel. Could you page him, please, and ask him to come?"

"I'll do that immediately," she said. Then she laid a hand on Jakob's arm. "I'm very sorry," she said.

Jakob crept into the annex. He stood at the end of the bed. Hans's head was bandaged and his eyelids fluttered a little.

"Hans," Inge whispered. "Hans, Hans," over and over again as she held his hand, massaging life into his fingers with a tenderness so acute that it bordered on violence. Jakob sat by her side and took Hans's other hand in his own. He wanted to call him too, but suddenly the name of Hans seemed to have become, at that moment, Inge's inalienable property. So he said nothing and he put Hans's hand to his own cheek and caressed it. So they sat there, the two of them, watching Hans as his life ebbed away, listening to each breath that he savored, aware of its rarity. He looked transparent, as if the shadow of sheer living had been lifted to point death on its undarkened way. He lay, his breathing quivering like a hummingbird, a faint burring sound, a polite chorale in death's overture.

After a while they felt a presence at the door, and turning, they saw Aaron, his face white and drawn with sadness. He tiptoed to the other side of the bed and gently took Hans's face in his hands. The eyelids fluttered as if in prelude to opening wide. Then Aaron spoke one word. "Papa," he said.

Tears veiled Jakob's eyes. From where had his brother plucked that word? From what hidden source had it echoed through Aaron's troubled heart? Had it lodged there since Auschwitz, on parole, as it were, waiting for its final release? And now the word had dropped from his brother's lips as if it had never been incarcerated at all.

A smile played erratically around Hans's mouth.

"Papa," Aaron said again.

Then Hans opened his eyes and all those at the bedside knew that it was for the last time. Inge bent to kiss him.

"Love, love," Hans whispered. Then he stared at Aaron and Jakob, and with the last traces of his smile, he said, "My two dear Bindels." Then his eyes closed, though the smile still hovered on his lips.

Aaron took his hand and searched for the pulse that no longer beat. "Papa is dead," he said.

Jakob took Inge in his arms. "No," he said. "He still lives in my son, for Hans will be his name."

Only that morning Hans had rejoiced in the name of Benjamin as a symbol of continuity. That continuity was what Hans, in his Bindel guardianship, had labored for most of all. Whatever the provenance of that principle, whether the pungent smell of gas in Auschwitz, or the small sniff of freedom in Mayakovsky Square, whether it was clothed in the name of Hans or Benjamin, it mattered not. For however it was called, it was a celebration of survival.

After Hans's death, Jakob and Deborah moved into the Dreiser apartment to live with Inge, and the presence of little Hans did much to alleviate the sorrow that had clouded all their lives. Aaron managed to secure Inge an administrative job in the hospital where he worked, and there she was able to make new friends. Aaron hoped that in time she would marry again, and indeed Inge hoped it for herself. She liked the state of marriage. She felt it was of her nature, and to continue to live alone, even with the company of little Hans, seemed to her unnatural. So when some eighteen months after Hans's death, she met Ivan Treger, a widower and one of the almoners in the hospital, she did not view him in any way as Hans's replacement, but as his continuation. They were married in the summer of that year, and Inge went to live in Ivan's apartment in the old city.

That time in Moscow, the mid-1960s, was a period of fervent dissidence. The poetry readings at the square had been officially banned, but the protest movement flourished. Writers managed to publish their works. Two of them, Andrei Sinyavsky and Yuri Daniel, were brought to trial on the charge of dissemination of anti-Soviet propaganda through their writings. Sinyavsky was sentenced to seven years' hard labor, and Daniel to five. The punishments were severe; the sentences made clear that the authorities would brook no opposition. Jakob and Deborah followed the trial from day to day, and they both eavesdropped in their respective places of work, to pick up the opinions of their colleagues. But the subject was surrounded by silence, either because of indifference or because of the fear of voicing sympathy for the accused. Aaron maintained the same silence when Jakob broached the subject with him.

One day, however, during the trial, he warned Jakob that dissidence should be none of his business. Aaron was more than irritated by Jakob's interest in the rebels. He was downright angry. He saw his brother's dissident connections as a serious threat to his own career. Earlier that year he had been elected to the Academy of Sciences, a highly distinguished honor for one so young. His work in immunology was well known to practitioners in his field throughout the world. It was rumored that he would soon be awarded the privilege of a country residence, and numerous other bonuses for which the Russian elite were eligible. A rebellious brother might well interfere with his prospects for promotion and advancement, and often he considered cutting himself off from Jakob entirely. But since Hans's death he had grown much closer to his brother, and it was because he loved him that he angered him so.

"I hear you went to the trial," Aaron said with displeasure.

"Yes," Jakob said. "I thought it was a historic occasion. Your father-in-law was there too. On the other side, of course. He actually smiled at me," Jakob said. "But I ignored him. I suppose he told you."

"He mentioned you were there," Aaron said. "He was not pleased."

"I am not in the business of keeping your father-in-law happy," Jakob shouted angrily. "He and his kind are my enemies."

"I urge you to be careful, brother," Aaron said. His use of the sibling term was rare, and it rang with a combination of concern and warning. Then, as if to underline his concern, he touched his brother's arm. "Sonia's pregnant," he said.

"Really?" Jakob was wide-eyed with excitement. He knew that Sonia and Aaron were trying for a baby, and from time to time he had glimpsed their despair at their failure. He was overjoyed for them both.

"When?" he asked.

"In five months," Aaron said.

"Hans will have a cousin," Jakob said. "May I tell Deborah?"

"Of course. Sonia will want her to know. I've told Inge. She was the first we told. She jumped up and down with excitement. It seemed worth it if only to give her that pleasure."

"You will change, Aaron," Jakob said. "Even you will be changed by fatherhood."

Aaron did not pursue the comment. He knew what Jakob meant.

"Maybe I will," he said. He turned to go. "I'd like you to be around for the birth, Jakob," he said. "Don't get yourself into trouble."

The baby was born in June. Aaron telephoned late one evening to give Jakob the news. "Hans has a cousin," he said. "Her name's Heidi." The announcement was over very quickly, pre-empting questioning or comment. Jakob understood that and inquired after Sonia's health and the baby's weight. He was glad for his brother. Aaron had made a certain peace with his past. As Hans had lay dying, he had called him Papa; his daughter he had called Heidi. Thus he had finally accepted his orphanhood, and in burying his parents, he had embraced continuity. Jakob now felt free to attend meetings once more and to play his part in his inherited battle of survival.

In the following summer, two events took place that were to put Jakob in the front line of the battle. Deborah had another child, and to Jakob's joy, it was a son. He named him Benjamin. Now he had donated to his tribe yet two more brothers Bindel, and it seemed as if a small burden had been lifted from his heart.

The second event of that summer, which was to conscript Jakob into the dissenting ranks, was the six-day Israeli war. Jakob had never ceased his correspondence with Aunt Sarah, although over the years it had become irregular. But her letters had kept alive Jakob's appetite for Judaism and for a knowledge of his past. The war reports on Russian radio and television were disturbing. They pointed to a total Israeli defeat. According to their bulletins, at the end of the six days, it would have appeared that Israel had been annihilated. But it was still possible to tune into the BBC World Service and between the jamming and the static, the truth could be learned. After a few days even the Russian News Agency could no longer mask the Israeli victory, but in their hamfisted attempts to do so, their hostile anti-Semitic face had been clearly shown. They called it anti-Zionism, but no Jew was deluded by that euphemism. The official press carried cartoons of the Israeli victors that recalled for Jakob those that had appeared in the Nazi paper *Der Stürmer* when he was a child. The effect of the war on Jakob, as on thousands of Russian Jews, was one of stunning change in his life. He began to think seriously of emigrating.

It seemed to Jakob that during those days, Aaron was avoiding

him. Whenever Jakob invited him over, he pleaded prior engage-
ments, and one day Jakob dropped into the hospital after school
and sought him out in his laboratory. Aaron was clearly not
pleased to see him, but he tried to hide his displeasure.

"It's ages since we met," Jakob apologized as he took the chair
that Aaron offered him.

"I've been busy," Aaron said.

He was prevaricating, Jakob knew, so he came straight to the
point. "What do you think of the war?"

"I don't think about it too much," Aaron lied, for the war had
threatened him profoundly. "But, as you know, I'm totally
against nationalism. It leads to Fascism. We've seen it in our own
lifetime."

There was no way Jakob knew how to argue with him. His
brother's premise was so brainwashed that to argue with him
would have been futile.

"I'm thinking of going to live there," Jakob said.

He was surprised at the violence of Aaron's reaction. "That's
impossible," he said, his face flushed with fury. "It would be an
outright anti-Soviet act. It would be treacherous."

Again Jakob felt he couldn't argue, and for the same reasons as
before. "How's Heidi?" he said.

"You mustn't go," Aaron said, almost pleading. "It will bring
shame to all of us."

"I'm sorry about your father-in-law," Jakob said, and he left
the room.

During that time both Deborah and Jakob achieved promotion
on their jobs. Deborah was appointed chief editor of the state
documentary film unit, and Jakob was promoted to head of the
mathematics department. These changes delayed their decision
for a while, even though many Russian Jews to their knowledge
had already emigrated to Israel.

The Soviet authorities, worried at the increasing numbers of
applications for Israel, called an international press conference.
Forty prominent Soviet Jews were invited to attend to testify to
the freedom and good fortune of the Jews in the USSR. The event
was heavily covered on radio and television. One evening Jakob
and Deborah had turned on their set to view an old film that had
been made by Deborah's father. But the program had been
changed and in its stead was a rerun of the press conference.
Those taking part were introduced around the table. They were

Russia's most prominent Jews in the fields of government, arts, and science.

"Traitors," Jakob muttered, turning away. Then he heard the announcer's voice behind his back. "Dr. Aaron Bindel of the National Hospital of Moscow, foremost immunologist of international repute." Jakob could hardly believe what he had heard. He looked at Deborah and saw confirmation in her disgusted glance. Then, turning, he saw his brother in full close-up. "Turn it off," Jakob said.

"You turn it off if you don't want to listen," Deborah said. "It's horrible, but I'm curious."

He sat by her side. The first to be introduced was the highest-ranking Jewish government official, who swore that his religion had in no way impeded his promotion. He had never in his whole life encountered anti-Semitism in the Soviet Union. This opinion was echoed by other token Jews around the table, a world-famous violinist, a ballerina, and a clutch of writers. Shortly it was Aaron's turn and Jakob was ashamed. Aaron reiterated much of what had already been said. But he went further. He attacked Israel for being anti-Soviet, and he suggested that rumors that Jews wished to leave Russia were sheer anti-Soviet propaganda. The Jews had every reason to be grateful to Russia, which had, after all, delivered them from the evils of Fascism.

Jakob turned the television off. He was sickened by his brother's treachery.

"His father-in-law wrote that speech," Deborah said.

"Yes, but Aaron delivered it. I don't want to talk to him again."

"We must try and change him," Deborah said.

"Hans used to tell me my father was like that. Stubborn, ostrichlike. He never believed that Hitler would stay in power."

"Yes, but he changed, didn't he?" Deborah said.

"He changed, all right." Jakob's voice was bitter. "But it was too late."

Jakob was deeply depressed by the television interview. The following week an incident took place at school that aggravated his depression. He was taking a class of fifteen-year-olds, when suddenly he was interrupted by the arrival of the headmaster. "I'm sorry to disturb you, Mr. Bindel," Dr. Kumysh said, "but I'd like a word with the class."

Jakob stood to one side. By the stern look on the headmaster's face, he knew there was trouble, and by some intuitive instinct he knew it was related to anti-Semitism. When the headmaster asked Isay Salmon to stand up, his guess was confirmed. Young Isay was one of Jakob's more talented students, but it was not on account of his promise that he had been singled out in class. He was also a Jew and known to Jakob to have Israeli sympathies. Jakob shuddered on his behalf. He marveled at the boy's coolness. Isay was clearly aware of why he had been called. He eyed the headmaster with a certain disdain.

"It has come to my notice," Dr. Kumysh said, "that there is a student in this class who is the son of a traitor. He stands before you. His father has relinquished his Soviet citizenship and applied to go to Israel, that country that is bent on maligning the highest ideals and principles by which we live in this blessed land. I have come here simply to make you aware of the treachery in your midst. As you know, one of the bases of our ideology is the strength and the power of the collective spirit. Traitors must learn their lesson, and it is the collective that is often the teacher. You may sit down now, Salmon," Dr. Kumysh said. Then he turned to Jakob. "Thank you, Mr. Bindel," he said, overpolitely. "I was delighted to see your brother on television." Then he left the room.

Salmon was still standing, proudly holding on to his status of outsider. If there was any fear in him, he was certainly hiding it. Indeed, a flicker of a smile played on his lips, as if in challenge.

"Sit down, Isay," Jakob said gently. "Now let us get on with the lesson."

It was the last lesson of the morning, after which came a playground recess and lunch break. Dr. Kumysh had timed his visit well. The break would come while the anger that he had instilled in his pupils was still hot upon them, and their spirits would be ripe for vengeance. They would lose no time in venting their spleen. Jakob dreaded the bell that would signal the end of the lesson. When it came, he asked Isay to stay behind. He did not know what he would say to him, but he knew that he would need some protection. He waited until the boys had left the classroom, and through the frosted glass of the window, he could see their shadows hovering in the corridor outside and hear the murmur of their belligerent voices.

"Where d'you eat your lunch?" Jakob asked.

"In the playground usually."

"I go to the park. D'you want to come with me?"

"I'm not afraid of them," Isay said. "In any case, you can't always be around. They'll get me one way or the other."

"I've never met your father," Jakob said, "but he has all my admiration and respect. And I don't mind who knows it." Jakob almost shouted this last remark, and there was a certain joy in it, for at that very moment he decided to take his family and leave the Soviet Union.

That evening he told Deborah of the school incident, and she insisted that he call Isay's father to inquire as to the boy's welfare.

"You're right," Jakob said. "But I would prefer to go to his house. I have his address. In any case, I should like to meet his father."

"Be careful," she said. "They're watching his house, I'm sure."

Deborah was right. One of Aaron's father-in-law's friends was idling outside Salmon's house with little attempt to disguise the small camera that recorded Jakob's entry. Jakob even smiled for him. Having made his decision to leave the country, he was aware of a sudden sense of freedom, and a total absence of fear. He knocked on Mr. Salmon's door. He heard scuffling behind it, and then silence. He waited, then knocked again.

"Who is it?" a woman's voice asked.

"Jakob Bindel. Isay's schoolmaster."

The door was opened almost immediately by Isay's mother, who welcomed him. "Isay has told us about you," she said.

"Is he all right?" Jakob asked.

"He's in bed. It's not too bad. A black eye and a cut lip."

"He put up quite a fight, I think." Mr. Salmon appeared behind her. "It's good to meet you," Mr. Salmon said, giving Jakob his hand. The tiny hall gave off into two rooms. The one they entered was the kitchen–living quarter, which also doubled as a bedroom. Mrs. Salmon offered Jakob tea and some sweets and biscuits from a small tin box. "You are good to come," Mr. Salmon said. "And brave, too."

"No, not brave," Jakob said. "I have decided to leave. I've come for your advice."

Mr. Salmon stared at him. "Are you sure?" he said. "It's a big decision and once you apply, they don't make it easy for you. You will lose your job. That's an automatic result of application. Have you got savings?"

"A little," Jakob said. "How soon do you expect to leave?"

"There are no rules," Mr. Salmon said. "Some people wait for months. Others get exit visas immediately."

"D'you have relatives in Israel?" Jakob asked.

"I have a sister there. She left Moscow ten years ago. She was widowed and alone. It was easy to get a visa in those days. She's married again and lives in Tel Aviv. I want Isay to go to the Hebrew University."

"D'you know Hebrew?" Jakob asked.

"We've been taking lessons for a year. There's a good teacher nearby. I could give you his address. But you must keep it quiet. It's illegal, you know, Hebrew lessons. Not officially, of course, but they harass him regularly. Raid his flat, take his books and papers and threaten him." Mr. Salmon shook his head. "We live in sad times, my friend. But since I applied, you know," Mr. Salmon went on, "I've never been happier. I've never felt more free. My wife is the same and so is Isay, despite the lesson they've tried to teach him. But now they've made their point, they'll leave him alone. Since I applied to leave, I've made many new friends. And lost some too. We all do. You can't blame them. They're just afraid to associate with us. But we know most of the people who apply for visas. We're a sort of secret fraternity. We compare notes. Some people apply secretly, and don't even tell their children."

"I shan't keep it a secret," Jakob said.

"Then I wish you luck, as I wish us all. But you must be in touch with us," Mr. Salmon went on. "We shall probably meet at Hebrew lessons. Wednesday is the beginner's class."

"I shall be there," Jakob said. "And my wife, too."

Jakob left shortly afterward, and went home and shared with Deborah the information he had received. They decided to make application right away, since there was likely to be a delay before visas were granted.

The following day was a Wednesday and Jakob's classes did not start till midday. He used his free time to go to the offices of OVIR, the Ministry of the Interior, where emigration details were processed. The official gave him the forms, his lip curling with contempt. Jakob filled them in with meticulous care, then he handed them back to the official, who gave him another set.

"These must be filled out by your parents," he said. "And the parents of your wife. You need to have their permission to leave."

"But by God," Jakob said. "We're over thirty."

"I don't care if you're over seventy. If your parents are alive, you cannot go without their permission. It's the law."

"My parents are dead," Jakob said.

The official looked up at him. "We can check on that," he said.

"Then check at Auschwitz," Jakob said. "In the gas chambers."

Jakob knew from the man's face that he had it in his heart to say that he was sorry, but some unwritten Russian law, unwritten since the czars, forbade it. "What about your wife's parents?" he said.

"I'll take the forms. They'll sign. How long will it take?" Jakob asked.

"Inquiries have to be made. They can take time."

"What inquiries?" Jakob asked.

"We will find something to inquire about," the official laughed. "We can always find something."

"How will I know when the visas are ready?"

"You will be told," the man said.

Jakob left the desk. Behind him was another applicant and Jakob hovered on the sidelines to overhear their exchange.

"You again, Mr. Levertov," the official said with a smile. "You were here only last week."

"And I'll be here next week, too, and the week after that, and every week until I get my visas. It's over a year now since I applied."

"Tell me, Mr. Levertov," the official said, leaning forward, "why are you so impatient to leave this country of ours?"

Mr. Levertov sat down and he too leaned forward. It was clear that the two men had a relationship of long standing. "Why do I want to leave, Volodya? I'll tell you. The trouble is, I'm tired of being happy here."

Volodya looked at Levertov for some elucidation.

"You see," Levertov went on. "I see a queue. I join it. I wait two hours and at the end of it, I can buy a pair of shoes. So I'm happy. I join another queue, and after an hour I can buy a lemon. Again I'm happy." He paused. "Listen, Volodya," he said, "to tell you the truth, I'm tired of being happy." He looked at the official with a smile, then sternly he said, "I'll be back next week."

Jakob followed him out of the office. Levertov knew he was

being followed. He had seen Jakob fill in his emigration forms. Even so, he did not trust him. The KGB had singular means of disguising their agents. After a whole year of being followed and harassed, after a year of nurtured paranoia, Levertov trusted nobody. He darted down a side street, out of Jakob's vision, then looked around furtively and saw that he had lost him. But Jakob had seen his detour and understood his flight. It saddened him that these were times when men were so wary of one another, an age in which suspicion had become a weapon for survival. He crisscrossed through a maze of streets to reach the river, where he could walk along the embankment that would eventually lead him to school. There were few people about.

But coming toward him, he saw Aaron. At first he was surprised, wondering what his brother was doing on the embankment, until he realized that his hospital was just across the nearest bridge. He did not want to meet with Aaron, but there was now no way to avoid him. They had had no contact since the press conference affair. Both brothers, for their own reasons, had avoided each other. As Aaron approached, Jakob saw that he was smiling, obviously pleased to see him. Aaron clapped his brother's shoulders.

"What are you doing in these parts?" he said.

"I've just come from the OVIR offices," he said.

Aaron's hand dropped from Jakob's shoulder. His face was white. "What for?" he asked, though with little hope, for there was only one reason why a Jew should go to OVIR.

"We've applied for emigration," Jakob said.

"But you can't leave," Aaron shouted. "What about my work?" He hadn't meant so crudely to reveal the cause of his objection. He could have bypassed it for a while. But his anger was extreme. He knew that anyone who applied for emigration was automatically victimized, and that victimization often extended to innocent relatives.

"I wouldn't worry about your job," Jakob said with contempt. "They won't touch you. They need you. You're one of their token Jews. You proved it yourself at their conference. I'm late. I must go," and with no leave-taking, Jakob left his brother agape on the embankment. When he reached the bend in the river, he looked around and saw Aaron still standing there, his shoulders hunched in despair. Jakob felt very sorry for him. Then suddenly

Aaron straightened and set off at a brisk rate, and it looked from his gait that he was smiling.

Which indeed he was. For he had had a very simple idea. He made his way to the OVIR office. There was no one waiting at Volodya's desk, and Aaron went straight toward him. Volodya raised his eyes to the ceiling. "Another one," he said.

"Another what?" Aaron said.

"Traitor, if you want it straight. I suppose you want to emigrate."

"No," Aaron said. "On the contrary. I like it here. I've come about my brother."

"It's your brother who wants to emigrate."

"Yes. He's already applied. This morning. Name of Jakob Bindel. Wife Deborah Bindel. Two children. Hans and Benjamin."

"Yes, I remember him well. He was here just now," the official said. "Parents died in Auschwitz. Your parents, too, of course."

"Yes," Aaron said, "but I am his older brother, and therefore, since we have no parents, I am his guardian. Yes?"

Volodya was not quite clear as to the direction of the argument.

"I do not give my permission," Aaron said.

Now Volodya understood. He'd never known a case like it, but there was little question in his mind as to its legality.

"You are a loyal Soviet citizen, sir," he said. "Here is the form. You should fill it in and send it to this office with a covering letter stating the nature of your guardianship."

Aaron collected the papers and made to leave. He felt Volodya staring at him.

"Didn't I see you on television the other night?" the official asked.

Aaron nodded.

"You see, I was right. You are a loyal citizen," he said.

The OVIR office did not inform Jakob of his brother's injunction. Nothing from that office on the matter of emigration was ever put in writing. Volodya expected the younger Bindel to return to the office about a week after handing in his application. They always did, the new ones. For the first six months or so, they would call regularly once a week, then it would fall off to a monthly visit, and then when a year had passed, there would be a clutch of desperate visits in a very short time. After that, from time to time, their steps would lead them automatically toward that place that they had come to hate with all their hearts, and on the OVIR threshold, despair would slacken their pace, and they would turn away without entering, unable to face yet another refusal.

And just as Volodya predicted, Jakob Bindel, the younger one, the sudden ward of his elder brother, Aaron, arrived at the office exactly one week after his first visit.

"Have you any news for me?" he asked.

"Name?" the official said, though he knew perfectly well who it was.

"Bindel," Jakob said impatiently. "Jakob Bindel. I sent the forms of permission from my wife's parents."

"Yes," Volodya said, checking needlessly on the file. "We've received those and they are quite in order. But it seems that you have been forbidden to leave."

"But my parents are dead," Jakob said. "I told you that last week."

"Yes, I know," Volodya said. "But you are still forbidden." He wanted to spin the tale out for all its worth.

"Who forbids it?" Jakob shouted.

"You have an elder brother," Volodya said slowly, "and since you have no parents, he is your legal guardian. It is within his rights to forbid you. Or, of course," he added, "to give you permission to leave. But I doubt he would ever do that. He is a loyal Soviet citizen. He came here and I was proud to shake his hand."

Jakob was trembling with anger and disbelief. "Does that mean," he spluttered, "that I cannot leave? Ever?"

"Not until your brother gives his permission," Volodya said. He leaned forward, confidentially. "Mr. Bindel," he said, "why can't you take an example from your brother?"

Jakob opened his mouth to try to tell him, but then he suddenly didn't want to involve this enemy with his family, even though there was enemy enough within. But Volodya's enmity was official. It was paid for, it was even, by dint of his upbringing, absolutely sincere. It was an enmity far cleaner than Aaron's. For Aaron's was expedient, self-seeking, and treacherous.

He left the office quickly. The need for fresh air was paramount, for he felt a nausea throughout his body. He darted into an alley near the office, and retched his heart out. The tears

streamed down his face, but he did not bother to ascribe them to
his retching, for he knew that they spelled out quite a separate
despair. He leaned against the wall and took deep breaths to
steady himself. He wondered what he should do. His instinct was
to go straight to the hospital and upbraid his brother. But when
he thought about it, he knew that that was probably what Aaron
was expecting, and he would be well prepared for it. He needed
urgently to see Deborah, but he was already late for his classes. It
would have to wait.

That evening, he was almost ashamed to tell Deborah. When
she had heard his story, she saw how it hurt him, and because of
that, her heart filled with hatred for Aaron. And anger, too, for
she knew that his refusal to sign would bind them to the Soviet
Union forever.

"I never want to see him again," Jakob was saying.

"No," Deborah said. "You must see him. You must try to
persuade him. It will be detrimental to us if you cut yourself off
from him. He expects you to come to him."

"He's waiting for me to beg," Jakob said.

"And if you have to beg," she said gently, "is that so terrible?
It would make the whole difference to our future. I would go to
him," she offered, "but it's you he wants. It's you he wants the
loving from, even if he has to torture you to get it."

"Then he'll have to wait," Jakob said.

"Yes. Let him wait awhile. But eventually you must go to him.
Plead with him if necessary."

"Never," Jakob shouted.

"Then you sentence us all to life in Russia."

"I'll find another way," Jakob said. "I'll ask around. There
must be loopholes in the law."

Over the course of the next few weeks, Jakob discovered that
his case was unique. There were sundry examples of parental
injunction, but no one had heard of the sibling maneuver. In itself
it was a loophole in the law, which the KGB would happily
exploit to their own advantage. Jakob's friends advised him to go
to his brother and persuade him to change his mind. Privately
they had little hope of it. They, too, had seen Aaron on television.
But they managed to talk Jakob into meeting with his brother,
and it was then only a question of choosing a place for their
meeting.

He decided against Aaron's apartment, for he did not wish to include Sonia in the encounter. He thought of going to the laboratory, but that would not appeal to Aaron because of its lack of privacy. They could meet in Gorki Square, he decided. It was large enough and peopled enough for privacy, and was not as yet suspected as a focal point for dissidents.

"When will you telephone him?" Deborah asked.

"Tomorrow," Jakob said, as he had said every day for a week.

"Shall I phone for you?" she asked, knowing that her offer would spur his decision.

"I'll do it," he said, and right away he went to the phone and dialed his brother's number.

He was relieved that Aaron himself answered the phone. "Can we meet?" Jakob asked.

"Of course." Aaron had clearly been waiting for the call. "Where? When?"

"Gorki Square. Three o'clock. Sunday."

"I'll see you there."

Jakob put the phone down. The worst part was over. His pride had been forfeited in the overture on the telephone.

Jakob arrived early at the square and so did Aaron, as if both were anxious to get the meeting over and done with. They came toward each other.

"How are you, brother?" Aaron said, his hand on Jakob's shoulder.

"How should I be?" he said, shrugging the hand away. "But you look well enough."

"I've had good news," Aaron said. "The government has given me extra finance for my research. A very large sum, in fact."

"Did that surprise you?" Jakob asked with disdain.

"Of course," Aaron said. "It came out of the blue."

"You sold your brother for it," Jakob shouted at him.

Aaron was shaken, but quickly recovered. "Rubbish," he said. "One thing has nothing to do with the other."

"They'll be giving you a country house next," Jakob said. "It flatters me in a way to think I'm worth all that. A country house, a research award, maybe in time even the Order of Lenin, just to keep me and my family in the Soviet Union. It's really rather pathetic, isn't it, such behavior from what we are told is the freest country in the world. I pity you, Aaron." He shouldn't have said that, he knew. That was a remark reserved for parting, and most certainly when the battle had been lost. "I've come to ask you to

change your mind. To give us permission to leave." There was no
other way he could ask him. No innuendo, no threat, no flattery.
Just the simple words of a straightforward request.

"I can't do that," Aaron said. "I don't want to do it. And even
if I did, for what reason should I suddenly change my mind?"

"Tell me, Aaron," Jakob asked, "why do you want me to stay?
It surely can't be brotherly love."

Aaron ignored that question. "I think you're misguided," he
said. "Israel is an enemy of the Soviet Union, and to take Israel's
side is to be a traitor."

"Then let me be a traitor," Jakob said, "and let me go." He
touched his brother's arm. "You don't mean that, Aaron, do you?
You're too intelligent to talk like that."

"Let's walk a little," Aaron said. He took Jakob's arm. "Don't
you see," he said, "how my hands are tied? You forget who my
father-in-law is."

Jakob had to laugh. "You're not serious," he said. "Is he going
to rule your life forever? Is he going to cost you the love of a
brother? What's happening to you, Aaron? They're laying a trap
for you, don't you see, with all kinds of bait—department grants,
cars, medals. And what for? You have no more faith in this country than I do." His voice was raised and Aaron squeezed his arm
in fear.

"Be quiet," he said.

"You are already afraid, brother. See how you tremble in this
great country of freedom. You are one of us. Leave this place.
Come with us."

"You are mad, brother," Aaron said. "I believe in this land. I
do," he shouted.

"Why are you shouting, Aaron?"

Aaron stopped and looked around at the passersby, who were
eyeing him with wonder. He grabbed Jakob by the sleeve. "Stay
away from me, brother," he whispered.

"How frightened you are, Aaron," Jakob said. Then out of the
corner of his eye, he saw a plainclothes KGB man. He did not
recognize him. He was someone he'd never seen before, and there
was no doubt in his mind that this new one was his brother's
keeper. He wondered whether he should tell Aaron, but he decided against it.

On his way home, Jakob wondered what the meeting had
achieved. Despite Aaron's refusal to retract his letter, Jakob had

the feeling that their conversation had little to do with his proposed emigration. The meeting had exposed Aaron's own fears, his own ostrichlike attitudes, and above all his vulnerability. Understanding all these things, Jakob found it very hard to dislike him. Indeed, he regretted that Aaron had ordered him to keep out of his way. He wanted to see him, because he wanted to help him. All this he explained to Deborah when he reached home, and all that she understood. But in the process, she was made more desolate, for there seemed no way that Aaron could be swayed.

"We must keep applying," she said. "We must make nuisances of ourselves. We must not give them rest. We will take it in turns to go. I wonder sometimes," she said helplessly, "whether anybody outside this country has any idea of what's going on. When you think of Stalin's time, when millions of people rotted and died in camps, and nobody outside the country, or even inside, ever knew. Could it happen to us, Jakob, d'you think?"

"We're not in any danger of our lives," Jakob said. "The worst that can happen is that we have to stay."

"What about all those dissident trials, the prisons, the labor camps and exile? People still disappear and are never heard of again."

They were silent for a while. Then Jakob said, "I'll leave it for a month or so, then I'll go and see him at the laboratory. He can't refuse me. We won't talk about emigration. I'll talk about his work. And there's nothing to stop you seeing Sonia. You know," he went on, "I wonder if your parents were aware of the risks they were taking when they gave you permission."

"Probably," Deborah said. "But despite Papa's status and his privileges, I think he is secretly sympathetic."

"I hope to God they leave him alone," Jakob said.

"Oh, Jakob," Deborah said suddenly. "What did we do when we opened our mouths?"

"D'you regret it?" Jakob asked. "D'you want to withdraw? We will if you want. I don't want to do it without you."

"No," she said, without hesitation. "We must think of our children."

He held her close. "It will happen," he said. "Sooner or later, we shall be free."

They went to bed early that night and fell asleep in that sweet safety of loving. But in the middle of the night, the phone rang. Jakob crawled out of bed to answer it. There was a curt apology for a wrong number. Jakob replaced the phone in its cradle. He knew that their term of harassment had begun.

About three weeks after Jakob's application, he was dismissed from his job. There was no explanation, no period of notice. Just a summary dismissal. It came as no surprise. Job dismissal was automatic after application for an exit visa. Deborah knew that eventually she too would be deemed unemployable. Neither of them was particularly worried. They had always saved money and they put aside a fund for the family fares so that they could leave as soon as permits were granted. For there was never any question in their minds that in time the visas would come through. The delay was part of their harassment. Both of them were surprised at their lack of anxiety. Indeed, instead of being constrained by the uncertainty of their livelihoods, they actually felt liberated, and this sense of freedom drove Jakob once more into the fray.

The dissident movement had been alive and active for many years in the Soviet Union, but the *refusenik* element was comparatively new. *Refusenik* was the term applied to those who had applied for exit and been refused. Most of these were Jews, and by the Law of Return promulgated by the State of Israel, any Jew who so wished was entitled to Israeli citizenship. Though in its infancy, the *refusenik* movement was already becoming a cause of international interest and concern, a fact that gave no pleasure to the authorities. For the Soviet regime was acutely concerned about its image abroad. When in the summer of 1972, Richard Nixon was paying a visit to the Soviet Union, the authorities were much concerned with the impressions he would take home. They could afford no leakings of discontent during his visit. Internal passports of malcontents were temporarily withdrawn, so that those living outside the capital were unable to travel to Moscow to demonstrate their protest. Those who lived in Moscow were warned to keep to their homes.

Some months before Nixon's visit, a group of activists had written an open letter to the American President, asking for a meeting with him. There were fifty-seven signatures to the letter, and among them was the name of Jakob Bindel. The authorities had been keeping an eye on him since his first appearance had been noted in Mayakovsky Square. Now, prior to the President's visit, their harassment increased.

One morning, Jakob was on his way to see a fellow *refusenik* to consider their course of action during the presidential visit. He traveled by underground. In the same compartment he noticed two men and a woman, who were eyeing him with undisguised surveillance. He alighted at Kursk station, and saw that they were following him. He was not easy with their shadows, and he quickened his pace. When he felt a hand on his shoulder, he trembled with fear. He stared into the face of the militiaman, then saw at his side his three shadows from the train. The woman was crying uncontrollably, mouthing unintelligible curses between her sobs. Her two escorts were looking at him with disgust.

"These witnesses," the militiaman said, "saw you molesting this woman. Come with me." He grabbed Jakob's arm and marched him off to the station militia department. There he awaited the van that would take him to the court. Since his arrest he had said not a word. He knew they had maneuvered a trumped-up charge, and no denial on his part could change the course of their injustice. Over the last few weeks he had heard of many such charges. Most common of all were those of drunkenness, and there was always a witness on hand to testify to disorderly behavior. He worried about Deborah. He asked his guard if he could make a phone call, but his request was brusquely refused. They bundled him into a van and took him to the Kalinsky District Court. There the woman and the two witnesses testified to Jakob's molestation. As he listened to their story, Jakob could not help but admire their barefaced audacity and the fluency with which each told his tale.

"I watched the accused leering at my friend with a look of such lecherous intent that I felt a shudder run through my whole body. I did nothing at the time, because I thought that that leer might be a natural look of his, and I wished to give him the benefit of the doubt. But I mentioned my fears to my friend." At this point his friend continued the story, reading it unashamedly from a sheet of paper in front of him.

"I shared the same feelings of revulsion as my friend," he read, "and as we approached Kursk station, the accused, on rising from his seat, shuffled toward our companion."

At this point in the narration the woman gave a cry that simulated a painful recollection, and she was offered a seat and excused from testimony. The second witness then continued his tale.

"As we were pulling into the station, the accused grabbed our companion by the buttocks"—this last in a stage whisper in deference to the feelings of the woman beside him—"and rubbed his body against hers. Then the train came to a stop, and the accused ran away down the platform."

The magistrate turned to Jakob. "Do you have anything to say?" he asked.

"I am innocent," Jakob said, and he heard the futility of his words as they echoed through the courtroom.

The magistrate sniffed and sentenced him to fifteen days for hooliganism. By the time of his release, the presidential visit would be over. Two militiamen took him from the dock, and as he turned he saw Deborah rush in through the court door. "Jakob," she shouted.

A policeman took her arm and spoke some words to her, and Jakob saw her laugh in his face, then he was dragged away from the court. On his way to the cells, he began to giggle, infected by Deborah's distant laughter. The ruse that they had played was so desperate and so amateurish that it could only be an object of mockery. But though he laughed at it, it incensed him too, and by the time he reached his appointed cell, he was filled with such a rage that he longed for a private place in which to scream aloud.

But there was no privacy. He took time to count the men who were already in residence. Because of their shaven heads, at first glance they all looked exactly the same. They stared at him in silence, their looks betraying nothing. He was shown his bunk. The guard threw a uniform on the bed, and told him to change his clothes, and nine pairs of lethargic eyes watched him as he undressed. The clothes were many sizes too big for him, and he had to roll up the trousers and the jacket sleeves. He hung his own clothes in the cupboard by the wall, and waited for further instructions. Then he was taken by the guard to have his head shaved. As he looked at the hair on the floor, he recalled Aunt Sarah's story of the milk-brothers' recruitment, and how the pi-

ous ringlets of the child-soldiers lay curled on the bathhouse
floor. Aunt Sarah had learned the story from Uncle David, who
had learned it from Grandpa Leon, who himself had heard it
from his father, Benjamin the milk-brother. Jakob marveled at
the tenacity of such an oral tradition, and he resolved that he
would tell it to his own sons as soon as they were ripe for inheritance. The shaving did not disturb him. Indeed, it gave him a
measure of relief, for now he would be no different from his
cellmates, and perhaps that would loosen their tongues. But he
returned to a silent cell, to a silence broken only by inward curses
and cries in the night. In a way Jakob welcomed the silence, but
he was unnerved by the looks of suspicion each man gave the
other. Then he remembered how a friend of his, Ivan, another
refusenik who had been imprisoned on a trumped-up charge, had
discovered that one of his cellmates was a planted KGB agent. So
when, on the second day of his incarceration, one of the men gave
Jakob a sickly smile, he shuddered and he turned his face away,
praying that the smile was not a true offer of friendship.

Three times a day they were released from the cell for their
meals, and once in early evening for exercise. Otherwise the men
remained in their cells all day with nothing to do but to stare
through each other or at the floor. It was a time for contemplation. For Jakob, his thoughts of Deborah and his children were a
welcome solace in his wretched situation and he tried to keep
them in the forefront of his mind. Not only for the comfort they
afforded, but because they took his mind off thoughts of Aaron.
He did not want to think about his brother because he knew he
would begin to hate him.

After a few days, two prisoners were released from his cell and
were not replaced by others. The silence that persisted now
seemed less oppressive, less confined. On the seventh day, three
more men were given their release, and now Jakob was alone in
the cell with the single other remaining prisoner. The man
watched the cell door close, then turned to face Jakob. The stare
was gone from his eyes.

"My name's Isaac," he said, and he held out his hand.

A Jewish name, Jakob thought, a little too Jewish perhaps, and
he looked at the man's face closely for the first time. The absence
of the frame of hair facilitated a careful examination of the features, and there was clearly nothing Jewish about them. The

man's hand still floated between them, and Jakob looked down at it and turned away.

"We've got a lot in common." The so-called Isaac was not put off by the snub. "I was on my way to Pavel's too when I got picked up." Pavel Revich was Jakob's contact for the presidential demonstration. He was a known *refusenik*. Jakob had visited him often, but never had he seen this man there.

"I'm new to the movement," Isaac went on, as if reading his thoughts. "They picked me up on a fake charge of drunkenness."

Jakob gave no response. He wondered how much longer the man would continue to seek his cooperation. He was inept at his job, Jakob thought, like all of his kind. They were not trained to be subtle, they did not even care if their real motives were discovered. Their job was to harass, to frighten, and to intimidate. Jakob debated now as to the best way to handle Isaac's presence. To continue to ignore him might lead to a dangerous antagonism. So he would be polite, he decided, and give nothing away.

"Who's Pavel?" Jakob asked. He was surprised at the sound of his own voice. For over a week now, apart from the occasional acknowledgment of food and exercise, he had not spoken at all. The sound pleased him and he wished to hear more of it.

"Pavel Revich," the man said. "He's a friend of yours. He told me so."

"I don't know any Pavel Revich. What does he do for a living?" Jakob asked.

"He's like us. Unemployed. A *refusenik.*"

Until that moment, the word had rung like a tribute in Jakob's ear. It sang of a certain courage, stubbornness, and fraternity. Now as it dropped so casually, so rehearsed from this man's lips, it was suddenly sullied, and Jakob wanted to strike him. But instead he said, "I don't know him. I was simply going to the park, and they picked me up on the underground."

Isaac smiled and lay down on his bunk.

That night Jakob couldn't sleep. He went over and over again in his mind each word he had given to his companion, to make sure that he had given nothing away. Toward dawn he fell into a deep sleep, and was awakened not by the usual clanging of doors and keys, but by a gush of hot air on his face. He opened his eyes wide to see his companion's face close to his own.

"The President comes tomorrow," he said. "What a pity we shall miss it all. Pavel had great plans for us."

"You lose no time," Jakob said, sitting up and brushing him aside.

"I'm getting out this morning," the man said. "And I need to know where we were supposed to meet. Pavel said he would tell me. But I never got there. Where is it?" he asked. "Who am I supposed to ask for?"

Jakob stared at him and couldn't help laughing. "You mean they faked a drunken charge on you, and now they're letting you out before the President's gone? Anyhow, how am I to know where you're supposed to meet? I've never heard of this Pavel you keep talking about. But if you hurry, you might still catch him," he laughed.

His companion's lower lip drooped into a sulk. "We Jews should stick together," he tried one more time.

The word *refusenik* out of his mouth had been offensive enough. But *Jew* was a far more insolent affront, for it embraced the whole of his tribe, and suddenly Jakob had the courage and the anger to call his bluff. "You're a Jew like I'm a KGB man," he said.

"You wait," Isaac said. "We'll meet again on the outside. We'll meet on the same demonstrations. And you'll be sorry," he added.

At that moment the cell door opened and Isaac was called outside.

"I hope you find your Pavel," Jakob shouted after him.

Now for the first time in over a week, he was alone. And he was afraid. He began to fear the next Isaac they would thrust upon him. All that day and night he waited in fearful anticipation, but nobody came. Slowly his fear left him, and he began to enjoy his solitary state. He thought of Aaron with less and less anger, and of Deborah with more and more love. He thought too of his own participation in the *refusenik* movement, and those thoughts led him to Hans. At the memory of Hans's death, he grew angry, and resolved that henceforth he would commit himself totally to dissidence. And that decision gave him a surprising sense of peace.

A peace that was rudely shattered on his last night of confinement. Another "Isaac" was let into his cell, and though he wore the convict's uniform, this one hadn't even bothered to shave his head. Nor did he bother with any preliminaries.

"Who were the leaders of the demonstration?" he shouted.

"They demonstrated?" Jakob asked, smiling. Somehow or other his friends had made a protest.

"I'm asking the questions," the man said.

"Why do you bother to put on convict's clothes?" Jakob asked. His recent decision had given him courage.

The man hit him across the face. "I told you I'm asking the questions," he said.

Jakob's cheeks stung with the blow and he was enraged. But he tried to keep calm. He did not want to be injured so early on in the struggle. So he sat on his bunk and breathed deeply to contain his pain and his anger.

"I asked you who were the leaders," the man said.

"I don't know." Jakob's voice was steady. He knew very well who they were. All of them, and he regretted this knowledge and he prayed for the courage to conceal it. But he couldn't understand why they were asking him. They must have known. All of the leaders were known *refuseniks*. All of them who had managed to avoid arrest must have been at the demonstration.

"Well, if you don't know, my friend," Isaac said. "I'll tell you." He took a piece of paper from his pocket and read out a list of names. Most of them were known to Jakob, and he winced when he heard the names of particularly close friends. "We know of their plans, too," Isaac went on. "The protest at Gorki Square next Thursday. They won't be there. Any of them. And I've come to make sure you won't be there either."

He opened the cell door and admitted two men. He nodded to them and left the cell, his duty done. The men took no time to examine their target. Jakob felt a sudden spurt of blood, and then a quick stab of pain, a pain so unbearable that his consciousness obliged by leaving him. Later, when he opened his eyes, he found himself alone in his cell, crouched on the floor. He located the pit of his stomach as the seat of his pain, and he felt on his groin the lingering imprint of a vicious knee. He touched his face with both his hands, feeling for the source of the blood. He knew he had to lie there and absorb his pain in deep and measured breathing. He wondered what time it was. He recalled that when the thugs had been let into the cell it had been twilight. Now, as he slowly raised his head to the window, it was twilight still, and he wondered whether only a few minutes had passed or perhaps a whole night. If the latter, then he would be released very soon. But the pain was so acute that he decided it must still be night, and he could sleep till morning. It seemed as if he had just closed his eyes when he heard his cell door open.

"Time's up, Bindel. You're free," a voice shouted. "Leave your clothes on the bunk."

He made to rise, but the movement was so painful he feared he might have an acute internal injury. The thought angered him, for it might put him out of combat for a while, and for him, the real battle had only just begun. He was determined now, at whatever cost, to devote himself totally to the *refusenik* cause, and his first battleground would be on Thursday at Gorki Square. He crawled to the bunk, and hoisted himself upright. Then he tried walking, but his progress was slow and painful. He would call on the doctor, he decided, on his way home from prison.

He undressed slowly and every movement was painful. He was shocked at the bruise on his upper thigh. A large spread of uncertain blue stretched from the knee to the hipbone and he could see the pulse throbbing beneath the mottled skin. He was glad he had some proof of his pain and evidence of the assault, though there was no one to whom he could complain.

The prison clock in the vestibule showed six o'clock in the morning. Earlier he had washed his face and noticed how the water had run red. He'd managed to stem the small amount of bleeding, but he felt swellings all over his face and he guessed at their uncertain tinge of blue. He lowered his head as he passed the mirror on the side wall. He knew that the sight of himself would depress him further. A warden stared at him as he approached the gates that led to the outside, and he could not disguise his look of horror.

"Don't want to see you again," he said, as he said to every outgoing prisoner.

Jakob stopped and looked him squarely in the face. "In my case," he said quietly, "it's entirely up to you and your lot."

The warden unlocked the gate. He had to have the last word. "You can take it from me," he said, "just in case you don't know. You're not a pretty sight." Then he shoved Jakob through the gate and bolted it after him.

The bright light of the early morning dazzled him, and so he did not recognize the figure of a solitary man waiting at the end of the prison drive—though his outline was familiar. Even as the figure started walking toward him, all he could decipher was its painful familiarity. Then, by his voice, he knew him, for he called aloud, "Jakob," and in the sound Jakob heard his brother. He was astonished that anyone had come to meet him, and Aaron most of all. As he waited, he could not deny his joy at seeing him, nor could he help being moved by the care and concern that Aaron showed in his coming. And by the risk that he took in the brazen and public association with one who in the eyes of all those who watched from the prison windows was nothing but a troublemaker. As Aaron neared him, he saw the look on his face and realized that his countenance must have seemed a battle-ground. Aaron stood in front of him. He did not offer a hand in welcome, or touch any part of him. The concern that Jakob had seen on his face in the distance was now transformed into anger.

"Look what you've done to yourself," he shouted.

"It's part payment for your research grant," Jakob said. He knew that what he had said was hurtful, so he stretched out his hand to offset the cruelty of his response, and touched his brother on the shoulder.

"I must get you to the hospital," Aaron said with his stiff, unyielding body, and he led the way to the car. He did not help his brother as he slowly and painfully maneuvered himself into the front seat, but Jakob noticed the painful concern on his face. Jakob wondered whether Aaron would be brazen enough to take him to his own hospital, but he noticed that they were not on that route. They were making for the outskirts of the city, and shortly they pulled up at a small building that Jakob knew as a private clinic for the privileged. Jakob was uneasy.

"*Must* we go here?" he asked.

Aaron ignored his objection. "I have friends here," he said. "We won't have to wait."

He strode into the clinic with an air of authority and immedi-ately arranged a series of X rays and examinations for his brother. None of the doctors asked any questions. Aaron had explained to them that Jakob had spent fifteen days in prison, and that information was enough to account for his condition. They made no comment. The examinations showed that nothing was broken but that there were bad bruises all over his body. The bones of his nose were intact, and the swellings would subside, they said, though it might take some weeks. They prescribed rest and quiet. "Keep off the streets," one of them said.

In the car on the way home, Aaron asked, "Who did it to you?"

"Friends of your father-in-law's," Jakob said. He didn't want Aaron to go home feeling he had totally squared his account by his care and concern for his brother's physical well-being.

"You should listen to that doctor," Aaron said. "Keep off the streets."

Jakob turned to face him. "Stop the car," he said. "I want to talk to you."

"We can talk as I'm driving," Aaron said.

"Please stop the car," Jakob said. "It's important."

Aaron pulled onto a side road. He looked in the rearview mirror before he stopped. Jakob had noticed how often during the drive his brother's eyes had been raised furtively to check on shadows. "Are you being followed, Aaron?" he asked as he brought the car to a halt.

Aaron laughed, rather too heartily, Jakob thought. "Of course not," he said. "Why should anyone follow me?"

"Because of the company you keep," Jakob said, and he laughed too, hoping to establish some affection between them, for what he had to ask of his brother presupposed friendship.

He came to the point right away. "We've got to get out of this country, Aaron," he said. "You have to withdraw your veto. I beg of you." He hadn't meant to so condense his request. He had wanted to serialize it, to give it style, cadence, and turns of phrase that would have softened the nature of its demand.

"I won't do that," Aaron said with some finality, and he turned the ignition key in the lock.

"Why not?" Jakob practically screamed at him.

"We're Russian citizens," Aaron said in a measured voice. "Our allegiance is to the Soviet Union. If you disagree with certain aspects of the system, you can fight it from within."

Jakob laughed aloud. "With what can you fight?" he asked. "With free elections? With open protest? Why, if you open a dissenting mouth in this place, you get clapped into jail. And even if you keep your mouth shut, you're not safe. Look at me. All I did was to go on the metro."

"Yes," Aaron said quietly. "But whom were you going to see?"

Jakob wondered whether he should argue with him. He wondered whether it was simply a question of political differences. Whether Aaron sincerely believed in his argument or whether it was a cover-up to protect his own livelihood and reputation. But was it even that? Jakob thought. Was Aaron so cold that he could

value his reputation above his sibling concern? Or was it more
than that? Was it ultimately a self-hate, one that had been born
all those years ago, when their parents had turned their backs on
the driveway of the Bindel home in Leipzig? Had such self-hate
been nurtured in those years in the dark attic in Halle, and
sprouted into full and poisonous flower when Inge and Hans had
gently confirmed their orphanhood? If that were true, when in
the name of God would his brother forgive God and His dark
and mysterious ways? He put his hand on Aaron's arm.

"Do you love me, brother?" he asked.

Aaron raised his foot from the clutch and put the car into jerky
forward motion. He pressed the accelerator, revving the engine,
so that its noise would drown his brother's simple plea. Jakob let
his question hover, for no amount of engine noise could mute its
elemental quest. For that was the only question that mattered
between them, and both of them knew it.

They drove in silence. After a while, Jakob asked, "How is
your work?" He did not want to estrange himself totally from his
brother and he could only maintain contact on levels that were
nonpartisan.

"It's exciting," Aaron answered. "There's an American immunologist arriving next week. We're working on the same lines. I'm
really looking forward to meeting him."

Jakob noticed how his brother's body slowly relaxed, how the
muscles of his face were less taut. He was even smiling, safe in
that area of his life.

"How will you manage for money, Jakob?" he asked.

Jakob was distrustful of the rare use of his name.

"I could let you have some money," Aaron was saying.

Jakob smiled. As long as you had it, money was the easiest
thing on earth to give, and the most comfortable, for it squared
the conscience and took little time. The essence of generosity was
the giving of one's time, of sharing one's thoughts and spirit—
pursuits that for Aaron were alien and unexplored.

"Thank you," Jakob said. "But Deborah is still working. And
I have some savings. That will keep us for a while. I have money
too that won't be touched. Enough for our fares to Israel."

"Will you get another job?"

"I shan't look for one," Jakob said. "I'm not planning any
future in this country. I'm going to spend all my time and energy
getting our visas. You could help, you know," he added quietly.

There was no response, and Jakob turned angrily toward him. "*Why* won't you let us go?" he asked, but again, both brothers knew that it was not a question. But rather a confirmation of the no-man's-land between them.

As they approached the district where he lived, Jakob noticed again how his brother kept glancing in the rearview mirror.

"Thank you for meeting me, Aaron," he said, for he was very conscious of the risk his brother had taken.

Aaron pulled up a few yards beyond Jakob's apartment block. Jakob struggled to get out of the car, delaying his movements a little to give Aaron time to suggest another meeting. But Aaron was silent.

"Good-bye," Jakob said. "And thanks again."

Aaron drove off in silence as a KGB car took off from the curb and followed in his shadow.

He expected to find the apartment empty. But as he put the key in the door, he heard Deborah singing from the kitchen. He opened the door and called her name. She rushed out to greet him.

"Jakob," she cried. "What have they done to you?" She held his face in her hands.

"I'm all right," he said. "I've seen a doctor. Nothing broken and the swellings will go down in a few days." He held her close, and knowing the answer, he asked, "Why aren't you at work?"

"For the same reasons as you," she smiled. "They fired me a week ago. It's nice being out of work," she said, leading him into the living room. "It gives me time to clear up the mess those thugs leave after their visits."

He looked around the room. It was tidy enough, overly tidy, in fact. He looked at the bookshelves and they were empty, as was the table that had once held the turntable and speakers.

"They took the equipment," Deborah explained. "And all our Hebrew books. The Beethoven symphonies as well," she laughed. "I suppose they're dangerous, too."

"When?" he said, enraged at the intrusion.

"The night they arrested you. They didn't lose any time."

"Where were the children?"

"In bed. They slept through it all."

"What did you tell them in the morning?"

"The truth. Where you were and why. It's better that they know everything."

"Has there been trouble at their school?" Jakob asked, sickened by the sudden memory of Isay Salmon and how he had been scapegoated for his father's so-called treachery.

"So far, nothing," Deborah said. She looked at him. "Oh, Jakob, how much longer will we have to wait?"

He took her in his arms. "Cry," he said. "Cry it out. We must not smother our feelings. We may have to wait a long time, and we must not allow the waiting to drive us mad. So cry," he urged her. "I'm home and we have each other." He held her for a long time. Then, "Aaron met me outside the prison," he said.

"I don't want to hear his name."

"He's in trouble, I think," Jakob said. "He's being followed."

"Of course he's being followed," Deborah said. "But not like you. He's being protected. He's one of their token Jews."

"But they're watching him nonetheless," Jakob said.

Aaron's kinship with his brother had in itself stained his reputation. They were watching him to decipher the nature of that kinship, its intensity and its endurance. By interfering with Jakob's visa application, Aaron had made a great mistake, for he had publicly acknowledged that kinship. Had he ignored it, he would probably not have been suspect. Perhaps now Aaron regretted his intrusion, but to recant at this stage would have drawn greater attention to himself. Jakob felt very sorry for him.

"I think he regrets what he's done," Jakob said.

"That's easily remedied," Deborah argued. "He could withdraw his letter and give you permission."

"Then he'll have the same harassment as us," Jakob said.

"Not with Koskin for a father-in-law," she laughed.

"It must be difficult for him anyway," Jakob said. He did not want to talk any more about Aaron, and he let Deborah lead him to the bed and gently undress him.

"You must rest," she said. "Tell me what it was like in prison."

He was glad that she had asked him. He felt the need to talk about it, to share it with another person, to record it and thus give it credence, for he was already doubting the silent events of the last fifteen days. He told it to her in as accurate a sequence as he could fashion, but days that were filled with silences did not lend themselves easily to accurate chronology. He had an idea that Deborah was not listening, that she had asked him the question simply for his own sake. When the story was told, she let him sleep, and then she phoned Inge and Ivan and invited them over that evening for supper. From Jakob's loyal defense of his brother, she sensed he had need for family, and Inge, with her love, untrammeled by expectation, would be solace for him.

That evening she kept the children up for supper. At that time, in the summer of 1972, in the first year of their father's application, they were eight and ten years old. Jakob hoped that the remainder of their childhood would be spent in Israel, and that, in their manhood, they would inherit in the land of their fathers. We shall all be going home, he thought. Perhaps old Grandpa Jakob's litany from the Odessa tavern would be obsolete once and for all. For surely home was no battleground for survival. That arena lay in the Exile. Home was safe. Home was for living. He raised his glass to the company around the table. "Next year in Jerusalem," he said, with such fervor and confidence that it was difficult to contradict him.

That Jerusalem toast, unfulfilled, tolled the passing of many years. Hans and Benjamin, the Bindel brothers of the sixth traceable generation, remained in the land of their buried forefathers, and lived out their childhood there. It had been seven years since Jakob Bindel had first applied for an exit visa, with his brother Aaron's veto still standing. But soon there would be a greater threat to their departure. Unless the Bindel brothers could get a study deferment, they would, in two or three years, be eligible for conscription, and as children of *refuseniks,* study deferment was likely to be denied them. Jakob and Deborah hid their panic from others. They maintained an outward face of optimism, but in private they gave way to their despair. Money was short. Their savings had dwindled. Over the years, Jakob had taken a variety of menial jobs, but even from these he was fired as soon as his employers felt the pressure of the KGB.

At that time, Jakob had been unemployed for three months, and the ominous threat, the newly invented charge of "parasitism" hung over him, a charge that related to continuous unemployment. One morning Jakob set out on his usual search for work, when he was picked up by two security officers and taken to the district court. His appearance was brief. The charge was parasitism and the magistrate gave him fifteen days to find employment or to suffer the consequences. He hinted at the same time that since the accused's political record bordered on the subversive, and because he was known to be a troublemaker, those consequences might be very severe. The penalty for parasitism was prison, and in some cases he had heard of, a term in a labor camp. The thought of a further postponement of his emigration and a separation from his family filled Jakob with a profound despair. And so, out of his desperation, he went to Aaron to ask for his help. There was always a vacancy as a menial in the various laboratories of a teaching hospital. When he entered the laboratory, he was relieved to find Aaron alone. Aaron was glad to see his brother, and since there were no witnesses, he was effusive in his welcome.

"I hope at last you've come for money, Jakob," he said.

Jakob shook his head. "I want a job," he said simply, coming to the point of his visit right away.

"What kind of job?" Aaron was on his guard.

"Something here. In a laboratory, I thought. Anything."

He saw his brother stiffen.

"I'm desperate, Aaron," he said.

"I'd rather give you money."

"I don't want money," Jakob fairly shouted. "Money won't help me. You know the charge of parasitism."

"I can't help you," Aaron said. "It's impossible for you to work here."

Jakob stared at him. His flat and swift refusal brooked no argument or pleading, and Jakob deeply regretted that he had asked at all. He had seen very little of his brother in the past few years. Jakob did not wish for complete estrangement, but now the bonds of their brotherhood were sorely stretched. At that moment he realized that he did not want to see his brother ever again. He turned and made for the door.

"Are you sure you don't want any money?" Aaron almost pleaded with him.

Jakob turned, and looked at him with disdain. "I pity you, brother," he said.

For a while Jakob walked aimlessly about the streets, envying those who went about their business. He didn't know where to turn. He joined a long line of people outside a shop, to give the appearance that he was doing something, and while he stood there, he made a sudden decision to give up the struggle. He would go right away to the OVIR offices, withdraw his application for exit visas, and confess the folly of his ways. He would resign himself and his family to a safe if joyless future in a land not of his choosing. And never, never again would he set eyes on his brother.

He left the line and made for the OVIR offices. On his way, his feet and his heartbeat quickened, and he noticed how his body sweated, and how his pace accelerated. It all seemed to be happening outside himself, as if he were viewing a stranger's raving.

He watched himself jostle people aside, he heard his loud exaggerated apologies. He thought he was probably laughing, though his body was buckled in a silent coiled scream. In his mind he heard the rehearsal of his confession. "I'm sorry. I was foolish. I can't imagine why I ever thought of leaving. There is no country in the world freer or fairer than the one in which I am privileged to live." He noticed how people stared at him as he made his demented way through the streets. By the time he reached Kolpachny Lane, his skin was crawling with the worms of his deception.

The office was crowded with renegade applicants, and Jakob was silenced by the sight of them. His eyes slowly focused on Volodya, sitting behind his desk, his face wreathed in a contemptuous smile. He was talking to an old Jew in a tone of infinite disdain. "My son's in Israel," the old man was pleading. "I want to join him."

Jakob rushed toward the desk, pushing past those who were waiting. Volodya looked up at him. "Bindel," he said wearily. "Again? You'll have to take your disgusting turn."

"No," Jakob said. The sweat was streaming down his face. "No," he shouted. "I've got something to say. I've got something to say."

"Well, say it, for God's sake," Volodya said.

"I've got something to say," Jakob faltered. "I know I've got something to say." Even in his raving mind he knew that what he had to say had nothing to do with his rehearsed speech. "Listen to me," he whispered. "Listen to me." Over and over again he said it, until a woman, sniffing the fever on him, took his arm gently and led him outside onto the street. "Listen to me," he kept saying, and she left him there, leaning against a lamppost, craving an audience. And they gathered, one by one, hearing the pleading in his voice. And as the crowd grew, so did the volume of Jakob's plea. He viewed the blurred sea of faces before him, and prophetlike he thundered into their midst. "Listen to me," and his voice was a trumpet, a last post for his despair. "We are living in a cursed land," he shouted, "a land without freedom. A land of torture and oppression. A land where men are in chains."

The crowd thinned suddenly, terrified to be caught eavesdropping on such subversion. They panicked, tumbling over each other, anxious to flee that polluted area, until within seconds it was emptied but vibrating still with his perilous and passionate syllables of dissent. But Jakob Bindel no longer needed an audience. He needed only himself as an ear, to hear his own shame that even for one moment he had been tempted to desert his cause.

"No country is free if you cannot leave it," he thundered across the streets. "I want to leave. I want to go to Israel with my family," he cried. "Let me go. Let me go."

And in his sobbing plea for freedom, he was rudely taken. Two security officers, who had all the while been listening as they stood at the entrance to OVIR, grabbed him, one on each side, and bundled him into a car that had silently pulled up at the curb. The crowd that had fled to the sidelines now reassembled for the kill, their anger and fear giving way to pity. "He's mad, poor devil," was the general murmur among the crowd, though some had heard an unerring ring of truth in his words, and pondered the nature of insanity.

In the back of the car, Jakob settled himself between his two guards. He made no protest. He felt a surge of relief. He tried to recall in detail the series of events since he had left his brother in the laboratory, but they were confused in his mind. But above all that confusion, he was aware of a sudden sense of freedom, the freedom that belongs to one who has nothing more to lose.

They took him to the police station and to the cells with which he was now familiar. And Jakob had a strange sense of homecoming. He leaned with ease against the bars of his cell and pondered once again the events of his day. In the course of a few hours, he felt, he had aged many years. In the short time since he had left home on his daily pursuit for work, he had flirted with hate, treachery, and madness. He examined each of them, each in their chronological order. Now he no longer needed to disguise his hatred of his brother, nor to find any excuses for Aaron's behavior. He had asked for his brother's help, and his brother had turned his back. "I hate him," Jakob whispered aloud. "I shall never see him again."

Jakob sat on the stone floor, and for the first time since leaving her that morning, he thought of Deborah, and his sense of freedom left him, and with it the small euphoria that came in its wake. In its stead he was overcome by a nagging fear as he thought of the charge that would be leveled against him, a charge more serious than parasitism and far more ominous than hooliganism. As he recalled the words of his lonely disordered oratory,

he knew that the charge was clear. That of anti-Soviet agitation.
It was a crime that carried unthinkable penalties. He shuddered
with fear.

He paced his cell to give himself something to do, measuring
its length with his tread. As he was pacing, a warder came to his
cell with a bowl of soup and a hunk of bread, and instructed him
to eat, for he would get nothing else until after his examination.
The word was ominous. Examination was not trial. It was a word
that pertained to medical care, an area so dark in the Soviet legal
system that it could not bear scrutiny.

"What examination?" he dared to ask.

"You'll see," the warder said, and he locked the cell door after
him. Jakob had not eaten all day, and until the warder's announcement, he had longed for some food. But now his appetite
evaporated. He looked at the thin gruel that the warder had
placed on the floor and he toyed with it with his metal spoon.
Slivers of onion and cabbage floated in the greasy water, and a
knob of mutton that he knew was inedible. He forced it down,
together with the bread, for he knew that hunger could unhinge a
man's mind. He nibbled on the hunk of bread, chewing it slowly,
and he tried to clarify his thoughts in preparation for the examination to come. But he knew how futile that was. Clarity of mind
in this society had nothing to do with sanity. Here, in the land of
freedom and equality, dissent was a diagnosable disease, and
there were plenty of dissenting words still echoing in the streets
to prove his malignancy. He felt already condemned with no
means of self-defense.

Shortly after his so-called lunch, they came for him. He did not
bother to ask where they were taking him. He did not want to
give them the satisfaction of ignoring his inquiry. In any case, he
didn't want to know. It would only add to his fear.

The police van drew up at a large building, which Jakob recognized as the Serbsky Institute of Forensic Psychiatry. "I am
sane," he kept whispering to himself as they shoved him in
through the door. "I am sane."

There were three doctors in the examining room, and they
treated him with courtesy. The preliminaries were as Jakob expected: blood pressure, pulse, heart, all formal postponements of
the serious business of diagnosis. Although they kept their findings to themselves, moving aside occasionally and whispering to

each other, Jakob was in no way worried about his physical condition. He knew he was fit.

They asked him to sit down opposite them and he placed his chair at the end of the table to avoid the triple wall of accusation. Aslant, the view of them was not so formidable. The doctors saw his move as significant, and one of them noted it on the pad before him. Jakob knew it was a bad mark, and would do well as a sign of madness. They would interpret his maneuver as fear, a need to conceal himself out of an obsession that he was being pursued. All that would do very nicely for the diagnosis of paranoia. He realized that whatever he said or did would be tailored to fit the unspoken, unwritten order from the authorities.

In front of the central doctor was a written document, which he now perused. After a while, he looked up at Jakob and said, "It appears you think there is no freedom in our country."

It was a question and he waited for a reply. Jakob knew that to answer in the affirmative would be an outright self-condemnation on political grounds. An answer in the negative would point to his mental instability, for if he said it, how could he not think it? There was no safe way to reply, so he remained silent.

"Yes or no?" the doctor asked.

"I'm not sure," Jakob whispered. He thought it was the safest thing to say, and again the note-taking doctor scribbled on his pad. Another appropriate symptom, Jakob thought.

"Tell me something." The interrogating doctor continued his probing. "What were we fighting against in the last war?"

"Fascism," Jakob said, safe in the knowledge that that answer could in no way incriminate him.

"And what were we fighting *for?*" He paused. "Was it freedom?" he asked, giving his patient a clue.

Jakob nodded. He did not trust his words anymore.

"Did we win?" the doctor asked.

Again Jakob nodded and again the doctor smiled. "Well," he said, "if we were fighting for freedom, and we won, then we have freedom." He paused. "No?" he inquired.

Jakob held his head and his tongue. He could not help but admire their brand of logic, which could be·fashioned to sentence anybody to any crime.

The doctor consulted the document once more. "We live in a land of torture and oppression," he quoted from Jakob's speech. "Torture? Oppression? Where is there torture and oppression?"

No. He would not answer that one, Jakob decided, neither with word nor with gesture.

"Do you remember the last dream you had?" the third doctor opened his mouth for the first time. It was clearly his job to pose the only question that was marginally related to a psychiatric investigation.

Automatically Jakob shook his head. He knew better than to offer any material for their partisan interpretation. Again the scribbling doctor made a note on his pad.

"That's all," the central doctor said suddenly, rising from his chair. The examination was over. It had taken them less than twenty minutes to diagnose their patient's mental aberrations, and only one token question had pertained to Jakob's state of mind.

The warders bundled him back into the van and returned him to his cell. This time they gave him his convict's uniform, as if he had already been tried and sentenced. For a whole week he languished there, ignorant of anything that took place outside his cell. Each day he waited for someone to come and read a charge to him and to tell him the date of his trial. Every day he asked his warder if there was any news, and the warder said he knew nothing, and given the strict hierarchy of the Soviet legal system, Jakob believed him.

At the end of the week the warder came to his cell and told him he had a visitor. Jakob was overjoyed at the prospect of seeing somebody, anybody who could give him news of the progress of his charge. But above all, painful as it would be for both of them, he wanted to see Deborah. The warder took him to the visitors' room, and there she sat, behind the table, with an officer standing at her side. Her face was pale and she looked frightened. Not on account of the guards or the prison, Jakob knew, but because of the knowledge that she held and feared to impart. She stood up as he approached and he went to embrace her. But the guard held out his hand.

"No touching," he said.

Jakob snatched at her hand and kissed it. He desperately needed some contact with her body, however small. The guard overlooked the gesture and told him to sit down.

"How are you?" he whispered. "How are the children?"

They appeared to him to be very personal questions and he did not want the guard to hear.

"No whispering," the guard said.

"I'm fine," Deborah said in a loud protesting voice. "And the children, too. They send their love, and all our friends," she stressed. "They wish you well."

Am I ill, then? Jakob feared.

"When is the trial?" he asked.

And it was then that she turned her eyes from him.

"When is it?" he asked again.

She looked up at him. "It's over," she said. "I've just come from the court."

"But I wasn't there," he shouted. "I wasn't told. I had no lawyer."

"Yes," she said. "You had a defense lawyer."

"But I never met him," Jakob practically screamed. Now the charge and his sentence seemed secondary to the gross injustice of his trial and it seemed now almost irrelevant to inquire about the judgment that had been passed on him.

"What was the charge?" he asked.

"Anti-Soviet agitation."

He trembled. From the despair on Deborah's face he knew he had been found guilty, and in his mind he cataloged the punishments for such a crime. Banishment, a long prison term, or detention in a labor camp. All were unthinkable. He was afraid to know his sentence. If only he could hold Deborah's hand. Her fingers were creeping along the table toward him. At the same time, she looked up at the guard, begging his permission, and he, knowing the terrible words that she had to say to him, nodded and looked away. She took his hand and caressed it against her cheek.

"They judged you insane," she whispered. "The doctors said you suffered from creeping schizophrenia."

"What will become of me?" His voice broke on the question, and he gripped her hand.

"They're sending you to a psychiatric hospital. It's in Minsk," she added wearily, for she knew that its location would make little difference to the pain of his sentence.

"For how long?" he asked, as if to punish himself further, for he knew that there was no time limit on such a judgment.

"Until you're better," she said.

He stared at her. For a moment he feared that she might really have believed in their judgment. "But I'm not ill," he shouted.

She nodded her head. "I know," she said, and she gripped his hand, and that certainty of hers heartened him, for he had, for a moment, become unsure of his own lucidity.

"When are they taking me?" he whispered.

She could barely answer, but she kept her sad eyes upon him. "Now," she said.

Jakob looked up at the guard, who once again nodded and turned away. Then he stood and took Deborah in his arms.

"Soon we shall all be together again," Deborah said.

That Bindel phrase once more.

"I love you," Jakob said. He held her close for a while, until the guard tapped his shoulder. Then he held her at arm's length.

"Kiss the children," he said.

"Next year in Jerusalem," she whispered.

Then they took him away, and she was glad that he did not turn again to look at her.

When Deborah reached home, she was relieved that the children were not there. They were with Inge. Now on her own, Deborah was able to give release to those tears that all day had seethed behind her eyes, during Jakob's mock trial, the prison visit, and the final separation. Once inside her front door, she let the tears flow, and with no preamble. No chair for her comfort, no support for her pain, but standing in the small hallway, and still in her hat and coat. Her heartbreak needed no setting, no backdrop, no direction. She knew that she must wring out her sorrow, just this one time, and then, dry-eyed, she could face her children, and together they would weather the years of separation. As she wept she reached into her pocket for a handkerchief and felt the familiar fidgetings of her mice. Moses and Aaron. She took them out and let them scurry about her hand, and as she watched them she knew that they were no longer part of her. They did not belong to the woman she had become, that person who, in this one long and terrible day, had aged a hundred years. They belonged to the days of her poetry and Mayakovsky Square and a freedom of a sort. They had no place in a cold and mean psychiatric ward that her vicarious world had now become. She took them into the kitchen. In the far corner between the skirting and the floor was a regular mousehole, a legitimate outlet for food forage in the winter months. Somewhere beyond that skirting, there must be a colony, and Moses and Aaron, with initial astonishment, would find their own tribe. She slipped them both into the opening, and they were gone before she had time to mourn them. She returned to the hallway and took off her hat and coat. The long plait slipped from her beret, and in the mirror she suddenly saw it as a foreign graft on her person. That, too, like Moses and Aaron, belonged to another country, another time, a strange anachronism in her present self-reflection. She took a pair of scissors from the drawer and, without style or production, she cut it off, plaited as it was, and she wondered where to put it. She knew that if she kept it, tissued in some drawer, it would be an invitation to nostalgia and perhaps regret. Unlike mice, she had no natural habitat for her own childhood. Except in the mind. So she wrapped it quickly and threw it in the dustbin, stuffing it into the rubbish, beyond retrieve. And so Deborah buried her childhood, casting off the last defense of her despair.

That evening Deborah took her boys in her arms and told them what had happened to their father. She explained it all in as much detail as they could understand with their tender years, and she told them too as much of the Bindel history as she had learned from Jakob. But she did not mention the inheritance. There would come a time for that telling, and the story would be told by Jakob. Later that evening, when the children were in bed, Inge and Ivan came to comfort her. They spoke about the past, for Deborah loved to hear from Inge stories of Jakob's hidden childhood in Germany. They talked about Hans, too, and of Benjamin and David, and of Grandpa Leon, and the stories served to comfort Deborah a little.

Inge left the apartment a little later. She was deeply saddened by Aaron's behavior. Only that afternoon she had gone from the court to visit Aaron in his laboratory, to apprise him of the court's findings, and of his brother's sentence. He had been visibly shocked, and for a moment had sat down with his head in his hands and said nothing. After a while he wanted to know where the offense had taken place, and at precisely what time. She wondered at his insistence on knowing the time of Jakob's arrest, and she had asked him why it seemed so important to him. He looked up at her, and she saw that he was crying. She went and put an arm around him. She was surprised at his tears, and tried to remember when last she had seen Aaron cry. Certainly not when she had told him he was an orphan. Those tears had been saved for many, many years. At Hans's deathbed, she remembered, he

had allowed them to the rim of his eyes. Now they fell freely, and
Inge knew that the only human being Aaron had ever truly loved
was his brother Jakob, and she knew, too, that he felt himself to
blame for Jakob's arrest and detention.

"Something happened between you. Tell me, Aaron." There
was a note of command in her voice, that tone she would occasionally use when they were children. And Aaron responded to it
exactly as he had when he was a child. He told her in self-punish-
ing detail of Jakob's visit to the laboratory, of how he had begged
for work, of how he, his elder brother, had turned him away.

Inge listened to his story, and was at pains to conceal her
horror. There was no doubt in her mind that Jakob's present
deprivation was entirely the result of his brother's rejection. She
wondered what Hans would have done had he lived to see the
terrible rift between his children. She had little doubt that he
would have ordered Aaron to withdraw his veto. Indeed, he
would have taken Aaron there himself to the OVIR offices and
witnessed its withdrawal, no matter at what cost to Hans's own
livelihood and reputation. But Inge knew that for Aaron, reputation was secondary. Foremost in his mind was the need for peace,
for an absence of disturbance in his life. His parents had deeply
offended him by dying in the camps, and he was sick, heartily
sick of the battle of survival, and of all the suffering that the
Bindel inheritance entailed. He wanted none of it, and the only
fight he would participate in was to keep it from his door. Yet he
wanted his brother's love and he feared he had forfeited it. Jakob,
the gentle forgiving one, would never forgive him.

"Does Deborah know?" Inge asked.

"Only if Jakob told her."

"Then she doesn't know," Inge said. It was a private sorrow
and Inge knew that Jakob would not share it. "And neither must
you tell her," she ordered. "But perhaps," she added gently, "you
could go and visit her. She's going to need friends."

But Aaron did not go to visit Deborah. Instead he went to see
his father-in-law. His relationship with Mr. Koskin was cordial.
As a high government official, Koskin was host to many parties
in his sumptuous apartment in the Hotel Ukrainia, but Aaron
was never invited. Indeed, Koskin discouraged any visits, pleading party business. But he would occasionally visit his daughter
in her own apartment, and he made a point of visiting during

laboratory hours when Aaron wasn't there. But on the rare occasions that they did meet, Koskin was polite and reticent. But Aaron knew his father-in-law kept an eye on him. Only once had Mr. Koskin directly referred to his reservations concerning his son-in-law's family. He had commented on Jakob's application for an exit visa with some disgust, and had hinted that it might well jeopardize Aaron's career if he did not do something quite positive to show which side he was on. But he had had nothing to do with Aaron's letter of veto. That had been Aaron's own idea, and he had written it with little thought of the consequences.

He rang the bell of his apartment and as he heard its echo, he realized that he had made no appointment. It was not a good beginning. Koskin was surprised to see him, but less displeased than Aaron had anticipated, for he was alone and seemingly unbusy. Yet his manner was businesslike.

"There's something you want to discuss?" he asked, leading him into the drawing room.

"My brother is in trouble," Aaron said, coming to the point right away.

"I know," Koskin said. "I know all about it. But I wouldn't call it trouble. Your poor brother is ill. He's very fortunate that he will receive treatment. In time he will be cured."

"There's nothing the matter with my brother," Aaron screamed at him.

"I would be grateful if you kept your voice down," Koskin ordered in measured tones. "I am not to blame for your brother's madness. I'm sorry for him, of course. It is especially hard on relatives to have to accept a strain of insanity in their blood. It worries me, too. Believe me, it worries me for Heidi."

"You're crazy," Aaron whispered.

Koskin ignored that comment, or perhaps he didn't hear it. "Take heart," he said. "Your brother will get better. We have cured dissidents before."

"You cannot really believe in the bottom of your heart that dissidence is a mental disease?"

"What else?" Koskin said. "How else can one describe it? We live in a society of equality and freedom. If one speaks out *against* equality, against justice, against freedom, then surely one is deranged. What is normal about injustice, inequality, imprisonment?"

Aaron opened his mouth to argue with him, but then he realized that his father-in-law was totally sincere in his beliefs. There was no doubt that he profoundly believed that a mind had to be disordered before dissent could find its lodging within. In Koskin's terms Jakob Bindel was mad, and in those same terms, the blessed system would make him better. Aaron had come to plead with his father-in-law to use his influence to engineer his brother's freedom. Now in the light of Koskin's arguments, there seemed no logic in that plea. Nevertheless, that was why he had visited him, and he could not go away without asking for some concession.

"Can't you use your influence?" he asked.

"To do what?"

"To free him, of course," Aaron said, his voice raised once more.

"Do you want your brother to get better?" Koskin asked. He put his hand on Aaron's shoulder in a rare gesture of contact with the man who had married his daughter. "Believe me," he said, "he's in the best hands. One year, maybe two, and he'll be among us again. We mustn't blame him, Aaron," he said. "That's the trouble with mental illness. We think it's their fault and we want to punish them. But it is an illness like any other. If I caught pneumonia, you wouldn't blame me, would you?"

Again the logic, Aaron thought, and again based on a totally illogical premise.

"But if you could get his release," Aaron begged, "I could talk to him. I could make him withdraw his application for a visa. He could go back to work and become a normal Soviet citizen." Whatever that meant, Aaron thought. He heard the futility of his argument, and he heard, too, how he diminished his brother by assuming that his waywardness was abnormal. It was Koskin and his kind who were crazy and brainwashed.

"Curing a disease is a professional job," Koskin was saying. "We should leave it to the professionals. I know it's hard on you," he said, touching his shoulder once more, but now Aaron felt it not as a gesture of sincere concern, but the ungentle touch of a KGB official. Had he imagined it, or was there a small hint of pressure in Koskin's touch, a pressure that had nothing to do with affection but that bore the weight of warning. He was relieved when he took his hand away.

Aaron got up to leave. There was no point in prolonging the meeting. In any case, he wanted to be by himself for a while to decide what he must do. For he had to do something. He wished now he'd never sent that letter of veto, but now, with Jakob incarcerated for an indefinite time, there would be little point in withdrawing it. He recalled their last meeting in his laboratory. In his mind he went over it in the greatest detail, and he knew that his rejection of his brother had for a while unhinged Jakob's reason. There was no doubt in his mind that he himself was entirely to blame. He must somehow make amends. But how? He had to accept that there was no way in which he could help his brother. He could offer his support to Deborah and the children, but she would, with good reason, reject it. He could ask his father-in-law to use his offices to get him a visitor's permit to the hospital and perhaps talk to the doctors there. He did, after all, have some standing in the medical profession. But he had heard from various sources, and with little surprise, that the doctors at the prison hospital were employed by the MVD and the KGB, and answerable to those authorities. In any case, it was more than likely that Jakob would refuse to see him.

He found himself nearing Mayakovsky Square. He rarely visited that quarter of the city, and he found it strange that as he was walking and deliberating with himself, his steps should take him to the scene of Hans's death. Certainly he had not been near the square since Hans died.

He sat on the stone steps beneath the statue on the square. He wondered at what spot Hans had made his sacrifice. He missed Hans terribly. His death had double-crossed him in orphanhood and sometimes he hated Hans as much as he hated his true father, and both for the same reason: that dying, they had rejected him. But Hans he could mourn and miss; his own father lay still uninterred in his heart. He knew as he sat there, with his mind full of questionings, that he was on the brink of self-confrontation, a precipice he had assiduously avoided his whole adult life. Now, at this time, and in this place, such confrontation was in season and so he took himself back to the attic in Halle, where his torment had begun—that dark breeding ground of all his pain, of all the fury that had finally sent him to war with his brother.

He thought of Jakob, probably at this moment handcuffed to a guard, huddled on a train on his way to Minsk. Was it possible that the guard was like Koskin, that he, too, viewed his prisoner as a dangerous lunatic who must be cured of his irrational thoughts, whose mind the devil had entered and there planted questions that were not supposed to be asked? But he himself had sometimes, in the dark and in the still small hours of the morning, asked himself those questions. Unlike Jakob, he could not run the risk of their answer, and he would turn to the woman sleeping by his side, and put his arms about her for his comfort. And wonder who she was. For she was a stranger to him. And always would be. For the first time, he confronted his reasons for marrying Sonia. He loved her. But it was more than that. His marriage was a strategy in the war against his brother, that man who had accepted the suffering of his tribe, that suffering that Aaron couldn't stomach; that man who had so peacefully accommodated his martyred inheritance, that inheritance whose words Aaron knew by heart, and each syllable of which stuck in his throat. That brother of his. That offensive survivor.

He smiled to himself. He could be relied upon, that brother of his, to resist the doctor's cure. The devil's questions would not be dislodged from his heart. Yet he would survive. For if Jakob had any disease at all, it was that of survival, and for that condition, there was no known cure. As he thought of Jakob, he saw the train going through a tunnel, yet it was he himself who was in the dark, and in that darkness he felt tears behind his eyes, and he rose quickly from the steps and went on his way.

He picked up a passing taxicab, and gave his home address. He knew he should go back to the laboratory. He had work to do there, work that until that time had totally involved him, the work that was his own homemade survival kit. Now he saw that weapon as futile, as unavailing as felling an oak with a razor blade. He felt he had lost his footing. Or rather, that the ground itself was shifting. He needed to talk to Sonia, though he knew that such an encounter, at this time, could well engender an earthquake.

She was surprised to see him at that time of day, troubled too by the worried look on his face.

"Is anything wrong?" she asked.

Everything was wrong, he thought. He was wrong, she was wrong, their whole life together was wrong. Yet there was comfort in that mutual incompatibility. She was a million miles from his Bessarabian beginnings, but in that unspannable distance there was so much excitement. Above all she was a daughter of the KGB, and there was a fearful eroticism in the rotten stock from which she came. He held her to him.

"What's the matter, Aaron?" she said. Sonia was aware of the
friction between the two brothers, but it was a subject that Aaron
assiduously avoided, and she knew it was too raw to touch. But
now she sensed that his unease lay in that quarter, and she asked,
"Is it about Jakob?"

He wanted so much to tell her, but if he were to tell her the
whole truth, she would hear their marriage crumble.

"I went to see your father," he said.

She was surprised. There must be a matter of some urgency if
he had made such a call. He must have needed a favor, and to ask
that of her father must have cost him some pride. Such a price
would only be paid in the name of his brother.

"Is Jakob in trouble?" she asked.

So he told her the whole story. He didn't even hesitate to tell
her how Jakob had come to him for a job and of how he had
refused to help.

"I am to blame," he told her.

"No," she said. "What was he charged with?"

So he continued with his story, of the fraudulent psychiatric
evidence, of the verdict and the judgment of the court. And when
it was told, he turned to her and said, "What do you think of all
that, Sonia?"

He was asking her a simple direct question, without any loopholes for escape or innuendo, for he felt it as basic and as elemental a question as "Do you love me?" Which, in effect, was exactly
what he was asking. Its answer would determine the course of his
future. He hoped she would pause to consider before answering,
that in her consideration, she would understand the desperate
importance of her response, and how much it could fray or ease
their loving. But she did not hesitate as he held his breath.

"What can one think?" she said. "Jakob is mad. I have always
thought so, and thanked God that you were so different. But
thank God too that he is in good hands. The Minsk hospital is
excellent, I have heard. In a year, two years maybe, he will be
well. He'll be back at work and you two can live together in some
kind of normal relationship. I know it's hard for you now,
Aaron," she said, "but in a way it's a blessing that it's come to a
head. Otherwise it would have been too late to cure him."

He stared at her, astonished, yet unsurprised by what she had
said. Her father's daughter. He went upstairs and packed a bag.
As he folded his suits and his shirts, he was aware each moment

of exactly what he was doing. He stowed his underwear in the separate compartment of the suitcase and checked that the drawers were empty. Then he left the room. As he closed the doors behind him, the thought came to him that in that room they had together made Heidi, and it was his only thought that touched on nostalgia.

He stood at the door of the living room, his suitcase in his hand.

"May I see Heidi once a week?" he asked. "I could collect her on a Saturday."

She stared at him, dumbfounded, astonished and bewildered by his move.

"What's the matter with you, Aaron?" She swallowed her words in her panic.

"Is it possible you don't know what is the matter?" he said quietly. Surely it was not possible, he thought. He stood there in the doorway, his body sweating with disgust. Was it possible she could not smell the stink of it upon him? He turned. "I'll be here on Saturday," he said. Then he left her. He stood for a while on the threshold of their apartment. His tears flowed freely now, and stung his cheeks with their truth. He knew that much had changed in his life that day, that priorities had shifted from their stubborn planting, that his past could no longer be denied, that the time was ripe at last for mourning. And for loving, too.

The psychiatric colony of the Minsk hospital was once a prison. Nowadays it is called a hospital for its implications of sickness and cure, but in effect it is an even more punitive institution than that of a prison. For once inside, the so-called patient loses all his legal rights. There is no avenue of protest, no machinery for redress. It is a place for toeing the line, for any protest only serves to confirm the initial and fraudulent diagnosis.

From his last incarceration Jakob Bindel remembered, above all, the silences. But this place, if he should survive to recall it, would be in the context of noise. Continuous noise, cacaphonic, demented—noise designed to drive the patients mad. He noticed the noise on his first entry as his guard led him down the long corridor to the receiving quarters. He tried to isolate the sounds, and found that they came from no human source. There were clanging of chains, slamming of doors, a buzzing of bells, the discordant sounds of efficient and rigid administration.

He was led into the medical room for his initial examination. The doctor asked him to sit down and to make himself comfortable and Jakob was angered by his excessive politeness.

"Why am I here?" he asked. "There's nothing the matter with my mind."

The doctor picked up the charge sheet. "I see from here," he said gently, "that your views are socially dangerous. That's why you must be put away."

"But my views have nothing to do with psychiatry," Jakob said.

"It is part of your mental condition that you should think that way. You are a mathematician. That is your profession. To engage in other activities as you have done is a sign of a split dissociated personality. Your mind is split, Mr. Bindel. You are rational and irrational at the same time. You dwell in fantasy and sometimes you cannot distinguish that from what is real. We call it schizophrenia." He pronounced the word slowly, as if he were speaking to a child. "Once you change your political views, you will be cured. The cure is up to you, Bindel," he said.

Jakob opened his mouth to comment on the utter stupidity of such an idea, but his instinct prompted him to hold his tongue. It warned him that to begin to argue on such a premise would give that premise some credence. He must ignore their speeches and hold his tongue. And if possible, avoid their treatment.

But it was clear to him on arrival at the ward that such avoidance was impossible. A line of patients waited at the drug trolley. A nurse handed a pill and a metal cup of water to the orderly beside him. The orderly would then place the pill on the patient's tongue and offer him the water. Then when the pill was presumably swallowed, he would examine the inside of the patient's mouth in case he had managed to avoid the dosage. With such a procedure, the doling out of drugs took some time, but the patients did not seem to mind the waiting. Indeed, some even appeared to be enjoying it, and later on in his stay, Jakob understood why. Because waiting for drugs, though intensely passive, was one of the few activities of the day. Jakob's guard showed him his bed, then pushed him into line and waited beside him, the order for his treatment in his hand. When, after an interminable wait, it was Jakob's turn, the warder handed the prescription to the nurse and left Jakob in his care. When his turn came, he asked the nurse what he'd been prescribed.

"You're new," the nurse said with a smile. Old-timers knew better than to ask questions. "Take it," he said. "It will make you well."

Jakob was on the point of declaring his perfect health, but such a declaration would have been taken as a common symptom of his illness. He took the pill obediently, with a terrible fear that by the time he got out of this place, he would be mad indeed.

When the trolley had been wheeled out of the ward, Jakob took time to look around him and at his company. He hoped that among them might be a familiar face, one that he had met in Moscow in the various clandestine meeting places where the *refuseniks* gathered. One or two of them seemed faintly familiar, although their shuffling gait and faintly zombielike appearance obscured the particularities of their features by which Jakob could have identified them, but one of the possibles was shuffling his way.

"We met at Victor's," he whispered, and his speech was drawled, and with great effort.

Jakob held out his hand. "Jakob Bindel," he said.

"Grigory," the man offered, but was clearly too tired or perhaps too unsure of his identity to offer anything further. There were so many questions that Jakob wanted to ask, but he could see from his friend's drawn and pale countenance that further conversation would have exhausted him. So he put his arm around his shoulder and squeezed it lightly, delighted that he had found a companion. Grigory put his hand on Jakob's and held it, like a child. Then he led him slowly down the ward to his bed. He almost collapsed on it and motioned Jakob to sit by his side. They looked at each other for a while, and then with enormous facial effort, it seemed, Grigory gave him a smile. Jakob tried to recall the details of their meeting. It had been some years ago, he thought, in the house of Victor Yakir, a *refusenik* who since that time had been lucky enough to emigrate. There had been about half a dozen of them there, and he tried to recall the specific purpose of the meeting, and to locate Grigory in its setting. Then he saw quite clearly in that picture a bearded man, slapping the table to make his point clear. A short brown beard he had had, Jakob recalled, and a shock of brown curly hair. He was certain Grigory was that man, that man of fire, audacity, and courage. He had never seen him again. He was told that he was in a labor camp for distributing illegal literature. Could this Grigory be the same? Jakob stared at him. "Did you have a beard?" he asked.

Grigory nodded.

"And a shock of hair?" He looked at his almost hairless head with fear, and a faint hope that he was mistaken.

Grigory nodded and in his eyes Jakob could see the faint flickering of the old fire.

"Were you in a labor camp?"

Again a nod.

"How long have you been here?" Jakob dared to ask.

"Two years," Grigory answered slowly. And then, after a long pause, "I think it's two years," he said.

His slow, unsure postscript was profoundly depressing, and Jakob raised his hand to his own head, stroking the hair gently as if he were touching it for the last time. He looked around the

ward and was relieved to see some patients with a good enough
head of hair, and some even had beards, but all seemed to share
Grigory's vacant look. He noticed how some of them made
moves to come toward him, but after a few steps in his direction,
they would return to their cots, exhausted. He thought that later
on he would do a round of the wards and talk to each patient in
turn, while he was still physically able to move around with ease,
for he knew that in time he would become exactly like them.

"What drug do they give us, Grigory?" Jakob asked.

"Triftazin," Grigory said.

It was the only word that had rolled with ease off his tongue.
He was more sure of it even than his own surname.

"What's it for?" Jakob asked.

"Punishment."

That word too rolled off the tongue. In his time, Grigory had
been in prison, in a labor camp, and now in a psychiatric hospital. He was familiar with every facet of the Soviet penal system.
He lay back on his cot and closed his eyes. "Morning," he
drawled. "Only time to talk."

From that information Jakob deduced that the effects of the
drug were less acute in the mornings. He looked around the ward
and saw that most of the men appeared to be sleeping. It was only
early afternoon, and he wondered if all their days were spent like
this one and how long a healthy mind could withstand such
abuse. He did not know what to do with himself. He listened to
the continuous din of noises. The patients seemed totally unaffected by them, the only bonus that the drug afforded. He walked
to the end of the ward, where the orderly had assigned him a bed.
He felt a drowsiness creep over him, but he tried to ignore it. He
was imagining it, he decided. He had been affected by the other
men's lethargy. Nevertheless he would sit on his bed, but not for
long, in case his imagined drowsiness would lead to sleep. After a
few minutes he forced himself to stand, but the action of pinning
his feet to the floor called for great physical effort. His whole
body was exhausted, but he knew that it had nothing to do with
fatigue. He was confident that if he lay on his cot, he would not
allow himself to sleep the day away. He must not, he thought,
because that way, madness lay. He lay down and felt the weight
of his eyelids, so heavy that they could not close. What in God's
name am I doing here, he thought, and then that same survival
instinct prompted him to speak those thoughts aloud and thus

release them into the air, else they would gather in his head and ferment there, and in time addle his brain. "What am I doing here?" he whispered aloud, dispersing that terrible thought into the air already polluted by other men's whispered fears. "They will not drive me mad," he said, over and over again, until he felt his tongue weighing heavily on the floor of his mouth. He longed for sleep, but he knew he must resist it. "I will not be driven mad," he drawled. The effort to speak was painful, but he forced his declaration from his lips, over and over again. A nurse passed his bed, and watched and listened.

"Talking to yourself?" he said with a sneer. Condemned, Jakob thought, but this thought he kept to himself, for to give it to the nurse would only reinforce their diagnosis. He raised his feet on his cot, pushed his feet to the ground, and forced himself to take a few steps. Slowly and with infinite effort, he ambled around the ward, but the weight of his eyelids was unbearable. He made for his cot again, lay back and put his hands over his eyes, as one would cover the stare of the dead. He felt them shutting and it was as if their closure had unturned the key of a projector, for it was then that the pictures began to run.

At first, as if in a pretitle sequence, he saw himself in Aaron's laboratory. In the background of his mind he could hear the hum of the projector, which seemed to be intensified by the silent nature of the film. And the film was not only silent; it was in slow motion, too, as Aaron turned his back on him in prolonged, interminable, unremitting rejection. Then the scene shifted suddenly to the attic in Halle, where he and Aaron, in the guise of Hermann and Heinrich, crouched silently on their beds, while below they carried the coffin of Hans's dead mother out of the front door. The film stuttered for a while, as if a sprocket had broken, and then a big black car came slowly into focus. He sat with his brother in the backseat, and through the window he could clearly see his parents as they turned their backs and walked up the drive of the house. It is enough, it is enough, Jakob cried in his mind, but the film recall was relentless. Vienna station now, and the departing train that robbed them of their freedom. In the tunnel, the film went black, and it was then that the silence ceased. Hermann, Heinrich, he heard his mother calling, and Aaron and Jakob from the gentle lips of Grandpa Leon. Oh, if only these doctors knew how split I really am, Jakob thought, and he longed for his eyes to open, to blind him to his cleft past, for that rerun,

in this place, he couldn't bear. He must have slept then, for the
screen whitened and there was silence.

When he awoke, his body was light and his mind clear. He
heard a bell ringing, and saw the men around him make their
way to the drug trolley and second drug round of the day. Their
walk was sprightly and full of hope, and now would have been
the time for talking. But the trolley waited to slacken their steps,
to numb their senses, to still their tongues. He joined the line next
to Grigory.

"How often do they drug us?" he whispered.

"Three times a day. One o'clock, five o'clock, eight o'clock.
Mornings are good here. Don't waste your talk now. In the
morning we will be human for a while."

Jakob took his turn with the others, resenting his own obedience. But he knew that any alternative would be to ask for trouble and that only mindless and blind obedience could work in this
place. He straightened his back like a good boy, and took his
medicine. Shortly afterward, he was again overcome with drowsiness and his mouth was very dry. He asked for water, but it did
not seem to assuage his thirst. He watched as the other men's
gaits slowly turned to shuffles. Some sat on their beds and stared
with disgust at their feet that had lost their function. There was
much sighing, and of a terrible resignation. He made for his cot
and he lay there, and though he struggled against it, he entered
once more the picture palace of his past. When the film had run
its nightmarish course, he slept in the uneasy dark, and woke,
purged and clear, once more to join the numbing line. After that
last dosage of the day, they were given a supper of thin broth, a
few sprats, and a hunk of bread, and though he was hungry, the
effort needed to raise the spoon to his mouth was greater than his
appetite. He put on the nightgown that the hospital had issued. It
was white but stained with all the colors of sickness. He wondered who had worn it before him, and whether he had died in it.
Such thoughts were not conducive to sleep, which he now so
craved, and he longed for a drug that would numb his mind for
the duration of his stay. He reached out for a mug of water, and
in his trembling and fragile holding, it dribbled down his chin.
He felt very old then, decrepit and disintegrating. But he did not
give way to self-pity, because he knew, with that old Bindel survival instinct, that the loss of self-esteem was the beginning of
despair, and perhaps even of the madness that they had prepared

for him. In time, he fell into a mercifully dreamless sleep, and so ended his first day as a government-licensed lunatic.

When he awoke in the morning, he wondered where and why and who he was. He took his time with his considerations because he sensed that their outcome would be depressing, and when his fears were confirmed as to his location and its cause, he took some comfort in the clarity of his thoughts and knew that this was a state of mind to be savored, every second of it, for it would not last for long.

He bounded out of bed, and looking around, saw that most of the men were already dressed and in conversation. He didn't want to miss one minute of it. There was so much he wanted to know, information that could only be gleaned from those who had experienced the hospital routine. He dressed quickly and went to join Grigory.

"Good morning, friend," Grigory said as he approached. "We meet for a short time in the land of the living. This is Yakov, Mikhail, and Ilya." He introduced the three men about him. "All from Kiev," Grigory went on. "There was an epidemic of schizophrenia in Kiev a few years ago."

"A few years?" Jakob asked, frightened. "How long have you been in this place."

"Two years," Ilya said. "All three of us. We came on the same day."

"People can be here two years?" Jakob asked in despair.

"Yuri over there," Grigory said, pointing to a man at the end of the ward. "He's been here almost four years. He's very stubborn," Grigory laughed. "He just refuses to get any better."

"What does better mean?" Jakob said.

"It depends," Ilya said. "Every six months they review your case. Then it's up to you."

Jakob refrained from asking for a clarification of Ilya's last remark. He had an idea of what it meant, with its overtones of surrender and abdication. That's why these men had been here for two years or more. They were, in their own terms, stubborn. He skirted to safer ground and asked about the hospital routine.

"We go to the dining room for a so-called breakfast," Grigory said, "and then there's an hour's exercise in the yard. Then a so-called lunch. Then after that we get on the old drug roundabout, and we don't come off till morning."

"Is that all the treatment we have?" Jakob asked.

"It's enough," Mikhail said. "The less treatment we get, the better for our sanity. As it is, one can go mad in here."

"Remember poor Evgeny," Ilya said.

But they did not pursue that subject, and Jakob knew that it was not in his interest to inquire further. He used the time before breakfast to discover how they had come to this place. Their stories were similar. All of them were *refuseniks,* some of them of six years' standing. All of them had been charged with anti-Soviet propaganda, and in each of their cases, the court had been generous and declared them insane.

"How does one survive here?" Jakob asked.

"We have each other," Grigory said.

Just then an orderly called them into line, shouting at them to hurry.

But the men took their time. The morning's clarity gave them the courage to dictate their own tempo. There was a refreshing arrogance about their gait, and Jakob caught it and ambled at his leisure. Then he was horrified to see the orderly crack a whip that he carried by his side. The men's paces quickened a little, but in some cases not enough, and those men felt a crack on their shins, and Jakob saw their faces wince with pride and pain. He was horrified.

"But they're not allowed to do that," he said to Grigory, who walked by his side. "We're supposed to be ill."

"That's a dangerous thought, my friend, and you must put it from your mind if you are to survive. Whatever they choose to think, we are not ill. There is nothing wrong with our minds. We are saner than all of them."

Jakob looked at the orderly and was unnerved by the uniform he was wearing. It was that of a convict, exactly the same as he himself had been obliged to wear during his prison term.

"He's a convict, isn't he," he whispered to Grigory.

"Yes. All the orderlies here are convicts," he said. "They're sent from the prisons to work here. It's a plum job for them. They can beat us up as a change from being beaten themselves. And they do. Believe me, they do. Keep out of their way if you can."

The line began to move and converge with the others on their way to the eating hall. There were about ten lines in all, and some of the men, Jakob noticed, looked very ill indeed, their bodies thin, and their faces yellow-pale, with hardly enough strength in their limbs to shuffle along the corridor. They frightened him, for they posed a picture of what he might in time become.

"Some of them look so ill," he whispered to Grigory.

"They are," Grigory said. "Too long on the drugs. They have no mornings anymore in their lives. They are riddled with lethargy."

"Who are they?" Jakob asked.

"They are dissidents like us," Grigory said. "But they're not *refuseniks*. They don't want to leave this country. They want to right its wrongs."

There were several long tables in the eating hall, and at the end of it a counter where the meal was dispensed. Jakob took his turn in the line, holding the metal plate and the cup that the orderly had given him. When his turn came, he was given three sprats, a hunk of bread, and a cup of thin gruel, together with his sugar ration for the whole day.

"Eat slowly," Grigory said as they moved toward a table. "It will satisfy you longer."

An orderly was posted at each table, and he watched his charges with a superior eye. He was probably a thief or a murderer, Jakob thought, but probably in this place, and for the first time in his wretched life, he enjoyed a sense of being a class above the others. And he was going to make sure that these lunatics knew their place. He barked at them to hurry with their food, almost before they were seated on the benches. But the men took their time nonetheless, most of them simply because they could not eat quickly. Their teeth were loose, or decayed perhaps from long lack of care, and their stomachs were shrunk to such proportions as to inhibit a swift intake of food. Indeed, some of them, Jakob noticed, had difficulty in swallowing even the tiny rations they were allowed.

"We're not allowed to talk during exercise," Grigory said. "So tell me about yourself and why you are here. And after our walk, you can give all of us news of the outside."

So Jakob told him his *refusenik* history, and as he unfolded each episode, he found it more ridiculous and more incredible than he had viewed it at the time. But Grigory was not surprised. It was a tale similar to hundreds of others.

"I remember when I first came here," he said. "I thought I was unique. I was caught distributing the *Chronicle*. Like you, I was taken to the Serbsky Institute. They said I had paranoid delu-

sions of reforming society and that I was suffering from something they called schizo-dissension. I thought they'd invented the
word just for me. Then when I arrived here, it seemed to be a
condition of epidemic proportions and I didn't feel so special
anymore. But for the first time since I'd been active, I realized
how nationwide our movement was. And that was heartening.
It's the brotherhood that keeps us sane."

"What happened to the one they call Evgeny?" Jakob asked.

"It's nearly exercise time," Grigory said quickly. "Finish your
food."

He must not ask about Evgeny, Jakob knew. Grigory's lack of
response had been for Jakob's own protection. Nevertheless
Evgeny's fate nagged at him. In time, he would ask one of the
others.

Most of the men took the exercise hour very seriously, and
they used every part of their bodies with as much vigor as their
health would allow. But toward the end of the first half hour,
most of them had flagged and were leaning against the walls,
their faces bitter with disappointment. For long and constant
drugging had abused their bodies as well as their minds, and
some men, knowing the pitiful outcome of their efforts, chose not
to exercise at all, thus avoiding the disappointment. Jakob's body
was fit, and he could with ease have spent the whole hour in
strenuous exercise, but after half an hour he felt ashamed to put
his rude health on show, so he lolled against the wall with the
rest of them. He was glad when the hour was over.

They returned to the ward. Some of the men lay on their cots
in sheer exhaustion. Their "mornings" were over. Others read or
wrote letters. That was a freedom that Jakob had not expected in
this place. But when he asked an orderly for writing materials, he
was refused. A month had to pass before he was allowed to make
contact with the outside world. He looked around for Grigory,
but found that even he had retired. He was fast asleep on his cot.
Jakob was afraid. How long would it be before he was like them,
before his body would betray him, and follow his mind into
numbness?

"No, no," he shouted.

It was an involuntary sound. Had he thought about it, he
would have kept his panic to himself, but it was already noted on
the nurse's pad. He thought of Deborah to take his mind off his
fears, and thoughts of her helped him for a while. He wondered

how he could pass a whole month without contact with her, and
he prayed that when permission was given, he would still have
the strength and, more crucial, the appetite to write to her.

There was a shelf of books at the end of the ward. From his bed
he could count them. Twenty-three in all. He resolved that he
would read every one of them, word by word, however weary
their matter or their style. I will start with the first book on the
top shelf, he thought, and he made his way across the ward.

It was a history of Marx and Lenin. He gave a cursory look at
the other titles, and they were no more promising. No matter, he
thought. They will keep my mind active. They will jog what is
left of my memory when the effect of the drugs wear off. He took
down the volume with some eagerness, grateful for the first item
of curative treatment that he had been offered. He took it back to
his bed and opened the first page. He read every word. The name
of the publisher, the copyright number, the dates of the first to
the twelfth printing. He read the small paragraph of acknowledg-
ments, over and over again, needing to memorize each meaningless name. Then he turned to the first page of the text. It was
clear from the first paragraph that it was a purely academic work,
turgid, heavy, and earnest, to the point of distraction. He forced
himself to read on, and when he came to the end of the page,
although he had understood each word, he had no sense of its
totality. He read it once again. And he felt his eyelids grow
heavy, and he realized that reading such matter was counter-
productive, for its effect was the same as the drugs.

He was woken by a slight shove on his shoulder. An orderly
gave him his lunch soup, and already a trolley was being wheeled
into the ward. My life is passing by, Jakob thought, shrinking in
sleep and idleness. I shall go mad here, he thought, and he wondered again about the man they called Evgeny.

That day passed like his first, and thereafter many days, until
he could reckon them in weeks. Each sleep was deeper and his
dreams were terrible. The exercise hour became a penance for
him, for it proved his growing frailty. Men left the ward and
never returned, and he was too afraid to ask where they had
gone. Then one morning he woke to find writing paper and a pen
at his bedside, and suddenly he was alive once more, and he
remembered Deborah and his children, to whom he realized he
had given no thought for many days. Now the recollection of
them gave him a small strength, a sense of his own being, so long

dormant. He was a husband and a father, and much more than
the wretch who slept his days away, and who peppered his nights
with terrible dreams. He grabbed the paper and took the pen in a
trembling hand.

My darling Deborah, Hans and Benjamin.

Their names were a shock to him. Who were these people
whose names he wrote with such fluent familiarity? For he could
not remember their faces. My God, he thought, and this is morning. Clarity time, conversation time. The pen shook in his hand.
Yet he could find no words to write, no style to couch his fear, no
grammar for the truth of his amnesia. He tried to picture
Deborah in certain events of their lives together, standing at the
plinth in Mayakovsky Square, under the wedding canopy in the
synagogue, in the hospital bed after Hans's birth. But even in
these identities, as lover, bride, and mother, he could not evoke
her features. But it was when he thought of their last meeting
that he saw her, as she gave him his verdict. It was then that he
heard her parting Bindel phrase, "Soon we shall all be together
again," and it was then that his fingers steadied on the pen, and
he began to write.

Soon we shall all be together again, my loved ones. It acted as a
sudden injection of his heritage, and it gave him strength. *You
remember the toast we give each other every year. That hope, in
time, will be fulfilled.* He was mindful of censorship. The word
Jerusalem would certainly not travel well from this place, but he
need not elucidate to Deborah and the children. *My life here is
calm and unmolested.* Both were close to the truth, though he
had occasionally been beaten by a vindictive warder for his keeper's pure diversion, and the calmness of which he wrote bordered
on despair. He was glad that there was a limited space in which
to write, for though he had volumes to tell Deborah, for his own
safety, and for the sake of her sanity, he would tell her nothing.
For if he were to describe the daily hospital routine, she would be
driven to despair. He wrote in unusually large letters, so that his
permitted space would soon be filled. He told her about the book
he was reading. Its title would happily pass the authorities, but
then he regretted having written it, for Deborah might deduce
from it his abdication. Indeed, there was nothing at all that he
could write that would not feed her anxieties.

Remember our toast, he wrote yet again. Even though he could
give small grounds for hope, they had to hold it in their hearts.

Write to me with news of our friends. And others, he rounded off his letter. He wanted mostly to hear about Aaron. But he could not bring himself to write his name, and he hoped that Deborah would know that he was the "other" of whom he wanted news. He sealed the letter and went to the end of the ward and put it in a box for that purpose. The box was half full, and he wondered how long the letters had been lying there, bursting with their truths half told, their longings and their pleas.

"When are these collected?" he asked the nurse on duty.

"Every Monday," he said.

He had no idea what day it was, and he refrained from asking the nurse, for he had learned to fear his note-taking. Grigory was dressing and he went over to his cot to ask him.

"How should I know what day it is?" Grigory laughed. "I only know it's morning."

Thereafter Jakob visited the letter box every day on waking, and after three days he knew that it was a Monday. He thought he would make a note of each day as it passed, or write a diary perhaps, since he now had writing materials. That thought cheered him a little and he went back to his cot to begin. But the problems he had with letter writing were far more acute in diary form. For they were but a confirmation to himself of the daily waste of his life, of the constant threat to his body and spirit. To write of such things to oneself precluded another's sympathy, another's encouragement not to give way to despair, another's view of possible recovery. So he quickly abandoned the idea of a journal, and instead he wrote on the top of the page, "Monday." That page he would keep under his pillow, and make of it a calendar, day by day. Thus time would tick through his sleep and his dreaming, and chronicle the passing of the days, and afford him some anchorage in the timeless sea of his despair.

He noticed that Ilya's bed was empty, and he could see him nowhere about the ward. Grigory was dressed and coming toward him.

"Where's Ilya?" Jakob asked.

"He's gone for his examination. They took him before you woke up."

"Might he be released?" Jakob's voice was full of hope.

"I doubt it," Grigory said. "It's his fourth examination since he's been here. He's not very good at passing. If he passes, he'll come back soon to say good-bye."

"And if he fails?" Jakob regretted his question, for he knew that Grigory would not give him a straight answer.

"He'll be back in a few days or so."

Jakob asked no more, but all that day he waited for Ilya's return, and as night fell, he accepted the fact that Ilya had failed again.

A whole week passed before Ilya returned. He was almost unrecognizable. It was morning, but the zombie look that clothed all the men after the first trolley had now settled on Ilya's face with hints of permanence. He walked very slowly, as if in great pain. The men went forward to welcome him, gentle with their embrace, for they knew that his body was bruised. But not one of them asked any questions, because most of them had had examinations and all of them had failed. Until that time, Jakob had itched for the review of his own case. Now he dreaded his failure. But that same day, he had a letter from Deborah, and it was as if he had been suddenly released. He fingered the envelope in his hands, delaying its opening. By the weight of it, it was brief and possibly censored and he wanted to prolong the simple pleasure of receiving. He put it under his pillow and let it lie there for a few minutes, each second a teasing temptation. Then he lifted the pillow, but first entered the day they had reached on his calendar. It was a Friday, and in his terms, marked the end of a week. So he drew a line underneath. Then he opened Deborah's letter.

He noticed first the authorities' deletions. They were blacked out and unreadable. About half the letter was censored, and he noticed how his knuckles whitened as he clutched the paper, and he felt the anger rise in him. But he knew he must contain it. The recent sight of Ilya was testimony to where anger and indignation could lead.

My darling, he read, and was suddenly grateful to the authorities that they had not blotted out that token of love. *Words from you at last made us all so happy, and we have read and shared your letter a hundred times.* There followed a blacked paragraph, one that Jakob surmised spoke of reactions of friends, and perhaps of "others." But the following lines lifted his spirits once more. *Every night the children and I make our toast, and Inge and Ivan are often with us. I have applied for a permit to visit you. I am told that it is straightforward. I long to see you once again, to bring you kisses from our sons, and to hold you in my arms.* Another deletion followed, and this one puzzled Jakob most of all.

He could not imagine what greater passion she could have expressed after her last sentence, so he supposed that it was a postscript of sorts, and such a cataloging could only concern the subject of Aaron. He was convinced that she had written news of him, and it was that news that the authorities wished to suppress. And that made him more curious than ever.

When they were summoned to breakfast, he joined the others to help Ilya into line. Ilya knew that he had to eat to preserve what strength was left to him, but he needed a great deal of assistance to get to the table. They walked on each side of him, crowding him to protect him from the warder's whip, and Jakob on the outside lent his back to the warder's zealous wrist. In time they reached the dining hall and the serving counter. Grigory held Ilya's tray, and they all urged him to eat. But he picked at his food with little appetite. "I'm so terribly hungry," he whispered.

He made no attempt to excuse himself from the exercise hour, probably knowing that such a plea would be refused. But he also knew that he had to nurture his body once more after the terrible assault it had suffered. Once in the open air, he was seen to rub himself gently, all over his limbs, and the guard took it for exercise and turned a blind eye. Toward the end of the hour, when most of the men were leaning exhausted against the wall, one of the guards told Ilya to run around the square. Ilya made no manner of protest. He picked up one leg after the other, and with monumental effort, paced them around the exercise area. It was his last act of obedience, for when the drug trolley appeared on its first round of the day, Ilya refused to join the line. He would not move from his cot, and none of the men did much to dissuade him. For they knew, as well as Ilya knew, that with more drugs in his present state, brain damage was not far away. They knew too that the punishment for drug refusal might well be worse. But Ilya, on his two unsupporting legs, was making a small stand for his rights as a human being.

It took little time for a guard to note his disobedience. He strutted across the ward, taking his time, no doubt savoring the prospect of a victim. The men saw a small but noble sign of struggle in the cot, and then Ilya was dragged bodily across the floor, his still-booted feet scraping a scream along the linoleum. The guard got him into the line, and tucked him under his arm, where Ilya lolled like a rag doll, and waited his reluctant turn.

When it came, he refused pill and water, using what little strength he had left to clamp his jaws shut. But another guard came to his side, and together with his mate, they squeezed Ilya's nose until he was forced to open his mouth. Then they held it wide with their fists while the nurse put the pill on Ilya's tongue and sloshed some water after it. But the nurse got it all back in his face for his pains, while Jakob stood with the other men, watching helpless on the sidelines. Then the nurse slapped Ilya hard across the face, and blood was seen to trickle from his nose.

"Once more," the nurse said to the guards, and they fisted his mouth again, while the nurse applied another pill. This time he added no water, and the guards clamped Ilya's mouth closed, gripping it in a fist-hold for a while. Then they opened it again, inspected its raw insides, and were satisfied. Then Ilya fell to the floor, and some of his friends ran to gather him up and to carry him back to his cot. Jakob dreaded the next trolley round.

But Ilya resisted again and again. And each time he gave and received the same treatment. In the evening, when the men finally carried him back to his cot, Grigory urged him in whispers to give in. "You will not survive another day of this," he said.

"I have to try to do it," Ilya whispered, "else I won't survive at all."

But the following morning, a doctor was seen to enter the ward and approach Ilya's bed. After a while, a stretcher trolley was wheeled to his cot and Ilya was carried out of the ward. Jakob wondered whether they would ever see him again.

"Thank God," he heard Grigory say. "They will take him off the drugs and give him proper treatment."

"What's proper treatment in this place," Jakob asked, "and what drugs are there to cure his courage?"

"Courage he has, my friend," Grigory said. "But he also has inflammation of the liver. I heard the doctor tell the nurse. Two years ago, Ilya Yakir entered this hospital a whole and healthy man. Even if he ever gets out of here alive, he will never be whole again."

"Is it worth it?" Jakob asked, and he whispered the question, for it was more of a question to himself than one that required an answer.

But Grigory had overheard. "Don't ever ask that question again," he said, and for the first time since Jakob had met him in this place, his voice was raised. "People make choices," he said.

"And those choices are private. Next week it's my turn for examination. I have failed three times. Perhaps next time I shall decide to pass. And if I do, I shall come and say good-bye to you without shame. We all choose our own ways of survival."

Jakob was stunned by the reverberating echoes of the Patriarch Jakob's litany. Grigory was its true inheritor, and he wondered when his review time came, whether he himself would have the courage to surrender.

But when, in the following week, Grigory was taken for his examination and did not return to the ward, Jakob wondered whether his shame was too great, or whether he had found another way to survive. One week later he shuffled back into the ward in the fashion of Ilya's return, zombied, fractured, but unbroken. Jakob was ashamed at the pleasure he took in seeing him again, for he had missed him terribly. For the next few days he sat by Grigory's bed, and did his best to comfort him. Unlike Ilya, Grigory obeyed all the rules. He dragged his fragile body to the drug trolley three times a day and he took his medicine. He lumbered around the exercise yard with no complaint, though his pain was clear for all to see. Sometimes Jakob would notice a glint of triumph in his eyes.

"Why do you do it, Grigory?" he asked one evening at his bedside.

"My friend," Grigory said, "the sweetest revenge is to live well, and to survive at all is revenge enough. One day I shall live well, too. That will come, Jakob. It will come for all of us."

The case-review examination that Jakob had dreaded, yet in many ways had been impatient for, came much earlier than he had expected. He was told that his first review would take place a week hence, barely three months after his arrival at the hospital. Grigory couldn't understand it, and could only ascribe it to pressure from the outside. At this suggestion, Jakob thought immediately of Aaron, who perhaps was using his connections in order to free him. And immediately he grew antagonistic, for he did not want his brother's help from whatever source, for his brother was different, and so were his sources. That same day, when they apprised him of this review, he received a letter from Deborah. It was a short letter and completely uncensored, and it announced that she had received a visitor's permit and hoped to arrange to see him within two weeks. The children were well and sent their love, and she, hers.

Her visit might not be necessary, Jakob thought, since his examination would precede it. Or would she come and find him zombied like Ilya? He went over to Grigory's bed. "What kind of examination is it?" he asked. "Blood? Heart? Pulse?" he asked hopefully.

"They don't touch you," Grigory said. "They only ask questions."

Jakob knew that he must not inquire further. As Grigory had told him, survival was a private matter. But he worried about Deborah's visit. He wished she were coming sooner. The brevity of her letter offered the promise of much news to impart on seeing him. He needed to sniff the outside world on her, to smell his home and his children, for as the drugged days passed, their pictures floated in his memory, swimming in and out of focus. He tried not to think of the impending examination. But its prematurity continued to worry him. He must not let that fact influence his behavior. He thought now of his Bindel inheritance and repeated to himself the old man Jakob's litany. There is not a cause on earth worth dying for, he had said. No God, no country, no ideology. Death was worthy only in the name of love and friendship. Ilya was on his way to dying, and there was no doubt that the altar of his sacrifice was cause and ideology. Did that make him less of a lover? Less of a friend? In his dying, he was marching for millions of people whom he didn't know. Did that mean he would not sing that same march of death for one he knew and loved? Jakob was confused. As Grigory had said, survival was a private matter.

He took his calendar from under his pillow. Almost three months had passed since his first entry. Each week's end was underlined, and as was his daily wont, he counted the days he had already spent in the hospital. But that morning, he did something very different. He began to count forward, adding the days until his review. It was the first time since he had been in this place that he had envisaged the future, and thus the beginnings of hope.

When Aaron left Sonia, he moved into an apartment near the hospital that belonged to a doctor friend who, at that time, had been transferred to a medical unit in Leningrad. He fully expected trouble. Koskin was not a man to let him get away with the desertion of his daughter. His revenge would take time perhaps, but when it came, it would be extreme. But nothing happened. His job remained secure, and when he looked in the rearview mirror of his car, as he did all the time from force of habit, he found no shadows there. It seemed that his father-in-law had let him off the hook, but he regarded it as the lull before the storm.

He was very lonely. His sights were fixed on Saturdays, the day he spent with Heidi. He missed Sonia, too, he had to confess to himself, and each time he saw her, the old forbidden longings were aroused. She was always polite to him, and very controlled, and he sensed that she was close to tears.

Aaron's desertion had in fact shattered her. She had kept it from her father in fear of his wrath and revenge. But after a week of painful loneliness and deliberation, she considered asking for his help. She was convinced that the central cause of their quarrel was Jakob, and the fact that he was in trouble. If Jakob could be released, set free, not only from the hospital but also from the country, Aaron's guilt would leave him and he would return to their home. She was surprised by her father's reaction. She had expected anger, and plans for revenge. But he was deeply distressed by his daughter's desolate state. Although his relationship with his son-in-law had been distant, he had secretly grown fond of him, and he had much respect for his achievements in his field. Dr. Aaron Bindel and his discoveries had often been talked about in the various official functions he had to attend, and although he would never volunteer his connection, he would admit to it whenever a Bindel-admirer inquired whether he knew him personally. But he had little room for that brother of his, and quickly dismissed Sonia's suggestion that he use his good offices to engineer his release.

"In any case, as you well know, my dear, he is ill. In his own interest he should not be released until he is better."

"But that might take years, Papa," she said.

"The law must take its course."

She began to cry then, and he realized how deeply distressed the parting had left her. "I can do nothing for his brother," Koskin said, "but I can see to it that Aaron is left alone to continue his work."

She was grateful for that. Harassment would only feed his antagonism toward her.

"What am I to do, Papa?" she asked.

"Wait and see, my dear. He will come back. You just have to give him time."

He had little confidence in his words, for he knew that Sonia was right. The core of Aaron's discontent lay with that offending brother of his. Koskin's whole being was revolted by the opinions such a man held. But his daughter's plight moved him, and when she was gone, he deliberated how he could intervene for Jakob's release. But she must never know it was his doing. As few people as possible would ever know, for Koskin had his own interests to safeguard. As a considerably influential party official, he had the seniority to act on his own authority, and forthwith, he contacted his minion in Minsk and he ordered him to go to the hospital where Jakob Bindel was held and to instruct the doctor in charge that suitable reasons must be found for the release of the patient. He stressed the importance of the latter. Reasons had to be found. Bindel was on no account to be given an unconditional release. That would totally invalidate their system of psychiatric treatment. There must be nothing in writing, he told his Minsk contact. "Do the job, comrade," he said. "Keep me informed, and when it is done, I want to hear no more about it."

He put the phone down, satisfied. The following day he phoned Sonia from his office simply to maintain contact. A few days later, his man from Minsk telephoned. It was too soon, he reported, to maneuver Bindel's release in any disguisable way. Three months was the minimum stay before a case review could be considered legitimate. The doctor in charge had suggested that

as soon as three months had passed, the Bindel case would receive sympathetic review.

Koskin was satisfied. In time, Dr. Aaron Bindel would return
to the fold that, by virtue of history and national consciousness,
did not belong to him. But his daughter loved him, as he himself
had once so deeply loved her mother. Such love, he knew from
his own philanderings, was never repeatable.

Some weeks passed, and Aaron was restless. The lull had begun to unnerve him. He should have been relieved, he knew, but
there was something within him that *needed* trouble, trouble that
would lead to punishment, or at least reprimand. It was his only
way of drawing near to his brother. So he went to the OVIR
offices, and withdrew his letter of veto. While he was there, the
thought occurred to him to make his own application for an exit
visa too, but that, at this stage, would have been too drastic, and
the thought of Heidi precluded any idea of emigration. One thing
at a time, he thought. The withdrawal of the veto was the first
stage. He left the offices and waited for the clap of thunder. But
even with that provocation, it never came.

It took little time for the withdrawal to come to Koskin's ear,
and he was much relieved by the news. For he had it in mind to
engineer the granting of exit visas to Jakob Bindel and his family
as soon as possible after the hospital release. And Aaron's veto
would have been something of an impediment. So he was pleased
with Aaron's move, although he was aware that it was motivated
by guilt. He knew that only if Jakob were allowed to leave the
country would his brother's guilt be finally assuaged. Then perhaps he would return to Sonia.

A few days later, Aaron telephoned Deborah. He had not seen
her for many weeks and he asked if he might call. She was welcoming, and suggested he come that evening for supper.

"Will you bring Sonia?" she asked.

"No. I'll come on my own."

Deborah was glad of it. Sonia's presence would have inhibited
conversation. She was an outsider to their family as much as
Aaron was to hers. Deborah looked forward to seeing him. Jakob
would be happy to know that he had come. After his phone call,
she went out to forage for food. For two hours she waited in line
for a small piece of meat, and she was overjoyed at her find.
When he arrived, he handed her flowers. It was the beginning of

his peace offering, and in case she should refuse them, he said right away, "I have withdrawn my letter of veto."

She threw her arms around him, unable to speak, so great was her relief and happiness.

"I shall write and tell Jakob," she said. "But I shall have to wait for his reply. He is not allowed to write letters for a month."

"Do you hear anything about him?" Aaron asked.

"Nothing," she said. "I know people who have been in the Minsk hospital, and I avoid them. They avoid me, too. I think they are afraid of the questions that I am too afraid to ask."

He tried to find words of comfort for her, but knew none. So he took her hand.

"I want to help you all I can. Though there's little enough I can do," he said. "I've left Sonia."

Deborah was shocked by a mixture of feelings compounded of relief and concern. But relief was uppermost among them. That Aaron had left Sonia was not merely a case of a husband leaving his wife. It was a greater desertion; that of ideology. And in Aaron's case, more than that even. More positive than that. It was a gesture of love toward his brother.

"Why?" she asked. "How did it happen?"

"Inge came to see me after Jakob's trial. Or so-called trial. And I went to see my father-in-law. I didn't doubt for one moment that he would help. He was in a position to free him. He has that kind of power. He was kind and polite. But he would do nothing. And d'you know why? He sincerely believed they were right. That Jakob is mad and needs treatment. In his opinion, dissent is a mental disease. And it's a sincere opinion, deeply sincere, so sincere that it's unarguable. I left him and I wandered around for a bit. Then I went home. I had to find out what Sonia thought, and in a way I was frightened of asking. Because her answers would be crucial. You know I loved Sonia. I love her still and in all the years of our marriage, I was conscious of the fact that there were certain questions that I would not ask, certain subjects I would not discuss. I was afraid that her answers might confirm the chasm between us and our marriage would collapse. Our love maintained itself simply because we never questioned it. I knew, and I think she knew, too, that we were bound together in our own lies and silences. Well, that time I could hold my tongue no longer, and I asked her what she thought. She didn't hesitate for one moment. She entirely agreed with her father. I couldn't stay

with her. D'you understand, Deborah?" he pleaded. "She was an
enemy. Always was, but I couldn't hide it from myself anymore."
He paused, fumbling with the tablecloth. Deborah put her hand
on his arm.

"You did all you could for Jakob," she said. "And even if it
didn't work, you did it. That's all that matters. What about
Heidi?" she said after a while.

"I see her every Saturday. She's upset, of course. I'd like to
bring her over to see the boys. She hardly knows her cousins."

"You must do that next Saturday," Deborah said. It was
Aaron who needed family, she knew.

"Does Inge know?" Deborah asked.

"I wanted to tell you first. But I shall go and see her."

"She'll come on Saturday," Deborah said. "We'll have a family
reunion."

"Without Jakob," Aaron said sadly.

"Not this time," Deborah said. "But there'll come a time.
There surely will."

Thereafter Aaron was a frequent visitor at Deborah's apartment. Once a week he brought Heidi, and Inge and Ivan would
join them. But the comfort that Aaron found within the family
circle only served to underline his monstrous part in separating
them, and he wondered how he could do penance for all the
wrongs he had perpetrated. He knew that ultimately, he too must
join his brother's struggle. But he also knew that the insurmountable impediment to that final move was his continuing love for
Sonia. He knew that there was no way they could be reconciled,
short of a radical change in Sonia's outlook. But he knew that
that was impossible. He himself had tried, had flirted with an
alien creed, had thrilled with shame to its taboo, but finally he
had returned to the fold because it was more comfortable there.

Aaron's logical course was to go to Israel. But there was Heidi,
and Heidi tied him forever to Moscow. Indeed, though Aaron did
not know, his own Grandfather Leon had once found himself in
the same trap of loving, in the name of one David in the
Senghenydd valley. Death had released him from that trap, else
he too would have been tied to a comfortless alien history.

A few weeks later, Deborah told him that she had received a
permit to go to Minsk and visit Jakob. He was happy for her and
envious, too, for he wished he could go with her. There were
almost two weeks before she would go, and during that time he

spent many hours with her, and Inge, too, recapturing for her his childhood in Halle, and Jakob's childhood, too, which was what Deborah delighted to hear.

"When you see him," Aaron said, "I want you to tell him everything."

"I've already written that you have left Sonia," Deborah said.

Aaron laughed. "I think that would merit their blue pencil," Aaron said.

He was happy while he was with them, but when he returned to his borrowed apartment, he felt very lonely and he longed for Sonia. He tried to immerse himself in his work, but most of the time he thought of Jakob, and he would have been happy and ashamed to know that in most of his idle time, Jakob thought of his brother.

Especially on that morning of his appointed examination. He was as nervous as he used to be at school in the Leipzig days before he was orphaned. And Aaron used to hold his hand and lead him into the classroom, and tell him not to be afraid. Now more than at any other time he needed a big brother, and those childhood memories stirred such fraternal love in his heart that for a moment he forgot how diligently his brother had sought to destroy it.

They came for him very early, while most of the men were still sleeping. He felt a slight touch on his shoulder, and he wondered why the guard was being so gentle.

"Wake up, Mr. Bindel," he whispered. "It's time for your examination." *Mr. Bindel?* Jakob thought, he who from that same guard had never merited a name of any kind except "scum," "traitor," or "criminal," names that in the guard's terms could apply to any one of the patients. But suddenly there was this gentle awakening and the courtesy of the summons. Jakob was now more nervous than ever. He was taken to the examination room, that same room he had entered when first arriving at the hospital. Since it was morning, his mind was relatively clear, and he thought he recognized the same three doctors who had initially received him: the questioner, the scribbler, and the diagnostician. But this time there was no pad in sight, and no interrogating table. Instead, the doctors were seated in armchairs and they invited him to take one too, as if they were going to partake in pleasant conversation. The doctors were anxious to set as informal a scene as possible, to give an air of friendliness and equality.

For the MVD had briefed them, "Use any pretext to release this man." They hoped he would give them no trouble.

They had a standard series of questions to ask each examinee and these they stated in time and turn. But they interlaced them with pleasantries that had nothing to do with the situation in hand.

"It's good to see you, Mr. Bindel," one of the doctors opened the proceedings. "You're looking well. And how are you feeling?"

"As well as can be expected." Jakob was polite but distant. He wanted none of their proffered friendship.

"What does that mean exactly, comrade?" the erstwhile scribbler asked. "As well as can be expected. Are you referring to the gravity of your mental condition?"

"Not at all," Jakob replied without hesitation. "I am as well as can be expected considering the drugs I am obliged to take."

"Obliged?" the diagnostician asked. "They're prescribed for your own good, and by the looks and the sound of you, they have ameliorated your condition."

"Mornings are different," Jakob replied. "The effect of the drugs wears off for a while. There is a certain clarity of mind."

"Then we are fortunate to have caught you in the morning, my friend," the interrogating doctor said. "We can have a pleasant discussion together. When you arrived," he said quickly, "you showed all the signs of what we termed creeping schizophrenia. Now, Jakob, you're an intelligent man."

Jakob was sickened by the use of his familiar name and he couldn't understand this friendliness.

"You had delusions of reforming society," the doctor went on, "an obsessive mania for truth-seeking. It was temporary, I'm sure of that, and yours was only a mild case. Which is why we are reviewing your situation earlier than is usual. The treatment you have been receiving should have had the desired effect by now. Let us say that your disease was a mild form of dissent. How have your opinions changed since you came here?"

He had delayed the vital question for as long as possible. He had created an atmosphere of amiable equality, a comfortable setting for the questions that had ultimately and legally to be asked. He waited for Jakob's reply and he was unnerved to see him smiling. It was not a good beginning. For not only was Jakob Bindel smiling, he was close to derisive laughter.

BROTHERS   513

"Why should my opinions have changed?" he asked. "On the contrary, in this place they have been mightily confirmed."

The doctors shuddered with dismay, knowing now that release was impossible. Even the MVD would understand that.

"When I was arrested," Jakob went on, "it was on the charge of saying that there was no freedom in this country. For what reason should I have changed my mind about that? The whole country's a prison, and parts of it are called psychiatric hospitals. It's a farce. It's you who are diseased. Not I. It's you whose brains are addled, and you and your kind dare to call me insane."

"Thank you, Bindel," the diagnostician said. The "Mr." had been quickly dropped. "That is enough."

But Jakob was unstoppable. As he spoke, his mind was racing with the words of the Patriarch Jakob's litany. That old and venerable namesake of his would not have approved of his tactics. "For whose love are you making this sacrifice?" he would have thundered. "For whose friendship? You are committing yourself to confinement in the name of a cause. That is called martyrdom, and that is not what I bequeathed you. My legacy was survival." But perhaps the old man had been wrong, and in this place and at this time, he would have said the same. For he would have known that personal survival was only secondary. That what was predominant was that ideas should not die, that notions of freedom must be kept alive for one's children and their future.

"I may not live to see freedom in this land," Jakob went on, "but it will come. In time the whole world shall hear of your evil and—"

One of the doctors, his face white with rage, clapped his hand over Jakob's mouth and screamed for the guard. He was enraged. "Take this scum away," he shouted. "Cell 4C."

Grigory would have known that location and would have shuddered at its name. So would Ilya and countless others. And the one they called Evgeny. They, like Jakob, had refused to get better. So they punished them.

It was called the "roll-up." Once in the cell, Jakob was thrown onto a bunk by two attendant guards, who then proceeded to roll him from neck to foot in strips of wet canvas, and so tightly that it was difficult to breathe. When they had thus embalmed him, they fastened him down to the bunk with rubber belts. Then they stood back and viewed their handiwork. They were smiling.

"Enjoy it while it lasts," one of them said, "because it won't last long."

Then they left him, bolting the door behind them.

Jakob was afraid. He wondered what they had meant by enjoyment, for his present situation was uncomfortable enough. When in the past he had been punished by the guards, he had resorted to deep breathing to contain his pain. But now, strapped down and swaddled, it was difficult to breathe at all. He closed his eyes, though he knew that sleep was impossible. It was very hot in the cell. He twisted his head toward the window, but it was closed and barred. Despite the wet cold canvas that swathed him, he felt a fever in his body and his heart palpitated and he was afraid. He kept thinking of Grigory and Ilya. Now he knew how and where they had spent their time away from the ward. Yet they had returned, both of them, to protest and survive once more. They had not died in their swaddling clothes. He would survive too. As he lay there, the canvas seemed to tighten around him, and he realized for the first time the point of the punishment. As the canvas dried, it would tighten itself around his body. Now he understood the guard's parting phrase. "Your enjoyment will not last long." Now he knew it would only get worse. He knew he must not lose consciousness, for that state was the carpeting before death's entry, and the thought of Great-great-grandfather Jakob came to his mind, as if that venerable figure could safeguard his survival. As he lay there, his body felt as if in a vise. He prayed that the canvas was by now absolutely dry, because he knew he could not bear it much longer. His heart thundered its struggle, and he felt a sickness in his stomach. He thought he saw the cell door open and the doctor approach, the diagnosing doctor who had been so disgusted at his lack of cooperation. He was not sure it was he, nor even whether he was there at all. He felt or thought he felt the doctor's hand on his wrist, as if he were taking his pulse. Then he saw the guards and felt the bonds loosen. They let him lie there for the rest of the day, while his body breathed and stretched itself. But the pain of the recovery was unspeakable. It was too quick, too sudden. The muscles sprang back to their accustomed span, tearing his body like nails. He thought how endless man's endurance was, offensively so, and he could not help but wonder what he had achieved by his martyrdom. For that's what the Patriarch would have called it and would have pointed to the painful "roll-up" as proof. But Grigory had come back, and so had Ilya, and countless others no doubt, and lived to tell the tale they would not tell.

That night they brought him some soup to his cell, and a hunk of black bread. He forced himself to eat it, though he feared vomiting. But he forced that down. He daren't weaken himself through lack of food. Grigory and Ilya had been absent for days from the ward. He wished now he could remember how many. He was sure that there was more punishment for him to come.

And as it turned out, he was right. For six successive days they treated him to the "roll-up," and released him only when his pulse threatened to surrender. On the seventh day, even those heathens rested, and returned him to the ward. Grigory helped him to his bed, a smile of joy on his face.

"We know how you feel," he whispered. "Don't talk. Just rest. Trust us. We'll look after you."

He plumped the pillow under Jakob's head. "Sleep now," he said. But one thing troubled Jakob, and he could not close his eyes for the sleep he so craved. If Grigory had asked him to trust them, all those former "roll-up" victims, then they must trust him, too.

"Grigory," he whispered. "What happened to the one they call Evgeny?"

Grigory clutched Jakob's hand. "After the 'roll-up,'" he said, "Evgeny went mad, really mad, the sort of madness they don't treat here. He hanged himself with one of the canvas strips they used to roll him."

Jakob sighed and closed his eyes. Though saddened by Evgeny's fate, there was a small satisfaction in knowing that he had now been fully accepted into that stubborn fraternity of *refuseniks*. He had paid his dues. He slept then, and the pain eased from his body.

On the first trolley round, he dragged himself across the ward, and on reaching his turn, he noted how the nurse checked on his treatment card.

"It seems you need more treatment," he said. "The doctors report you're not responding. I have orders to double the dosage."

Jakob opened his mouth obediently while they slid two pills inside. Helplessly he washed them down with water, and as he did so, he knew that from that time, his life would be robbed of mornings.

Over the next few days he became like Ilya, walking around in a daze. It was an effort for him to speak, and though he was always tired, he could never sleep. He had continual headaches and his mouth was always dry, with a thirst that no amount of water could assuage. Often in those days, he wanted very much to die. It was during that time that they came to his bed and told him that he had a visitor.

"I can't," he whispered.

"It's your wife," the guard said.

He knew it was Deborah, which was why he couldn't see her. It would be too painful for both of them.

"Get up," the guard shouted. "She's come all the way from Moscow. You have twenty minutes. You're wasting time."

Jakob dragged himself out of bed, straightened his hair, and tried to compose himself. Then he shuffled behind the guard to the visitors' room. He wished he could walk upright with the brisk tread that she had last seen. He wished he had a mind to talk and an ear to listen. He wished above all that she hadn't come. Yet his heart raced to see her.

As he entered the room, he registered the look of horror on her face when she saw him.

"Jakob," she cried, and ran toward him, holding his body gently and wondering where all its flesh had gone. For now, even holding him loosely, her own hands overlapped each other on his back. She took them away quickly, afraid that his frame would crack. She helped him to a chair. It seemed pointless to ask how he was. It was plain from his appearance that he had been abused, maltreated, and possibly tortured. She would not ask him.

"Don't talk," she said, taking his face in her hands. "Let me do the talking."

She took a chair and sat alongside him, holding his hand the while as she spoke, caressing his cheek with her fingers and her lips. He was totally without response, seeming almost not to recognize her. Though he was staring at her, Deborah felt that he did not see her, that her face was but a blurred interruption of his vision of oblivion.

"Aaron has left Sonia" was the first piece of news that she gave him.

He heard the words, and the fact that they spelled out, but his mind, fuzzed by drugs, had lost the talent of deduction, inference, or perception of innuendo. His brother had left his wife. A piece of information. She realized, as she looked at him, and by his complete lack of response, that he had no idea of the import of that news.

She tried again. "He has withdrawn his letter of veto, Jakob," she said.

Again he heard it as a piece of information, but he could not consider its cause, and certainly not its effect.

"That means we'll get exit visas when you come out."

It was her last phrase that registered with more clarity than any of the others. He knew that he could never leave the hospital, that loyalty to his friends was a bond stronger than any canvas "roll-up" strip. How could he tell her that? He nodded his head as a signal of his understanding.

"Pavel has gone," she was saying. "They called him up and told him he had forty-eight hours to get out. He was astonished. They had a farewell party."

She looked at his nonregistering face. "You remember Pavel," she said, reminding him of his closest friend. "The engineer. They were holding him because he's had access to government secrets. You remember Pavel? And Mikhail's gone, too. You remember Mikhail, Jakob? They kept him because he only had an uncle in Israel. Not sufficient kinship, they said." She was trying to remind him of all the aspects of the *refusenik* struggle, to confirm that once he had been a part of it, and would be again.

"There was another letter from Aunt Sarah," she was saying. "She looks forward to our coming. Jakob," she pleaded, gripping his hand. "Don't lose hope. Don't despair."

The tears rolled down her cheeks, and those he saw with blinding clarity and clear deduction. He wished that she would go away. He could not bear her pain. He could not bear the humiliation of his own frailty.

"I love you," she was saying. "However you are."

Inference. Deduction. What did she mean by that? However I am. Does she too begin to believe that I am mad? He looked at her, painfully focusing his eyes on her face, and the name that went with that face struck his tongue.

"Deborah," he said, and there was a small relief in saying it. "Deborah," he whispered again. "Please go. Please."

Those were the first words he had spoken to her. She rose. "The children are well," she said. "They send their love." He hadn't asked about them. He had asked no questions at all. But she knew that later on, when he was alone, he would wonder about his home and those he had left behind, and he would be glad that they had not forgotten him. She took his face in her hands and kissed him gently. Then she watched him being led away, with half his visiting time still to run.

The guard, who had eavesdropped on the one-sided visit, was angry. Once out of the waiting room, he gripped Jakob's arm. "She came all the way from Moscow," he said.

Jakob was grateful for that rare show of concern, for that, he knew, was the cause of the guard's anger. "I'm ill," he said.

Whether that guard called the doctor, or whether it was a routine visit, Jakob never discovered. But shortly after he returned to his bed, a doctor arrived and gave him an authentic physical examination. He ordered the ward nurse to keep Jakob in bed for a week, and to take him off all drugs. He was adamant about that order, shouting it at the nurse, as if Jakob's condition was entirely his fault. The doctor was clearly disturbed by the state of his patient. In a supposedly remedial institution, it did not do to have too many deaths on their hands. Even if dissidence was a state-licensed disease, it was hardly fatal, and death, from its cause, carried uncomfortable overtones of murder.

"No drugs," he ordered again. "And extra rations. And don't let him leave his bed."

All this, Jakob heard in a blur of sound, deciphering the occasional word and its meaning. Out of it all, he experienced a surge of gratitude that they would save his life in this place, they who had been so bent on destroying it, pill by numbing pill. He would survive, and that word, that anchorage to his past, suffused him with joy.

For a whole week he lay there, fed, undrugged, and undisturbed. From time to time he saw Grigory's face hovering above him, his lips moving with words of comfort. At the end of the week, Jakob woke, stretched his limbs, and got out of bed, knowing that his "mornings" had returned. At least this morning, for later on that day, the drug trolley that for the past week he had not heard or noticed now wheeled its way across the ward, and the nurse shouted to him that from today, he was back to normal. Jakob smiled. Normal, he said to himself. Language was so abusable, he thought. Fashion could dishonor it, and manners, but most corrupting of all was ideology.

For the first few days after his rest cure, before the normal course of drugging began to take its toll, Jakob experienced a sense of physical well-being and a clarity of mind that he remembered from his prehospital days. During that time he thought a great deal about Deborah's visit, and always with terrible soundings of regret. He knew that she would understand, but he knew too that she had returned to Moscow in despair. He recalled all that she had told him. All the facts of it had registered, but now, in his clear state, he could understand the ramifications of the news that she had given him. Aaron had left Sonia and had withdrawn his letter of veto. Now he could read the subtitling of those news items and from them he could understand that his brother had returned to the fold. But Deborah's face as he had left her, or rather as he had sent her away, remained to haunt him. He thought of his inheritance, and for some reason it was Deborah's face that crystallized its whole meaning. She was love, she was friendship. Only in her name would he die. No other. No other, he kept repeating to himself. The old Odessa Patriarch had been right. Survive, he had said, in order to fight. In order to win. Survive, he had ordered the milk-brothers before they had entered the pagan service of the Czar. "They will force you into baptism," he had said, "and you must not resist them. Let them sprinkle their holy water on your brows. Let them flood your bodies with their purging priesthood. They cannot lay hands on your Jewish soul."

His words sang in Jakob's ear. The old Patriarch might well have been talking to him. Because in a way, to claim that he was better, that he had changed his views, was to admit to a baptism of sorts. And there would be a joy in deceiving them, for their baptism too could not touch his spirit. At his next case review, he would recant, with as much sincerity, piety, and obsequiousness as he could muster, and he would return to the ward and say his farewells without shame. Then he caught sight of Grigory walking toward him. It would be hardest of all to part from Grigory, and he wondered how long that old activist would hold out in this place. Perhaps he should tell him about Jakob's litany, and recruit him into his own brand of subversion. But Jakob knew that finally it was a question of language that divided them. Both of them colored words according to their needs. Words like *principle, cause, commitment,* even the word *survival* itself, could be cast in different lights.

"I have news for you," Grigory said as he approached. "I have another review of my case."

"Have you decided this time to be cured?" Jakob whispered.

"I want to see my wife and children," Grigory said.

"They are cause," Jakob told him. "They are principles, they are ideals, they are love, they are friendship. They are worth lying for and perhaps dying for. So lie and live, my friend. We have both of us paid our dues."

They made their way to the drug trolley.

"Pavel has gone, you know. And Mikhail," Jakob said. "We have to join them."

"If I choose to leave this place," Grigory said, "will you shake my hand and wish me well?"

"As long as you offer it without shame," Jakob said.

A week later, Grigory returned from his case review. His face was wreathed in smiles.

"I've passed," he said, "and they were delighted with their cure. They fell over themselves with gratitude. They called me 'comrade,' that word I so often use to you with all my affection. Words, my friend," Grigory said. "We're all of us in the cutthroat business of words. The only truth is silence." He held out his hand and Jakob clasped it.

"Farewell, my friend," Jakob said. "We shall meet on the outside. I, too, deal in words."

"Then fashion them," Grigory said, embracing him, "and we shall meet again in Jerusalem."

Deborah returned from the hospital visit in a mood of deep despair. Apart from their total lack of communication, she was profoundly disturbed by the state of Jakob's health. He had lost much weight and, it seemed, all of his spirit. She was anxious to get home and see Aaron. Over the past few weeks he had been a frequent visitor, and she had grown very close to him. She had wanted to tell Jakob how Aaron had changed, giving him all the details that indicated a turning-away from his former life. For Aaron had changed radically. He was becoming like Jakob in many ways, Deborah thought, as each day he released the Bindelhood within him and allowed it to assume its natural contours. He was gentle, supportive, and repentant, but Deborah knew that his guilt still nagged at him, and that he continually sought ways of assuaging it.

She telephoned Aaron as soon as she returned to Moscow and arranged to meet him that evening. She lied to the children about their father. She told them he was well and had every hope of release. She hated herself for the deception, but she did not wish to burden them with her own profound pessimism. But to Aaron she told the whole truth. He was able to comfort her a little by explaining that his condition, as she described it, was wholly due to the drug that he was obliged to take. He had made inquiries as to its nature, he told her, and he stressed that though the effects were worrying, they were not irreversible. He stressed that factor over and over again, as much for himself as for Deborah, but in his heart he feared he might be wrong. When he left her, her spirits had lifted a little, but his own had sunk considerably. He knew from Deborah's description that Jakob's health could not withstand such treatment for very long. He wished he could see him. Just to be with him. He wished most of all that he could share his sentence. He hadn't known why he'd never thought of it before, that obvious solution to his guilt.

He had to avail his own self to punishment. It was the only way to atonement. The following morning, before going to his laboratory, he walked with determined and almost euphoric stride to the offices of OVIR. And there, in a loud voice, and to the very official to whom he had long ago handed his letter of veto against his brother, he announced his application for an exit visa. It was how his brother had entered the struggle. He filled in the required forms and returned to his laboratory. He opened his drawers and packed a few personal belongings. He had left Sonia and he had withdrawn his letter of veto. And Koskin had all the time held his tongue and his power. This last move, this visa application, Koskin could not ignore. He would be summarily dismissed from his job and his struggle would follow his brother's course. He worked that day in his laboratory, convinced that it would be his last.

But Koskin had other plans. Words came to him soon enough about his son-in-law's application. He knew Aaron's motive. It had nothing to do with leaving the Soviet Union. It had less to do with going to Israel. It was his bid to join his brother, to penalize himself and thus lodge in his brother's skin. So he issued orders that Dr. Aaron Bindel's latest move was to be ignored. Moreover, he once again telephoned his minion in Minsk. Koskin knew in his heart that nothing short of Jakob Bindel's release, and possibly nothing short of his emigration—and he would engineer that, too—would ease Aaron's heart and possibly urge him back to Sonia and Heidi. Sonia's unhappiness did not seem available to time's healing, and almost every day she came to his apartment or even to his offices and begged him to use his influence for Jakob's release. Each time he refused, and with all the ideology that he could muster, for he dared not let her know that he was using his powers to weaken the system that he served. He carefully covered his tracks with each move. He had no intention of jeopardizing his position on account of Aaron Bindel. Though he had to admit to a certain fascination with the man, a certain pride, a certain excitement in the taboos that clothed him. Like any self-respecting racist, Koskin had to have his pet Yid, and Aaron fit that role exactly. He made a note on his file and dated it. October 1979. Two months from Christmas. By that time he could effect a family reunion. Jakob Bindel's release could be scheduled for November. Meanwhile he would start cutting through the bureaucratic tape of the emigration process. So by Christmas, Sonia would smile again and he could boast of his son-in-law at official functions. He read the notes he had made, memorized them, and tore them up into tiny pieces.

Meanwhile, Aaron waited. He went every day to his laboratory expecting minute by minute an indignant visit from the hospital director. He even arranged a comfortable chair for him, though he doubted whether his words of angry dismissal would have been at ease in a chair. Day after day he waited, and after some weeks he had to accept the fact that they had chosen to ignore his trespass. He was after all, their token Jew, as Jakob was always so fond of calling him. He was their pet Yid, their Judas, and such tokens could get away with anything. But he would think of something. He would find a manner of trespass that they could not ignore.

He went to the stationery department of the hospital and collected a sheaf of graph papers, together with tape, and he wrapped them furtively under his coat, and returned to his apartment. All that night he roughed out his design. "Free Jakob Bindel" was his first attempt. But, somehow in his eyes, it lacked something. It was too impersonal and as such, minimized the seriousness of his plea. "Free Jakob Bindel from the Hospital," was his next example, but that, too, though more specific, was still neutral. It was not until the morning light broke over his balcony that he found the word he had been seeking. Though indeed he had never lost it. It was a question only of its expression. He roughed it out on a piece of paper. "Free my brother, Jakob Bindel." It said everything he wanted to say.

It took him some time to paint out the letters, boldly and with clarity, so that they could be read by the passersby from his balcony only two floors above street level. When it was done, inscribed across four large taped sheets of graph paper, he gummed each side to batons of wood that he had bought for that purpose, and stood it against the living room wall to judge its effect. Its design did not bear too close an examination, nor did its calligraphy. But its message was loud and clear. They could not ignore it. Not even Koskin. It was too public a protest. He waited for the hour when people would start going to work, then he secured the banner across the balcony, returned to the room, put on his overcoat in readiness, and waited. After a short while

he heard murmurings in the street and he crawled to the balcony
doors and peeped outside. Across the road he could see that a
small crowd had gathered, and he watched for a while as the
crowd grew. It would not be long now before the police would
arrive and the plainclothes-uniformed KGB in their wake. He
returned to his armchair and waited. He knew that he would not
have to wait for long. He listened with joy to the crowd noises
outside. He listened to their cries of disgust with infinite pleasure,
and when he heard the boots outside his door, he almost rushed
forward to let his captors in.

"Open up," they shouted.

But Aaron was already at the door, his hand on the knob. He
turned it quickly and opened the door wide. Three of them stood
there, jackbooted in fury.

"Aaron Bindel?" one of them said.

"Yes," Aaron said. *"Dr.* Aaron Bindel," he insisted. They were
not arresting a nobody, he wanted them to know. They were
taking into custody their system's token Jew, who had stood
them in good if misguided stead in the past. "Dr. Aaron Bindel,"
he said again. "Fellow of the Moscow Academy of Sciences."

The thugs were unimpressed. Two of them grabbed Aaron by
the arms, while the other stormed to the balcony and tore down
the offensive protest, stamping it with disgust under his foot.
Then he closed the balcony doors, and joined his colleagues. Together they shoved Aaron into the lift and down into the street,
where a police van was waiting. They took him straight to the
Kalinsky District Court, where he was arraigned on a charge of
anti-Soviet agitation. When the magistrate realized the identity of
the accused, he ordered the court cleared and a defense counsel
to be called. He summoned the advocate to his desk, and suggested that in view of the reputation of the accused he should
plead for mitigation of sentence rather than seek an acquittal. To
take the latter course would involve many hearings, and could
not escape public attention. The former course of action could be
dealt with without any delay. He promised a light sentence. And
so the defense lawyer, without a word of consultation with his
client, by whom in any case he had never been appointed, agreed
to the validity of the charge and asked for the lightest sentence
that such a charge carried. The magistrate was satisfied and he
sentenced Aaron to prison for six months. He was to be held in
Moscow.

They put him back in the van and handcuffed him. He was astonished that it was all so quickly over and that the wheels of Soviet law rolled with such speed that any possibility of justice must be bypassed. He looked at his watch. It was barely two hours since he had first stolen out on his balcony and erected his protest. They had been quick to hush it all up, out of the public eye. He did not doubt that the speed and the cover-up were on account of his reputation, and he regretted it. But he also had no doubt that in time Deborah would hear of it, and Sonia as well, who might hear of it on that very day from her father. But it was Deborah most of all whom he wanted to know. Because through Deborah, Jakob would hear of it, and would know at last that his brother had asked forgiveness.

When they reached the prison, they speeded him through all the formalities and then stowed him solitary in a cell. He sat on his bunk fingering the rough serge of his prison uniform, and for the first time in many years, he felt at peace with himself.

That evening, Koskin himself came to Sonia's apartment, and broke the news. Again he stressed that he could not use his influence to free him. That his act had been too public. It would jeopardize his own career were he to intervene. But he suggested that Sonia apply for a visit.

"Believe me, my dear, prison life is so dull and monotonous, he will be glad to see you. Although I disagree with all he's done, you're still his wife and you owe him your support," he said.

"Everything he did was because of Jakob," Sonia said. "If only he were free."

She began to cry uncontrollably. He sat by her side and whispered, "I am doing what I can. But not a word. Never. Never. Or I shall end up where Jakob Bindel is, or your husband."

She looked up at him and smiled.

"No questions," he said quickly. "And if you love your father, not a word to a living soul."

She shook her head vigorously.

"Don't worry," he said. "I'll keep you informed."

A month later, Aaron was called from the prison workshop.

"You've got a visitor, Bindel," the guard said.

Aaron hoped it would be Deborah. That was a possibility. He dared not hope for Sonia for he knew that she would not come. Sonia was ever present in his thoughts. But he was pessimistic about their future together. It saddened him, for their years with each other had been an expenditure of such passion. He could not live with her unless she changed, and if she changed, he would no longer love her.

When he saw her there, sitting in the visitors' room, he went toward her, full of forbidden love, and wondered at her courage that she had come at all. "It was brave of you to come, Sonia," he said. He dared not touch her. The heat of her body would have sent him to sure and swift recantation. But she touched him, running her long fingers along his hand, and her touch seared his skin with longing.

"I know you only did it for Jakob," she said.

Her first words to him, and each syllable of them was wrong, misguided, misunderstood.

He shook his head. "It was more than that," he said. "You see, I'm not like you. I don't believe there's anything wrong with Jakob. If a man wants his freedom, that doesn't make him mad. I didn't do it just for Jakob." He had to make that very clear to her, though it hurt him, for he knew that as she looked at him she saw their future fade. Then he took her hand.

"Then what am I to do?" she said. It wasn't a question. It was a declaration of a future without him. "What will you do when Jakob is released?" she asked.

"There seems to be little chance of that," he said.

But she held her tongue on her father's maneuvers, as she had promised him. "But what will you do, Aaron, when you are free?"

He shrugged his shoulders for he really didn't know.

"Do you honestly want to go to Israel? I heard about your application."

He didn't know, but to admit to that would cast doubt on his visa request and thus prove that he had done it solely for Jakob's sake.

"Would you leave Heidi?" she asked.

He gripped her hand. "It would be harder to leave you," he said. "And that's the truth."

Her eyes lightened. "We could come with you," she said.

He had to laugh at that, because he could not bear the shattering inference of sacrifice in her offer.

"Your father wouldn't give you permission," he joked.

"He would," she said. "And I'm serious. We could go with you."

"Then it would be you who would be living a lie."

"What does it matter," she said helplessly, "as long as I'm with you?"

"It would matter," he said, as he knew full well its cost.

She stared at him, the question on her lips that she knew she must not ask, but had, for her own confusion, to put to him. "Will you never come back?" she said.

And with utter honesty he said, "I don't know."

For in truth, Aaron was confused. He wasn't sure that he wanted to go to Israel. If he had to leave the Soviet Union, he would prefer to emigrate to America. From a work point of view, it would have been more exciting. And for Sonia, too. But he knew that finally places of settlement were only peripheral to the choice and commitment to identity, and it was that area that lay still undefined and blurred and sometimes tormented in his spirit. No. He didn't know, and *that* was the truth of it and *that* truth he gave her. And if she chose to take hope from it, it was her risk.

"I don't know," he said again. "I really don't know." He smiled at her, hoping to offset the pain of his ambivalence. He had a sudden desire to make love to her. But he wouldn't look at her face. He would not want to know who she was. He would not smell their past on her. Oh, God, he thought to himself, I wish that she would go.

"How's Heidi?" he said.

"She's well. She misses you. I often take her to Deborah's. She gets on well with Hans and Benjamin. I'm getting closer to Deborah, too."

He smiled, though his feelings were ambivalent. He was happy with the idea of family contact, but he could not help but suspect Sonia's motivation and he hated himself for such doubts.

"Have you told her?" he asked.

"She knows where you are, and why. She's old enough to understand. The other day she said to Hans, 'My father's a *refuse-nik* too.'" Both of them, Sonia and Heidi, in their own ways, Aaron thought, were leading him back into his fold, even though it might cost them their own isolation.

"Has Deborah heard from Jakob?" he asked.

"Yes. I saw the letter. It was censored, of course. But he's much better now, he says, and he's recovered from the illness he had when she last saw him."

"Recovered? Illness?" Aaron asked. "Do you never stop to think, Sonia, what all that means?"

"I'm different from you, Aaron," she said. "I was born here. I went to school here. All my life I have known no other way. I have not been taught the ways of other people."

Aaron heard her words with a sudden flash of understanding. The whole massive body of the Russian people knew no other way. Why should they not think, then, that their way was right? They had no access to knowledge of any other choices. Nor ever would in their entire lifetimes.

"In his letter Jakob sent you his love," she said quickly. Then he took her face in his hands and kissed her for the great gift she had brought him.

"Time's up," the warder said, and Aaron was grateful, for after that piece of news there really was no more to say. They rose together and he kissed her once again.

"Shall I come again?" she asked timidly.

He nodded. "There will never be a time when I wouldn't want to see you," he said.

He watched her go, relieved, yet impatient for her next visit, and he returned to the prison workshop and thought about the gift she had brought him. Jakob's love. It had been worth all his torment.

So the two women, widowed by prison, waited in their separate apartments, the one knowing the exact duration of her widowhood, but unsure of its outcome. The other, Deborah, waited with only hope for company, for she knew there need be no end to Jakob's incarceration.

But in the Minsk hospital, some weeks later, Jakob was inwardly rehearsing his second case review. For the warder had told him that he was to be given another chance. Those were the warder's exact words. He, like the doctors, made no attempt to cover the speciousness of the examination. If Jakob was prepared to be better, then better he would be. And on this premise, Jakob rehearsed his apostasy. He had been wrong in his criticism of Soviet society. He had seen the light. As he spoke the words to himself, he heard the Patriarch Jakob prompting him and saw how he nodded his head in benign approval. "Survival," he kept whispering. "Remember that. Each word is given in its name." So when the time came for Jakob's review, he walked to the doctor's room, his mouth full of the vocabulary of recantation, and he prayed to the Patriarch to use his cunning wisdom to guide Jakob's lies from his throat.

They welcomed him as before. The long examining table had been removed and armchairs were in its place. They resuscitated the "Mr." of his name, and asked him politely to sit down. Once he was settled, they joined him.

"We're going to have a bad winter this year, it seems," one of the doctors opened the proceedings.

Jakob was unnerved by this introduction to the examination and was afraid to react to it in any way, lest they diagnose from his reaction some further aberration in his mind. So he said nothing.

"Well, it will have its advantages," the diagnostician said. "It will be easier on the police. There'll be less demonstration. People do not like hanging around in the streets if they are cold."

So that's what it's all about. So childish, Jakob thought, and he risked a look at them, hoping that the hatred and contempt that he felt did not show on his face.

"How are you feeling, Mr. Bindel?" the third doctor asked.

"Much better, thank you," Jakob said.

"Better than what?" the doctor probed.

"Better than when I was here before," Jakob said. He was as wary of their game as they no doubt were of his. But they had had their instructions from the MVD. This review had to work, and they found its opening promising.

"D'you want me to read you the speech you made in Kolpachny Lane?"

Jakob manufactured a shiver. "No," he said.

"And why not?"

Jakob was grateful for the easy cue. "I would now be ashamed of those words," he said, and the sound of his sincerity sickened him.

"How do you now regard your former behavior?" the scribbling doctor asked.

"I regret it," Jakob said. He was going to add, "with all my heart," but he curbed his enthusiasm, for an excess of protest often betrayed a lie.

"If you regret such behavior," the diagnostician said, "you are not likely to act in the same way again."

"Never," Jakob said. "I do not hold those opinions anymore.

The doctor was right," he said, "when he first examined me. In the war we fought for freedom and we won. Therefore we have freedom." He thought he heard the Patriarch chuckle in his ear.

"Then we can assume that when you return to Moscow, you will withdraw your application for an exit visa."

Jakob was prepared for that question, the hardest of all to dissemble. But he did not hesitate, for hesitation at that point would have given the lie to all the lies he had already told.

"Of course," he said. "I want to stay in the Soviet Union." Say anything, he thought, just to get out of here. Grigory had told him that. The point, Grigory had explained, is to get out, if only for a while, and resume the struggle. At that point the Patriarch must have put the thought of Deborah in Jakob's mind, for the prospect of reunion with her and their sons was worth all the falsehoods he could muster.

"There would be no reason now for me to leave this country," he added for good measure.

They smiled at each other, clearly satisfied. No questions remained to be asked. Jakob Bindel was cured. He had entered the hospital with the disease of dissent, and their clever and constant administration of drugs had destroyed his intellectual capacity to the extent that he was now incapable of holding dissident opinions. And that they sincerely believed. They rarely questioned that premise, possibly out of fear of discovering its flaws. Now that they had satisfied themselves with the state of his mind, it only remained for them to check his physical health.

"Would you open your jacket?" the examining doctor said, putting his stethoscope to his ear.

He gave Jakob a cursory examination of heart, pulse, and blood pressure, and pronounced him fit.

"Normally," the doctor said, and Jakob shuddered at the word, "you would have to revisit the Serbsky Institute in Moscow for your checkout, and then appear at court for your discharge. But all that will be waived in your case. You are free, Mr. Bindel," he said.

What a farce it all was, Jakob thought. Yet there was some justice in it. He had been charged and sentenced in his absence. It seemed right and proper that his discharge did not require his presence either.

The doctors showed him to the door, proffering their hands. He shook them each in turn.

"You will be given a train ticket back to Moscow," one of them said. "And we rely on you to uphold the honor of Soviet citizenship."

Jakob nodded his head in false promise. He could hardly suppress his feelings of joy. As he was leaving, one of the doctors put his hand on his arm.

"Ilya Yakir died, you know," he said. "Yesterday. Inflammation of the liver."

Yes, from all your drugs, Jakob thought. He was glad that they had not given him that information in the beginning of the interview, for all of the Patriarch's wisdom could not have persuaded him to hold a truthful tongue. His heart was leaden.

"I'm sorry," he said. "He was a friend."

"You will no longer have such friends," the doctor said.

Jakob clenched his fists and pinned them to his side, lest he strike him.

The warder returned him to the ward, where he collected his clothes. He sat on his bed. The news of Ilya's death had deeply shaken him. He was offended by the futility of it all, the indignity of such a death for a man of such honor and nobility. He looked around at the other men in the ward. Most of them were sleeping, some ambled around aimlessly, and it was still only morning. He couldn't bring himself to say good-bye to them. It wasn't because of shame of his recantation. That had not humiliated him. It was because of Ilya's death. That news had numbed his tongue to farewells. As he walked out of the ward, it seemed that none of them noticed his departure and he wondered whether they would ever remark on his absence.

In the train he could not put Ilya from his mind. Even thoughts of Deborah and his children could not erase Ilya's image. He had known the punishment that killed his friend, that remedial "roll-up" meant to squeeze all dissidence out of the body. But Ilya had known it too, and many times before, yet still he had returned to it, defiant, stubborn, proud. Finally it had broken him. He wondered what the Patriarch Jakob would have thought of Ilya. Did he die for love, he would have asked? Or friendship? Indeed, Ilya had died for all those, Jakob thought, for he had loved and befriended mankind, and for the first time in that lie-riddled day, Jakob felt a pang of shame. He was glad to be alone in the compartment, for he needed no witness to his guilt. He tried to sleep, but Ilya's face haunted him behind his eyes. After a while he did not try to blind himself from it; indeed, he came to be glad of it, for he needed that beautiful vision for his own resolve. Soon he fell asleep, and woke as the train was pulling into Moscow station and for the first time that day, he could think exclusively of Deborah and his sons, and though he was impatient to see them, the prospect frightened him a little. She would not be expecting him. His arrival would be a shock. Somehow or other he must cushion it.

As he stood outside his apartment door, he decided he would not use his key. His entry would be too sudden. He knocked on the door.

"Who is it?" He heard Deborah's voice.

"Jakob."

There was silence then, and in the silence he heard her fear. He remembered then that a knock on a *refusenik*'s door could be a prelude to a search, an interrogation, or an arrest.

"It's Jakob," he said again.

Again a silence, then after a while, with a voice full of hope, she said, "I don't believe it. Jakob has his own key."

He took it out of his pocket and inserted it in the lock. Gently he turned it, knowing that she stood terrified at the door.

"It's Jakob," he kept saying as he turned the key. "It's really Jakob."

Then he opened the door wide. Proof of him. Proof of the recanted Jakob Bindel. She stared at him.

"Hans, Benjamin," she screamed, as if she needed protection, protection from her own overwhelming bewilderment, relief and loving. The boys ran from the back room, and rushed toward him without any crippling astonishment, and embraced him lovingly. Then they made room for Deborah. She went to him and took him in her arms.

"I don't want to know why they freed you," she said. "It's enough that you are here."

She knew of course, and that he understood. For she knew that in a psychiatric colony the doctor diagnosed the sentence and the patient pronounced the cure. She knew he had had to pay a price for such a freedom, but she didn't care. She would help him to live with it.

I have to tell her about Ilya, Jakob thought. Then she will understand everything.

She prepared a festive supper and asked for his help in the

preparation, easing him back into his domestic scene. She gave him all the news of all the events of his absence, news of the children, Inge, and their friends. But she did not mention Aaron. He would know nothing of his story. Certainly not in Minsk, for even in Moscow the trial and sentence had been covered with silence. No newspaper had reported it, and outside the family, few people knew that it had happened at all. His sentence had been short enough, so that by the time people missed him and had begun to inquire as to his whereabouts, he would be free and it would be as if nothing had happened. Which would have pleased Aaron, for he had not made his protest for publicity's sake. He'd made it only for himself and that it should come to Jakob's ears. And now it was for Deborah to inform him. But she waited. She was waiting for Jakob to inquire of his brother. But on that subject he was silent, too, and it was not until late that evening, when the supper was cleared away, and the boys were in bed, that he sat by her side and asked of his brother.

"A great deal has happened to him since you left," she began, and slowly, step by step, she told him Aaron's story. As he listened, his face registered pleasure and concern, at times indignation and anger, but always it registered compassion.

"I must see him," he said. Visits to local prisons were not hard to organize, especially for a close relation. He would make inquiries in the morning, he decided.

Deborah told him she had already visited, and he had talked of nothing but Jakob. "I said you had forgiven him," she said, "but a visit from you would greatly ease his heart."

"I can't wait to see him," Jakob said. "We'll be close again. It will be like the old days in Halle when we were threatened and hidden, and our danger united us."

"Those are strange grounds for loving," Deborah said.

"Perhaps you're right, but they will have to do. At least for the time being," Jakob answered her.

That night when they were in bed, he told her the story of Ilya, but he refrained from telling her about the one they called Evgeny. That story was sealed in the "roll-up" brotherhood and he would share it with nobody.

The following morning, when the boys had gone to school, Jakob told her something of the life in the hospital. It was a relief to share the story with another, one who didn't find it unbelievable. For even as he unfolded his tale, he found it hard to credit and he wondered how he had managed to survive at all. As they were talking, the telephone rang.

"It must be for you," Jakob said. "No one knows I'm home."

Deborah went to the telephone. "Hello," she said, and waited, while Jakob saw her face grow pale. "Just a minute," she said. She turned to Jakob, trembling. "It's for you," she said.

"Who is it?" he whispered.

"I don't know the voice," she said. "I was afraid to ask."

What do I have to fear? he thought to himself. I've just been released. I've been in no trouble. But just to be Jakob Bindel, and in this land, was to be in trouble. Deborah took his arm and led him to the phone and watched his face for clues.

"This is Jakob Bindel," he said.

· There was a long pause while Jakob listened and while Deborah watched and on his face she saw a mixture of total astonishment and pleasure. And she hovered impatiently until he put the phone down. Then when he had finished he turned and looked at her.

"That was OVIR," he said.

She gripped his hand.

"The exit visas have been granted. I'm to pick them up. They're giving us forty-eight hours to leave the country."

"It's seven years," she said quietly. She was stunned. "Seven years of waiting. Somehow it's become a way of life. But why? Why now?"

"Who knows?" Jakob said. "There seems no reason for anything. Except perhaps Koskin," he added. "I have to see Aaron, and I have to see him today. And I must see Inge and we must pack and . . ." He took her in his arms. "I can't believe it," he said. She held him, and felt the sobbing in his body.

"How can I leave Aaron?" he said.

She knew he expected no answer. He was simply stating his pain. He would leave Aaron, and he would know that he would never see him again, but he would leave nonetheless, because he was a Bindel survivor.

"You go now to OVIR," she said. "I'll ask Sonia to arrange a visit. And I'll call Inge, too. And my parents. I'll ask them to come this evening. And Yosif and Gadaly and Irena and Abram."

"It will be hard to say good-bye to them," he said.

"Go," she urged him, "before they change their minds."

"I'll talk to Inge first," he said.

When that was done, and Jakob was gone, Deborah toyed with the idea of calling Sonia, but then decided against it. There was little scruple in speaking to friends from one tapped phone to another, but Sonia's phone was clean, and it would be safer to visit her, so she took a tram trolley to Sonia's apartment.

Sonia was happy to see her. Deborah rarely came on a visit. Sonia listened as Deborah told of Jakob's sudden release from the hospital and the equally sudden granting of the exit visas. Deborah was surprised at Sonia's reaction. She had expected pleasure, but Sonia's delighted response was overwhelming and as she embraced her sister-in-law, Deborah sensed that her pleasure was less on Jakob's behalf than on her own, that in Jakob's freedom and absence she saw an avenue of encounter with Aaron. Then she understood why Aaron had left her, why he had made his protest, and she understood, too, that Jakob's suspicions of Koskin's hand in the events were more than confirmed. Sonia said that she herself had a prison visit that afternoon, but she would gladly waive it and arrange for Jakob to go in her stead.

"He comes out soon," she said. "Another two months, then we have all the time in the world to be together."

Deborah was a little disturbed by Sonia's confidence in her future with Aaron. But she said nothing. Aaron himself was confused as to his future and she suspected that Jakob's emigration would confuse him further.

"Come this evening," Deborah said, "and bring Heidi. We'll have a farewell party." She turned to leave.

"Wait a minute," Sonia said. There was pleading in her voice and its tone was unavoidable.

Deborah went toward her. "What is it?" she asked.

"What shall I do?" Sonia said helplessly.

"I don't know." Deborah did not want to hold out any hope. When Aaron had left Sonia, he had relinquished a way of life. Yet he had chosen no alternative. He was in a limbo, a tenuous arena for Aaron's and Sonia's kind of loving.

"I don't know," she said again, but she knew that politics were irrelevant to Sonia's present pain. She thought of how desolate she herself would be if she were to lose Jakob's love. She took Sonia in her arms. "I shall miss you very much," she said.

On her way home, she went to the savings bank and withdrew the money that they had safely guarded for their fares. And once having taken that money out, that untouchable, almost holy sum, she realized for the first time that they were leaving, and her heart filled with sadness. She would miss her parents, and Inge. Especially Inge. She would miss Aaron, too. And Sonia. But most of all she would miss Russia, for after all, it was her cradle.

Jakob was home when she returned. He was examining the permits closely. He could still hardly believe that they were his. He showed them to Deborah—those papers that had been the object of all their waiting, all their torment. She took them and put them with the money.

"You must go to Aaron," she said, "and I must start to pack." She behaved in a businesslike fashion, a totally uncharacteristic trait in her, but both of them were so close to tears that the whole day could have passed in regret.

"Give my love to Aaron," she said.

Jakob stood outside the prison, that same prison where he himself had been silently incarcerated almost eight years ago. He stood still on the gravel path leading to the prison gates and he remembered how Aaron had met him there on his release, that stern, unyielding man, full of concern and rage, rigid in his suit of self-deception. He longed to see him, yet he lingered, in postponement of a meeting that would probably be their last. For Aaron was fettered to this land as Grandpa Leon had been bound to the valley of Senghenydd. What a legion of partings had littered the Bindel line, he thought, and had bred that hopeful coda of "Soon we shall be together again." He walked slowly toward the prison door.

"Bindel," the warder shouted in the workshop. "A visitor."

Aaron rose excitedly, stirred by a passion that he knew would evaporate at the sight of Sonia, and that would surely return when she had gone. As he neared the door of the visiting room, he began to tremble, and when the guard opened it, he gave an audible cry of delight, for however much he wanted to see Sonia, there was no one on earth with whom he more wanted to be. He practically flew to Jakob's side.

"Where have you come from, brother. And why? And how? You are free at last."

"I am more than that," Jakob said, embracing him, and he led him to a chair at the table. "But tell me first how you are."

"No, no," Aaron said, sitting down but not letting go of

Jakob's hand. "There is nothing to say about me. They treat me well here, and I shall be free shortly. But you, Jakob, what has happened?"

Jakob noticed how his brother's body trembled and he was filled with such pain for him, for all the love that Aaron was at last able to release.

"I was freed yesterday," Jakob said, "and this morning they telephoned from OVIR to say that the visas had been granted. They gave us forty-eight hours to leave." He paused then. "We leave tomorrow," he said, as gently as he could. He thought it best to tell him right away, so that Aaron would know from the beginning that they were not likely to meet again. Jakob saw his brother's eyes fill with tears.

"I'm glad," Aaron said. "I'm glad for you. I'm glad for all of us. I'm glad for the Bindels. The line will be secure."

How radically he had changed, Jakob thought, and how dearly he had paid for the transformation.

"What will you do, Aaron? Will you stay here?"

Aaron shrugged. "I really don't know," he said. "But I'll tell you a story. Some years ago, when Sonia and I were first married, we were invited to a dinner at Koskin's apartment. There were just the three of us. It was his birthday, I remember, and he opened a rare bottle of wine. No Georgian stuff for him, of course. It was imported and the very best, as he and his kind are privileged to acquire." He smiled with a twist of irony. "It was a claret, a Château Mouton-Rothschild. The wine was superb, but what fascinated me was the label on the bottle. Old Koskin couldn't understand my fascination with its design, but he gave me the label to take home. I have it somewhere still among my papers. The pattern is in the form of a shield. A red shield, which is a direct translation of the family name. Within that shield are five arrows that branch in different directions. Old Mayer Rothschild, the founder of the firm, had five sons, and when they grew, he sent them to different parts of Europe to establish in each place a branch of the Rothschild banking tree. Frankfurt, Vienna, Paris, London, Rome. It was his way of insuring continuity. You see, that old man from Frankfurt, old Mayer Rothschild, knew about survival. We're not Rothschilds," Aaron said, "but our history is as long. Our wanderings are as worldwide. Go to Israel and be happy there."

"And you?" Jakob asked again.

"I don't know. I really don't know," Aaron said. "My application might have been just a gesture. I'm beginning to understand, but I'm still confused, you see. Then there's Heidi. There's Sonia. There's all of my loving."

Jakob looked at him tenderly. "You mustn't turn away from that," he said.

For a while there was silence between them, then Aaron asked, "Will you go via Vienna?"

"Yes," Jakob said.

"I remember that railway station so vividly, and how glad I was that I was not on that train, and that I was going back to Leipzig."

"I shall think of you on that platform," Jakob said.

"D'you remember how Mama hugged us when we returned, how she held us in her arms and wouldn't let us go? D'you remember . . . d'you remember? There are so many memories I'm now ready to share with you. Will you write?"

"Of course," Jakob said. "And so will the boys to Heidi."

And again there was silence between them, but each unspoken moment was a cementing of their brotherhood and it was as audible and as resonant as words between them. So that when they heard the guard's voice, it was as if he had interrupted their conversation.

"Time's up," he said.

They smiled at each other. They had said all that they needed to say. They held each other close and for as long as the guard allowed. Then he tapped Aaron's shoulder. Neither Aaron nor Jakob could turn his back on the other, so they walked away from each other backward, each holding the other's face in his eyes. Aaron to prison, Jakob to freedom. Then they stood for a moment on their distant and separate thresholds.

"Shalom," Aaron shouted. Out of his enforced Jewish childhood, he recalled that word that would do for greeting or farewell.

"Shalom," Jakob said.

Outside the prison, Jakob stood for a while and said his own farewell to his brother. Inside the prison workshop, Aaron was doing the same. Soon we shall be together again, each said to himself. In every generation, from Russia to England, from England to Germany, and from Germany back to Russia, no Bindel could part from another without that phrase. Over the years it had lost its overtones of reunion. It was stated simply as a confirmation of Bindel continuity.

They were catching the night train to Vienna and Inge and Ivan saw them off at the station. Inge could not hold back her tears. It was a terrible parting for her. It seemed to her as final as Hans's dying. Which it was, for she was unlikely to see them again.

"You still have Aaron," Jakob said.

"I'll look after him, don't you worry," she said. "Sonia, too, and Heidi." In her heart she had reunited them and that gave Jakob a measure of comfort.

The journey was long and they slept most of the way. They reached Vienna early the next morning. Jakob stood on the platform and breathed freedom. He remembered when he and Aaron had last stood on that same platform. It was not freedom that they breathed at that time, but captivity. The official from the Israeli embassy, who met all trains bound from Moscow, was there to greet them.

"Welcome to freedom," he said, and for some reason Jakob felt a shiver of resentment. What did this man know about freedom, he wondered, he who had probably never known bondage? He thought then of all those friends he had left behind in their involuntary servitude, and he thought of Aaron, too, in his own thrall, and he hoped that he was sleeping.

They traveled by El Al to Tel Aviv, and when four hours later the plane touched down, the pilot made an announcement. He gave it first in Hebrew, only a few words of which Jakob could understand. But a German translation followed in deference to the plane's port of embarkation, and from it Jakob gleaned the message. He translated it for Deborah and the children as the pilot was speaking.

"He apologizes," Jakob said, "but there will be a delay in passing through customs and immigration. There has been a bomb scare in the airport, and it is being cleared. The police are searching the area. The delay will last about two hours. Meanwhile passengers will be taken to a building on the far side of the airport, and given refreshment." The Bindels looked at each other. Had they left Russia for this? Had their long struggle resulted only in the exchange of one peril for another?

"Whose bombs?" Benjamin asked.

"Palestinians," Hans said.

They knew about the PLO. Over the past few years Russian radio and television had given much time and praise to the activities of the Palestinians, not so much that they applauded their cause, for in truth they cared little for their fate, but that they were a convenient peg on which to hang their incessant anti-Israel propaganda.

"What a welcome home," Hans said.

They were taken by bus to a building on the fringes of the airport. It seemed to be a conference room of sorts, for it was huge and richly appointed. The Bindels took chairs at the far end of the room, away from the other passengers. He wanted to sit privately with Deborah and his sons. Coffee was brought to them, and refreshments. It would be a long wait, the server told them.

Jakob looked at his two sons. Fifteen and seventeen years old, uncircumcised, too late for bar mitzvah, and still uninherited. What was there Jewish about them, he thought, except the vicarious and fragile thread connecting them to their past? Yet, alien as they were, they were going to a land that by virtue of that same history was their home, their family, and he pondered on the wisdom of their uprooting.

"It was safer in Moscow," Hans was saying.

"That's stupid," Benjamin said. "What is safe in not being free? At least in Israel we're home."

"It's the Palestinians' home, too," Hans said with some indignation.

A terrible peal of warning bells chimed in Jakob's ear. For in his children's argument, he heard the rumblings of that fraternal conflict that had dogged every generation of Bindels since the milk-brothers, whose love for each other had not been clotted by fraternal blood. His children had to learn that Bindel history. They must be told. They had wandered for so many generations over the earth's surface, and had finally come home, and even before entering they were threatened. It was surely the time, and certainly the place, for his children to inherit.

"It's not safer in Moscow," Jakob said again, "nor ever was. Nor in the whole of Russia. The Bindels knew that generations ago. It was from Russia that they started their wanderings."

"Where? And who?" Benjamin asked.

"It's a long story," Jakob said, smiling.

"Then tell us," Hans said. "We've plenty of time."

Jakob wished that Aaron were with him, that they could bequeath together, in the same way as the milk-brothers had together consigned their inheritance in the woods behind the Odessa tavern. At that moment he felt very much alone. He took Deborah's hand.

"It all started, as far as is known, over a hundred years ago in Odessa. But first I must tell you a little of the history at that time."

And as his father, Benjamin, before him, and Grandpa Leon before his father, and as Benjamin the milk-brother had spoken to Grandpa Leon, Jakob began his story. He told them first of the great Patriarch himself, of the recruitment of children in the service of the Czar, and the birth of the great Bindel inheritance. Word for word he repeated it, as it had been learned by rote by all the Bindel brothers of each generation.

"That is your inheritance," he said to his sons, "the gift you will bequeath to your children, and they to theirs." He looked at them, and like all Bindel fathers before him, he wondered whether his sons had understood.

"Did they come back, the milk-brothers?" Benjamin asked.

"They survived," Jakob said, "but while they were away, Reuben's father died."

Then he told them the story of the gentle Leon who had died imprisoned on the Siberian wastes. And he told them of the first pogrom and the tavern fire.

"That was the beginning of the Bindel wanderings. They made their way across Europe to Hamburg. That was the beginning of the German Bindels. But not until later, and then, of course, it was too late. But let me first tell you about Hamburg."

He told them Zelda's story then and Aaron's and of how Leon had turned away from his tribe. He hesitated when he came to the Senghenydd tale, but he felt that that too must now be told, for all parts of the past enriched their legacy. Then the Bindel story shifted uneasily to Germany and Jakob told it with pain, for it was the tale of his own parents and his orphanhood. But Hans and Inge livened that story and took his tale to Moscow, the life that his children already knew.

"The Bindels have come a long way from Odessa," Benjamin said.

"Yes," Jakob said. "But now we're home."

"Then we're safe," Hans said. "We need no longer struggle for survival." He saw his father's questioning look. "Well, need we, Papa?" he asked.

"I can only answer you with another question," Jakob said. "Why are we waiting here? Perhaps in each and every step from Odessa, the struggle for survival was only a long and grueling rehearsal. For the real battle begins at home."

"We're ready now," the steward called the passengers. "The bus is waiting to take you to the airport."

Thus Hans and Benjamin, of the sixth traceable Bindel generations, from Bessarabia to England, from England to Germany, and from Germany to Russia, entered the land of their forefathers, not of their bones but of their spirit. Jakob followed them. He recalled the old man who had led Aunt Sarah and himself to the graves of their past in Odessa. Living Judaism belongs to the Diaspora, he had said. Did survival, too? Jakob wondered. He thought he heard the minstrel singing.

EPILOGUE

Come stranger. We have eaten of the bread of affliction and the bitter herbs. We have recounted the plagues of Egypt and given thanks for our deliverance. Now between us we may break unleavened bread, and share the feast that celebrates our freedom. We will be here next year, too, and every year to come. "In every generation each man must regard himself as if he himself had gone forth from Egypt." That phrase will echo in many places and in many tongues, that refrain of the minstrel's song, that tone poem of almost six thousand years of Jewish history. Know stranger of our survival. Know stranger of our stubborn continuity. Know stranger of our chronic permanence.

Then come stranger. Any year, any place, any tongue.